The Complete Strategy & War Collection (Vol. 5)

The Arthashastra & Machiavelli's Art of War — Statecraft from Court to Battlefield

A Modern Translation

Adapted for the Contemporary Reader

Kautilya (Chanakya) | Sun Tzu

Translated by Tim Zengerink

Table of Contents

Preface - Message to the Reader

What If You Could Help Rebuild the Greatest Library in Human History?

Thousands of years ago, the Library of Alexandria stood as the crown jewel of human achievement — a sanctuary where the collected wisdom of every known civilization was gathered, preserved, and shared freely.

And then, it was lost.

Through fire, conquest, and the slow erosion of time, humanity lost not just books — but ideas, dreams, discoveries, and stories that could have changed the world forever.

Today, the Library of Alexandria lives again — and you are invited to be a part of its restoration.

Our mission is simple yet profound:

To rebuild the greatest library the world has ever known, and to translate all timeless works into every language and dialect, so that no seeker of knowledge is ever left behind again.

By joining our movement to rebuild the modern Library of Alexandria, you become part of an unprecedented mission:

- **Unlimited Access to the Greatest Audiobooks & eBooks Ever Written:**

  Instantly explore thousands of legendary works—Plato, Shakespeare, Jane Austen, Leo Tolstoy, and countless more. All instantly available to read or listen, placing a complete literary universe at your fingertips.

- **Beautiful Paperback & Deluxe Editions at Printing Cost**

  Own any title as an elegant paperback, deluxe hardcover, or stunning collectible boxset—offered to you at true printing cost, delivered straight to your door. Build your personal Library of Alexandria, crafted for beauty, built for durability, and worthy of proud display.

- **Fresh Translations for Modern Readers—in Every Language & Dialect**

  Enjoy timeless masterpieces reimagined in clear, contemporary language—no more outdated phrases or obscure references. Alongside the original versions, we're tirelessly translating these classics into every language and dialect imaginable, ensuring accessibility and understanding across cultures and generations.

- **Join a Global Renaissance of Literature & Knowledge**

  You directly support expanding our library, publishing deluxe editions at true cost, translating works into all global languages, and bringing humanity's greatest stories to people everywhere. By joining today, you're not just preserving a legacy of masterpieces; you set in motion a powerful wave of literary accessibility.

Become a Torchbearer of Knowledge.

Join us for free now at **LibraryofAlexandria.com**

Together, we will ensure that the light of human wisdom never fades again.

With gratitude and a shared love of knowledge,
The Modern Library of Alexandria Team

Visit:

www.libraryofalexandria.com

Or scan the code below:

Introduction

Two Faces of Strategy:
Kautilya and Machiavelli on War, Power, and Political Control

In the vast landscape of political philosophy and military theory, two towering figures stand out for their unapologetic realism, their granular detail, and their profound influence on how we understand power: Kautilya (also known as Chanakya), the ancient Indian advisor to Emperor Chandragupta Maurya, and Niccolò Machiavelli, the Florentine diplomat and thinker who witnessed the turbulence of Renaissance Italy. In The Complete Strategy & War Collection (Vol. 5), we present two foundational works that span cultures and centuries but converge in purpose: Kautilya's Arthashastra and Machiavelli's Art of War.

These texts are not only manuals for statecraft—they are comprehensive blueprints for how to survive, stabilize, and dominate in a world governed by uncertainty and ambition. Both authors are concerned with far more than warfare. They analyze the inner workings of government, the role of law, the psychology of rulers, the instruments of coercion, the legitimacy of violence, and the value of public perception. They do not shy away from difficult truths: power is preserved not merely by virtue, but by vigilance, deception, adaptability, and force.

Kautilya, writing over two millennia ago, offers one of the oldest surviving treatises on political economy and military strategy. His Arthashastra is encyclopedic, covering everything from espionage to taxation, urban planning to battlefield logistics. Machiavelli, more focused in scope but equally incisive, lays out in The Art of War his vision of a citizen-army, republican virtue, and the indispensable role of military preparedness in securing political freedom.

This introduction explores the themes and insights of both authors in depth. Though their worlds are different, they share a common project: to understand how power functions, how it fails, and how it can be wielded effectively in the pursuit of lasting order. Their relevance today is not diminished—it is amplified in an age of instability, disinformation, and global competition. Their writings challenge us to confront the hard edge of politics without illusions, and to lead not with sentiment, but with strategy.

Kautilya's Arthashastra: The Architecture of Imperial Power

Composed sometime between the 4th and 3rd centuries BCE, Kautilya's Arthashastra is arguably the most comprehensive guide to statecraft ever written. Attributed to Chanakya, the mastermind behind the rise of the Mauryan Empire in India, the Arthashastra offers a vision of governance that is at once administrative, economic, military, and philosophical.

The work opens with a bold statement: "The end justifies the means." This sets the tone for what follows—a pragmatic, results-driven approach to political life. The king, according to Kautilya, is the axis around which the state revolves, and his success depends on knowledge, strategy, and the careful use of power. Governance, in this model, is not a moral enterprise—it is a technical one.

Kautilya structures his text into books that address a wide range of issues: the duties of kings, the appointment and surveillance of officials, taxation and trade, agriculture, law enforcement, and the administration of justice. But central to the work is the concept of the mandala theory, a strategic model of interstate relations. According to this theory, neighboring states are natural enemies, while states separated by intervening powers are natural allies. Foreign policy, then, is a shifting web of alliances, espionage, subversion, and war.

The Arthashastra emphasizes intelligence above all. Espionage is not a sideline—it is a central institution. Kautilya describes networks of spies, counter-spies, and informants. He advocates misinformation campaigns, false flag operations, and the covert manipulation of enemy leadership. No detail is too small. The idea is simple: knowledge is power, and secrecy is survival.

On military matters, Kautilya is equally detailed. He describes the composition of armies, the importance of morale, and the use of strategic deception. He divides warfare into open battle, covert war, and silent war—fought through destabilization and psychological manipulation. The best ruler is the one who wins without fighting, subduing his enemies through strategy rather than brute force.

Yet despite its ruthlessness, the Arthashastra is not chaotic or anarchic. It is rooted in order, law, and the long-term sustainability of the state. Its vision is authoritarian, but also utilitarian. The ruler must secure prosperity, peace, and loyalty—not through moral appeal, but through well-managed systems.

Kautilya's genius lies in his clarity. He understood human nature—its greed, ambition, and fear—and built a system that channels those traits toward stable governance. His advice remains strikingly modern, and his conception of the state as a dynamic, competitive organism remains foundational in geopolitics.

Machiavelli's Art of War: Civic Virtue and Military Readiness

While Kautilya operated in an imperial monarchy, Niccolò Machiavelli (1469–1527) wrote during the political fragmentation and cultural ferment of Renaissance Italy. His Art of War (1521) is a dialogue in seven books that explores the relationship between military power and political freedom, placing particular emphasis on the role of a well-trained, citizen-based militia.

Where The Prince is a study in political cunning, The Art of War is an exhortation to civic responsibility. Machiavelli argues that military strength is not only necessary for survival, but for virtue. A republic that relies on mercenaries or foreign troops will lose both its liberty and its soul. True security, he claims, depends on a citizen-army: disciplined, patriotic, and deeply connected to the state it defends.

Machiavelli is not nostalgic. He admires the Roman Republic not for its rituals, but for its institutions. He sees warfare as the school of discipline, a crucible in which civic virtue is forged. War, for him, is not only a necessity—it is a moral force that shapes character and preserves liberty.

The Art of War blends classical sources—especially Roman writers like Vegetius and Livy—with Machiavelli's firsthand experience as a diplomat and official. He dissects the failures of Italy's mercenary armies and criticizes the complacency of its elites. He warns that without preparedness, a state invites conquest and collapse.

While his analysis is often martial, it is also political. Military structure must align with political structure. A virtuous army depends on virtuous citizens, and virtuous citizens require a republic that rewards service, merit, and sacrifice. The state, then, must not only defend its borders but cultivate the moral strength of its people.

Machiavelli's realism is matched by a sense of possibility. He believes that greatness is still attainable—but only if leaders abandon illusions and commit to the hard work of reform. The Art of War is a guide for nations in decline, offering a pathway to renewal through discipline, unity, and strategic clarity.

Between Court and Republic:
Two Traditions of Strategic Thought

Kautilya and Machiavelli approach power from different angles— one from the palace, the other from the republic. But both share core convictions:

- Security is the foundation of political life. No state can endure without military preparedness, internal order, and the ability to respond to threats with speed and precision.
- Leadership must be realistic, not idealistic. Human nature is self-interested, often irrational, and subject to manipulation. Leaders must anticipate betrayal, understand psychology, and act preemptively.
- Power must be organized, not improvised. Strategy requires

foresight, structure, and doctrine. Whether it's the spy networks of Kautilya or the militias of Machiavelli, both thinkers stress the importance of systems over spontaneity.

• The health of the state depends on disciplined citizens and institutions. Kautilya's hierarchical state and Machiavelli's participatory republic both rely on trained, morally grounded leadership and civic virtue.

Their legacies endure not because they appeal to sentiment, but because they force us to confront the raw mechanics of governance. They do not peddle utopias—they build models that work in the real world.

In our age of complex geopolitics, digital warfare, and fragile institutions, the insights of Kautilya and Machiavelli offer clarity. They remind us that strategy is not the province of the battlefield alone—it begins in the mind, in the law, in the morale of the people, and in the long view of the state.

Welcome to The Complete Strategy & War Collection (Vol. 5). May the sharp intelligence of Kautilya and the bold vision of Machiavelli guide you through the intricacies of power—so you can lead with wisdom, plan with foresight, and build not just victories, but enduring strength.

Arthashastra

Kautilya

Book 1

˙CHAPTER I & II. THE LIFE OF A KING & THE END OF SCIENCES.

Anvikshaki, the three Vedas (Trayi), Varta (agriculture, cattle-breeding, and trade), and Danda-Niti (the science of government) are what are referred to as the four sciences.

The school of Manu (Manava) holds that there are only three sciences: the three Vedas, Varta, and the science of government, as they consider Anvikshaki to be merely a specialized branch of the Vedas.

The school of Brihaspati argues that there are only two sciences: Varta and the science of government, as they see the three Vedas as simply an abridgment or a pretext for one experienced in worldly affairs.

The school of Usanas asserts that there is only one science: the science of government, claiming that all other sciences find their beginning and end within it.

However, Kautilya contends that there are four and only four sciences, from which all knowledge concerning righteousness and wealth is derived, and therefore they are so named.

Anvikshaki encompasses the philosophies of Sankhya, Yoga, and Lokayata.

Righteous and unrighteous deeds (Dharmadharmau) are learned from the three Vedas; wealth and non-wealth from Varta; the expedient and inexpedient (Nayanayau), as well as strength and weakness (Balabale), from the science of government.

When viewed through the lens of these sciences, Anvikshaki is seen as highly beneficial to the world. It steadies the mind in times of both prosperity and adversity, and it grants clarity in foresight, speech, and action.

The Science of Anvikshaki is regarded as the light to all forms of knowledge, a simple means to accomplish all tasks, and the holder of all virtues.

[Thus ends Chapter II, "Determination of the place of Anvikshaki among Sciences" in Book I, "Concerning Discipline" of the Arthasástra of Kautilya.]

CHAPTER III. THE END OF SCIENCES.

Determination of the place of the Triple Vedas.

The three Vedas—Sama, Rik, and Yajus—are known as the triple Vedas. Together with the Atharvaveda and the Itihasaveda, they constitute the Vedas.

The Angas (limbs of the Vedas) include Siksha (Phonetics), Kalpa (Ceremonial injunctions), Vyakarana (Grammar), Nirukta (Glossarial explanation of obscure Vedic terms), Chandas (Prosody), and Astronomy.

As the triple Vedas clearly define the respective duties of the four castes and the four stages of religious life, they are considered the most useful.

The duty of a Brahman is to study, teach, perform sacrifices, officiate in others' sacrifices, and give and receive gifts.

The duty of a Kshatriya is to study, perform sacrifices, give gifts, engage in military service, and protect life.

The duty of a Vaisya is to study, perform sacrifices, give gifts, engage in agriculture, cattle-breeding, and trade.

The duty of a Sudra is to serve the twice-born (dvijati), engage in agriculture, cattle-breeding, trade (varta), and practice the professions of artisans and court-bards (karukusilavakarma).

The duty of a householder is to earn a livelihood through his profession, marry within his equal class of different ancestral Rishis, have intercourse with his wife after her monthly ablution, give gifts to gods, ancestors, guests, and servants, and consume the remaining offerings.

The duty of a student (Brahmacharin) is to learn the Vedas, perform fire-worship, practice ablution, live by begging, and devote himself to his teacher, even at the cost of his own life—or in the absence of his teacher, to the teacher's son or elder classmate.

The duty of a Vanaprastha (forest recluse) is to observe chastity, sleep on the bare ground, wear twisted locks and deer-skin, perform fire-worship, practice ablution, worship gods, ancestors, and guests, and subsist on food from the forest.

The duty of an ascetic (Parivrajaka) is to exercise complete control over the senses, abstain from all kinds of work, disown wealth, withdraw from society, beg from various places, dwell in forests, and maintain purity, both internal and external.

Harmlessness, truthfulness, purity, freedom from spite, abstinence from cruelty, and forgiveness are duties common to all.

The observance of one's own duty leads to Svarga (heaven) and eternal bliss (Anantya). If violated, the world will fall into chaos due to confusion of castes and duties.

Thus, the king must ensure that people do not stray from their duties. Whoever upholds their duty, adheres to the customs of the Aryas, and follows the rules of caste and religious life, will find happiness in this life and the next. The world, when sustained by the principles of the triple Vedas, will flourish and never perish.

[Thus ends Chapter III, "Determination of the place of the Triple Vedas" among Sciences in Book I, "Concerning Discipline" of the Arthasástra of Kautilya.]

CHAPTER IV. THE END OF SCIENCES.

Varta and Dandaniti.

Agriculture, cattle-breeding, and trade constitute Varta. It is highly valuable as it provides grains, cattle, gold, forest produce (kupya), and free labor (vishti). It is through the treasury and the army, which are solely acquired through Varta, that the king can control both his own forces and those of his enemies.

The sceptre, on which the welfare and advancement of the sciences of Anvikshaki, the triple Vedas, and Varta depend, is called Danda (punishment). The science of punishment, or the law of governance, is known as Dandaniti.

Dandaniti is the means to acquire possessions, to secure them, to improve them, and to distribute the benefits of such improvements among those who deserve them. The progress of the world relies on this science of government.

"Hence," says my teacher, "whoever desires the progress of the world must always keep the sceptre raised (udyatadanda). There is no better tool than the sceptre to bring people under control."

Kautilya, however, disagrees: whoever imposes overly harsh punishment becomes hated by the people, while one who imposes overly mild punishment becomes disrespected. But a ruler who enforces punishment fairly, according to what is deserved, earns respect. When punishment is administered with proper consideration, it encourages people to follow righteousness and pursue productive works that generate wealth and enjoyment. On the other hand, punishment given out of greed, anger, or ignorance sparks outrage, even among hermits and ascetics in the forests—let alone among householders.

When the law of punishment is neglected, disorder arises, as the proverb of the fish (matsyanyayamudbhavayati) suggests: without a magistrate (dandadharabhave), the strong will devour the weak. Under the protection of the sceptre, however, the weak can resist the strong.

The people (loka), consisting of the four castes and the four stages of religious life, will stay true to their duties and occupations when governed by the king with his sceptre, remaining devoted to their respective paths.

[Thus ends Chapter IV, "Determination of the Place of Varta and of Dandaniti" among Sciences in Book I, "Concerning Discipline" of the Arthasástra of Kautilya. "The End of Sciences" is completed.]

CHAPTER V. ASSOCIATION WITH THE AGED.

Thus, the first three sciences (of the four) depend on the science of government for their proper functioning. Danda, or punishment, which ensures safety and security of life, is itself reliant on discipline (vinaya).

Discipline is of two types: artificial and natural. Instruction (kriya) can only bring a docile being into conformity with the rules of discipline, but not an undocile being (adravyam). The study of sciences can only educate those with the mental faculties of obedience, listening, grasping, memory, discrimination, inference, and deliberation, but not those who lack such qualities.

Sciences must be studied and their teachings strictly followed under the guidance of specialized teachers.

After undergoing the ceremony of tonsure, the student must learn the alphabet (lipi) and arithmetic. Upon receiving the sacred thread, he must study the triple Vedas, the science of Anvikshaki from acknowledged teachers (sishta), the science of Varta from government superintendents, and the science of Dandaniti from both theoreticians and practical politicians (vaktriprayoktribhyah).

The prince shall observe celibacy until he reaches the age of sixteen. Then, he shall undergo the tonsure ceremony (godana) and marry.

To maintain effective discipline, the prince must always remain in the company of aged professors of the sciences, for in them alone discipline is firmly rooted.

He shall spend his mornings receiving lessons in military arts, including those related to elephants, horses, chariots, and weapons, and his afternoons listening to the Itihasa.

Itihasa includes Purana, Itivritta (history), Akhyayika (tales), Udaharana (illustrative stories), Dharmasastra, and Arthasastra.

During the rest of the day and night, the prince shall not only receive new lessons and revise old ones, but also repeatedly hear anything that has not been clearly understood.

For knowledge arises from hearing (sutra); from knowledge, steady application (yoga) becomes possible; and from application, self-possession (atmavatta) can be attained. This is what is meant by the efficiency of learning (vidhyasamarthyam).

A king who is well educated, disciplined in the sciences, dedicated to the good governance of his subjects, and committed to the welfare of all people will enjoy the earth without opposition.

[Thus ends Chapter V, "Association with the Aged" in Book I, "Concerning Discipline" of the Arthasástra of Kautilya.]

CHAPTER VI. RESTRAINT OF THE ORGANS OF SENSE.

The Shaking Off of the Aggregate of the Six Enemies.

Restraint of the organs of sense, on which success in study and discipline depends, can be achieved by abandoning lust, anger, greed, vanity (mána), haughtiness (mada), and overjoy (harsha).

The absence of confusion (avipratipatti) in the perception of sound, touch, color, taste, and scent—through the ear, skin, eyes, tongue, and nose—is what is meant by the restraint of the organs of sense. Strict adherence to the precepts of the sciences also signifies this, for the sole aim of all the sciences is the restraint of the senses.

Anyone of contrary character, who does not control their organs of sense, will perish swiftly, even if they possess the entire world.

For example: Bhoja, also known as Dándakya, perished along with his kingdom and relations after attempting to act lasciviously toward a Brahman maiden.

Similarly, Karála, the Vaideha, met the same fate. Likewise, Janamejaya was consumed by his anger against Brahmans, and Tálajangha for his vengeance against the family of the Bhrigus.

Aila, driven by greed to extract wealth from the Brahmans, and Ajabindu, the Sauvíra, faced their downfall in similar circumstances.

Ravana, driven by vanity and unwilling to return another man's wife, and Duryodhana, unwilling to part with even a portion of his kingdom, also perished.

Dambhodbhava and Arjuna of the Haihaya dynasty, in their arrogance and disdain for others, likewise fell.

Vátápi, in his overjoyed attempt to attack Agastya, and the corporation of the Vrishnis in their attempt against Dvaipáyana, also perished.

These kings, along with others, fell victim to the aggregate of the six enemies and failed to restrain their senses, leading to the downfall of their kingdoms and families.

By driving out the six enemies, kings like Ambarísha of the Jámadagnya dynasty, famous for his restraint of the senses, and Nábhága, were able to enjoy long reigns over the earth.

[Thus ends Chapter VI, "The Shaking Off of the Aggregate of the Six Enemies" in the section on "Restraint of the Organs of Sense" in Book I, "Concerning Discipline" of the Arthasástra of Kautilya.]

CHAPTER VII. RESTRAINT OF THE ORGANS OF SENSE.

The Life of a Saintly King.

By conquering the aggregate of the six enemies, the king shall restrain his organs of sense; gain wisdom through association with the aged; gain insight through his spies; ensure safety and security through constant activity; maintain his subjects in their respective duties through the exercise of authority; uphold his personal discipline through continuous study of the sciences; and win the affection of the people by connecting them with wealth and doing good deeds for them.

With his senses under control, the king shall avoid harming the women and property of others, stay free not only from lust, even in dreams, but also from falsehood, arrogance, and evil tendencies. He will steer clear of unrighteous and uneconomical activities.

By adhering to righteousness and economy, he will enjoy his desires without transgressing limits. He will never be without happiness. He may enjoy in equal measure the three pursuits of life—charity, wealth, and desire—which are all interdependent. When one of these pursuits is indulged excessively, it harms not only the other two but also itself.

Kautilya asserts that wealth, and wealth alone, is the most important, as both charity and desire rely on wealth for their fulfillment.

Those teachers and ministers who protect the king from falling prey to dangers, and who, by striking the hours of the day as determined by measuring shadows (chháyánálikápratodena), warn him of any carelessness, even in secret, shall always be respected.

Sovereignty (rájatva) is possible only with assistance. A single wheel cannot move alone. Therefore, the king must employ ministers and listen to their opinions.

[Thus ends Chapter VII, "The Life of a Saintly King," in the section of the "Restraint of the Organs of Sense," in Book I, "Concerning Discipline" of the Arthasástra of Kautilya; "Restraint of the Organs of Sense" is completed.]

CHAPTER VIII. CREATION OF MINISTERS.

"The king," says Bháradvája, "should appoint his classmates as ministers, for they can be trusted since he personally knows their honesty and ability."

"No," says Visáláksha, "because they were also his playmates and may despise him. Instead, he should appoint those whose secrets are shared with him and well-known to both. Having shared vices and habits with the king, they would not harm him for fear of betrayal."

"Such fear is common," says Parásara, "because under the threat of revealing his secrets, the king may follow their good and bad deeds. By disclosing his secrets, the king could humble himself before as many people as he confides in. Therefore, the king should appoint ministers who have demonstrated loyalty during life-threatening situations and have proven devotion."

"No," says Pisuna, "this shows devotion, but not intelligence (buddhigunah). The king should choose ministers who, when handling finances, produce as much or more than the expected revenue, demonstrating their capability."

"No," says Kaunapadanta, "such individuals may lack other essential ministerial qualities. Therefore, the king should appoint ministers whose fathers and grandfathers were also ministers. These individuals, due to their knowledge of past events and established loyalty, will never desert the king, even if offended. Faithfulness, even among animals, shows this—cows, for example, stay with their familiar herds."

"No," says Vátavyádhi, "such individuals might gain excessive influence over the king and act as though they were the king themselves. Instead, the king should appoint new individuals who are proficient in the science of politics. These new ministers will see the king as the true sceptre-bearer (dandadhara) and will not dare to offend him."

"No," says the son of Báhudantí (a woman), "a person with only theoretical knowledge and no experience in practical politics may make serious mistakes when dealing with real issues. Therefore, the king should appoint ministers from high-born families, who are wise, pure in intent, brave, and loyal, as ministerial appointments should be based solely on qualifications."

Kautilya concludes: "This is satisfactory in all respects. A person's ability is proven through their demonstrated capacity in work.

Accordingly, based on differences in their abilities, their powers should be divided, and the time and place of their duties clearly determined. Such individuals should not be appointed as councillors (mantrinah) but as ministerial officers (amátyah)."

[Thus ends Chapter VIII, "Creation of Ministers" in Book I, "Concerning Discipline" of the Arthasástra of Kautilya.]

CHAPTER IX. THE CREATION OF COUNCILLORS AND PRIESTS.

A person who is native-born, from a respected family, influential, well-educated in various skills, forward-thinking, wise, has a good memory, courageous, eloquent, skilled, intelligent, enthusiastic, dignified, persistent, of pure character, approachable, firm in loyalty, and possessing good behavior, strength, health, and bravery, without procrastination or indecisiveness, affectionate, and free from qualities that cause hatred or hostility—these are the traits of a qualified minister.

Those who have only half or even a quarter of these traits belong to the middle or lower ranks.

Of these traits, native birth and influence should be verified by reliable people; education and skills by professors of the same field; practical and theoretical knowledge, foresight, memory, and approachability should be judged from successful work outcomes; eloquence, skill, and quick intelligence from how well they tell stories in conversations; endurance, enthusiasm, and bravery in times of trouble; purity of life, friendliness, and loyal devotion by regular interaction; behavior, strength, health, dignity, and freedom from laziness and indecision from close friends; and an affectionate and generous nature through personal experience.

A king's actions can be direct, indirect, or inferred.

What he directly sees is visible; what others teach him is indirect; and drawing conclusions about what hasn't been done yet from what has been accomplished is inferred.

Since actions don't all happen at the same time, come in different forms, and may occur in distant and varied places, the king must appoint his ministers to carry them out, keeping in mind the right time and place. This is the duty of the ministers.

A person whose family and character are highly praised, who is well educated in the Vedas and the six Angas, skilled in interpreting signs whether natural or accidental, knowledgeable in the science of government, obedient, and capable of preventing disasters, whether caused by nature or humans, by performing rituals from the Atharvaveda, should be appointed by the king as the high priest. The king should follow him as a student follows his teacher, as a son follows his father, and as a servant follows his master.

A Kshatriya, raised by Brahmans, guided by wise advisors, and faithfully following the teachings of the scriptures, becomes unbeatable and achieves success, even without the help of weapons.

CHAPTER X. ASCERTAINING BY TEMPTATIONS PURITY OR IMPURITY IN THE CHARACTER OF MINISTERS.

Assisted by his prime minister (mantri) and his high priest, the king shall, by offering temptations, examine the character of ministers (amátya) appointed in government departments of ordinary nature.

The king shall dismiss a priest who, when ordered, refuses to teach the Vedas to an outcaste person or to officiate in a sacrificial performance (apparently) undertaken by an outcaste person (ayájya).

Then the dismissed priest shall, through the medium of spies under the guise of classmates (satri), instigate each minister one after another, saying on oath, "This king is unrighteous; well, let us set up in his place another king who is righteous, or who is born of the same family as of this king, or who is kept imprisoned, or a neighboring king of his family and of self-sufficiency (ekapragraha), or a wild chief (atavika), or an upstart (aupapádika); this attempt is to the liking of all of us; what dost thou think?"

If any one or all of the ministers refuse to acquiesce in such a measure, he or they shall be considered pure. This is what is called religious allurement.

A commander of the army, dismissed from service for receiving condemnable things (asatpragraha), may, through the agency of spies under the guise of classmates (satri), incite each minister to murder the king in view of acquiring immense wealth, each minister being asked, "This attempt is to the liking of all of us; what dost thou think?"

If they refuse to agree, they are to be considered pure. This is what is termed monetary allurement.

A woman-spy under the guise of an ascetic and highly esteemed in the harem of the king may allure each prime minister (mahámátra) one after another, saying, "The queen is enamored of thee and has made arrangements for thy entrance into her chamber; besides this, there is also the certainty of large acquisitions of wealth."

If they discard the proposal, they are pure. This is what is styled love-allurement.

With the intention of sailing on a commercial vessel (prahavananimittam), a minister may induce all other ministers to follow him. Apprehensive of danger, the king may arrest them all. A spy under the guise of a fraudulent disciple, pretending to have suffered imprisonment, may incite each of the ministers thus deprived of wealth and rank, saying, "The king has betaken himself to an unwise course; well, having murdered him, let us put another in his stead. We all like this; what dost thou think?"

If they refuse to agree, they are pure. This is what is termed allurement under fear.

Of these tried ministers, those whose character has been tested under religious allurements shall be employed in civil and criminal courts (dharmasthaníyakantaka sodhaneshu); those whose purity has been tested under monetary allurements shall be employed in the work of a revenue collector and chamberlain; those who have been tried under love-allurements shall be appointed to superintend the pleasure-grounds (vihára) both external and internal; those who have been tested by allurements under fear shall be appointed to immediate service; and those whose character has been tested under all kinds of allurements shall be employed as prime ministers (mantrinah), while those who are proved impure under one or all of these allurements shall be appointed in mines, timber and elephant forests, and manufactories.

Teachers have decided that in accordance with ascertained purity, the king shall employ in corresponding works those ministers whose character has been tested under the three pursuits of life, religion, wealth, and love, and under fear.

Never, in the view of Kautilya, shall the king make himself or his queen an object (laksham, butt) of testing the character of his councillors, nor shall he vitiate the pure like water with poison.

Sometimes the prescribed medicine may fail to reach the person of moral disease; the mind of the valiant, though naturally kept steadfast, may not, when once vitiated and repelled under the four kinds of allurements, return to and recover its original form.

Hence, having set up an external object as the butt for all the four kinds of allurements, the king shall, through the agency of spies (satri), find out the pure or impure character of his ministers (amátya).

CHAPTER XI. THE INSTITUTION OF SPIES.

Assisted by the council of his ministers, who have been tested through espionage, the king shall proceed to create spies: spies under the guise of a fraudulent disciple (kápatika-chhátra), a recluse (udásthita), a householder (grihapaitika), a merchant (vaidehaka), an ascetic practicing austerities (tápasa), a classmate or colleague (satri), a fire-brand (tíkshna), a poisoner (rasada), and a mendicant woman (bhikshuki).

A skillful person capable of reading others' thoughts is a fraudulent disciple. After honoring such a spy with rewards of money and respect, the minister shall instruct him, "Sworn to the king and me, you shall inform us of any wickedness you discover in others."

One who is initiated into asceticism and has foresight and a pure character is called a recluse. This spy, provided with substantial funds and many disciples, shall engage in agriculture, cattle-rearing, and trade (vártakarma) on the lands assigned to him for this purpose. From the produce and profits thus earned, he shall provide all the ascetics with food, clothing, and shelter. He will also send those under his care who wish to earn a livelihood (vrittikáma) on espionage, directing each to detect a specific crime related to the king's wealth and to report it when they come to collect their wages and sustenance. Each ascetic (under the recluse) shall, in turn, send their followers on similar missions.

A farmer, fallen from his profession but possessing foresight and a pure character, is termed a householder spy. This spy shall cultivate the lands assigned to him for this purpose and maintain the farmers and others involved, as previously described.

A trader, fallen from his profession but possessing foresight and pure character, is a merchant spy. This spy shall engage in the production of merchandise on the lands allotted to him for this purpose, etc., as before.

A man with a shaved head (munda) or braided hair (jatila), desiring to earn a livelihood, is a spy disguised as an ascetic practicing austerities. Such a spy, accompanied by a group of disciples with shaved heads or braided hair, may settle in the outskirts of a city, pretending to survive on a handful of vegetables or meadow grass (yavasamushti) taken once every month or two, while secretly consuming his preferred food (gúdhamishtamáháram).

Merchant spies, pretending to be his disciples, may worship him as if he possesses supernatural powers. His other disciples may publicly declare, "This ascetic is a master of extraordinary powers."

Regarding those who, eager to learn about their future, gather around him, the ascetic may, through palmistry, predict future events based on the signals and gestures of his disciples (angavidyayá sishyasanjnábhischa) concerning the affairs of prominent people in the country—such as minor gains, destruction by fire, fear of robbers, execution of rebels, rewards for the virtuous, and forecasts of foreign matters (videsa pravrittivijnánam), saying, "This will happen today, that tomorrow, and the king will do this." His disciples shall corroborate these predictions by providing supporting facts and details.

He shall also predict not only the rewards that people with foresight, eloquence, and bravery are likely to receive from the king, but also possible changes in the appointments of ministers.

The king's minister shall conduct his duties in accordance with the predictions made by the ascetic. He shall appease, with offers of wealth and honor, those who have known reasons to be disaffected, and secretly punish those who are discontented without cause or who are conspiring against the king.

Honored by the king with rewards of money and titles, these five institutes of espionage (samstháh) shall determine the purity of character of the king's servants.

CHAPTER XII. INSTITUTION OF SPIES.

Creation of Wandering Spies.

Those orphans (asambandhinah), who must be supported by the state and are trained in the sciences, palmistry (angavidya), sorcery (máyágata), the duties of various religious orders, sleight of hand (jambhakavidya), and the reading of omens and augury (antara-chakra), are classmate spies or spies learning by social interaction (samsargavidyasatrinah).

Brave desperados from the country, who risk their lives fighting elephants or tigers primarily to earn money, are called firebrands or fiery spies (tíkshna).

Those who have no trace of filial affection, who are exceptionally cruel and lazy, are considered poisoners (rasada).

A poor widow of the Bráhman caste, who is very clever and seeks to earn her livelihood, is called a woman ascetic (parivrájiká). Honored within the king's harem, such a woman shall visit the residences of the king's prime ministers (mahámátrakuláni).

The same rule applies to women with shaved heads (munda), as well as those of the súdra caste. All of these are wandering spies (sancháráh).

Of these spies, those who are from good families, loyal, reliable, well-trained in the art of disguising themselves according to different countries and professions, and who possess knowledge of many languages and arts, shall be sent by the king to spy within his own country on the activities of his ministers, priests, army commanders, the heir-apparent, the gatekeepers, the officer in charge of the harem, the magistrate (prasástri), the collector-general (samáhartri), the chamberlain (sannidhátri), the commissioner (pradeshtri), the city constable (náyaka), the officer in charge of the city (paura), the superintendent of transactions (vyávahárika), the superintendent of manufactories (karmántika), the assembly of councillors (mantriparishad), heads of departments (adhyaksháh), the commissary-general (dandapála), and officers in charge of fortifications, borders, and wild tracts.

Fiery spies, such as those employed to hold the royal umbrella, vase, fan, and shoes, or to attend to the throne, chariot, and conveyance, shall observe the public behavior (báhyam cháram) of these officers.

Classmate spies shall report this information (i.e., that gathered by the fiery spies) to the institutes of espionage (samsthásvarpayeyuh).

Poisoners, such as a sauce-maker (súda), a cook (arálika), a water-bath attendant (snápaka), a shampooer, a bed-spreader (ástaraka), a barber (kalpaka), a toilet attendant (prasádaka), a water-servant, and servants disguised as a hunchback, a dwarf, a pigmy (kiráta), the dumb, the deaf, the simpleton, the blind; as well as artisans such as actors, dancers, singers, musicians, comedians, and a bard, along with women, shall observe the private behavior of these officers.

A mendicant woman shall report this information to the institute of espionage.

The immediate officers of the institutes of espionage (samsthánámantevásinah) shall activate their own spies using signs or written communication (samjnálipibhih) to verify the information.

Neither the institutes of espionage nor the wandering spies shall know each other.

If a mendicant woman is blocked at the entrance, the line of doorkeepers, spies disguised as parents (mátápitri vyanjanáh), women artisans, court-bards, or prostitutes shall, under the pretense of delivering musical instruments, or by using cipher-writing (gudhalekhya), or by signs, convey the information to its intended destination (cháram nirhareyuh).

Spies from the institutes of espionage may suddenly leave under the pretense of suffering from a long-standing illness, lunacy, or by causing a fire or administering poison to someone.

When the information received from these three different sources is consistent, it shall be considered reliable. If these sources frequently differ, the spies involved shall either be secretly punished or dismissed.

The spies referred to in Book IV, "Removal of Thorns," shall receive their salaries from the foreign kings (para) with whom they are employed as servants. However, if they assist both states in catching robbers, they shall receive salaries from both states (ubhayavetanáh).

Those whose sons and wives are kept as hostages shall receive salaries from two states and be regarded as under the mission of enemies. The purity of character of such individuals shall be verified through people of the same profession.

Thus, regarding kings who are enemies, allies, intermediaries, of low rank, or neutral, and concerning their eighteen government departments (ashtáldasa-tírtha), spies shall be deployed.

The hump-backed, the dwarf, the eunuch, accomplished women, the mute, and various ranks of the Mlechcha caste shall serve as spies within their households.

Merchant spies shall operate within forts; saints and ascetics shall reside in the suburbs of forts; farmers and recluses shall be positioned in the rural areas; herdsmen at the country's borders; and in forests, forest-dwellers, sramanas, and chiefs of wild tribes shall be stationed to monitor enemy movements. All these spies shall execute their duties with great speed.

Spies sent by foreign kings shall also be identified by local spies; spies will detect other spies of similar professions. It is the institutes of espionage, whether secret or open, that will activate these spies.

Those chiefs whose hostile intentions have been discovered by spies loyal to the king shall be made to live on the borders of the state, providing an opportunity to identify the spies of foreign kings.

CHAPTER XIII. PROTECTION OF PARTIES FOR OR AGAINST ONE'S OWN CAUSE IN ONE'S OWN STATE.

Having set up spies over his prime ministers (mahámátra), the king shall proceed to spy on both citizens and country people.

Classmate spies (satri) formed into opposing factions shall engage in debates in places of pilgrimage (tírtha), in assemblies, houses, corporations (púga), and among gatherings of people. One spy may begin by saying:

"This king is said to possess all the desirable qualities; he seems unfamiliar with tendencies that would cause him to oppress the citizens and country people with heavy fines and taxes."

In response to those who seem to agree with this statement, another spy may interrupt and say:

"People suffering under anarchy, as seen in the proverb of the large fish swallowing the small one (mátsyanyáyábhibhútah prajáh), first chose Manu, the Vaivasvata, as their king and allotted him one-sixth of the grains produced and one-tenth of the merchandise as sovereign dues. Supported by these payments, kings took on the responsibility of ensuring the safety and well-being (yogakshemavaháh) of their subjects and being accountable for their subjects' sins if they violated the principles of fair punishments and taxes. That is why even hermits give the king one-sixth of the grains they collect, believing it is a tax paid to the one who protects them. The king embodies both the duties of Indra (the rewarder) and Yama (the punisher), acting as a visible dispenser of punishments and rewards (heda-prasáda). Anyone who disrespects the king will also face divine punishments. Thus, kings should never be disrespected."

In this way, treacherous opponents of the sovereignty shall be silenced.

Spies shall also be aware of the rumors circulating within the state. Spies with shaved heads or braided hair shall investigate whether there is contentment or discontent among those who depend on the king's grains, cattle, and gold, among those who supply these to the king in both good and bad times, those who restrain a disaffected relative of the king or a rebellious district, and those who fend off an invading enemy or a wild tribe. The more content such people are, the more honor they shall receive; while those who are disaffected shall be won over by rewards or conciliation. Alternatively, dissension may be sown among them so that they alienate themselves from each other, from a neighboring enemy, from a wild tribe, or from a banished or imprisoned prince. If these measures fail, they may be employed in collecting fines and taxes, making them incur the displeasure of the people. Those who are overcome with enmity may be secretly punished or made to incur the anger of the entire country. Alternatively, by taking the sons and wives of such treacherous persons into state protection, they may be forced to live in mines, preventing them from offering shelter to enemies.

Those who are angry, greedy, fearful, or who despise the king serve as instruments for enemies. Spies disguised as astrologers and fortune-tellers shall ascertain the connections these individuals have with each other and with foreign kings.

Honors and rewards shall be given to those who are content, while those who are disaffected shall be brought around through conciliation, gifts, sowing dissension, or punishment.

Thus, in his own state, a wise king shall protect factions among his people, whether friendly or hostile, powerful or powerless, against the intrigues of foreign kings.

CHAPTER XIV. WINNING OVER FACTIONS FOR OR AGAINST AN ENEMY'S CAUSE IN AN ENEMY'S STATE.

The protection of parties for or against one's own cause in one's own state has been discussed. Now, similar measures concerning parties in a foreign state are to be addressed.

Those who are misled with false promises of large rewards; those whose party, although equally skillful as another in artistic work or in producing useful or profitable works, is overlooked in favor of their rival, who receives larger rewards; those who are oppressed by courtiers (Vallabhá-varuddháh); those who are invited only to be insulted; those who are harassed through banishment; those who, despite investing large sums of money, have failed in their undertakings; those who are prevented from exercising their rights or claiming their inheritance; those who have lost their rank and honors in government service; those who are marginalized by their own relatives; those whose women are violently assaulted; those who are imprisoned; those who are secretly punished; those who are warned of their wrongdoings; those whose property has been completely confiscated; those who have endured long imprisonment; and those whose relatives have been banished—these all belong to the group of provoked persons.

Those who have fallen into misfortune through their own misdeeds; those who are offended by the king; those whose sinful actions have been exposed; those who are fearful after seeing punishment given to someone guilty of the same offense; those whose lands have been confiscated; those whose rebellious nature has been suppressed by force; those who, as superintendents of government departments, have suddenly amassed great wealth; those who, as relatives of such wealthy individuals, aspire to inherit their fortune; those who are disliked by the king; and those who hate the king—all of these come under the group of alarmed persons.

He who is impoverished; he who has lost much wealth; he who is niggardly; he who is addicted to evil propensities; and he who is engaged in dangerous transactions—all these constitute the group of ambitious persons.

He who is self-sufficient; he who is fond of honors; he who is intolerant of his rival's honor; he who is esteemed low; he who is of a fiery spirit; he who is foolhardy, as well as he who is not content with what he has been enjoying—all these come under the group of haughty persons.

Of these, he who clings to a particular faction shall be so deluded by spies with shaved heads or braided hair as to believe that he is intriguing with that party. Partisans under provocation, for example, may be won over by saying, "Just as an elephant in rut, mounted by a driver under intoxication, tramples whatever it encounters, so this king, deprived of the eye of knowledge, blindly oppresses both citizens and country people with taxes and fines; it is possible to restrain him by setting up a rival elephant against him. Therefore, have the patience to wait."

Likewise, alarmed persons may be won over by telling them, "Just as a hidden snake strikes and emits venom over anything that frightens it, so this king, fearful of danger from you, will soon unleash his anger on you. So, it would be wise for you to seek safety elsewhere."

Similarly, ambitious persons may be persuaded by telling them, "Just as a cow raised by dog-keepers gives milk to the dogs but not to Bráhmans, so this king grants rewards to those without valor, foresight, eloquence, or bravery, but not to those of noble character.

Therefore, another king, who is capable of distinguishing men of worth, should be sought."

In like manner, haughty persons may be swayed by telling them, "Just as a water reservoir owned by Chándálas serves only the Chándálas and not others, so this low-born king grants his favor only to people of low birth, not to Aryas like you. Therefore, another king, who is capable of recognizing the differences between men, should be sought."

All these disaffected persons, once they have agreed to these proposals, may be bound under a solemn agreement (panakarmaná) to form a coalition with the spies to achieve their aims.

Likewise, friends of a foreign king may also be won over through persuasion and rewards, while implacable enemies may be brought around by sowing discord, by threats, or by pointing out the faults of their master.

CHAPTER XV. THE BUSINESS OF COUNCIL MEETING.

Having secured the loyalty of both local and foreign parties, both within his own and the enemy's state, the king shall proceed to consider administrative measures.

All kinds of administrative actions must be preceded by careful deliberation in a well-formed council. The discussions within the council must remain entirely secret, and the deliberations must be conducted in such a way that not even birds can witness them; for it is said that the secrecy of counsels was once betrayed by parrots, minas, dogs, and other low creatures of insignificant birth. Therefore, without ensuring sufficient safeguards against any potential leaks, the king should never enter into council deliberations.

Whoever reveals the content of these counsels shall be torn to pieces. The disclosure of secrets can be detected by observing changes in the behavior and expressions of envoys, ministers, and leaders. Changes in behavior are referred to as a change in attitude (ingitamanyathávrittih), and observation of facial expressions is known as reading countenance (ákritigrahanamákárah).

Strict secrecy regarding the council's discussions must be maintained, and vigilance must be exercised over the officers involved in these deliberations until the time to act on the decisions made in the council approaches.

Carelessness, intoxication, talking during sleep, love affairs, and other vices among council members are often the causes of the betrayal of secrets.

Those who are secretive by nature or feel disregarded may reveal counsels. Therefore, it is essential to take precautions against these dangers. The disclosure of secret matters benefits people other than the king and his officials.

"Hence," says Bháradvája, "the king should deliberate on secret matters alone; for ministers have their own confidants, and those confidants, in turn, have theirs. This chain of ministers tends to the leakage of secrets.

"Thus, no outsider should be aware of the king's plans. Only those directly involved in executing the plan should know of it, either when it begins or when it is completed."

"No deliberation," says Visáláksha, "made by a single person will be successful. The nature of the work a sovereign must undertake is to be understood by considering both visible and invisible factors. The ability to perceive what is not seen, to make conclusive decisions about what is visible, to clear up doubts in matters where two opinions are possible, and to infer the whole from seeing only a part—all this is possible only through ministers. Therefore, the king should deliberate with people of wide intellect.

He should not disregard anyone but listen to the opinions of all. A wise man should even make use of the sensible utterance of a child.

"This," says Parásara, "is about gathering the opinions of others, not about keeping counsels. He should ask his ministers for their opinion on a matter similar to the one he has in mind, saying, 'This is the situation; it happened in this way; what should be done if it turns out like this?' and he should act according to their decision. In this way, both the gathering of opinions and the maintenance of secrecy can be achieved."

"Not so," says Pisuna, "because when ministers are asked for their opinions about a distant task or an accomplished or unaccomplished work, they either approach it with indifference or offer half-hearted opinions. This is a significant flaw. Therefore, the king should consult only those people who are known to provide decisive opinions about the work for which he seeks advice. By doing so, he will secure both good advice and the secrecy of counsel."

"Not so," says Kautilya, "because this kind of advice-seeking is infinite and endless. The king should consult three or four ministers. Consultation with a single minister may not lead to any definite conclusion, especially in complicated matters. A single minister may act willfully and without restraint. When deliberating with two ministers, the king may be either overpowered by their combined action or endangered by their mutual dissension. However, with three or four ministers, he will avoid serious trouble and reach satisfactory results. With more than four ministers, reaching a decision becomes burdensome, and maintaining the secrecy of counsel becomes much more difficult. Depending on the situation, time, and nature of the work in question, the king may, as he sees fit, deliberate with one or two ministers, or even by himself.

The five essential elements of every council deliberation are: means to carry out the work, command over plenty of men and wealth, allocation of time and place, remedies against dangers, and final success."

The king may ask his ministers for their opinion either individually or collectively and evaluate their competence by examining the reasons they provide for their opinions.

He should not delay when the awaited opportunity arises, nor should he engage in lengthy consultations with those whose interests he plans to harm.

The school of Manu suggests that the assembly of ministers (mantriparishad) should consist of twelve members.

The school of Brihaspati proposes that it should consist of sixteen members.

The school of Usanas recommends that it should have twenty members.

However, Kautilya asserts that the assembly should consist of as many members as the needs of the kingdom require (yathásámarthyam).

These ministers must consider all matters concerning the interests of both the king and his enemies. They should initiate work that has yet to begin, complete what has been started, improve what has already been achieved, and ensure strict compliance with orders (niyogasampadam).

The king should supervise works alongside his close officers (ásannaih), and consult with those who are distant by sending written messages (patrasampreshanena).

Indra's assembly of ministers (mantriparishad) consists of a thousand sages. They are his eyes, which is why he is called "thousand-eyed" though he possesses only two eyes.

In emergencies, the king shall summon both his ministers and the assembly of ministers (mantrino mantriparishadam cha) to inform them of the situation. He shall act according to the majority's (bhúyishtháh) suggestion or follow the course of action that leads to success (káryasiddhikaram va) they recommend.

And while performing any task, none of his enemies (pare) should know his secret, but he shall know the vulnerabilities of his enemy. Like a tortoise retracting its limbs, he should withdraw any exposed actions.

Just as offerings of food made to ancestors by someone ignorant of the Vedas are unfit for wise men to eat, so too is a person unlearned in the sciences unfit to participate in council deliberations.

CHAPTER XVI. THE MISSION OF ENVOYS.

Whoever has succeeded as a councillor is an envoy.

Whoever possesses the qualifications of a minister is a chargé-d'affaires (nisrishtárthah).

Whoever possesses the same qualifications, but with one-quarter less, is an agent entrusted with a specific mission (parimitárthah).

Whoever possesses the same qualifications, but with one-half less, is a conveyer of royal writs (sásanaharah).

Having made excellent arrangements for transportation, conveyance, servants, and sustenance, the envoy shall embark on his mission, thinking: "The enemy shall be told this; the enemy (para) will respond like this; this shall be my reply; and this is how he shall be deceived."

The envoy shall form friendships with the enemy's officers, such as those in charge of wild tracts, boundaries, cities, and rural areas. He shall also compare the military posts, war resources, and fortresses of the enemy with those of his own master. He shall assess the size and area of the forts and the state, as well as the strongholds where valuables are stored and identify the assailable and unassailable points.

Once permission has been granted, he shall enter the enemy's capital and deliver the mission exactly as entrusted to him, even if it costs him his life.

A brightness in the tone, face, and eyes of the enemy; a respectful reception of the mission; inquiries about the health of friends; participation in discussions of virtues; being given a seat close to the throne; courteous treatment of the envoy; remembrance of friends; and a conclusion of the mission with satisfaction—all these are signs of the enemy's goodwill, while their absence signifies his displeasure.

In the case of a displeased enemy, he may be told: --

"Messengers are the mouthpieces of kings, not only of you but of all; therefore, messengers, who, even in the face of weapons raised against them, must deliver their mission exactly as they were entrusted, do not deserve death, even if they are outcasts. Where, then, is the justification for putting messengers of the Bráhman caste to death? This is the speech of another. The duty of messengers is to deliver that speech exactly."

Not carried away by the respect shown to him, the envoy shall remain there until he is permitted to leave. He shall not be intimidated by the enemy's power, shall strictly avoid women and liquor, and shall sleep alone. It is well known that the intentions of envoys are often discovered while they are asleep or under the influence of alcohol.

Through the help of spies disguised as ascetics, merchants, or their disciples, or through spies posing as physicians and heretics, or through those who receive salaries from two states (ubhayavétana), the envoy shall gather information about the intrigues among those loyal to his master, the conspiracies of hostile factions, and assess the people's loyalty or disloyalty to the enemy, as well as any vulnerable points.

If there is no possibility of directly engaging in such conversations (regarding the people's loyalty), he may attempt to gather such information by listening to the talk of beggars, intoxicated and insane people, or those babbling in their sleep. He may also observe signs made at places of pilgrimage and temples or decipher paintings and secret writings (chitra-gúdha-lékhya-samjñá-bhih).

Whatever information he gathers in this way, he shall verify through further intrigues.

He shall not refute the enemy's assessment of the elements of sovereignty in his own master's kingdom but shall simply respond with, "All is known to you." Nor shall he disclose the methods employed by his master to achieve a certain goal.

If he has not succeeded in his mission but is still detained, he shall consider the situation, pondering:

Whether the enemy, recognizing the danger my master faces, seeks to avoid his own peril; whether he intends to incite an enemy or a neighboring king against my master; whether he aims to stir up internal rebellion in my master's state or provoke a wild chief (átavika) against him; whether he seeks to destroy my master by employing a friend or a king whose domain borders my master's state (ákranda); whether he aims to prevent internal troubles in his own state or avoid a foreign invasion or incursions by wild tribes; whether he intends to delay the timing of my master's military expedition; whether he seeks to gather raw materials and merchandise, repair his fortifications, or recruit a powerful army; whether he waits for the right moment to fully train his own army; or whether he seeks an alliance to remedy the current contempt caused by his carelessness—what could be the reason for detaining me like this?

Based on his assessment, the envoy may choose to stay or depart as he sees fit, or he may demand a quick resolution of his mission.

Alternatively, after delivering an unfavorable message (sásana) to the enemy and feigning fear of imprisonment or death, he may return without permission; otherwise, he may face punishment.

The duties of an envoy (dúta) include the transmission of missions, the maintenance of treaties, the issuance of ultimatums (pratápa), gaining friends, executing intrigues, sowing discord among allies, assembling secret forces, secretly removing relatives or valuable items, gathering intelligence about the movements of spies, displaying bravery, breaking peace treaties, winning the favor of the enemy's envoy and officials.

The king shall employ his own envoys to carry out such tasks and guard himself against the mischief of foreign envoys by employing counter-envoys, spies, and visible and invisible watchmen.

CHAPTER XVII. PROTECTION OF PRINCES.

Protection of Princes

Having first secured his own personal safety from his wives and sons, the king can then ensure the security of his kingdom against both immediate enemies and foreign kings.

We shall discuss "Protection of Wives" in the section on "Duties toward the Harem."

From the time of the princes' birth, the king shall take special care of them.

"For," says Bháradvája, "princes, like crabs, have a notorious tendency to devour their begetter. When they lack filial affection, it is better to punish them in secret (upámsudandah)."

"This," says Visáláksha, "is cruelty, the destruction of fortune, and the extinction of the Kshatriya race. Therefore, it is better to keep the princes under guard in a designated place."

"This," says the school of Parásara, "is like the fear of a lurking snake (ahibhayam); for a prince may suspect that his father, fearful of danger, has confined him, and may attempt to destroy his father. Therefore, it is better to keep a prince under the custody of boundary guards or inside a fort."

"This," says Pisuna, "is akin to the fear of a wolf among a flock of sheep (aurabhrakam bhayam); for after realizing the reason for his confinement, the prince may ally with the boundary guards against his father. Therefore, it is better to send him to a fort belonging to a foreign king far away from his own state."

"This," says Kaunapadanta, "is like the position of a calf (vatsasthánam); just as a man milks a cow with the help of its calf, so the foreign king may exploit the prince's father. Therefore, it is better to have the prince live with his maternal relatives."

"This," says Vátavyádhi, "is akin to the position of a flag (dhvajasthánamétat); just as in the case of Aditi and Kausika, the prince's maternal relatives may use him as a banner and continue to beg favors. Therefore, it is better to let princes dissipate their lives in sensual pleasures (grámyadharma), as indulgent sons do not oppose their permissive father."

"This," says Kautilya, "is a living death; for no sooner is a royal family with a prince or princes given to dissipation attacked than it collapses, like wood infested with worms. Therefore, when the queen reaches the age favorable for conception, priests shall offer the necessary oblations to Indra and Brihaspati. When she becomes pregnant, the king shall observe the instructions of midwifery concerning gestation and delivery. After the birth, the priests shall perform the prescribed purification ceremonies. When the prince reaches the proper age, experts shall train him under the correct discipline."

"Any one of the classmate spies," say the Ambhíyas (politicians), "may lure the prince towards hunting, gambling, liquor, and women, and provoke him to rebel against his father and seize control of the kingdom. Another spy, however, shall prevent him from committing such acts."

"There can be," says Kautilya, "no greater crime or sin than corrupting an innocent mind; just as a fresh object is stained by whatever it comes into contact with, so a young prince with a fresh mind is inclined to accept everything he is told as a legitimate teaching. Therefore, he should only be taught about righteousness and wealth (artha), not unrighteousness or non-wealth. Classmate spies should be so courteous towards him as to say, 'We are yours.' When, under the influence of youth, he turns his attention to women, impure women disguised as Aryas shall terrify him in the night and in lonely places. If he indulges in liquor, he shall be frightened by making him drink liquor adulterated with narcotics (yógapána). When fond of gambling, spies disguised as fraudulent gamblers shall terrify him. If he enjoys hunting, he shall be scared by spies posing as highway robbers. And when he desires to rebel against his father, he shall, under the pretense of compliance, be gradually dissuaded from such actions by being told: 'A king is not made by mere desire; failure in your attempt will bring your death, and success will lead you to hell, causing the people to grieve (for your father) and condemn you, the only clod (ekalóshtavadhascha).'"

When a king has an only son, who is either indifferent to worldly pleasures or is his favored child, the king may keep him under restraint. If the king has several sons, he may send some of them to places where there is no heir apparent, nor any child recently born or still in the womb.

If a prince possesses good and friendly qualities, he may be made the commander-in-chief or appointed as the heir apparent.

Sons are of three kinds: those of sharp intelligence, those of stagnant intelligence, and those of a perverted mind.

Whoever diligently practices what he has been taught regarding righteousness and wealth is of sharp intelligence. Whoever does not put into practice the good teachings he has received is of stagnant intelligence. And whoever gets entangled in dangers and despises righteousness and wealth is of a perverted mind.

If a king has an only son of the last type, efforts should be made to produce another son; or sons may be begotten through his daughters.

When a king is too old or ill to beget sons, he may appoint a maternal relative or a blood relative (kulya) of his, or a neighboring king of good and friendly qualities, to "sow the seed in his field" (kshétrebíjam, i.e., to beget a son with his wife).

But a wicked and only son shall never be placed on the royal throne.

A royal father, who serves as the only support for many people, should be favorably inclined towards his son. Except in times of danger, sovereignty falling to the eldest son is always respected. Sometimes, however, sovereignty may belong to a clan; for the corporation of clans, invincible in nature and free from the chaos of anarchy, can maintain a permanent existence on earth.

CHAPTER XVIII. THE CONDUCT OF A PRINCE KEPT UNDER RESTRAINT AND THE TREATMENT OF A RESTRAINED PRINCE.

A prince, though subjected to difficulties and assigned an unfair task, shall still loyally follow his father unless the task threatens his life, enrages the people, or causes other serious calamities. If he is given a noble or beneficial duty, he shall strive to gain the favor of the superintendent in charge of the work, complete the task with better results than expected, and present his father with both the expected profits from the work and any excess profit due to his skill. If, despite this, the king remains displeased with him and shows undue favor to another prince or other wives, the prince may request permission from the king to retire to a forest life.

If the prince fears imprisonment or death, he may seek refuge with a neighboring king known for being righteous, charitable, truthful, and not cunning, but also one who welcomes and respects guests of good character. Living under such a king's protection, he can gather men and money, establish marriage ties with influential individuals, form alliances with wild tribes, and win over factions in his father's state.

Alternatively, traveling alone, he may earn his livelihood by working in gold or ruby mines, or by crafting gold and silver ornaments or other trade goods. By forming close connections with heretics (páshanda), wealthy widows, or merchants engaged in ocean trade, he may, through the use of poison (madanarasa), rob them of their wealth and the wealth of the gods, except when such wealth is reserved for Bráhmans learned in the Vedas. He may also adopt measures used to capture villages from a foreign king. Or he may move against his father with the help of his mother's servants.

The prince, disguising himself as a painter, carpenter, court-bard, physician, buffoon, or heretic, and assisted by spies similarly disguised, may seize an opportunity to present himself armed with weapons and poison before the king, declaring: "I am the heir-apparent; it is not fitting that you alone enjoy the kingdom, which is meant for both of us, or which others rightly desire to share. I should not be excluded simply by being given double the subsistence and salary."

These are the measures that a prince under restraint might undertake.

Spies or his mother, whether natural or adoptive, may reconcile a restrained heir-apparent and bring him back to court.

Alternatively, secret emissaries armed with weapons and poison may kill a prince who has been abandoned. If the prince has not been abandoned, he may be captured at night by women prepared for the task, or by the use of liquor, or during a hunting expedition, and brought back to court.

Once brought back, the king may appease the prince with a promise of sovereignty after the king's death and keep him under guard in a designated place. If the king has many sons, a rebellious prince may be banished.

CHAPTER XIX. THE DUTIES OF A KING.

If a king is energetic, his subjects will also be energetic. If he is reckless, not only will they become reckless, but they will also undermine his efforts. Furthermore, a reckless king will easily fall into the hands of his enemies. Therefore, the king must always remain vigilant.

He shall divide both day and night into eight nálikas (1½ hours each), or according to the length of the shadow cast by a gnomon standing in the sun: a shadow of three purushás (36 angulás or inches), one purushá (12 inches), four angulás (4 inches), and no shadow, indicating midday, are the four divisions of the forenoon; the same divisions (in reverse order) are used for the afternoon.

Of these divisions, during the first one-eighth part of the day, the king shall post watchmen and attend to accounts of receipts and expenditures; during the second part, he shall look after the affairs of both the citizens and the rural population; during the third part, he shall bathe, dine, and study; during the fourth part, he shall receive revenue in gold (hiranya) and manage the appointments of superintendents; during the fifth part, he shall correspond by writs (patrasampreshanena) with his ministers and receive secret information from his spies; during the sixth part, he may engage in his favorite pastimes or personal contemplation; during the seventh part, he shall supervise elephants, horses, chariots, and infantry; and during the eighth part, he shall discuss military operations with his commander-in-chief.

At the close of the day, he shall perform the evening prayer (sandhya).

During the first one-eighth part of the night, he shall receive secret emissaries; during the second part, he shall bathe, have supper, and study; during the third part, he shall enter the bedchamber to the sound of trumpets and sleep during the fourth and fifth parts; awakened by the sound of trumpets during the sixth part, he shall recall to mind the teachings of the sciences and his duties for the day; during the seventh part, he shall consider administrative matters and dispatch spies; and during the eighth part of the night, he shall receive blessings from sacrificial priests, teachers, and the high priest. Afterward, he shall meet his physician, chief cook, and astrologer, and salute a cow with its calf and a bull by circumambulating around them before entering his court.

Or, according to his capacity, the king may modify the timetable and attend to his duties accordingly.

When in the court, he shall never keep petitioners waiting at the door, for if a king becomes inaccessible to his people and delegates his responsibilities to immediate officers, it is certain to create confusion in business, cause public dissatisfaction, and make him vulnerable to his enemies.

Therefore, he shall personally attend to the matters of the gods, heretics, Bráhmans learned in the Vedas, cattle, sacred places, minors, the elderly, the afflicted, the helpless, and women—each in the order of importance or according to the urgency of the matter.

He shall address urgent matters immediately and never delay them, for when postponed, they may become too difficult or impossible to resolve.

Seated in the room where the sacred fire is kept, the king shall attend to the concerns of physicians and ascetics practicing austerities, doing so in the presence of his high priest and teacher and after offering preliminary salutations to the petitioners.

Accompanied by those proficient in the three sciences (trividya)—but never alone, lest the petitioners be offended—he shall consider the matters of those practicing austerities, as well as those knowledgeable in witchcraft and Yóga.

For a king, his religious vow is his readiness for action; his performance of duties is his sacrifice; giving equal attention to all is his offering of fees and ablution towards consecration.

The happiness of his subjects is his happiness; their welfare is his welfare. He shall not consider what pleases him personally as good, but rather what pleases his subjects.

Therefore, the king shall always be active and diligent in his duties; the root of wealth is activity, and the root of misfortune is its opposite.

Without activity, current and future acquisitions will be lost; through activity, he can achieve both his desired goals and abundant wealth.

CHAPTER XX. DUTY TOWARDS THE HAREM.

On a site naturally best suited for the purpose, the king shall construct his harem, consisting of many compartments, one within another, surrounded by a parapet and a ditch, and secured with a door.

He shall build his own residential palace following the model of his treasury-house; or he may have his residence in the center of the delusive chamber (móhanagriha), which is equipped with secret passages built into the walls; or in an underground chamber adorned with figures of goddesses and altars (chaitya) carved into the wooden door-frame, with multiple underground exits. Another option is an upper story with a hidden staircase inside the wall and an escape passage concealed in a hollow pillar, with the entire structure designed with mechanical contrivances so it can collapse when needed.

If he fears danger from his own classmates (sahádhyáyi), such contrivances and safeguards against peril may be employed during times of danger or at other times, as he deems necessary.

No other kind of fire can burn the harem that is thrice circumambulated from right to left by a fire of human origin (manushénágnina); no other fire can be kindled there. Fire also cannot harm a harem whose walls are made of mud mixed with ashes from lightning and soaked in hail-water (karaka-vári).

Poisonous snakes will not enter buildings protected by plants like Jívanti (Fæderia Fœtida), svéta (Aconitum Ferox), mushkakapushpa (?), and vandáka (Epidendrum Tesselatum), and branches of péjáta (?) and asvattha (Ficus Religiosa).

Cats, peacocks, mongooses, and spotted deer will eat snakes. Parrots, minas (sárika), and Malabar birds (bhringarája) will shriek when they detect the smell of snake venom. The heron (crauncha) faints in the presence of poison, the pheasant (jívanjívaka) feels distress, the young cuckoo (mattakókila) dies, and the eyes of the partridge (chakóra) turn red. Thus, precautions against fire and poison shall be taken.

On one side, behind the harem, there shall be compartments for the women, equipped with all necessary medicines for midwifery and illnesses, as well as well-known pot-herbs (prakhyátasamsthávriksha) and a water reservoir. Outside these compartments shall be the residences of princes and princesses. In front of these buildings will be the toilet ground (alankára bhúmih), the council ground (mantrabhúmib), the court, and the offices of the heir-apparent and superintendents.

Between the compartments, the army under the command of the officer in charge of the harem shall be stationed for security.

When inside the harem, the king shall only see the queen after her personal purity has been assured by an old maid-servant. He shall not touch any woman unless her purity is verified, for many dangers have arisen from within the queen's chambers. For example, King

Bhadrasena was slain by his own brother who hid in the queen's chamber; King Kárusa was killed by his son who hid under his mother's bed; Queen Kásirája poisoned her king by mixing poison with fried rice disguised as honey; Queen Vairantya killed her king using an anklet coated with poison; Queen Sauvíra murdered her king with a gem from her waist, smeared with poison; Queen Jálútha killed her king with a looking glass tainted with poison; and Queen Vidúratha killed her king with a weapon concealed in her hair.

Therefore, the king must always be cautious to avoid such hidden dangers. He shall prevent his wives from associating with ascetics, whether with shaved heads or braided hair, buffoons, and outside prostitutes (dási). Women of high birth should not have the opportunity to see his wives, except for the designated midwives.

Prostitutes (rúpájíva), attending the harem, must always maintain personal cleanliness by bathing frequently, and wear fresh garments and ornaments.

Eighty men and fifty women disguised as fathers, mothers, elderly persons, and eunuchs shall oversee the purity and conduct within the harem. They shall ensure that the affairs of the harem are managed in a way that brings happiness to the king.

Each person in the harem must live in the area assigned to them and shall never move into the spaces assigned to others. No one in the harem shall associate with any outsiders at any time.

The movement of all goods, whether entering or leaving the harem, shall be strictly controlled. After careful examination, these items may only reach their destination—inside or outside the harem—based on the seal-mark (mudrá) provided.

CHAPTER XXI. PERSONAL SAFETY.

On rising from bed, the king shall be greeted by groups of women armed with bows. In the second compartment, he shall be received by the Kanchuki (the one who presents the king's coat), the Ushnisi (the one who presents the king's head-dress), elderly attendants, and other members of the harem.

In the third compartment, he shall be greeted by crooked and dwarfish persons, and in the fourth compartment, by prime ministers, kinsmen, and doorkeepers holding barbed missiles in their hands.

The king shall employ as his personal attendants those whose fathers and grandfathers had served the royal family, those who are closely related to the king, those who are well-trained and loyal, and those who have provided distinguished service.

Foreigners, those who have not earned rewards or honor through good service, and even natives who are known to be engaged in inimical activities shall not be part of the king's bodyguard or the troops of the officers in charge of the harem.

In a well-guarded area, the head cook (máhánasika) shall oversee the preparation of a variety of relishing dishes. The king shall partake of these freshly prepared dishes only after first offering them as an oblation to the fire and then to birds.

The presence of poison in the dish can be inferred if the flame and smoke from the fire turn blue and crackle, or if the birds (that eat the offering) die. Other signs include: when the steam rising from cooked rice has the color of a peacock's neck and appears suddenly cool; when vegetables show an unnatural color, are watery, hardened, and seem to have dried suddenly, with blackish foam layers, lacking their natural smell, touch, and taste; when utensils reflect more or less light than usual and have a foam layer at the edges; when liquids develop surface streaks; when milk has a bluish streak in the center of its surface; when liquor or water shows reddish streaks; when curd shows black or dark streaks, and honey shows white streaks; when watery substances seem overcooked, appear blue and swollen; when dry substances shrink and change color; when hard things seem soft and soft things become hard; when tiny creatures near the dishes die; when carpets and curtains show black circular spots with loose threads and hair falling off; and when metallic vessels set with gems become tarnished as though roasted, losing their polish, color, shine, and softness to the touch— poison should be suspected in all these cases.

As for the person who has administered poison, the telltale signs include a dry and parched mouth, hesitation in speech, excessive sweating, frequent yawning, intense bodily tremors, frequent stumbling, evasion in conversation, careless work, and reluctance to remain in the place assigned to them.

Thus, physicians and experts skilled in detecting poison must always attend to the king.

After taking medicine from the storeroom, the purity of which has been confirmed through experimentation, and after both the physician, the decoctioner (páchaka), and the purveyor (póshaka) have tasted it themselves, the physician shall deliver the medicine to the king. The same procedure applies to liquor and other beverages.

Servants in charge of clothing and toiletries, after having bathed and cleaned themselves and dressed in freshly washed garments, shall provide the king with clothing and toiletries that have been sealed and received from the officer in charge of the harem.

Prostitutes shall be responsible for duties in the bathhouse, as shampooers, bedding-room attendants, washermen, and garland-makers. When presenting water, scents, fragrant powders, clothing, and garlands to the king, the servants, along with the prostitutes, must first touch these items with their eyes, arms, and breasts to ensure they are safe.

This same rule applies to anything received from someone outside the palace.

Musicians shall entertain the king only with performances that do not involve weapons, fire, or poison. Musical instruments, as well as the ornaments of horses, chariots, and elephants, must always be kept within the confines of the harem.

The king shall mount chariots or beasts of burden only after they have first been mounted by his hereditary driver or rider.

He shall board a boat only when it is piloted by a trustworthy sailor and attached to a second boat for safety. He shall never sail on a ship that has previously been weatherbeaten, and even when on a good ship, his army shall stand guard on the shore.

He shall enter water only when it is free from large fish (matsya) and crocodiles. He shall wander in forests only if they are cleared of snakes and crocodiles (gráha).

To gain proficiency in shooting arrows at moving targets, the king shall engage in sports in forests that have been cleared by hunters and hound-keepers of the dangers of highway robbers, snakes, and enemies.

He shall give audiences to saints and ascetics only when he is attended by a trustworthy bodyguard armed with weapons. When receiving envoys from foreign states, he shall be surrounded by his assembly of ministers.

When inspecting his army, he shall be attired in military dress and mount a horse, chariot, or elephant to review his troops prepared in military formation.

On occasions of entering or leaving the capital, the king's road shall be guarded on both sides by staff-bearers and cleared of armed persons, ascetics, and the crippled (vyanga).

He shall only attend festivals, fairs (yátra), processions, or sacrificial performances when these events are policed by bands of 'The Ten Communities' (dasavargikadhishthitáni).

Just as the king ensures the personal safety of others through the use of spies, a wise king shall also take care to secure his own person from external dangers.

Book 2

CHAPTER I. FORMATION OF VILLAGES.

Either by encouraging foreigners to immigrate (paradesapravåhanena) or by reducing the excessive population from the densely populated areas of his own kingdom (svadésábhishyandavámanéna vá), the king may establish new villages either on uninhabited sites or on the ruins of old settlements (bhútapúrvama vá).

Villages shall be composed of no fewer than one hundred families and no more than five hundred families of agricultural people from the súdra caste. The boundaries of these villages shall extend as far as one or two krósas (2250 yards or more) and be capable of providing mutual protection. Boundaries may be marked by natural features like rivers, mountains, forests, bulbous plants (grishti), caves, artificial constructions (sétubandha), or trees such as the sálmali (silk cotton tree), samí (Acacia Suma), and kshíravriksha (milky trees).

In the center of eight hundred villages, a stháníya (a fortress) shall be constructed; in the center of four hundred villages, a drónamukha; in the center of two hundred villages, a khárvátika; and a sangrahana in the midst of a group of ten villages.

At the borders of the kingdom, forts shall be built and manned by boundary-guards (antapála), whose duty will be to control access into the kingdom. The interior of the kingdom shall be secured by trap-keepers (vágurika), archers (sábara), hunters (pulinda), chandálas, and wild tribes (aranyachára).

Those who perform sacrifices (ritvik), spiritual guides, priests, and those learned in the Vedas shall be granted Brahmadaya lands that yield sufficient produce and are exempt from taxes and fines (adandkaráni).

Superintendents, accountants, gopas (village heads), sthánikas (regional officers), veterinary surgeons (Aníkastha), physicians, horse trainers, and messengers shall also be endowed with lands, but they shall not have the right to sell or mortgage these lands.

Prepared lands shall be given to taxpayers (karada) for their lifetime use (ekapurushikáni).

Lands that are being prepared for cultivation shall not be taken away from those who are working on them.

Lands may be confiscated from those who fail to cultivate them properly and given to others; or they may be cultivated by village laborers (grámabhritaka) and traders (vaidehaka) to prevent the original owners from paying less than they should to the government. If cultivators pay their taxes without difficulty, they may be favorably provided with grains, cattle, and money.

The king shall bestow on cultivators only such favor and tax remission (anugrahaparihárau) as will increase the treasury, avoiding any measures that might deplete it.

A king with a depleted treasury will drain the vitality of both the citizens and rural population. In the case of opening new settlements or during other emergencies, remissions of taxes may be granted.

He shall treat with fatherly kindness those who have passed the period of tax remission.

The king shall engage in mining operations and manufacturing, exploit timber and elephant forests, facilitate cattle breeding and commerce, construct roads for land and water traffic, and establish market towns (panyapattana).

He shall also build reservoirs (sétu) filled with either perennial water or water from another source. Alternatively, he may provide sites, roads, timber, and other necessary materials for those who wish to construct reservoirs on their own. The same applies to the construction of places of pilgrimage (punyasthána) and groves.

Anyone who abstains from cooperative construction (sambhúya setubhandhát) must send his servants and bullocks to carry out the work, contribute to the expenses, but will have no claim to the profits.

The king shall exercise his ownership rights (swámyam) over fishing, ferrying, and trading in vegetables (haritapanya) in reservoirs or lakes (sétushu).

Those who neglect the rightful claims of their slaves (dása), hirelings (áhitaka), and relatives shall be reminded of their duties.

The king shall provide for the maintenance of orphans (bála), the elderly, the infirm, the afflicted, and the helpless. He shall also offer support to helpless pregnant women and provide for the care of the children they give birth to.

Elders among the villagers shall be responsible for managing and improving the property of bereaved minors until they reach maturity; this applies to the property of Gods as well.

If a capable person, other than an apostate (patita) or a mother, neglects to provide for the maintenance of his or her child, spouse, mother, father, minor brothers or sisters, or widowed girls (kanyá vidhaváscha), that person shall be punished with a fine of twelve panas.

If a person adopts asceticism without making provisions for the maintenance of his wife and sons, he shall be punished with the first amercement. Similarly, anyone who converts a woman to asceticism (pravrájayatah) without providing for her will be fined.

Only those who have passed the age of reproduction may become ascetics after distributing their property among their sons. If they fail to do so, they will be punished.

No ascetic other than a vánaprastha (forest hermit), no community other than local communities (sajátádanyassanghah), and no guilds except for local cooperative guilds (sámutthávViká-danyassamayánubandhah) shall be allowed entry into the kingdom's villages. Furthermore, villages shall not have buildings (sáláh) intended for sports and entertainment.

For the sake of maintaining peace and avoiding disturbances, actors, dancers, singers, drummers, buffoons (vágjívana), and bards (kusílava) shall not interfere with the daily work of the villagers, nor shall they attempt to exploit the villagers by seeking money, free labor, commodities, grains, or liquids in abundance. Helpless villagers are always dependent on their fields and must not be disturbed.

The king shall refrain from taking possession of any territory that is prone to invasions by enemies and wild tribes or that suffers from frequent famines and pestilence. He shall also avoid indulging in expensive and lavish sports.

The king must protect agriculture from oppressive fines, forced labor, and excessive taxes (dandavishtikarábádhaih), and he shall safeguard herds of cattle from thieves, tigers, poisonous creatures, and cattle diseases.

Furthermore, he shall ensure that roads are free from the interference of courtiers (vallabha), workmen (kármika), robbers, and boundary guards. He must also prevent roads from being damaged by herds of cattle.

In this way, the king shall not only maintain and repair the timber and elephant forests, buildings, and mines established in the past but also create new ones.

CHAPTER II. DIVISION OF LAND.

The king shall make provision for pasture grounds on uncultivable lands.

Bráhmans shall be provided with forests for the cultivation of sóma, for religious learning, and for the performance of penance. Such forests shall be made safe from dangers posed by both animate and inanimate objects, and they shall be named after the tribal lineage (gótra) of the Bráhmans residing within them.

A forest as large as the aforementioned, with only one entrance, made inaccessible by surrounding ditches, filled with plantations of delicious fruit trees, bushes, bowers, and thornless trees, with a large lake full of water and harmless animals, as well as tigers (vyála), beasts of prey (márgáyuka), male and female elephants, young elephants, and bisons—all with their claws and teeth removed—shall be established for the king's sports.

At the extreme border of the kingdom or in another suitable location, another game forest, containing game animals and open to all, shall be created. In order to obtain all types of forest produce, as mentioned elsewhere, one or several forests shall be specially designated for this purpose.

Manufactories for preparing goods from forest produce shall also be established.

Wild tracts of land shall be separated from timber forests. Elephant forests shall be created at the farthest limits of the kingdom, separated from wild areas.

The superintendent of forests, along with his team of forest guards, shall not only maintain the forests but also be aware of all the entrance and exit routes for forests that are mountainous, swampy, or contain rivers or lakes.

Anyone who kills an elephant shall be sentenced to death.

Anyone who brings in the tusks of an elephant that has died from natural causes shall be rewarded with four-and-a-half panas.

The guards of the elephant forests, along with elephant keepers, those who chain the legs of elephants, boundary guards, forest-dwellers, and those who nurse elephants, shall track herds of elephants by following the trails of urine and dung left by elephants, and by observing forest paths covered by branches of Bhallátaki (Semicarpus Anacardium). They will also look for places where elephants have slept or sat, left droppings, or destroyed the banks of rivers or lakes. They shall determine whether these signs come from herds of elephants, a single roaming elephant, a stray elephant, a leader of herds, a tusker, a rogue elephant, an elephant in rut, a young elephant, or an elephant that has escaped from captivity.

Experts in catching elephants shall follow the instructions of the elephant doctor (aníkastha) and capture elephants that possess auspicious characteristics and a good temperament.

The victory of kings in battle primarily depends on elephants, as their large size enables them to destroy the enemy's army formations, fortifications, and encampments, as well as to carry out dangerous tasks.

Elephants bred in regions such as Kálinga, Anga, Karúsa, and the East are considered the best. Those from Dasárna and western regions are of middle quality, while those from Sauráshtra and Panchajana regions are of lower quality. However, the strength and energy of all elephants can be improved through proper training.

CHAPTER III. CONSTRUCTION OF FORTS

On all four sides of the kingdom's boundaries, defensive fortifications against enemy attacks in times of war shall be constructed in areas best suited for the purpose: a water fortification (audaka), such as an island in the middle of a river or a plain surrounded by lower ground; a mountainous fortification (párvata), such as a rocky area or a cave; a desert fortification (dhánvana), such as a wild tract devoid of water and overgrown with thickets in barren soil; or a forest fortification (vanadurga) filled with wagtails (khajana), water, and dense thickets.

Of these, water and mountain fortifications are best suited for defending populous centers, while desert and forest fortifications are suited for habitation in wilderness areas (atavísthánam).

Alternatively, with preparations ready for retreat, the king may establish his fortified capital (sthán/ya) as the center of his sovereignty (samudayásthánam) in the middle of his kingdom. This capital should be located in a naturally strategic area, such as the bank of a river confluence, a deep pool of perennial water, or near a lake or tank. The fort may be circular, rectangular, or square in shape, surrounded by an artificial water canal and connected to both land and water routes.

Around this fort, three ditches, spaced one danda (6 ft.) apart from each other, shall be dug. These ditches shall be fourteen, twelve, and ten dandas wide, respectively, and their depth shall be one-quarter to one-half of their width. The ditches shall be square at the bottom, one-third as wide as the top, with sides constructed of stones or bricks. These ditches shall be filled with perennial flowing water or water drawn from another source, and they shall contain crocodiles and lotus plants.

At a distance of four dandas (24 ft.) from the innermost ditch, a rampart six dandas high and twice as wide shall be constructed by heaping up mud. The rampart shall be square at the bottom, oval in the center, and pressed down by the trampling of elephants and bulls. It shall be planted with thorny and poisonous bushes. Any gaps in the rampart shall be filled with fresh earth.

Above the rampart, parapets, either in odd or even numbers, with an intermediate space of 12 to 24 hastas between them, shall be built of bricks and raised to a height twice their breadth.

The passage for chariots shall be constructed from palm tree trunks or broad and thick slabs of stone, with spheres resembling the heads of monkeys carved on their surface, but never from wood, as wood is vulnerable to fire.

Square towers, uniform in shape and equipped with moveable staircases or ladders equal to their height, shall also be built.

In the 30 danda space between two towers, there shall be a broad street divided into two compartments, covered with a roof, and two and a half times as long as it is wide.

Between the towers and the broad street, an Indrakósa shall be constructed, which is made of wooden planks providing seating for three archers.

A road for the gods shall also be built, measuring two hastas wide inside (perhaps within the towers), four times as wide on the sides, and eight hastas along the parapet.

Paths (chárya) to ascend the parapet, as wide as one danda (6 feet) or two, shall also be constructed.

In an unassailable section of the rampart, a passage for escape (pradhávitikám) and an exit door (nishkuradwáram) shall be made.

Outside the rampart, movement passages shall be blocked by forming various obstacles, such as a knee-breaker (jánubhanjaní), tridents, mounds of earth, pits, wreaths of thorns, tools resembling the tail of a snake, palm leaf, triangle, dog's teeth, rods, ditches filled with thorns and covered with sand, frying pans, and water pools.

On both sides of the rampart, circular holes with a diameter of one and a half dandas shall be made, and an entrance gate, one-sixth as wide as the street, shall be fixed.

A square (chaturásra) shall be formed by successively adding one danda up to eight dandas, starting from five, or in the ratio of one-sixth the length up to one-eighth.

The rise in elevation (talotsedhah) shall be formed by adding one hasta at a time, starting from 15 hastas up to 18 hastas.

In constructing a pillar, six parts of it shall form its visible height, with twice as much (12 parts) buried in the ground, and one-fourth of the height reserved for its capital.

For the first floor, five parts shall be allocated for the formation of a hall (sálá), a well, and a boundary house; two-tenths of the floor space shall be used for two platforms opposite each other (pratimanchau). The upper storey shall be twice as high as its width, and carvings of images shall adorn it. The top-most storey shall be half or three-fourths as wide as the first floor. The side walls shall be built of bricks, and on the left side, a staircase shall circumambulate from left to right, while on the right side, a secret staircase hidden within the wall shall be constructed. A top-support with ornamental arches (toranasirah) shall extend two hastas outward. Two door panels shall each occupy three-fourths of the door space. Two sets of crossbars (parigha) shall be used to fasten the door, and an iron bolt (indrakila) the length of an aratni (24 angulas) shall secure it. A boundary gate (ánidváram) shall be five hastas wide, and four beams shall be used to secure the door against elephants. Turrets (hastinakha), raised to the height of a man's face, may be either movable or fixed, or constructed of earth in areas without water.

A turret above the gate, beginning from the top of the parapet, shall be constructed, with its front resembling an alligator for three-fourths of its height.

In the center of the parapets, a deep lotus pool shall be constructed, as well as a rectangular building with four compartments, one inside the other. A residence for the Goddess Kumiri (Kumárípuram) shall be built, with its external area one-and-a-half times the size of the innermost room. A circular building with an archway shall also be constructed. According to the space and materials available, canals (kulyá) shall be built to store weapons, and they shall be three times as long as they are broad.

These canals shall hold stones, spades (kuddála), axes (kuthári), various staffs, cudgels (musrinthi), hammers (mudgara), clubs, discus, machines (yantra), and weapons capable of killing a hundred men at once (sataghni). They shall also store spears, tridents, bamboo sticks with iron-pointed edges, camel-necked weapons, explosives (agnisamyógas), and whatever other weapons can be designed and created from the available materials.

CHAPTER IV. BUILDINGS WITHIN THE FORT.

The demarcation of the ground inside the fort shall begin by laying out three royal roads running from west to east and three from south to north.

The fort shall have twelve gates, each provided with both land and water access, kept secret.

Chariot roads, royal roads, and roads leading to drónamukha, stháníya, rural areas, and pasture grounds shall each be four dandas (24 feet) in width.

Roads leading to sayóníya (?), military stations (vyúha), burial or cremation grounds, and villages shall be eight dandas in width.

Roads to gardens, groves, and forests shall be four dandas wide.

Roads leading to elephant forests shall be two dandas wide.

Chariot roads shall measure five aratnis (7½ feet). Roads for cattle shall measure four aratnis, and roads for smaller quadrupeds and men shall measure two aratnis.

Royal buildings shall be constructed on strong, stable ground.

In the midst of the houses of people from all four castes, and to the north from the center of the ground inside the fort, the king's palace shall be built, facing either north or east, occupying one-ninth of the total area inside the fort, as described elsewhere (Chapter XX, Book I).

The royal teachers, priests, sacrificial grounds, water reservoir, and ministers shall be located to the east by north of the palace.

The royal kitchen, elephant stables, and the storehouse shall be situated to the east by south.

On the eastern side of the fort, merchants dealing in scents, garlands, grains, and liquids, along with expert artisans and people of the Kshatriya caste, shall have their residences.

The treasury, the accountant's office, and various manufacturing sites (karmanishadyáscha) shall be located south by east.

The storehouse for forest produce and the arsenal shall be situated south by west.

To the south of the city, the superintendents of the city, commerce, manufactories, and the army shall live, as well as those who trade in cooked rice, liquor, and meat, along with prostitutes, musicians, and the people of the Vaisya caste.

To the west by south, stables for asses, camels, and working horses shall be located.

To the west by north, stables for conveyances and chariots shall be situated.

To the west, artisans manufacturing worsted threads, cotton threads, bamboo mats, skins, armor, weapons, and gloves, as well as the people of the Súdra caste, shall have their dwellings.

To the north by west, shops and hospitals shall be established.

To the north by east, the treasury and stables for cows and horses shall be located.

To the north, the royal tutelary deity of the city, ironsmiths, artisans working on precious stones, and Bráhmans shall reside.

In various corners of the city, guilds and corporations of workmen shall have their residences.

At the center of the city, temples or apartments for gods such as Aparájita, Apratihata, Jayanta, Vaijayanta, Siva, Vaisravana, Asvina (divine physicians), and the honorable liquor house (Srí-madiragriham) shall be situated.

In the corners, the guardian deities of the land shall be appropriately installed.

Likewise, the principal gates—Bráhma, Aindra, Yámya, and Sainápatya—shall be constructed; and at a distance of 100 bows (dhanus = 108 angulas) from the ditch (on the counterscarp side), places of worship, pilgrimage, groves, and buildings shall be constructed.

Guardian deities for all quarters shall also be installed in their respective quarters.

Burial or cremation grounds shall be situated either to the north or east, but the burial grounds for the highest caste people shall be located to the south of the city.

Violation of this rule shall result in the first amercement as punishment.

Heretics and Chandálas shall live beyond the burial grounds.

Families of workmen shall be provided with sites suitable to their occupation and fieldwork. In addition to working in flower gardens, fruit gardens, vegetable gardens, and paddy fields assigned to them, these families shall gather grains and merchandise in abundance, as authorized.

There shall be one water well for every ten houses.

Oils, grains, sugar, salt, medicinal articles, dried or fresh vegetables, meadow grass, dried meat, haystacks, firewood, metals, skins, charcoal, tendons (snáyu), poison, horns, bamboo, fibrous garments, strong timber, weapons, armor, and stones shall also be stored in the fort in such quantities that they can last for years without causing any shortage. Old supplies shall be replaced with new ones when fresh stock is received.

Elephants, cavalry, chariots, and infantry shall each be commanded by several chiefs, as having many chiefs ensures they remain fearful of betrayal from one another and are less vulnerable to enemy plots and intrigue.

The same principle shall apply to the appointment of boundary guards and those responsible for repairing fortifications.

People dangerous to the safety of cities and countries (báhirikas) shall never be allowed to reside in forts. They may either be relocated to rural areas or forced to pay taxes.

CHAPTER V. THE DUTIES OF THE CHAMBERLAIN.

The Chamberlain (sannidhátá, meaning one who always attends upon the king) shall oversee the construction of the treasury house, trading house, grain storehouse, forest produce storehouse, armory, and jail.

He shall dig a square well, not too deep but moist with water, and pave both the bottom and sides with stone slabs. In this well, using strong timber, he shall construct a cage-like underground chamber with three stories, the topmost story at ground level. This chamber shall have multiple compartments of various designs, with floors plastered with small stones, one door, a movable staircase, and it shall be consecrated by the presence of a guardian deity.

Above this chamber, the treasury house shall be built, enclosed on both sides, with projecting roofs, and it shall open extensively into the storehouse. It shall be constructed of bricks.

The Chamberlain may employ outcast men (abhityakta-purusha) to build, at the extreme boundary of the kingdom, a grand mansion to store substantial treasure for safeguarding against dangers and calamities.

The trading house shall be a quadrangle, enclosed by four buildings with one door. It shall have pillars built of burnt bricks, many compartments, and rows of pillars on both sides, spaced apart.

The storehouse shall consist of many spacious rooms, enclosing the forest produce storehouse, which shall be separated by a wall and connected to both the underground chamber and the armory.

The court (dharmasthíya) and the office of the ministers (mahámátríya) shall be constructed in a separate location.

A jail shall also be constructed, with separate accommodations for men and women, both kept apart, and with many compartments that are well guarded.

All these buildings shall be equipped with halls (sála), pits (kháta— possibly privies), water wells, bathrooms, protections against fire and poison, as well as cats and mongooses. They shall also include the necessary provisions to worship the guardian deities appropriate to each location.

In front of the storehouse, a bowl (kunda) with a mouth as wide as an aratni (24 angulas) shall be set up as a rain-gauge (varshamána).

Assisted by experts with the necessary qualifications and equipped with tools and instruments, the Chamberlain shall attend to the reception of gems, whether old or new, as well as raw materials of superior or inferior value.

In cases of deception involving gems, both the deceiver and the accomplice shall be punished with the highest amercement. In cases involving superior commodities, they shall be punished with the middle-most amercement. For inferior commodities, the offenders shall not only be compelled to return the same but also pay a fine equal to the value of the goods.

The Chamberlain shall accept only those gold coins that have been verified as pure by the coin examiner.

Counterfeit coins shall be cut into pieces, and whoever brings in counterfeit coins shall be punished with the first amercement.

Grains that are pure and fresh shall be accepted in full measures; otherwise, a fine of twice the value of the grains shall be imposed.

The same rules shall apply to the receipt of merchandise, raw materials, and weapons.

In all departments, whether an officer (yukta), a clerk (upayukta), or a servant (tatpurusha), anyone who misappropriates amounts from one to four panas or other valuable items shall be punished with the first, middlemost, or highest amercement or even death, depending on the severity of the offense.

If the officer in charge of the treasury causes a loss of money, he shall be whipped (ghátah), while his accomplices shall receive half the punishment. If the loss is due to ignorance, he shall be censured.

If guards frighten robbers with the intent of giving them a hint, the guards shall be tortured to death.

Therefore, the Chamberlain shall, with the assistance of trustworthy individuals, handle the business of revenue collection.

He shall have such thorough knowledge of both external and internal incomes extending up to a hundred years that, when questioned, he can state without hesitation the exact amount of net balance remaining after all expenditures have been met.

CHAPTER VI. THE BUSINESS OF COLLECTION OF REVENUE BY THE COLLECTOR-GENERAL.

The Collector-General shall oversee the collection of revenue from forts (durga), rural areas (ráshtra), mines (khani), buildings and gardens (setu), forests (vana), herds of cattle (vraja), and roads of traffic (vanikpatha).

Revenue from tolls, fines, weights and measures, the town-clerk (nágaraka), the superintendent of coinage (lakshanádhyakshah), the superintendent of seals and passports, liquor sales, the slaughter of animals, threads, oils, ghee, sugar (kshára), the state goldsmith (sauvarnika), warehouses, prostitutes, gambling, building sites (vástuka), the guild of artisans and craftsmen (kárusilpiganah), the superintendent of gods, and taxes collected at the city gates or from external inhabitants (Báhirikas) all come under the category of forts.

Produce from crown lands (sita), the government's share of the produce (bhága), religious taxes (bali), taxes paid in cash (kara), taxes from merchants, the superintendent of rivers, ferries, boats, ships, towns, pasture grounds, road cess (vartani), ropes (rajjú), and ropes for binding thieves (chórarajjú) fall under the category of rural areas.

Gold, silver, diamonds, gems, pearls, corals, conch shells, metals (loha), salt, and other minerals extracted from plains and mountain slopes fall under the category of mines.

Flower gardens, fruit gardens, vegetable gardens, wet fields, and fields where crops are grown by sowing roots or seeds (múlavápáh, such as sugarcane crops) fall under the category of gardens (sétu).

Game forests, timber forests, and elephant forests come under the category of forests.

Cows, buffaloes, goats, sheep, asses, camels, horses, and mules come under the category of herds.

Land and waterways fall under the category of roads of traffic.

All of these form the body of income (áyasaríram).

Capital (múla), shares (bhága), premia (vyáji), parigha (?), fixed taxes (klripta), premia on coins (rúpika), and fixed fines (atyaya) are the various forms of revenue (áyamukha), the sources from which income flows.

The chanting of auspicious hymns during the worship of gods and ancestors, gifts, the harem, the kitchen, the messengers' establishment, the storehouse, the armory, the warehouse, the storehouse for raw materials, manufactories (karmánta), free laborers (vishti), maintenance of infantry, cavalry, chariots, elephants, herds of cows, the museum of animals, deer, birds, and snakes, as well as the storage of firewood and fodder, all constitute the body of expenditure (vyayasaríram).

The royal year, month, fortnight (paksha), day, dawn (vyushta), the third and seventh fortnights of the rainy, winter, and summer seasons (which are shorter in days), the remaining months that are complete, and the separate intercalary month are the divisions of time.

The Collector-General shall also pay attention to the work in hand (karaníya), completed work (siddham), partial work (sésha), receipts, expenditures, and the net balance.

The work of maintaining the government (samsthánam), daily routine tasks (prachárah), gathering life necessities, collecting, and auditing all forms of revenue—these are considered the tasks at hand.

What has been credited to the treasury, what has been taken by the king, what has been spent in connection with the capital and not entered into the register or carried over from the previous year, and royal commands either written or orally communicated to be entered—these constitute completed work.

Preparation of plans for profitable works, recovery of unpaid fines, demands for arrears of revenue kept in abeyance, and the examination of accounts—these tasks fall under what is called partial work in hand, which may sometimes be of little or no value.

Receipts can be classified into three types: (1) current, (2) last balance, and (3) accidental (anyajátah, received from external sources).

Current receipts (vartamána) are those collected day by day.

Last balance (puryushita) refers to whatever has been carried over from the previous year, what is held by others, or what has changed hands.

Accidental receipts include what has been lost and forgotten by others, fines levied on government servants, marginal revenue (pársva), compensation collected for damage (párihínikam), gifts to the king, the property of those who have died due to epidemics (damaragatakasvam) without leaving any heirs, and treasure-troves.

The investment of capital (vikshépa), the remnants of a failed undertaking, and savings from estimated expenditures are all means to monitor and control spending (vyayapratyayah).

The rise in the price of merchandise due to the use of varying weights and measures during sales is called vyáji. Another source of profit comes from price increases driven by competitive bidding among buyers.

Expenditure is divided into two types—daily expenditure and profitable expenditure.

Daily expenditure refers to what is spent regularly every day.

Profitable expenditure refers to what is earned or spent periodically, such as once per paksha (fortnight), month, or year.

The amount spent on these two categories is termed daily expenditure and profitable expenditure, respectively.

The net balance (nívi) is what remains after deducting all incurred expenses and excluding all future revenue yet to be realized. This net balance may be newly realized or carried forward from a previous period.

Thus, a wise Collector-General shall manage the task of revenue collection, focusing on increasing income and reducing expenses.

CHAPTER VII. THE BUSINESS OF KEEPING UP ACCOUNTS IN THE OFFICE OF ACCOUNTANTS.

The superintendent of accounts shall ensure that the accountant's office is constructed with its door facing either north or east, with seats for clerks arranged separately, and with shelves for account books neatly organized.

In this office, records shall be maintained regarding the following: the number of various departments; a description of the work being carried out and the results achieved in the various manufactories (Karmánta); the amount of profit, loss, expenditure, delayed earnings, and vyáji (premia in kind or cash) realized; the status of the government agency employed; the amount of wages paid; the number of free laborers (vishti) engaged in relation to the capital invested in any work. Likewise, for gems and commodities of superior or inferior value, records shall detail their prices, the rate of barter, the counterweights (pratimána) used in weighing them, their quantity, weight, and cubical measure.

Records shall also include information about the customs, professions, and transactions of countries, villages, families, and corporations; the gains in the form of gifts given to the king's courtiers; their rights to own and enjoy lands; tax remissions granted to them; and provisions and salaries paid to them. The gains provided to the king's wives and sons in the form of gems, lands, and prerogatives, as well as provisions made to counteract evil portents, shall also be recorded. Additionally, the treaties with friendly or hostile kings, issues of ultimatum, and the payments of tribute either received from or paid to them shall be regularly entered into the prescribed registers.

From these account books, the superintendent shall provide reports on the status of work in progress, completed work, partial works, receipts, expenditures, net balances, and tasks yet to be undertaken in each of the departments.

Supervisors with corresponding qualifications shall be employed to oversee high, middling, and low-level works.

The king will ultimately suffer if he reduces the fixed expenditure for profitable works.

If a person engaged by the government for any work is absent, his sureties, who jointly received wages from the government, or his sons, brothers, wives, daughters, or servants benefiting from his work, shall bear the loss caused to the government.

The work of 354 days and nights constitutes a full year. Payment for such work shall be made in proportion to the amount completed at the end of the month of Ashádha (around mid-July). The work done during the intercalary month shall be calculated separately.

A government officer, who neglects to understand the information gathered through espionage or fails to properly supervise the work in his department as required, may cause a loss of revenue to the government. This could be due to ignorance, idleness when he is too weak to engage in active duties, inadvertence in perceiving sounds and other sensory objects, timidity when afraid of public outcry or unrighteous actions, selfish desires when he is inclined towards those pursuing their own selfish ends, cruelty resulting from anger, lack of dignity when surrounded by sycophants and needy flatterers, or by using false balances, measures, and calculations out of greed.

The school of Manu holds that the fine imposed on such an officer should equal the amount of the lost revenue multiplied by the serial number of the offense committed.

The school of Parásara maintains that the fine should be eight times the amount lost.

The school of Brihaspati suggests that it should be ten times the amount.

The school of Usanas proposes that it should be twenty times the amount.

However, Kautilya argues that the fine should be proportional to the severity of the guilt.

Accounts should be submitted during the month of Ashádha. When the accountants from different districts present themselves with sealed books, commodities, and the net revenue, they shall be kept apart in a single location to prevent any conversation among them. After hearing the totals for receipts, expenditure, and net revenue, the net amount shall be received.

If the superintendent of a department increases the net total of revenue by raising any one of the items of receipts or reducing any item of expenditure, he shall be rewarded eight times that amount. However, if the net total is decreased, the same penalty shall apply—he will be required to pay eight times the amount of the decrease.

Accountants who fail to present themselves on time or who do not submit their account books along with the net revenue shall be fined ten times the amount due from them.

If the superintendent of accounts (káranika) does not promptly proceed to receive and verify the accounts when the clerks (kármika) are ready, he shall be punished with the first amercement. If the clerks are not ready, they shall be punished with double the first amercement.

All the ministers (mahámátras) shall together report the complete and accurate accounts pertaining to each department.

Whoever among these individuals (whether ministers or clerks) offers divided counsel, remains aloof, or speaks falsehoods shall be punished with the highest amercement.

If an accountant has not prepared the table of daily accounts (akritáhorúpaharam), he may be granted one additional month for its preparation. After the lapse of that month, he shall be fined 200 panas for each additional month of delay.

If an accountant has only a small portion of the accounts concerning net revenue to prepare, he may be allowed five nights to complete it.

The table of daily accounts, along with the net revenue submitted by the accountant, shall be scrutinized by verifying it with righteous transaction norms, precedents, and through the application of arithmetical processes such as addition, subtraction, and inference, as well as through espionage. It shall be cross-checked with regard to divisions of time such as days, five nights, pakshas (fortnights), months, four-month periods, and the year.

Receipts shall be verified by considering the place and time of collection, the form of their collection (whether capital or share), the current and past production levels, the person who made the payment, the one who facilitated the payment, the officer who determined the payable amount, and the officer who received it. Expenditure shall be verified by examining the cause of profit from any source, the relevant place and time, the amount payable and paid, the officer who ordered the collection, the person who remitted the payment, the individual who delivered it, and the person who received it.

Similarly, the net revenue shall be verified in terms of place, time, and source, along with its standard of fineness, quantity, and the personnel assigned to guard the deposits and magazines (grains, etc.).

If an officer (káranika) does not facilitate, or actively prevents, the execution of the king's orders, or if he renders the receipts and expenditure in a manner other than prescribed, he shall be punished with the first amercement.

Any clerk who deviates from the prescribed format for writing accounts, enters information unknown to him, or makes double or triple entries (punaruktam), shall be fined 12 panas.

Anyone who scrapes off the net total shall face double the punishment.

If anyone consumes or conceals it, they shall be fined eight times the amount.

Anyone causing a loss of revenue shall be fined five times the amount lost (panchabandha) and be required to make good the loss. If a lie is spoken, the punishment for theft shall be imposed. If an omitted or lost entry is later entered, or is made to appear as forgotten but added after recollection, the punishment shall be double the original.

The king shall forgive minor offenses, show satisfaction even if the revenue is low, and reward (with pragraha) those superintendents who bring immense benefit to him.

CHAPTER VIII. DETECTION OF WHAT IS EMBEZZLED BY GOVERNMENT SERVANTS OUT OF STATE REVENUE.

All undertakings rely on financial resources. Therefore, primary attention shall be directed toward maintaining the treasury.

Public prosperity (prachárasamriddhih), rewarding good conduct (charitránugrahah), capturing thieves, reducing the number of unnecessary government employees, abundant harvests, prosperous commerce, freedom from troubles and calamities (upasargapramokshah), reduction in tax remissions, and income from gold (hiranyópáyanam) all contribute to financial prosperity.

On the other hand, the following are the causes of financial depletion: obstruction (pratibandha), loans (prayóga), trading (vyavahára), fabrication of accounts (avastára), causing revenue loss (parihápana), self-enjoyment (upabhóga), barter (parivartana), and defalcation (apahára).

Obstruction refers to the failure to begin an undertaking or realize its results, or to credit its profits to the treasury. In such cases, a fine of ten times the amount involved shall be imposed.

Loan refers to lending treasury money with periodic interest.

Trading refers to conducting business using government funds. Both these offenses shall be punished with a fine of twice the profit earned.

Fabrication of accounts occurs when one misrepresents the proper timing of revenue collection, either accelerating or delaying it inappropriately. Here, a fine of ten times the amount (panchabandha) shall be imposed.

Causing revenue loss refers to reducing a fixed amount of income or increasing expenditure without authorization. The punishment shall be a fine of four times the loss incurred.

Self-enjoyment occurs when one personally uses or causes others to use what belongs to the king. The penalty for this offense varies: for enjoying gems, the death sentence shall be imposed; for enjoying valuable articles, the middlemost amercement shall apply; and for articles of lesser value, they must be restored along with a fine equal to their value.

Barter refers to exchanging government-owned articles for similar articles of others, and it is covered under the same rules as self-enjoyment.

Defalcation occurs when one fails to deposit the fixed amount of revenue collected into the treasury, does not spend what has been ordered to be spent, or falsifies the net revenue collected. For defalcation, a fine of twelve times the amount shall be imposed.

There are about forty ways of embezzlement: what is realized earlier is entered later on; what is realized later is entered earlier; what ought to be realized is not realized; what is hard to realize is shown as realized; what is collected is shown as not collected; what has not been collected is shown as collected; what is collected in part is entered as collected in full; what is collected in full is entered as collected in part; what is collected is of one sort, while what is entered is of another sort; what is realized from one source is shown as realized from another; what is payable is not paid; what is not payable is paid; not paid in time; paid untimely; small gifts made large gifts; large gifts made small gifts; what is gifted is of one sort while what is entered is of another; the real donee is one while the person entered (in the register) as donee is another; what has been taken into (the treasury) is removed while what has not been credited to it is shown as credited; raw materials that are not paid for are entered, while those that are paid for are not entered; an aggregate is scattered in pieces; scattered items are converted into an aggregate; commodities of greater value are bartered for those of small value; what is of smaller value is bartered for one of greater value; price of commodities enhanced; price of commodities lowered; number of nights increased; number of nights decreased; the year not in harmony with its months; the month not in harmony with its days; inconsistency in the transactions carried on with personal supervision (samágamavishánah); misrepresentation of the source of income; inconsistency in giving charities; incongruity in representing the work turned out; inconsistency in dealing with fixed items; misrepresentation of test marks or the standard of fineness (of gold and silver); misrepresentation of prices of commodities; making use of false weight and measures; deception in counting articles; and making use of false cubic measures such as bhájan—these are the several ways of embezzlement.

Under the above circumstances, the persons concerned, such as the treasurer (nidháyaka), the prescriber (nibandhaka), the receiver (pratigráhaka), the payer (dáyaka), the person who caused the payment (dápaka), and the ministerial servants of the officer (mantri-vaiyávrityakara), shall each be separately examined. If any one of these tells a lie, he shall receive the same punishment as the chief officer (yukta) who committed the offense. A proclamation in public (prachára) shall be made to the effect, "whoever has suffered at the hands of this offender may make their grievances known to the king." Those who respond to the call shall receive compensation equal to the loss they have sustained.

When there are a number of offenses in which a single officer is involved, and when his guilt of parókta (embezzlement or misappropriation) in any one of those charges has been established, he shall be answerable for all those offenses. Otherwise (i.e., when it is not established), he shall be tried for each of the charges separately. When a government servant has been proven guilty of misappropriating part of a large sum in question, he shall be held accountable for the entire amount.

Any informant (súchaka) who supplies information about embezzlement just about to be perpetrated shall, if successful in proving it, receive as a reward one-sixth of the amount in question. If the informant happens to be a government servant (bhritaka), he shall receive one-twelfth of the amount for the same act. If an informant succeeds in proving only a part of a significant embezzlement, he shall still receive the prescribed share of the part of the embezzled amount proven.

An informant who fails to prove his claim shall be subject to monetary or corporal punishment and shall never be acquitted. When the charge is proven, the informant may attribute the tale-bearing to someone else or clear himself in any other way from blame. Any informant who withdraws his assertion after being influenced by the insinuations of the accused shall be condemned to death.

CHAPTER IX. EXAMINATION OF THE CONDUCT OF GOVERNMENT SERVANTS.

Those who are possessed of ministerial qualifications shall, in accordance with their individual capacity, be appointed as superintendents of government departments. While engaged in work, they shall be daily examined; for men are naturally fickle-minded and like horses at work exhibit constant change in their temper. Hence the agency and tools which they make use of, the place and time of the work they are engaged in, as well as the precise form of the work, the outlay, and the results shall always be ascertained. Without dissension and without any concert among themselves, they shall carry on their work as ordered. When in concert, they eat up (the revenue). When in disunion, they mar the work. Without bringing to the knowledge of their master (bhartri, the king), they shall undertake nothing except remedial measures against imminent dangers.

A fine of twice the amount of their daily pay and of the expenditure (incurred by them) shall be fixed for any inadvertence on their part. Whoever of the superintendents makes as much as, or more than, the amount of fixed revenue shall be honoured with promotion and rewards. My teacher holds that that officer who spends too much and brings in little revenue eats it up; while he who proves the revenue (i.e., brings in more than he spends) as well as the officer who brings in as much as he spends does not eat up the revenue. But Kautilya holds that cases of embezzlement or no embezzlement can be ascertained through spies alone. Whoever lessens the revenue eats the king's wealth. If owing to inadvertence he causes diminution in revenue, he shall be compelled to make good the loss.

Whoever doubles the revenue eats into the vitality of the country. If he brings in double the amount to the king, he shall, if the offence is small, be warned not to repeat the same; but if the offence be grave he should proportionally be punished. Whoever spends the revenue (without bringing in any profit) eats up the labour of workmen. Such an officer shall be punished in proportion to the value of the work done, the number of days taken, the amount of capital spent, and the amount of daily wages paid. Hence the chief officer of each department (adhikarana) shall thoroughly scrutinise the real amount of the work done, the receipts realised from, and the expenditure incurred in that departmental work both in detail and in the aggregate. He shall also check (pratishedhayet) prodigal, spend-thrift and niggardly persons. Whoever unjustly eats up the property left by his father and grandfather is a prodigal person (múlahara). Whoever eats all that he earns is a spendthrift (tádátvika). Whoever hoards money, entailing hardship both on himself and his servants is niggardly.

Whoever among these three types of people has the support of a strong party shall not be disturbed; but whoever does not have such support shall be captured (paryádátavyah). Whoever is stingy, despite possessing immense wealth, hoarding, depositing, or sending it out— hoarding in their own house, depositing with local citizens or country people, or sending it to foreign countries—a spy will find out the advisors, friends, servants, relatives, partisans, as well as the income and expenditure of such a stingy person. Whoever, in a foreign country, carries out the business of such a stingy person shall be persuaded to reveal the secret. When the secret is exposed, the stingy person shall be murdered, seemingly under the orders of (his) declared enemy.

Therefore, the superintendents of all departments shall carry on their respective duties together with accountants, writers, coin-examiners, treasurers, and military officers (uttarádhyaksha). Those who serve military officers and are known for their honesty and good behavior shall be spies to observe the conduct of accountants and other clerks. Each department shall be managed by several temporary heads. Just as it is impossible to avoid tasting the honey or poison that finds itself on the tip of one's tongue, it is also impossible for a government worker not to take at least a small part of the king's revenue. Just as it is impossible to see whether fish swimming under the water are drinking or not drinking, it is also impossible to detect whether government workers employed in the service are taking money for themselves.

It is possible to observe the movements of birds flying high in the sky, but it is not possible to detect the hidden motives of government workers. Government workers shall not only have their ill-gotten gains confiscated, but they shall also be transferred from one position to another, so that they cannot either misappropriate government money or keep what they have already taken. Those who increase the king's revenue rather than stealing it, and who are loyally devoted to him, shall be made permanent in their service.

CHAPTER X. THE PROCEDURE OF FORMING ROYAL WRITS.

Teachers say that the word "sásana," meaning command, is only used when referring to royal writs (sásana). Writs hold great importance for kings, as treaties and events leading to war rely on these writs.

Therefore, a person who possesses the skills of a minister, is knowledgeable about all types of customs, proficient in writing, capable of producing legible script, and quick in reading should be appointed as a writer (lékhaka).

This writer, after carefully listening to the king's orders and thoroughly considering the matter at hand, should write down the king's command.

When writing a writ addressed to a lord (ísvara), it should include a respectful mention of the lord's country, possessions, family, and name. For a writ addressed to a common man (anisvara), it should include a polite mention of the person's country and name.

The writer must take into account the addressee's caste, family, social rank, age, education (sruta), occupation, property, character (síla), blood relations (yaunánubandha), and also the place and time of writing, to create a writ that suits the position of the person being addressed.

The organization of the subject matter (arthakrama), relevance (sambandha), completeness, elegance, and clarity are the essential qualities of a writ.

The act of presenting facts in order of importance is called arrangement. When the following facts are not contradictory to the previous facts, continuing until the completion of the letter, it is called relevance.

Avoiding redundancy or a lack of words or letters, offering an impressive explanation of the subject by providing reasons, examples, and illustrations, and using appropriate, suitably strong words (asrántapada) makes for completeness.

Describing a meaningful subject in an elegant style that has a pleasing effect is sweetness.

Using words that are not colloquial (agrámya) is dignity.

The use of common and well-known words brings lucidity.

There are sixty-three alphabetical letters, starting with Akára.

The combination of letters forms a word (pada). Words are of four types—nouns, verbs, verb prefixes, and particles (nipáta).

A noun is something that represents an essence (satva).

A verb is something that does not have a fixed gender and represents an action.

'Pra' and similar words are prefixes to verbs.

'Cha' and other words that do not change are particles.

A group of words that conveys a complete meaning is called a sentence (vákya).

A combination of words (varga) consisting of no more than three words and no fewer than one word should be arranged in such a way that it harmonizes with the meaning of the words that follow.

The word "iti" is used to indicate the completion of a writ and also to mark an oral message, as in the phrase "váchikamasyeti," meaning an oral message along with this (writ).

There are thirteen purposes for which writs are issued: calumniation (nindá), commendation, inquiry, narration, request, refusal, censure, prohibition, command, conciliation, promise of help, threat, and persuasion.

Calumniation (nindá) involves speaking badly about someone's family, appearance, and actions.

Commendation (prasamsá) involves praising someone's family, person, and actions.

Asking, "How is this?" is inquiry.

Explaining something as "this way" is narration (ákhyána).

Requesting by saying "give" is a request.

Saying, "I do not give" is refusal.

Saying, "This is not worthy of you" is censure (upálambhah).

Telling someone "do not do this" is prohibition (pratishedha).

Saying "this must be done" is a command (chódaná).

Saying "what I am, you are too; whatever I own, you own as well" is conciliation (sántvam).

Offering help in a difficult situation is a promise of help (abhyavapattih).

Pointing out potential future harm is a threat (abhibartsanam).

Persuasion comes in three forms: persuasion for the purpose of gaining money, persuasion when someone fails to fulfill a promise, and persuasion during times of trouble.

There are also different types of writs: writs of information, writs of command, and writs of gift. Additionally, there are writs of remission, writs of license, writs of guidance, writs of reply, and writs of general proclamation.

"This is what the messenger says," and "this is what the king says." If there is truth in what the messenger has said, then the agreed-upon item should be handed over immediately. The messenger has informed the king about all the enemy's actions (Parakára). This is the writ of information, which is said to take many forms.

Whenever, and especially when it concerns government officials, the king issues an order either for punishment or reward, it is called a writ of command (ájnálékha).

When the intention is to bestow honor upon someone who has earned it, either to help ease their suffering (ádhi) or as a gift (paridána), writs of gift (upagrahalekha) are issued.

Whenever a favor (anugraha) is announced in accordance with the king's orders for specific castes, cities, villages, or countries, it is known as a writ of remission (pariháralékha) by those familiar with it.

Similarly, permission (nisrishti) is either given verbally or in writing, and it is called a verbal order or a writ of license.

When various natural disasters or confirmed human-made troubles are believed to be the reason for taking action, writs of guidance (pravrittilékha) are issued to attempt remedies.

After reading a letter and discussing how to respond to it, a reply made according to the king's orders is called a writ of reply (pratilékha).

When the king commands his viceroys (isvara) and other officers to protect and provide material assistance to travelers, whether on roads or within the country, it is called a writ of general proclamation (sarvatraga lekha).

Negotiation, bribery, causing dissension, and open attack are methods of strategy (upáya).

Negotiation comes in five types: praising the qualities of the enemy, discussing shared relationships, pointing out mutual benefits, highlighting future opportunities, and emphasizing shared interests.

When the family, person, occupation, behavior, education, property, and other qualities of the enemy are acknowledged with careful attention to their merit, it is called praising the qualities (gunasankírthana).

When it is shown that both parties share relatives, blood relations, teachers (maukha), a priestly hierarchy (srauva), family, and friends, it is known as narrating mutual relationships (sambandhópakhyána).

When both sides—the king's party and the enemy's party—are shown to be helpful to each other, it is called pointing out mutual benefit (parasparópakárasamdarsanam).

Inducement such as saying, "If this is done in this way, such results will benefit both of us," is called showing vast future prospects (Ayátipradarsanam).

Saying, "What I am, you are as well; you may use whatever is mine in your works," is called identity of interests (átmópanidhánam).

Offering money is known as bribery (upapradána).

Creating fear, suspicion, and making threats is called sowing dissension.

Killing, harassing, and looting is considered attack (danda).

The faults in a writ include clumsiness, contradictions, repetition, poor grammar, and misarrangement.

Writing on a black and ugly leaf (kálapatrakamacháru) or with uneven and uncolored (virága) writing causes clumsiness (akánti).

If one part of a letter contradicts an earlier part, it causes contradiction (vyágháta).

Repeating something that has already been stated before is considered repetition.

Using words incorrectly in terms of gender, number, tense, or case is poor grammar (apasabda).

Improper paragraph divisions (varga), omitting necessary divisions, and violating any other essential qualities of a writ are considered misarrangement (samplava).

Having studied all sciences and having carefully observed the forms of writing in use, these rules for writing royal writs have been laid down by Kautilya for the benefit of kings.

[Thus ends Chapter X, "The Procedure of Forming Royal Writs," in Book II, "The Duties of Government Superintendents," of the Arthasástra of Kautilya. End of the thirty-first chapter from the beginning.]

CHAPTER XI. EXAMINATION OF GEMS THAT ARE TO BE ENTERED INTO THE TREASURY.

The Superintendent of the treasury, in the presence of qualified individuals, shall accept into the treasury whatever should be admitted, including gems (ratna) and items of both high and low value.

Támraparnika refers to pearls produced in the Támraparni; Pándyakavátaka refers to pearls obtained in Pándyakavata; Pásikya refers to those produced in the Pása; Kauleya refers to those produced in the Kúla; Chaurneya refers to those produced in the Chúrna; Mahéndra refers to pearls obtained near the Mahéndra mountain; Kárdamika refers to those produced in the Kárdama; Srautasíya refers to those produced in the Srótasi; Hrádíya refers to those found in the deep pool of water known as Hrada; and Haimavata refers to pearls obtained near the Himalayas. These are the various types of pearls.

Pearls are found in oyster shells, conch shells, and other miscellaneous sources.

Pearls that resemble the lentil (masúra), those made of three segments (triputaka), those resembling a tortoise (kúrmaka), semi-circular pearls, multi-layered pearls, double pearls (yámaka), scratched pearls, rough-surfaced pearls, spotted pearls (siktakam), those resembling the water-pot of an ascetic, those that are dark brown or blue in color, and those poorly drilled are considered inauspicious.

The best pearls are those that are large, round, without a flat bottom (nistalam), bright, white, heavy, smooth to the touch, and well-drilled.

There are several types of pearl necklaces: Sirshaka, Upasirshaka, Prakándaka, Avaghátaka, and Taralapratibandha.

A necklace made of 1,008 strings of pearls is called Indrachchhanda.

Half of that, or 504 strings, is called Vijayachchhanda.

Sixty-four strings form an Ardhahára.

Fifty-four strings form a Rasmikalápa.

Thirty-two strings form a Guchchha.

Twenty-seven strings form a Nakshatramála.

Twenty-four strings form an Ardhaguchchha.

Twenty strings form a Mánavaka, and half of that, or ten strings, is called Ardhamánavaka.

The same necklaces, when containing a gem at the center, retain their names with "Mánavaka" added to their respective titles.

When all the strings in a necklace are of the sirshaka pattern, it is called a pure necklace (suddhahára), and the same applies to strings of other patterns. A necklace with a gem in the center is also called Ardhamánavaka.

A necklace with three slab-like gems (triphalaka) or five slab-like gems (panchaphalaka) in the center is called Phalakahára.

A single string of pearls is called a pure Ekávali, and with a gem in the center, it is called Yashti. When the string is adorned with gold globules, it is called Ratnávali.

A string made of alternating pearls and gold globules is called Apavartaka.

Strings of pearls with a gold wire between two strings are called Sopánaka.

When this type of string has a gem in the center, it is called Manisópánaka.

The above descriptions also apply to the formation of head-strings, bracelets, anklets, waist-bands, and other similar varieties of jewelry.

Kauta, which is obtained from Kúta; Mauleyaka, which is found in Múleya; and Párasamudraka, which is found beyond the ocean, are several varieties of gems.

A gem that has a pleasant color like that of the red lotus flower, the Párijáta flower (Erithrina Indica), or the rising sun is called the Saugandhika gem.

A gem that is the color of the blue lotus flower, sirísha (Acacia Sirisa), water, fresh bamboo, or the feathers of a parrot is known as the Vaidúrya gem. Pushyarága, Gómútraka, and Gómédika are other varieties of this type.

A gem characterized by blue lines, one that is the color of the Kaláya flower (a type of phraseolus), or one that is intensely blue, as blue as the Jambu fruit (rose apple), or as blue as the clouds is called the Indraníla gem. Other types of gems include Nandaka (pleasing gem), Sravanmadhya (which appears to pour water from its center), Sítavrishti (which appears to pour a cold shower), and Súryakánta (sunstone).

Gems may be hexagonal, quadrangular, or circular. They are dazzling, pure, smooth, heavy, brilliant, transparent (antargataprabha), and illuminating. These are the qualities of fine gems.

However, gems with a faint color, sandy layers, spots, holes, poor perforation, or scratches are considered defective.

Inferior gems include Vimalaka (pure), Sasyaka (plant-like), Anjanamúlaka (deep-dark), Pittaka (like the bile of a cow), Sulabhaka (easily obtainable), Lohitaka (red), Amritámsuka (with white rays), Jyótírasaka (glowing), Maileyaka, Ahichchhatraka (found in the country of Ahichchhatra), Kúrpa, Pútikúrpa, Sugandhikúrpa, Kshírapaka, Suktichúrnaka (like the powder of an oyster shell), Silápraválaka (coral-like), Pulaka, and Súkrapulaka.

The remaining ones are metallic beads (káchamani).

Sabháráshtraka, which is found in the country of Sabháráshtra; Madhyamaráshtraka, found in the Central Province; Kásmaka, from the country of Kásmaka; Sríkatanaka, found near the mountain Vedótkata; Manimantaka, from the vicinity of the mountain Maniman or Manimanta; and Indravánaká are varieties of diamonds.

Diamonds are sourced from mines, streams, and other miscellaneous locations.

The color of a diamond may resemble that of a cat's eye, the Sirísha flower (Acacia Sirísa), cow urine, cow bile, alum (sphatika), the Málati flower, or any of the previously mentioned gems.

The best diamonds are those that are large, heavy, hard (prahárasaham, capable of withstanding blows), regular in shape (samakóna), able to scratch the surface of vessels (bhájanalékhi), refractive of light (kubrámi), and brilliant.

Inauspicious diamonds are those that lack angles, are uneven (nirasríkam), or are bent to one side (pársvápavrittam).

Alakandaka and Vaivarnaka are the two types of coral that have a ruby-like color, are very hard, and are free from internal contamination by other substances.

Sátana coral is red and smells like earth; Gósirshaka is dark red and has a fishy smell; Harichandana is the color of parrot feathers and smells like tamarind or mango fruit, as does Tárnasa; Grámeruka coral is red or dark red and smells like goat urine; Daivasabheya is red and smells like a lotus flower, as does Aupaka (Jápaka); Jongaka and Taurupa corals are red or dark red and soft; Maleyaka coral is reddish-white; Kuchandana coral is as black as Agaru (resin of the aloe), or red, or dark red, and is very rough; Kála-parvataka coral has a pleasant appearance; Kosákaraparvataka, which comes from a mountain shaped like a bud, is black or variegated black; Sítódakíya coral is black and soft, with a lotus-flower scent; Nágaparvataka, from the Naga mountain, is rough and has the color of Saivala (Vallisneria); and Sákala coral is brown.

Light, soft, moist (asyána, not dry), as greasy as ghee, pleasantly fragrant, adhesive to the skin, mildly scented, long-retaining both its color and scent, tolerant of heat, absorptive of heat, and comfortable on the skin—these are the characteristics of sandalwood (chandana).

As for Agaru (Agallochum, resin of aloe): Jongaka is black or variegated black with spots; Dongaka is black; and Párasamudraka is variegated in color and smells like cascus or Navamálika (jasmine).

Agaru is heavy, soft, greasy, has a long-lasting fragrance that can be detected from afar, burns slowly with continuous smoke, has a uniform scent, absorbs heat, and adheres so firmly to the skin that it cannot be easily removed by rubbing. These are the qualities of Agaru.

Regarding Tailaparnika: Asókagrámika, from Asókagráma, is meat-colored and smells like a lotus flower. Jongaka is reddish-yellow and smells like a blue lotus flower or cow's urine. Grameruka is greasy and smells like cow's urine. Sauvarnakudyaka, from the land of Suvarnakudya, is reddish-yellow and smells like Mátulunga (citron fruit or sweet lime). Púrnadvipaka, from the island of Púrnadviipa, smells like a lotus flower or butter. Bhadrasríya and Páralauhityaka are nutmeg-colored, and both smell like Kushtha (Costus Speciosus). Antarvatya is the color of cascus and also smells like Kushtha. Kaleyaka, from the land of Svarna-bhúmi, is yellow and greasy. Auttaraparvataka, from the northern mountain, is reddish-yellow.

These fragrant substances are considered commodities of superior value (Sára).

The fragrance of Tailaparnika substances lasts regardless of whether they are made into a paste, boiled, or burned. Their scent remains unchanged and unaffected even when mixed with other substances. These substances share similar qualities with sandalwood and Agaru.

Kántanávaka, Praiyaka, and Auttaraparvataka are varieties of skins.

Kántanávaka is peacock-neck-colored, and Praiyaka is variegated with blue, yellow, and white spots. Both are eight angulas (inches) long.

Bisí and Mahábisí are products of Dvádasagráma (twelve villages).

Bisí is of indistinct color, hairy, and variegated with spots. Mahábisí (great Bisí) is rough and almost white. Both are twelve angulas long.

Syámika, Kálika, Kadali, Chandrottara, and Sákulá are other types of skins obtained from Aroha (Arohaja).

Syámika is brown with variegated spots, and Kálika is brown or the color of a pigeon. Both of these are eight angulas long. Kadali is rough and two feet long; when Kadali has variegated, moonlike spots, it is called Chandrottarakadali and is one-third of its length. Sákulá is variegated with large, round spots similar to those seen in a type of leprosy (kushtha) or has tendrils and is spotted like a deer's skin.

Sámúra, Chínasi, and Sámúli are skins procured from Báhlava (Bahlaveya).

Sámúra is thirty-six angulas long and black; Chínasi is reddish-black or blackish-white; and Sámúli is wheat-colored.

Sátina, Nalatúla, and Vrittapuchchha are skins from aquatic animals (Audra).

Sátina is black; Nalatúla is the color of Nala grass fibers; and Vrittapuchchha, which has a round tail, is brown.

These are the varieties of skins.

Among skins, the best are those that are soft, smooth, and hairy.

Blankets made of sheep's wool may be white, purely red, or as red as a lotus flower. They may be made by sewing worsted threads (khachita), woven with woolen threads of various colors (vánachitra), made from different pieces (khandasanghátya), or woven with uniform woolen threads (tantuvichchhinna).

There are ten types of woolen blankets: Kambala, Kauchapaka, Kulamitika, Saumitika, Turagastarana, Varnaka, Talichchhaka, Váravána, Paristoma, and Samantabhadraka.

Among these, the best blanket is the one that is as slippery (pichchhila) as a wet surface, has fine hair, and is soft.

That blanket which is made up of eight pieces and is black in color is called Bhingisi, used as rainproof; similarly, Apasáraka serves the same purpose. Both of these blankets are products of Nepal.

Samputika, Chaturasrika, Lambara, Katavánaka, Praváraka, and Sattalika are blankets made from the wool of wild animals.

The fabric produced in the country of Vanga (Vangaka) is a white and soft fabric (dukúla). That produced in the Pándya region (Paundraka) is black and as soft as the surface of a gem. The fabric from Suvarnakudya is red like the sun, as soft as a gem's surface, woven while the threads are very wet, and of either uniform (chaturasra) or mixed texture (vyámisravána).

There are single, half, double, treble, and quadruple garments, which are various forms of the same fabric.

The above explanation applies to other types of fabrics, such as Kásika, Benarese products, and Kshauma, which is manufactured in Pándya (Paundraka).

Mágadhika (a product of the Magadha country), Paundraka, and Sauvarnakudyaka are fibrous fabrics.

Nágavriksha (a species of tree), Likucha (Artocarpus Lakucha), Vakula (Mimusops Elengi), and Vata (Ficus Indica) are the sources of their fibers.

The fiber from Nágavriksha is yellow (pita); that from Likucha is wheat-colored; that from Vakula is white, and the rest is butter-colored.

Of these, the fiber produced in Suvarnakudya is considered the best.

This also explains fabrics such as kauseya (silk cloth) and chinapatta (fabrics of Chinese manufacture).

Regarding cotton fabrics, those from Madhura, Aparánta (the western parts), Kálinga, Kási, Vanga, Vatsa, and Mahisha are considered the best.

For other kinds of gems (not previously mentioned), the superintendent shall determine their size, value, species, form, utility, treatment, and repair of old gems, as well as any undetectable adulteration. The superintendent shall also assess their wear and tear over time and location, as well as remedies for those that are inauspicious (himsra).

[Thus ends Chapter XI, "Examination of Gems that are to be entered into the Treasury," in Book II, "The Duties of Government Superintendents," of the Arthasástra of Kautilya. End of the thirty-second chapter from the beginning.]

CHAPTER XII. CONDUCTING MINING OPERATIONS AND MANUFACTURE.

Possessed of knowledge in the science of copper and other minerals (Sulbádhátusástra), experienced in the processes of distillation and condensation of mercury (rasapáka), and skilled in testing gems, the superintendent of mines, aided by experts in mineralogy and equipped with mining laborers and the necessary tools, shall examine mines. These mines may show signs of having been exploited before, indicated by mineral waste (kitta), crucibles, charcoal, and ashes, or they may be newly discovered in plains or mountain slopes containing mineral ores. The richness of these ores can be determined by their weight, deep color, strong smell, and taste.

Liquids that seep from pits, caves, slopes, or deep excavations of known mountains, which have the color of the fruit of rose-apple (jambu), mango, or fan palm, which are yellow like ripe turmeric, sulphur of arsenic (haritála), honeycomb, or vermilion, which shine like the petals of a lotus or the feathers of a parrot or peacock, and which are near bodies of water or shrubs of similar color, and are greasy (chikkana), clear (visada), and heavy, are ores of gold (kánchanika). Similarly, liquids that spread like oil when dropped in water, to which dirt and filth adhere, and which amalgamate with copper or silver more than one hundred percent (satádupari veddhárah) are also gold ores.

Substances that have a similar appearance to the above but with a piercing smell and taste are Bitumen.

Ores that are found in plains or on mountain slopes, which are yellow, copper-red, or reddish-yellow in color, marked with blue lines, and resemble black beans (masha, Phraseolus Radiatus), green beans (mudga, Phraseolus Mungo), or sesame seeds; those that are marked with spots like curd drops and shine like turmeric, yellow myrobalan, lotus petals, aquatic plants, liver, or spleen; those containing sandy layers within and marked with circular or svastika-shaped figures; and those containing globular masses (sagulika), which, when roasted, do not crack but emit much foam and smoke, are gold ores (suvarnadhátavah) used to form amalgams with copper or silver (prativápárthasté stámrarúpyavedharáh).

Those ores that have the color of a conch-shell, camphor, alum, butter, pigeon, turtle-dove, Vimalaka (a kind of precious stone), or the neck of a peacock; which shine like opal (sasyaka), agate (gomédaka), cane sugar (guda), and granulated sugar (matsyandika); those with the color of the kovidára flower (Bauhinia Variegata), lotus, patali flower (Bignonia Suaveolens), kalaya (a kind of phraseolus), kshauma (flax), and atasi (Linum Usitatissimum); those found combined with lead or iron (anjana); those that smell like raw meat, are disjointed gray or blackish-white, and are marked with lines or spots; and those which, when roasted, do not crack but emit foam and smoke—these are silver ores.

The heavier the ores, the greater the quantity of metal they contain (satvavriddhih).

Impurities in ores, whether superficial or deeply embedded, can be removed, and the metal extracted when the ores are chemically treated with Tikshna urine (mútra) and alkalies (kshára). The ores are also smeared with a mixture of the powder of Rajavriksha (Clitoria Ternatea), Vata (Ficus Indica), and Pelu (Carnea Arborea), along with cow's bile, and the urine and dung of a buffalo, an ass, and an elephant.

Metals become soft when treated with the powder of kandali (mushroom) and vajrakanda (Antiquorum), together with the ashes of barley, black beans, palása (Butea Frondosa), and pelu (Carnea Arborea), or with the milk of both cows and sheep. Any metal split into a hundred thousand parts can be softened when it is soaked three times in a mixture made from honey (madhu), madhuka (Bassia Latifolia), sheep's milk, sesame oil, clarified butter, jaggery, kinva (ferment), and mushroom.

Permanent softness (mridustambhana) can also be achieved when the metal is treated with the powder of cow's teeth and horn.

Ores found in plains or on mountain slopes, which are heavy, greasy, soft, tawny, green, dark, bluish-yellow (harita), pale-red, or red, are copper ores.

Ores that are the color of kákamechaka (Solanum Indica), pigeon, or cow's bile, and are marked with white lines and smell like raw meat, are the ores of lead.

Those ores that are variegated in color like saline soil or have the color of a burnt lump of earth are the ores of tin.

Those ores that are orange (kurumba), pale-red (pándurohita), or the color of the flower of sinduvára (Vitex Trifolia) are the ores of tíkshna (steel or iron).

Those ores that are the color of the leaf of kánda (Artemisia Indica) or the leaf of birch are the ores of vaikrintaka.

Precious stones are those that are pure, smooth, effulgent, resonant (when struck), very hard (satatívrah), and of light color (tanurága).

The yield of mines may be used for purposes that are commonly practiced.

The commerce in commodities made from mineral products shall be centralized, and there should be established punishments for the manufacturing, selling, or purchasing of such commodities outside the prescribed areas.

A mine laborer who steals mineral products, except for precious stones, shall be punished with a fine of eight times their value.

Any person who steals mineral products or carries on mining operations without a license shall be bound in chains and forced to work as a prisoner.

Mines that yield minerals used for making vessels (bhánda) or that require a large investment to extract may be leased out for a fixed share of the output or a fixed rent (bhágena prakrayena va). Mines that can be worked without much outlay shall be exploited directly by government agencies.

The superintendent of metals (lóhádhyakshah) shall oversee the production of copper, lead, tin, vaikrintaka (possibly mercury), árakúta (brass), vritta (?), kamsa (bronze or bell-metal), tála (sulphur of arsenic), and lodhra (?), as well as the manufacturing of commodities (bhánda) from these metals.

The superintendent of mint (lakshnádhyakshah) shall manage the production of silver coins (rúpyarúpa) composed of four parts copper and one-sixteenth part (mása) of one of the metals: tíkshna (steel or iron), trapu (tin), sisa (lead), or anjana (antimony). The coins shall be in denominations of a pana, half a pana, a quarter, and one-eighth.

Copper coins (támrarúpa), made of four parts of an alloy (pádajívam), shall be issued in denominations of a máshaka, half a máshaka, a kákani, and half a kákani.

The examiner of coins (rúpadarsaka) shall regulate currency both as a medium of exchange (vyávahárikim) and as legal tender admissible into the treasury (kosapravesyám). The premia levied on coins paid into the treasury shall be: 8 percent, known as rúpika; 5 percent, known as vyáji; one-eighth pana per cent, as páríkshika (testing charge); along with a fine of 25 panas to be imposed on offenders, excluding the manufacturer, seller, purchaser, and examiner. The superintendent of ocean-mines (khanyadhyakshah) shall oversee the collection of conch-shells, diamonds, precious stones, pearls, corals, and salt (kshára) and regulate commerce in these commodities. Once the crystallization of salt is complete, the superintendent of salt shall promptly collect both the money-rent (prakraya) and the government's share of salt. By selling the government's share of salt, he shall realize not only its value (múlyam) but also a 5 percent premium (vyájím), both in cash (rúpa). Imported salt (ágantulavanam) shall pay one-sixth of its value (shadbhága) to the king. The sale of this share (bhágavibhága) shall fetch a 5 percent premium (vyáji) and an 8 percent premium (rúpika), both in cash (rúpa). Purchasers of this salt shall also pay a toll (sulka) and compensation (vaidharana) equivalent to the loss caused to the king's commerce. If they fail to pay, they shall be fined 600 panas. Adulteration of salt shall be punished with the highest amercement, as will the unauthorized manufacture of salt by individuals other than hermits (vánaprastha). Men learned in the Vedas, those engaged in penance, and laborers may carry salt for their own food, but salt and alkalies for any other purposes shall be subject to toll payment. Thus, in addition to collecting from mines the ten kinds of revenue, such as: value of the output (múlya), the share of the output (vibhága), a 5 percent premium (vyáji), the testing charge on coins (parigha), fines previously announced (atyaya), toll (sulka), compensation for losses entailed on the king's commerce (vaidharana), fines determined based on the severity of crimes (danda), coinage (rúpa), an 8 percent premium (rúpika), the government shall maintain a state monopoly over both mining and commerce in minerals. Thus, taxes (mukhasangraha) on all commodities intended for sale shall be prescribed once and for all.

[Thus ends Chapter XII, "Conducting Mining Operations and Manufacture," in Book II, "The Duties of Government Superintendents," of the Arthasástra of Kautilya. End of the thirty-third chapter from the beginning.]

CHAPTER XIII. SUPERINTENDENT OF GOLD IN THE GOLDSMITH'S OFFICE.

In order to manufacture gold and silver jewelry, keeping each material separate, the superintendent of gold shall establish a goldsmith's office (akshasála) consisting of four rooms and one door. In the center of the high road, a trained, skilled goldsmith of high birth and reliable character shall be appointed to run the shop.

Jámbúnada, which is the product of the Jambu river; Sátakumbha, extracted from the mountain of Satakumba; Hátaka, from the mines known as Hátaka; Vainava, from the mountain Vénu; and Sringasúktija, extracted from sringasúkti (?) are the varieties of gold.

Gold may be found either pure, amalgamated with mercury or silver, or alloyed with other impurities as mine gold (ákaródgata). The best gold is that which is the color of lotus petals, ductile, glossy, produces no continuous sound (anádi), and glittering. Gold that is reddish-yellow (raktapíta) is of middle quality, while red-colored gold is of low quality. Impure gold is of a whitish color.

Impure gold shall be fused with lead in a quantity four times that of the impurity. When gold becomes brittle due to contamination with lead, it shall be heated with dry cow dung (sushkapatala). If the gold splits into pieces due to hardness, it should be heated and then drenched in oil mixed with cow dung (taila-gomaye).

Mine gold that becomes brittle due to contamination with lead shall be heated while wrapped in cloth (pákapatráni kritvá) and hammered on a wooden anvil. Alternatively, it can be drenched in a mixture made of mushroom and vajrakhanda (Antiquorum).

Tutthodgata, extracted from the mountain Tuttha; Gaudika, a product of the country known as Gauda; Kámbuka, extracted from the mountain Kambu; and Chákraválika, from the mountain Chakravála, are the varieties of silver.

The best silver is white, glossy, and ductile, while silver of the reverse quality is considered bad.

Impure silver shall be heated with lead, using one-fourth the quantity of the impurity. When the silver becomes full of globules, white, glowing, and the color of curd, it is considered pure.

When the streak of pure gold made on a touchstone is the color of turmeric, it is termed suvarna. If one to sixteen kákanis of gold in a suvarna (of sixteen máshakas) are replaced with one to sixteen kákanis of copper, and the copper becomes inseparably alloyed with the rest of the gold, the sixteen varieties (carats) representing the standard of the purity of gold (shodasavarnakáh) will be achieved.

First, a streak with suvarna should be made on a touchstone, and then, next to it, a streak with a piece of the gold to be compared. If a uniform streak made on the smooth surface of the touchstone can be wiped off, swept away, or appears due to the sprinkling of glittering powder (gairika) using the nail, an attempt at deception can be inferred.

If the edge of the palm dipped in a solution of vermilion (játihinguláka) or sulphate of iron (pushpakásísa) in cow's urine touches gold (suvarna), it turns white.

A touchstone with a soft, shining luster is considered the best. The touchstone from the Kálinga country, which is the color of green beans, is also the best. A touchstone of even or uniform color is ideal for the sale or purchase of gold. The one that has the color of an elephant, tinged with green and capable of reflecting light (pratirági), is good for selling gold. The touchstone that is hard, durable, uneven in color, and does not reflect light is good for purchasers (krayahitah). The best touchstone is grey, greasy, uniformly colored, soft, and glossy.

Gold that maintains the same color when heated (tápo bahirantascha samah), is as glittering as tender sprouts, or is the color of the flower of kárandaka (?), is considered the best.

Black or blue discoloration in gold is considered an impurity (apráptaka).

We will discuss the balance and weights under the "Superintendent of Weights and Measures" (Chapter XIX, Book II). In accordance with the instructions provided there, silver and gold (rúpyasuvarnam) may be exchanged.

No person who is not an employee shall enter the goldsmiths' office. Any person who enters without permission shall be executed (uchchhedyah). Any workman who enters the office carrying gold or silver shall forfeit the same.

Goldsmiths engaged in preparing various types of ornaments, such as kánchana (pure gold), prishita (hollow ornaments), tvashtri (gem-setting in gold), and tapaníya, as well as blowers and sweepers, shall only enter or exit the office after a thorough examination of their person and dress. All their instruments, along with their unfinished work, shall remain where they were working. The amount of gold they received and the ornamental work they were crafting shall be placed in the center of the office. Finished items shall be examined in both the morning and evening, and then locked up with the seals of both the manufacturer and the superintendent (kárayatri, the person commissioning the work).

Kshepana, guna, and kshudra are three kinds of ornamental work.

Setting jewels (kácha, glass beads) in gold is called kshepana.

Thread-making or string-making is called guna.

Solid work (ghana), hollow work (sushira), and the manufacture of globules with rounded orifices are considered kshudra, which refers to basic or ordinary work.

For setting jewels in gold, five parts of káñchana (pure gold) and ten parts of gold alloyed with four parts of copper or silver shall be used. Here, the pure gold shall be kept separate from impure gold.

For setting jewels in hollow ornaments (prishitakácha karmanah), three parts of gold will hold the jewel, and four parts will be used for the base.

For tvashtri work, copper and gold shall be mixed in equal quantities.

For solid or hollow silver articles, silver may be mixed with half the amount of gold; alternatively, using a powder or solution of vermilion, gold equal to one-fourth the amount of the silver ornament may be applied (vásayet) as a coating.

Pure and glittering gold is called tapaníya. When tapaníya is combined with an equal quantity of lead and heated with rock salt (saindhav'ika) until it reaches its melting point under dry cow dung, it becomes the basis for gold alloys of various colors such as blue, red, white, yellow (harita), parrot green, and pigeon gray.

The coloring ingredient for gold is one kákaní of tíkshna, which has the color of a peacock's neck, tinged with white, and is dazzling, being full of copper (pitapúrnitam).

Pure or impure silver (tára) may be heated four times with asthituttha (copper sulfate mixed with powdered bone), then four more times with an equal quantity of lead, again four times with dry copper sulfate (sushkatuttha), followed by three times in a skull (kapála), and lastly twice in cow dung. Silver that has undergone these seventeen stages of treatment with tuttha (shodasatutthátikrántam), and is finally heated to a white light with rock salt, can be alloyed with suvarna in proportions ranging from one kákani to two máshas. The resulting suvarna takes on a white color and is called sveta-tára.

When three parts of tapaníya (pure gold) are melted with thirty-two parts of sveta-tára, the alloy becomes reddish-white (svetalohitakam). When three parts of tapaníya are combined with thirty-two parts of copper, the alloy becomes yellow (píta, red!). When three parts of the coloring ingredient (rágatribhága, i.e., tíkshna mentioned earlier) are heated with tapaníya, the compound turns yellowish-red (píta). When two parts of sveta-tára and one part of tapaníya are heated together, the alloy turns as green as mudga (Phraseolus Mungo). When tapaníya is soaked in a solution containing half the quantity of black iron (káláyasa), it turns black.

If tapaníya is twice soaked in this solution mixed with mercury (rasa), it takes on the color of a parrot's feathers.

Before these varieties of gold are put to use, their test streaks shall be taken on a touchstone. The process of assaying tíkshna and copper shall be thoroughly understood. Consequently, the various counterweights (avaneyimána) used in weighing diamonds, rubies, pearls, corals, and coins (rúpa), as well as the proportional amounts of gold and silver needed for various types of ornaments, can be properly understood.

Uniform in color, equal in the color of its test streak to standard gold, free from hollow bulbs, ductile (sthira), very smooth, free from alloys, pleasing to wear as an ornament, not overly dazzling yet glittering, appealing in its consistency of mass, and pleasing to the mind and eyes—these are the qualities of tapaníya, pure gold.

[Thus ends Chapter XIII, "The Superintendent of Gold in the Goldsmiths' Office," in Book II, "The Duties of Government Superintendents," of the Arthasástra of Kautilya. End of the thirty-fourth chapter from the beginning.]

CHAPTER XIV. THE DUTIES OF THE STATE GOLDSMITH IN THE HIGH ROAD.

The State Goldsmith shall employ artisans to manufacture gold and silver coins (rúpyasuvarna) from the bullion of citizens and country people. The artisans employed in the office shall perform their tasks as ordered and within the prescribed time. If, using the excuse that no specific time or nature of the work was given, they spoil the work, they shall forfeit their wages and pay a fine equal to twice the amount of their wages. If they delay the work, they shall forfeit one-fourth of their wages and pay a fine equal to twice the forfeited amount.

The goldsmith of the mint shall return coins or ornaments of the same weight and quality (varna) as the bullion (nikshepa) received at the mint. Except for coins that have been worn out or have diminished in value (kshínaparisírna), the same coins may be returned to the mint even after many years.

The state goldsmith shall gather from the artisans employed in the mint information regarding pure gold, metallic mass (pudgala), coins (lakshana), and the rate of exchange (prayóga).

When a suvarna coin (weighing 16 máshas) is manufactured from gold or silver, an additional one kákani (one-fourth másha) of the metal shall be given to the mint to account for the loss during the manufacturing process. The coloring ingredient (rágaprakshépa) shall be two kákanis of tíkshna (copper sulfate?), with one-sixth being lost during the manufacturing process.

If the quality (varna) of a coin weighing less than the standard másha is lowered, the artisans responsible shall be punished with the first amercement. If the weight of the coin is less than the standard weight, they shall be punished with the middlemost amercement. Deception involving balances or weights shall result in the highest amercement. Deception in the exchange of manufactured coins (kritabhándopadhau) shall also be punished with the highest amercement.

Anyone who causes gold or silver items to be manufactured anywhere other than the mint, or without being observed by the state goldsmith, shall be fined 12 panás. The artisan who performs such work shall, if caught, be fined twice that amount. If not caught, measures described in Book IV shall be taken to detect the offense. Once detected, the artisan shall either be fined 200 panás or have his fingers cut off.

Weighing balances and counterweights must be purchased from the superintendent responsible for them; otherwise, a fine of 12 panás shall be imposed.

The types of artisan work (kárukasma) include compact work (ghana), compact and hollow work (ghanasushira), soldering (samyúhya), amalgamation (avalepya), enclosing (samghátya), and gilding (vásitakam).

False balances (tulávishama), removal (apasárana), dropping (visrávana), folding (petaka), and confounding (pinka) are various means employed by goldsmiths to deceive the public.

False balances include those with bending arms (sannámini), those with a high helm or pivot (utkarnika), those with a broken head (bhinnamastaka), those with a hollow neck (upakanthi), those with faulty strings (kusikya), those with defective cups or pans (sakatukakshya), those that are crooked or shaky (párivellya), and those combined with a magnet (ayaskánta).

When pure alluvial gold is replaced with an equal portion of Triputaka (a mixture of two parts silver and one part copper), this deceitful practice is termed copper-removal (triputakávasáritam). When an equal portion of gold is replaced with copper, it is also termed copper-removal (sulbávasáritam). If vellaka is used to replace an equal portion of gold, it is called vellaka-removal. When pure alluvial gold is replaced with gold half mixed with copper, it is called gold removal (hemávasáritam).

Goldsmiths use various tools and methods for stealing gold, including a crucible with a hidden base metal, metallic excrement, pincers, tongs, metallic pieces (jongani), and borax (sauvarchikálavanam).

When, by intentionally causing the crucible containing bullion to burst, a few sand-like particles of gold are mixed with other particles of a base metal and formed into a mass, this deceitful act is called dropping (visrávana). Likewise, when examining the folded or inlaid leaves of an ornament (áchitakapatrapariksháyám), if silver is substituted for gold or if base metal particles are substituted for gold, it is also termed dropping (visrávana).

Folding (petaka), whether firm (gádha) or loose (abhyuddhárya), is employed in soldering, preparing amalgams, and enclosing a piece of base metal between two pieces of superior metal.

When a lead piece (sísarúpa—lead coin) is firmly covered with gold leaf using wax (ashtaka), this act is called gádhapetaka, or firm folding. When it is loosely covered, it is called loose folding.

In amalgams, a single or double layer of superior metal is used to cover a piece of base metal. Copper or silver may be placed between two leaves of superior metal. A copper piece (sulbarúpya) may be covered with gold leaf, with the surface and edges smoothened. Similarly, a piece of any base metal may be covered with a double layer of copper or silver, with the surface and edges smoothened.

The two forms of folding may be detected by heating, by testing on a touchstone (nikasha), or by noticing the absence of sound when it is rubbed (nissabdollekhana). Loose folding can be identified using the acid juice of badarámla (Flacourtia Cataphracta or jujube fruit) or in saltwater. This covers folding (petaka).

In a compact and hollow piece (ghana-sushire rúpe), small particles of gold-like mud (suvarnamrinválukáh) or bits of vermilion (hingulakalkah) are heated to adhere firmly inside the piece. Even in a solid piece (dridhavástuke rúpe), wax-like mud from Gándhára mixed with particles of gold-like sand is heated to make it stick. These impurities can be removed by hammering the pieces while they are red hot.

In an ornament or coin (sapari-bhánde vá rúpe), salt mixed with hard sand (katusarkará) is heated in flame to make it firmly adhere to the item. This salt and sand can be removed by boiling (kváthana).

In some pieces, mica may be firmly fixed inside using wax and covered with a double leaf of gold or silver. When such a piece with mica or glass inside is suspended in water (udake), one side dips more than the other. Alternatively, if pierced by a pin, the pin moves easily through the layers of mica inside (patalántareshu).

Spurious stones and counterfeit gold and silver may be substituted for real ones in compact and hollow pieces (ghanasushira). They can be detected by hammering the pieces while red hot. This is the process of confounding (pinka).

Therefore, the state goldsmith must have a thorough knowledge of the species, characteristics, color, weight, and composition (pudgala-lakshana) of diamonds, precious stones (mani), pearls, corals, and coins (rúpa).

There are four ways deception can occur when examining new pieces or repairing old ones: hammering, cutting, scratching, and rubbing.

When, under the excuse of detecting the deception known as folding (petaka) in hollow pieces or in threads or cups made of gold or silver, the articles in question are hammered, this act is termed hammering.

When a lead piece (covered over with gold or silver leaf) is substituted for a real one and its interior is cut out, this is termed cutting (avachchhedanam).

When compact pieces are scratched using tíkshna (copper sulfate?), the act is called scratching (ullekhana).

When gold or silver articles are rubbed with a piece of cloth that has been painted with the powder of sulphuret of arsenic (haritála), red arsenic (manassila), vermilion, or with the powder of kuruvinda (black salt?), this is termed rubbing.

Through these acts, gold and silver articles (bhándáni) undergo diminution, but no other kind of damage is inflicted on them.

In all articles that are hammered, cut, scratched, or rubbed, the loss can be determined by comparing them with intact pieces of the same type. In amalgamated pieces (avalepya) that are cut off, the loss can be identified by cutting off an equal portion of a similar piece. For pieces whose appearance has changed, they should be frequently heated and drenched in water.

The state goldsmith shall infer deception (kácham vidyát) when the artisan preparing the articles exhibits undue attention to throwing away materials, counterweights, fire, anvils (gandika), working instruments (bhandika), the seat (adhikarani), the assaying balance, folds of their dress (chellachollakam), their head, thigh, or if they appear preoccupied with flies, are eager to examine their own body, or closely monitor the water-pot or firepot.

Regarding silver, a bad smell like that of rotten meat, hardness due to any alloy (mala), projection (prastína), and discoloration may be signs of adulteration.

Thus, articles of gold and silver, whether new, old, or of bad or unusual color, must be examined, and appropriate fines as described above shall be imposed.

[Thus ends Chapter XIV, "The Duties of the State Goldsmith in the High Road" in Book II, "The Duties of Government Superintendents" of the Arthasástra of Kautilya. End of the thirty-fifth chapter from the beginning.]

CHAPTER XV. THE SUPERINTENDENT OF STOREHOUSE.

The superintendent of the storehouse (Koshthágára) shall supervise the accounts related to agricultural produce (síta); taxes under Ráshtra (country parts); commerce (krayima); barter (parivartna); grains obtained through begging (prámityaka); grains borrowed with a promise to repay (ápamityaka); production of rice, oils, and similar products (simhanika); accidental revenue (anyajáta); reports to verify expenditures (vyayapratyaya); and recovery of past arrears (upasthánam). Whatever agricultural produce is brought in by the superintendent of agriculture (from crown lands) is referred to as sítá.

Taxes such as fixed taxes (pindakara); taxes paid as one-sixth of the produce (shadbhága); provisions provided by the people for the army (senábhakta); taxes levied for religious purposes (bali); taxes or subsidies paid by vassal kings and others (kara); taxes collected on the occasion of the birth of a prince (utsanga); taxes collected when there is a margin for such collection (pársva); compensation in the form of grain for damage done by cattle to crops (párihínaka); gifts presented to the king (aupáyanika); and taxes levied on lands below tanks, lakes, etc., constructed by the king (kaushtheyaka)—all fall under the category of 'Ráshtra.'

The sale proceeds of grains, purchased grains, and the collection of interest on grain debts (prayogapratyádána) are considered commerce. The profitable exchange of grains for other grains is termed barter (parivarthana). Grains obtained through begging are termed prámityaka. Grains borrowed with a promise to repay them are referred to as ápamityaka.

The pounding of rice, the splitting of pulses, the frying of grains and beans, the production of beverages (suktakarma), the preparation of flour by those who depend on such work, the extraction of oil by employing shepherds and oil-makers, and the manufacture of sugar from sugarcane juice are known as simhanika.

Anything lost, forgotten, or found forms accidental revenue (anyajáta). Investment, remnants of a failed venture, and savings from an estimated outlay serve as ways to verify and check expenditures (vyayapratyaya). The amount or quantity of compensation claimed for using a different balance or for any error in taking a handful is called vyáji. The collection of past dues is termed 'upasthána' or 'recovery of past arrears.'

Regarding grains, oils, sugar, and salt, the section on grains will be covered under the duties of the 'Superintendent of Agriculture.'

[Thus ends Chapter XV, "The Duties of the Superintendent of Storehouse" in Book II, "The Duties of Government Superintendents" of the Arthasástra of Kautilya.]

Clarified butter, oil, serum of flesh, and pith or sap (of plants, etc.) are termed oils (sneha). Decoction (phánita), jaggery, granulated sugar, and sugar-candy are termed kshára.

Sáindhava, which is the product of the Sindhu region; Sámudra, produced from seawater; Bida; Yavakshara, nitre; Sauvarchala, the product of the country of Suvarchala; and udbhedaja, extracted from saline soil, are termed lavana, or salt.

The honey of bees, as well as the juice extracted from grapes, is called madhu.

A mixture made by combining one of the following substances—sugarcane juice, jaggery, honey, grape juice, the essence of the fruits of jambu (Eugenia Jambolana) and the jaka tree—with the essence of meshasringa (a type of plant) and long pepper, with or without the addition of the essence of chirbhita (a kind of gourd), cucumber, sugarcane, mango fruit, and the fruit of myrobalam, the mixture being prepared to last for a month, six months, or a year, constitutes the group of astringents (sukta-varga).

The fruits of trees bearing acid fruits, such as karamarda (Carissa Carandas), vidalámalka (myrobalam), matulanga (citron tree), kola (small jujube), badara (Flacourtia Cataphracta), sauvíra (large jujube), and parushaka (Grewia Asiatica), come under the group of acid fruits.

Curds, acids prepared from grains, and similar items are classified as acids in liquid form.

Long pepper, black pepper, ginger, cumin seed, kiratatikta (Agathotes Chirayta), white mustard, coriander, choraka (a plant), damanaka (Artemisia Indica), maruvaka (Vangueria Spinosa), sigru (Hyperanthera Moringa), and similar substances, including their roots (kánda), are classified under the group of pungent substances (tiktavarga).

Dried fish, bulbous roots (kándamúla), fruits, and vegetables form the group of edibles (sakavarga).

Of the store thus collected, half shall be kept in reserve to ward off the calamities of the people, and only the other half shall be used. Old collections shall be replaced by new supplies.

The superintendent shall also personally supervise the increase or decrease sustained in grains when they are pounded (kshunna), frayed (ghrishta), reduced to flour (pishta), fried (bhrashta), or dried after being soaked in water.

The essential part (sára, i.e., the portion fit for food) of kodrava (Paspalam Scrobiculatum) and vrihi (rice) is one-half; for sáli (a kind of rice), it is less by one-eighth part; for varaka (Phraseolus Trilobus), it is less by one-third part; for priyangu (panic seed or millet), it is one-half; for chamasi (barley), mudga (Phraseolus Mungo), and masha (Phraseolus Radiatus), it is less by one-eighth part; for saibya (simbi), it is one-half; for masúra (Ervum Hirsutum), it is less by one-third part compared to the raw material or grains from which it is prepared.

Raw flour and kulmasha (boiled and forced rice) will amount to one and a half times the original quantity of the grains. Barley gruel and its flour, when baked, will yield twice the original quantity.

Kodrava (Paspalam Scrobiculatum), varaka (Phraseolus Trilobus), udáraka (Panicum), and priyangu (millet) will increase three times the original quantity when cooked. Vríhi (rice) will increase four times when cooked. Sáli (a type of rice) will increase five times when cooked.

Grains will increase twice the original quantity when moistened, and two and a half times when soaked to the point of sprouting.

Grains, when fried, will increase by one-fifth of the original quantity, and leguminous seeds (kaláya) will double in quantity when fried, as will rice.

Oil extracted from atasi (linseed) will be one-sixth of the seed quantity; oil from seeds such as nimba (Azadirachta Indica), kusámra (?), and kapittha (Feronia Elephantum) will yield one-fifth; and oil from tila (sesame), kusumba (a type of kidney bean), madhúka (Bassia Latifolia), and ingudi (Terminalia Catappa) will yield one-fourth.

Five palas of kárpása (cotton) or kshauma (flax) will yield one pala of threads.

Rice prepared in such a way that five drónas of sáli yield ten ádhakas of rice is suitable for feeding young elephants; eleven ádhakas from five drónas are fit for elephants with a bad temper (vyála); ten ádhakas from the same amount are for elephants trained for riding; nine ádhakas for war elephants; eight ádhakas for infantry; eleven ádhakas for army chiefs; six ádhakas for queens and princes; and five ádhakas from the same quantity are for kings.

One prastha of pure, unsplit rice, one-fourth prastha of súpa (soup or broth), and clarified butter or oil equal to one-fourth part of the súpa will suffice to form one meal for an Arya.

For low castes (avara), one-sixth prastha of súpa and half the quantity of oil will be sufficient for one meal.

For women, the same rations, reduced by one-fourth, will form a meal. For children, half the above rations will suffice.

For cooking twenty palas of meat, half a kutumba of oil, one pala of salt, one pala of sugar (kshára), two dharanas of pungent substances (katuka, spices), and half a prastha of curd will be necessary. For larger quantities of meat, the same ingredients should be proportionally increased.

For cooking sákas (dried fish and vegetables), the above ingredients should be added in one and a half times the quantity. For dried fish, the ingredients are to be doubled.

Rations for elephants and horses will be described in connection with the "Duties of Their Respective Superintendents."

For bullocks, one drona of masha (Phraseolus Radiatus) or one drona of barley, cooked with other ingredients prescribed for horses, is the requisite quantity of food, in addition to one tula of oilcakes (ghánapinyaka) or ten ádhakas of bran (kanakuttana-kundaka). For buffaloes and camels, the quantity is doubled.

For asses, red spotted deer, and deer with white stripes, half a drona.

For antelopes and large red deer, one ádhaka.

For goats, rams, and boars, half an ádhaka or one ádhaka of grain, along with bran.

For dogs, one prastha of cooked rice. For hamsa (geese), krauncha (herons), and peacocks, half a prastha.

From the above measures, the quantity of rations sufficient for one meal for other beasts, cattle, birds, and rogue elephants (vyála) can be inferred.

Charcoal and chaff may be provided for iron smelting and lime-kilns (bhittilepya).

Bran and flour (kánika) may be given to slaves, laborers, and cooks. Surplus bran and flour may also be given to those who prepare cooked rice and rice cakes.

The necessary instruments include weighing balances, weights, measures, millstones (rochani), pestles, mortars, wooden contrivances for pounding rice (kuttakayantra), contrivances for splitting seeds (rochakayantra), winnowing fans, sieves (chálani), grain baskets (kandoli), boxes, and brooms.

Sweepers, preservers, those who weigh (dharaka), those who measure grains (mápaka), supervisors of grain measuring, those in charge of the supply of commodities to the storehouse (dápaka), suppliers (dáyaka), workers who receive compensation for errors in grain measuring (sálákáipratigráhaka), slaves, and laborers are collectively referred to as vishti.

Grains are heaped on the floor; jaggery (kshára) is bound with grass-rope (múta); oils are stored in earthenware or wooden vessels; and salt is heaped on the ground.

[Thus ends Chapter XV, "The Superintendent of Storehouse," in Book II, "The Duties of Government Superintendents," of the Arthasástra of Kautilya. End of the thirty-sixth chapter from the beginning.]

CHAPTER XVI. THE SUPERINTENDENT OF COMMERCE.

The Superintendent of Commerce shall ascertain the demand or absence of demand, and the rise or fall in the price of various kinds of merchandise, whether produced on land or in water, and whether transported by land or water routes. He shall also determine the appropriate time for the distribution, centralization, purchase, and sale of these goods.

Merchandise that is widely distributed shall be centralized, and its price increased. Once the increased price becomes widely accepted, a new rate shall be declared. Merchandise produced locally by the king shall be centralized, while imported goods shall be distributed to various markets for sale. Both types of goods shall be sold at favorable prices to the public.

The Superintendent shall avoid setting profits so high as to cause harm to the people.

Commodities for which there is frequent demand shall not be restricted by time limits for sale, nor shall they suffer from the disadvantages of centralization (sankuladosha). Alternatively, peddlers may sell the king's merchandise at a fixed price in multiple markets, paying necessary compensation (vaidharana) proportional to any losses incurred (chhedánurúpam).

The amount of vyáji (profit margin) due on commodities sold by cubical measure is one-sixteenth of the total quantity (shodasabhágo mánavyáji); for commodities sold by weight, it is one-twentieth; and for those sold by number, it is one-eleventh of the total.

The Superintendent shall show favor to those who import foreign merchandise. Mariners (návika) and merchants who import foreign goods shall be granted a remission of trade taxes so that they may derive some profit (áyatikshamam pariháram dadyát).

Foreigners importing merchandise shall not be sued for debts unless they are part of local associations or partners (anabhiyogaschárthesshvágantúnámanyatassabhyopakári bhyah).

Those selling the king's merchandise must always deposit their sale proceeds in a wooden box placed in a designated location, with a single aperture at the top. During the eighth part of the day, they shall submit a sales report to the superintendent, stating, "This much has been sold, and this much remains." They must also hand over the weights and measures. These are the rules for local commerce.

Regarding the sale of the king's merchandise in foreign countries:—

The superintendent must first compare the value of local produce with that of foreign produce that can be obtained in barter. He will then calculate whether there is any profit left after covering the necessary payments to the foreign king, such as tolls (sulka), road-cess (vartaní), conveyance-cess (átiváhika), tax payable at military stations (gulmadeya), ferry charges (taradeya), subsistence for the merchant and his followers (bhakta), and the portion of merchandise owed to the foreign king (bhága).

If no profit can be made by selling local produce in foreign countries, the superintendent must consider whether any local produce can be profitably bartered for foreign goods. He may then send one-quarter of his valuable merchandise via safe routes to different markets on land. To maximize profits, the deputed merchant may build friendships with forest guards, boundary guards, and the officers in charge of cities and country parts under the foreign king. The merchant must take precautions to protect both his treasure (sára) and his life from danger. If he cannot reach the intended market, he may sell the merchandise at any market free from all dues (sarvadeyavisuddham).

Alternatively, the merchant may take his merchandise to other countries by river routes (nadípatha).

The merchant must also gather information about conveyance charges (yánabhágaka), subsistence during the journey (pathyadana), the value of foreign goods that can be obtained in exchange for local merchandise, occasions of pilgrimages (yátrakála), methods to ward off journey dangers, and the history of commercial towns (panyapattanacháritra).

Having gathered information about transactions in commercial towns along riverbanks, the merchant should transport his goods to profitable markets and avoid unprofitable ones.

[Thus ends Chapter XVI, "The Superintendent of Commerce," in Book II, "The Duties of Government Superintendents," of the Arthasástra of Kautilya. End of the thirty-seventh chapter from the beginning.]

CHAPTER XVII. THE SUPERINTENDENT OF FOREST PRODUCE.

The Superintendent of Forest Produce shall collect timber and other products from the forests by employing those who guard the productive forests. He shall initiate productive works in the forests and impose appropriate fines and compensations for any damage caused to productive forests, except in cases of natural calamities.

The following are classified as forest products:

Sáka (teak), tinisa (Dalbergia Ougeinensis), dhanvana (?), arjuna (Terminalia Arjuna), madhúka (Bassia Latifolia), tilaka (Barleria

Cristata), tála (palmyra), simsúpa (Dalbergia Sissu), arimeda (Fetid Mimosa), rájádana (Mimosops Kauki), sirisha (Mimosa Sirísha), khadira (Mimosa Catechu), sarala (Pinus Longifolia), tálasarja (sal tree or Shorea Robesta), asvakarna (Vatica Robesta), somavalka (a kind of white khadíra), kasámra (?), priyaka (yellow sal tree), dhava (Mimosa Hexandra), and others are considered strong timber (sáradáruvarga).

The bamboo group includes utaja, chimiya, chava, vénu, vamsa, sátina, kantaka, and bhállúka.

The creeper group includes vetra (cane), sokavalli, vási (Justicia Ganderussa?), syámalatá (Ichnocarpus), and nágalata (betel).

The fibrous plant group (valkavarga) includes málati (Jasminum Grandiflorum), dúrvá (panic grass), arka (Calotropis Gigantea), sana (hemp), gavedhuka (Coix Barbata), and atasí (Linum Usitatissimum).

Plants used for making ropes (rajjubhánda) include munja (Saccharum Munja) and balbaja (Eleusine Indica).

Táli (Corypha Taliera), tála (palmyra or Borassus Flabelliformis), and bhúrja (birch) yield leaves (patram).

Flowers are yielded by kimsuka (Butea Frondosa), kusumbha (Carthamus Tinctorius), and kumkuma (Crocus Sativus).

Bulbous roots and fruits form the group of medicinal plants.

Poisons include kálakúta, vatsanábha, háláhala, meshasringa, mustá (Cyperus Rotundus), kushtha, mahávisha, vellitaka, gaurárdra, bálaka, márkata, haimavata, kálingaka, daradaka, kolasáraka, ushtraka, and others. Snakes and worms kept in pots also constitute the group of poisons.

Skins include those from animals such as godha (alligator), seraka (?), dvípi (leopard), simsumára (porpoise), simha (lion), vyághra (tiger), hasti (elephant), mahisha (buffalo), chamara (bos grunniens), gomriga (bos gavaeus), and gavaya (the gayal).

Other animal products include bones, bile (pittha), snáyu (?), teeth, horn, hooves, and tails of the above animals, as well as other beasts, cattle, birds, and snakes (vyála).

Metals include káláyasa (iron), támra (copper), vritta (?), kámsya (bronze), sísa (lead), trapu (tin), vaikrintaka (mercury?), and árakuata (brass).

Utensils (bhanda) are made from cane, bark (vidala), and clay (mrittiká).

Other forest products include charcoal, bran, and ashes.

The forest produce also includes menageries of beasts, cattle, and birds, as well as the collection of firewood and fodder.

The Superintendent of Forest Produce shall carry out the manufacture of all kinds of articles, either within or outside the capital city, that are essential for daily life or for the defense of forts.

[Thus ends Chapter XVII, "The Superintendent of Forest Produce," in Book II, "The Duties of Government Superintendents," of the Arthasástra of Kautilya. End of the thirty-eighth chapter from the beginning.]

CHAPTER XVIII. THE SUPERINTENDENT OF THE ARMOURY.

The Superintendent of the Armoury shall employ skilled and experienced workmen to manufacture wheels, weapons, mail armor, and other related instruments within a specified time and for fixed wages. These items are to be used in battles, for the construction or defense of forts, or for destroying the cities or strongholds of enemies.

All weapons and instruments shall be stored in places properly designated for them. They shall be regularly dusted, moved from one location to another, and exposed to the sun. Weapons susceptible to heat and moisture (úshmopasneha) or prone to being eaten by worms shall be stored in secure locations. They shall also be inspected periodically in terms of their category, shape, characteristics, size, source, value, and total quantity.

The following are immovable machines (sthirayantrám): Sarvatobhadra, Jamadagnya, Bahumukha, Visvásagháti, Samgháti, Yánaka, Parjanyaka, Ardhabáhu, and Úrdhvabáhu.

The following are movable machines: Pánchálika, Devadanda, Súkarika, Musala, Yashti, Hastiváraka, Tálavrinta, Mudgara, Gada, Spriktala, Kuddála, Ásphátima, Audhghátima, Sataghni, Trisúla, and Chakra.

Weapons with ploughshare-like edges (halamukháni) include Sakti, Prása, Kunta, Hátaka, Bhindivála, Súla, Tomara, Varáhakarna, Kanaya, Karpana, and Trásika.

Bows are made from different materials: tála (palmyra), chápa (a kind of bamboo), dáru (a type of wood), and sringa (bone or horn), and are known as kármuka, kodanda, druna, and dhanus, respectively.

Bow-strings are made from múrva (Sansviera Roxburghiana), arka (Catotropis Gigantea), sána (hemp), gavedhu (Coix Barbata), venu (bamboo bark), and snáyu (sinew).

Different kinds of arrows include Venu, Sara, Saláka, Dandásana, and Nárácha. The arrowheads are made of iron, bone, or wood and are designed to cut, rend, or pierce.

Swords include Nistrimsa, Mandalágra, and Asiyashti, with handles made of rhinoceros or buffalo horn, elephant tusk, wood, or bamboo root.

Razor-like weapons include Parasu, Kuthára, Pattasa, Khanitra, Kuddála, Chakra, and Kándachchhedana.

Other weapons include Yantrapáshána, Goshpanapáshána, Mushtipáshána, Rochaní (mill-stone), and stones.

Armor varieties include Lohajáliká, Patta, Kavacha, and Sútraka, made from iron or skins combined with the hoofs and horns of porpoise, rhinoceros, bison, elephant, or cow.

Likewise, sirastrána (cover for the head), kanthatrána (cover for the neck), kúrpása (cover for the trunk), kanchuka (a coat extending as far as the knee joints), váravána (a coat extending as far as the heels), patta (a coat without cover for the arms), and nágodariká (gloves) are varieties of armor.

Veti, charma, hastikarna, tálamúla, dharmanika, kaváta, kitika, apratihata, and valáhakánta are instruments used in self-defense (ávaranáni).

Ornaments for elephants, chariots, and horses, as well as goads and hooks to guide them in battlefields, are considered accessory items (upakaranáni).

In addition to these, other delusive and destructive contrivances (as discussed in Book XIV) and any new inventions by expert workmen shall also be kept in stock.

The Superintendent of Armoury shall carefully assess the demand and supply of weapons, their application, their wear and tear, as well as their decay and loss.

[Thus ends Chapter XVIII, "The Superintendent of the Armoury," in Book II, "The Duties of Government Superintendents," of the Arthasástra of Kautilya. End of the thirty-ninth chapter from the beginning.]

CHAPTER XIX. THE SUPERINTENDENT OF WEIGHTS AND MEASURES.

The Superintendent of Weights and Measures shall oversee the manufacturing of standardized weights. Ten seeds of másha (Phraseolus Radiatus) or five gunja (Cabrus Precatorius) equal one suvarna-másha. Sixteen máshas equal one suvarna or karsha. Four karshas equal one pala. Eighty-eight white mustard seeds equal one silver-másha. Sixteen silver máshas or twenty saibya seeds equal one dharana. Twenty grains of rice equal one dharana of a diamond.

The various units of weight include: Ardha-másha (half a másha), one másha, two máshas, four máshas, eight máshas, one suvarna, two suvarnas, four suvarnas, eight suvarnas, ten suvarnas, twenty suvarnas, thirty suvarnas, forty suvarnas, and one hundred suvarnas.

A similar series of weights shall also be created in dharanas.

Weights (pratimánáni) shall be made from iron or stones found in the regions of Magadha and Mekala, or from materials that neither contract when wetted nor expand under heat.

Starting with a lever that is six angulas long and weighs one pala, ten balances shall be made, with each successive balance increasing by one pala in weight and eight angulas in length. Each balance will have a scale-pan attached on one or both sides.

A balance known as samavrittá, with a lever 72 angulas long and weighing 53 palas in its metallic mass, shall also be made. A scale-pan weighing five palas will be attached to its edge. The horizontal position of the lever (samakarana) when weighing a karsha shall be marked at the point where, when held by a thread, it balances horizontally. To the left of this mark, symbols for 1 pala, 12, 15, and 20 palas shall be indicated. After this, each place of tens up to 100 shall be marked. In the place of Akshas, the sign of Nándi shall be inscribed.

Likewise, a balance called parimáni, with twice the metallic mass of samavrittá and measuring 96 angulas in length, shall be made. On its lever, markings for 20, 50, and 100, in addition to the initial weight of 100, shall be engraved. Twenty tulas equal one bhára, and ten dharanas equal one pala. One hundred such palas equal one áyamáni, which is a measure of royal income.

The public balance (vyávaháriká), servants' balance (bhájiní), and harem balance (antahpurabhájiní) shall decrease successively by five palas when compared to áyamáni. Each pala in these balances will fall short of the áyamáni by half a dharana. The metallic mass of the levers in each balance will successively decrease in weight by two ordinary palas and in length by six angulas.

With the exception of flesh, metals, salt, and precious stones, all other commodities weighed in the two first-named balances shall have an excess of five palas (prayáma) given to the king.

A wooden balance with an 8-hand-long lever, equipped with measuring marks and counterpoise weights, shall be erected on a pedestal resembling that of a peacock.

Twenty-five palas of firewood will be required to cook one prastha of rice. This is the unit for calculating any greater or lesser quantity of firewood.

Thus, the weighing balance and weights are discussed. Then, with 200 palas of másha grains, one drona becomes an áyamána (a measure of royal income). A public drona will contain 187½ palas; a servants' drona (bhájaníya) will contain 175 palas; and a harem drona (antahpurabhájaníya) will contain 162½ palas.

Adhaka, prastha, and kudumba are each one-quarter of the unit before them. Sixteen dronas equal one várí, twenty dronas equal one kumbha, and ten kumbhas equal one vaha.

Cubic measures shall be made of dry and strong wood, so that when filled with grains, the conically heaped-up portion standing above the mouth of the measure equals one-fourth of the measured grains. Alternatively, measures may be made so that the heaped-up portion can fit inside the measure. Liquids, however, shall always be measured level to the mouth of the measure.

For wine, flowers, fruits, bran, charcoal, and slaked lime, twice the quantity of the heaped-up portion (i.e., one-fourth of the measure) shall be given as excess. The price of a drona is 1¼ panas, an ádhaka is ¾ pana, a prastha is 6 máshas, and a kudumba is 1 másha.

The price of liquid measures will be double the price of dry measures. The price of a set of counter-weights is 20 panas, and the price of a tulá (balance) is 6⅔ panas.

The Superintendent shall charge 4 máshas for stamping weights or measures. A fine of 27¼ panas shall be imposed for using unstamped weights or measures.

Traders shall pay one kákaní per day to the Superintendent as a charge for stamping weights and measures.

Those who trade in clarified butter shall give to purchasers 1/32 part more as taptavyáji (i.e., compensation for the decrease in the quantity of ghee due to its liquid condition). Those who trade in oil shall give 1/64 part more as taptavyáji.

While selling liquids, traders shall give 1/50 part more as mánasráva (i.e., compensation for the decrease in quantity due to overflow or adhesion to the measuring can).

Half, one-fourth, and one-eighth portions of the kumbha measure shall also be manufactured. Eighty-four kudumbas of clarified butter are considered equal to one wáraka of ghee, while sixty-four kudumbas of clarified butter are equal to one wáraka of oil (taila). One-quarter of a wáraka is referred to as ghatika, either of ghee or oil.

[Thus ends Chapter XIX, "Balance, Weights and Measures," in Book II, "The Duties of Government Superintendents," of the Arthasástra of Kautilya. End of the fortieth chapter from the beginning.]

CHAPTER XX. MEASUREMENT OF SPACE AND TIME.

The Superintendent of Lineal Measure shall possess knowledge of measuring both space and time. Eight atoms (paramánavah) are equal to one particle thrown off by the wheel of a chariot. Eight such particles are equal to one likshá. Eight likshás are equal to the middle of a yúka (louse) of medium size. Eight yúkas are equal to one yava (barley) of medium size. Eight yavas are equal to one angula (¾ of an English inch), or the middle joint of the middle finger of a man of medium size may be taken as equal to one angula. Four angulas are equal to one dhanurgraha. Eight angulas are equal to one dhanurmushti. Twelve angulas are equal to one vitasti, or one chháyápaurusha. Fourteen angulas are equal to one sama, sala, pariraya, or pada.

Two vitastis are equal to one aratni or one prájápatya hasta. Two vitastis plus one dhanurgraha are equal to one hasta, used in measuring balances, cubic measures, and pasture lands. Two vitastis plus one dhanurmushti equal one kishku or one kamsa. Forty-two angulas are equal to one kishku, as used by sawyers and blacksmiths for measuring the grounds for army encampments, forts, and palaces. Fifty-four angulas equal one hasta, used in measuring timber forests. Eighty-four angulas are equal to one vyáma, used in measuring ropes and digging depth in terms of a man's height. Four aratnis are equal to one danda, dhanus, nálika, or paurusha. One hundred and eight angulas are equal to one garhapatya dhanus (a measure used by carpenters called grihapati), used for measuring roads and fort walls. The same 108 angulas are equal to one paurusha, a measure used in building sacrificial altars. Six kamsas or 192 angulas are equal to one danda, used in measuring lands gifted to Bráhmans. Ten dandas are equal to one rajju. Two rajjus are equal to one paridesa (square measure). Three rajjus are equal to one nivartana (square measure). The same three rajjus, plus two dandas on one side, equal one báhu (arm). One thousand dhanus are equal to one goruta (the sound of a cow). Four gorutas are equal to one yojana.

Thus, lineal and square measures are dealt with.

Then, with regard to measures of time:

The divisions of time are: truti, lava, nimesha, káshthá, kalá, náliká, muhúrta, forenoon, afternoon, day, night, paksha (fortnight), month, ritu (season), ayana (solstice), samvatsara (year), and yuga (age). Two trutis are equal to one lava. Two lavas are equal to one nimesha. Five nimeshas are equal to one káshthá. Thirty káshthás are equal to one kalá. Forty kalás are equal to one náliká, which is the time taken for one ádhaka of water to flow out of a pot through an aperture the same diameter as a 4-angula-long wire made of 4 máshas of gold. Two nálikas are equal to one muhúrta. Fifteen muhúrtas are equal to one day or one night.

Such a day and night occur in the months of Chaitra and Asvayuja. After six months, the duration of day and night increases or decreases by three muhúrtas.

When the shadow is eight paurushas (96 angulas), it is 1/18th of the day. When it is six paurushas (72 angulas), it is 1/14th of the day. When four paurushas, it is 1/8th. When two paurushas, it is 1/6th. When one paurusha, it is ¼th. When the shadow is eight angulas, it is 3/10th of the day (trayodasabhágah); when four angulas, it is 3/8th. When no shadow is cast, it is considered midday.

Likewise, when the day declines, the same process in reverse order shall be observed. It is in the month of Ashádha that no shadow is cast at midday. After Ashádha, during the six months from Srávana onward, the length of the shadow successively increases by two angulas. During the next six months from Mágha onward, it successively decreases by two angulas.

Fifteen days and nights together make up one paksha. The paksha during which the moon waxes is called sukla (white), and the paksha during which the moon wanes is called bahula.

Two pakshas make one month (mása). Thirty days and nights together make one prakarmamása (work-a-month). The same 30 days and nights, with an additional half day, make one solar month (saura). The same 30 days and nights, less by half a day, make one lunar month (chandramása). Twenty-seven days and nights make a sidereal month (nakshatramása).

Once in thirty-two months, there comes one malamása, a "profane month" (an extra month added to the lunar year to harmonize it with the solar). Once in thirty-five months, there is a malamása for Asvaváhas. Once in forty months, there is a malamása for hastiváhas.

Two months make one ritu (season). Srávana and Proshthapada make the rainy season (varshá). Asvayuja and Kárthíka make the autumn (sarad). Márgasírsha and Phausha make the winter (hemanta). Mágha and Phalguna make the dewy season (sisira). Chaitra and Vaisákha make the spring (vasanta). Jyeshthámúlíya and Ashádha make the summer (grishma).

The seasons from sisira and upward are the summer solstice (uttaráyana), and those from varshá and upward are the winter solstice (dakshináyana). Two solstices (ayanas) make one year (samvatsara). Five years make one yuga.

The sun "carries off" (harati) 1/60th of a whole day every day, thus completing one full day every two months (ritau). Likewise, the moon falls behind by 1/60th of a whole day every day, falling behind by one day every two months. Thus, in the middle of every third year, they (the sun and the moon) make one adhimása (additional month), the first in the summer season and the second at the end of five years.

[Thus ends Chapter XX, "Measurement of Space and Time," in Book II, "The Duties of Government Superintendents," of the Arthasástra of Kautilya. End of the forty-first chapter from the beginning.]

CHAPTER XXI. THE SUPERINTENDENT OF TOLLS.

The Superintendent of Tolls shall establish both the toll-house and its flag near the large gate of the city, with the flag facing either the north or the south. When merchants arrive at the toll gate with their merchandise, four or five collectors shall record who the merchants are, where they come from, the amount of merchandise they are bringing, and where the sealmark (abhijnánamudrá) was first placed on the merchandise.

Merchants whose merchandise has not been stamped with the sealmark shall pay double the toll. For using counterfeit seals, they shall pay eight times the toll. If the sealmark is effaced or torn, the merchants in question shall be compelled to stand in the ghatikásthána (a place for public punishment). When a seal meant for one type of merchandise is used for another or when the merchandise is falsely named (námakrite), the merchants shall pay a fine of 1¼ panás for each load (sapádapanikam vahanam dápayet).

The merchandise shall be placed near the flag of the toll-house, and the merchants shall declare its quantity and price, then cry out three times, "Who will purchase this quantity of merchandise for this price?" They shall hand over the merchandise to anyone who demands it for that price. If buyers offer a higher price, the enhanced amount, along with the toll on the merchandise, shall be paid into the king's treasury. If the merchants reduce the quantity or price of the merchandise to avoid a high toll, the excess shall be taken by the king, or the merchants shall be made to pay eight times the toll. The same punishment shall apply if the price of merchandise packed in bags is lowered by showing an inferior sample or when valuable goods are covered with a layer of inferior ones.

If the price of merchandise is increased beyond its proper value due to fear of bidders raising the price, the king shall receive the enhanced amount or twice the toll on it. The same punishment or eight times the toll shall be imposed on the Superintendent of Tolls if he conceals merchandise.

Therefore, commodities shall be sold only after they are accurately weighed, measured, or numbered.

In the case of inferior goods or those exempt from tolls, the toll amount due shall be determined after careful consideration.

Merchants who pass beyond the flag of the toll-house without paying the toll shall be fined eight times the amount of the toll due from them. Those traveling to and from the city shall ascertain whether the toll has been paid on any merchandise going along the road.

Commodities intended for marriages, or taken by a bride from her parents' house to her husband's (anváyanam), or intended for presentation, or taken for the purpose of performing sacrifices, confinement of women, worship of gods, the ceremony of tonsure, investiture with the sacred thread, gift of cows (godána, made before marriage), any religious rite, consecration ceremony (dikshá), and other special ceremonies, shall be exempt from tolls.

Those who lie about such goods shall be punished as thieves.

Anyone smuggling part of their goods without paying toll, mixing it with goods on which toll has already been paid, or breaking open a bag to hide goods in order to use the same toll pass for a second portion of merchandise, shall lose the smuggled goods and be fined the value of the smuggled amount.

Someone who, after falsely swearing by cow dung, smuggles goods shall face the highest penalty.

If a person imports banned items like weapons, armor, metals, chariots, precious stones, grains, or cattle, they will not only be punished according to other laws but will also have to forfeit the goods. If these items were brought in to be sold, they must be sold outside the city walls, toll-free.

The officer in charge of boundaries (antapála) shall collect a pana-and-a-quarter as road tax (vartani) for each load of goods.

They shall charge one pana for each single-hoofed animal, half a pana for each head of cattle, and a quarter of a pana for smaller four-legged animals.

They will also collect a másha for each head-load of merchandise.

The officer is responsible for compensating merchants for any losses suffered within their region.

After thoroughly inspecting foreign goods for quality, the officer shall stamp them with a seal and send them to the toll superintendent.

Alternatively, they may send a spy disguised as a merchant to inform the king about the amount and quality of the goods. The king will then pass this information to the toll superintendent to show the king's all-knowing power. The superintendent will tell the merchants that a certain merchant has brought in a certain amount of high or low-quality merchandise, which cannot be hidden, emphasizing that this knowledge is due to the king's wisdom.

For hiding inferior goods, eight times the toll shall be charged; for hiding or covering up superior goods, they shall be confiscated.

Anything harmful or useless to the country will be blocked, while goods of great benefit, including rare seeds, will be allowed in without paying tolls.

CHAPTER XXII. REGULATION OF TOLL-DUES.

Merchandise, whether it comes from outside the city (báhyam, i.e., from country parts), is produced inside the city (ábhyantaram, i.e., manufactured inside forts), or is imported from foreign countries (átithyani), shall all be subject to tolls, both when exported (nishkrámya) and imported (pravésyam).

Imported goods shall pay 1/5th of their value as a toll.

For flowers, fruits, vegetables (sáka), roots (múla), bulbous roots (kanda), pallikya (?), seeds, dried fish, and dried meat, the superintendent shall collect 1/6th of their value as toll.

For conch-shells, diamonds, precious stones, pearls, corals, and necklaces, experts familiar with the production cost, timing, and quality of the items shall determine the toll amount.

For fibrous garments (kshauma), cotton cloths (dukúla), silk (krimitána), mail armor (kankata), sulphuret of arsenic (haritála), red arsenic (manassilá), vermilion (hingulaka), metals (lóha), and coloring materials (varnadhátu); as well as sandalwood, agarwood (agaru), spices (katuka), ferments (kinva), clothing (ávarana), and similar items; wine, ivory, skins, raw materials for making fiber or cotton garments, carpets, curtains (právarana), and products derived from worms (krimijáta); and wool and other products from goats and sheep, he shall collect 1/10th or 1/15th as toll.

For cloths (vastra), quadrupeds, bipeds, threads, cotton, scents, medicines, wood, bamboo, fibers (valkala), skins, and clay pots; as well as grains, oils, sugar (kshára), salt, liquor (madya), cooked rice, and similar items, he shall collect 1/20th or 1/25th as toll.

Gate dues (dvárádeya) shall be 1/5th of toll dues, though this tax may be waived if circumstances call for such a favor. Goods shall not be sold where they are grown or produced.

When minerals and other goods are purchased from mines, a fine of 600 panás shall be imposed.

When flowers or fruits are purchased from flower or fruit gardens, a fine of 54 panas shall be imposed.

When vegetables, roots, or bulbous roots are purchased from vegetable gardens, a fine of 51¾ panas shall be imposed.

When any type of grass or grain is purchased from a field, a fine of 53 panas shall be imposed.

Permanent fines of 1 pana and 1½ panas shall be collected on agricultural produce (sítátyayah).

Therefore, based on the customs of the country or community, the rate of tolls shall be set for both new and old commodities, and fines shall be proportionate to the seriousness of the offenses.

CHAPTER XXIII. SUPERINTENDENT OF WEAVING.

The Superintendent of Weaving shall employ qualified persons to manufacture threads, coats, cloths, and ropes.

Widows, crippled women, young girls, mendicant or ascetic women, women forced to work due to failure to pay fines, mothers of prostitutes, elderly female servants of the king, and temple dancers who have ceased to attend temple service shall be employed to cut wool, fiber, cotton, fluff, hemp, and flax.

Wages shall be determined according to whether the threads spun are fine, coarse, or of medium quality, in proportion to the amount of work done, and the quantity of thread produced. Those who produce a greater quantity shall be rewarded with oil and dried myrobalan fruit cakes. They may also be employed to work on holidays with the promise of additional rewards.

If the amount of thread spun falls short, considering the quality of the raw material, wages shall be reduced accordingly.

Weaving can also be done by artisans who are capable of producing a set quantity of work within a specified time and for a fixed wage.

The superintendent shall closely associate with the workmen.

Those who manufacture fibrous cloths, garments, silk-cloths, woolen cloths, and cotton fabrics shall be rewarded with presentations such as scents, garlands of flowers, or any other prizes of encouragement.

Various kinds of garments, blankets, and curtains shall be produced.

Those skilled in the craft shall manufacture mail armor.

Women who do not leave their homes, whose husbands are away, or those who are disabled or young girls may, when compelled to work for their livelihood, be given work through the courtesy of maid-servants of the weaving establishment.

Women who can present themselves at the weaving house shall, at dawn, be allowed to exchange their spun threads for wages. Only enough light as is necessary to examine the threads shall be used. If the superintendent looks at the face of these women or discusses any other work, he shall be punished with the first amercement. Delay in paying wages shall result in the middle amercement, and the same punishment shall apply when wages are paid for incomplete work.

A woman who, after receiving wages, does not turn out the required work shall have her thumb cut off.

Those who misappropriate, steal, or run away with the raw materials shall be punished in the same way.

Weavers, when guilty of offenses, shall be fined from their wages in proportion to their offenses.

The superintendent shall closely associate with those who manufacture ropes and mail armor, and he shall also oversee the manufacture of straps and other necessary items.

He shall oversee the production of ropes from threads and fibers and the production of straps from cane and bamboo bark, which are used for training or tethering draft animals.

[Thus ends the section on "The Superintendent of Weaving."]

CHAPTER XXIV. THE SUPERINTENDENT OF AGRICULTURE.

Being knowledgeable in the science of agriculture, which deals with the planting of bushes and trees (krishitantragulmavrikshsháyurvedajñah), or with the help of those trained in these sciences, the Superintendent of Agriculture shall collect seeds at the proper time from all kinds of grains, flowers, fruits, vegetables, bulbous roots, roots, pállikya (?), fibre-producing plants, and cotton.

He shall employ slaves, laborers, and prisoners (dandapratikartri) to sow these seeds on crown-lands that have been regularly and thoroughly ploughed.

The work of these individuals shall not be disrupted by any shortage of plows (karshanayantra) or other essential tools, nor by the lack of bullocks. Nor shall there be any delay in securing for them the services of blacksmiths, carpenters, drillers (medaka), ropemakers, and those skilled in catching snakes or similar tasks.

Any loss caused by negligence on the part of these workers shall result in a fine equal to the value of the loss.

The average rainfall in the Jangala region is 16 dronas; it is one and a half times greater in moist regions (anúpánám). For countries that are agriculturally suited (désavápánam), the rainfall is 13½ dronas in the Asmaka region, 23 dronas in Avanti, and immense amounts in the western regions (aparántánám), the borders of the Himalayas, and regions where water channels are used for agriculture (kulyávápánám).

When one-third of the necessary rainfall occurs both in the early and late months of the rainy season and two-thirds falls in the middle, the rainfall is considered evenly distributed (sushumárúpam).

A forecast of such rainfall can be made by observing the position, movement, and "pregnancy" (garbhádána) of Jupiter (Brihaspati), as well as the rise, set, and movement of Venus, and the natural or unnatural appearance of the sun.

From the sun, the sprouting of seeds can be predicted; from the position of Jupiter, the formation of grains (stambakarita) can be foretold; and from the movement of Venus, the likelihood of rainfall can be inferred.

Three are the clouds that continuously rain for seven days; eighty are they that pour minute drops; and sixty are they that appear with the sunshine—this is termed rainfall. Where rain, free from wind and unmingled with sunshine, falls so as to render three turns of ploughing possible, there the reaping of a good harvest is certain.

Hence, according as the rainfall is more or less, the superintendent shall sow the seeds which require either more or less water.

Sáli (a kind of rice), vríhi (rice), kodrava (Paspalum Scrobiculatum), tila (sesamum), priyangu (panic seeds), dáraka (?), and varaka (Phraseolus Trilobus) are to be sown at the commencement (púrvávápah) of the rainy season.

Mudga (Phraseolus Mungo), másha (Phraseolus Radiatus), and saibya (?) are to be sown in the middle of the season.

Kusumbha (safflower), masúra (Ervum Hirsutum), kuluttha (Dolichos Uniflorus), yava (barley), godhúma (wheat), kaláya (leguminous seeds), atasi (linseed), and sarshapa (mustard) are to be sown last.

Or seeds may be sown according to the changes of the season.

Fields that are left unsown (vápátiriktam, i.e., owing to the inadequacy of hands) may be brought under cultivation by employing those who cultivate for half the share in the produce (ardhasítiká); or those who live by their own physical exertion (svavíryopajívinah) may cultivate such fields for ¼th or 1/5th of the produce grown; or they may pay (to the king) as much as they can without entailing any hardship upon themselves (anavasitam bhágam), with the exception of their own private lands that are difficult to cultivate.

Those who cultivate irrigating by manual labour (hastaprávartimam) shall pay 1/5th of the produce as water-rate (udakabhágam); by carrying water on shoulders (skandhaprávartimam)

¼th of the produce; by water-lifts (srotoyantraprávartimam), ⅓rd of the produce; and by raising water from rivers, lakes, tanks, and wells (nadisarastatákakúpodghátam), ⅓rd or ¼th of the produce.

The superintendent shall cultivate wet crops (kedára), winter crops (haimana), or summer crops (graishmika) based on the availability of laborers and water. Rice and similar crops are considered the best to grow (jyáshtha), vegetables (shanda) are of medium difficulty, and sugarcane (ikshu) is the most challenging (pratyavarah) because it is prone to various issues and requires significant care and cost to harvest.

Lands that are beaten by river foam (phenághátah), such as riverbanks, are ideal for growing plants like pumpkins, gourds, and other vines (vallíphala). Areas frequently flooded (paríváhánta) are good for growing long pepper, grapes (mridvíká), and sugarcane. The areas near wells are best suited for growing vegetables and roots, while low-lying grounds (haríníparyantáh) are suitable for growing green crops. The spaces between rows of crops are suitable for planting fragrant plants, medicinal herbs, cascus roots (usínara), híra (?), beraka (?), pindáluka (lac), and similar plants.

Medicinal herbs that typically grow in marshy areas should be planted not only in suitable grounds but also in pots (sthályam). Grain seeds need to be exposed to mist and heat (tushárapáyanamushnam cha) for seven nights, while kosi seeds should be treated the same way for three nights. The cut ends of sugarcane and similar seeds (kándabíjánam) should be coated with a mixture of honey, clarified butter, hog fat, and cow dung. Bulbous root seeds (kanda) should be coated with honey and clarified butter, while cotton seeds (asthibíja) should be treated with cow dung. Water pits at the roots of trees should be burned and manured with cow bones and dung at the appropriate times.

Once the seeds sprout, they should be fertilized with a fresh haul of small fish and watered with the milk of the snuhi plant (Euphorbia Antiquorum).

Where there is the smoke caused by burning tWhere there is smoke created by burning the essence of cotton seeds and the shed skin of a snake, snakes will not stay in that area.

When sowing seeds, always begin by planting a handful of seeds soaked in water along with a piece of gold. While doing this, recite the following mantra:

"Prajápatye Kasyapáya déváya namah. Sadá Sítá medhyatám déví bíjéshu cha dhanéshu cha. Chandaváta hé."

This means: "Salutations to the god Prajápati Kasyapa. May agriculture always thrive, and may the Goddess reside in both seeds and wealth. Channdavata he."

Provisions should be provided to watchmen, slaves, and laborers according to the amount of work they complete. They shall receive a monthly wage of one and a quarter pana. Artisans shall also be compensated with wages and provisions based on the amount of work they do.

People who are well-versed in the Vedas and those practicing penance may take ripe flowers and fruits from the fields to worship their gods, as well as rice and barley for performing the ágrayana, a sacrificial ceremony marking the beginning of the harvest season. Similarly, those who make a living by gleaning grains from fields may collect leftover grains after the main harvest has been removed.

Grains and other crops should be gathered immediately after each harvest. A wise person leaves nothing behind in the fields, not even chaff. Once harvested, crops should be stacked in tall piles or shaped into turrets. The piles should not be packed too tightly, and their tops should not be small or low. Threshing floors from different fields should be located near each other. Workers in the fields should always have access to water but not to fire.

[Thus ends Chapter XXIV, "The Superintendent of Agriculture" in Book II, "The Duties of Government Superintendents" of the Arthasástra of Kautilya. End of the forty-fifth chapter from the beginning.]

CHAPTER XXV. THE SUPERINTENDENT OF LIQUOR.

By employing men skilled in the production of liquor and ferments (kinva), the Superintendent of Liquor will manage the liquor trade not only in forts and rural areas but also in military camps. Based on the supply and demand (krayavikrayavasena), the sale of liquor can either be centralized or spread out.

A fine of 600 panas will be imposed on all violators involved in the liquor trade, except for those who are manufacturers, buyers, or sellers. Liquor must not be taken out of villages, and liquor shops should not be located too close to each other.

To prevent workers from neglecting their tasks, and Aryas (noble people) from compromising their dignity and virtuous conduct, and to avoid irresponsible behavior by troublemakers, liquor should only be sold to trustworthy individuals in small quantities—one-fourth or half-a-kudumba, one kudumba, half-a-prastha, or one prastha. People of known good character may be permitted to take liquor out of the shop.

Alternatively, everyone may be required to consume liquor inside the shops to detect any stolen goods or items of value like sealed deposits, unsealed deposits, items given for repair, or stolen goods that customers may have obtained unlawfully. If customers are found with gold or other possessions that do not belong to them, the superintendent will arrange for their arrest outside the shop. Similarly, those who spend excessively or beyond their means will also be arrested.

Fresh liquor should not be sold below its proper price, except for low-quality liquor, which may be sold elsewhere or given to slaves or workers as payment. It can also be used as a drink for draft animals or as food for pigs.

Liquor shops should have several rooms, each with separate beds and seats. The drinking room should have fragrances, flower garlands, water, and other amenities suitable to the season to ensure customers' comfort.

Spies positioned in the shops will observe whether the customers' spending is normal or unusual and whether there are any unfamiliar faces. They will also assess the value of the clothing, jewelry, and gold left by customers who may be intoxicated.

When customers under intoxication lose any of their belongings, the merchants of the shop shall not only make good the loss but also pay an equivalent fine. Merchants seated in half-closed rooms shall observe the appearance of local and foreign customers who, in real or false guise of Aryas, lie down in intoxication along with their beautiful mistresses.

Of various kinds of liquor such as medaka, prasanna, ásava, arista, maireya, and madhu:

Medaka is manufactured with one drona of water, half an ádaka of rice, and three prastha of kinva (ferment).

Twelve ádhakas of flour (pishta), five prastha of kinva (ferment), with the addition of spices (játisambhára) together with the bark and fruits of putraká (a species of tree), constitute prasanná.

One hundred palas of kapittha (Feronia Elephantum), 500 palas of phánita (sugar), and one prastha of honey (madhu) form ásava.

With an increase of one-quarter of the above ingredients, a superior kind of ásava is manufactured; and when the same ingredients are lessened to the extent of one-quarter each, it becomes of an inferior quality.

The preparation of various kinds of arista for various diseases is to be learned from physicians.

A sour gruel or decoction of the bark of meshasringi (a kind of poison) mixed with jaggery (guda) and with the powder of long pepper and black pepper or with the powder of triphala (a mixture of 1 Terminalia Chebula, 2 Terminalia Bellerica, and 3 Phyllanthus Emblica) forms Maireya.

To all kinds of liquor mixed with jaggery, the powder of triphala is always added.

The juice of grapes is termed madhu. Its own native place (svadesa) is the commentary on such of its various forms as kápisáyana and hárahúraka.

One drona of either boiled or unboiled paste of másha (Phraseolus Radiatus), three parts more of rice, and one karsha of morata (Alangium Hexapetalum) and similar ingredients form kinva (ferment).

In the making of medaka and prasanna, five karshas of the powder of each of páthá (Clypea Hermandifolia), lodhra (Symplocos Racemosa), tejovati (Piper Chaba), eláváluka (Solanum Melongena), honey, the juice of grapes (madhurasa), priyangu (panic seeds), dáruharidra (a species of turmeric), black pepper, and long pepper are added as sambhára, the necessary spices.

The decoction of madhúka (Bassia Latifolia) mixed with granulated sugar (katasarkará), when added to prasanna, gives it a pleasing color.

For ásava, the required amount of spices includes one karsha of the powder of each of chocha (bark of cinnamon), chitraka (Plumbago Zeylanica), vilanga, and gajapippalí (Scindapsus Officinalis), and two karshas of the powder of each of kramuka (betel nut), madhúka (Bassia Latifolia), mustá (Cyprus Rotundus), and lodhra (Symplocos Racemosa).

The addition of one-tenth of the above ingredients (such as chocha, kramuka, etc.) is referred to as bíjabandha.

The same spices that are added to prasanná are also added to white liquor (svetasurá).

The liquor that is produced from mango fruits (sahakárasurá) may have a higher concentration of mango essence (rasottara) or spices (bíjottara). It is called mahásura when it contains sambhára (the spices described above).

When a handful (antarnakho mushtih, meaning as much as can be held in the hand while bending the fingers so the nails are hidden) of the powder of granulated sugar dissolved in the decoction of moratá (Alangium Hexapetalum), palása (Butea Frondosa), dattúra (Datura Fastuosa), karanja (Robinia Mitis), meshasringa (a kind of poison), and the bark of milky trees (kshiravriksha), mixed with half of the paste made from the powders of lodhra (Symplocos Racemosa), chitraka (Plumbago Zeylanica), vilanga, páthá (Clypea Hermandifolia), mustá (Cyprus Rotundus), kaláya (leguminous seeds), dáruharidra (Amomum Xanthorrhizon), indívara (blue lotus), satapushpa (Anethum Sowa), apámárga (Achyranthes Aspera), saptaparna (Echites Scholaris), and nimba (Nimba Melia) is added to a kumbha of liquor payable by the king, it makes the liquor very pleasant. Five palas of phánita (sugar) are added to the above mixture to enhance its flavor.

On special occasions (krityeshu), families (kutumbinah) shall be permitted to make white liquor (svetasura), arishta for medicinal use, and other types of liquor.

During festivals, fairs (samája), and pilgrimages, the right to manufacture liquor for four days (chaturahassaurikah) shall be granted.

The Superintendent shall collect daily fines (daivasikamatyayam), or license fees, from those who are allowed to produce liquor on these occasions.

Women and children shall be assigned the task of collecting 'sura' and 'kinva' (ferment).

Those who deal in liquor other than that made by the king shall pay a five percent toll.

Regarding sura, medaka, arishta, wine, phalámla (acid drinks made from fruits), and ámlasídhu (spirit distilled from molasses):

After determining the day's sale of these types of liquor, the difference between royal and public measures (mánavyáji), and the surplus profit made from such sales, the Superintendent shall set the amount of compensation (vaidharana) owed to the king. This compensation applies to local or foreign merchants who cause loss to the king's liquor trade. The Superintendent shall always choose the most beneficial course of action.

[Thus ends Chapter XXV, "The Superintendent of Liquor" in Book II, "The Duties of Government Superintendents," of the Arthasástra of Kautilya. End of the forty-sixth chapter from the beginning.]

CHAPTER XXVI. THE SUPERINTENDENT OF SLAUGHTER-HOUSE.

When a person traps, kills, or harms deer, bison, birds, and fish that are protected by the state or live in state-protected forests (abhayáranya), they shall be punished with the highest fine.

Householders who trespass in protected forests will be punished with the middlemost fine.

If someone traps, kills, or harms either fish or birds that do not prey on other animals, they shall be fined 26¾ panas. If the same is done to deer or other animals, the fine will be twice as much.

For captured wild animals, the superintendent shall take one-sixth; for fish and birds of prey, they will take one-tenth or more, and for deer and other animals (mrigapasu), one-tenth or more as toll.

One-sixth of live animals, such as birds and beasts, shall be released in state-protected forests.

Elephants, horses, or animals resembling a human, bull, or donkey living in oceans, as well as fish in tanks, lakes, channels, and rivers, and game-birds such as krauncha (a kind of heron), utkrosaka (osprey), dátyúha (a type of cuckoo), hamsa (flamingo), chakraváka (brahmany duck), jivanjívaka (a type of pheasant), bhringarája (Lanius Malabaricus), chakora (partridge), mattakokila (cuckoo), peacocks, parrots, and maina (madanasárika), along with other auspicious animals, both birds and beasts, shall be protected from any harm.

Those who break this rule shall be punished with the first level of amercement.

Butchers must sell only fresh and boneless meat of animals (mrigapasu) that were just killed.

If they sell bony meat, they shall provide an equal compensation (pratipákam). If any weight is lost due to using a false balance, they shall pay eight times the weight difference.

Calves, bulls, and milch cows are not to be slaughtered. Those who slaughter or torture them to death shall be fined 50 panas.

The meat of animals killed outside the slaughterhouse (parisúnam), headless, legless, or boneless meat, rotten meat, and the meat of animals that have suddenly died shall not be sold. Otherwise, a fine of 12 panas will be imposed.

Vicious animals such as cattle, wild beasts, elephants (vyala), and fish living in state-protected forests shall, if they become dangerous, be trapped and killed outside the forest preserve.

[Thus ends Chapter XXVI, "The Superintendent of Slaughterhouse" in Book II, "The Duties of Government Superintendents" of the Arthasástra of Kautilya. End of the forty-seventh chapter from the beginning.]

CHAPTER XXVII. THE SUPERINTENDENT OF PROSTITUTES.

The Superintendent of Prostitutes shall appoint a prostitute (ganiká), whether born into a prostitute's family or not, and known for her beauty, youth, and accomplishments, to the king's court with an annual salary of 1,000 panas.

A rival prostitute (pratiganiká) shall also be appointed with half that salary (kutumbárdhéna).

If the appointed prostitute goes abroad or dies, her daughter or sister shall take her place and receive her property and salary. Alternatively, her mother may substitute another prostitute. If none of these are available, the king shall take possession of her property.

To enhance the prestige of the prostitutes serving the king, who hold the royal umbrella, golden pitcher, and fan while attending him on his litter, throne, or chariot, they shall be ranked according to their beauty and splendid jewelry, into first, middle, and highest ranks. Their salaries shall be fixed accordingly, in thousands of panas.

A prostitute who has lost her beauty shall be appointed as a nurse (mátriká).

To regain her freedom, a prostitute shall pay 24,000 panas as ransom, and the son of a prostitute shall pay 12,000 panas.

From the age of eight, a prostitute shall perform music before the king.

Those prostitutes, female slaves, and elderly women who are no longer able to serve in terms of enjoyment (bhagnabhogáh) shall work in the king's storehouse or kitchen.

A prostitute who chooses to place herself under the protection of a private individual and stops attending the king's court must pay a monthly fee of one pana-and-a-quarter to the government.

The superintendent shall oversee the earnings, inheritance, income (áya), expenditure, and future income (áyati) of every prostitute and also curb their extravagant spending.

If a prostitute entrusts her jewelry to anyone other than her mother, she shall be fined 4¼ panas.

If she sells or mortgages her property (svapateyam), she shall be fined 50¼ panas.

A prostitute shall be fined 24 panas for defamation, twice that amount for causing injury, and 50¼ panas, along with 1½ panas, for cutting off someone's ear.

When a man forces a prostitute against her will or has relations with a prostitute girl (kumári), he shall be punished with the highest amercement. However, if he has relations with a willing underage prostitute, he shall be punished with the first amercement.

If a man confines or abducts a prostitute against her will, or disfigures her by causing injury, he shall be fined 1,000 panas or more, up to twice the amount of her ransom (nishkraya), depending on the severity of the crime and the social position of the prostitute (sthánaviseshena).

If a man harms a prostitute appointed at the court (praptádhikáram), he shall be fined three times the amount of her ransom.

If a man harms the mother, young daughter, or rúpadási (a female attendant) of a prostitute, he shall be punished with the highest amercement.

In all cases, for a first-time offense, the punishment shall be the first amercement; for a second-time offense, twice that amount; for a third-time offense, three times that amount. For a fourth offense, the king may impose any punishment he deems appropriate.

If a prostitute refuses to yield her person under the king's orders, she shall receive 1,000 lashes with a whip or pay a fine of 5,000 panas.

If a prostitute refuses to provide her services after receiving payment, she shall be fined twice the amount of the fees.

If, in her own house, a prostitute denies her paramour enjoyment, she shall be fined eight times the amount of the fees unless the paramour is unassociable due to disease or personal defects.

If a prostitute murders her paramour, she shall be burned alive or thrown into water.

If a paramour steals the jewelry or money of a prostitute, or deceives her by not paying the agreed fees, he shall be fined eight times that amount.

Every prostitute shall report her daily earnings (bhoga), future income (áyati), and the identity of her paramour (under her influence) to the superintendent.

These same rules shall apply to actors, dancers, singers, musicians, buffoons (vágjivana), mimics (kusílava), rope-dancers (plavaka), jugglers (saubhika), wandering bards or heralds (chárana), pimps, and unchaste women.

When performers of these types come from foreign lands to hold shows, they shall pay 5 panas as a license fee (prekshávetana).

Every prostitute (rúpájivá) shall pay twice the amount of one day's earnings (bhogadvigunam) to the government each month.

Those who teach prostitutes, female slaves, and actresses in arts such as singing, playing musical instruments, reading, dancing, acting, writing, painting, playing instruments like the vina, pipe, and drum, reading the thoughts of others, making scents and garlands, massage techniques, and the art of attracting and captivating others, shall be provided maintenance by the state.

They (the teachers) shall train the sons of prostitutes to become chief performers (rangopajívi) on the stage.

The wives of actors and others of similar professions, who have been taught various languages and the use of signals (sanja), shall, along with their relatives, be employed to detect wrongdoers and to eliminate or mislead foreign spies.

[Thus ends Chapter XXVII, "The Superintendent of Prostitutes" in Book II, "The Duties of Government Superintendents," of the Arthasástra of Kautilya. End of the forty-eighth chapter from the beginning.]

CHAPTER XXVIII. THE SUPERINTENDENT OF SHIPS.

THE Superintendent of Ships shall oversee the records related to navigation, not only on oceans and river mouths but also on natural or artificial lakes and rivers near fortified cities such as sthániya and others.

Villages located on seashores or riverbanks and lakes shall pay a fixed amount of tax (kliptam). Fishermen must give one-sixth of their catch as a fee for their fishing license (naukáhátakam). Merchants shall pay the customary toll levied in port towns, and passengers arriving on the king's ship shall pay the appropriate sailing fees (yátrávetanam). Those who use the king's boats for gathering conch shells and pearls shall pay the appropriate hire (naukáhátakam), or they may use their own boats.

The duties of the superintendent of mines will also apply to the superintendent of conch shells and pearls. The superintendent of ships must closely follow the customs of commercial towns and the orders of the superintendent of towns (pattana, or port town). When a ship battered by weather arrives at a port, he shall show it fatherly care and concern.

Ships carrying merchandise that has been damaged by water may either be exempted from tolls or have their tolls reduced by half, allowing them to depart when it is time to sail. Ships that dock at harbors along their journey may be asked to pay tolls. Pirate ships (himsríká), vessels bound for enemy territories, and those violating the rules and customs of port towns shall be destroyed.

Large boats (mahánávah) equipped with a captain (sásaka), a steersman (niyámaka), and crew members to handle the ropes, hold the sickle, and pour out water, shall be launched on large rivers that cannot be forded even during winter and summer. Small boats shall be used in rivers that overflow during the rainy season.

Fording or crossing rivers without permission shall be prohibited to prevent traitors from escaping. If someone crosses a river at an improper place or during unusual times, they shall be punished with the first amercement. If a person crosses a river at the regular place and time without permission, they shall be fined 26¾ panas.

Exemptions to cross rivers at any time and place shall be granted to fishermen, carriers of firewood, grass, flowers, and fruits, gardeners, vegetable dealers, herdsmen, people pursuing suspected criminals, messengers following other messengers, servants delivering supplies, provisions, and orders to the army, those using their own ferries, and those supplying villages in marshy districts with seeds, essentials, commodities, and other necessary items.

Bráhmans, ascetics (pravrajita), children, the elderly, the afflicted, royal messengers, and pregnant women shall be provided with free passes by the superintendent to cross rivers.

Foreign merchants who frequently visit the country and are known to local merchants shall be permitted to land in port towns.

The following individuals shall be arrested: anyone abducting another's wife or daughter, someone carrying off another's wealth, a suspicious person, someone with a disturbed appearance, anyone without baggage, a person attempting to conceal or evade notice of a valuable load, someone who has just changed their attire, anyone who has renounced or removed their usual garb, someone pretending to be an ascetic, someone feigning illness, anyone who appears alarmed, someone secretly carrying valuable items or on a secret mission, anyone carrying weapons or explosives (agniyoga), someone holding poison, and anyone who has traveled a long distance without a pass.

A minor quadruped, as well as a man carrying some load, shall pay one másha. A head-load, a load carried on shoulders (káyabhárah), a cow, and a horse shall each pay 2 máshas. A camel and a buffalo shall each pay 4 máshas. A small cart (laghuyána) shall pay 5 máshas, and a cart of medium size drawn by bulls (golingam) shall pay 6 máshas, while a big cart (sakata) shall pay 7 máshas. A head-load of merchandise shall pay ¼ másha, which explains the toll for other types of loads. In big rivers, ferry-fees are double the amounts listed above.

Villages near marshy areas shall provide the ferry-men with the prescribed amount of food and wages. At boundaries, ferry-men shall collect tolls, carriage-cess, and road-cess. They shall also confiscate the property of anyone traveling without a pass. The Superintendent of Boats shall compensate for losses caused by a boat's failure due to overloading, sailing at the wrong time or place, lack of ferry-men, or inadequate repairs. Boats should be launched between the months of Ashádha (excluding the first seven days) and Kártika, with the ferryman's evidence recorded and the daily income remitted.

[Thus ends Chapter XXVIII, "The Superintendent of Ships" in Book II, "The Duties of Government Superintendents" of the

Arthasástra of Kautilya. End of the forty-ninth chapter from the beginning.]

CHAPTER XXIX. THE SUPERINTENDENT OF COWS.

The Superintendent of Cows shall supervise the following:

(1) Herds maintained for wages (vétanópagráhikam), (2) Herds surrendered for a fixed amount of dairy produce (karapratikara), (3) Useless and abandoned herds (bhagnotsrishtakam), (4) Herds maintained for a share in dairy produce (bhágánupravishtam), (5) Classes of herds (vrajaparyagram), (6) Cattle that strayed (nashtam), (7) Cattle that are irrecoverably lost (vinashtam), and (8) The amassed quantity of milk and clarified butter.

(1) When a cowherd, buffalo-herdsman, milker, churner, and hunter (lubdhaka), all fed by wages, graze milch cows (dhenu) in groups of hundreds (satam satam)—since if they graze the herds for the profit of milk and ghee, they might starve the calves to death—this system of rearing cattle is termed "herds maintained for wages."

(2) When a single person rears a hundred heads of cattle (rúpasatam), comprising equal numbers of aged cows, milch cows, pregnant cows, heifers, and calves (vatsatari), and gives the owner 8 várakas of clarified butter annually along with the branded skin of any dead cows, this system is called "herds surrendered for a fixed amount of dairy produce."

(3) When those who rear a hundred heads of cattle, made up of equal numbers of afflicted cattle, crippled cattle, cattle that can only be milked by a familiar person, cattle that are difficult to milk, and cattle that kill their own calves, give a share of the dairy produce in return to the owner, it is termed "useless and abandoned herd."

(4) When, out of fear of cattle-lifting enemies (parachakrátavibhayát), cattle are placed under the protection of the superintendent, who receives 1/10th of the dairy produce for this service, it is termed "herds maintained for a share in dairy produce."

(5) When the superintendent classifies cattle into categories such as calves, steers, tameable ones, draught oxen, bulls to be trained for yoking, bulls kept for breeding, cattle fit only for meat supply, buffaloes, and draught buffaloes; and female calves, female steers, heifers, pregnant cows, milch cows, barren cows—whether cows or buffaloes—calves that are one or two months old, as well as those that are even younger; and when he brands all of them, including the calves that are one or two months old, along with any stray cattle that have remained unclaimed for a month or two in the herds; and when he registers their branded marks, natural marks, color, and the distance between their horns, that system is known as "class of herds."

(6) When an animal is carried off by thieves, ends up in another herd, or strays without being recognized, it is considered "lost."

(7) When an animal gets stuck in a quagmire or falls off a precipice, dies from disease or old age, drowns in water, is killed by the fall of a tree or riverbank, is beaten to death with a staff or stone, struck by lightning, devoured by a tiger, bitten by a cobra, carried off by a crocodile, or caught in a forest fire, it is deemed "irrecoverably lost."

Cowherds shall make every effort to keep their cattle safe from such dangers.

Anyone who injures or causes harm to a cow, or who steals or helps another steal a cow, shall be sentenced to death.

If a person substitutes an animal bearing the royal brand with a privately owned one, they shall be punished with the first amercement.

When someone retrieves local cattle from thieves, they shall receive the promised reward (panitam rúpam), and if someone rescues foreign cattle from thieves, they shall receive half its value.

Cowherds must provide care and remedies to calves, elderly cows, or cows suffering from diseases.

They shall graze the herds in forests that are specifically assigned as pasture grounds for various seasons, where thieves, tigers, and other dangerous animals are driven away by hunters with the help of their hounds. To keep away snakes and tigers and as a way to track the location of the herds, bells shall be tied around the necks of timid cattle. Cowherds shall allow their cattle to enter rivers or lakes that are uniformly deep, wide, and free from mud and crocodiles, and they must protect them from any dangers in these circumstances.

Whenever an animal is captured by a thief, a tiger, a snake, or a crocodile, or if the animal becomes weak due to old age or illness, cowherds must report it; otherwise, they will be required to compensate for the loss.

If an animal dies naturally, the cowherds shall surrender the skin with the brand mark if it is a cow or buffalo; the skin with the ear (karnalakshanam) if it is a goat or sheep; the tail with the branded skin if it is a donkey or camel; and simply the skin if it is a young animal. In addition to the above, they must also return the fat (vasti), bile, marrow (snáyu), teeth, hooves, horns, and bones.

Cowherds may sell either fresh or dried meat. They shall give buttermilk to the dogs and hogs as drink, and keep a small amount of buttermilk in a bronze vessel for preparing their own meal. They may also use curdled milk or cheese (kíláta) to make their oilcakes more appetizing (ghánapinyáka-kledartha).

Anyone who sells a cow from the herds shall pay the king one-fourth of the cow's value (rúpa). During the rainy season, autumn, and the first part of winter (hemanta), the cows shall be milked twice a day (morning and evening). During the latter part of winter, as well as spring and summer, they shall be milked only once in the morning. Any cowherd who milks a cow a second time during these seasons shall have their thumb cut off.

If a cowherd misses the proper time for milking, he will lose the profit from that milk. The same rule applies if a cowherd neglects the opportune time to pierce a bull's nose for a ring, or to tame or train it for the yoke.

When one drona of cow's milk is churned, it will yield one prastha of butter. The same quantity of buffalo's milk will yield one-seventh prastha more, and milk from goats or sheep will yield half a prastha more. The exact amount of butter in all types of milk should be determined by churning, since the supply of milk and butter depends on factors such as the nature of the soil and the quality and quantity of the fodder and water.

If someone causes a bull from a herd to fight with another bull, he shall be punished with the first amercement. If the bull is injured in such a fight, the person will be punished with the highest amercement.

When grazing, cattle should be grouped into herds of ten, organized by color. Depending on the protective strength of the cowherds and the capacity of the cattle to travel, cowherds should decide whether to graze the cattle near or far.

Sheep and other animals should be shorn of their wool every six months. The same rules apply to herds of horses, donkeys, camels, and pigs.

For bulls fitted with nose-rings and capable of carrying heavy loads or traveling as fast as horses, the daily diet should consist of half a bhára of meadow grass (yavasa), twice that amount of ordinary grass (trina), one tulá (100 palas) of oilcakes, ten ádhakas of bran, five palas of salt (mukhalavanam), one kudumba of oil for rubbing on the nose (nasya), one prastha of drink (pána), one tulá of meat, one ádhaka of curis, one drona of barley or cooked másha (Phaseolus radiatus), and one drona of milk. In place of milk, half an ádhaka of surá (liquor), one prastha of oil or ghee (sneha), ten palas of sugar or jaggery, and one pala of ginger root (sringibera) may be given.

The same provisions, reduced by one-quarter, will serve for mules, cows, and donkeys, while buffaloes and camels should be provided with double the quantity of these rations. Draught oxen and milk cows should receive food based on how long the oxen are worked and how much milk the cows produce. All cattle should be given plenty of fodder and water.

This is how herds of cattle should be raised and maintained.

A herd of 100 donkeys or mules should contain five male animals, a herd of goats or sheep should have ten, and a herd of ten cows or buffaloes should have four male animals.

[Thus ends Chapter XXIX, "The Superintendent of Cows" in Book II, "The Duties of Government Superintendents" of the Arthasástra of Kautilya. End of the fiftieth chapter from the beginning.]

CHAPTER XXX. THE SUPERINTENDENT OF HORSES.

The Superintendent of Horses shall record the breed, age, color, identifying marks, group or class, and the native place of each horse. He shall categorize the horses as follows: (1) those kept in sale-houses for sale (panyágárikam), (2) those recently purchased (krayopágatam), (3) those captured in wars (áhavalabdham), (4) those of local breed (ájátam), (5) those sent there for assistance (sáháyyakágatam), (6) those mortgaged (panasthitam), and (7) those temporarily housed in stables (yávatkálikam).

He shall report to the king about horses that are considered inauspicious, crippled, or diseased.

Every horseman shall know how to properly manage and make economic use of whatever provisions he has received from the king's treasury and storehouse.

The superintendent shall have stables constructed that are spacious enough to accommodate the number of horses to be kept. The stables should be twice as wide as the length of a horse, with four doors facing the four cardinal directions. The central floor should be designed for horses to roll on, and the front of the stable should have wooden seats at the entrance. The stable should house animals like monkeys, peacocks, red spotted deer (prishata), mongoose, partridges (chakora), parrots, and maina birds (sárika).

Each horse's room should be four times as wide or long as the length of the horse, with a central floor paved with smooth wooden planks, and separate compartments for fodder (khádanakoshthakam).

There should also be passages for the removal of urine and dung, and the door should face either north or east. The orientation of the quarters (digvibhága) may be based on practical considerations or in relation to the position of the building.

Steeds, stallions, and colts shall be housed separately.

A horse that has just given birth to a colt shall be given a drink of 1 prastha of clarified butter for the first three days. Afterward, it shall be fed 1 prastha of flour (saktu) and made to drink oil mixed with medicine for ten nights. Following this period, it shall be given cooked grains, meadow grass, and other food appropriate for the season.

A colt that is ten days old shall be given a kudumba of flour mixed with ¼ kudumba of clarified butter and 1 prastha of milk until it is six months old. Afterward, the rations shall be increased by half as much each month, with the addition of 1 prastha of barley until it turns three years old. From three to four years old, it shall be fed one drona of barley. By the age of four or five, the colt reaches full development and becomes fit for work.

The face (mukha) of the best horse measures 32 angulas; its body length is five times the length of its face, its shank measures 20 angulas, and its height is four times the length of its shank. Horses of medium and lower sizes are shorter by two and three angulas respectively in these measurements.

The circumference (parínáha) of the best horse is 100 angulas, while medium and smaller horses are five parts (panchabhágávaram) smaller in measurement.

The diet for the best horse consists of 2 dronas of any grain, such as rice (sáli or vríhi), barley, or panic seeds (priyangu), which may be soaked or cooked, as well as cooked mudga (Phraseolus Mungo) or másha (Phraseolus Radiatus). Additionally, the horse should receive 1 prastha of oil, 5 palas of salt, 50 palas of flesh, 1 ádhaka of broth (rasa) or 2 ádhakas of curd, and 5 palas of sugar (kshára) to make its diet more palatable, along with 1 prastha of liquor (súrá) or 2 prasthas of milk.

This same quantity of food and drink shall be provided to horses that are fatigued from long journeys or from carrying loads.

For care, 1 prastha of oil should be given for enema (anuvásana), 1 kudumba of oil for rubbing over the nose, and 1,000 palas of meadow grass. Twice as much ordinary grass (trina) shall also be provided, and hay or grass shall be spread over an area of 6 aratnis.

The same quantity of rations, less by one-quarter, is given to horses of medium and smaller sizes. A draught horse or stallion of medium size should receive the same amount as the best horse, while those of smaller size will receive the same quantity as a horse of medium size. Steeds and párasamas are provided with one-quarter less rations. Colts are given half the rations provided to steeds. This outlines how rations are distributed.

Those who prepare the food for horses, grooms, and veterinary surgeons are also entitled to a share of the rations (pratisvádabhajah). Stallions that have become incapacitated due to old age, illness, or the hardships of war, and are thus no longer fit for battle but only consume food, should be allowed to mate with mares for breeding purposes in the interest of the citizens and the country.

The best horse breeds come from the regions of Kámbhoja, Sindhu, Aratta, and Vanáyu. Those from Báhlíka, Pápeya, Sauvira, and Taitala are of middle quality, and all others are considered ordinary (avaráh). These three types of horses—best, middle, and ordinary— can be trained for war or riding, depending on whether they are fierce (tíkshna), gentle (bhadra), or slow (manda).

The regular training of a horse is meant to prepare it for war (sánnáhyam karma). The different types of riding are circular movement (valgana), slow movement (níchairgata), jumping (langhana), gallop (dhorana), and responding to signals (nároshtra).

There are different styles of circular movement (valgana): Aupavenuka, vardhmánaka, yamaka, álídhapluta, vrithatta, and trivacháli. The same types of movements, but with the head and ears kept upright, are called slow movements. These are performed in sixteen ways: Prakírnaka, prakírnottara, nishanna, pársvánuvritta, úrmimárga, sarabhakrídita, sarabhapluta, tritála, báhyánuvritta, panchapáni, simháyata, svádhúta, klishta, slághita, brimhita, and pushpábhikírna.

Different forms of jumping include jumping like a monkey (kapipluta), jumping like a frog (bhekapluta), sudden jumping (ekapluta), jumping with one leg (ekapádapluta), leaping like a cuckoo (kokila-samchári), dashing with the chest almost touching the ground (urasya), and leaping like a crane (bakasamchari).

Galloping is classified as flying like a vulture (kánka), dashing like a water-duck (várikánaka), running like a peacock (máyúra), half the speed of a peacock (ardhmáyúra), dashing like a mangoose (nákula), half the speed of a mangoose (ardha-nákula), running like a hog (váráha), and half the speed of a hog (ardha-váráha).

Movement that follows a signal is called nároshtra. Carriage horses can travel distances of six, nine, or twelve yojanas in a day.

Five, eight, and ten yojanas are the distances that should be covered by riding horses. Trotting according to its strength, trotting with good breathing, and trotting while carrying a load on its back are the three kinds of trot. Trotting according to strength, trotting combined with circular movement, ordinary trotting, medium-speed trotting, and regular speed are also different types of trotting.

Qualified instructors shall give directions for making proper ropes that will be used to tether the horses. Charioteers shall take care of the manufacturing of all necessary war equipment for horses. Veterinary surgeons shall administer the required treatments to prevent the horse's body from growing too much or shrinking and adjust the horse's diet according to seasonal changes.

Those who move the horses, those who tie them in the stables, those responsible for supplying meadow grass, those who cook grains for the horses, stable guards, grooms, and those responsible for treating poisons should perform their assigned duties properly, or they will forfeit their daily wages.

Anyone who rides a horse that is kept inside the stables either for rituals like waving lights or for medical treatment will be fined 12 panas. If, due to defects in medicine or carelessness in treatment, a disease worsens, a fine of twice the cost of the treatment shall be imposed. If the wrong medicine is administered, or if the treatment is neglected, resulting in an adverse outcome, the fine will be equivalent to the value of the horse. The same rule applies to cows, buffaloes, goats, and sheep.

Horses must be washed, covered with sandalwood powder, and adorned with garlands twice a day. On new moon days, sacrifices should be made to Bhútas, and on full moon days, auspicious hymns should be chanted. Not only on the ninth day of the Asvayuja month, but also at the start and end of journeys, and during times of illness, priests should wave lights to invoke blessings on the horses.

CHAPTER XXXI. THE SUPERINTENDENT OF ELEPHANTS.

The Superintendent of Elephants shall take proper steps to protect elephant forests and supervise the operations regarding the standing or lying in stables of elephants, whether male, female, or young, when they are tired after training. He shall also examine the proportional quantity of rations and grass, the extent of training given to them, their accoutrements and ornaments, as well as the work of elephant doctors, trainers of elephants in warlike feats, and grooms such as drivers, binders, and others.

An elephant stable shall be constructed to be twice as broad and twice as high as the length of the elephant, with separate apartments for female elephants, a projected entrance, and posts called kumári, with the door facing either east or north.

The space in front of the smooth posts, where elephants are tied, shall form a square with one side equal to the length of the elephant and shall be paved with smooth wooden planks and provided with holes for the removal of urine and dung.

The space where an elephant lies down shall be as broad as the length of the elephant and be equipped with a flat form raised to half the height of the elephant for leaning on.

Elephants used in war or for riding shall be kept inside the fort, while those still being tamed or of bad temper shall be kept outside.

The first and the seventh of the eight divisions of the day are the two times for bathing the elephants. The time following these two periods is for their food. Forenoon is designated for exercise, while the afternoon is the time for drinking. Two parts of the night are reserved for sleep, and one-third of the night is spent in staying alert.

Summer is the season for capturing elephants.

Only elephants that are 20 years old should be captured.

Young elephants (bikka), infatuated elephants (mugdha), elephants without tusks, diseased elephants, those suckling their young (dhenuká), and female elephants (hastiní) shall not be captured.

An elephant that is seven aratnis tall, nine aratnis long, and ten aratnis in circumference, and is therefore inferred to be 40 years old, is considered the best.

An elephant that is 30 years old is of middle quality, while one that is 25 years old is of the lowest class.

The diet for the last two classes of elephants shall be reduced by one-quarter based on their classification.

For an elephant measuring seven aratnis in height, the rations shall include 1 drona of rice, ½ ádhaka of oil, 3 prasthas of ghee, 10 palas of salt, 50 palas of meat, 1 ádhaka of broth (rasa), or twice that quantity (2 ádhakas) of curd. To make the food flavorful, 10 palas of sugar (kshára), 1 ádhaka of liquor, or twice the quantity of milk (payah), shall be added. For external use, 1 prastha of oil shall be used to smear over the body, and 1/8 prastha of oil for the head and for lighting the stables. Additionally, 2 bháras of meadow grass, 2¼ bháras of ordinary grass (sashpa), 2½ bháras of dry grass, and any amount of stalks of various pulses (kadankara) shall be given.

An elephant in rut (atyarála) and 8 aratnis tall shall receive the same rations as an elephant of 7 aratnis.

The rest of the elephants, measuring 6 or 5 aratnis in height, shall receive rations proportionate to their size.

A young elephant (bikka) captured for the mere purpose of playing with it shall be fed milk and meadow grass.

The physical attributes of an elephant's splendor are classified as follows: one that is blood-red (samjátalóhita), one that is fleshy, one whose sides are evenly grown (samaliptapakshá), one whose girths are full or equal (samakakshyá), one whose flesh is evenly distributed, one with a smooth back (samatalpatala), and one with a rough surface (játadrónika).

Depending on the seasons and their physical splendor, elephants, whether sharp or slow of sense (bhadra and mandra), as well as elephants possessing characteristics of other beasts, shall be trained and taught to perform suitable tasks.

CHAPTER XXXII. TRAINING OF ELEPHANTS.

Elephants are classified into four categories based on their training: tameable (damya), those trained for war (sánnáhya), those trained for riding (aupaváhya), and rogue elephants (vyála).

Tameable elephants are divided into five groups: those that allow a person to sit on their withers (skandhagata), those that permit being tethered to a post (stambhagata), those that can be taken to water (várigata), those that lie down in pits (apapátagata), and those attached to their herd (yúthagata). All of these elephants should be cared for as attentively as a young elephant (bikka).

Military training consists of seven types: drill (upasthána), turning (samvartana), advancing (samyána), trampling down and killing (vadhávadha), fighting other elephants (hastiyuddha), attacking forts and cities (nágaráyanam), and general warfare.

The first steps in this training include binding the elephants with girths (kakshyákarma), putting on collars (graiveyakakarma), and making them work with their herd (yúthakarma).

Elephants trained for riding are categorized into seven types: those that allow a person to mount while in the company of another elephant (kunjaropaváhya), those that allow riding when led by a war elephant (sánnáhyopaváhya), those taught to trot (dhorana), those trained in various movements (ádhánagatika), those that move with the use of a staff (yashtyupaváhya), those that move with an iron hook (totropaváhya), those that move without the use of whips (suddhopaváhya), and those helpful in hunting.

The initial training steps for these include autumnal work (sáradakarma), rough or mean work (hínakarma), and learning to respond to signals.

Rogue elephants can only be controlled in one way—through punishment. These elephants exhibit a deep distrust of work, are stubborn, unruly, unstable, willful, or behave erratically due to the influence of rut.

Rogue elephants whose training is unsuccessful may be classified as purely roguish (suddha), clever in roguery (suvrata), perverse (vishama), or exhibiting all kinds of vices.

Rogue elephants whose training fails may be classified as purely roguish (suddha), clever in roguery (suvrata), perverse (vishama), or possessing all kinds of vices.

The appropriate types of fetters and other necessary means to control them shall be determined by the elephant doctor. Tether posts (álána), collars, girths, bridles, leg chains, and frontal fetters are some of the different binding instruments used for control.

Hooks, bamboo staffs, and machines (yantra) are also instruments used for handling elephants. Necklaces such as vaijavantí and kshurapramála, along with litters and housings, are the ornaments for elephants.

War accoutrements include mail armor (varma), clubs (totra), arrow bags, and machines. Elephant doctors, trainers, expert riders, and others involved in taking care of elephants, including those who groom them, prepare their food, provide grass, tether them, clean the stables, and watch the stables at night, all have responsibilities in maintaining elephants' well-being.

Elephant doctors, watchmen, sweepers, cooks, and others involved in elephant care shall receive 1 prastha of cooked rice, a handful of oil, and 2 palas of sugar and salt from the storehouse. Additionally, except for the doctors, others shall also receive 10 palas of meat.

Elephant doctors shall provide necessary medical care to elephants that, during journeys, suffer from disease, exhaustion, rut, or old age.

Offenses such as allowing stables to accumulate dirt, failing to provide grass, making an elephant lie on hard, unprepared ground, striking its vital parts, allowing a stranger to ride it, riding it at improper times, leading it through impassable water routes, or letting it enter thick forests are punishable with fines. These fines shall be deducted from the rations and wages owed to the offenders.

During the Cháturmásya period (July, August, September, and October) and at the junction of two seasons, a ritual of waving lights shall be performed three times. Sacrifices to Bhútas for the safety of elephants shall also be carried out on new-moon and full-moon days by commanders.

When it comes to tusks, leaving a portion of the tusk near its root, equal to twice its circumference, the remaining part of the tusk shall be cut off once every 2½ years for elephants born in river-irrigated regions (nadija), and once every 5 years for mountain elephants.

[Thus ends Chapter XXXII, "The Training of Elephants" in Book II, "The Duties of Government Superintendents" of the Arthasástra of Kautilya. End of the fifty-third chapter from the beginning.]

CHAPTER XXXIII. THE SUPERINTENDENT OF CHARIOTS; THE SUPERINTENDENT OF

INFANTRY AND THE DUTY OF THE COMMANDER-IN-CHIEF.

The duties of the Superintendent of Horses will also explain those of the Superintendent of Chariots. The Superintendent of Chariots shall oversee the construction of chariots.

The best chariot shall be 10 purushas in height (which is 120 angulas) and 12 purushas in width. Following this model, seven more chariots with the width decreasing by one purusha each time, down to a chariot of 6 purushas in width, shall be made. He shall also construct chariots for gods (devaratha), festal chariots (pushyaratha), battle chariots (sángrámika), travelling chariots (páriyánika), chariots for attacking enemy strongholds (parapurabhiyánika), and training chariots.

He shall assess the skills of troops in shooting arrows, hurling clubs and cudgels, wearing armor, using equipment, driving chariots, fighting while seated in a chariot, and controlling the chariot horses.

He shall also handle the accounts for provisions and wages paid to those either permanently or temporarily employed to make chariots and other necessary items. He must ensure that the workers are content and well-rewarded (yogyarakshanushthánam) and measure the distance of roads.

The same rules apply to the Superintendent of Infantry. This superintendent must understand the exact strength or weakness of hereditary troops (maula), hired troops (bhrita), corporate troops (sreni), as well as the armies of friendly or hostile kings and wild tribes.

He must also be familiar with fighting in lowlands, open battle, fraudulent attacks, fighting under cover of trenches (khanakayuddha), or from heights (ákásayuddha), and fighting during the day and night. Additionally, he must be trained in the necessary drills for such warfare.

He shall be able to assess whether troops are fit or unfit for emergency situations.

With attention to the position of the entire army (chaturangabala), trained in handling all kinds of weapons and leading elephants, horses, and chariots, the Commander-in-Chief must be capable of ordering advance or retreat (áyogamayógam cha).

He must know what type of terrain is more advantageous for his army, the most favorable time for battle, the enemy's strength, how to cause dissension in a united enemy force, how to rally his own scattered troops, how to scatter an enemy's forces, how to lay siege to a fortress, and when to launch a full-scale attack.

Always mindful of the discipline his army must maintain, not just in camping and marching, but in the heat of battle, he shall name the regiments (vyúha) after trumpets, boards, banners, or flags.

[Thus ends Chapter XXXIII, "The Superintendent of Chariots, the Superintendent of Infantry, and the Duties of the Commander-in-Chief" in Book II, "The Duties of Government Superintendents" of the Arthasástra of Kautilya. End of the fifty-fourth chapter from the beginning.]

CHAPTER XXXIV. THE SUPERINTENDENT OF PASSPORTS.

The Superintendent of Passports shall issue passes at the rate of one masha per pass. Whoever holds a pass shall have the freedom to either enter or leave the country. Whoever, being a native of the country, enters or leaves without a pass shall be fined twelve panas. If someone presents a false pass, they shall be punished with the first amercement. A foreigner who commits the same offense shall be punished with the highest amercement.

The Superintendent of Pasture Lands shall check the passes. Pasture grounds will be established between any two dangerous areas. Valleys will be cleared of the threat of thieves, elephants, and other wild animals.

In barren areas of the country, tanks, shelter buildings, and wells shall be constructed, along with flower gardens and fruit gardens. Hunters with their hounds shall scout the forests. When thieves or enemies are approaching, they must hide by climbing trees or mountains to avoid capture, and blow conch-shells or beat drums to give warning. Regarding the movements of enemies or wild tribes, hunters may send messages by releasing the pigeons of the royal household with passes (mudrá), or by setting fires and creating smoke signals at different intervals.

The superintendent shall also be responsible for the protection of timber and elephant forests, keeping roads in good condition, arresting thieves, ensuring the safety of merchant travel, protecting cows, and overseeing the transactions of the people.

[Thus ends Chapter XXXIV, "The Superintendent of Passports, and the Superintendent of Pasture Lands," in Book II, "The Duties of Government Superintendents," of the Arthasástra of Kautilya. End of the fifty-fifth chapter from the beginning.]

CHAPTER XXXV. THE DUTY OF REVENUE-COLLECTORS; SPIES IN THE GUISE OF HOUSEHOLDERS, MERCHANTS AND ASCETICS.

After dividing the kingdom (janapada) into four districts and further classifying the villages (gráma) into three ranks—first, middle, and lowest—he shall assign them to one of the following categories: villages exempt from taxation (pariháraka); those that supply soldiers (áyudhíya); those that pay their taxes in the form of grains, cattle, gold (hiranya), or raw materials (kupya); and those that provide free labor (vishti) or dairy products in place of taxes (karapratikara).

It is the duty of the Gopa, the village accountant, to manage the accounts of five or ten villages as instructed by the Collector-General. The Gopa shall establish village boundaries, mark plots of land as cultivated, uncultivated, plains, wet lands, gardens, vegetable gardens, fences (váta), forests, altars, temples, irrigation works, cremation grounds, feeding houses (sattra), places where water is provided to travelers (prapá), pilgrimage sites, pasture grounds, and roads. By doing so, he will define the boundaries of various villages, fields, forests, and roads, and he will record the details of gifts, sales, charities, and any remission of taxes related to fields.

Additionally, after numbering the houses as either taxpaying or non-taxpaying, the Gopa shall record the total number of inhabitants in all four castes in each village, and he shall also account for the number of cultivators, cowherds, merchants, artisans, laborers, slaves, and both biped and quadruped animals. At the same time, he shall calculate the amount of gold, free labor, tolls, and fines that can be collected from each house.

He shall also keep records of the number of young and old men living in each house, along with their personal history (charitra), occupation (ájíva), income (áya), and expenditures (vyaya).

Similarly, the Sthánika, the district officer, shall oversee the accounts of one-quarter of the kingdom. In the areas under the supervision of the Gopa and Sthánika, commissioners (prodeshtárah) specially appointed by the Collector-General will not only inspect the work and methods used by the village and district officers but will also collect the special religious tax known as bali (balipragraham kuryuh).

Spies disguised as householders (grihapatika), acting under the orders of the collector-general for espionage, shall verify the accuracy of the accounts kept by village and district officers regarding the fields, houses, and families in each village. This includes the area and yield of crops in the fields, ownership rights and any tax remissions related to houses, and the caste and profession of each family.

They shall also assess the total number of people and animals (janghágra) as well as the income and expenditures of each household. They will investigate the reasons behind the migration of people, whether leaving or arriving, especially those who are habitual wanderers, and monitor the movement of men and women of questionable character (anarthya), as well as foreign spies.

Similarly, spies disguised as merchants will assess the quantity and price of royal merchandise such as minerals, products from gardens, forests, and fields, or manufactured goods. Regarding foreign merchandise of superior or inferior quality arriving by land or water, they will investigate the tolls, road taxes, transportation fees, military taxes, ferry charges, and the one-sixth portion merchants are required to pay. They will also check the expenses merchants incur for their own sustenance and for storing their goods in warehouses (panyágára).

Spies disguised as ascetics, under the collector-general's orders, will gather information on the actions, whether honest or dishonest, of farmers, cowherds, merchants, and heads of government departments.

In locations such as places of worship, crossroads, ancient ruins, near tanks, rivers, bathing areas, pilgrimage sites, hermitages, desert regions, mountains, and dense forests, spies disguised as old and notorious thieves, along with their band of students, shall investigate the reasons for the arrival, departure, and resting of thieves, enemies, and overly brave individuals.

The collector-general shall diligently attend to the kingdom's affairs. Likewise, his subordinates, as part of the espionage network, shall work with their colleagues and followers to carry out their duties.

[Thus ends Chapter XXXV, "The Duty of Revenue Collectors; Spies under the Guise of Householders, Merchants, and Ascetics," in Book II, "The Duties of Government Superintendents" of the Arthasástra of Kautilya. End of the fifty-sixth chapter from the beginning.]

CHAPTER XXXVI. THE DUTY OF A CITY SUPERINTENDENT.

Like the Collector-general, the Officer in charge of the Capital City (*Nágaraka*) shall look to the affairs of the capital.

A *Gopa* shall keep the accounts of ten households, twenty households, or forty households.

He shall not only know the caste, *gotra*, the name, and occupation of both men and women in those households, but also ascertain their income and expenditure.

Likewise, the officer known as *Sthánika* shall attend to the accounts of the four quarters of the capital.

Managers of charitable institutions shall send information (to *Gopa* or *Sthánika*) as to any heretics (*Páshanda*) and travellers arriving to reside therein.

They shall allow ascetics and men learned in the Vedas to reside in such places only when those persons are known to be of reliable character.

Artisans and other handicraftsmen may, on their own responsibility, allow others of their own profession to reside where they carry on their own work (i.e., in their own houses).

Similarly, merchants may on their own responsibility allow other merchants to reside where they themselves carry on their mercantile work (i.e., their own houses or shops).

They (the merchants) shall make a report of those who sell any merchandise in forbidden places or at forbidden times, as well as of those who are in possession of any merchandise other than their own.

Vintners, sellers of cooked flesh, and sellers of cooked rice, as well as prostitutes, may allow any other person to reside with them only when that person is well-known to them.

They (vintners, etc.) shall make a report of spendthrifts and fool-hardy persons who engage themselves in risky undertakings.

Any physician who treats in secret a patient suffering from ulcers or the effects of unwholesome food or drink, as well as the master of the house where such treatment occurs, will only be considered innocent if they report the situation to either the *Gopa* or *Sthánika*. Otherwise, both the physician and the master of the house will be held equally guilty along with the patient.

Householders must report any strangers arriving at or departing from their homes; failing to do so will make them guilty of any crime committed during that night. Even when no crime seems to have been committed, they will still be fined 3 panas for failing to report such movements.

Travelers on highways or footpaths must apprehend any person they come across who is injured, carrying weapons, struggling with a heavy load, avoiding others timidly, indulging in excessive sleep, appearing fatigued from a long journey, or seeming unfamiliar with the place, particularly within or outside the capital, in temples, places of pilgrimage, or burial grounds.

Spies shall also search for suspicious individuals in deserted houses, the workshops or homes of vintners, sellers of cooked rice and flesh, gambling houses, and in the abodes of heretics.

The lighting of fires is prohibited during the middle two parts of the day, divided into four equal parts during the summer. A fine of 1/8th of a pana shall be imposed for starting a fire during this time.

Householders may carry out cooking operations outside their homes.

If a house-owner does not have ready at hand five water pots, a *kumbha* (large pot), a *dróna* (large vessel), a ladder, an axe, a winnowing basket, an elephant-driving hook, pincers, and a leather bag, he shall be fined ¼th of a pana.

They must also remove thatched roofs. Blacksmiths and others who work with fire must live together in a single designated area.

Every houseowner must remain by the door of their house at night. Water vessels must be kept in rows, in the thousands, without causing disorder. These vessels should be placed not only along big streets and at intersections but also in front of royal buildings.

Any houseowner who does not run to help extinguish a fire, regardless of what is burning, shall be fined 12 panas. A renter (one who occupies a rented house) shall be fined 6 panas for not helping to put out the fire.

Whoever carelessly sets a fire shall be fined 54 panas. Whoever intentionally sets a fire shall be thrown into the fire as punishment.

Whoever throws dirt in the street shall be fined 1/8th of a pana. Whoever causes mud or water to accumulate in the street shall be fined ¼th of a pana. Whoever commits the above offenses on the king's road shall be fined double the amount.

Whoever excretes feces in places of pilgrimage, water reservoirs, temples, and royal buildings shall be fined beginning with one pana, with the fines increasing according to the severity of the offense. But when such excretions are due to the use of medicine or disease, no punishment shall be imposed.

Whoever throws inside the city the carcass of animals such as a cat, dog, mongoose, or snake shall be fined 3 panas. Whoever throws in the carcass of an ass, camel, mule, or cattle shall be fined 6 panas. Whoever throws in a human corpse shall be fined 50 panas.

When a dead body is taken out of the city through a gate other than the prescribed one or through a path other than the usual path, the first amercement shall be imposed; and those who guard the gates through which the dead body is taken out shall be fined 200 panas.

When a dead body is buried or cremated outside the designated burial or cremation grounds, a fine of 12 panas shall be imposed.

The time interval between six *nálikas* (2 2/5 hours) after nightfall and six *nálikas* before dawn shall be marked by the sound of a trumpet, signaling a prohibition on public movement.

Once the trumpet has been sounded, anyone moving near the royal buildings during the first or last *yáma* (3 hours) of the restricted period shall be fined one pana and a quarter. During the middle *yámas*, the fine shall be double that amount. Anyone found moving outside the royal buildings or the fort shall be fined four times that amount.

Anyone arrested in suspicious places or caught committing a criminal act shall be examined.

Anyone found moving near royal buildings or climbing the fortifications of the capital shall be punished with the middlemost amercement.

However, those who go out at night for the purpose of midwifery or medical treatment, to carry a dead body to the burial or cremation grounds, to walk with a lamp in hand, to visit the city officer, to investigate the cause of a trumpet sound, to extinguish a fire, or with the authority of a pass shall not be arrested.

On nights when movement is allowed (chárarátrishu), those who go out in disguise, those who venture out despite being forbidden, and those who carry clubs or weapons shall be punished in accordance with the seriousness of their crime.

Those watchmen who stop someone they should not stop, or who fail to stop someone they should stop, shall be punished with twice the amount of the fine levied for untimely movement.

When a watchman has carnal connection with a slave woman, he shall be punished with the first amercement; when he has such connection with a free woman, he shall be punished with the middlemost amercement; when he has carnal connection with a woman arrested for untimely movement, he shall be punished with the highest amercement; and when he has such connection with a woman of high birth (kulastrí), he shall be put to death.

When the officer in charge of the city (nágaraka) fails to report to the king whatever nocturnal disturbance of animate or inanimate nature (chetanâchetana) has occurred, or when he is careless in performing his duties, he shall be punished according to the gravity of his offense.

He shall conduct daily inspections of reservoirs of water, roads, secret passages for going out of the city, forts, fort walls, and other defensive structures. He shall also keep in his custody any objects he finds that have been lost, forgotten, or left behind by others.

On days corresponding to the king's birth star, as well as on full moon days, young, old, sick, or helpless prisoners (anátha) shall be released from the jail (bandhanâgâra); or those who are of charitable disposition or who have made agreements with the prisoners may release them by paying an appropriate ransom.

Once a day or once every five nights, prisoners may be released from jail, taking into account the work they have completed, the whipping they have undergone, or an adequate ransom paid in gold.

Whenever a new country is conquered, when an heir apparent is installed on the throne, or when a prince is born to the king, prisoners are generally set free.

Book 3

CHAPTER I. DETERMINATION OF FORMS OF AGREEMENT; DETERMINATION OF LEGAL DISPUTES.

In the cities of Sangrahana, Dronamukha, and Sthániya, and at places where districts meet, three individuals who are well-versed in Sacred Law (dharmasthas) and three ministers of the king (amátyas) shall oversee the administration of justice.

(Valid and Invalid Transactions)

They shall consider as invalid any agreements (vyavahára) made in secret, inside homes, during the night, in forests, in secluded areas, or through fraudulent means.

The proposer of such an agreement and any accomplices shall be punished with the first amercement. [A fine ranging from 48 to 96 panas is called the first amercement; from 200 to 500 panas, the middlemost amercement; and from 500 to 1,000 panas, the highest amercement. See Chap. XVII, Book III.]

The witnesses (srotri = voluntary hearers) shall each be fined half of the above amount, and the persons who accepted the agreement shall bear any loss they have incurred.

However, agreements made in the presence of others, or those that do not have any other grounds for invalidation, shall be considered valid.

Agreements concerning matters like inheritance division, sealed or unsealed deposits, or marriage, or those involving women who are either suffering from illness or do not leave their homes, and agreements made by individuals who are not known to be of unsound mind, shall be valid, even if they were entered into inside homes.

Transactions involving robbery, duels, marriages, or the execution of the king's orders, as well as agreements made by individuals who typically conduct their business during the early part of the night, shall be valid even if they take place at night.

For those who spend most of their lives in forests, whether they are merchants, cowherds, hermits, hunters, or spies, their agreements, even if made in the forests, will be considered valid. If fraudulent agreements are involved, only those entered into by spies will be valid.

Agreements made by members of any association among themselves will also be valid, even if made in private. However, any other agreements made in seclusion or under similar conditions, unless specified otherwise, will be considered void.

Similarly, agreements made by dependent or unauthorized individuals, such as a father's mother, a son, a father who has a son, an outcast brother, the youngest brother in a family with shared interests, a wife who has a husband or son, a slave, a hired laborer, anyone too young or too old to manage business, a convict (abhisasta), a cripple, or an afflicted person, will not be considered valid unless the individual is specifically authorized to do so.

Even if an authorized person enters into an agreement, it will be void if at the time of making the agreement they were provoked, anxious, intoxicated, or if they were a lunatic or haunted. In all of these cases, the person who proposed the agreement, their accessory, and the witnesses will each be punished according to the rules specified above.

However, agreements entered into personally by someone within their community at the right place and time will be valid, as long as the circumstances, the nature of the agreement, its description, and the qualities of the case are believable.

Such agreements, with the exception of orders (Adesa, likely referring to a bill of exchange) and hypothecations, can still be binding even if made by a third person. This concludes the determination of the forms of agreement.

(The Trial.)

The year, season, month, fortnight (paksha), date, nature, and location of the event, the amount of the debt, as well as the country, residence, caste, gotra, name, and occupation of both the plaintiff and the defendant—both of whom must be capable of suing or defending (kritasamarthávasthayoh)—must first be recorded. After that, the statements of both parties will be taken in the order appropriate to the case. These statements will then undergo a thorough examination.

(The offence of Parokta.)

If either party, instead of addressing the main issue, brings up unrelated matters; if their previous statements contradict their later ones; if they insist on considering the opinion of a third person, even when it's not relevant; if, after starting to answer the main question, they abruptly stop despite being ordered to continue; if they introduce topics other than those they initially raised; if they retract their own statements; if they reject the testimony given by their own witnesses; or if they secretly converse with their witnesses when they shouldn't— these actions constitute the offence of "Parokta."

(Punishment for Parokta.)

The fine for *Parokta* (bringing up unrelated matters or changing the subject during a trial) is five times the amount in question. The fine for *Svayambadi* (making claims without evidence) is ten times the amount.

(Payments for Witnesses.)

Fees for witnesses (*purushabhritih*) shall amount to 1/8th of the total sum in dispute (*astánga*). Additionally, provisions may be made to cover the travel expenses of the witnesses, based on the amount of the lawsuit. These two types of costs shall be borne by the losing party.

(Countersuits.)

In cases other than duels, robbery, or disputes among merchants or trade-guilds, the defendant is not allowed to file a counterclaim against the plaintiff. Similarly, no counterclaim can be made on behalf of the defendant.

(Adjournments.)

The plaintiff must respond quickly after the defendant has answered the questions at issue. If not, the plaintiff will be guilty of parokta, as they are expected to know the key details of the case, while the defendant may not. The defendant is allowed three or seven nights to prepare their defense. If the defendant is not ready within that time, they will be fined between 3 and 12 panas. If they still fail to respond after three fortnights, they will be fined for parokta, and the plaintiff will be able to recover the amount in question from the defendant's property. However, if the plaintiff is suing only for the return of a favor (pratyupakarana), no decree will be passed.

The same punishment will apply to defendants who fail to defend their case.

If the plaintiff is unable to prove their case, they will also be guilty of parokta. If the plaintiff cannot substantiate the case against a defendant who has passed away or is ill, they will need to pay a fine and perform the defendant's funeral rites as determined by the witnesses. However, if the plaintiff successfully proves the case, they may be allowed to take possession of the property pledged to them. If the plaintiff is not a Bráhman and fails to prove their case, they may be required to perform ceremonies to drive out demons (rakshoghna rakshitakam).

- In virtue of the king's power to ensure that the duties of the four castes and the four stages of religious life are observed, and to prevent the violation of these duties, the king is seen as the fountain of justice (dharmapravartaka).
- Sacred law (Dharma), evidence (Vyavahára), history (Charitra), and royal edicts (Rájasásana) are the four pillars of Law. In

order of importance, each is superior to the one preceding it.

- Dharma represents eternal truth governing the world; Vyavahára is based on the testimony of witnesses; Charitra refers to historical tradition (sangraha) upheld by the people; and Rájasásana is the order or edict of the king.

- The duty of a king is to protect his subjects with justice, and by doing so, he secures his place in heaven. A king who neglects this duty or disturbs social order wields his power (danda) in vain.

- It is power, and power alone, exercised impartially and in proportion to guilt—whether against his own son or his enemy—that sustains both this world and the next.

- A king who administers justice in accordance with sacred law (Dharma), evidence (Vyavahára), history (Samsthá), and royal edicts (Nyáya) will be able to conquer the world within the four quarters (Chaturantám mahím).

- If there is a disagreement between history and sacred law, or between evidence and sacred law, the matter should be resolved according to sacred law.

- However, if sacred law (sástra) conflicts with rational law (Dharmanyáya, or the king's law), reason should take precedence, as the original text of sacred law may not always be available.

- Self-assertion (svayamváda) by either party has often proven faulty. Only through examination (anuyoga), honesty (árjava), evidence (hetu), and oath-taking (sapatha) can a person win their case.

- If witness testimony reveals contradictions in the statements of either party, or if spies discover that one party's cause is false, the judgment shall go against that party.

CHAPTER II. CONCERNING MARRIAGE. THE DUTY OF MARRIAGE, THE PROPERTY OF A

WOMAN, AND COMPENSATIONS FOR REMARRIAGE.

Marriage comes before all other transactions in life (vyavahára). The giving of a well-adorned maiden in marriage is called Bráhma marriage. The union of a man and a woman to jointly perform sacred duties is known as Prájápatya marriage.

When a maiden is given in marriage in exchange for a couple of cows, it is called Arsha. When a maiden is given to a priest who officiates in a sacrifice, it is called Daiva. The voluntary union of a maiden with her lover is referred to as Gándharva marriage. When a maiden is given after receiving a significant amount of wealth (súlka), it is known as Asura. The abduction of a maiden is called Rákshasa, and if the abduction happens while she is asleep or intoxicated, it is called Paisácha marriage.

Of these, the first four types are ancient ancestral customs and are considered valid when approved by the father. The remaining types require approval from both the father and the mother, as they receive the súlka, or bride price, given by the bridegroom for their daughter. If one parent has passed away, the surviving parent will receive the súlka. If both parents have died, the maiden herself shall receive it. Any form of marriage is acceptable as long as it pleases all parties involved.

(Property of Women.)

A woman's property includes her means of living (vritti) or jewelry (ábadhya). If her means of living are worth more than two thousand, they should be officially given to her. There is no limit to the amount of jewelry she can own. A wife is not wrong to use this property to support her son, daughter-in-law, or herself when her husband is away and has not left anything for her care. In times of trouble, like illness, famine, or danger, or for charitable acts, her husband can also use this property. No one can complain if this property is used with the mutual agreement of a couple who have twins. Likewise, no complaint will be made if this property is used for three years by couples married under the first four types of marriage. However, in Gándharva and Asura marriages, the use of this property must be paid back with interest. In Rákshasa and Paisacha marriages, using this property will be treated as theft. This is how the responsibility of marriage is handled.

When her husband dies, a woman who wishes to live a religious life should immediately receive both her endowment and jewelry (sthápyábharanam) and any remaining súlka owed to her. If she does not already have these in her possession, even though they were supposed to be given to her, she will get both of them along with any interest that has accumulated. If she wants to remarry (kutumbakáma), she will be given whatever her father-in-law, her husband, or both gave her at the time of her remarriage (nivesakále). The right time for a woman to remarry will be explained when talking about the long absence of husbands.

If a widow marries a man who was not chosen by her father-in-law, she will lose whatever her father-in-law or husband gave her. The relatives (gnátis) of a woman must return to her any property she left with them. Whoever fairly takes a woman under his care must also take care of her property. No woman will succeed in claiming her husband's property. If she lives a religious life, she may enjoy it (dharmakámá bhunjíta). A woman with sons cannot freely use her own property (strídhana), as it will be passed on to her sons. If a woman tries to take her own property for the purpose of supporting her sons, she must set it aside in their name. If a woman has several sons, she must keep her property in the same condition as it was when her husband gave it to her. Even if the property was given to her with the freedom to enjoy and manage it, she must still put it in her sons' names.

A widow who has no children but stays loyal to her deceased husband may, under the care of her teacher, enjoy her property for as long she lives, as property is given to women to protect them from misfortune. After her death, her property will go to her relatives (dáyáda). If the husband is still alive and the wife dies, her sons and daughters will split her property. If there are no sons, the daughters will inherit it. If there are no daughters either, the husband will take back the súlka, which he gave to her, and her relatives will take back any gifts or dowry they had given her. This is how a woman's property is handled.

(Re-marriage of Males.)

If a woman has no children, no male children, or is barren, her husband must wait for eight years before marrying another. If she only gives birth to a dead child, he has to wait for ten years. If she only has daughters, he must wait for twelve years. After this time, if he wants to have sons, he may marry another woman. If he breaks this rule, he must pay her not only the sulka (the dowry), her property (strídhana), and an appropriate monetary compensation (ádhivedanikamartham), but also a fine of 24 panas to the government. He must give the sulka and property (strídhana) even to women who didn't receive these things when they married him, as well as giving his wives their proper compensation and enough to live on (vritti). Then he can marry as many women as he wants because women are meant to bear sons. If many or all of his wives are having their period at the same time, he must lie with the wife he married first or with the one who has given birth to a living son. If he hides the fact that a wife is menstruating or neglects to lie with any of them after their menstruation, he will be fined 96 panas.

None of his wives who either have sons, are pious, barren, give birth to a dead child, or are beyond the age of menstruation should be forced to sleep with him if she doesn't want to. If the man doesn't want to, he doesn't have to lie with his wife if she has leprosy or is mentally ill. However, if a woman wishes to have sons, she may lie with men who have such diseases.

- If a husband has a bad character, is away for a long time, becomes a traitor to his king, endangers his wife's life, falls from his caste, or loses his virility, his wife can leave him.

[Thus ends Chapter II, "The Duty of Marriage, the Property of a Woman, and Compensation for Remarriage," in Book III, "Concerning Law," of the Arthasástra of Kautilya. End of the fifty-ninth chapter from the beginning.]

CHAPTER III. THE DUTY OF A WIFE; MAINTENANCE OF A WOMAN; CRUELTY TO WOMEN; ENMITY BETWEEN HUSBAND AND WIFE; A WIFE's TRANSGRESSION; HER KINDNESS TO ANOTHER; AND FORBIDDEN TRANSACTIONS.

Women reach their legal majority at the age of twelve, and men at the age of sixteen. If, after reaching adulthood, they disobey lawful authority (asusrúsháyám), women shall be fined 15 panas, while men shall be fined twice that amount.

(Maintenance of a woman.)

A woman who is entitled to claim maintenance for an unlimited period shall be provided with as much food and clothing (grásacchádana) as necessary or even more, based on the income of the person responsible for maintaining her (yatha-purushaparivápam vá). If the period for which she is entitled to support is limited, then a fixed amount of money, determined in proportion to the maintainer's income, shall be given to her. This also applies if she has not received her sulka, property, or compensation (due to her if her husband remarries). If, after separating from her husband, she places herself under the protection of someone from her father-in-law's family (svasrakula) or chooses to live independently, then her husband shall not be liable for her maintenance. Thus, the determination of maintenance is addressed.

(Cruelty to women.)

Women of disobedient nature shall be taught proper behavior through general expressions such as "You, half naked; you, fully naked; you, cripple; you, fatherless; you, motherless" (nagne vinagne nyange pitrke matrke vinagne ityanirdesena vinayagrahanam). Alternatively, three light blows, either with bamboo bark, a rope, or the palm of the hand, may be given on her hips. Any violation of these guidelines will be punished with half the penalty for defamation or physical harm. The same punishment applies to a woman who, driven by jealousy or hatred, acts cruelly toward her husband. Penalties for engaging in inappropriate behavior, either at the door or outside her husband's house, are addressed elsewhere. Thus, cruelty to women is addressed.

(Enmity between husband and wife.)

A woman who despises her husband, has gone through seven cycles of her menses, and loves another man must immediately return to her husband both the endowment and jewelry she received from him and allow him to lie with another woman. A man who dislikes his wife must let her seek refuge either in the house of a mendicant woman, with her legal guardians, or with her relatives. If a man falsely accuses his wife of adultery with one of her or his relatives, or with a spy—an accusation that can only be proven by eyewitnesses (drishtilinge)—or accuses her of trying to leave him unjustly, he shall be fined 12 panas. A woman who despises her husband cannot end their marriage without his consent, nor can a man divorce his wife against her will. However, if there is mutual hatred, divorce may be agreed upon (parasparam dveshánmokshah). If a man fears harm from his wife and desires a divorce, he must return to her everything he gave her at the time of marriage. If a woman, fearing danger from her husband, seeks a divorce, she will forfeit her claim to her property. Marriages performed in accordance with the customs of the first four types of marriages cannot be dissolved.

(Transgression.)

If a woman engages herself in amorous sports, For drinking against an order, a woman shall be fined 3 panas. She shall pay a fine of 6 panas for going out during the day to attend sports or visit a woman or watch a spectacle. If she goes out to see another man or for sports, the fine shall be 12 panas. For the same offenses committed at night, the fines shall be doubled. If a woman abducts another woman while she is asleep or intoxicated (suptamatta-pravrajane), or if she drags her husband to the door of the house, she shall be fined 12 panas. If she leaves her house at night, the fine shall be double the previous amount. If a man and a woman exchange signals for the purpose of sensual enjoyment or carry on secret conversations for the same reason, the woman shall be fined 24 panas, and the man shall pay double that amount. A woman showing off her hair, the tie of her dress around her waist, her teeth, or her nails shall pay the first amercement, and a man doing the same shall pay twice the first amercement.

For having conversations in suspicious places, whips may be used as punishment instead of fines. In the center of the village, an outcaste (chandála) may whip such women five times on each side of their bodies. A woman can avoid being whipped by paying a pana for each whip (panikam vá praharam mokshayet). Thus, transgression is dealt with.

(Forbidden transactions.)

For a man and a woman who, though forbidden, engage in any mutual transaction, the woman shall be fined 12, 24, and 54 panas, depending on whether the help consists of (i) small items, (ii) heavy items, or (iii) gold or gold coins (hiranyasuvarnayoh); the man shall be fined double the above amounts. For a similar transaction between a man and a woman who are forbidden to associate (agamvayoh), half of the above punishment shall be imposed. The same punishment applies for any other forbidden transaction between men and women. Thus, forbidden transactions are addressed.

- Treason, transgression, and wandering at will shall cause a woman to lose her rights not only to (i) strídhana, her personal property of over 2,000 panas and her jewelry, (ii) áhita, compensation she received for allowing her husband to marry another woman, but also (iii) sulka, the money her parents received from her husband.

Thus concludes the section on "The Duty of a Wife; Maintenance of a Woman; Enmity between Husband and Wife; a Wife's Transgression; and Forbidden Transactions" in the portion "Concerning Marriage" from the book "Concerning Law" of the Arthasástra of Kautilya.

CHAPTER IV. VAGRANCY, ELOPEMENT AND SHORT AND LONG SOJOURNMENTS.

If a woman leaves her husband's house for any reason other than danger, she shall be fined 6 panas. If she leaves against her husband's direct order, she shall be fined 12 panas. If she goes beyond her neighbor's house (prativesagrihatigatáyah), she shall be fined 6 panas. If she allows her neighbor into her house, accepts alms from a mendicant, or brings in the goods of a merchant, she shall be fined 12 panas. If she continues to do so even after being explicitly forbidden, she shall be punished with the first amercement. If she goes beyond the surrounding houses (parigrihátigatáyam), she shall be fined 24 panas. If she takes another man's wife into her house without any legitimate reason, she shall be fined 100 panas. However, if this happens without her knowledge or against her orders, she will not be held accountable.

My teacher says: For the sake of avoiding danger, it is not wrong for a woman to seek the help of a man who is a kinsman of her husband, a wealthy and respectable man (sukhávastha), the head of the village, one of her legal guardians (anvádhikula), or someone from the family of a mendicant woman, or any of her own male relatives.

But Kautilya raises the question: How can good women (sádhvíjana) even know if the family of her own male relatives is virtuous? It is not an offense for a woman to go to her relatives' houses under situations like death, illness, calamities, or childbirth. Whoever stops her from going in such situations shall be fined 12 panas. If a woman hides herself during such events, she will forfeit her endowment. If her relatives hide her to exempt her from aiding in such situations, they shall lose the remaining balance of sulka, the money due to them from her husband for her marriage. Thus, issues of vagrancy are addressed.

(Elopement or Criminal Rendezvous.)

If a woman leaves her husband's house and goes to another village, she shall not only pay a fine of 12 panas but also forfeit her endowment and jewelry (sthápyábharanalopascha). If she goes to any other place under any pretense other than for subsistence or pilgrimage (bharmádánatirthagamanábhyámanyatra), even if she is in the company of a suitable man, she shall pay a fine of 24 panas and lose all social privileges (sarvadharmalopascha). The man who permits such a woman to accompany him on his journey shall be punished with the first amercement. If both the man and woman share similar sinful ideals in life (tulyasreyasoh) and live a corrupt life (pápiyasoh), each of them shall be punished with the middle-most amercement. However, if the man she accompanies is a near relative, he shall not be punished. If a relative takes a woman with him despite being forbidden, he shall be fined half of the middlemost amercement.

If, on the road, in a forest, or in any hidden place, a woman falls into the company of another man or, for the purpose of pleasure, joins a suspicious or forbidden man, she shall be guilty of elopement (sangrahanam vidyát). It is no offense for women to be in the company of actors, performers, singers, fishermen, hunters, herdsmen, vintners, or other men who usually travel with their women. If a man takes a woman with him on his journey despite being forbidden to do so, or if a woman accompanies a man despite being forbidden, half of the fines previously mentioned shall apply to both of them. Thus, the issue of elopement is dealt with.

(Re-marriage of women.)

Wives belonging to the Súdra, Vaisya, Kshatriya, or Bráhman caste, who have not borne children, should wait for their husbands who have gone abroad for a short time for at least a year. However, if they have given birth to children, they should wait for their absent husbands for more than a year. If they have been provided with maintenance, they should wait twice the length of time mentioned. If they are not provided for, their well-to-do relatives (gnátis) should maintain them for either four or eight years. After this period, the relatives should allow them to remarry, after taking what was given to them at the time of their marriage.

If the husband is a Bráhman who is studying abroad, his wife, if childless, should wait for him for ten years; if she has borne children, she should wait for twelve years. If the husband is of the Kshatriya caste, his wife should wait for him until her death. Even if she has children with a second husband of the same caste (savarna) to prevent the extinction of her family line, she will not face disgrace for this (savarnatascha prajátá ná pavádam labheta).

If the wife of an absent husband lacks maintenance and is neglected by her wealthy relatives, she may remarry someone of her choice who can support her and alleviate her suffering.

A young wife (kumárí) married according to the customs of the first four kinds of marriage (dharmaviváhát), whose husband has gone abroad and is heard from, should wait for him for seven menstrual cycles (saptatirthányákánksheta), provided she has not publicly mentioned his name. If she has announced his name, she should wait for him for a year. If the husband has gone abroad and is not heard from, the wife should wait for him for five menstrual cycles. However, if the husband has not been heard from, the wife should wait for ten menstrual cycles.

If the wife has only received a part of the marriage payment (sulka) from her absent husband who is not heard from, she should wait for him for three menstrual cycles. If he is heard from, she should wait for seven cycles. If she has received the full marriage payment, she should wait for five cycles if the husband is not heard from, and ten cycles if he is heard from. Afterward, with the permission of judges (dharma-sthairvisrishtá), she may marry a man of her choice, as neglecting his wife after her monthly purification is, according to Kautilya, a failure in duty (tirthoparodho hi dharmavadha iti Kautilyah).

For husbands who have been away for a long time (dirgrhapravásinah), who have become ascetics, or who have passed away, their childless wives should wait for seven menstrual cycles. If they have children, they should wait for a year. Afterward, the wife may marry her husband's brother. If her husband had multiple brothers, she should marry the next in age to her late husband, someone virtuous who can protect her, or the youngest unmarried brother. If no brothers are available, she may marry someone from her husband's gotra or a close relative. If there are several suitable candidates, she should choose the closest relation to her deceased husband.

- If a woman remarries someone who is not a relative (dáyáda) of her late husband, she and the man she marries, along with those who arranged and consented to the marriage, will be punished as if they had eloped.

[Thus ends Chapter IV, "Vagrancy; Elopement; and Short and Long Sojournments," in the section "Concerning Marriage" in Book III, "Concerning Law" of the Arthasástra of Kautilya. End of the Section "Concerning Marriage". End of the sixty-first chapter from the beginning.]

CHAPTER V. DIVISION OF INHERITANCE.

Sons whose fathers, mothers, or ancestors are still alive cannot act independently (anísvarah). After the time of the parents or ancestors, the division of ancestral property among the descendants from the same ancestor will occur, calculating the shares based on lineage (per stirpes, meaning according to fathers).

Any self-acquired property of the sons, except that which was gained using the parental property, is not subject to division. Sons or grandsons up to the fourth generation from the first ancestor also have designated shares (amsabhájah) in the property acquired through their undivided ancestral property, as the line of descent (pindah) remains unbroken up to the fourth generation (avichchhinnah). However, those whose lineage from the first ancestor has been broken (vichchhinnapindáh, i.e., beyond the fourth generation) shall divide the property equally. Those who have been living together shall redistribute their property, regardless of whether they had previously divided their ancestral property or had never received such property at all. Among the sons, the one who has brought prosperity to the ancestral property will also receive a share of the profit.

If a man dies without male children, his brothers or those who have been living with him (saha jívino vá) shall inherit his movable property (dravyam), while his daughters (born of marriages other than the first four types) will inherit his immovable property (riktham). If he has sons, they will inherit the property. If he has only daughters born from marriages following the customs of the first four types of marriage, these daughters will inherit the property. If there are neither sons nor daughters of such marriages, the deceased man's father will inherit the property if he is alive. If the father is also deceased, the deceased's brothers and their sons will inherit it. If there are many fatherless brothers, they will divide the property among themselves, and each of the sons of these brothers will receive the share due to his father (piturekamamsam). If the brothers (sodarya) are the sons of different fathers, they will divide the property according to their paternal lines.

Among a deceased man's father, brother, and brother's sons, the latter shall depend on the former for their shares if the former are still living. This also applies to the youngest or eldest claiming their own share of the inheritance.

When a father distributes his property while still alive, he shall not make any distinction when dividing it among his sons. He must not deprive any of his sons of their rightful share without sufficient reason. After the father's death, the elder sons shall show kindness and consideration to the younger ones, as long as the younger ones are not of bad character.

(Time of dividing inheritance.)

The division of inheritance shall take place when all inheritors have reached their legal age. If the division occurs before this, the minors shall receive their shares free from any debts. The shares belonging to the minors shall be kept in the safe custody of their maternal relatives or trustworthy elders from the village until the minors reach maturity. The same rule applies to those who have gone abroad. Unmarried brothers shall also receive the same amount for marriage expenses as was spent on their married brothers. Likewise, unmarried daughters shall receive an appropriate dowry, payable at the time of their marriage.

Both assets and liabilities must be divided equally.

My teacher suggests that even the smallest items, such as mud vessels, should be equally divided among the poor. However, Kautilya holds that this is unnecessary, as the rule is that all existing property is to be divided, but nothing that does not exist. After declaring before witnesses the total amount of shared property, as well as the property that constitutes additional shares for the brothers (based on birth order), the division of inheritance shall proceed. Any property that was divided unfairly, deceptively, or concealed shall be redivided.

Property that has no rightful heir shall be given to the king, except for the property of a woman, a deceased person for whom no funeral rites have been performed, or a miserly man—excluding property belonging to a Bráhman learned in the Vedas. The property of the learned shall be given to those well-versed in the three Vedas.

Persons who have fallen from their caste, those born of outcastes, and eunuchs shall have no share in the inheritance. This also applies to idiots, lunatics, the blind, and lepers. However, if such individuals have wives with property, their children who are not afflicted by the same conditions shall inherit. All these individuals, except for those who have fallen from caste, shall be entitled only to food and clothing.

- If any of these individuals were married before falling from caste or suffering from these afflictions, and if their family line risks becoming extinct, their relatives may beget sons for them and allot these sons a proportionate share of the inheritance.

[Thus ends Chapter V, "Procedure of Portioning Inheritance" in the section of "Division of Inheritance" in Book III, "Concerning law" of the Arthasástra of Kautilya. End of the sixty-second chapter from the beginning.]

CHAPTER VI. SPECIAL SHARES IN INHERITANCE.

Goats shall be the special shares of the eldest sons born of the same mother among Bráhmans; horses among Kshatriyas; cows among Vaisyas; and sheep among Súdras. Blind animals of the same type shall be the special shares of the middle sons; animals with a variegated color shall be the special shares of the youngest sons. In the absence of quadrupeds, the eldest shall receive an additional share of the whole property, excluding precious stones, as this act alone will bind him to his duty to his ancestors.

This method follows the rules observed among the followers of Usanas.

When the father passes away, his carriage and jewelry shall be the special share of the eldest son; his bed, seat, and the bronze plate from which he took his meals shall go to the middle son, while black grains, iron, household utensils, cows, and a cart shall go to the youngest. The remaining property, or even the aforementioned items, may be divided equally among the sons. Sisters shall not have a claim to inheritance but will receive their mother's bronze plate and jewelry after her death.

If the eldest son is impotent, he shall receive only one-third of the special share usually given to the eldest. If he follows a condemnable occupation or has abandoned religious duties, he shall receive only one-quarter of the special share. If he is reckless in his actions, he shall receive nothing.

This rule also applies to the middle and youngest sons. Of these two, the one who demonstrates manliness shall receive half of the special share usually given to the eldest.

Regarding sons born of different wives:

Of sons born to two wives, if only one wife has gone through all the necessary religious ceremonies, or if neither wife observed the necessary rites as maidens, or if one of the wives gave birth to twins, primogeniture is decided by birth.

Shares in inheritance for sons such as Súta, Mágadha, Vrátya, and Rathakára depend on the abundance of paternal property. Other sons of inferior birth, not among the aforementioned categories, shall depend on the eldest for their subsistence. Dependent sons shall receive equal divisions.

For sons born to a Bráhman father from the four castes, the son of a Bráhman woman shall take four shares; the son of a Kshatriya woman shall take three shares; the son of a Vaisya woman shall take two shares; and the son of a Súdra woman shall take one share.

The same rule applies to Kshatriya and Vaisya fathers who have begotten sons in three or two castes, respectively.

An Anantara son of a Bráhman, meaning a son begotten by a Bráhman with a woman of the next lower caste, shall, if endowed with manly or superior qualities (mánushopetah), take an equal share with other sons of lesser qualities. Similarly, Anantara sons of Kshatriya or Vaisya fathers, if they possess manly or superior qualities, shall take either half or equal shares with others.

An only son born to two mothers from different castes shall inherit the entire property and be responsible for maintaining the relatives of his father.

A Palrasava son, begotten by a Bráhman on a Súdra woman, shall receive one-third of the share. A sapinda (agnate) or a kulya (nearest cognate) of the Bráhman shall take the remaining two-thirds, being obliged to perform funeral rites. In the absence of agnates or cognates, the deceased father's teacher or student shall take the remaining shares.

- Alternatively, on the wife of such a Bráhman, a sagotra (relative from the same family name) or a mátribandha (relative from the mother's side) may beget a natural son (kshetraja), and this son may inherit the wealth.

[Thus ends Chapter VI, "Special Shares of Inheritance" in the section of "Division of inheritance" in Book III, "Concerning law" of the Arthasástra of Kautilya. End of the sixty-third chapter from the beginning.]

CHAPTER VII. DISTINCTION BETWEEN SONS.

My teacher says that the seed sown in another's field shall belong to the owner of that field. Others argue that, since the mother is merely the receptacle for the seed (mátá bhastrá), the child must belong to the one whose seed it is. Kautilya, however, says that the child belongs to both living parents.

The son born to a man from his wife who has gone through all the necessary ceremonies is called aurasa, a natural son. Equal to him is the son of an appointed daughter (putrikáputra). The son begotten on a wife by another man, appointed for the purpose, who is of the same gotra as the husband or of a different gotra, is called kshetraja. Upon the begetter's death, the kshetraja son will be the son to both fathers, follow the gotras of both, offer funeral libations to both, and inherit the immovable property (ríktha) of both. Of the same status as the kshetraja is he who is secretly begotten in the house of relatives and is called gúdhaja, the secretly born.

The son cast off by his natural parents is called apaviddha and belongs to the man who performs the necessary religious ceremonies for him. The son born of a maiden before wedlock is called kánína. The son born to a woman married while carrying is called sahodha. The son of a remarried woman (punarbhátáyáh) is called paunarbhava. A natural son can claim relationships with both his father and his father's relatives, but a son born to another man can have relationships only with his adopter.

Of the same status as the latter is he who is given in adoption with water by both the father and mother, known as datta. The son who, either by his own will or following his relatives' intent, offers himself as the son of another is called upagata. He who is appointed as a son is called kritaka, and the one who is purchased is called kríta.

Upon the birth of a natural son, savarna sons will inherit only one-third of the property, while the asavarna sons will receive only food and clothing.

Sons begotten by Bráhmans or Kshatriyas on women of the next lower caste (anantaráputráh) are called savarnas, but sons born of women two castes lower are called asavarnas. The son begotten by a Bráhman on a Vaisya woman is called Ambashtha, and the son of a Bráhman on a Súdra woman is called Nisháda or Párasava. The son begotten by a Kshatriya on a Súdra woman is known as Ugra, while the son of a Vaisya on a Súdra woman is considered a Súdra. Sons begotten by men of impure life, from any of the four castes, on women of lower castes next to their own are called Vrátyas. The above types of sons are called anuloma, sons begotten by men of higher castes on women of lower castes.

Sons begotten by a Súdra on women of higher castes are called Ayogava, Kshatta, and Chandála. When begotten by a Vaisya, they are Mágadha and Vaidehaka, and by a Kshatriya, they are called Súta. However, the individuals known as Súta and Mágadha in the Puránas are distinct and hold greater merit than either Bráhmans or Kshatriyas. The above types of sons are pratiloma, meaning sons born from men of lower castes and women of higher castes, originating from kings who violate all dharmas.

The son begotten by an Ugra on a Nisháda woman is called Kukkuta, and in reverse, when begotten by a Nisháda on an Ugra woman, the son is called Pulkasa. The son begotten by an Ambhashtha on a Vaidehaka woman is named Vaina, and the reverse order of that combination produces a son called Kusílava. An Ugra fathering a child with a Kshatta woman creates a son named Vapáka. These and other such sons are known as Antarálas, or mixed castes.

A Vainya becomes a Rathakára or chariot-maker by profession. Members of this caste shall marry within their own group. They should continue to follow the customs and occupations of their ancestors. They may either become Súdras or join other lower castes, except for Chandálas.

A king who guides his subjects according to these rules will ascend to heaven; otherwise, he will fall into hell.

- The offspring of mixed castes (Antarálas) shall receive equal shares of inheritance. Partition of inheritance shall follow the customs of the country, caste, guild (sangha), or village of the inheritors.

[Thus ends Chapter VII "Distinction between Sons" in the section of "Division of Inheritance" in Book III, "Concerning law" of the Arthasástra of Kautilya. End of "Division of Inheritance". End of the sixty-fourth chapter from the beginning.]

CHAPTER VIII. BUILDINGS.

Disputes concerning property (Vástu) are to be settled based on evidence provided by people living in the neighborhood. Houses, fields, gardens, buildings of any kind (setubandhah), lakes, and tanks are all considered Vástu.

The attachment of a house's roof to the transverse beam using iron bolts is called setu (karna-kílaya-sabandho'anugriham setuh). Houses must be constructed according to the stability of the setu, and new houses should be built without encroaching on the property of others.

The foundation (pade bandhah) should measure 2 aratnis by 3 padas. All permanent houses, except for temporary structures built for the confinement of women for ten days, must be equipped with a dunghill (avaskara), a water course (bhrama), and a well (udapánum). Failure to comply with this rule will result in the first amercement.

This rule also applies to the construction of closets, pits, and water courses for festive occasions.

Each house should have a water course with sufficient slope and a length of 3 padas or 11 aratnis, ensuring that water either flows continuously or falls directly into the drain. Violating this rule will incur a fine of 54 panas.

An apartment, starting with a pada or an aratni, should be built measuring 3 padas by 4 padas for placing a fire for worship (agnishtham), a waterbutt (udanjaram), a corn mill (rochaním), or a mortar (kuttinín). Non-compliance with this rule will result in a fine of 24 panas.

The space between any two houses or between the extended portions of any two houses shall be 4 padas, or 3 padas. The roofs of neighboring houses may either be 4 angulas apart, or one of them may overlap the other. The front door (anidváram) should measure a kishku, and there should be no obstacle inside the house that blocks the opening of either leaf of the door. The upper story must have a small but high window. If the window obstructs a nearby house, it must be closed. The owners of houses can build their homes in whatever way they mutually agree upon, as long as they avoid anything harmful. To prevent rain from causing damage, the roof should be covered with a broad mat that cannot be blown away by the wind. The roof should also not be of a type that easily bends or breaks. If this rule is violated, it shall be punished with the first amercement. The same punishment applies for causing inconvenience by constructing doors or windows that face those of neighboring houses, except when these houses are separated by the king's road or a public road.

If any pit, steps, water-course, ladder, dung-hill, or any other part of a house causes inconvenience to outsiders, blocks their enjoyment, or results in water collecting and damaging the wall of a neighboring house, the owner shall be fined 12 panas. If the inconvenience is caused by feces or urine, the fine shall be doubled. Watercourses or gutters must allow free passage for water; otherwise, the fine will be 12 panas.

The same fine of 12 panas shall apply not only to a tenant who refuses to leave after being asked but also to a homeowner who evicts a renter who has paid their rent, unless the renter is involved in defamation, theft, robbery, abduction, or falsely claiming ownership. Anyone who voluntarily leaves a house must pay the remaining balance of the annual rent.

If any member of a group does not participate in building a structure meant for the common use of all members, or if anyone obstructs another member from using any part of that structure, they shall be fined 12 panas. Similarly, if someone interferes with another's enjoyment of such a structure, they shall be fined double that amount.

- With the exception of private rooms and parlors (angana), all other open areas of houses, as well as any rooms where a fire is kept burning for worship or where a mortar is located, should be made available for common use.

[Thus ends Chapter VIII, "House-building" in the section of "Buildings" in Book III, "Concerning Law" of the Arthasástra of Kautilya. End of the sixty-fifth chapter from the beginning.]

CHAPTER IX. SALE OF BUILDINGS, BOUNDARY DISPUTES, DETERMINATION OF BOUNDARIES, AND MISCELLANEOUS HINDRANCES.

Wealthy individuals among relatives or neighbors shall, one after another, take the opportunity to purchase land or other holdings. Neighbors of good standing, numbering forty and different from the buyers mentioned earlier, shall gather in front of the property up for sale and announce its availability. An accurate description of the exact boundaries of fields, gardens, buildings, lakes, or tanks must be declared in front of the village elders or elders of the neighborhood. If, after shouting three times, "Who will purchase this at such and such a price?" no objections are raised, the buyer may proceed with the purchase of the property in question. If, at this point, the value of the property increases due to bidding even among members of the same community, the increased amount, along with the toll on the value, shall be handed over to the king's treasury. The person bidding (vikrayapratikroshtá) shall pay the toll. Bidding for a property in the absence of its owner shall be punished with a fine of 24 panas. If the owner does not come forward even after seven nights, the bidder may take possession of the property. Selling the property or buildings (vástu) to anyone other than the bidder shall be punished with a fine of 200 panas; if the property in question is other than buildings (vástu), the fine for the offense shall be 24 panas. Thus, the rules for the sale of buildings are outlined.

(Boundary disputes.)

In all disputes over boundaries between two villages, the neighboring elders from five or ten nearby villages (panchagrámí or dasagrámí) shall investigate the case, using evidence drawn from natural or man-made boundary markers. Senior cultivators and herdsmen, or others with prior knowledge of the area, as well as any individuals familiar or unfamiliar with the disputed boundary markers, shall first describe the markers in question. Then, dressed in unusual attire (viparítaveshah), they shall lead the group to the location. If the boundary markers they described are not located, a fine of 1,000 panas shall be imposed on the person providing false or misleading information. However, if they reach the correct location, the party that has encroached on the boundary or destroyed the markers shall be fined similarly. The king shall then distribute for beneficial use any landholdings without boundary markers or those that have ceased to be maintained by any individual.

(Disputes about fields.)

Disputes over fields shall be resolved by the elders of the neighborhood or village. If their opinions differ, a decision shall be sought from a group of honest and respected individuals, or the disputants may choose to divide the disputed holding equally. If neither of these methods succeeds, the king shall take possession of the holding (vástu) in question. The same rule applies to holdings for which no claimant comes forward; such holdings may also be beneficially distributed among the people. Any forcible occupation of a holding shall be punished as theft.

If someone occupies a holding on justifiable grounds, they shall pay the rightful owner a rent, with the amount set based on what is reasonably needed for the subsistence of the cultivator working the holding. Encroachment upon boundaries shall be punished with the first amercement. Destroying boundary markers shall be fined 24 panas. These rules also apply to disputes concerning forest hermitages, pasture lands, main roads, cremation grounds, temples, sacrificial sites, and places of pilgrimage. Thus, the determination of boundaries is addressed.

(Miscellaneous hindrances.)

All kinds of disputes will be settled based on the evidence provided by neighbors. Regarding pasture lands, fields, flower gardens, threshing floors, houses, and stables for horses, priority will be given to resolving issues for the first person in line before addressing those of anyone who comes afterward. Exceptions are made for forests belonging to Brahmins, places with Soma plants, temples, and sites of sacrifice and pilgrimage. Anyone who causes damage to seeds sown in someone else's fields by using a shortcut to reach tanks, rivers, or fields must pay the affected party compensation equal to the amount of the damage.

If the owner of any wet fields, parks, or buildings causes harm to similar property owned by others, the fine will be double the amount of the damage caused.

The water from a lower tank should not be allowed to flood any field that is irrigated by a higher tank.

The natural flow of water from a higher tank to a lower one must not be stopped unless the lower tank has remained unused for three continuous years. Anyone breaking this rule will be punished with the first level of penalty. The same punishment applies to draining a tank of its water. Any type of structure, including bridges or dams, that has been neglected for five consecutive years will be forfeited, except in cases of natural disaster.

(Remission of taxes.)

When constructing new works, such as tanks or lakes, taxes on the lands below these tanks will be waived for five years. For repairs on neglected or ruined works of this kind, a four-year tax exemption is given. Improvements or expansions of waterworks will have a three-year tax exemption. For new works acquired by mortgage or purchase, a two-year tax exemption will apply on lands below these works. If uncultivated land is acquired for farming, whether by mortgage, purchase, or any other means, the tax exemption will last for two years.

Out of the crops grown by irrigation using wind power, bullocks, or from tanks, fields, parks, flower gardens, or any other method, a portion of the produce, not so large as to burden the cultivators, should be provided to the Government.

Individuals who cultivate lands below tanks or similar works owned by others, either by paying a fixed price, an annual rent, or a share of the crops grown, or who are permitted to cultivate the land rent-free, must maintain these tanks and structures in good condition; otherwise, they will be fined double the amount of the damage caused.

- Those who divert the water of tanks or similar works at any place other than the designated sluice gate will be fined 6 panas; those who block the water flow from the sluice gate of a tank carelessly will be fined the same amount.

[Thus ends Chapter IX, "Sale of buildings, boundary disputes, determination of boundaries, and miscellaneous hindrances" in the section of "Buildings" in Book III, "Concerning Law" of the Arthasástra of Kautilya. End of the sixty-sixth chapter from the beginning.]

CHAPTER X. DESTRUCTION OF PASTURE-LANDS, FIELDS AND ROADS, AND NON-PERFORMANCE OF AGREEMENTS.

People who block or interfere with the flow of water intended for farming will face the first level of punishment. Anyone constructing buildings on someone else's property to attract pilgrims, including places of worship or temples, or who sells, mortgages, or causes the sale or mortgage of long-established charitable structures, will be subject to the middle level of punishment. Witnesses to such actions will face the highest level of punishment, except in cases involving neglected or ruined buildings. If there are no claimants for rundown religious buildings, villagers or charitable individuals are allowed to repair them.

(Blocking the roads.)

The rules regarding types of roads and paths were covered in the section on fort construction.

Blocking roads meant for common animals or people will incur a fine of 12 panas; blocking roads for superior animals, 24 panas; for roads used by elephants or leading to fields, 54 panas; for roads leading to buildings or forests, 600 panas; for roads to burial grounds or villages, 200 panas; for roads to a fortress, 500 panas; and for roads leading to regions, pasture grounds, or district centers, 1,000 panas. These fines also apply to excessively deep plowing on any of these roads, and a quarter of these fines apply if the plowing only affects the surface.

If a cultivator or neighbor encroaches on a field during the sowing season, they will be fined 12 panas, except when the encroachment results from unavoidable disasters, other disturbances, or extreme hardship coming from the field itself.

(Settling in villages.)

Taxpayers may sell or mortgage their fields only to other taxpayers; Brahmins may sell or mortgage their Brahmadaya, or gifted lands, only to those who also possess such lands. Otherwise, they will face the first level of punishment. The same penalty applies to any taxpayer who settles in a village where taxpayers do not reside. If one taxpayer takes over the place of another, they shall have rights to all holdings except the house of the previous owner, although the house itself may also be granted to the new resident.

If someone cultivates another person's inalienable land when the owner is not farming it, that person must return the land after enjoying its use for five years, receiving fair compensation for any improvements made on the land. Individuals who are not taxpayers and live abroad will retain ownership rights to their lands.

(The Head-man of the village.)

When the headman of a village needs to travel for business concerning the entire village, the villagers shall take turns accompanying him. Those unable to accompany him must pay a fee of 1½ panas for every yojana.

If the headman expels anyone from the village, except in cases involving a thief or an adulterer, he will be fined 24 panas, and the villagers will face the first level of punishment if they do the same.

The re-entry of a person previously expelled from the village is clarified in the section on the "settlement of people in villages."

Around each village, an enclosure of timber posts must be constructed, extending 800 angulas in distance from the village boundary.

(Trespassing cattle.)

Pasture lands, plains, and forests may be used for grazing cattle.

For camels or buffaloes that are allowed to stray after grazing in pasture grounds, the fine will be ¼ of a pana; for cows, horses, or asses, it will be 1/8 of a pana; for smaller animals, 1/16 of a pana. If cattle are found lying on these lands after grazing, the fines will be double the above amounts. For cattle that continually stay near the pasture grounds, the fines will be four times the above rates.

Bulls released in the name of the village deity, cows within ten days of calving that remain in the enclosure, or bulls kept specifically for breeding purposes will not be fined. If animals are proven guilty of eating crops, their owner or owners will pay double the amount of the crop loss. People driving their cattle through a field without informing the owner will be fined 12 panas. If someone allows their cattle to stray, they will be fined 24 panas, and cowherds allowing cattle under their care to stray will be fined half of that. The same penalty applies to letting cattle graze in flower gardens.

Breaking the fence of a field will incur twice the previous fine. If cattle stray and consume grains stored in a house, on a threshing floor, or in a courtyard, the owners of the cattle will have to provide adequate compensation.

If animals kept in reserve forests are found grazing in a field, it should be reported to the forest officers, and the animals will be driven out without harm. Stray cattle should be driven away with ropes or whips, and anyone who harms them will face punishment for assault or violence. Those who encourage cattle to graze in others' fields or are caught in the act must be thoroughly prevented. This concludes the guidelines for preventing damage to pasture lands, fields, and roads.

(Non-performance of agreement.)

The fine imposed on a cultivator who comes to a village for work but does not fulfill his duties will go to the village. He must return double the wages he accepted with the promise to work, along with double the value of any food and drink he was provided. If the work involves a sacrificial ceremony, he must also pay double the wages for not participating.

Anyone who does not contribute to the preparations for a public show will lose, along with their family, the right to attend the event. If someone who did not help prepare for a public performance is caught secretly listening or watching, or if anyone refuses to contribute to a project beneficial to all, they will be required to pay double the value of their expected contribution. The orders of any person acting for the common good must be respected. Disobedience in such a case will result in a fine of 12 panas. If others unite to harm or beat the person giving orders for the public benefit, each participant will pay twice the standard fine for such an offense.

If one of the offenders is a Brahmin or someone of higher status, they will face punishment first. A Brahmin who chooses not to join a village sacrificial ceremony will not be forced but may be persuaded to contribute his share.

These rules also apply to any failure to fulfill agreements among regions, castes, families, and assemblies.

- Those who work together to construct public buildings along roads, which benefit the entire country, and those who not only beautify their villages but also guard them will receive favorable recognition from the king.

[Thus ends Chapter X "Destruction of pasture lands, fields, and roads," in the section of "Buildings" in Book III, "Concerning Law" of the Arthasástra of Kautilya; end of "Buildings"; and of non-performance of agreements.' End of the sixty-seventh chapter from the beginning.]

CHAPTER XI. RECOVERY OF DEBTS.

An interest rate of one and a quarter panas per month per cent is considered fair. A rate of five panas per month per cent constitutes commercial interest. An interest rate of ten panas per month per cent is common among forest regions, while twenty panas per month per cent is usual among sea traders. Any person who exceeds, or causes another to exceed, the above rates of interest shall be punished with the first level of punishment; and those who are witnesses to such transactions shall each pay half the amount of the fine imposed.

The nature of the transactions between creditors and debtors, upon which the welfare of the kingdom depends, shall be thoroughly scrutinized at all times. In times of a good harvest, interest on grains shall not exceed half of its value in money. Interest on investments in stocks (prakshepa) shall be set at one-half of the profit and should be paid as each year expires. If it is allowed to accumulate due to either intention or the absence of the receiver or payer abroad, the amount to be paid shall be twice the share or the original principal.

A person who demands interest before it is due, or who attempts to represent the total amount of both the principal and its interest as the principal alone, shall be fined four times the amount under dispute. A creditor who sues for four times the amount they initially lent shall also pay a fine of four times the unjust amount. Of this fine, the creditor shall pay three-fourths, while the debtor shall pay the remaining one-fourth.

Interest on debts owed by persons engaged in prolonged sacrifices (dírghasatra), suffering from illness, detained in the houses of their teachers for learning, or who are minors or too impoverished, shall not accumulate.

A creditor who refuses to receive payment of his debt shall pay a fine of 12 panas. If this refusal is due to some justifiable reason, then the amount, free from any further interest, shall be held in safe custody by others. Debts neglected for ten years, except in the cases of minors, elderly persons, sick individuals, those involved in calamities, those traveling abroad or fleeing the country, and in cases of national disturbances (rájyavibhrama), shall not be reclaimed.

Sons of a deceased debtor are responsible for repaying the principal with interest. In the absence of sons, the deceased's kinsmen who claim a share of his estate, or any sureties such as joint partners in the debt, shall repay the debt. No other kind of surety shall be considered valid; the surety of a minor is weak and ineffective.

A debt for which there is no specified time or place for repayment shall be paid by the sons, grandsons, or any other heirs of the deceased debtor. Any debt with no specified time or place for repayment, and for which life, marriage, or land has been pledged, shall be borne by the debtor's sons or grandsons.

(Regarding many debts against one.)

Except when a debtor is going abroad, no debtor shall be sued simultaneously for more than one debt by one or two creditors. Even if the debtor is going abroad, he shall repay his debts in the order in which they were borrowed or shall first settle debts owed to the king or a learned Brahmin.

Debts contracted mutually by a husband and wife, a son and father, or between brothers with undivided interests shall be deemed irrecoverable.

Cultivators or government servants shall not be detained for debts while engaged in their official duties or work.

A wife, even if unaware of the debt (pratisrávaní), shall not be detained for a debt contracted by her husband, except in cases involving herdsmen or joint cultivators. However, a husband may be detained for a debt contracted by his wife. If it is confirmed that a man fled the country without addressing the debt contracted by his wife, he shall be subject to the highest level of punishment; if this is disputed, reliance shall be placed on witnesses.

(Witnesses.)

It is required to present three witnesses who are reliable, honest, and respected. A minimum of two witnesses acceptable to both parties is necessary in debt cases; never shall one witness alone be considered sufficient.

The following individuals are not eligible to serve as witnesses: brothers of the wife, co-partners, prisoners, creditors, debtors, enemies, dependents, or those previously punished by the Government. Also ineligible are persons legally barred from transactions, the king, those learned in the Vedas, those dependent on village provisions, lepers, individuals with bodily eruptions, outcasts, individuals of low occupation, the blind, the deaf, the mute, egotistical individuals, females, or government servants, except in cases involving dealings within their own community.

In disputes involving assault, theft, or abduction, individuals other than a wife's brothers, enemies, or co-partners can act as witnesses. In cases of secret dealings, a single woman or man who has privately seen or heard them may testify, except if they are the king or an ascetic. In cases of prosecution, masters can testify against servants, priests or teachers against disciples, and parents against sons. Other individuals may also act as witnesses in criminal cases.

If masters, servants, or other similarly related persons sue each other, they will be punished with the highest level of penalty. Creditors found guilty of making false claims (parokta) shall be fined ten times the amount involved, but if unable to pay such a fine, they shall pay at least five times the amount claimed. Thus concludes the section on witnesses.

(Taking oaths.)

Witnesses shall be presented before Brahmins, along with vessels of water and fire. A Brahmin witness shall be instructed, "Tell the truth." A Kshatriya or a Vaisya witness shall be told, "If you speak falsehood, may you fail to receive the rewards of your sacrificial and charitable deeds; but, after defeating your enemies in battle, may you become a beggar, carrying a skull in your hand."

A Sudra witness shall be warned as follows: "If you speak falsely, may all your good deeds, whether from a previous life or after your death, go to the king, and may any sins the king has committed fall upon you. Fines will also be levied on you, for facts as they were heard or seen will certainly be revealed in time."

If witnesses are found to have made a unanimous false agreement within seven nights, a fine of 12 panas shall be imposed. If they are found to have done so within three fortnights, they shall pay the full amount being claimed in the dispute.

If witnesses disagree in their testimonies, judgment shall be based on the statements of a majority of pure and respectable witnesses; or the average of their statements may be followed; or the amount in dispute may be claimed by the king. If witnesses testify to a lesser amount than claimed, the plaintiff shall be fined in proportion to the extra amount claimed; if they testify to a greater amount, the excess shall go to the king. In cases where the plaintiff proves himself ignorant or foolish, or when difficulty arises due to the witnesses' poor hearing at the time of the transaction or due to unclear writing, or where the debtor is deceased, only the evidence of witnesses shall be relied upon.

The followers of Usanas state: "Only in cases where witnesses prove themselves senseless or foolish, and when investigating the place, time, or nature of the transaction proves futile, shall the three levels of fines be imposed."

The followers of Manu assert: "False witnesses shall pay a fine ten times the amount, whether the sum lost is true or false."

The followers of Brihaspati declare: "When witnesses have muddied a case due to their ignorance, they shall be tortured to death."

"No," says Kautilya. "Witnesses must pay attention to the truth of what they hear when they are called to testify in any matter; if they did not pay attention, they shall be fined 24 panas; if they testified to a false case without thorough scrutiny, they shall be fined half of this amount."

- Each party shall produce witnesses who are not far removed either by time or place from the event in question; witnesses who are greatly removed either by time or place, or who are unwilling to appear, shall be compelled to present themselves by order of the judges.

[Thus ends Chapter XI, "Recovery of debts" in Book III, "Concerning Law" of the Arthasástra of Kautilya. End of the sixty-eighth chapter from the beginning.]

CHAPTER XII. CONCERNING DEPOSITS.

The rules concerning debts shall also apply to deposits. In cases where forts or regions of the kingdom are destroyed by enemies or wild tribes, where villages, merchants, or herds of cattle suffer attacks from invaders, where the kingdom itself is devastated, where widespread fires or floods result in the complete destruction of villages or partially damage immovable properties, with movable properties having been saved beforehand, or where sudden fires or floods prevent even movable properties from being salvaged, or when a ship loaded with goods is either sunk or looted by pirates, deposits lost in any of these situations shall not be reclaimed.

If the depositary has used the deposit for personal comfort, they shall not only pay compensation (bhogavetanam) determined according to the circumstances of place and time but shall also pay a fine of 12 panas. Any loss in the value of the deposit due to its use shall also be restored, along with an additional fine of 24 panas. Deposits that are damaged or lost through any cause must also be compensated in full.

When the depositary is either deceased or suffering from calamities, the deposit shall not be claimed. If the deposit has been mortgaged, sold, or lost, the depositary shall not only restore four times its value but shall also pay a fine equal to five times the value stipulated (pancbabandho dandah). If the deposit has been exchanged for a similar one by the depositary or lost in any other manner, its value shall be compensated.

(Pledges.)

The same rules shall apply in cases involving pledges whenever they are lost, consumed, sold, mortgaged, or misappropriated. A pledge that is productive, known as a usufructuary mortgage, shall never be lost to the debtor, nor shall any interest on the debt be charged. However, if the pledge is unproductive, as in the case of hypothecation, it may be lost, and interest on the debt shall continue to accumulate. A pledgee who does not return the pledge when the debtor is ready to redeem it shall be fined 12 panas.

In the absence of the creditor or mediator, the debt amount may be placed in the safekeeping of the village elders, allowing the debtor to reclaim the pledged property; alternatively, with its current value established and no future interest accruing, the pledge may be left where it is. If there is an increase in the value of the pledge or if there is reason to believe it may depreciate or be lost soon, the pledgee may, with permission from the judges or based on evidence from the officer responsible for pledges, sell the pledge either in the presence of the debtor or under the oversight of experts who can assess the validity of such concerns.

An immovable property pledged for enjoyment, whether through labor or without labor, shall not be allowed to lose its value while generating interest on the loaned amount and covering the maintenance expenses.

A pledgee who enjoys the pledged property without permission shall forfeit both the debt and shall pay the net profit they derived from it. The rules concerning deposits shall also be applicable to other matters related to pledges.

(Property entrusted to another for delivery to a third party)

The same rules shall apply to orders (ádesa) and property entrusted for delivery to a third party (anvádhi).

If a merchant entrusts a messenger with property for delivery to a third person and the messenger does not reach the intended destination or is robbed by thieves, the merchant shall bear no responsibility for the property; similarly, the family of a messenger who dies while en route shall not be held liable for the entrusted property.

For all other matters, the rules regarding deposits shall also apply here.

(Borrowed or hired properties.)

Properties either borrowed (yáchitakam) or hired (avakrítakam) must be returned in the same intact condition as when they were received. If, due to a long passage of time or distance, or because of inherent defects in the properties themselves, or due to unforeseen accidents, borrowed or hired properties are lost or destroyed, they need not be compensated for. The rules concerning deposits shall also apply here.

(Retail sale.)

Retail dealers who sell merchandise belonging to others, at prices specific to particular localities and times, shall hand over to the wholesale dealers the full amount of the sale proceeds and profit they have realized. The rules regarding pledges shall apply in this context as well. If, due to time or distance, there is a decrease in the value of the merchandise, retail dealers shall pay the value and profit at the rate that was in effect when they originally received the merchandise.

Servants who sell commodities at prices set by their masters shall not make any profit. They shall only return the actual sale proceeds. If prices decline, they shall only return as much of the sale proceeds as they receive at the lower rate.

However, merchants who are members of trade guilds (samvyavaharikeshu), or who are known to be trustworthy and are not condemned by the king, need not repay the value of merchandise that is lost or destroyed due to its inherent defects or unforeseen accidents. But for merchandise affected by time or distance, they shall return as much of its value and profit as remains after accounting for the wear and tear of the goods.

For all other matters, the rules regarding deposits shall also apply here. This explains retail sales.

(Sealed deposits.)

The rules established concerning unsealed deposits (upanidhis) shall also apply to sealed deposits. A person who hands over a sealed deposit to anyone other than the rightful depositor shall be punished. In the event that a depositary denies having received a deposit, the previous circumstances (púrvápadánam) surrounding the deposit, as well as the character and social standing of the depositor, shall serve as the only evidence. Artisans (káravah) are considered to naturally possess an impure character, and it is not customary for them to make deposits for valid reasons.

When a depositary denies having received a sealed deposit that was not deposited for a credible reason, the depositor may be granted secret permission from the judges to present witnesses whom he might have discreetly stationed behind a wall (gúdhabhitti) during the deposit.

In the midst of a forest or on a voyage, an elderly or ailing merchant might entrust a valuable article with a specific secret mark to a depositary and proceed on his way. Upon sending details of this deposit to his son or brother, the latter may request the sealed deposit. If the depositary does not return it without issue, he shall not only lose his credibility but shall also face punishment for theft in addition to being required to return the deposit.

A trustworthy individual, intending to renounce worldly life and become an ascetic, may leave a sealed deposit marked with a secret sign in the custody of another and, after several years, return to claim it. If the depositary denies it dishonestly, he shall be made to restore the deposit and shall also face punishment for theft.

If a person with a sealed deposit marked with a secret sign becomes fearful while passing through a street at night and, fearing capture by the police for walking at an odd hour, entrusts the deposit to someone before continuing on his way, and is subsequently jailed, he may later request the deposit back. Should the depositary deny this claim dishonestly, he shall be forced to restore it and will face punishment for theft.

A member of the depositor's family may recognize the sealed deposit in another person's possession and may request not only the deposit but also information about the depositor's whereabouts. If the custodian denies either request, he shall be treated in the same way as in the previous cases.

In all these situations, it is essential to inquire how the disputed property came into the depositary's possession, the circumstances connected to the transactions surrounding the property, and the plaintiff's social standing and wealth (arthasámarthyam).

The above rules shall apply to all types of transactions between any two people (mithassamaváyah).

- Therefore, all agreements should be entered into openly and in the presence of witnesses, without secrecy. Whether dealing with one's own people or others, the circumstances of the time and place should first be carefully considered.

[Thus ends Chapter XII "Concerning Deposits" in Book III, "Concernig Law" of the Arthasástra of Kautilya. End of the sixty-ninth chapter from the beginning.]

CHAPTER XIII. RULES REGARDING SLAVES AND LABOURERS.

The selling or mortgaging of the life of a Sudra who is not a born slave, has not reached adulthood, and is Arya by birth shall be punished by a fine of 12 panas; for a Vaisya, the fine is 24 panas; for a Kshatriya, 36 panas; and for a Brahmin, 48 panas. If persons who are not kin engage in the sale or mortgage of such individuals, they shall face the three levels of amercement, and in severe cases, capital punishment. Purchasers and those who abet these actions shall also be punished. It is not considered a crime for Mlechchhas to sell or mortgage the life of their own children. However, an Arya shall never be subjected to slavery.

If the life of an Arya is mortgaged to alleviate family difficulties, to obtain money for fines or legal decrees, or to reclaim confiscated household goods, the family members must redeem him as soon as possible, especially if he is a youth or an adult capable of providing assistance.

A person who has willingly enslaved himself once shall, if guilty of an offense (nishpatitah), remain a slave for life. Likewise, any person whose life has been twice mortgaged by others shall, if found guilty of an offense, be enslaved for life. Both types of individuals shall be bound to lifelong servitude if they are found attempting to flee to foreign lands.

Deceiving a slave of his earnings or denying him the rights he has as an Arya shall be punished by half the fine normally levied for enslaving the life of an Arya.

A person who unknowingly mortgages the life of a convict, deceased person, or an afflicted individual shall be entitled to recover the value paid for the slave from the original mortgager.

Employing a slave to handle the dead, clean waste, or clear away food remnants; forcing a slave to remain unclothed; harming or insulting them; or violating the chastity of a female slave shall result in the forfeiture of the amount paid for that slave. Violating the chastity of nurses, female cooks, or female servants who are joint cultivators or of similar class shall immediately grant them freedom. Any act of violence toward an attendant of high birth entitles him to escape servitude. If a master has relations with a nurse or pledged female slave against her will, he shall face the first level of amercement, while a stranger doing the same shall face the middle level of amercement.

If a man commits or assists in committing rape with a girl or female slave pledged to him, he shall forfeit the purchase value and pay a monetary sum (sulka) to her, in addition to a fine double that amount to the Government.

The offspring of a man who has sold himself into slavery shall be considered Arya. A slave shall have the right to retain not only his earnings, provided they do not interfere with his master's work, but also any inheritance received from his father.

By paying the amount for which one was enslaved, a slave shall regain Arya status. This rule applies equally to those who were born into slavery or pledged as slaves.

The amount required for a slave to secure freedom shall be equivalent to the price for which he was originally sold.

Any person enslaved for fines or court decrees (dandapranítah) shall earn the amount through labor. An Arya captured in war shall pay for his freedom a sum proportional to the risk endured during his capture, or half of that amount.

If a slave under eight years old, who has no relatives—whether born in the master's household, inherited, purchased, or acquired by any other means—is employed in menial tasks against his will, or is sold or mortgaged in a foreign land; or if a pregnant female slave is sold or pledged without arrangements made for her confinement, the master shall face the first level of amercement. The buyer and any abettors shall also be punished similarly.

Failing to release a slave upon receipt of the required ransom shall be penalized with a fine of 12 panas; confining a slave without valid reason (samrodhaschákaranát) shall also carry the same punishment.

A slave's property shall pass to his kinsmen; if no relatives are present, the master shall inherit it.

If a master begets a child by a female slave, both the child and the mother shall immediately be recognized as free. If, for subsistence, the mother must remain in servitude, her brother and sister shall be freed.

Selling or mortgaging the life of a male or female slave once freed shall result in a fine of 12 panas, except in cases of voluntary enslavement. Thus concludes the rules regarding slaves.

(Power of Masters over their hired servants.)

Neighbors shall be aware of the terms of agreement between a master and his servant. The servant shall receive the wages that were promised. If wages were not agreed upon in advance, the amount shall be determined based on the work completed and the time spent on it (karmakálánurúpam—according to the prevailing rate). When wages have not been previously set, a cultivator shall receive one-tenth of the crops grown, a herdsman one-tenth of the clarified butter produced, and a trader one-tenth of the sale proceeds. Wages that were agreed upon beforehand shall be paid and received as promised.

Artisans, musicians, physicians, entertainers, cooks, and other workers who voluntarily offer their services shall be paid the same wages as others in similar positions, or as determined by skilled persons (kusaláh) in that profession.

Disputes concerning wages shall be resolved based on evidence provided by witnesses. If no witnesses are available, the master who assigned work to the servant shall be questioned. Failure to pay agreed wages shall incur a fine of ten times the amount due (dasabandhah), or 6 panas; misappropriation of wages shall be punished with a fine of 12 panas or five times the amount of wages (panchabandho vá).

If a person, while being swept away by floods, trapped in a fire, or in peril from elephants or tigers, is rescued on the condition that he would give his rescuer all his property and even offer his sons, wife, and himself as slaves, he shall instead pay only an amount as determined by experts. This rule shall apply to all situations in which assistance is provided to a person in distress.

- A public woman shall honor her agreements, as promised;

however, insistence on fulfilling an agreement that is ill-considered or inappropriate shall not be enforced.

[Thus ends Chapter XIII, "Rules regarding slaves" in the section of "Rules regarding slaves" and the "Right of Masters" in the section of "Rules regarding Labourers" in Book III, "Concerning Law" of the Arthasástra of Kautilya. End of the seventieth chapter from the beginning.]

CHAPTER XIV. RULES REGARDING LABOURERS; AND CO-OPERATIVE UNDERTAKING.

A servant who neglects or unreasonably delays work after receiving wages shall be fined 12 panas and detained until the work is completed. However, if a worker is incapable of performing the task, is engaged in a low-level job, is suffering from illness, or is affected by calamities, they shall be given some leniency or allowed to have the work done by a substitute. Any loss caused to the employer due to this delay shall be compensated by additional work from the servant.

An employer may freely engage another person to complete the work, provided there are no restrictive conditions preventing the original employee from taking on other work, nor shall the employee seek work elsewhere.

An employer who does not assign work to his laborer, or an employee who does not complete the employer's task, shall be fined 12 panas. An employee who has received wages for specific work that remains incomplete shall not leave to take up other work on his own accord.

My preceptor asserts that an employer not assigning work when the employee is prepared should be considered as if the work has been performed by the employee.

However, Kautilya disagrees, arguing that wages should only be paid for work actually completed, not for work left undone. If an employer assigns only a portion of the work to the laborer and does not assign the rest, though the laborer is ready to finish it, then the incomplete portion of work shall still be considered finished. Yet, if circumstances, such as changes in time or place, or if the work quality by the laborer is unsatisfactory, the employer may reasonably withhold satisfaction with the work performed. Moreover, if the laborer is left unchecked, he may exceed the agreed amount of work, resulting in a loss for the employer.

The same rules shall apply to guilds of workmen (sanghabhritáh).

Workmen guilds shall have a grace period of seven nights beyond the agreed deadline to fulfill their contracts. Beyond this time, they shall find substitutes to ensure the work is completed. Without their employer's permission, guild members shall neither leave any work unfinished nor take anything from the worksite. A fine of 24 panas shall be imposed for taking anything, and 12 panas for leaving work incomplete. Thus conclude the rules regarding laborers.

Guilds of workmen (sanghabhritáh, those employed by companies) as well as those engaged in cooperative work (sambhúya samutthátarah) shall divide their earnings (vetanam, or wages) either equally or as agreed among themselves.

Cultivators or merchants shall, either at the end or midway through their cultivation or manufacturing process, pay their laborers a share proportional to the work completed. If the laborers, upon leaving work midway, provide suitable replacements, they shall receive their wages in full.

In the case of commodities being manufactured, wages shall be paid according to the amount of work completed, as such payment is unaffected by any potential gains or losses in the subsequent sale of merchandise (by peddlers or otherwise).

A healthy person who abandons his company after work has begun shall be fined 12 panas, as no one shall leave the company of his own accord. Any individual found secretly neglecting his share of work shall be pardoned (abhayam) for the first offense and be assigned a proportionate amount of new work, with the promise of a corresponding share of earnings. In cases of repeated negligence or if the person seeks employment elsewhere, they shall be expelled from the company (pravásanam). If the offense is severe (maháparádhe), the person shall be treated as condemned.

(Co-operation in sacrificial acts.)

Priests cooperating in a sacrifice shall divide their earnings either equally or according to a prior agreement, except for specific portions that are due to any individual priest. If a priest participating in sacrifices such as Agnishtoma, etc., passes away after the consecration ceremony, his claimant shall receive 1/5th of the promised or prescribed gift (dakshiná); after the ceremony consecrating the purchase of Soma, 1/4th; after the Madhyamopasad or Pravargyodvásana ceremony, 1/3rd; and after the Maya ceremony, 1/2 of the share. In the Sutya sacrifice, if the priest passes after the Prátassavana ceremony, 3/4ths of the share shall be paid; after the Madhyandina ceremony, the full present shall be given, as the payment of presents shall be completed by that stage. In every sacrifice, except Brihaspatisavana, it is customary to provide presents. The same rule shall apply to the presents due in Aharganas, sacrifices by this name.

The remaining priests, retaining the remainder of the present, or any other relatives of a deceased priest, shall perform the funeral rites for the deceased for a period of ten days and nights.

If the sacrificer (the one who initiated the sacrifice) dies, the remaining priests shall complete the sacrifice and retain the presents. If a sacrificer dismisses a priest before completing the sacrifice, he shall be punished with the first amercement. If the sacrificer who dismisses a priest has not kept the sacrificial fire, or is a preceptor, or one who has already performed sacrifices, the fines shall be 100, 1000, and 1000 panas respectively.

Since sacrificial merits diminish when performed in the company of certain individuals—such as a drunkard, a man married to a Sudra woman, a Brahmin murderer, one who has violated the chastity of his preceptor's wife, a recipient of condemnable gifts, a thief, or one whose sacrificial acts are reproachable—it is permissible to dismiss such a priest without penalty.

[Thus ends Chapter XIV, "Rules regarding labourers, and Co-operative undertaking" in the section of "Rules regarding slaves and labourers," in Book III, "Concerning Law" of the Arthasástra of Kautilya. End of the seventy-first chapter from the beginning.]

CHAPTER XV. RESCISSION OF PURCHASE AND SALE.

A merchant who refuses to deliver merchandise that he has sold shall be fined 12 panas unless the merchandise is inherently defective, hazardous, or unsuitable.

Merchandise with inherent flaws is termed naturally bad; items liable to confiscation by the king, or susceptible to loss from thieves, fire, or floods, are deemed dangerous; and goods lacking all good qualities or made by deceased persons are considered intolerable.

The time allowed for rescinding a sale is one night for merchants, three nights for cultivators, five nights for herdsmen, and seven nights for transactions involving precious items or goods of mixed qualities (vivrittivikraye).

Merchandise likely to perish soon may, if it does not result in a loss to others, be granted early disposal privileges by restricting the sale of similar merchandise elsewhere that is not as perishable. Violation of this rule shall result in a fine of 24 panas or one-tenth of the value of merchandise sold in contravention of this rule.

If a buyer attempts to return a purchased item and it is neither naturally bad, dangerous, nor intolerable, he shall be fined 12 panas. The rescission rules applying to a seller shall likewise apply to the purchaser.

(Marriage Contracts)

As regards marriages among the three higher castes, the rejection of a bride before the rite of pánigrahana (the clasping of hands) is considered valid; similarly, among the Sudras, when observing religious rites. Even in cases where the rite of pánigrahana has taken place, the rejection of a bride is valid if it is later discovered that she has previously lain with another man. However, this rule does not apply to brides and bridegrooms of pure character and high family. Any person who has given a girl in marriage without disclosing her guilt of having been with another man shall be fined 96 panas and shall also be required to return the sulka and strídhana. Similarly, any person who accepts a girl in marriage without revealing the faults of the bridegroom shall pay double the aforementioned fine and forfeit the sulka and strídhana paid for the bride.

(Sale of bipeds and quadrupeds)

If bipeds or quadrupeds are sold as strong, healthy, and clean when they are actually unclean or suffering from leprosy or other diseases, the seller shall be fined 12 panas. The period allowed for rescinding the sale is three fortnights for quadrupeds and one year for humans, as it is possible to ascertain their true condition within this time.

- An assembly convened for this purpose shall, in cases of rescinding sales or gifts, make a decision that ensures neither the giver nor the receiver is harmed by the outcome.

[Thus ends Chapter XV, "Rescission of purchase and sale" in Book III, "Concerning Law" of the Arthasástra of Kautilya. End of the seventy-second chapter from the beginning.]

CHAPTER XVI. RESUMPTION OF GIFTS, SALE WITHOUT OWNERSHIP AND OWNERSHIP.

Rules concerning the recovery of debts shall also apply to the resumption of gifts. Invalid gifts shall be kept in the safe custody of designated individuals. Anyone who has given away not only his entire property but also his sons, wife, and even his own life as a gift shall bring this for consideration by those authorized to annul such gifts. Gifts or charitable donations made to wicked individuals or for unworthy purposes, financial support to malevolent or cruel persons, and promises of sexual enjoyment to the unworthy shall be settled by these authorized individuals so that neither the giver nor the receiver is harmed by the outcome.

Those who extort any kind of assistance from timid individuals by threatening them with legal punishment, defamation, or financial loss shall be punished as if guilty of theft, and the individuals who yield such assistance shall likewise be penalized.

Cooperating in harming a person and showing insolence towards the king shall be punished with the highest amercement. No son or heir claiming the property of a deceased person shall be obliged, against his will, to pay the value of any bail borne by the deceased (prátibhávyadanda), any remaining balance of a dowry (sulkasesha), or gambling stakes, nor shall he be bound to fulfill promises of gifts made by the deceased under the influence of alcohol or love. Thus concludes the section on resumption of gifts.

(Sale without ownership.)

As regards the sale of property by someone without ownership: Upon discovering a lost item in another person's possession, the rightful owner shall arrange for the offender's arrest through the court's judges. If time or location does not allow for this, the owner shall personally apprehend the offender and bring him before the judges. The judge shall inquire as to how the offender acquired the property. If the offender explains how he obtained it but cannot produce the person who sold it to him, he shall be released and forfeit the property. However, if the seller is produced, he shall not only repay the value of the property but also face the punishment for theft.

If someone in possession of stolen property flees or hides until the property is entirely consumed, he shall pay its full value and also receive the punishment for theft.

After proving his claim to the lost property (svakaranam kritva), the rightful owner shall be permitted to reclaim it. If he cannot substantiate his title, he shall be fined five times the value of the property (panchabandhadandah), and the property shall be seized by the king.

If the owner reclaims a lost item without obtaining court permission, he shall be subject to the first level of amercement.

Stolen or lost items, when discovered, shall be held at the toll-gate. If no claimant appears within three fortnights, the items shall be taken by the king.

The rightful owner of a lost or stolen biped shall pay a ransom of 5 panas before reclaiming it. Likewise, the ransom for a single-hoofed animal shall be 4 panas; for a cow or buffalo, 2 panas; for minor animals, 1/4 of a pana; and for items such as precious stones or raw materials, five percent of their value.

Any property of his subjects that the king recovers from enemy forests or territories shall be returned to its rightful owner. Any property stolen by thieves that the king cannot retrieve shall be compensated from the king's treasury. If the king is unable to compensate for these losses, he shall either authorize a self-appointed agent (svayamgráha) to retrieve them or provide an equivalent ransom to the affected party. An adventurer may keep whatever the king generously grants him from the spoils taken from an enemy's land, excluding the life of an Arya and the property of gods, Brahmins, or ascetics.

Thus concludes the rules regarding the sale of property by someone without ownership.

(Ownership.)

As to the title of an owner to his property: Owners who have left their country where their property lies shall continue to retain their title to it. When owners—excluding minors, the elderly, those afflicted with disease or calamities, those sojourning abroad, or those who have abandoned their country during national disturbances—neglect their property, allowing it to remain under the enjoyment of others for ten years, they shall forfeit their title to it.

Buildings left in the enjoyment of others for a period of 20 years shall not be reclaimed. However, the mere occupation of buildings belonging to others by kinsmen, priests, or heretics during the absence of the king shall not entitle them to a right of possession. The same rule applies with regard to open deposits, pledges, treasure troves (nidhi), boundary markers, or any property belonging to kings or priests (srotriyas).

Ascetics and heretics shall reside in a large area without disturbing each other. However, a new resident shall be provided with space occupied by an old resident. If the old resident is unwilling to yield the space, he shall be removed.

The property of hermits (vánaprastha), ascetics (yati), or bachelors learning the Vedas (Brahmachári) shall, upon their death, be inherited in succession by their preceptors, disciples, spiritual brothers (dharmabhrátri), or classmates.

Whenever hermits, ascetics, or similar individuals are required to pay any fines, they may perform penance, offer oblations to the gods, conduct fire worship, or perform the ritual known as Mahákachchhavardhana in the name of the king, observing the ritual for as many nights as the number of panas required to satisfy the fine. Heretics (páshandáh) who lack either gold or gold-coins shall observe fasting in the same manner, except in cases involving defamation, theft, assault, and the abduction of women. In these instances, they shall be compelled to undergo conventional punishment.

- The king shall, under the penalty of fines, prohibit any willful or improper actions by ascetics, as vice overwhelming righteousness will, in the long run, bring ruin upon the ruler himself.

[Thus ends Chapter XVI, "Resumption of gifts, sale without ownership, and ownership" in Book III, "Concerning Law" of the Arthasástra of Kautilya. End of the seventy-third chapter from the beginning.]

CHAPTER XVII. ROBBERY.

Sudden and direct seizure (of person or property) is termed sáhasa, while fraudulent or indirect seizure (niranvaye'pavyayanecha) is regarded as theft.

The school of Manu holds that the fine for the direct seizure of precious stones and superior or inferior raw materials shall equal their value. According to the followers of Usanas, it should be twice the value of the items. However, Kautilya asserts that the fine should correspond to the severity of the crime.

For articles of small value, such as flowers, fruits, vegetables, roots, turnips, cooked rice, skins, bamboo, and earthenware pots, the fine shall range from 12 to 24 panas. For items of moderate value, like iron (káláyasa), wood, roping materials, and herds of smaller animals, the fine shall range from 24 to 48 panas. For items of higher value, such as copper, brass, bronze, glass, ivory, and vessels, the fine shall range from 48 to 96 panas. This is termed the first amercement.

In cases of seizure involving large animals, people, fields, houses, gold, gold coins, or fine fabrics, the fine shall range from 200 to 500 panas, known as the middlemost amercement.

My preceptor holds that forcibly detaining or causing others to detain men or women in prison or forcibly releasing them from imprisonment shall be punished with fines ranging from 500 to 1,000 panas. This is termed the highest amercement.

A person who induces another to commit sáhasa according to a plan devised by themselves shall be fined double the value of the person or property seized. An instigator who hires someone to commit sáhasa with the promise, "I shall pay you as much gold as you require," shall be fined four times the value.

The school of Brihaspati believes that if an abettor, with the promise, "I will pay you this amount of gold," induces someone else to commit sáhasa, the abettor shall be required to pay the promised amount of gold along with an additional fine. However, Kautilya holds that if an abettor justifies their actions by claiming anger, intoxication, or loss of sense (moham), they shall be punished as previously described.

- In all fines below one hundred panas, the king shall collect an additional eight percent as rúpa, and in fines exceeding one hundred panas, an additional five percent. These two forms of exaction are deemed just, given that people are prone to sin on one hand, and kings are naturally subject to misguidance on the other.

[Thus ends Chapter XVII, "Robbery" in Book III, "Concerning Law" of the Arthasástra of Kautilya. End of the seventy-fourth chapter from the beginning.]

CHAPTER XVIII. DEFAMATION.

Calumny, contemptuous speech, or intimidation constitutes defamation.

Among insulting expressions directed at one's physical attributes, habits, education, occupation, or nationality, calling a person with a deformity by their true name, such as "the blind" or "the lame," shall be punished with a fine of 3 panas; calling them by a false name incurs a fine of 6 panas. If the blind, the lame, etc., are mocked with ironic terms, such as "a man of beautiful eyes" or "a man of beautiful teeth," the fine shall be 12 panas. The same applies when a person is insulted with terms referring to conditions such as leprosy, lunacy, or impotency. Insulting expressions in general, whether true, false, or sarcastic toward the insulted person, shall be punished with fines exceeding 12 panas when directed at individuals of equal rank.

If the insulted persons are of superior rank, the fines shall be doubled; if of lower rank, they shall be halved. For defaming the wives of others, the fines shall be doubled.

If the abuse arises from carelessness, intoxication, or loss of sense, the fines shall be halved.

Regarding the verification of leprosy or lunacy, physicians or neighbors shall serve as authorities.

For evidence of impotency, testimony may come from women, the examination of urine scum, or the low specific gravity of feces in water (i.e., the sinking of feces in water).

(Speaking ill of habits.)

If, among Brahmins, Kshatriyas, Vaisyas, Sudras, and outcastes (antávasáyins), any person of a lower caste abuses the habits of someone of a higher caste, the fines imposed shall increase, beginning from 3 panas and upward, with the progression starting from the lowest caste. If any person of a higher caste abuses someone of a lower caste, the fines imposed shall decrease, beginning from 2 panas.

Contemptuous expressions such as "a bad Brahmin" shall also be punished according to the above rule.

The same rules shall apply to defamatory remarks regarding learning (sruta), the professions of buffoons (vágjívana), artisans, or musicians, as well as relating to specific nationalities such as Prájjunaka or Gándhára.

(Intimidation)

If a person intimidates another by using expressions like "I shall render thee thus," the bravado shall be punished with a fine that is half of what would be imposed on a person who actually carries out such an act.

If a person, being unable to fulfill his threat, claims provocation, intoxication, or loss of sense as his excuse, he shall be fined 12 panas.

If a person who is capable of causing harm and acts under the influence of enmity intimidates another, he shall be compelled to provide lifelong security for the well-being of the intimidated person.

- Defamation of one's own nation or village shall be punished with the first amercement; defamation of one's own caste or assembly shall incur the middlemost amercement; and defamation of gods or temples (chaitya) shall be penalized with the highest amercement.

[Thus ends Chapter XVIII, "Defamtion" in Book III, "Concerning Law" of the Arthasástra of Kautilya. End of the seventy-fifth chapter from the beginning.]

CHAPTER XIX. ASSAULT.

Touching, hitting, or injuring someone is considered assault.

When a person touches another person's body below the navel with a hand, mud, ashes, or dust, he will be fined 3 panas. If the touch involves something unclean, like the foot or spit, the fine is 6 panas. If touched with saliva, urine, feces, or similar substances, the fine is 12 panas. If this action happens above the navel, the fines are doubled, and if on the head, the fines are quadrupled.

If the same offense is committed against a person of higher rank, the fine will be twice as much; if against a person of lower rank, the fine will be half the amount stated. If the offense is directed toward another person's wife, the fine is doubled.

If the offense happens because of carelessness, intoxication, or loss of reason, the fines are reduced by half.

For grabbing someone by the legs, clothes, hands, or hair, the fines will be more than 6 panas. Actions like squeezing, wrapping arms around, pushing, dragging, or sitting on another person will be punished with the first level of amercement.

Running away after making someone fall will result in a fine equal to half of those listed above.

The limb of a Sudra used to strike a Brahmin will be cut off.

(Striking.)

For striking, compensation must be paid, and the fine imposed will be half of what is levied for touching. This rule also applies to Chandalas and other persons considered profane when committing the same offense. Striking with the hand shall incur a fine of less than 3 panas; striking with the leg will result in a fine twice that amount; and striking with an instrument that causes swelling shall be punished with the first level of amercement. Striking in a way that endangers life shall be punished with the middle level of amercement.

(Hurting.)

Causing a bloodless wound with a stick, mud, a stone, an iron bar, or a rope shall be punished with a fine of 24 panas. Causing the blood to gush out, excepting cases where it is diseased or bad blood, shall be punished with double the fine.

Beating a person nearly to the point of death, though without causing blood, or breaking a person's hands, legs, or teeth, tearing off the ear or the nose, or breaking open the flesh of a person except in cases of ulcers or boils, shall be punished with the first amercement. Causing injury to the thigh or the neck, wounding the eye, or harming in such a way as to impede eating, speaking, or any other bodily movement shall not only be punished with the middlemost amercement but shall also require the payment of compensation (to the sufferer) sufficient to cover his treatment and cure. If circumstances of time or place do not permit the immediate arrest of an offender, he shall be handled as described in Book IV, which treats the measures to suppress the wicked.

Each individual in a confederacy of persons who have inflicted harm on another person shall be punished with double the usual fine.

My preceptor holds that quarrels or assaults of a remote date shall not be grounds for a complaint.

However, Kautilya holds that there shall be no acquittal for an offender. My preceptor believes that he who is the first to bring a complaint of a quarrel should win, as it is the pain that drives one to seek justice.

However, Kautilya disagrees; whether a complaint is lodged first or last, it is the testimony of witnesses that must be relied upon. In the absence of witnesses, the nature of the injury and other circumstances connected with the quarrel in question shall serve as evidence. A sentence of punishment shall be passed on the very day that a defendant accused of assault fails to answer the charge made against him.

(Robbery in quarrels.)

A person stealing anything amidst the commotion of a quarrel shall be fined 10 panas. The destruction of articles of small value shall be punished with a fine equal to the value of the articles, in addition to an adequate compensation paid to the sufferer. Destruction of large items shall require compensation equal to their value and a fine twice the value of the items. In cases involving the destruction of items such as clothes, gold, gold coins, vessels, or merchandise, the first amercement along with the value of the articles shall be imposed.

Causing damage to the wall of another man's house by striking it shall be fined 3 panas; breaking open or demolishing it shall result in a fine of 6 panas, in addition to the cost of restoring the wall. Throwing harmful substances into someone's house shall incur a fine of 12 panas; throwing objects that endanger the lives of the inhabitants shall be punished with the first amercement.

For causing pain with sticks or similar objects to minor animals, a fine of one or two panas shall be imposed; if blood is drawn, the fine shall be doubled. For larger animals, double the fines stated above shall be imposed, along with adequate compensation to cover the animals' treatment and recovery.

Cutting off the tender sprouts of fruit-bearing, flowering, or shade-providing trees in city parks shall result in a fine of 6 panas; cutting minor branches of such trees shall result in a fine of 12 panas; and cutting large branches shall result in a fine of 24 panas. Cutting the trunks of these trees shall be punished with the first amercement, and felling them shall incur the middlemost amercement.

For plants that bear flowers, fruits, or provide shade, half of the above fines shall be levied.

The same fines shall apply in cases involving trees grown in places of pilgrimage, forests dedicated to hermits, or in cremation or burial grounds.

- For similar offenses related to trees marking boundaries, those which are worshipped or marked for observation (chaityeshválakshiteshucha), or trees grown in royal forests, double the aforementioned fines shall be imposed.

[Thus ends Chapter XIX, "Assault" in Book III, "Concerning law" of the Arthasástra of Kautilya. End of the seventy-sixth chapter from the beginning.]

CHAPTER XX. GAMBLING AND BETTING AND MISCELLANEOUS OFFENCES.

With the purpose of identifying spies or thieves, the Superintendent of Gambling shall centralize all gambling activities and impose a fine of 12 panas if gambling takes place elsewhere.

My preceptor believes that in disputes concerning gambling, the winner should be punished with the first amercement and the loser with the middlemost amercement, as the loser, though not skillful enough to achieve his desire to win, cannot tolerate his defeat.

However, Kautilya disagrees: if the penalty for the loser were doubled, no one would dare to bring complaints to the king. Nevertheless, gamblers are naturally inclined to play deceitfully.

Therefore, the Superintendents of Gambling shall be upright and provide dice at a rental rate of one kákani per pair. If any player substitutes dice through sleight of hand instead of using the provided ones, he shall be fined 12 panas. A deceitful player shall be punished with the first amercement, pay fines applicable for theft and deception, and forfeit the stakes he has won.

The Superintendent shall collect not only 5 percent of the stakes won by each winner, along with the rental for supplying dice and other necessary items, but also fees for providing water, accommodation, and the license fee.

Additionally, the Superintendent may manage transactions involving the sale or mortgage of items. If he neglects to prevent sleight-of-hand tricks and other deceptive practices, he shall be fined twice the amount levied on the deceitful gamblers.

These rules shall also apply to betting and challenges, except in cases related to learning and art.

(Miscellaneous offences.)

As regards miscellaneous offenses:

When a person fails to return borrowed, hired, or deposited property at the required place or time; sits in the shade for more than one and a quarter hours (ayáma) beyond the prescribed time; evades payment at military stations or river crossings by claiming to be a Brahmin; or loudly invites others to engage in disputes with his neighbors, he shall be fined 12 panas.

When a person fails to deliver property entrusted to him for another, drags the wife of his brother by the hand, has relations with a public woman kept by another, sells merchandise known for its bad reputation, breaks open the sealed door of a house, or harms any of the forty householders or neighbors, a fine of 48 panas shall be imposed.

When a person misappropriates funds collected as a household agent, forcibly violates the chastity of an independently living widow, when an outcast (Chandála) touches an Arya woman, when a person fails to assist another in danger without cause, or invites to a religious feast Buddhists (Sákya), Ajívakas, Sudras, or exiled persons (pravrajita), a fine of 100 panas shall be imposed.

When an unauthorized person administers an oath to an offender, undertakes government work without authorization, renders minor animals impotent, or induces a female slave to miscarry through medicine, he shall be punished with the first amercement.

If between father and son, husband and wife, brother and sister, maternal uncle and nephew, or teacher and student, one abandons the other when neither has renounced their duties, or if a person leaves behind another in the center of a village after bringing them there for help, the first amercement shall be levied.

If a person abandons a companion in the middle of a forest, he shall be punished with the middlemost amercement.

If a person threatens and abandons a companion in the forest, he shall be fined with the highest amercement.

When individuals who started a journey together abandon each other as described above, half the corresponding fine shall be imposed.

When a person illegally confines another, releases someone from prison, or detains a minor unlawfully, a fine of 1,000 panas shall be imposed.

Fines shall vary according to the ranks of the people involved and the severity of the crimes.

Mercy shall be shown to pilgrims, ascetics engaged in penance, the diseased, those suffering from hunger, thirst, or travel fatigue, villagers from rural areas, those who have endured much punishment, and those without means.

Transactions involving gods, Brahmins, ascetics, women, minors, the elderly, the sick, and the helpless shall, even if not complained of, be settled by the judges themselves, and excuses of time, place, or possession shall not be considered in such cases.

Individuals known for learning, intelligence, bravery, noble birth, or great works shall be shown honor.

• Judges shall settle disputes impartially, without circumvention, with minds unaffected by moods or circumstances, remaining pleasant and accessible to all.

Book 4

CHAPTER I. PROTECTION OF ARTISANS.

Three Commissioners (pradeshtárah) or three ministers shall be responsible for implementing measures to suppress disturbances to peace (kantakasodhanam kuryuh).

Those individuals who are expected to relieve hardship, who can instruct artisans, who are trustworthy with deposits, who can design and plan artistic work, and who are relied upon by artisan guilds, may receive deposits from the guilds. The guilds (sreni) shall have their deposits returned to them in times of distress.

Artisans shall fulfill their engagements according to the agreed-upon time, place, and form of work. Those who delay their commitments, claiming no agreement on time, place, and form of work, shall, except in cases of trouble or calamity, forfeit one-fourth of their wages and be fined an amount equal to twice their wages. They shall also compensate for any resulting losses or damages. Artisans who work against given instructions shall not only forfeit their wages but also be fined an amount equal to twice their wages.

(Weavers.)

Weavers shall increase the threads supplied to them for weaving cloths in the proportion of 10 to 11 (dasaikádasikam). If they fail to do so, they shall not only pay a fine equal to twice the loss in threads or the value of the entire yarn but also forfeit their wages. In weaving linen or silk cloths (kshaumakauseyánam), the increase shall be in the ratio of 1 to 1½. In weaving fibrous or woolen garments or blankets (patronakambáladukúlánám), the increase shall be 1 to 2.

If there is any loss in length, the value of the loss shall be deducted from the wages, and a fine equal to twice the loss shall be imposed. Any loss in weight (tuláhíne) shall be punished with a fine equal to four times the amount of the loss. If different types of yarn are substituted, the fine shall be twice the value of the original yarn.

The same rules shall apply to the weaving of broad cloths (dvipatavánam).

The acceptable loss in weight of woolen threads due to threshing or shedding of hair is 5 palas.

(Washermen.)

Washermen shall wash clothes either on wooden planks or on stones with a smooth surface. Washing on any other surface shall result in a fine of 6 panas, along with the payment of compensation equal to the damage caused.

If washermen wear clothes other than those marked with the symbol of a cudgel, they shall be fined 3 panas. A fine of 12 panas shall be imposed for selling, mortgaging, or renting out the clothes of others.

In cases of substituting clothes with others, they shall be fined an amount equal to twice the value of the clothes and be required to return the original ones.

For keeping clothes overnight that are to be made as white as a jasmine flower, or are meant to attain their natural color after washing on smooth stones, or are to be made simply whiter by dirt removal, proportional fines shall be levied. For keeping clothes intended for a light tinting more than five nights, clothes meant to be made blue more than six nights, or clothes to be made as white as flowers or as glossy as lac, saffron, or blood and requiring significant skill for brilliance more than seven nights, the wages shall be forfeited.

Trustworthy individuals shall act as judges in disputes regarding color, and experts shall assess the appropriate wages.

For washing high-quality garments, the wage shall be one pana; for garments of medium quality, half a pana; and for lower-quality garments, one-fourth of a pana.

For rough washing on large stones, the wage shall be one-eighth of a pana.

In the first wash of red-colored clothes, a loss of one-fourth of the color is expected; in the second wash, one-fifth of the color is lost, explaining the color losses in subsequent washes. The rules concerning washermen also apply to weavers.

Goldsmiths who, without informing the government, purchase silver or golden articles from unclean sources without altering the form of the articles shall be fined 12 panas; if they purchase such articles and alter their form (e.g., by melting), they shall be fined 24 panas. If they purchase these items from a thief, they shall be fined 48 panas. If they secretly melt an item and purchase it below its value, they shall face the penalty for theft, as they would for deception involving manufactured articles. When a goldsmith steals gold equal to the weight of a másha (1/16th of a suvarna) from a suvarna, he shall be fined 200 panas; if he steals silver equal to the value of a másha from a silver dharana, the fine shall be 12 panas. This illustrates the proportional increase of penalties. When a goldsmith removes the entire weight of gold (karsha) from a suvarna by the apasárana method or any other deceptive combination (yoga), he shall be fined 500 panas. Contaminating gold or silver in any way shall be regarded as a loss of their intrinsic color.

One másha shall be the fee for crafting a silver dharana; for a suvarna, it shall be one-eighth of that amount, with fees doubling based on the skill of the craftsman. This indicates the proportional rise in fees.

The fee for crafting articles from copper, brass, vaikrinataka, and árakúta shall be five percent. In crafting items from copper, a loss of one-tenth of the material is expected. If the weight loss amounts to a pala, a fine equal to twice the value of the loss shall be imposed. This shows the increase in penalties based on loss. In crafting items from lead or tin, a loss of one-twentieth of the mass is expected. For each pala of these materials, a fee of one kákani shall be charged. In crafting iron articles, one-fifth of the mass will be lost, with a fee of two kákanis for each pala. This further explains the proportional increase in fees.

When a coin examiner declares an unacceptable current coin as suitable for entry into the treasury or rejects an acceptable coin, he shall be fined 12 panas. If the examiner misappropriates a másha from a current coin of a pana, after the tax (Vyájí) of five percent on the coin has been paid, he shall be fined 12 panas. This demonstrates the proportional rise in fines. When someone manufactures, accepts, or exchanges a counterfeit coin, he shall be fined 1,000 panas; if a counterfeit coin is placed into the treasury, the offender shall be sentenced to death.

(Scavengers.)

Of any precious items that sweepers come across while sweeping, one-third shall be kept by them, and two-thirds shall go to the king.

However, any precious stones found shall be fully surrendered to the king. Seizing precious stones shall incur the highest amercement.

A discoverer of mines, precious stones, or treasure troves shall, upon reporting the find to the king, receive one-sixth of it as their share. However, if the discoverer is a peon (bhritaka), his share shall be only one-twelfth of it.

Treasure troves valued beyond 100,000 shall be taken entirely by the king. If of lesser value, the discoverer shall receive one-sixth as his share.

Treasure troves that a person of pure and honest life can prove to be their ancestral property shall be taken in full by that person. Claiming a treasure trove without such proof shall incur a fine of 500 panas. Secretly taking possession of a treasure trove shall be punished with a fine of 1,000 panas.

(Medical Practice).

Physicians who undertake medical treatment without informing the government of the disease's dangerous nature shall, if the patient dies, be punished with the first amercement. If a patient under treatment dies due to the physician's carelessness, the physician shall face the middlemost amercement. If a disease worsens due to a physician's negligence or indifference (karmavadha), it shall be regarded as assault or violence.

(Musicians)

Bands of musicians (kúsílavah) shall reside in a fixed place during the rainy season. They shall be careful not to give excessive indulgence or cause excessive loss (atipátam) to anyone. Violation of this rule shall be punished with a fine of 12 panas. They may hold performances as they wish, following the customs of their region, caste, family, profession, or association.

The same rules shall apply to dancers, mime artists, and other mendicants.

For offenses, mendicants shall receive as many lashes with an iron rod as the number of panas imposed on them.

Wages for the works of other types of artisans shall be similarly determined.

Thus, traders, artisans, musicians, beggars, buffoons, and other idlers—who are thieves in effect, though not in name—shall be restrained from oppressing the country.

[Thus ends Chapter I, "Protection of artisans" in Book IV, "The Removal of Thorns" of the Arthasástra of Kautilya. End of the seventy-eighth chapter from the beginning.]

CHAPTER II. PROTECTION OF MERCHANTS.

The Superintendent of Commerce shall allow the sale or mortgage of any old commodities (purána bhándanám) only when the seller or mortgagor of such articles proves his ownership of the same. With a view to prevent deception, he shall also supervise weights and measures.

A difference of half a pala in such measures as are called parimáni and drona is not considered an offense. However, a difference of a full pala in these measures shall be punished with a fine of 12 panas. Fines for greater differences shall be increased proportionally.

A difference of one karsha in the balance called tulá is not an offense. However, a difference of two karshas shall incur a fine of 6 panas, with fines for greater differences increased proportionally.

A difference of half a karsha in the measure called ádhaka is not an offense; however, a difference of one karsha shall incur a fine of 3 panas. For greater differences, fines shall be increased proportionally. Fines for differences in weight in other types of balances shall be inferred based on this rule.

If a merchant, using a false balance, buys a greater quantity of a commodity and sells a lesser quantity under the same nominal weight by using the same or another false balance, he shall be punished with double the fines stated above.

Any deception by a seller to the extent of one-eighth part of articles valued at a pana and sold by number shall incur a fine of 96 panas.

The sale or mortgage of articles such as timber, iron, gemstones, ropes, skins, earthenware, threads, fibrous garments, and woolen clothes as superior when they are actually inferior shall be punished with a fine of eight times the value of the articles thus sold.

If a trader sells or mortgages inferior items as superior, goods from one region as if they were from another, adulterated products, or deceitful mixtures, or if he subtly substitutes other items for those just sold (samutparivartimam), he shall be fined 54 panas and shall also be required to compensate for the loss.

To determine fines for any such fraudulent sales, the rate shall be two panas for a loss valued at one pana, and 200 panas for a loss valued at 100 panas.

Those who conspire to lower the quality of artisans' work, obstruct their income, or interfere with their sale or purchase shall be fined 1,000 panas.

Merchants who conspire either to prevent the sale of goods or to manipulate the buying or selling prices of commodities shall be fined 1,000 panas.

Middlemen who cause a merchant or a purchaser to lose one-eighth of a pana by substituting, through tricks of hand, false weights or measures or other inferior items shall be punished with a fine of 200 panas. Fines for greater losses shall be proportionally increased, beginning from 200 panas.

The adulteration of grains, oils, alkalis, salts, scents, and medicinal articles with similar items of no quality shall be punished with a fine of 12 panas.

It is the responsibility of the trader to calculate the daily earnings of middlemen and to fix that amount on which they are authorized to live, as the income which falls between sellers and purchasers (i.e., brokerage) differs from profit.

Only authorized persons shall collect grains and other merchandise; any collection of such items without permission shall be confiscated by the Superintendent of Commerce.

Therefore, merchants shall display a favorable attitude toward the people in the sale of grains and other commodities.

The Superintendent of Commerce shall fix a profit margin of five percent above the set price for local commodities and ten percent on foreign produce. Merchants who raise the price or realize profit even to the extent of half a pana above this on the sale or purchase of commodities shall be punished with a fine starting from five panas for realizing 100 panas up to 200 panas.

Fines for greater price enhancements shall be increased proportionally.

If there is a failure to sell collected merchandise wholesale at the established rate, the rate shall be adjusted.

In cases of obstruction to traffic, the Superintendent shall grant necessary concessions.

When there is an oversupply of merchandise, the Superintendent shall centralize its sale and prohibit the sale of similar merchandise elsewhere until the centralized stock is cleared.

Showing goodwill towards the public, merchants shall sell this centralized stock for daily wages.

The Superintendent shall, considering the cost of outlay, quantity manufactured, amount of toll, interest on the outlay, hire, and other kinds of accessory expenses, determine the price of such merchandise, taking into account whether it was manufactured long ago or imported from a distant country (desakálántaritánám panyánám).

[Thus ends Chapter II, "Protection of merchants" in Book IV "The Removal of Thorns" of the Arthasástra of Kautilya. End of the seventy-ninth chapter from the beginning.]

CHAPTER III. REMEDIES AGAINST NATIONAL CALAMITIES.

There are eight kinds of providential visitations: they are fire, floods, pestilential diseases, famine, rats, tigers (vyáláh), serpents, and demons. From these calamities shall the king protect his kingdom.

(Fire.)

During the summer, villages shall conduct cooking activities outdoors. Alternatively, they shall equip themselves with the ten remedial instruments (dasamúlî).

Precautionary measures against fire have been discussed in the context of the duties assigned to the superintendents of villages as well as those related to the king's harem and retinue.

On regular days, and especially on full-moon days, offerings, oblations, and prayers shall be made to honor fire.

(Floods.)

Villagers residing along riverbanks shall, during the rainy season, relocate to higher grounds. They shall prepare wooden planks, bamboos, and boats. Through bottle gourds, canoes, tree trunks, or boats, they shall rescue individuals being swept away by floods. Persons neglecting rescue efforts, except those lacking boats or other means, shall be fined 12 panas. On new and full-moon days, rivers shall be worshipped. Those skilled in sacred magic and mysticism (máyáyogavidah), as well as individuals learned in the Vedas, shall perform incantations to guard against excessive rain.

During drought shall Indra (sachínátha), the Ganges, mountains, and Mahákachchha be worshipped.

(Pestilences.)

Such remedial measures as will be treated of in the 14th book shall be taken against pestilences. Physicians with their medicines, and ascetics and prophets with their auspicious and purificatory ceremonials shall also overcome pestilences. The same remedial measures shall be taken against epidemics (maraka = killer). Besides the above measures, oblations to gods, the ceremonial called, Mahá-kachchhavardhana, milking the cows on cremation or burial grounds, burning the trunk of a corpse, and spending nights in devotion to gods shall also be observed.

With regard to cattle diseases (pasuvyádhimarake), not only the ceremony of waving lights in cowsheds (nirájanam) shall be half done, but also the worship of family-gods be carried out.

(Famines.)

During famine, the king shall show favour to his people by providing them with seeds and provision (bíjabhaktopagráham).

He may either do such works as are usually resorted to in calamities; he may show favour by distributing either his own collection of provisions or the hoarded income of the rich among the people; or seek for help from his friends among kings.

Or the policy of thinning the rich by exacting excessive revenue (karsanam), or causing them to vomit their accumulated wealth (vamanam) may be resorted to.

Or the king with his subjects may emigrate to another kingdom with abundant harvest.

Or he may remove himself with his subjects to seashores or to the banks of rivers or lakes. He may cause his subjects to grow grains, vegetables, roots, and fruits wherever water is available. He may, by hunting and fishing on a large scale, provide the people with wild beasts, birds, elephants, tigers or fish.

(Rats.)

To ward off the danger from rats, cats and mongooses may be let loose. Destruction of rats that have been caught shall be punished with a fine of 12 panas. The same punishment shall be meted out to those who, with the exception of wild tribes, do not hold their dogs in check.

To destroy rats, grains mixed with the milk of the milk-hedge plant (snuhi: Euphorbia Antiquorum), or grains combined with ingredients discussed in the 14th book may be left on the ground. Ascetics and prophets may perform auspicious ceremonies, and on new and full-moon days, rats may be worshipped.

Similar measures may also be taken to counter threats from locusts, birds, and insects.

(Snakes.)

When facing a threat from snakes, experts skilled in remedies for snake poison shall use incantations and medicines. Alternatively, snakes may be destroyed collectively, or those learned in the Atharvaveda may perform auspicious rites. On new and full-moon days, snakes may be worshipped. This outlines the measures to be taken against threats from water-dwelling animals.

(Tigers.)

To eliminate tigers, the carcasses of cattle mixed with the juice of the madana plant, or calves' carcasses filled with the juices of madana and kodrava plants, may be placed in appropriate locations. Hunters or keepers of hounds may capture tigers by entrapping them in nets. Armed individuals in protective armor may also kill tigers using weapons.

Failure to aid a person seized by a tiger shall be punished with a fine of 12 panas, and an equal reward shall be given to anyone who kills a tiger. On new and full-moon days, mountains may be worshipped.

Similar methods may be employed against attacks from wild animals, birds, or crocodiles.

(Demons.)

Individuals acquainted with Atharvaveda rituals and experts in sacred magic and mysticism shall perform ceremonies to ward off dangers from demons. On full-moon days, the worship of Chaityas shall be conducted by placing offerings on a verandah, including an umbrella, a picture of an arm, a flag, and some goat's flesh.

In all situations of demonic threat, the incantation "we offer thee cooked rice" shall be used.

The king shall always protect the afflicted among his people as a father would protect his sons.

Ascetics skilled in magical arts, who possess supernatural powers to ward off natural visitations, shall therefore be honored by the king and encouraged to reside within his kingdom.

[Thus ends Chapter III, "Remedies against national Calamities" in Book IV, "The Removal of Thorns," of the Arthasástra of Kautilya. End of the eightieth chapter from the beginning.]

CHAPTER IV. SUPPRESSION OF THE WICKED LIVING BY FOUL MEANS.

Measures necessary for the protection of countries were briefly addressed in the description of the duties of the Collector-general. Now, we shall discuss in detail such measures as are effective in removing disturbances to peace.

The Collector-general shall employ spies disguised as people endowed with supernatural abilities, those engaged in penance, ascetics, travelers of the world (chakra-chara), bards, buffoons, mystics (prachchhandaka), astrologers, prophets foretelling the future, individuals skilled in reading auspicious or inauspicious times, physicians, lunatics, the dumb, the deaf, the intellectually disabled, the blind, traders, painters, carpenters, musicians, dancers, vintners, and manufacturers of cakes, meat dishes, and cooked rice, and send them throughout the country to gather intelligence.

These spies shall determine the integrity or corruption of villagers or the Superintendents of villages and report accordingly.

If any person is discovered to live a concealed life of corruption (gúdhajívi), a spy familiar with such conduct shall be deployed to engage with him.

By forming a connection with the suspect, who may be either a judge or a commissioner, the spy may ask that a misfortune involving a friend of the spy be averted in exchange for a certain amount of money. If the judge agrees to the arrangement, he shall be proclaimed a receiver of bribes and banished. The same rule shall apply to commissioners.

A spy may inform the village assembly (grámakútam) or its superintendent that a wealthy but wicked man is facing difficulties and suggest that they take advantage of the situation to extract money from him. If either the assembly or the superintendent complies with the spy's suggestion, banishment shall be imposed with a proclamation of "extortion."

By pretending to be accused of a crime, a spy may approach false witnesses, offering them substantial sums of money. If they agree, they shall be declared as false witnesses and banished.

Manufacturers of counterfeit coins shall be dealt with in the same manner.

If any person is believed to use magical charms, drugs, or rituals performed on cremation grounds to obtain the love of women for others, a spy may approach him and ask for assistance in winning back the affections of a wife, daughter, or daughter-in-law, whom the spy claims to love, in exchange for a sum of money. If the individual consents, he shall be proclaimed as one practicing witchcraft (samvadanakáraka) and banished.

Similar actions may be taken against those engaged in harmful witchcraft practices that are detrimental to others.

Anyone suspected of using poison (rasa = mercury) on others, due to their talk of it, selling or purchasing mercury, or using it to prepare medicines, may be approached by a spy with a request to poison a particular enemy in exchange for a sum of money. If he agrees, he shall be proclaimed a poisoner (rasada) and banished.

Similar measures may be applied to those who handle medicines prepared from the madana plant.

Anyone suspected of manufacturing counterfeit coins, evidenced by frequent purchases of various metals, alkalis, charcoal, bellows, pincers, crucibles, stoves, and hammers, having hands and clothing stained with ashes and smoke, or possessing other necessary tools for illegal minting, may be approached by a spy posing as an apprentice. Gradually betraying him, the spy shall expose his guilt, and the accused, upon being proclaimed a manufacturer of false coins, shall be banished.

Similar actions may be taken against those who dilute gold by mixing it with alloys or deal with counterfeit gold (suvarna = coin?).

There are thirteen types of criminals who, secretly attempting to live by dishonest means, disrupt the peace of the country. Depending on whether their offenses are minor or severe, they shall either be banished or made to pay an adequate compensation.

[Thus ends Chapter IV, "Suppression of the wicked living by foul means" in Book IV "The Removal Thorns" of the Arthasástra of Kautilya. End of the eighty-first chapter from the beginning.]

CHAPTER V. DETECTION OF YOUTHS OF CRIMINAL TENDENCY BY ASCETIC SPIES.

On using the opportunities provided by ordinary spies sent in advance, special spies pretending to be endowed with supernatural powers may, under the pretense of knowing incantations that allow rapid escape, invisibility, or the unsealing of tightly fastened doors, entice highway robbers into committing robberies. Similarly, under the guise of knowing incantations that attract the love of women, they may lure adulterers into engaging in criminal activities intended to expose their criminal intentions.

These enthusiastic recruits, thus persuaded, may then be taken to a village where persons disguised as men and women have been pre-positioned, and which is a different village than the one intended to be reached. The youths may be told that reaching the desired village on time is difficult and that the power of incantation must be demonstrated here and now.

Pretending to open doors with the power of incantation, the youths may be invited to enter. In the midst of alert watchmen, who are actually acting in concert, the youths may be rendered "invisible" by incantation and directed to proceed further inside. Making the watchmen appear sleepy, the youths may be instructed to move the beds of the watchmen confidently, believing in the spell's protection. Individuals disguised as wives of others may then, under the apparent influence of incantation, interact favorably with the youths.

Once the youths have seemingly experienced these magical powers, they may be taught recitations and other procedures as part of this art. They may then be asked to test the effectiveness of their new knowledge by looting houses containing marked valuables or money, and subsequently apprehended in the act. They may also be captured while attempting to sell, buy, or mortgage items marked with identifying symbols, or while under intoxication induced by medicinal drinks (yogasurámatta).

From these apprehended youths, details of their past activities and the identities of their accomplices may be gathered.

Spies disguised as old and notorious thieves may similarly infiltrate robber gangs and, through similar strategies, lead to the robbers' arrests.

The Collector-general shall present these arrested robbers to the public and announce that their capture is due to the king's instructions, as the king has mastered the divine art of catching robbers. He shall proclaim, "I will continue to apprehend other robbers repeatedly, and it is your duty, citizens, to prevent any of your kin from engaging in wicked deeds."

Any person identified through spy reports as having been a robber of yoking ropes, whips, or other agricultural implements may be detained and informed that their capture is the result of the king's omniscient power. Spies, disguised as old and notorious robbers, herdsmen, hunters, or hound keepers, may infiltrate criminal groups living in forests and conspire with them to raid villages or caravanserais that, according to a prior arrangement, are stocked with counterfeit gold and other items. During the ensuing chaos, these criminals may be killed by armed men positioned there for this purpose. Or, when these robbers have secured a haul of stolen treasure, they may be given food laced with the intoxicating juice of the madana plant or apprehended either while sleeping, exhausted from constant movement, or while under the influence of intoxicating medicinal beverages consumed during religious festivals.

The Collector-general shall publicly display these and other apprehended criminals, proclaiming the omniscient power of the king to the people at large.

[Thus ends Chapter V, "Detection of youths of criminal tendency by ascetic spies," in Book IV, "The Removal Thorns" of the Arthasástra of Kautilya. End of the eighty-second chapter from the beginning.]

CHAPTER VI. SEIZURE OF CRIMINALS ON SUSPICION OR IN THE VERY ACT.

In addition to the measures taken by spies posing as prophets, further actions based on suspicious behavior or possession of stolen items may also be undertaken.

(Suspicion.)

Persons to be suspected include those whose families subsist on limited inheritance; who have little comfort; who frequently change their residence, caste, or names, including those of their family (gotra); who conceal their occupations; who have adopted a lavish lifestyle involving meat, condiments, alcohol, perfumes, garlands, fine clothing, and jewelry; who spend money extravagantly; who often associate with promiscuous women, gamblers, or vintners; who frequently leave their place of residence; whose business dealings, journeys, or destinations are hard to decipher; who travel alone in secluded areas like forests and mountainous regions; who hold private meetings in isolated locations close to or far from their homes; who rush to treat fresh wounds or boils; who constantly hide in the inner rooms of their homes; who are overly devoted to women; who are keen to gather information about the women and property of others; who associate with people of questionable knowledge and work; who loiter in the dark behind walls or under cover; who buy rare or suspicious items at odd times or places; who are known for hostile behavior; whose caste and occupation are disreputable; who maintain false appearances or wear different caste symbols; who abandon their ancestral customs with false justifications; whose notoriety is well-known; who, though overseeing villages, are fearful of appearing before the prime minister and either hide or go elsewhere; who breathe heavily from fear while sitting alone; who display unusual anxiety or heart palpitations; whose faces are pale and dry, with indistinct and stammering voices; who frequently travel with armed companions; or who present a threatening demeanor.

These and other individuals may be suspected of being murderers, robbers, or offenders guilty of misappropriating treasure troves or deposits, or of being any other kind of deceivers secretly engaged in foul means for survival.

Thus, the capture of criminals based on suspicion is addressed.

(Seizure of Stolen Articles.)

Concerning the capture of criminals caught in the very act: Information regarding items that are either lost or stolen shall, if these items are not located, be shared with those who deal in similar goods. Traders who conceal items about which they have previously received such information shall be condemned as accomplices. If they are found to have been unaware of the item's loss, they may be acquitted upon returning the item.

No one shall, without informing the Superintendent of Commerce, mortgage or purchase any old or second-hand item for personal use.

Upon receiving information about the sale or mortgage of old items, the Superintendent shall question the seller about the item's origin. The seller may state: it is an inheritance; it was received from a third party; it was purchased by him; it was made to order; or it is a secret pledge. He may then specify the time and place where it was obtained. Alternatively, he may provide evidence concerning the price and commission (kshanamúlyam) for which it was acquired. If his account of the item's background is verified, he shall be acquitted.

If, however, the item is identified as one lost by another person whose description of the item's background matches the prior account, the item shall be deemed to belong to that individual who is proven to have owned it for an extended period and whose life is known to be pure. For, while even animals are found to bear identifying features such as color, gait, and form, there should be no difficulty in identifying items like raw materials, jewels, or vessels, which are products of a unique source, specific materials, a particular manufacturer, and intended for a definite purpose.

The possessor of the disputed item may argue that the item is either borrowed or hired, a pledge or sealed deposit, or an article obtained from a certain person for resale. If he substantiates his claim by presenting a reference person, he shall be released; otherwise, the reference person may deny any involvement in the matter.

In cases where a person is found in possession of an article lost by another and claims to have received it as a gift from a third person, he must support this by presenting as witnesses not only those who gave or facilitated the transfer of the article to him but also those who, as mediators, custodians, bearers, or witnesses, arranged for the transfer.

If a person claims that the item in his possession was thrown away, lost, or forgotten by a third party, he must establish his innocence by providing evidence regarding the time, location, and circumstances of finding the item. Failing to do so, he must return the item and pay a fine equal to its value, or he may be punished as a thief.

Thus, the seizure of criminals caught in the act is addressed.

(Circumstantial Evidence.)

Concerning the apprehension of criminals based on circumstantial evidence:

In instances of housebreaking and theft, circumstances such as entry and exit through means other than doors, breaking a door with specialized tools, breaking windows with or without latticework, removing the roof in multi-story houses, ascending and descending stairs, breaking walls, tunneling, or utilizing techniques needed to access secret hoards of treasure (known only from internal sources) shall indicate the involvement of insiders in the crime. Conversely, when these clues do not suggest insider involvement, they indicate external agents. When both types of clues are present, they imply the participation of both internal and external individuals.

Regarding crimes suspected to be committed by internal agents:

Any individual of a miserable appearance, present at the scene, associated with known rogues or thieves, and found with tools used in theft; a woman from a poor family or one who has placed her affections elsewhere; servants of similarly questionable character; any person overly prone to sleep or suffering from lack of sleep; any individual showing signs of exhaustion, with a pale, dry face, a stammering and unclear voice, watching others or excessively grieving; any person bearing signs of climbing heights; anyone with a scratched or wounded body or torn clothing; anyone whose legs and hands show evidence of scraping or scratching; anyone with hair and nails dirty or freshly broken; anyone who has just bathed and applied sandalwood paste; anyone who has oiled their body and recently washed hands and feet; anyone with identifiable footprints matching those left near the house; anyone whose broken garlands, sandalwood marks, or pieces of clothing match fragments found in or near the house; anyone whose sweat or scent of drink matches fragments of dress left in or near the house—these individuals and others fitting this description shall be thoroughly examined.

A citizen or someone known for adulterous habits may also be under suspicion.

- A commissioner (pradeshtá), along with his team of gopas and sthánikas, shall work to uncover external thieves; meanwhile, the city officer (nágaraka) shall investigate internal suspects within fortified towns under these outlined circumstances.

[Thus ends Chapter VI, "Seizure of criminals on suspicion or in the very act," in Book IV, "'The Removal of Thorns" of the Arthasástra of Kautilya. End of the eighty-third chapter from the beginning.]

CHAPTER VII. EXAMINATION OF SUDDEN DEATH.

In cases of sudden death, the corpse shall be smeared with oil and examined.

A body showing traces of mucus and urine, with bloated organs, swollen hands and legs, open eyes, and ligature marks around the neck, may indicate death by suffocation and suppression of breathing.

A body with contracted arms and thighs may suggest death by hanging.

A corpse with swollen hands, legs, and belly, sunken eyes, and an inflated navel may also point to death by hanging.

A body with a stiff rectum and eyes, tongue bitten between the teeth, and a swollen belly may indicate drowning.

A corpse covered in blood, with injured or broken limbs, may be evidence of death caused by beatings with sticks or ropes.

A body with fractures and broken limbs may suggest it was thrown down from a height.

A corpse with darkened hands, legs, teeth, and nails, loose skin, fallen hair, reduced flesh, and a face marked with foam and saliva may indicate poisoning.

A body with similar symptoms but with bleeding bite marks may suggest death from bites by serpents or other venomous creatures.

A corpse found sprawled, with disheveled clothing, showing signs of severe vomiting and purging, may indicate death due to the administration of the juice of the madana plant.

Death from any of the above causes is sometimes disguised as voluntary hanging, with ligature marks placed around the neck to create the appearance of self-inflicted death.

In suspected cases of poisoning, the undigested portion of meat may be tested in milk. If extracted from the stomach and thrown into a fire, the sample may be declared poisoned if it produces a "chitchita" sound and shows rainbow-colored flames. Additionally, if the stomach (hridayam) remains unburnt while the rest of the body has turned to ashes, the dead man's servants may be questioned about any violent or cruel treatment they may have received from the deceased. Similarly, relatives of the dead, such as a person living in misery, a woman who may have placed her affections elsewhere, or any relative defending a woman who was deprived of her inheritance by the deceased, may also be examined.

The same examination shall apply to cases where an already deceased body has been staged to look as if it were hanged.

Any investigation into death from alleged voluntary hanging shall consider past harm or wrongdoings committed by the deceased.

All instances of sudden death typically involve one or more of the following motives: offense to women or kin, inheritance disputes, professional competition, rivalry, commerce, guilds, or any legal disputes—each a source of anger, and anger, in turn, is a cause of death.

When, due to mistaken identity, one is murdered by hired hands, thieves for money, or the enemies of another, the relatives of the deceased shall be questioned as follows:

Who summoned the deceased? Who was with him? Who accompanied him on his journey? And who took him to the place where he was found dead?

Those present in the area of the murder shall also be individually questioned as follows:

By whom was the deceased brought there? Did they (the witnesses) notice any armed person hiding nearby and showing signs of distress?

Any lead provided by these witnesses shall be pursued in the subsequent investigation.

- After examining the personal belongings of the deceased, such as travel items, clothing, jewelry, or other possessions found on the body, those who supplied or were involved with these items shall be questioned regarding the deceased's companions, place of residence, reasons for the journey, profession, and other activities.

- If a man or woman, driven by passions like love, anger, or other sinful impulses, commits or incites suicide by ropes, weapons, or poison, their body shall be dragged by a Chandala along the public road with a rope.
- Such individuals shall not receive cremation rites, nor any traditional funeral ceremonies normally performed by relatives.
- Any relative who conducts funeral rites for such persons shall either forfeit the right to their own funeral rites or be abandoned by their family and kin.
- Anyone associating with persons who perform forbidden rites shall, along with any other associates, lose within a year the right to conduct or oversee sacrifices, to teach, and to give or receive gifts.

[Thus ends Chapter VII, "Examination of sudden death," in Book IV, "The Removal of Thorns" of the Arthasásatra of Kautilya. End of the eighty-fourth chapter from the beginning.]

CHAPTER VIII. TRIAL AND TORTURE TO ELICIT CONFESSION.

Whether the accused is a stranger or a relative of the complainant, the defendant's defense witness shall be questioned thoroughly in the presence of the complainant. These questions will cover detailed aspects of the defendant's life, including his country of origin, caste, family background, full name, occupation, assets or property, close friends, and usual place of residence. The responses provided by the defense witness will then be carefully cross-checked against the defendant's own statements on these same points to ensure consistency. Any discrepancies between the witness's account and the defendant's statements may affect the credibility of the defense.

Next, the defendant will be asked for a detailed account of his actions during the day leading up to the alleged crime, covering both the specific tasks he engaged in and the people he interacted with.

Furthermore, he will need to specify where he spent the night prior to his apprehension, including any individuals he may have been with or places he visited. If the defendant's answers to these questions are substantiated by credible and reliable referees or witnesses, he shall be exonerated of the charges. However, if his statements lack reliable corroboration, he may be subjected to more rigorous interrogation, which may include torture if there is substantial reason to suspect guilt (anyatha karmapráptah).

If more than three days have passed since the commission of a crime, any person suspected of the crime shall not be detained solely on the basis of suspicion, as, after this time, there may be too few details to justify a full questioning unless there exists strong evidence that establishes a link between the suspect and the alleged crime.

Further, individuals who wrongfully accuse an innocent person of theft, or those who knowingly conceal a thief and prevent their apprehension, shall be held accountable and subject to the same penalties as if they had committed the theft themselves. This rule is in place to discourage false accusations and to ensure that no innocent individual is subjected to undue punishment based on deceit or malice.

Moreover, if a person accused of theft can demonstrate that the complainant has personal enmity, rivalry, or longstanding hatred towards him, then this established motive of animosity shall be enough to acquit the accused, as it casts reasonable doubt on the legitimacy of the Any person who unlawfully confines an innocent individual (parivásayatah suddham) shall be penalized with the first amercement.

Establishing guilt against a suspected individual shall require the presentation of concrete evidence. This may include instruments or tools linked to the accused, involvement of any accomplices or abettors, the stolen items themselves, and any middlemen involved in the selling or purchase of the stolen goods. The credibility of these evidences shall be carefully assessed in relation to the location of the theft, the circumstances surrounding the possession of the stolen article, and the means by which it was circulated or disposed of.

If none of these evidences are present and the accused expresses significant distress, he shall be considered innocent. Often, innocent individuals are wrongly accused due to unfortunate circumstances, such as merely being near the scene of the crime, having a similar appearance, attire, or weapons as the true thief, or possessing items resembling those that were stolen. Cases like that of Mándavya, who under the threat of torture admitted to theft despite his innocence, illustrate that accidental coincidences often lead to wrongful detainment. Therefore, only definitive and conclusive evidence shall be required to confirm guilt (tasmátsamáptakaranam niyamayet).

Certain individuals are exempt from torture, including the uneducated, minors, the elderly, the infirm, intoxicated individuals, the mentally unwell, those suffering from hunger or thirst, travelers fatigued from long journeys, those who have overeaten, those who have confessed willingly (átmakásitam), and those who are physically very weak. None of these groups shall be subjected to physical coercion.

Among the group of spies, including courtesans, those providing water and other refreshments to travelers, storytellers, innkeepers offering accommodations, any spy who shares a similar skill or background to the suspect may be released to discreetly observe the suspect's activities, as discussed in the context of misappropriation involving sealed deposits.

Those individuals whose guilt is strongly suspected shall be subjected to physical examination through torture (áptadosham karma kárayet), provided that evidence or behavior has raised substantial suspicion of their involvement in the alleged crime. However, certain groups are exempt from these harsher measures. Women who are currently pregnant or who have recently given birth—specifically within one month postpartum—shall be entirely spared from any form of physical torture due to their condition. In cases where women are involved, the extent of physical examination or punishment shall be set to half of the standard severity prescribed for men. Alternatively, women, with no exceptions, may be subjected to a thorough process of cross-examination (vákyanuyogo vá) in order to verify their statements or gather information, thus avoiding any physical punishment.

Furthermore, individuals of the Brahman caste, especially those esteemed for their knowledge of the Vedas, along with ascetics who have renounced worldly affairs, shall be exempt from physical punishment altogether. Instead, they shall only be subject to surveillance and espionage to gather evidence of any alleged wrongdoing, given the high respect accorded to their roles in society.

Anyone who disregards or violates these protective regulations shall face the first amercement as punishment, demonstrating the state's commitment to enforcing these exemptions responsibly. The same level of penalty shall be applied if any person, regardless of status, suffers fatal consequences from the use of torture, underscoring the gravity of inflicting excessive harm.

There are four main categories of torture (karma) utilized for punitive purposes: these include six different types of fines or penalties (shatdandáh), seven specific forms of whipping or flogging (kasa), two methods of suspension from above (upari nibandhau), and one particular method involving water known as the water-tube (udakanáliká cha).

In cases where individuals are deemed to have committed particularly serious or grave offenses, a series of nine types of blows using a cane shall be administered as part of the physical penalty: these include 12 hard strikes to each thigh, which is intended to induce pain without permanent harm; 28 targeted blows with a specially designated stick from the naktamála tree, whose wood is traditionally used for its punitive impact; 32 strikes to each palm and each sole of the feet, to inflict controlled pain without disabling injury; and two strikes specifically aimed at the knuckles, with the hands clasped together in such a way that the position resembles a scorpion.

Further methods of disciplinary suspension include two types where the individual is suspended face-down (ullambane chale), a method designed to disorient and discomfort. Additionally, the punishment may involve burning one joint of a finger after making the accused drink rice gruel as a way to increase sensitivity to the burning sensation. In other cases, the accused may be subjected to heating of the body for an entire day after being made to drink oil, which heightens the body's sensitivity to the heat. Another form of torture involves forcing the individual to lie on coarse green grass overnight during the cold winter season, exposing them to the discomfort of the rough surface and low temperatures.

Together, these methods constitute the full range of 18 types of physical punishment, carefully outlined to address different levels of perceived offenses, while aiming to balance the punitive and deterrent effects of these forms of punishment.

The instruments used by the accused in the commission of their crime, such as ropes, clubs, arrows, spades, knives, and similar items, shall be publicly displayed on the back of an ass as a mark of disgrace and a warning to others. Each day, a different form of torture may be employed as a means of progressively intensifying the punishment.

For those criminals who have acted with prior threats, robbing after having announced their intentions, or those who have partially used the stolen goods, been apprehended in the very act, or caught with the stolen items in their possession, stricter punishments apply. Criminals who have attempted to seize the king's treasury or committed a severe crime against the state or society may, by the king's order, be subjected repeatedly to any or all of the forms of torture previously described, depending on the gravity and impact of their offenses.

Regardless of the crime, a Bráhman offender shall not be subjected to physical torture. Instead, their punishment involves marking their crime in a manner that makes their transgressions known to society. The face of a convicted Bráhman shall be branded with a symbol that signifies the nature of their offense. For theft, a symbol of a dog shall be used; for murder, a mark of a headless body shall indicate the crime; for committing sexual misconduct with the wife of a teacher, the image of the female part (bhaga) shall be branded; and for drinking liquor, the emblem of a vintner's flag shall be imprinted.

After the branding has created a lasting wound and the offense has been publicly proclaimed, the king shall determine the Bráhman's ultimate fate. He may be banished from the kingdom, casting him out of society, or sentenced to a life of forced labor in the mines, where he shall remain permanently as a punishment befitting his crime. This approach ensures that justice is served while observing the societal norms and respecting the unique position of Bráhmans within the law.

[Thus ends Chapter VIII, "Trial and Torture to Elicit Confession" in Book IV, "The Removal of Thorns" of the Arthasástra of Kautilya. End of the eighty-fifth chapter from the beginning.]

CHAPTER IX. PROTECTION OF ALL KINDS OF GOVERNMENT DEPARTMENTS.

COMMISSIONERS appointed by the Collector-general shall first check (the proceedings of) Superintendents and their subordinates.

Those who unlawfully seize valuable articles or precious stones from either mines or large-scale manufactories shall face the punishment of beheading, as their crime is deemed a significant offense. For individuals who take ordinary items or essential goods from manufactories producing items of lesser value, the penalty shall be the first amercement, aligning the severity of punishment with the relative value of the seized items.

If anyone takes items valued between 1/16 and 1/4 of a pana from manufactories or from the king's granary, the fine imposed shall be 12 panas. For items valued from 1/4 to 1/2 a pana, the fine shall be 24 panas. Seizing items valued from 1/2 to 3/4 of a pana shall result in a fine of 36 panas, and for items valued between 3/4 and 1 pana, the penalty shall be 48 panas.

Those who seize items valued between 1 and 2 panas shall face the first amercement. For items valued between 2 and 4 panas, the penalty shall be the middle amercement, and for items valued between 4 and 8 panas, the highest amercement shall apply. Should anyone seize items worth between 8 and 10 panas, they shall be sentenced to death due to the gravity of the offense.

When a person unlawfully takes raw materials, finished goods, or similar commodities valued at half the above amount from courtyards, shops, or arsenals, the penalties outlined above shall apply similarly. Should an individual seize items of only 1/4 of the listed values from the government treasury, granaries, or the offices of superintendents, they shall be fined at double the amount indicated in the original penalties.

It has already been established within the laws of the king's harem that anyone who attempts to intimidate or signal thieves to escape shall be punished with torture leading to death, as this act facilitates crime.

If anyone other than a government official commits theft during daylight hours, stealing from fields, threshing yards, houses, or shops, and takes items such as raw materials, finished goods, or everyday necessities valued between 1/16 and 1/4 of a pana, they shall either be fined 3 panas or be paraded through the streets. During this procession, their body shall be smeared with cow dung, and an earthenware pan containing a burning light shall be tied around their waist (sarávamekhalayá), serving as a public mark of disgrace for their offense.

When any person steals articles valued between 1/4 and 1/2 of a pana, they shall face a fine of 6 panas. Alternatively, they may be punished by having their head shaved or by being exiled (mundanam pravrajanam vá). If someone steals articles valued between 1/2 and 1/3 of a pana, the fine imposed shall be 9 panas, or the offender may be publicly paraded through the streets, with their body covered in cow dung or ashes, or an earthenware pan with a blazing light tied around their waist as a mark of disgrace. For theft of items worth between 1/3 and 1 pana, the penalty shall be a fine of 12 panas, or the offender may have their head shaved or face banishment.

When a person is caught stealing goods valued between 1 and 2 panas, they shall be fined 24 panas, or alternatively, their head may be shaved with a piece of brick, or they may be exiled. For theft of items valued between 2 and 4 panas, the fine shall be 36 panas; for items between 4 and 5 panas, the fine shall be 48 panas. If the value of the stolen articles ranges between 5 and 10 panas, the offender shall face the first amercement. If the stolen items are worth between 10 and 20 panas, the penalty shall be a fine of 200 panas; for goods worth 20 to 30 panas, the fine shall rise to 500 panas; for articles worth 30 to 40 panas, the fine shall reach 1,000 panas. Any person stealing articles valued between 40 and 50 panas shall be condemned to death, as this is considered an extreme offense.

If a person forcibly seizes items, whether during the early part of the day or night, valued at half the amounts specified above, they shall face double the fines previously outlined. If an armed individual seizes goods by force, regardless of the time of day, valued at 1/4 of the amounts listed, they shall be subject to the same fines.

A master of a household (kutumbádhyaksha), a superintendent, or an independent officer (mukhyaswámi) who issues or utilizes unauthorized orders or seals shall be punished based on the severity of their transgression, either with the first, middlemost, or highest amercement, or they may face the death penalty or another appropriate punishment reflecting the gravity of the offense.

A judge who threatens, intimidates, ejects, or unjustly silences one of the disputants in their court shall first be punished with the first amercement. Should the judge defame or abuse either disputant, the punishment shall be doubled. A judge who fails to inquire about essential matters, asks irrelevant questions, omits previously asked questions, or improperly aids a party by suggesting answers shall face the middlemost amercement as punishment.

If a judge neglects to investigate necessary details, delves into irrelevant matters, causes delays out of spite, unnecessarily prolongs a case to exhaust the involved parties, avoids or sidesteps statements leading to a case's resolution, assists witnesses by providing hints, or reopens cases that have already been settled, they shall be subject to the highest amercement. A judge who repeats any of these offenses shall be both fined double the previous amount and dismissed from their position to prevent further judicial misconduct.

If a clerk fails to record exactly what the parties have stated, instead entering details that were not actually said, or disregards statements that were poorly worded (duruktam), or changes statements that were clearly expressed to make them seem contradictory or ambiguous, he shall be penalized with either the first amercement or a fine proportionate to the seriousness of his error.

When a judge or commissioner levies an unjust fine in gold, they shall be required to pay a fine either double the amount unjustly levied or, if they have imposed a sum either exceeding or falling short of the legal limits, they shall be fined eight times the amount of the improper imposition.

If a judge or commissioner enforces an unjust corporal punishment, they shall either face the same punishment or be fined twice the ransom amount that would typically be applied for such an offense. Should a judge intentionally misstate the correct sum or endorse as true an amount that is actually false, the penalty shall be eight times that amount.

If an officer releases or causes the release of detainees from confinement (cháraka), or interferes with prisoners' access to basic activities such as sleeping, sitting, eating, or other necessary actions, they shall be subject to fines starting from 3 panas and increasing with the severity of the infraction.

If anyone releases or facilitates the release of debtors from confinement, they shall not only be fined with the middlemost amercement but shall also be held responsible for covering the full debt owed by the released debtor.

Anyone who releases or arranges the release of prisoners from formal jails (bandhanágára) shall face the death penalty, and all of their property shall be confiscated as part of the punishment.

If the superintendent of jails detains anyone without clearly stating the cause or justification for the detention (samkrudhakamanákhyáya), he shall be fined 24 panas. If he imposes any form of unjust torture, the fine shall be 48 panas. For transferring a prisoner to another location or depriving a detainee of necessary food and water, the penalty shall be 96 panas. If the superintendent harasses or extorts bribes from a prisoner, he shall face the middlemost amercement. Should he beat a prisoner to the point of death, the fine shall be a substantial 1,000 panas.

In cases where a person commits sexual assault with a female prisoner, slave, or a woman hired for work within the jail, the first amercement shall apply. If he commits this offense against the widow of a thief or any man who has died in an epidemic (dámara), the penalty shall be the middlemost amercement. However, if an Arya woman in detention is assaulted, the offender shall receive the highest amercement.

If an inmate in lock-up commits assault upon an Arya woman in the same facility, he shall face the death penalty on the very grounds of the offense. Similarly, any officer who assaults an Arya woman detained for improper movement at night (akshanagrihitáyám) shall also be hanged at the scene. When such an offense is committed with a woman who is enslaved, the punishment shall be the first amercement.

An officer who facilitates a prisoner's escape from lock-up without breaking it open shall be subjected to the middlemost amercement. If the officer breaks open the lock-up to allow a prisoner to escape, he shall be condemned to death. Should he permit a prisoner to escape from a more secure jail facility, the sentence is death, with complete confiscation of his property.

Through enforcing such suitable punishments, the king shall rigorously test the conduct of government officials. Once officials of proven integrity are established, they shall, in turn, oversee the conduct of the people in both urban and rural settings.

[Thus ends Chapter IX, "Protection of all kinds of Government Departments" in Book IV, "The Removal of Thorns" of the

Arthasástra of Kautilya. End of the eighty-sixth chapter from the beginning.]

CHAPTER X. FINES IN LIEU OF MUTILATION OF LIMBS.

When government servants (arthachara) commit certain offenses, such as violating a sacred institution (tírthághata) or engaging in pickpocketing (granthibheda), the penalties they face increase in severity with repeated infractions. On the first offense, they may either have their index finger amputated or pay a fine of 54 panas, depending on the discretion of the ruling authority or the legal severity attributed to the crime. Should these individuals repeat the offense a second time, they shall either lose another finger or pay a heightened fine of 100 panas. With a third offense, the consequences escalate even further: they shall forfeit their right hand or be subject to a substantial fine of 400 panas. Upon a fourth offense, no leniency is offered, and they shall be subject to execution, the means of which may vary according to the king's directive or the established customs governing capital punishment.

If a person steals or harms animals, such as roosters, mongooses, cats, dogs, or pigs, valued at less than 54 panas, they face a penalty reflecting both the offense and the value of the animals. For the initial infraction, they shall have the tip of their nose cut off, or alternatively, pay a fine of 54 panas. Should these animals belong to individuals of the Chandala caste or wild tribes, the fine shall be reduced by half, reflecting a lesser severity.

Further provisions address those who steal or capture animals of greater value or specific rarity. Anyone found guilty of taking wild animals, livestock, birds, elephants, tigers, fish, or other animals confined in traps, enclosures, or pits must return the stolen animals and pay a fine equal to their value to compensate for the loss and any potential distress caused by their absence.

In cases where forest resources are stolen—be it valuable raw materials, wild animals, or plants—a fine of 100 panas shall be imposed as a penalty. Should anyone be guilty of theft or destruction involving animals kept in infirmaries or other welfare institutions, the imposed fine will be twice that amount, signaling the elevated consequence due to the intended purpose of the animals' care.

When individuals steal minor tools, personal belongings, or other valuable items from artisans, musicians, or ascetics, they will face a fine of 100 panas. For larger items, or agricultural implements crucial to a trade or livelihood, the imposed fine shall be twice this amount.

If a person enters a fort without authorization, especially with an intent to remove valuables through a concealed passage or an opening in the walls, this intrusion shall be punished by beheading. Alternatively, the offender may pay a substantial fine of 200 panas, the choice of which may depend on the surrounding circumstances or the individual's intent.

For the theft of carts, boats, or smaller animals such as minor livestock, the penalty involves the amputation of one leg or payment of a fine totaling 300 panas.

In cases involving fraudulent gambling activities, such as where a gambler substitutes or manipulates dice rented for a kákaní or employs sleight of hand to deceive the opponent, they shall have their hand amputated or pay a penalty amounting to 400 panas.

Those who serve as accomplices, either to a thief or to an adulterer, will face significant penalties. The accomplice, along with any woman who voluntarily engages in adultery with the knowledge of its nature, shall have both their ears and noses removed or, alternatively, pay a fine of 500 panas each. Meanwhile, the primary offender—the thief or adulterer—will face double this penalty, further establishing accountability.

If an individual is caught stealing larger animals, kidnapping a male or female slave, or seizing items belonging to a deceased person, also known as pretabhándam, they shall face severe repercussions. Both of the offender's legs will be amputated, or they may choose to pay a hefty fine of 600 panas as retribution for the gravity of the offense.

Should a person brazenly attack or cause injury to the limbs of someone from a higher caste, or a teacher, or if they display disrespect by climbing onto the horse, elephant, or coach of the king, this individual shall lose one leg and one hand or be fined 700 panas.

When a Súdra falsely claims the identity of a Bráhman, it is considered a serious offense. Additionally, those who commit acts of theft involving property consecrated to deities, who conspire against the king, or who intentionally blind another person shall face the ultimate form of retribution: either the blinding of their own eyes through a poisonous ointment, or the imposition of an exorbitant fine of 800 panas to fully account for their crime.

When a person enables the release of a thief or an adulterer, falsifies or omits portions when transcribing the king's orders, abducts a girl or a slave who is carrying gold, engages in deceitful transactions, or sells spoiled meat, they shall face severe penalties. The offender may have two legs and one hand amputated or pay a substantial fine of 900 panas, reflecting the gravity of these transgressions.

Should anyone be found selling human flesh, the punishment shall be death, as this crime is seen as utterly reprehensible and deserving the highest level of punitive response.

If an individual steals images of deities or animals, abducts people, or unlawfully seizes another person's fields, houses, gold, coins, precious stones, or crops, they too shall face severe consequences. They may either be sentenced to beheading or required to pay the highest level of amercement, depending on the specific context of the offense.

- In determining the suitable penalties, several factors must be carefully considered: the social standing of the individuals involved, the specific nature and seriousness of the offense, whether the motivation behind the crime was substantial or minor, and the context of past and present circumstances. The timing and location of the offense are also important, as they can influence the assessment of intent and impact.
- Furthermore, the commissioner is tasked with making a fair

and balanced judgment, taking into account the distinctions among offenders, whether they are members of the royal family or commoners. This deliberate approach ensures that the severity of punishment is properly aligned with the first, middlemost, or highest amercements, reflecting a just response to the nature of each crime and the individuals involved.

[Thus ends Chapter X, "Fines in lieu of mutilation of limbs" in Book IV, "The Removal of Thorns" of the Arthasástra of Kautilya. End of the eighty-seventh chapter from the. beginning.]

CHAPTER XI. DEATH WITH OR WITHOUT TORTURE.

If a man kills another during a quarrel, he shall be subjected to death by torture. If someone is wounded in a fight and dies within seven nights, the person responsible for the wound shall face immediate execution. Should the wounded individual die within a fortnight, the offender shall be required to pay the highest level of amercement. If the wounded person succumbs to the injury within a month, the responsible party shall pay a fine of 500 panas along with an appropriate compensation to the bereaved family.

When someone injures another using a weapon, the highest amercement shall apply. If the act was committed under intoxication, the offender's hand shall be amputated; if the injury results in immediate death, the perpetrator shall be executed.

In cases where a person causes a woman to miscarry by physical harm, medication, or repeated harassment, the punishments are staggered: the highest amercement for physical harm, the middlemost for causing abortion through medication, and the first amercement for harassment that leads to miscarriage.

Individuals who bring violent death to others, frequent prostitutes, inflict unjust penalties, spread false or defamatory rumors, assault or obstruct travelers, engage in housebreaking, or harm royal animals such as elephants, horses, or carriages shall face hanging.

Anyone who attempts to destroy or steal the remains of those executed for these offenses shall face the same punishment or be subject to the highest amercement.

If a person provides support to murderers or thieves—be it food, clothing, materials, shelter, guidance, or any other form of assistance—they shall be fined with the highest amercement. If such support was given without knowledge of the criminal activities, the individual shall receive a public reprimand.

If the sons or wives of murderers or thieves are found innocent of involvement, they shall be acquitted. However, if any evidence shows their cooperation in the crime, they will be taken into custody.

Anyone who conspires against the kingdom, forces entry into the king's private quarters, incites wild tribes or enemies to rebel, or spreads discontent in forts, villages, or the army shall be burned alive from head to toe. If a Bráhman is guilty of such actions, he shall instead be drowned.

Anyone who kills their father, mother, son, brother, teacher, or an ascetic shall face execution by burning of both head and skin. If they insult any of these individuals, their tongue shall be cut out; if they bite or injure any body part of these persons, the corresponding limb shall be removed.

When a man kills another without cause or steals a group of cattle, he shall be beheaded. For these purposes, a group or herd of cattle is defined as ten or fewer animals.

If someone intentionally breaches the dam of a full tank, they shall be drowned in that same tank. If the tank was empty, they shall pay the highest amercement, and if it was already in disrepair due to neglect, they shall pay the middlemost amercement.

Anyone who administers poison to another or a woman who murders someone shall be sentenced to drowning.

A woman who kills her husband, teacher, or child; sets fire to property; administers poison; or mutilates another's body shall be torn apart by bulls. This punishment shall apply regardless of whether she is pregnant or within a month of childbirth.

Anyone who sets fire to pasture lands, grain fields, threshing yards, houses, or forests (whether for timber or shelter for elephants) shall be cast into flames.

Any person who insults the king, reveals confidential information from the royal council, attempts to harm the king, or desecrates the kitchens of Bráhmans shall have their tongue cut out.

If a civilian steals weapons or armor, they shall be executed by archers. A soldier committing the same act shall face the highest amercement.

Anyone who castrates another shall face the removal of their own generative organ.

Anyone who mutilates another's tongue or nose shall have their fingers cut off.

- Such severe punishments as these are recorded in the texts of wise sages, but it is advised that if the crime is not especially cruel, the offender may be given a simple execution instead.

[Thus ends Chapter XI, "Death with or without torture" in Book IV, "The Removal of Thorns" of the Arthasástra of Kautilya. End of the eighty-eighth chapter from the beginning.]

CHAPTER XII. SEXUAL INTERCOURSE WITH IMMATURE GIRLS.

Anyone who defiles a young maiden of equal caste before she reaches maturity shall either lose his hand or be fined 400 panas; should the maiden lose her life as a result, the offender shall face the death penalty.

Anyone who defiles a maiden who has reached maturity shall either lose his middle finger or pay a fine of 200 panas, in addition to providing adequate compensation to her father.

No one is permitted to engage in sexual relations with a woman without her consent.

If a man defiles a consenting maiden, he shall be fined 54 panas, while the maiden shall pay half that amount.

When a man impersonates someone who has already paid the marriage fee to a woman (to deceive her into intercourse), he shall either lose his hand or pay a fine of 400 panas, in addition to reimbursing the marriage fee.

If a man has relations with a maiden who has reached maturity but remains unwed after seven cycles of menses, and she was betrothed to him but not yet married, he shall neither be considered guilty nor owe her father compensation, for her father has forfeited authority over her by delaying the marriage.

It is not an offense for a man of equal caste and rank to engage with a maiden who has remained unmarried three years after her first menses. Nor is it an offense for a man of another caste to engage with a maiden who has been without marriage and jewelry for more than three years after her first menses, as this lack of paternal provision constitutes neglect of her rightful dowry, akin to theft.

Anyone who, under the guise of securing a bride for someone else, instead obtains her for a third party shall pay a fine of 200 panas.

No man shall engage in sexual intercourse with a woman against her will.

If a man replaces the bride initially promised with another woman, he shall be fined 100 panas if the substituted bride is of the same rank, and 200 panas if she is of a lower rank. The substituted bride shall also be fined 54 panas, and the man shall be required to return the marriage fee along with any additional expenses the bridegroom incurred in preparation for the marriage.

If a man, after agreeing to marry a particular maiden, later refuses to do so, he shall be fined double the amount previously specified for such substitutions.

In cases where a man marries a woman of a different bloodline than he originally agreed to or makes false claims about her qualities, he shall pay a fine of 200 panas, return the marriage fee, and cover any expenses related to the marriage preparations.

It is strictly prohibited for a man to force a woman into a relationship or sexual act against her will, regardless of circumstances.

If a woman willingly consents to be with a man of her own caste and social rank, she shall be fined 12 panas, while any other woman who encourages or assists in this situation shall be fined double, paying 24 panas. A woman who aids a man in coercing a maiden into a relationship against her will shall be fined 100 panas, and she must also compensate the maiden with an appropriate marriage fee as a form of restitution.

A woman who voluntarily offers herself to a man without any prior marriage arrangement shall become a slave to the king, forfeiting her freedom as a consequence.

When a man engages in relations with a woman outside of the village boundaries or spreads false stories regarding such matters, the fines imposed shall be doubled.

In the case of a man forcibly abducting a maiden, he shall be fined 200 panas. However, if the maiden was adorned with valuable golden jewelry, the offender shall face the maximum possible fine. If several men are involved in the abduction of a maiden, each individual shall be subject to the same penalty.

When a man engages in relations with the daughter of a harlot, he shall pay a fine of 54 panas and additionally provide the girl's mother with a sum equivalent to sixteen times her daily income, acknowledging the impact of his actions.

If a man violates the daughter of his male or female slave, he shall pay a fine of 24 panas and also provide the maiden with an adequate marriage fee and suitable jewelry, ensuring she has the means for her future well-being and social standing.

When a man engages in a relationship with a woman held in servitude due to an unpaid ransom, he shall not only pay a fine of 12 panas, but also provide her with appropriate clothing and necessary support for her well-being.

In all such cases, anyone who aids or encourages the principal offender shall receive the same punishment as the offender himself.

If a relative or servant of a man who is absent takes under his protection a woman of questionable character who is the absentee's wife, he may do so legally (in effect, marrying her). However, while under such protection, the woman must wait for her husband's return. If the husband returns and has no objections, both the protector and the woman shall be acquitted of any wrongdoing. If the husband objects, the woman shall have her ears and nose cut off as punishment, while her protector shall be put to death as an adulterer.

If a man falsely accuses someone of theft while the true issue is adultery, the false accuser shall be fined 500 panas.

A person who lets an adulterer go free by accepting a bribe shall pay a fine amounting to eight times the value of the gold or payment received.

The occurrence of adultery may be proven by evidence such as physical confrontation, abduction, visible marks on the bodies of those involved, expert evaluations based on the situation, or testimonies from the women implicated.

When a man rescues a woman from enemies, dense forests, or floodwaters, or when he saves the life of a woman abandoned in a forest, left helpless in times of famine, or discarded as if she were deceased, he may have her companionship if both parties consented during the rescue.

However, if the woman is of high caste, has children, and shows no inclination for a romantic relationship, she may be freed from any obligations to him upon payment of an adequate ransom.

- Women who have been saved from thieves, floodwaters, famine, national disasters, or from abandonment or being lost in forests, or those cast out as though dead and later brought to safety, may become the companion of their rescuer if both have mutually agreed upon it.

- However, women who have been cast out by royal decree or by their own families, as well as those of high caste, those unwilling to be rescued, or women with children, shall not be taken either for ransom or for companionship.

[Thus ends Chapter XII, "Sexual Intercourse with Immature Girls," in Book IV, "The Removal of Thorns" of the Arthasástra of Kautilya. End of the eighty-ninth chapter from the beginning.]

CHAPTER XIII. PUNISHMENT FOR VIOLATING JUSTICE.

Anyone who forces a Bráhman to consume forbidden food or drink shall be subject to the highest penalty. For compelling a Kshatriya to do so, the penalty shall be the middle amercement; for a Vaisya, the first amercement; and for a Súdra, a fine of 54 panas.

Those who willingly consume any food or drink that is condemned shall be declared outcasts.

If anyone forces entry into another's home during the day, they shall be fined with the first amercement; if it happens at night, the fine shall be the middlemost amercement. If someone enters another's home with a weapon, whether day or night, they shall face the highest amercement.

If beggars, peddlers, lunatics, or disturbed individuals try to enter a house by force, or if neighbors force entry into a home during an emergency, they will not be penalized provided there was no explicit prohibition against such entry.

Those who go onto their own roof after midnight shall be fined with the first amercement; those who climb onto another's roof will face the middlemost amercement.

Breaking the fences of villages, gardens, or fields shall also incur the middlemost amercement.

Traders are to inform the headman of the village regarding the value and nature of their merchandise before halting in any area of a village. If any portion of their goods, not securely transported out of the village during the night, is stolen or lost, the headman shall compensate for the loss.

Merchandise stolen or lost on routes between villages shall be the responsibility of the superintendent of pasture lands. If there is no such pasture officer, the Chorarajjuka officer shall cover the loss. If merchandise is lost in an area without even this level of protection, the people on the boundary of that area shall compensate. If there are no boundary people, residents from the five or ten nearest villages shall make up for the loss.

Harm caused by building weak houses, using carts with no support, or carts with broken beams, sharp objects hanging above, damaged support, or missing coverings, as well as harm caused by a cart falling into a pit, a tank, or off a dam, shall be considered assault.

Cutting down trees, stealing the rope used to tie a tameable animal, using untrained animals, and throwing sticks, mud, stones, rods, or arrows at chariots or elephants, as well as raising or waving an arm against chariots or elephants, will also be treated as assault.

If the driver of a chariot shouts "get out" to a passerby, he will not be held responsible for any collision.

If a person is killed by an elephant because they provoked it, the person who died is considered responsible. The family of the deceased should offer nearly a full kumbha of liquor, along with garlands, scents, and enough cloth to wash the tusks of the elephant. This is because death caused by an elephant is seen as having the same honor as taking a sacred bath after a horse-sacrifice. This offering is known as "washing the legs."

However, if an innocent passerby is killed by an elephant, the driver shall be fined the highest penalty.

If the owner of a horned or tusked animal fails to prevent their animal from harming someone, they shall be fined the first amercement. If the owner refuses to help after being asked to, the fine will be doubled.

If a person causes or permits animals with horns or tusks to harm or kill each other, he is responsible for paying a fine equal to the value of the animals that were harmed or lost, and he must also compensate the owner or any other person who suffered a loss. When someone rides over an animal that has been released in the name of the gods, or over a bull, ox, or young female calf, they will face a fine of 500 panas. Anyone who drives away these animals will be penalized with the highest amercement.

When a person takes away lesser animals that are valuable for their wool or milk, or for carrying or riding purposes, they must pay a fine equal to the animal's worth and also return it. The same fine and restitution apply if someone drives these animals away for reasons unrelated to religious ceremonies for gods or ancestors.

In cases where an animal with a broken or removed nose-ring, or one not properly trained for yoking, injures someone, or when an animal charges at a person or causes harm by pulling backward with its cart, or if it becomes confused due to crowding of people or other animals, the owner is not held responsible. However, when injuries are caused in any other circumstance, fines are applied according to prior rules, and any loss of animal life due to such incidents must be compensated. If the driver of the cart or carriage that caused harm is underage, the responsible adult in the cart will be fined. If there is no adult present, any passenger of age will be fined, or the driver himself if he is an adult. Carts driven by minors or unaccompanied by any person of age will be seized by the king.

Any actions involving witchcraft that are intended to harm others will have the same harm inflicted back on the person responsible. If witchcraft is done only to inspire love between a wife and her husband or to help a lover gain affection from a maiden, it is not considered an offense. However, when such acts cause harm to others, the perpetrator will face a fine set at the middlemost amercement.

If someone uses witchcraft to try to win the affections of his father's or mother's sister, his maternal uncle's wife, his teacher's wife, or his own daughter-in-law, daughter, or sister, he will have a limb cut off and be put to death. Any woman who willingly consents to such a relationship with the offender will face the same punishment. A woman who chooses to engage with a slave, servant, or hired worker will receive the same penalty.

If a Kshatriya is found guilty of adultery with a Bráhman woman who is unprotected, he will be punished with the highest amercement. If a Vaisya commits the same act, he will lose all his property. If a Súdra is guilty of this offense, he will be wrapped in mats and burned alive.

Anyone found guilty of adultery with the queen of the kingdom will be punished by being burned alive in a vessel (kumbhílpákah). If a man engages in adultery with a woman of a lower caste, he will be branded on his forehead with a mark indicating his punishment and banished, or he will be reduced to the same caste as the woman. Should a Súdra or svapáka commit adultery with a woman of a low caste, that man shall be sentenced to death, and the woman will have her ears and nose cut off as punishment.

Adultery involving a nun (pravrajitá) is punishable with a fine of 24 panas, which the nun herself must also pay if she consents to the act. If a man forces himself upon a harlot, he will face a fine of 12 panas. In cases where several people attempt to use witchcraft to influence a single woman, each person involved will be fined 24 panas.

Any man who engages in intimate acts with a woman in a way that goes against the natural order (a-yonau) will be subject to the first amercement. Likewise, a man found having relations with another man will also face the first amercement.

- A person who, in a senseless state, engages in intimate acts with animals will face a fine of 12 panas. If the same act is committed with idols representing goddesses (daivatapratimá), the fine will be doubled.
- If the king imposes punishment on an innocent person, he

must dedicate a fine equal to thirty times the amount of the wrongful penalty to the god Varuna by casting it into water. This amount will subsequently be distributed among the Bráhmans.

- Through this act of atonement, the king will be absolved of the sin of unjust punishment, as King Varuna is considered the ruler over the sins of men.

Book 5

CHAPTER I. CONCERNING THE AWARDS OF PUNISHMENTS.

Actions necessary to remove disturbances to public order, both in fortified cities and rural areas, have been discussed. Now, we will proceed to address measures to suppress acts of treason against the king and his kingdom.

For those officials who serve the king but hold hostile feelings or who have aligned with his enemies, a spy on a secret mission or one disguised as an ascetic, loyal to the king's cause, shall act as previously described. Alternatively, a spy skilled in creating discord may be deployed, as will be explained in the section on "Invasion of an Enemy's Villages."

The king, in the name of righteousness, may discreetly punish those courtiers or groups of influential officials who pose a threat to the kingdom and who cannot be dealt with openly in daylight.

A spy may instigate the brother of a disloyal minister and, with suitable incentives, bring him to the king for a meeting. The king, after bestowing upon him the right to control and enjoy the wealth of his treacherous brother, may arrange for him to confront his brother; and if he murders his brother with a weapon or poison, he shall also be executed on the same spot, under the charge of committing parricide.

This measure illustrates the approach for dealing with a disloyal Pârasava (offspring of a Bráhman and a Sûdra wife) and a seditious son of a servant.

Alternatively, under the influence of a spy, the brother of a disloyal minister may claim inheritance rights. If the claimant, while resting at night near his brother's residence or elsewhere, is killed by an aggressive spy (tîshna), it may then be declared, "Alas! the claimant to inheritance has been murdered (by his own brother)." The king, aligning himself with the aggrieved party, may proceed to punish the disloyal minister.

Spies, in the presence of a seditious minister, may openly threaten to strike his inheritance-claiming brother. Then, as "the claimant lies by the door, etc.," the procedure continues as outlined.

This tactic also applies to causing a fraudulent conflict between two disloyal ministers within a family where a father or son has had improper relations with a daughter-in-law, or a brother with the wife of another brother.

A spy may appeal to the ego of a seditious minister's son, who is known for his gentle demeanor and respectable conduct, by telling him, "Although you are like a prince, you are held here in fear of enemies." The king may privately honor this misguided individual, saying, "Fearing harm from the minister, I have delayed your official appointment, even though you have reached the age to be recognized as my heir." The spy may then encourage him to kill the minister. Once the task is completed, the son, too, will be executed in the same place on the charge of parricide.

A wandering woman, skilled in deception, may enchant the wife of a rebellious minister by using particular herbs or potions that stir feelings of love. Through this influence, the woman might persuade the minister's wife to act against him, potentially leading to his poisoning.

If this method proves ineffective, the king has other ways to address the disloyalty of the minister. He might assign him to lead a regiment of poorly trained soldiers along with fiery spies on a high-risk mission. Such tasks could include suppressing a rebellious wild tribe or an unruly village, setting up a new local governor in a region close to the wilderness, controlling a highly rebellious city, or securing a caravan carrying tributes to the king from a neighboring territory. During the disorder that might arise in any of these missions, whether during the day or at night, the fiery spies or those disguised as robbers may kill the minister and declare to all that he perished in the line of duty.

In another strategy, while preparing for a military expedition or engaging in a royal game, the king may summon his disloyal ministers for a meeting. Fiery spies with concealed weapons may accompany the ministers and, upon reaching the royal pavilion, will offer themselves for a search to enter the inner chamber. When the guards find weapons on these spies, they will declare them as accomplices of the seditious ministers. This incident will be made public, and the ministers will be executed, with replacements hanged in place of the fiery spies, protecting the king's plan from any exposure.

During recreational outings outside the city, the king may house disloyal ministers in accommodations adjacent to his own. Here, a woman of disrepute, posing as the queen, could be planted in their quarters to tarnish their reputations. Once discovered, the ministers could be publicly disgraced and punished according to the prior instructions, linking them to a scandal.

Another plan involves a sauce maker or sweetmeat maker gaining the trust of a disloyal minister by saying, "Only someone of your status deserves such special delicacies." Once the minister approves, the cook may lace a small amount of sauce, sweetmeat, or water with poison, secretly switching these with items in the king's lunch when he is outside the city. Upon public revelation of this incident, the king may order the execution of both the minister and the cook, branding them as poisoners and traitors to the crown.

If a disloyal minister shows a fascination with witchcraft, a spy pretending to be a skilled sorcerer may deceive him into believing that certain ritualistic objects, like a pot containing an alligator, a tortoise, or a crab, could help him achieve his ambitions. The spy could convince him that by performing rituals using these items, he could obtain supernatural assistance. While the minister becomes absorbed in this supposed ritual, the spy could seize the opportunity to end his life, either by poisoning him or striking him with a concealed iron rod. Publicly, it would be announced that the minister's own fixation on dangerous witchcraft led to his untimely end.

A spy disguised as a physician might deceive a disloyal minister into thinking he has a terminal or incurable illness. This way, the spy can secretly administer poison while pretending to prescribe medicine or dietary advice. Likewise, spies posing as sauce-makers or sweetmeat vendors may seek any opportunity to poison him when they find a chance.

These are covert techniques for dealing with traitorous individuals who pose a threat to peace and stability. When dealing with individuals conspiring against both the king and his realm:

If a dangerous conspirator needs to be eliminated, another similarly disloyal figure can be enlisted, accompanied by a group of untrained soldiers and fiery spies. They might be given a complex assignment such as, "Travel to this fort or district, assemble an army or gather taxes; confiscate wealth from a courtier; bring the daughter of a noble by force; build a new fortress; lay out a garden; construct a trade route; establish a settlement; set up a mine; establish timber or elephant reserves; demarcate a new district or frontier; and restrain or punish anyone who defies or hinders your tasks." A second conspirator or group may then be sent to counter the first group's activities under similar instructions. If a conflict arises between the two parties, spies in the guise of fiery or undercover operatives may throw weapons, causing death and chaos. They can then arrest others and use the scene as grounds for their punishment.

When disputes erupt in rebellious towns, villages, or families—perhaps over boundaries, land yields, property damages, livestock injuries, or even during public celebrations or festivals—whether the disputes are genuine or ignited by spies, the spies may throw weapons and declare, "This is what happens to those who defy this leader." The conspirators can then be arrested and penalized.

Similarly, when conflicts arise between disloyal factions, fiery spies may set their fields, granaries, or homes ablaze, assault their family members or livestock, and claim that their actions were done on orders from the rebels themselves. As a result, others will face arrest and punishment. Spies can also arrange for meetings between conspirators in strongholds or rural areas under the guise of shared feasts, during which poisoners could act, resulting in poisonings that lead to further arrests and penalties.

A mendicant woman could skillfully deceive a disloyal district chief by convincing him that the wife, daughter, or daughter-in-law of a rival seditious chief is enamored with him. She could accept any jewelry the misled chief gives her for this supposed love interest and then present it to the rival chief, alleging that the first chief, in youthful arrogance, is pursuing his wife or daughter. This deception may spark a bitter feud between the two chiefs, potentially leading to a deadly night duel and retribution against both sides.

In cases where loyalty needs to be tested, the prince or a commander might show favor to a group of enemies subdued by one faction, only to later show disapproval. Meanwhile, others subdued by a separate faction could be dispatched to confront the first group, accompanied by a mix of untrained soldiers and undercover operatives, helping to turn the disloyal groups against each other in the process.

In this way, any surviving sons of these conspirators who remain calm and unaffected by these events will inherit their father's wealth and property, proving their loyalty. By managing disloyal factions with these consistent methods, the kingdom will establish loyalty among the people. This process will ensure the enduring loyalty of the population to the king's descendants and prevent any unrest or troubles caused by seditious elements.

With patience and foresight, the king, assured of stability both now and in the future, may choose to enforce punishments discreetly. These punishments may apply not only to his own subjects who pose a threat but also to those who support or act on behalf of the enemy's cause. By doing so, the king maintains a secure realm, ensuring peace while dealing with threats quietly and effectively.

[Thus ends Chapter I, "Concerning the Awards of Punishments" in Book V. "The Conduct of Courtiers" of the Arthasástra of Kautilya. End of the ninety-first chapter from the beginning.]

CHAPTER II. REPLENISHMENT OF THE TREASURY.

If the king finds himself in urgent need of funds and faces significant financial strain, he may resort to additional revenue collection from his subjects. In areas where the primary livelihood depends on rainfall and grain is abundant, he may request either one-third or one-fourth of the grain harvest based on the resources and capacity of the people there. However, he must refrain from placing demands on subjects residing in regions of moderate or lower productivity. This exemption also extends to people who contribute substantially to the kingdom, such as those aiding in the construction of fortifications, public gardens, buildings, trade routes, the development of unused lands, the mining sector, and forest preservation efforts for timber and elephant habitats. Similarly, he must not impose extra demands on border residents or individuals struggling to maintain basic sustenance. Instead, he should offer grain and livestock to support those involved in reclaiming and cultivating barren lands.

The king may consider purchasing a quarter of the remaining grain stock from his subjects, ensuring sufficient reserves for seeds and personal sustenance are set aside. The property and resources of forest-dwelling tribes and Bráhmans skilled in Vedic knowledge should be avoided entirely for revenue collection; however, if their goods are needed, they should be bought at a fair market price. Should these methods prove insufficient, the collector-general's officials might encourage the farming communities to cultivate crops during the summer. To ensure compliance, they may issue a notice that doubled fines will be imposed for violations among the peasantry and facilitate the sowing of seeds during planting seasons. Upon the ripening of crops, officials may respectfully request a share of ripened produce, while refraining from gleaning or disturbing grains and vegetables that have naturally fallen to the ground. These scattered grains serve an important role in offerings to gods and ancestors, feeding livestock, and supporting mendicants and village staff.

For those who attempt to hide their harvested grain, a penalty of eight times the concealed amount in each variety is due. Anyone caught stealing crops from another's field must pay a fine of fifty times the value if the thief belongs to the same community; however, a foreign thief shall face a death sentence. Officials may levy one-fourth of the grain yield from cultivators and one-sixth of forest produce and resources such as cotton, wax, woven materials, tree bark, hemp, wool, silk, medicinal herbs, sandalwood, flowers, fruits, vegetables, firewood, bamboo, meat, and dried meat. Half of all ivory and animal hides may also be claimed. Those trading any goods without the king's permission shall face the first level of amercement. This encompasses the guidelines for revenue collection among cultivators.

Merchants who trade in valuable goods like gold, silver, diamonds, precious stones, pearls, coral, horses, and elephants must contribute 50 karas. Those dealing in cotton threads, cloth, copper, brass, bronze, sandalwood, medicinal products, and alcohol are required to pay 40 karas. Traders in grains, liquids, metals, and those dealing in carts must pay 30 karas. For those trading in glass or engaging in fine craftsmanship, the fee is 20 karas. Artisans of lesser-quality goods, along with those who manage brothels, are to pay 10 karas. Those trading in firewood, bamboo, stones, pottery, cooked foods, and vegetables are expected to pay 5 karas. Performers and prostitutes shall contribute half of their earnings. Goldsmiths, however, will have their entire stock confiscated, with no leniency shown for their offenses, as their trade is known for dishonesty under the guise of respectability. Thus are the levies upon merchants established.

People raising poultry and pigs must hand over half of their livestock to the government. Those raising smaller animals are expected to give up one-sixth of their animals. Herdsmen keeping cows, buffaloes, mules, donkeys, and camels are to offer one-tenth of their herds. Those who manage brothels are to collect revenue with the help of women renowned for beauty and youth serving under the king's command. These are the obligations for livestock keepers.

These demands are intended to be imposed only once and not to be repeated. In the absence of such demands, the collector-general may seek contributions from both citizens and rural inhabitants by using pretexts related to various governmental projects. Leading citizens, brought in through agreement, should publicly provide notable donations, thereby encouraging others to contribute similarly. Undercover agents posing as common citizens may publicly criticize those who give less, stirring competition among contributors. Affluent individuals may be encouraged to offer as much gold as they can spare. Those who willingly or charitably offer their wealth to the king should be honored with positions in court or tokens of prestige like an umbrella, turban, or valuable ornaments as thanks for their generosity.

Spies, disguised as mystics or sorcerers, may collect funds for the supposed safety of the state. They are permitted to collect money not only from societies of heretics or temples but also from estates of deceased persons or households affected by fires, provided that these funds are not designated for the enjoyment or use of Bráhmans.

The Superintendent of Religious Institutions may consolidate various properties belonging to the deities of both cities and rural areas and transfer this wealth to the king's treasury. Alternatively, under the cover of religious events, such as establishing a deity's shrine, setting up an altar, opening an ascetic's sacred space, or interpreting omens, the king may collect resources through ceremonies or gatherings. Another means might include proclaiming the miraculous presence of a god, highlighted by a sacred tree in the royal gardens that has produced untimely blooms or fruit.

Or, by sparking a false panic over an "evil spirit" residing in a prominent city tree, where a person is hidden and making eerie, unsettling sounds, the king's spies, disguised as holy ascetics, could initiate a campaign to collect offerings. Claiming that the offerings are necessary to appease this spirit and send it away, they could draw funds from the people. Similarly, spies might invite the public to witness a supposedly mythical serpent with multiple heads in a well connected to an underground tunnel system, charging a fee for those who wish to catch a glimpse of this "rare" creature. To add authenticity, they could plant a drugged cobra in a borehole within an idol of a serpent, a temple corner, or even in the hollow of an anthill, using the sedated snake to heighten the sense of mystique and power. Believers would be enticed to pay to view this serpent. For those who are skeptical by nature, spies could prepare a special "sacred water," subtly mixed with anesthetic ingredients. When these nonbelievers drink it, their sudden lethargy and drowsiness would be blamed on a divine presence, supposedly cursing those who doubt.

If the people remain unconvinced, an outcast could be secretly bitten by a cobra, an incident spies would later use as an example of the dangers of ignoring or defying these sacred events. With this, more revenue could be gathered to "appease the gods."

Meanwhile, a royal spy disguised as a wealthy merchant could pose as the business partner of a real, affluent merchant. Together, they would gather a large sum from sales, deposits, and loans. Once the fund grew to a significant amount, the spy could arrange to be "robbed" of all their collective assets. This strategy would also apply to officials like the royal coin examiner or the state goldsmith, who could stage similar thefts by pretending they'd lost significant assets in the course of their duties.

Alternatively, a spy, posing as a trader, or even an established merchant widely known for his dealings, could take loans or valuables from other traders, requesting gold and goods in pledges for foreign trade. After obtaining a sizable amount of resources, this supposed merchant would also arrange for a sudden nighttime robbery, claiming to be a victim of thieves.

In another tactic, prostitute-spies posing as virtuous women could captivate seditious individuals, luring them with their charms. As soon as these rebellious individuals are seen within the residences of these women, they could be arrested, and all their wealth confiscated. Or, in cases where rival seditious groups within a family argue or clash, spies trained as poisoners could target one faction, using the altercation to accuse the other group, confiscating their property as punishment.

A planted outcast might act as though he were a high-born man demanding repayment of a "large debt" supposedly left with the seditious person, or he could lay claim to an inheritance. He could also claim to be a servant or slave of the person and assert ownership over his wife, daughter, or daughter-in-law. Stationing himself outside the target's residence or nearby at night, he could await his moment, at which point a spy would arrange his death, declaring loudly, "This is the fate of one claiming what is rightfully his." In turn, this accusation could be used to strip the seditious person and his associates of their possessions, effectively neutralizing both the immediate threat and future unrest from similar groups.

Or a spy disguised as an ascetic may approach a seditious individual, tempting him with promises of great wealth or influence through the use of witchcraft, saying, "I am skilled in witchcraft that can bring endless wealth, gain entry into the king's court, win the love of any woman, eliminate one's enemies, prolong life, or grant a son if desired." If the seditious person agrees to pursue this forbidden magic, the spy could set up an elaborate scene involving ritual offerings. This might take place near an altar in a burial ground, where a small amount of money and the body of a man or child had already been hidden. The spy would offer up rich sacrifices of meat, wine, and perfume, claiming these offerings are essential for success. Once the ritual is over, the buried treasure is uncovered, but it is made to appear minimal. The spy would then explain that the wealth gained was small because the offerings weren't grand enough, suggesting that the seditious person should buy more valuable offerings to increase his gains. The spy would then catch him in the act of buying these extravagant items, providing ample evidence of his activities.

In a further twist, a female spy, disguised as a grieving mother, might raise an alarm, crying out that her child has been sacrificed for witchcraft, drawing public condemnation on the seditious person involved.

If a seditious person secretly practices sorcery at night, performs rituals in the forest, or indulges in amusements in a secluded park, fiery spies could eliminate him under cover of night and dispose of the body as though it were that of a social outcast.

Alternatively, a spy disguised as the servant of a seditious person could mix counterfeit coins with his own wages, planting them to be found, leading to the seditious person's arrest. Another spy, posing as a goldsmith, might work within the household of a rebellious individual and accumulate various tools needed to make counterfeit coins, setting up the seditious person for arrest on charges of fraud.

In another strategy, a spy disguised as a physician might declare a healthy yet seditious person to be ill and administer poison under the guise of medicine. Or a spy acting as the servant of a suspected person could ask another spy—disguised as a trustworthy friend—for an explanation of how letters from the king's enemies or items essential to a royal ceremony ended up in his master's possession. The spy himself could even pretend to offer explanations, further sowing doubt about the seditious person's loyalty.

These measures, as intricate as they may seem, are reserved strictly for dealing with the seditious and the wicked, ensuring that innocent individuals are never subjected to these severe tactics.

Just as fruits are picked from a garden only when they have fully ripened, so too should revenue be collected only when it becomes due or "ripe." Gathering taxes or revenue prematurely, just like harvesting unripe fruit, can harm the source, potentially leading to significant losses and creating a great deal of unnecessary hardship. Therefore, it is essential that revenue collection is timed carefully, ensuring that the source remains undisturbed and productive, so it may continue to yield resources without interruption.

[Thus ends Chapter II, "Replenishment of the Treasury" in Book V, "The Conduct of Courtiers" of the Arthasástra of Kautilya. End of the ninety-second chapter from the beginning.]

CHAPTER III. CONCERNING SUBSISTENCE TO GOVERNMENT SERVANTS.

In line with the needs of his forts and provinces, the king should allocate a portion, ideally less than one-fourth of the total revenue, to support his officials and retainers. Their well-being should be secured through suitable compensation to keep them motivated and dedicated to their duties. Importantly, this allocation should not compromise principles of righteousness or sound financial practices.

The sacrificial priest, the royal teacher, the minister, the court priest, the commander of the army, the crown prince, the queen, and the king's mother are each to receive an annual allowance of 48,000 panas. This generous provision helps ensure they remain steadfast, avoiding temptations that could lead to disloyalty or dissatisfaction.

Door-keepers, the superintendent of the royal harem, chief officials overseeing governance, the chief chamberlain, and the head of financial collection should each receive 24,000 panas. This amount supports their role, making them reliable and effective in their duties.

For the prince, his nurse, the chief constable, the town overseer, the superintendent of judicial or trade matters, heads of manufacturing, council ministers, as well as superintendents of territories and borders, an annual allocation of 12,000 panas is advised. This amount aims to strengthen their loyalty and make them formidable allies of the king.

Leaders of various military divisions, including those heading elephant, cavalry, chariot, and infantry units, along with commissioners, are each to be allotted 8,000 panas, enabling them to command respect within their respective ranks.

Lastly, superintendents responsible for managing infantry, cavalry, chariots, elephants, and the guards overseeing forests for timber and elephants should each receive 4,000 panas.

The chariot driver, the army physician, the horse trainer, the carpenter, and those responsible for rearing animals are each to receive 2,000 panas annually, recognizing their essential contributions to military operations and animal care.

Individuals who offer counsel, including the foreteller, omen reader, astrologer, storyteller, bard, and members of the priest's retinue, along with various departmental heads, are to be allocated 1,000 panas each. This ensures these roles are honored for their cultural and administrative importance.

For trained soldiers and the accounting and writing staff, an annual wage of 500 panas is appropriate to support their diligent and accurate service. Musicians are granted 250 panas, though trumpeters are awarded double this amount in acknowledgment of their skill in ceremonial music. Artisans and carpenters, who are crucial for both construction and maintenance, are to be given 120 panas each.

Lower-ranked support staff, including caretakers for animals and attendants tasked with miscellaneous duties, those serving the king directly, bodyguards, and coordinators of free labor, are designated an annual wage of 60 panas to reflect their support roles.

The king's chosen companion, the elephant driver, sorcerers, mountain miners, attendants of various types, teachers, and scholars are given a special honorarium that ranges from 500 to 1,000 panas based on their skill and merit.

Messengers are compensated by the distance they travel, with a rate of 10 panas per yojana. If their journey spans from 10 to 100 yojanas, their rate doubles to ensure the strenuous travel is rewarded adequately.

Any representative of the king participating in royal sacrifices like the Rájasúya ceremony will receive three times the amount that others of similar learning would be given, highlighting their elevated role. Meanwhile, the charioteer of the king in these sacrifices is awarded 1,000 panas for his role.

Spies, whether they are disguised as tricksters, impartial observers, householders, merchants, or ascetics, are granted 1,000 panas each, recognizing the value of their intelligence gathering. Lower-ranked spies, including village servants, fiery spies, poisoners, and wandering mendicant women, are compensated with 500 panas, acknowledging their work in gathering and reporting information essential for the king's security and strategy.

Servants who lead spies are to be compensated with 250 panas, or adjusted according to the level of work they complete. Superintendents responsible for overseeing one hundred or one thousand community units (vargas) will regulate the subsistence, wages, profits, appointments, and transfers of the people under their command.

However, officers appointed to guard the royal palaces, forts, and rural areas are exempt from reassignment. Chief officers, tasked with overseeing these secure locations, should be numerous and maintain long-term, stable appointments in these roles.

When a servant dies while on duty, provisions will be made for their surviving family members, including their children, spouses, and dependent relatives. Furthermore, during times of mourning, illness, or childbirth, the king shall show favor and generosity to these affected families. In times of financial constraint, the king may distribute forest goods, livestock, or even portions of land along with a small monetary gift. If he wishes to encourage settlement on undeveloped lands, payments will be made solely in currency; however, to ensure fairness across all villages, no single village shall be exclusively allocated to any servant.

Through these measures, the king not only ensures the livelihood of his servants but also rewards them according to their skills, knowledge, and dedication. For payments, the king may substitute one adhaka in place of the standard 60 panas, allowing for compensation in kind.

Foot soldiers, horses, chariots, and elephants will undergo thorough military training at sunrise on all days except those marked by planetary conjunctions. The king will be present to observe and assess the readiness of his forces during each training session. Weapons and armor must bear the royal seal before being entered into the armory, ensuring that they are accounted for and securely maintained. Armed individuals are restricted in movement unless they possess a valid passport permitting them to carry weapons.

If any weapons are lost or damaged, the superintendent responsible will bear the cost, reimbursing double the value of each lost or spoiled item, with records kept of all damaged or disposed weapons. Boundary guards are instructed to confiscate weapons and armor from caravans lacking the required travel passport.

When preparing for a military campaign, the king will activate his army. On these missions, spies disguised as merchants will deliver essential supplies to military outposts, doubling the supplies with a promise of repayment later. This strategy allows the king's merchandise to reach a wider market, simultaneously ensuring profitable returns on wages paid out.

By maintaining careful oversight of income and expenses, the king will prevent financial and military challenges. These arrangements ensure both subsistence and fair wages for all in service.

- Spies, prostitutes, craftsmen, singers, and senior military officers are tasked with closely observing the behavior of military personnel, assessing whether their actions are honorable or dishonorable.

[Thus ends Chapter III, "Concerning Subsistence to Government Servants" in Book V, "The Conduct of Courtiers" of the Arthasástra of Kautilya. End of the ninety-third chapter from the beginning.]

CHAPTER IV. THE CONDUCT OF A COURTIER.

Anyone with worldly experience and understanding of its affairs might, through the help of a trusted ally, seek the patronage of a king who is known for his pleasant nature and possesses all the qualities of a true ruler. He may consider aligning himself with any king whom he perceives as appreciative of wise counsel and good-hearted in character, even if that king lacks great wealth or the full strength of sovereignty. However, he should avoid associating with a king of a corrupt nature, for no matter how vast his power, a ruler devoid of good temperament and driven by a dislike for the science of governance and an inclination towards wrongful deeds cannot sustain his rule.

Upon gaining an audience with a virtuous king, he should provide the king with instruction in the sciences, and the king's silent acceptance of his teachings will strengthen his standing. When consulted on important matters, present or future, that require insight and deliberation, he may confidently and wisely offer his advice without fear of opposition from the council, ensuring that his guidance aligns with principles of righteousness and prudence. He may further advise the king, saying, "According to the principle that delays in quelling strong alliances of wrongdoers should be avoided, you should act firmly against the wicked, especially if they are well-supported. Also, refrain from disregarding my counsel, character, or secrets, and allow me to signal you with subtle gestures if you are about to deliver a punishment under impulse or anger."

With these understandings, the courtier may begin his duties. He should sit close to the king, distinguished from the seats of other courtiers. He must refrain from subtle criticisms of any assembly member's opinions, making unbelievable statements, laughing loudly without reason, or causing excessive noise. He should avoid speaking in whispers, private exchanges within the council, appearing publicly in royal attire, showing arrogance, jesting inappropriately, openly seeking gifts or promotions, looking sidelong or biting his lips, frowning at others, interrupting the king, making enemies of powerful factions, or associating with women, go-betweens, messengers of foreign rulers, foes, dismissed officers, or those of questionable character. He must avoid excessive adherence to a single course of action and contact with any union or alliance of men.

- Without missing timely moments, he should advocate for the king's interests; in the presence of trusted friends, he may speak of his own interests, and discuss the concerns of others when the time and place are fitting, all while upholding the principles of righteousness and economy.

- When consulted, he should advise the king on matters that are both beneficial and pleasing, avoiding the suggestion of anything harmful even if it might appeal to the king. If the king is open to it, he may, in private, offer guidance that, though unwelcome, is in the king's best interest.

- He may choose silence over sharing anything offensive and should refrain from mentioning topics the king dislikes, as many, even those who are otherwise unfavored, have gained influence simply by avoiding such subjects. When a king seeks only pleasing news, indifferent to its negative effects, a wise advisor will observe this and act accordingly.

- In moments of jest, he should restrain his laughter, avoiding hurtful remarks or blaming others unfairly. He should demonstrate patience towards personal slights and cultivate a resilience as steadfast as the earth itself.

- A wise person will keep self-preservation at the forefront of his mind, understanding that service to a king is akin to living within fire—where fire may harm parts of the body, the king has the ability to shape or even destroy the lives of his servants, impacting not only the individual but also his family, including his children and wife.

[Thus ends Chapter IV, "The Conduct of a Courtier" in Book V, "The Conduct of Courtiers" of the Arthasástra of Kautilya. End of the ninety-fourth chapter from the beginning.]

CHAPTER V. TIME-SERVING.

When serving as a minister, the courtier must present the king with an accurate account of the net revenue after all forms of expenditure are covered. He should give detailed information, clarifying specifics like the nature of work that is either external or internal, secretive or open, costly or trivial. In all the king's pursuits, be it hunting, gambling, drinking, or pleasures, he should be close at hand, striving through careful persuasion to prevent the king from succumbing to negative habits or falling victim to the plots, schemes, or deceit of enemies. At all times, he must attempt to interpret the king's thoughts and expressions.

In guiding the king's scattered thoughts toward resolution, the courtier should pay close attention to the cues the king displays—indications of his inclinations, anger, joy, sadness, resolve, fear, or his shifts between opposing emotions.

When the king is favorably disposed towards the courtier, he displays it through particular gestures and actions: he shows enjoyment in recognizing the courtier's insights; listens attentively; offers him a seat and welcomes him in private; shows trust even in uncertain situations; engages in pleasant conversation; takes initiative in noticing details without needing reminders; tolerates reasonable suggestions; gives orders with a gentle demeanor; extends his hand in friendly gestures; refrains from ridicule when commendable things are said; praises the courtier's qualities when he is not present; recalls the courtier at mealtime; seeks his company in leisure; consults him when faced with concerns; respects those who follow him; confides in him; honors him increasingly; provides him with wealth; and alleviates his burdens. Each of these actions serves as a sign of the king's satisfaction with the courtier.

When the opposite occurs, the courtier should recognize the king's displeasure. Here are further indications, expressed clearly:

Signs of dissatisfaction include the king's angry demeanor when the courtier is near; avoidance or refusal to hear him; reluctance to offer him a seat or grant him audience; a noticeable change in tone or expression while conversing with him; seeing him with one eye or brow furrowed; biting the lips; visible perspiration; heavy breathing or unexplained smiles; talking to himself; sudden shifts in body posture; reaching for another's hand or chair; unsettling another person present; mocking the courtier's knowledge, background, or heritage; criticizing his colleague with similar flaws; condemning a person of opposite character flaws; censuring his adversary; ignoring his accomplishments; fixating on his shortcomings; paying undue attention to others entering the room; excessive gifting; dishonesty; and noting changes in how visitors to the court behave.

In observing signs of change, the courtier should even consider the behavior of animals around the king, as these too may reveal the underlying disposition of his sovereign.

- Kátyáyana asserts that this king dispenses his favors generously, extending them to all.
- Kaninka Bháradvája observes that the Krauncha bird has moved from the right to the left, implying a subtle change in fortune or direction.
- Dírgha Chárayana remarks that this king is like grass, likely suggesting pliability or being easily influenced.
- Ghotamukha compares him to a damp cloth, indicating softness or perhaps yielding nature.
- Kinjalka likens him to an elephant pouring out water, a symbol of power and grandeur, yet potentially wasteful in the process.
- Pisuna advises to consider him as a chariot-horse, suggesting he serves as a vehicle for others' ambitions. Pisuna's son adds that seeking favor with the king's opponent may lead to personal hardship or disapproval.

When the flow of wealth and honor ceases, such a king may indeed be left behind; alternatively, one might gain insight into both the king's character and his own shortcomings and adjust his behavior accordingly. Another option is to align with one of the king's most trusted allies for protection and favor.

- Living with the king's trusted friend, the courtier must strive to eliminate his master's flaws by leveraging his own network of friends to influence matters indirectly. Once this is achieved, he should return to his original position, regardless of whether the king remains in power or has passed away.

[Thus ends Chapter V "Time-serving" in Book V, "The Conduct of Courtiers" of the Arthasástra of Kautilya. End of the ninety-fifth chapter from the beginning.]

CHAPTER VI. CONSOLIDATION OF THE KINGDOM AND ABSOLUTE SOVEREIGNTY.

The minister shall skillfully deflect any dangers threatening the king. Long before any risk to the king's life appears imminent, the minister should, in collaboration with his own allies and followers, allow visitors to see the king only once a month or every two months. On other occasions, he may excuse the king's absence by claiming the king is involved in rituals meant to prevent national calamities, eliminate enemies, extend life, or ensure an heir.

When appropriate, the minister may even show a false king to the public or to messengers from allies or adversaries. This false king would direct all communication through the minister, making him the spokesperson in every interaction. Orders from the king would appear to come through the minister, channeled via the gatekeeper and the officer of the harem, and any decisions of mercy or punishment towards wrongdoers would be delivered indirectly.

Both the treasury and the military forces shall be overseen by two reliable and confidential officials, centralized in a single, secure location within the fort or on the kingdom's boundary. Members of the royal family, including princes and other close kin, may be deployed for challenging assignments, such as seizing a commander who has become a threat along with his followers, leading expeditions, or carrying out visits to the families of the king's allies.

Any neighboring king who appears likely to invade can be invited under the pretense of a festival, wedding, elephant capture, horse trade, or other land dealings, and captured. Alternatively, an ally might be enlisted to keep this potential invader occupied until a suitable agreement can be negotiated. Or the neighboring ruler could be encouraged to quarrel with hostile tribes or rivals. Should any member of his family be held in captivity, an offer of territorial gains could turn him against his own.

By garnering support from the nobility and princes of the royal family, the minister may install and publicly present the heir-apparent. Or, having eliminated all threats to the kingdom as outlined in the instructions on punishment, he might take charge of administration himself.

If, however, one of the neighboring kings continues to cause trouble, the minister might invite him with the promise, "Come here, and I shall make you king," and then dispose of him; or he might restrain this king through strategic means to keep him from posing any threat.

Finally, having gradually shifted the responsibilities of governance to the heir-apparent, the minister may formally announce the king's passing to the people.

If the king passes away while in enemy territory, the minister may form an alliance between the enemy and a trusted ally posing as the deceased king's adversary and then withdraw. Alternatively, he might install one of the neighboring kings in the fort of the deceased ruler and then withdraw. He could also set up the rightful heir on the throne and direct the army to face the enemy, using all available defensive strategies if the enemy advances, as laid out in other teachings on averting danger.

Kautilya states, "In such situations, the minister should assume full powers of sovereignty."

Bháradvája disagrees, arguing, "If the king is on his deathbed, the minister might instead provoke discord between the royal family's princes and influential nobles, allowing them to weaken each other. Any who then threaten the kingdom could be executed under the justification of preserving public order. By secretly disciplining the key members of the royal family and securing control, the minister may rightfully claim the throne. After all, in matters of power, even fathers and sons are known to turn against each other for the sake of the kingdom. Why should the minister, the chief guardian of the realm, be an exception?

"Moreover," Bháradvája continues, "one should not reject what has fallen into their hands through circumstance, for people say that a woman who pursues a man out of her own volition, if later dismissed, may turn to curse him."

- "An opportunity will present itself only once to a man who is vigilant and prepared, and it will not come again if he later wishes to complete his endeavor."

"But it is unrighteous," says Kautilya, "to undertake actions that provoke the anger of the people, nor is it a recognized standard. Therefore, he should appoint as ruler a son of the king who possesses virtuous qualities. If there is no prince of good character, he may put forward a less favorable prince, a princess, or the pregnant queen and say to the other ministers: 'This is your lineage (kshepa); consider both the heritage of this (child) and your own bravery and descent; this (child) is merely a symbol, and you are the leaders; now, how should I proceed?'"

While he speaks, those already taken into confidence should reply: "Who else, other than someone under your guidance, is fit to safeguard the multitude of the kingdom's four castes?" The remaining ministers will undoubtedly agree. Thus, he should install a prince, princess, or the pregnant queen and present them to the royal kin as well as to emissaries from allies or adversaries. He should grant the ministers and military officers enhanced stipends and wages, assuring them, "This (child) will further elevate your standing upon reaching adulthood." He should also make similar promises to the chief officers governing the forts and provincial areas, as well as to parties aligned with both allies and foes. Afterward, he should make all necessary arrangements for the prince's education and training.

Alternatively, he may install as the successor a child born of the princess by a man of her own caste. He should appoint as the prince's representative someone from the same family who is of modest valor and attractive appearance, to prevent the mother from being distressed with undue anxieties. He should ensure she is protected justly and refrain from indulging himself in luxuries. For the king, he may provide new chariots, horses, jewels, clothing, attendants, and residences.

- When the prince reaches maturity, the minister may suggest to the prince that he take over the responsibilities of governance, thus relieving the minister of the intellectual burden. He may choose to step away from his position if the king shows dissatisfaction but remain in his role if the king is pleased with his service.
- If he finds himself disillusioned with the life of a minister, he may choose to withdraw to a secluded forest or embark on a prolonged sacrificial ritual, ensuring that he informs the queen of all the measures and persons assigned to guide and protect the prince's upbringing.
- Even if the king is heavily influenced by powerful chiefs, the minister can, through the king's trusted advisors, guide him in the principles of governance, using stories and examples from the ancient texts, such as the Itihása and Purána, to reinforce his teachings.
- Should circumstances require, the minister may assume the guise of a skilled ascetic to endear himself to the king further. Once he has secured the king's trust, he can take effective steps to curb any seditious influences that might threaten the stability of the kingdom.

Book 6

CHAPTER I. THE ELEMENTS OF SOVEREIGNTY.

The elements of sovereignty consist of the king, the minister, the country, the fort, the treasury, the army, and the friend.

The foremost qualities of an ideal king include the following: He should come from a noble lineage, possess a godly disposition, and be endowed with valor. He seeks wisdom from the experience of elders, is virtuous, honest, and consistent in nature, showing gratitude and commitment to large and noble ambitions. His zeal is strong, he avoids procrastination, and he commands power to influence neighboring rulers. The king's mind is resolute, supported by a council of skilled ministers, and he values discipline—qualities that make his character both inviting and admirable.

In regard to intellectual qualities, a king should demonstrate inquiry, attentive listening, perceptiveness, a strong memory, thoughtful reflection, careful deliberation, insightful inference, and unwavering adherence to decisions.

Enthusiasm manifests in valor, a firm purpose, swift action, and moral integrity.

A ruler of self-possession exhibits a keen intellect, an impressive memory, and an alert mind. He is energetic, powerful, skilled in various arts, virtuous, and discerning in matters of rewards and punishment. Such a king maintains dignity, identifies dangers and solutions, exercises foresight, and seizes opportunities wisely based on place, time, and effort. He understands when treaties or warfare are necessary and maneuvers deftly with treaties and obligations to exploit his enemy's weaknesses. This king makes lighthearted jokes without compromising his dignity or confidentiality, remains calm, avoids anger, greed, and stubbornness, and is not prone to rashness or gossip. He addresses others with a pleasant demeanor, respects customs and traditions, and upholds the wisdom imparted by the elderly.

The qualifications of a minister have been previously discussed at various stages in this work.

A good country is defined by strategic capital cities, centrally and at the kingdom's borders, capable of providing sustenance not only to residents but also to outsiders in times of crisis. It deters enemies and possesses the strength to withstand neighboring threats. Such a region is free from muddy, rocky, uneven, or desert terrains, and avoids issues with conspirators, wild beasts, or vast wilderness. A prosperous country is visually appealing, blessed with fertile lands, rich mines, abundant timber and elephants, and vast grazing lands. It is artfully structured, with concealed passageways, plentiful livestock, reliable water sources independent of rain, an integrated network of land and waterways, and is enriched with varied commercial goods. It bears the capacity for a large army and supports significant taxation, while being populated by diligent and ethical farmers, intelligent landowners, skilled laborers, and a citizenry renowned for loyalty and high character.

The qualities of ideal forts have already been discussed in detail.

An exemplary treasury is one that is acquired justly, whether through inheritance or self-earned, and is rich in gold, silver, and an array of large, colorful gems and gold coins. Such a treasury is capable of supporting the kingdom through long periods of hardship or calamity.

The best kind of army is one that has been consistently maintained over generations, directly from the king's father and grandfather. It is strong and devoted, with soldiers who are well-respected and content with their families. This army is loyal and willing to stay in distant locations as required, standing invincible in all circumstances. Its soldiers are skilled in various combat techniques, proficient with multiple forms of weaponry, and are ready to share in the king's fortunes, whether for better or worse. Due to their loyalty, they are never prone to internal disputes with the king. Furthermore, an ideal army is comprised entirely of warriors from the Kshatriya caste, emphasizing its strength and commitment.

The best kind of ally or friend, also handed down from father and grandfather, is one who has stood the test of time. This friend is rational, steadfast, always open to reasonable persuasion, and unshakable in their loyalty. Such an ally is capable of swiftly organizing and preparing for warfare on a large scale, adding resilience and reliability to the kingdom's support network.

On the other hand, the most dangerous enemy is one who lacks royal heritage, who is driven by greed, possesses a weak council of ministers, and leads a populace that is disloyal and discontented. This enemy is frequently engaged in unjust actions, shows poor character, indulges in unworthy pleasures, and lacks zeal and strategic insight. Their actions are marked by indiscretion, helplessness, and ultimately cause harm to themselves and those they lead. Such an enemy is feeble and thus easily overthrown, for they are already weakened from within.

- Apart from the enemy, these seven elements—each possessing the ideal qualities described—are regarded as the essential limbs of sovereignty.
- A wise king has the capability to uplift and transform even the weakest, poorest, and most troubled parts of his sovereignty into ones that are thriving and content. Conversely, a ruler with wicked intentions and poor judgment will undoubtedly ruin even the most prosperous, loyal, and stable elements of his kingdom.
- Therefore, a king who lacks integrity and engages in corrupt habits, regardless of his power or status as an emperor, will inevitably face downfall, either through the uprising of his own people or at the hands of his enemies.
- On the other hand, a wise and politically astute king, even one ruling over a modest territory, can harness the strength of these essential elements to extend his influence across the entire earth, securing victories without experiencing defeat.
- [Thus, ends Chapter I "The Elements of Sovereignty" in Book VI, "The Source of Sovereign States" of the Arthasástra of Kautilya. End of the ninety-seventh chapter from the beginning.]

CHAPTER II. CONCERNING PEACE AND EXERTION.

The acquisition and safeguarding of property rely on the stability of peace and the vigor of industry.

Industry, or vyayama, is the effort put forth to accomplish the goals of any undertaking. Peace, on the other hand, is the condition where the results of these efforts are enjoyed without disruption. Together, peace and industry are secured through the wise application of six-fold royal policy.

Positions in sovereignty can experience three possible states: deterioration, stagnation, or progress. These states are influenced by both human and providential causes. Human-driven influences are represented by policy (naya) and impolicy (apanaya), while fortune (aya) and misfortune (anaya) reflect the providential.

Providential events are those that are unforeseen; fortune here is described as the attainment of a sought-after outcome that once seemed unreachable. Human causes are those anticipated or driven by foresight; when goals are reached as anticipated, they are the result of good policy. Impolicy, on the other hand, brings harmful outcomes, which can sometimes be foreseen, while providential misfortunes are entirely beyond foresight.

The conqueror is the king whose good character and well-composed sovereignty make him the source of wise policy. The king situated immediately on the boundary of the conqueror's land is termed the enemy, while the king lying just beyond the enemy, separated from the conqueror only by the enemy, is called the friend of the conqueror.

An adversary of nearby and substantial strength is an enemy, and he becomes vulnerable when facing hardship or when he has strayed into corrupt actions. Such an enemy becomes susceptible to attack when he lacks support, but if equipped with some assistance, he is only subject to harassment or weakening. These various states represent different approaches to an enemy.

In front of the conqueror and in proximity to the enemy, other kings are aligned: first, the conqueror's friend; next, the enemy's ally; followed by the conqueror's friend's friend, and finally, the ally of the enemy's friend.

Behind the conqueror's position are situated a rearward enemy (parshnigraha), a rearward friend (akranda), the ally of the rearward enemy (parshnigrahasara), and the ally of the rearward friend (akrandasara).

A rival of equal noble lineage, positioned directly beside the conqueror, is regarded as a natural enemy, while one who opposes the conqueror indirectly by stirring up antagonism and creating adversaries is considered an artificial, or factitious, enemy.

A king who has inherited a long-standing alliance, established by his forefathers and situated next to the territory of the conqueror's immediate adversary, is a natural ally. On the other hand, an ally whose friendship is based primarily on self-preservation and security is regarded as an acquired friend.

The king whose territory lies between both the conqueror and his primary enemy, and who is strong enough to assist either side in unity or in separation, or to resist either one independently, is called the Madhyama or mediatory king.

Beyond the reach of these local powers lies a more distant, highly powerful king capable of extending support or opposition to the conqueror, his enemy, or the Madhyama king, either individually or collectively. This figure, wielding considerable influence, is known as the neutral king (udasina). Together, these roles comprise the twelve primary kings within the geopolitical framework.

A "Circle of States" includes the conqueror, his friend, and the friend of that friend, forming a triplet of primary kings. Each of these kings has five foundational elements of sovereignty—namely, a trusted minister, a secure country, a fortified stronghold, a wealthy treasury, and a capable army. In this arrangement, a single Circle of States contains eighteen primary elements. Similarly, other circles are structured with different central figures, such as the conqueror's enemy, the Madhyama king, or the neutral king, thereby forming three additional Circles of States, each with its distinct configuration.

Altogether, these formations create four essential Circles of States, composed of twelve primary kings, sixty sovereign elements, and a combined seventy-two elements of statecraft and governance.

Each of the twelve kings in these Circles must be considered with regard to their sovereignty, strength, and ultimate objectives. Here, strength represents power, and happiness is seen as the end goal of sovereignty.

Strength is classified into three types: first, intellectual strength, which is rooted in wisdom and careful planning; second, the strength of sovereignty, represented by a well-funded treasury and a robust army; and third, physical strength, which is manifest through martial prowess and combat capability.

The end of statecraft is similarly divided into three kinds: the end of deliberation, achieved through wise counsel and planning; the end of sovereignty, attained by leveraging the power of governance; and the end of martial power, secured through steadfast perseverance and military force.

A king's standing is determined by the extent of his power and his capacity for ensuring happiness: if he possesses both in greater measure than another, he is deemed superior; if in lesser measure, he is inferior; and if equal, he stands on par. Thus, a wise king must always strive to enhance his power and elevate his state's happiness to gain advantage over rivals.

A king whose elements of sovereignty are on par with those of his enemy should utilize his righteous conduct and the influence of allies or those hostile to his enemy to eclipse his opponent's power. Alternatively, he may assess the potential for his enemy's self-undoing, contemplating: "Though my enemy may have great power now, his own actions—such as using harsh language, imposing severe penalties, and mismanaging wealth—will likely damage his rule. Even if he achieves some short-term victories, he may succumb to his own vices, such as indulging in excessive hunting, gambling, drinking, or women. If his subjects are already discontented, he may become weak and arrogant, making him vulnerable to my advance."

The conqueror may also consider the likelihood of his enemy retreating, thinking, "Should he be attacked, my enemy might flee with his resources to a fort or remote area. Though his army is strong, his lack of loyal friends or a secure fortification may still render him vulnerable to my strategies."

Furthermore, if a distant king is eager to subdue his own rival and would also support my cause in defeating this enemy when my resources are stretched, then it may be strategic for me to momentarily permit my enemy to consolidate his strength and enjoy temporary success, anticipating future opportunities. In situations where I am called upon to act as a Madhyama king or mediating force, I can better position myself to take advantage of my opponent's vulnerabilities as they unfold.

- By extending the boundaries of his Circle of States to encompass his friend's lands, the conqueror can align the neighboring kings as the spokes of this circle, positioning himself firmly as its central axis. This arrangement places the conqueror at the heart of a network, directing influence outward with the support of allies.

- An enemy who can be weakened or subdued will, when situated between the conqueror and his allied friend, seem to gather power, yet this apparent growth in strength is merely a fleeting illusion, as his position is strategically vulnerable within the conqueror's expanding circle.

Book 7

CHAPTER I. THE SIX-FOLD POLICY, AND DETERMINATION OF DETERIORATION, STAGNATION AND PROGRESS.

The Circle of States serves as the foundation for six principal forms of strategy in statecraft, shaping how rulers interact with allies, enemies, and those they govern. My teacher identifies these six forms as peace (sandhi), war (vigraha), neutrality (ásana), preparations for conflict (yána), alliance (samsraya), and a combined approach involving peace with one side and war with another, often referred to as a double policy (dvaidhíbháva). However, Vátavyádhi posits that all six ultimately derive from two fundamental strategies—peace and war—as each of the six approaches originates from these two primary forms of statecraft. In contrast, Kautilya holds that these six approaches, given their unique functions and respective applications, merit individual recognition as distinct strategies.

Each of these six forms of policy has a particular purpose. Peace involves agreements and assurances to avoid conflict, while war comprises offensive measures and direct confrontation. Neutrality is a stance of non-engagement, whereby the ruler refrains from favoring any side in a conflict. Marching or making preparations involves mobilizing resources and readiness to engage in conflict should circumstances require it. Alliance signifies reliance on a stronger power for protection and support. Lastly, a double policy allows a ruler to maintain peace with one faction while pursuing conflict with another. Together, these six forms offer a range of choices for navigating complex relationships with other states.

Each form of policy is best suited to a specific situation. A ruler who finds himself weaker than an adversary should seek peace to avoid unnecessary losses. Conversely, a ruler confident in his superior strength may consider war as a means to expand his influence. When a king believes he is neither vulnerable to threats nor capable of overcoming his enemy, neutrality provides a safe course. A ruler with abundant resources and an advantageous position may decide to march forward and assert dominance over a foe. A ruler lacking sufficient power to protect himself may best secure his survival by aligning with a stronger ally, while a king who sees strategic merit in supporting one side and opposing another may choose the double policy, balancing peace with one ally while confronting a shared adversary. Each of these forms serves a distinct role, allowing a ruler to respond with flexibility to a variety of circumstances.

A wise king will select whichever policy aligns best with his goals, enabling him to construct fortifications, improve infrastructure, establish roads, expand agriculture, found new settlements, exploit mineral and forest resources, and hinder similar developments by his enemies. When a king observes his strength increasing in both quality and quantity faster than that of his adversary, he may temporarily ignore his rival's attempts to advance, knowing that his own growth will soon outpace the competition.

If two rival kings find themselves progressing toward their respective goals at an equal rate, they may see mutual benefit in negotiating peace. In contrast, no ruler should engage in any strategy that brings about a reduction in his own gains without producing an equivalent disadvantage for his enemy. Such a situation leads to deterioration and risks weakening his own kingdom over time. However, if the king foresees that his temporary losses will be offset by future gains that ultimately surpass his rival's, he may accept minor setbacks to secure a longer-term advantage.

When two rulers, though facing difficulties, anticipate an equal benefit in the future, they, too, may find peace preferable to prolonged conflict. The state in which neither growth nor decline is evident, where the kingdom neither advances nor recedes, is termed stagnation, a condition that a wise ruler will seek to avoid, ensuring that his policies and efforts always serve to strengthen and expand his power and influence over time.

Whoever thinks his stagnancy to be of a shorter duration and his prosperity in the long run to be greater than his enemy's may neglect his temporary stagnation.

My teacher says that if any two kings, who are hostile to each other and are in a stationary condition expect to acquire equal amount of wealth and power in equal time, they shall make peace with each other.

"Of course," says Kautilya, "there is no other alternative."

Or if a king thinks:--

"That keeping the agreement of peace, I can undertake productive works of considerable importance and destroy at the same time those of my enemy; or apart from enjoying the results of my own works, I shall also enjoy those of my enemy in virtue of the agreement of peace; or I can destroy the works of my enemy by employing spies and other secret means; or by holding out such inducements as a happy dwelling, rewards, remission of taxes, little work and large profits and wages, I can empty my enemy's country of its population, with which he has been able to carry his own works; or being allied with a king of considerable power, my enemy will have his own works destroyed; or I can prolong my enemy's hostility with another king whose threats have driven my enemy to seek my protection; or being allied with me, my enemy can harass the country of another king who hates me; or oppressed by another king, the subjects of my enemy will immigrate into my country, and I can, therefore, achieve the results of my own works very easily; or being in a precarious condition due to the destruction of his works, my enemy will not be so powerful as to attack me; or by exploiting my own resources in alliance with any two (friendly) kings, I can augment my resources; or if a Circle of States is formed by my enemy as one of its members, I can divide them and combine with the others; or by threats or favour, I can catch hold of my enemy, and when he desires to be a member of my own Circle of States, I can make him incur the displeasure of the other members. and fall a victim to their own fury,"--if a king thinks thus, then he may increase his resources by keeping peace.

Or if a king considers:

"My land is naturally well-defended with mountains, forests, rivers, and strategically placed forts with only one secure entrance, and it is populated with experienced soldiers and established groups of fighters. Therefore, it can easily repel any assault from my enemy. Or, by positioning myself within my stronghold at the border, I can effectively hinder my enemy's efforts. Additionally, internal conflicts and diminished morale may soon weaken my enemy, causing his projects to fail on their own. Or, should he face an attack from another ruler, I could encourage his people to migrate to my land." With such thoughts, he might decide to maintain open hostilities to expand his resources at the enemy's expense.

Alternatively, a king might reason:

"My enemy lacks the strength to disrupt my undertakings, just as I am not strong enough to damage his. Even if he attempts an attack, he will suffer greatly, like a dog fighting a boar, while my resources remain intact." In this case, the king could maintain neutrality, confident that his resources would grow as his enemy weakens himself.

Or, a king might think:

"By mobilizing my army, I could successfully damage my enemy's enterprises, and I have solid arrangements to protect my own." This would allow him to increase his resources by moving forward with a campaign.

Yet, if a king concludes:

"I am not strong enough either to weaken my enemy's efforts or to shield my own resources against his attacks," he would be wise to seek protection from a more powerful ruler, aiming to improve his condition gradually, moving from deterioration to stability, and from stability to advancement.

Finally, a king might assess:

"By forming an alliance with one ruler, I can continue strengthening my own resources, while engaging in warfare with another enables me to hinder my enemy's progress." This would allow him to follow a dual policy of selective peace and war, thereby enhancing his resources and strategic influence.

- • Therefore, a king within the circle of sovereign states should utilize the six-fold policy with strategic wisdom, aiming to transition his kingdom from a state of decline to stability and, from there, towards a state of flourishing progress.

[Thus ends Chapter I, "The Six-fold Policy and Determination of Deterioration, Stagnation and Progress" in Book VII, "The end of the Six-fold Policy" of the Arthasástra of Kautilya. End of the ninety-ninth chapter from the beginning.]

CHAPTER II. THE NATURE OF ALLIANCE.

When the benefits of peace and war are evenly matched, peace should be chosen, as the disadvantages—such as loss of strength, wealth depletion, prolonged absence from home, and moral repercussions—are always linked to war.

This principle also applies when comparing neutrality with war. Between dual policy (pursuing peace with one while engaging in war with another) and alliance, dual policy is preferable; for by adopting dual policy, a king can strengthen his position while remaining focused on his own objectives, whereas a king in an alliance is bound to support his ally at his own expense.

An alliance should be formed with a king stronger than the neighboring adversary; if such a king is unavailable, then it is wise to foster goodwill with the neighboring enemy. This can be achieved through strategic support, either financially, militarily, or by ceding a portion of territory while maintaining a cautious distance. For kings, there is no greater danger than forming an alliance with a considerably powerful king, except in situations where an enemy is actively attacking.

A king without strength should adopt the stance of a defeated ruler towards his closest enemy. However, when signs of his own rising influence become evident—such as his enemy's vulnerability due to severe illness, internal strife, the growth of other enemies, or misfortune affecting a friend of the enemy—then he can find a reason to free himself from subordination. For example, he could feign a need for ritual purification to protect his enemy from impending calamity, using it as an opportunity to escape the enemy's court. If in his own lands, he should avoid contact with his ailing foe, and if in close proximity, he may seize the chance to eliminate the enemy whenever circumstances allow.

A king positioned between two powerful neighboring rulers should seek protection from the stronger of the two or align with the one he finds most trustworthy. Alternatively, he may establish peace with both on equal terms and then work to create rivalry between them, telling each that the other is a threat whose tyranny could lead to their downfall, thus sowing discord. Once divided, he may try to subdue each of them separately using secretive or indirect methods.

If necessary, he may seek refuge with two nearby kings of significant power, allowing them to help him counter an immediate enemy. He could also forge an alliance with a leader fortified in a stronghold, adopting a dual strategy—making peace with one king while waging war with the other. Alternatively, he may adapt his actions based on the changing dynamics of peace and war, acting as circumstances dictate. Aligning himself with traitors, adversaries, and tribal chiefs plotting against both neighboring kings could also prove advantageous.

Pretending to be closely allied with one of the kings, he might exploit the other's vulnerabilities by employing the help of enemies and tribal forces. Forming a Circle of States by befriending both kings is another option. Alternatively, he could ally with a mediating king or a neutral ruler, using their support to overpower one or even both of the neighboring kings. Should both kings cause him harm, he may seek the protection of a just and righteous king, whether from the mediating, neutral, or allied circles. This protector should be one whose subjects are loyal and support the ruler's happiness and peace, someone who can help him regain his lost standing, who shares a historical or familial bond with his ancestors, and in whose realm he can rely on numerous powerful allies.

- When faced with two powerful kings who are friendly with one another, a ruler should establish an alliance with the one he both favors and who favors him in return. This mutual preference and goodwill form the most reliable basis for forging a strong and beneficial alliance.

[Thus ends Chapter II, "The Nature of Alliance" in Book VII, "The end of the Six-fold Policy" of the Arthasástra of Kautilya. End of the hundredth chapter from the beginning.]

CHAPTER III. THE CHARACTER OF EQUAL, INFERIOR AND SUPERIOR KINGS; AND FORMS OF AGREEMENT MADE BY AN INFERIOR KING.

A king who seeks to expand his own power should apply the six-fold policy carefully.

Agreements of peace should be made with those kings of equal or superior strength, while a weaker king may be engaged in battle. A king who wages war against one much stronger will be as vulnerable as a foot-soldier challenging an elephant, risking inevitable defeat. Similarly, when two kings of equal power clash, the outcome is likely to damage both, just as two clay pots striking each other would break. In contrast, when a stronger king confronts a weaker one, the outcome resembles a stone shattering an earthen pot, ensuring the stronger king's victory.

If a stronger king dismisses a weaker one's proposal for peace, the lesser king should adopt the stance of a vassal, showing humility as a subordinate before a superior. But when two kings of equal might resist peace, then one should return to the other the same level of opposition he has received, since peace between two equals only emerges when they possess comparable strength. As iron can only meld with iron when heated, so too does equal force forge harmony between kings.

When a weaker king shows complete submission, peace should be granted; for an overly troubled or angered lesser king, much like an uncontrolled fire, may retaliate fiercely and find support from nearby allies. If a king perceives that his ally's subjects, despite being overtaxed and impoverished, have not yet fled to his own domain due to fear of being called back, he may choose, even with limited strength, to challenge his ally openly. Likewise, if a king locked in battle with another observes that the suffering populace of his enemy does not rally to him due to the hardships of war, he should, though stronger, consider peace or lessen the burdens of conflict.

When two kings are equally matched in battle and one sees his difficulties as more severe than his opponent's, realizing that resolving his enemy's issues might lead to an increased threat, he should seek peace despite his resources. If a king experiences neither harm to his rival nor benefit to himself, he should adopt a stance of neutrality, even if he holds an advantage.

Lastly, if a king assesses his enemy's problems as impossible to fix, he may advance against that foe, confident of victory, regardless of his own inferior power.

When a king perceives himself beset by impending dangers or significant troubles, he should, despite his superior strength, seek the protection of another for stability. If he recognizes that his goals can be best met by forming peace with one ruler while engaging in conflict with another, he should—even with greater power—adopt a dual strategy, balancing both alliance and opposition.

In this way, the six forms of state policy come into play, each used in combination as circumstances demand.

Now, as for their specific application:

- When a king of lesser power finds himself under attack by a stronger ruler leading a Circle of States, he should humbly seek peace by offering resources such as treasure, troops, himself, or even his land.
- If the agreement includes the condition that a set number of troops or the elite of his army must be presented upon request, this type of peace is called átmámisha, or "offering himself as flesh."
- An agreement where the commander of the army, along with the heir-apparent, is required to present themselves upon request is termed purushántarasandhi, or "peace with hostages other than the king himself." This type is beneficial for self-preservation since it does not necessitate the king's direct attendance.
- If the terms require that the king himself or another delegate should march with the army to a designated place when needed, it is called adrishtapurusha, or "peace without a specific individual as a representative." This arrangement contributes to the safety of both the king and the principal commanders of his army.
- In the first two forms of peace, a woman of status may be given as a pledge, while in the last form, there should be a

covert plan to seize the enemy. These describe the various peace arrangements that hinge upon the provision of the king's forces.

- When wealth is offered to free the other elements of sovereignty, such peace is known as parikraya, or "price."
- Likewise, when peace is reached by giving an amount of money that can be carried on a person's shoulders, it's termed upagraha, or "subsidy," and this form comes in various arrangements. Due to distance or prolonged storage, sometimes the promised tribute may accrue arrears. Nevertheless, since this type of payment can be reasonably postponed, it's considered preferable to agreements where a woman is given as a pledge.
- When both parties reach peace through amicable union, it's called suvarnasandhi, or "golden peace." The opposite of this is kapála, meaning "half of a pot," a type of peace involving the payment of a vast sum of money.
- In the first two forms, one should provide materials, elephants, horses, and troops; in the third, gold; and in the fourth, one should avoid payment by citing losses incurred from previous efforts. These illustrate types of peace agreements reached through monetary terms.
- When a part of the territory is ceded to keep the rest of the kingdom and its people secure, this is known as ádishta, or "ceded," and benefits a ruler who seeks to rid the ceded area of thieves and other malefactors.
- When the entire territory, excluding the capital and weakened by resource exploitation, is ceded, it's called uchchhinnasandhi, or "peace cut off from profit," which serves a king wishing to bring hardship upon his adversary.
- When freedom for the kingdom is secured by agreeing to pay the produce of the land, this agreement is called avakraya, or "rent." An agreement involving the promise to pay even more than the land produces is known as paribhúshana, or "ornament."
- Among these options, the first is preferable; however, the last

two, which are based on yielding the land's produce, should only be agreed upon when circumstances force one to submit to a stronger power. These illustrate types of peace achieved by ceding territory.

- These three kinds of peace are to be concluded by a lesser king who must yield to the strength of a more powerful ruler due to the specific conditions of his resources, prevailing circumstances, and the timing involved.

[Thus ends Chapter III, "The Character of Equal, Inferior, and Superior Kings; and Forms of Agreement made by an Inferior King" in Book VII, "The end of the Six-fold Policy" of the Arthasástra of Kautilya. End of the hundred and first chapter from the beginning.]

CHAPTER IV. NEUTRALITY AFTER PROCLAIMING WAR OR AFTER CONCLUDING A TREATY OF PEACE; MARCHING AFTER PROCLAIMING WAR OR AFTER MAKING PEACE; AND THE MARCH OF COMBINED POWERS.

Remaining neutral, or deciding to proceed with action only after declaring either peace or war, has been outlined. Sthána (remaining quiet), ásana (withdrawing from hostility), and upekshana (neglect) all align with the concept of ásana, or neutrality. As for the distinctions between these three aspects: Sthána involves remaining steady with a specific policy; ásana is the act of holding back from hostilities to serve one's own interests; and upekshana means taking no steps at all against an opponent.

When two rulers are both interested in extending their power but also desire peace, and neither can advance successfully against the other, they may each decide to maintain a stance of quiet after either declaring war or reaching a peaceful understanding.

When a ruler sees he has the means to defeat an enemy of equal or greater power—either through his own forces, with support from allies, or using wild tribes—then, having fortified his defenses against both internal and external threats, he may decide to remain quiet after declaring a state of war.

When a king is confident that his people are brave, united, and prosperous enough to sustain their own work without interruption, while also able to interfere with the enemy's efforts, he may then choose to stay neutral after declaring war.

Should a ruler recognize that his enemy's subjects are mistreated, impoverished, greedy, and often harassed by hostile armies, thieves, or wild tribes, and might thus be won over through intrigue; or that his own agricultural and commercial sectors are thriving while those of his enemy are dwindling; or that the enemy's people, suffering from famine, might relocate to his own lands; or that, despite any declines in his own agricultural or trade returns and any growth in his enemy's, his people will remain loyal and not defect to the enemy; or that by declaring war he could seize the enemy's grain, cattle, and gold by force; or that he could halt the enemy's damaging trade imports to protect his own economy; or that valuable trade could flow toward his lands instead of the enemy's; or that war would prevent the enemy from dealing with traitors, enemies, wild tribes, and rebels and would lead to conflict among them; or that his own ally would swiftly accumulate wealth without significant losses and would stand by him on his march, since no ally would miss the chance to acquire fertile land and a prosperous ally like himself—then, with a view to weakening his enemy and showcasing his strength, he may choose to stay neutral after proclaiming a state of war.

However, my teacher contends that if a king takes such a passive approach, his enemy might use this opportunity to overpower him.

Kautilya disagrees, saying, "The aim in maintaining quiet after proclaiming war is to weaken the enemy's resources rather than allowing him to grow stronger." He believes that once a king gains enough strength, he will be ready to confront and defeat his enemy. Additionally, any adversary of this enemy will likely support the quiet king to protect their own interests. For this reason, any king with adequate resources may consider staying quiet after proclaiming war.

If this strategy of remaining neutral after declaring war brings about negative results, then switching to neutrality after making peace might be more favorable.

When a king finds his strength bolstered by keeping quiet post-declaration of war, he should consider launching an attack on his enemy.

If a king notices that his enemy has become entangled in difficulties, that these troubles are beyond the enemy's control to fix, and that the enemy's subjects are suffering, mistreated, unhappy, impoverished, or disunited, thus making them prone to deserting their ruler; or that his enemy's land has succumbed to devastating calamities like fire, floods, diseases, epidemics, or famine, weakening its defenses and draining its resources—then it may be time to move forward with an attack after proclaiming war.

If a king is fortunate enough to have a strong ally ahead and a dependable supporter behind him, both with loyal and courageous citizens, while his foes lack these strengths, then he can feel secure in advancing with his powerful ally holding back the enemy in the front and the supporter containing any threats from behind. With these favorable conditions, he can march forward after proclaiming war against the primary enemy ahead.

Should a king see the chance to achieve victory swiftly on his own, he may press on against the main enemy while proclaiming war on those behind him; otherwise, he should secure peace with those rearward enemies before advancing.

If a king feels he cannot confront his enemy alone but finds it necessary to proceed, he should arrange to march with the support of kings of comparable, greater, or lesser power, depending on the needs of his campaign.

For objectives with clearly defined goals, the distribution of spoils should be set in advance; however, if the objective involves numerous or varied targets, the spoils should be divided as circumstances demand. When it's not possible to forge such an alliance, he might request assistance in the form of an army for a fixed portion of the spoils or ask an ally to accompany him, agreeing to an equal share.

If the prospect of gain is highly probable, the shares should be fixed; if uncertain, they should remain flexible.

- A share of profit based on the strength of the army provided is the first approach; assigning shares according to the effort each participant contributes is the most effective. Profits may also be divided in proportion to the success achieved or the resources initially invested.
- [Thus ends Chapter IV, "Neutrality after Proclaiming War or after Concluding a Treaty of Peace; Marching after Proclaiming War or after Making Peace; and the March of Combined Powers," in Book VII, "The end of the Six-fold Policy" of the Arthasástra of Kautilya. End of the hundred and second chapter from the beginning.]

CHAPTER V. CONSIDERATIONS ABOUT MARCHING AGAINST AN ASSAILABLE ENEMY AND A STRONG ENEMY; CAUSES LEADING TO THE DWINDLING, GREED, AND DISLOYALTY OF THE ARMY; AND CONSIDERATIONS ABOUT THE COMBINATION OF POWERS.

If a king has two enemies—one weaker but vulnerable and one stronger, and both are struggling—which one should he attack first?

The stronger enemy should be attacked first. Once this enemy is defeated, the weaker enemy can then be targeted, as this one will likely surrender willingly to the conqueror after seeing the powerful opponent fall. The stronger enemy, however, would never surrender so easily.

Now, if faced with a choice between a weaker enemy in serious trouble or a stronger enemy facing only minor difficulties, which one should the conqueror go after first? My teacher suggests that, for an easier conquest, the vulnerable enemy facing worse troubles should be attacked first.

Kautilya, however, disagrees. He argues that the conqueror should aim for the stronger enemy with minor troubles. Even if the troubles of this stronger enemy are less severe, they will increase under attack. While attacking the weaker enemy may worsen that enemy's troubles, leaving the stronger one alone might allow him to overcome his issues and unite with the weaker enemy or another rival positioned behind the conqueror.

When there are two vulnerable enemies, one known for integrity but facing serious troubles, and another of vicious character facing lighter troubles, but with unfaithful subjects, which one should be attacked first?

If the conqueror attacks the virtuous enemy with serious troubles, that enemy's loyal subjects will likely come to his aid. In contrast, the vicious enemy's subjects—disloyal and unmotivated—will probably not support their ruler. These disloyal subjects could even weaken a strong ruler. For this reason, the conqueror should go after the enemy whose subjects cannot be trusted.

Now, given a choice between an enemy whose subjects are poor and greedy and another whose subjects feel oppressed, which one should he attack first?

My teacher suggests that the conqueror should march against the enemy whose subjects are poor and greedy, as they are more easily won over by schemes and can be quickly stirred up. However, the subjects who feel oppressed are less likely to be swayed and can be calmed by punishing their leaders.

Kautilya disagrees. He argues that, although these subjects may be poor and greedy, they remain loyal to their ruler and will stand firmly by his side, ready to counter any intrigue against him. Loyalty, he notes, is the foundation of all other virtues. Therefore, the conqueror should focus his attack on the enemy whose subjects feel oppressed.

Next, which enemy should be targeted: a powerful but corrupt enemy or a weaker but righteous one? The answer is the powerful enemy with a corrupt nature. When this enemy is attacked, his subjects are unlikely to support him; instead, they may even work against him or join forces with the conqueror. In contrast, if the virtuous enemy is attacked, his subjects will stand by him, or even die with him.

- By disrespecting the virtuous and praising the corrupt; by allowing unjust and unnatural killings to occur;
- by disregarding the observance of moral and just traditions; by engaging in unjust deeds and ignoring just actions;
- by doing things that should be avoided and failing to do what should be done; by withholding rightful payments and demanding what should not be taken;
- by failing to punish the guilty and harshly punishing the less guilty; by arresting the innocent and letting those who should be caught go free;
- by taking on dangerous tasks while neglecting profitable ones; by failing to protect people from thieves and by seizing their wealth;
- by abandoning courageous efforts and discouraging noble deeds; by offending the leaders of the people and looking down upon those who are honorable;
- by disrespecting the elderly, by acting deceitfully and lying; by failing to address issues and neglecting ongoing tasks;
- and by being careless in ensuring the security and welfare of his people and their property, the king fosters poverty, greed, and resentment among his subjects;
- when people are impoverished, they become greedy; when they become greedy, they grow discontented; when discontented, they willingly side with the enemy or turn against their own ruler.

Therefore, no king should allow situations to arise that lead to poverty, greed, or disaffection among his people. If such issues do arise, he must act swiftly to address them.

Of the three—impoverished people, greedy people, or disaffected people—which is the most dangerous?

An impoverished population constantly fears oppression and ruin, whether through excessive taxation or other means, and will naturally seek relief from poverty, support rebellion, or even consider fleeing elsewhere.

A greedy population remains perpetually unsatisfied and is susceptible to enemy manipulation.

A disaffected population will rise against its ruler, especially in collaboration with the enemy.

If the decline in population arises from a lack of resources, such as gold or grain, it signals a kingdom-wide threat and is difficult to resolve. However, a shortage of capable people can be offset by acquiring wealth and supplies. Greed, though limited to a few high-ranking officials, can be resolved or appeased by allowing them to acquire spoils from an enemy. Disaffection or disloyalty can be quelled by eliminating key leaders, as without leadership, the people are more manageable and less likely to be swayed by external enemies. When a population is too fearful to withstand hardships, it may scatter if its leaders are subdued, but when controlled, it can endure difficulties.

After thoroughly assessing the reasons for making peace or engaging in war, a king should form alliances with rulers who are both powerful and of good moral character to act against an enemy.

A "king of considerable power" refers to one who has the strength either to defeat or capture an enemy behind his ally or to offer sufficient support to his ally during a campaign.

A "king of righteous character" is one who remains committed to fulfilling promises, regardless of whether the outcome is favorable or not.

Should the conqueror march with a single, stronger ally or with two allies of equal strength?

It is generally more advantageous to march with two allies of equal strength. If aligned with a superior king, an ally might seem under the influence of that stronger power. Marching with two equally powerful allies allows for flexibility, and should those allies be skilled in tactics, they can be split if necessary. Moreover, if one of these allies proves untrustworthy, the other two can work together to counter any betrayal or discord caused by the third.

Should a king march with a single ally of equal power or two allies of lesser strength?

Marching with two allies of lesser power is preferable; the conqueror can assign different tasks to each, maintaining command over both. Once the primary objective is achieved, the lesser allies are more likely to withdraw respectfully, satisfied by their support for a more dominant partner.

- To ensure the reliable behavior of an ally known for inconsistent character, the conqueror should carefully monitor the ally's conduct until the mission is complete. This can be done by making surprise inspections at critical moments or by securing the ally's loyalty with his family, such as by holding his wife as a pledge.
- Even when genuinely motivated by friendship, a conqueror should exercise caution with an ally of equal power, especially if that ally achieves notable success. Success can often shift an ally's approach, and an ally who feels empowered may alter his stance, even towards a stronger conqueror.
- An ally of greater strength should be trusted with caution since prosperity has the potential to change intentions. Such an ally, even if content with a modest share of the gains, may later take advantage, perhaps even claiming twice what was initially agreed.
- The primary conqueror, pleased with victory, should ensure the fair dismissal of his allies by providing their rightful shares. Rather than competing with them for the rewards, he should be willing to yield when necessary. By doing so, the king can cultivate respect and loyalty from the entire Circle of States.

[Thus ends Chapter V, "Considerations about Marching against an Assailable Enemy and a Strong Enemy; Causes Leading to the Dwindling, Greed, and Disloyalty of the Army; and Considerations about the Combination of Powers" in Book VII, "The end of the Six-fold Policy" of the Arthasástra of Kautilya. End of the hundred and third chapter from the beginning.]

CHAPTER VI. THE MARCH OF COMBINED POWERS; AGREEMENT OF PEACE WITH OR WITHOUT DEFINITE TERMS; AND PEACE WITH RENEGADES.

In this way, the conqueror can effectively manage the second key factor in his strategy: the neighboring enemy. He should prompt his nearby rival to join him in a joint campaign, proposing, "You advance in that direction, and I will move in this direction. We will share the spoils equally."

If the loot is to be shared equally, it represents a peace agreement; if divided otherwise, it signals dominance over the enemy. A peace agreement can either include a clear commitment to achieve a specific goal (paripanita) or have no concrete objectives (aparipanita).

When the agreement specifies, "You proceed to that region, and I shall proceed here," it is a peace agreement aimed at achieving a set objective in a particular location.

If the terms involve, "You remain engaged for this duration, while I remain engaged similarly," it constitutes an agreement with a fixed timeframe.

Where the terms are, "You aim to complete that task, and I will focus on this one," it becomes an agreement to achieve distinct goals.

When the conqueror reasons, "My ally (formerly my rival) must cross unfamiliar terrain filled with mountains, forests, rivers, forts, and deserts, lacking food supplies, inhabitants, grazing areas, firewood, and water, and distant and unlike other lands, making it challenging for his army to operate; while I will travel through a territory offering the complete opposite advantages," he should form an agreement centered on a specific location.

Similarly, if the conqueror considers, "My ally must engage in action without sufficient supplies and endure harsh weather—rainy, hot, or cold seasons—that hinder his forces over an ill-suited period, whereas I can work in ideal conditions," then he should base the agreement on timing.

If the conqueror sees that "my ally's task is temporary and insignificant, irritating his people, consuming excessive time and resources, and potentially causing harm, going against righteousness, alienating the Madhyama and neutral kings, and risking friendships, whereas my task yields opposite results," he should structure the agreement around achieving specific goals.

Additionally, agreements may combine location and time, time and objective, location and objective, or all three elements—location, time, and objective. This approach produces a total of seven possible forms of peace agreements.

Long before making such an agreement, the conqueror has to fix his own work and then attempt to overreach his enemy.

When a peace agreement is made with a hasty, careless, and short-sighted enemy who has fallen into hardship, without specifying exact terms regarding time, location, or objectives—solely for the purpose of mutual peace—the conqueror can exploit the situation to catch the enemy off guard at their weak points. This approach is referred to as peace with no definite terms (aparipanita). An old saying illustrates this strategy:

"By keeping one neighboring enemy entangled with another, a wise king can then turn his attention to a third king. After defeating this third adversary of equal power, he can claim his territory."

There are several additional forms of peace: peace with no specific objective (akritachikírshá), peace with binding conditions (kritasleshana), breaking of peace (kritavidúshana), and the restoration of broken peace (apasírnakriyá).

Battles also come in three varieties: open battle, deceptive battle, and silent battle, in which the enemy is covertly eliminated, without any formal declaration or mention of war.

When a new peace agreement is established using tactics like negotiation, and when the rights of the parties—whether they are equal, inferior, or superior in power—are clearly defined, it is called peace with no specific end, meaning it aims solely for security and stability.

Peace with binding terms occurs when allies secure the agreement by ensuring its conditions are strictly followed, maintaining unity and avoiding any risk of discord.

Breaking of peace arises when, through spies or traitors, proof of the other king's breach of trust or treachery is established, justifying the annulment of the agreement.

Restoration of broken peace refers to the act of reconciling and reinstating cooperation with a servant, ally, or other former member who had defected.

There are four types of those who leave their master and later return: the first has a reason both for leaving and returning; the second has no reason for either; the third has a reason for leaving but none for returning; and the fourth has no reason for leaving, but a reason to come back.

Anyone who left due to the master's own shortcomings and returns upon recognizing the master's good character or realizing flaws in the enemy's kindness is to be accepted back. Such a person, after weighing his circumstances, has legitimate reasons both for leaving and returning. Recognizing the value of this judgment, he should be reconciled and welcomed, as his return signals respect for the master's virtues or a desire to amend past misjudgments.

If a person deserted because of his own failings and returns without regard for the kindness or merits of either his old or new master, he shows a lack of loyalty and stability. This type of fickle behavior, coupled with the absence of a compelling reason for his actions, indicates he does not merit the trust or forgiveness of reconciliation, as his unpredictable nature could disrupt the harmony within the court.

A person who abandoned his master due to the master's faults but returned out of his own inadequacies or difficulties should be considered a deserter. Since he had a reason to leave but not a genuine reason to return, his motives must be thoroughly scrutinized. Welcoming back someone in this category should be approached cautiously, ensuring the interests of the court are not compromised by one who left only to return in unfavorable circumstances.

In the case of one who returns under the influence of the enemy or with intentions of undermining his former master, the situation requires a meticulous examination. This person may harbor ill will toward his former master, either through natural inclination or by fear of retribution, should the former master regain power over his current master. Additionally, he may return after realizing that his new master's aims might be harmful or ruthless, reflecting his apprehension for his own safety. Such individuals need careful scrutiny. If their motives are honest, they should be welcomed respectfully; if not, it is best to keep them at a distance to protect the court from potential harm.

Individuals who left of their own fault but returned due to the cruelty or ill nature of their new master should be considered deserters who had no valid reason to leave initially but developed a legitimate reason to return. Their actions suggest they are more likely to follow a leader of good character, and such individuals require careful assessment to determine their loyalty before any decision is made regarding their return.

If a king determines, "This deserter brings me valuable information about my enemy's weaknesses, is aligned with my allies, and can be easily rallied against cruel and corrupt figures or groups," he may deem this individual worthy of trust and retain him as an asset within his service. Such a person's awareness of enemy flaws and potential usefulness could outweigh concerns about his past desertion.

My teacher advises that any person who has failed to achieve results in his duties, weakened in strength, sought personal gain from his skills instead of devotion, was driven by greed, overly inquisitive about foreign lands, indifferent to the bonds of friendship, or entangled with strong enemies, should be disregarded. Such individuals are considered unfit for service as they lack the virtues required for steadfast loyalty and allegiance to the court.

However, Kautilya counters this view, suggesting that abandoning individuals for these reasons shows timidity, poor management, and lack of patience in discerning true potential. He proposes that only those who pose harm to the king's interests should be removed, while those who threaten the enemy's interests could be useful allies. If an individual's actions seem harmful to both parties, then a thorough investigation should precede any decision.

- In situations where peace with an otherwise unworthy king becomes necessary, the conqueror must establish defenses at points where his power might pose a risk. By fortifying vulnerable positions, the conqueror can ensure that his interests are protected while still maintaining an alliance of convenience.

- To restore broken peace, a renegade or anyone showing sympathy toward the enemy should be kept at a strategic distance, where they remain valuable to the state but are not a direct threat. This positioning allows the state to utilize the renegade's skills or influence while minimizing risks, ensuring he contributes to the state until the end of his life.

- Alternatively, such an individual could be directed to oppose the enemy directly, perhaps as a captain of the army responsible for guarding remote or wild areas vulnerable to enemy incursions. Placing him in a boundary role serves both as an act of control and as a practical use of his skills, keeping him from the heart of state affairs.

- Another option might involve sending him on missions to engage in discreet trade dealings involving either new or old goods in foreign territories. This covert operation, intended to keep him preoccupied with complex overseas dealings, could later be used as a means to accuse him of conspiracy with the enemy, should the need arise.

- In cases where the future peace of the state absolutely requires it, a renegade deemed dangerous may be removed without delay. Swift, decisive action can neutralize any further threats that he might pose, preventing long-term repercussions.

- A deeply ingrained, wicked nature that has developed from ongoing association with enemies is as hazardous as the untrustworthy presence of a snake close by. Just as a pigeon feeding on the seeds of the plaksha (holy fig-tree) endangers the salmali (silk-cotton) tree by threatening its habitat, so too does a person of a corrupt nature continuously menace the peace and safety of the state.

- When battle is waged openly in broad daylight and within a specific location, it is classified as open battle. However, strategies that involve pretending to attack from one direction while planning an assault from another, or capturing and eliminating an enemy when he is least prepared or when he is already troubled, fall under the category of treacherous combat.

- Treachery also includes bribing a section of the enemy's army while methodically destroying another section. Meanwhile, silent warfare is characterized by cunning efforts to sway the principal officers of the enemy's forces through subtle intrigue, rather than direct confrontation. This tactic undermines the enemy's structure from within, silently destabilizing their power.

[Thus ends Chapter VI, "The March of Combined Powers; Agreement of Peace with or without Definite Terms; and Peace with Renegades," in Book VII, "The end of the Six-fold Policy" of the Arthasástra of Kautilya. End of the hundred and fourth chapter from the beginning.]

CHAPTER VII. PEACE AND WAR BY ADOPTING THE DOUBLE POLICY.

The conqueror can outmaneuver his closest enemy as follows:

By forming an alliance with a neighboring king, the conqueror can initiate a campaign against another nearby ruler. If the conqueror anticipates that the enemy will not target his rear nor join forces with any vulnerable foe he intends to attack, he considers himself safe from facing unfavorable odds. In this arrangement, the ally not only aids in gathering revenue and resources but also suppresses any internal dissidents troubling the conqueror, deals with wild tribes and their strongholds, and destabilizes the targeted enemy, either pushing them toward a vulnerable state or forcing them into a peace agreement. Moreover, the ally, once satisfied with his share of benefits, may even assist in converting other potential foes of the conqueror into friendly entities. In this way, the conqueror can declare war on one adversary while making peace with another, securing either military support through funds or financial backing to support his army from neighboring kings.

When kings of varying strength—superior, equal, or inferior—agree to an alliance with the conqueror and provide him with armies or wealth in amounts directly proportional to the strength they lend, this arrangement is known as an "even peace." Conversely, if the contributions differ from what the situation demands, this is called "uneven peace," and if the contributions are particularly advantageous to one side, it is termed "deceptive peace" or "atisandhi."

When a powerful king finds himself beset by challenges or unfortunate events, a weaker king may propose an arrangement where the powerful king lends military support in exchange for a portion of the profits, proportional to the strength he contributes. Should the more powerful king find such terms insulting or opportunistic, he may respond with an act of war; otherwise, he might agree to the arrangement if it serves his interests.

In another instance, a weaker king, intending to strengthen his own resources and revenue, may approach a stronger ruler for military assistance to secure his rear and protect his home territories during his campaign, offering a larger share of the profits than the strength of the army lent would usually warrant. If the superior king considers the weaker ruler sincere, he may accept the proposal; however, if suspicions arise, he might instead initiate a counterattack.

A weaker king, who is fortified with defensive strongholds and alliances, may need to make a brief advance to capture an enemy or secure a valuable prize without an all-out battle. In this situation, he may seek assistance from a more powerful but troubled ally, proposing a smaller profit share than the worth of the army provided would usually justify. If the stronger ruler feels disrespected or sees an opportunity, he may retaliate, but if he sees the benefit, he may instead accept the offer and provide his support.

When a powerful king, who is unburdened by any troubles, wishes to bring about losses in men and resources to his enemy through that enemy's unwise actions, or intends to send his own army abroad under the guise of assistance, or aims to entangle his enemy in a conflict with a hostile force, or to stir up troubles for a vulnerable and weakened enemy by setting an inferior king against him, or if he genuinely desires peace for its own sake with sincere intentions, he may agree to accept a smaller portion of the profit (in exchange for providing an army to another). This way, he gains financially through his alliance, assuming his ally shares his good intentions; otherwise, he may simply declare war on the ally.

A king may also deceive or support an equal in the following ways:

When a king offers peace to an equal in strength, with a condition that he receives that ally's army—one strong enough to counter a rival force, or to secure his territory's front, center, and rear, or to protect his friend, or to defend any other vulnerable region of his land—in exchange for a profit share proportional to the army's strength, the latter king may accept if he believes the offer is sincere. Otherwise, he may resort to war.

When an equal in power, who has access to an alternate military force, seeks an ally's army due to weakened sovereignty and multiple threats, and requests this in return for a smaller share of profit than the contribution deserves, the stronger ally may reject the request or accept it if necessary.

When a king, currently under duress, with his plans vulnerable to the ambitions of nearby rulers, and who is still gathering his forces, seeks assistance from an equal in strength, offering a larger share of profit than the army's worth warrants, his ally may choose to assist him if the proposal appears genuine. If not, a declaration of war remains a possibility.

Moreover, if a king wishes to weaken a rival king who is already struggling due to diminished resources, or to ruin his otherwise highly profitable ventures, or if he plans to strike when the rival is within reach or during a campaign, he may increase demands on an assailable rival (whether that rival is equal, inferior, or even superior in power) by repeatedly requesting aid. The targeted king may agree to these demands if he believes doing so will help him preserve his power by using the ally's army to destroy an enemy's stronghold or pillage an ally of the enemy, or to devastate that enemy's outlying territories. Alternatively, he may use his ally's forces to strengthen his own through their exposure to battles in favorable conditions, thereby positioning himself to either subdue his ally or persuade the ally's army to his side.

When a king wishes to control another king, whether stronger or weaker, by holding him as an assailable enemy to be overpowered later, especially after utilizing his help to defeat a third opponent, or if he wants to reclaim funds previously paid out (like subsidies), he may propose a peace agreement to that king with terms offering to pay more than the cost of his army. If the king receiving this proposal is strong enough to retaliate, he may respond with a declaration of war; if he is not as powerful, he may either accept the terms or choose to remain allied with the assailable enemy instead. Alternatively, he could offer troops filled with traitors, hostile elements, and unpredictable forces.

When a king of greater power finds himself in trouble due to weakened resources or allies and seeks assistance from a lesser king's army, offering a profit share equal to the value of the troops provided, the lesser king, if he has the strength to resist, might declare war; otherwise, he might agree to the proposal.

Similarly, a stronger king might ask a weaker king for troops in return for a profit share less than the cost of the army provided. The weaker king, if powerful enough to oppose this, may opt to declare war; if not, he may simply accept the terms as they are.

- Both the king being approached for peace and the king proposing peace should carefully evaluate the intentions behind the peace proposal. After considering the potential benefits and outcomes, each should decide on the course of action that promises the most favorable results.

[Thus ends Chapter VII "Peace and War by Adopting the Double Policy" in Book VII, "The end of the Six-fold Policy" of the Arthasástra of Kautilya. End of the hundred and fifth chapter from the beginning.]

CHAPTER VIII. THE ATTITUDE OF AN ASSAILABLE ENEMY; AND FRIENDS THAT DESERVE HELP.

If an assailable enemy at risk of being attacked wishes to assume the conditions that led two kings to ally against him or to drive a wedge between them, he may propose peace to one of these kings by offering twice the profit expected from their current alliance. Once an agreement is reached, the enemy can then emphasize the toll of war, such as the loss of men and wealth, the difficulty of fighting abroad, the moral consequences, and the personal hardships that the king would otherwise endure. If the king accepts this reasoning, the promised amount may be paid, or the agreement may be dissolved by sowing distrust between that king and other rulers.

If a king's objective is to see his ally suffer loss in a poorly planned venture, to disrupt a rival's successful enterprises, or to strike his enemy while he's off-guard or on the march, he may agree to take only a small gain for now and plan to ask for additional support later, potentially in alliance with the vulnerable enemy's foe.

When a king's primary aim is to support a friend, to weaken an adversary, or to secure substantial returns down the line by ensuring his ally's success now, he may be wise to set aside the offer of immediate profit in favor of smaller, future gains from his ally.

In cases where a king wishes to defend his ally from internal conspirators, other enemies, or a stronger ruler who threatens his ally's survival, and he hopes to set a precedent for reciprocal aid in the future, he may take no present or future compensation.

However, if a king intends to undermine an enemy's subjects, disrupt an ally's peace, or break an alliance due to suspicion of betrayal or pending attacks, he may preemptively demand a larger payment than usual. Under these circumstances, his ally may request a delay or installment plan, either now or later, which can also apply to prior situations discussed.

The conqueror and his rival each support their allies based on how steadfast and loyal those allies are, how feasible and beneficial their projects seem, and the dedication of their subjects to these causes.

Whoever undertakes a feasible task begins a manageable endeavor; whoever starts a task that is unblemished by poor reputation begins a commendable project; whoever initiates a task promising substantial returns begins a profitable effort; and whoever remains dedicated without rest until the task is completed shows true resolve. The one who enjoys loyal, devoted subjects has the advantage of securing assistance and seeing any project through to success without risking his favor or influence. Friends with these qualities, when won over by the conqueror or his enemy, provide immense support. Friends who lack these qualities, however, should not be aided.

Between two kings—the conqueror and his rival—who share the same ally, the king who supports a truly loyal friend has the upper hand. By supporting a genuine ally, he not only strengthens his position but avoids the losses of men, resources, and the strains of campaigning abroad. Meanwhile, the other king, who may inadvertently aid an ungrateful rival, risks wasting resources and even emboldening an enemy who resents any perceived favoritism.

If the conqueror and his rival both find an ally in the same mediatory (Madhyama) king, the one who assists a loyal and genuine friend gains an advantage. Helping a trustworthy ally brings mutual benefit and security, while the other king risks losing resources, enduring the burdens of distant ventures, and inadvertently empowering a resentful enemy. However, when the Madhyama king is unreliable and misuses assistance, investing his energies in futile endeavors and providing little in return, the rival gains an edge over the conqueror.

This principle equally applies to a neutral king under the same conditions.

In situations where a king considers aiding either a Madhyama or a neutral king with part of his army, it's wise to discern the ally's qualities carefully. If the king chooses to support an ally who is courageous, adept with weapons, resilient, and genuinely loyal, he may unintentionally put himself at risk, especially if his enemy, by contrast, supports someone with opposing, less dependable qualities—allowing the enemy to gain a strategic advantage.

When a king successfully accomplishes an objective with the aid of a friend who expects future military assistance in return, he may select among his different types of armies—be it his own hereditary army, hired forces, a collective army of regional groups, his ally's troops, or an army of wild tribes. He should consider sending those troops that are well-prepared for diverse terrains and seasons or, alternatively, select forces such as those from an enemy or wild tribes located far enough to avoid immediate repercussions.

If the king suspects his ally might misuse his forces by deploying them into hazardous or hostile regions, unfavorable wilderness, or during challenging seasons that would weaken his own military, he could defer sending his troops, citing other pressing uses for them, and instead offer assistance by other means. However, if he must lend his army, he should send only units accustomed to the prevailing conditions, ensuring they'll remain stationed until the ally's objective is fulfilled and that they'll be protected from undue risk. When his ally's task is completed, the king should seek a valid reason to recall his troops. Alternatively, he might send forces filled with those harboring animosity, traitors, or wild tribes—forces potentially unreliable to the ally—or, by establishing a truce with the ally's vulnerable enemy, subtly undermine the alliance.

- When all kings involved in an agreement, regardless of whether they hold equal, lesser, or greater power, gain an equal benefit from the alliance, this arrangement is known as peace (sandhi). However, if the benefit gained is uneven, with one party profiting less than others, it is regarded as defeat (vikrama). This principle defines the nature of peace and war.
- [Thus ends Chapter VIII, "The Attitude of an Assailable Enemy; and Friends that Deserve Help," in Book VII, "The end of the Six-fold Policy" of the Arthasástra of Kautilya. End of the hundred and sixth chapter from the beginning.]

CHAPTER IX. AGREEMENT FOR THE ACQUISITION OF A FRIEND OR GOLD.

Among the three gains—gaining a friend, acquiring gold, and securing territory—which result from the march of allied forces, the gain mentioned last is more valuable than the previous ones. Territory is prioritized since it can enable the acquisition of both friends and wealth. Between the acquisition of a friend and that of gold, each can be used to obtain the other, and both hold their distinct advantages.

An agreement made on the terms "let us gain a friend," for instance, is known as even peace. If one party acquires a friend while the other is left with an adversary, this is seen as uneven peace, and if one side benefits more significantly than the other, it is viewed as deception. In the case of even peace, the one who gains a friend of strong character or assists an old friend out of difficulties is ultimately the greater beneficiary, for support given in challenging times strengthens the friendship.

Now, of the two—an enduring but somewhat unyielding friend or a more recent, submissive ally, each secured by helping them in difficult times—which is preferable? My teacher believes a long-standing friend of independent nature is better, as they may not be as supportive but will also not cause harm. However, Kautilya argues that a recent friend who shows submissive qualities is better, as such a friend is more likely to provide meaningful help when needed; for, after all, the essence of friendship lies in assistance.

When comparing two equally loyal friends—one a new ally with substantial resources and potential for mutual gain, and the other a long-standing ally with limited resources—my teacher asserts that a new friend with ample resources is preferable because such a friend can offer significant support swiftly and help sustain larger ventures. Kautilya, however, disagrees, favoring the long-standing friend of more limited means. He argues that a new, wealthy friend might waver in their loyalty if they encounter significant material loss from their help or might seek a reciprocal arrangement. Meanwhile, a loyal, enduring friend, even if less resourceful, will provide sustained support over the long term due to the strength of the long-established relationship.

Which is preferable: a powerful but slow-to-respond ally, or a smaller, more responsive ally? My teacher suggests that a powerful ally, though slow to act, brings an impressive strength that can achieve large goals when finally moved to action. However, Kautilya argues that a smaller, more easily mobilized ally is preferable, as such a friend is ready at the right moment to act and, due to limited power, can be directed by the conqueror as needed. A powerful ally, in contrast, cannot be so easily maneuvered.

Next, which is better: scattered forces, or a standing army that is not entirely loyal? My teacher maintains that scattered forces are preferable because, though spread out, they are more likely to obey when summoned. Kautilya disagrees, favoring a standing army that, even if not immediately loyal, can be won over through diplomatic and strategic measures. Gathering scattered forces in time is more challenging, as their individual lives and duties often delay their collective mobilization.

Is it better to have a friend with a large population or a friend with abundant gold? My teacher believes that a friend with a vast population is better because such a friend wields considerable power and can undertake any mission when needed. Kautilya, however, values a friend rich in gold, as wealth is always useful, whereas an army is not always essential. Gold can procure troops and other desired resources as necessary.

Between an ally with gold and one with extensive territory, which is preferable? My teacher asserts that a friend with gold is advantageous, as they can support heavy expenses wisely. But Kautilya argues that territory is superior, as it can yield both friends and wealth. Therefore, an ally with vast land is ultimately more valuable.

Even when the allies of both the conqueror and his enemy have similarly sized populations, they may still differ in traits like bravery, resilience, willingness to cooperate, and readiness for military formation. Similarly, when both allies are equally wealthy, they may differ in qualities such as willingness to grant requests, generosity, and consistent availability.

Regarding this topic, the following sayings are well known:

- A truly good friend possesses six qualities: being long-standing, submissive, easily motivated, connected through family ties, powerful, and of a harmonious nature.
- A long-standing friend is one who values the relationship out of genuine, disinterested motives, upholding the friendship simply for the sake of friendship itself and preserving its legacy over generations.
- A submissive friend is one whose generosity can be enjoyed in various ways and is of three types: one who offers benefits exclusively to a single ally, one who benefits both the conqueror and the enemy, and a third type who offers benefits

that extend to everyone.

- A steadfast friend, though less yielding, is one who stands firm, whether in offering or receiving help, maintaining a forceful stance toward adversaries, possessing numerous strongholds, and commanding a large army that includes wild tribes, demonstrating a lasting but resolute and independent nature.

- A friend who seeks alliance primarily for self-preservation during times of threat or trouble is a temporary and submissive friend.

- A true friend remains aligned with a single purpose, providing support reliably, staying unchanged, and maintaining a friendly nature even in hardship.

- An amicable friend is one who is inherently loyal. A friend who also sides with the enemy is changeable, while one who is neutral toward both the conqueror and his enemy is considered a friend to both.

- A friend who holds hostility toward the conqueror or is equally loyal to the conqueror's enemy is harmful, regardless of whether he actively helps or simply possesses the capacity to assist.

- A friend who aids the enemy's allies, dependents, vulnerable persons, or relatives is a mutual friend, valued by both the enemy and the conqueror.

- A friend with expansive and fertile lands, who is self-sufficient, strong but somewhat idle, tends to withdraw support if his ally falls into disrepute or hardship.

- A weaker ally, cautious and adaptive to both the conqueror's and enemy's influence without forming enmities, is known as a common friend.

- Lastly, one who ignores a friend's request for help, whether the need is clear or not, disregards his own potential danger by neglecting loyalty.

The question arises: which is preferable—a quick, smaller gain or a distant, larger gain?

My teacher argues that a quick, smaller gain is better since it enables the fulfillment of immediate objectives.

Kautilya, however, disagrees: a distant, larger gain that continually yields benefits, like a productive seed, is preferable; otherwise, only then should an immediate smaller gain be considered.

- Thus, when deciding, a king who wishes to fortify his power should carefully evaluate the lasting benefits of a continuous gain or a share in such a lasting gain before marching in alliance with others.

[Thus ends Chapter IX, "Agreement for the Acquisition of a Friend or Gold" in the section of "Agreement for the Acquisition of a Friend, Gold, or Land and Agreement for Undertaking a Work," in Book VII, "The end of the Six-fold Policy" of the Arthasástra of Kautilya. End of the hundred and seventh chapter from the beginning.]

CHAPTER X. AGREEMENT OF PEACE FOR THE ACQUISITION OF LAND.

The agreement to acquire land is termed a peace agreement for the acquisition of territory.

Of the two kings entering this agreement, the one who acquires a fertile, productive land rich with crops gains the upper hand.

If both kings acquire similarly fertile lands, the one who takes such land by defeating a powerful enemy gains the advantage; not only does he acquire land, but he also weakens an adversary and thereby strengthens his own position. True, conquering a weaker enemy offers its own merit, but the land gained is often poor, and former allies in the vicinity may now become adversaries.

When enemies are equally powerful, the one who secures land after conquering a fortified opponent gains the edge; capturing a fortress not only secures the territory but also helps contain wild tribes.

Acquiring land from a wandering foe has a further distinction— whether the acquired land borders a powerful or powerless enemy. Land near a powerless enemy is more manageable, while that bordering a powerful adversary requires constant defense, draining men and resources.

Which is preferable: gaining fertile land near a persistent enemy or sterile land near a temporary one?

My teacher suggests fertile land near a persistent enemy is preferable since it yields resources to maintain a strong army capable of subduing the enemy.

Kautilya, however, disagrees: rich land attracts many adversaries, and a constant enemy will remain hostile, whether or not conciliated with men and money. A temporary enemy, on the other hand, may remain calm due to either fear or favor. Land bordered by multiple forts sheltering bandits, foreigners, and wild tribes is land with a persistent enemy; land of the opposite character has only a temporary enemy.

Which is better, a small, nearby piece of land or an extensive, distant one?

A small, nearby territory is better, as it can be more easily acquired, secured, and defended, unlike the other, which is challenging on all fronts.

Of these two types of land, which is preferable—one self-sustaining or one that requires external defense?

Self-sustaining land is preferable, as it supports its own military and financial needs, unlike the latter, which serves merely as a remote military outpost.

Finally, is it better to acquire land from a foolish king or a wise one?

Acquiring land from a foolish king is better, as it can be easily gained and held without fear of it being reclaimed, whereas land obtained from a wise and beloved king presents a far greater challenge.

Of two enemies—one that can only be harassed and another that is fully reducible—acquiring land from the reducible one is the better choice. When this enemy is attacked, having little to no external aid, he tends to flee, taking his army and wealth along, often abandoned by his subjects. In contrast, the other enemy, who can only be harassed, remains steady with the support of his forts and allies.

Among two fortified kings, the one with forts on flat land is easier to subdue than one whose fort lies within a river's embrace; a fort on a plain is accessible, vulnerable to assault, and may be taken with the enemy inside. However, a fort surrounded by a river demands double the effort to overcome and offers a natural supply of water and other essentials to sustain its defenders.

When choosing between capturing land from a king with a river fort and another with mountainous fortifications, taking land from the former is preferable. A river fort can be attacked using elephants aligned to form a bridge across the river, wooden bridges, or boats. Additionally, the river may not always have a deep flow and can potentially be drained. In contrast, a mountain fort is inherently defensive and challenging to besiege or climb; even if one part of its defense falls, the remaining forces can retreat safely. Such a fort provides strategic advantages, allowing defenders to hurl rocks or trees down onto attackers.

Which is easier: taking land from those fighting on plains or from those defending from low grounds? Land is easier to seize from the latter, as they battle under challenging conditions of both timing and terrain, whereas those on the plains can readily fight at any moment and location.

Between two enemies, one who defends from ditches and another from elevated ground, seizing land from the former is advantageous. Defenders in ditches can be valuable as they are accustomed to fighting both from within trenches and with weapons in hand, whereas those fighting from higher ground depend solely on their weapons.

- Whoever, well-versed in political strategy, captures land from these and other types of enemies will stand out in strength, overshadowing both allied partners and any rivals outside the alliance.

[Thus ends Chapter X, "Agreement of Peace for the Acquisition of Land" in the section of "Agreement for the Acquisition of a Friend, Gold, or Land and Agreement for Undertaking a Work," in Book VII, "The End of the Six-fold Policy" of the Arthasástra of Kautilya. End of the hundred and eighth chapter from the beginning.]

CHAPTER XI. INTERMINABLE AGREEMENT.

The agreement that is established under the mutual understanding, "Let us cultivate and settle on this unused or waste land," is known as an interminable agreement. This type of agreement involves both parties contributing to develop a previously uncultivated or deserted tract of land, with each party aiming to gain advantages, whether in terms of crop production, revenue, or strategic control.

When one of the parties takes the lead in colonizing a fertile portion of this land, managing to sow and gather a harvest earlier than the other, that party gains a marked advantage, as it can reap immediate benefits, secure resources, and assert a stronger presence on the land. This initial success in securing crops is likely to make the cultivating party less dependent on external resources, enhancing their standing in the partnership and strengthening their claim over the cultivated area.

Now, if a choice has to be made between colonizing an extensive plain or a smaller area rich in water sources, the latter option is generally preferable. A limited but well-watered area is advantageous as it allows for continual crop and fruit cultivation year-round, without the reliance on seasonal rains. This sustained productivity supports a dependable source of income and food, which in turn sustains population growth and stability. The smaller, well-watered land also requires fewer resources to manage, whereas vast plains, although expansive, may demand substantial investment for irrigation and infrastructure.

Of the various plains available for colonization, one that supports the cultivation of both early and late-season crops, requires minimal labor, and has low irrigation needs is ideal. Such land provides a continuous yield, increasing food security and economic stability for the settlers. In contrast, a plain with higher water needs and limited crop cycles is less favorable, as it might demand greater investment in both labor and water resources for a sustainable return.

When considering watery lands, one that enables the cultivation of grains is more valuable than one that primarily yields other types of crops. Grains serve as a staple food and can be stored over long periods, providing sustenance in times of scarcity. Additionally, a steady grain supply reduces dependency on external sources, strengthening the colony's independence. However, if two watery areas are compared—one small and grain-rich, and the other extensive but producing a range of crops other than grains—the larger area may offer greater benefits. With its vast expanse, the larger area not only supports specialized agricultural practices, such as the cultivation of spices or medicinal plants, but also provides ample room for constructing forts and defensive structures, which enhance security and stability. Moreover, this diversity in agricultural output and available space supports the growth of trade, which can generate additional revenue and help sustain the population.

If a choice is presented between land rich in grains and land abundant in mineral resources, the latter contributes significantly to the treasury, while the former can support both the treasury and essential stockpiles of food. A supply of grains is critical for maintaining storehouses that feed both civilians and soldiers, especially during extended military campaigns or in times of crisis. However, territory with rich mineral deposits, especially those yielding precious metals, holds considerable value as it allows for wealth accumulation, which can be used to fund further territorial expansion or other strategic investments.

My teacher argues that when choosing between two types of forests, one that produces timber and another home to elephants, the timber forest should be prioritized, as it provides resources for constructing essential infrastructure, stockpiling for emergencies, and supporting general livelihood needs. Timber forests are invaluable for building, and with timber supplies readily available, a kingdom can ensure its infrastructural needs are met.

Kautilya, however, counters this view by emphasizing that while timber forests are indeed valuable, they can be cultivated and grown in various locations. An elephant forest, however, is unique and cannot simply be replicated. Elephants are crucial for military purposes, and they contribute significantly to a kingdom's ability to conquer and defend against powerful enemies. The strength of an army is amplified by having trained elephants, which can overpower cavalry and infantry alike, playing a decisive role in warfare. Hence, an elephant forest is strategically indispensable, especially for a kingdom intending to expand its influence.

Among different types of routes, land routes are preferable as they are long-standing, reliable, and can be maintained more effectively over time, whereas water routes, though sometimes useful, may be less dependable due to changing conditions, navigability, and seasonal restrictions.

Another important consideration is whether to settle a land with a dispersed population or one with an organized community. The former, with scattered inhabitants, is easier to control and manage. Such populations are generally less prone to internal discord and are more resilient against the influence of external enemies. In contrast, a community of closely-knit people may be more vulnerable to collective anger, influenced easily by charismatic figures or external pressures, making them more susceptible to manipulation by enemies. In the event of calamities, these populations may also struggle with coping as a group, while a dispersed population is more resilient and adaptable.

Lastly, when colonizing a land with people of varying social classes, it is advantageous to begin with the lowest caste, as these individuals are versatile, highly serviceable, and numerous. The lowest caste can perform a wide array of essential functions that support the colony's development and provide a stable workforce for various tasks, ensuring the colony's productivity and longevity. This foundation provides a secure base for further settlement, allowing for a gradual expansion that sustains economic and social stability.

Between cultivated and uncultivated areas, the uncultivated land is often more valuable, especially if it has rich soil suitable for various types of farming activities. When it's fertile, able to support pasturelands, manufacturing, mercantile activities like lending and borrowing, and attracts wealthy merchants, it holds even more potential than already cultivated land.

When comparing a tract of land that has forts with one that is densely populated, the latter is more beneficial. A well-populated area embodies a complete kingdom, full of life and productivity. In contrast, an unpopulated region, like a barren cow, offers little in terms of prosperity or productivity.

If a king seeks to reclaim land previously sold to another for colonization, particularly after the purchaser has depleted his resources in the attempt, he should strategically make an agreement with a buyer who is weak, of low birth, lacking in vigor, isolated, unprincipled, inclined toward wrongful behavior, resigned to fate, and careless in actions. Such a buyer, if unfit for colonization, will struggle and likely fail, losing both his men and money. A man born to a low position may initially attract a following due to wealth or power, but his subjects may abandon him to avoid being adversely affected by his weakness. A leader who lacks vitality won't be able to command his forces effectively, resulting in an army that dwindles due to his inability to support it. Similarly, a person with wealth who is unwilling to spend or show generosity will struggle to rally support or find assistance. A colonizer with a poor moral character or one addicted to harmful habits is easily removable from a settlement and may even endanger its security. Furthermore, one who resigns himself to fate without taking bold, deliberate action will achieve nothing, and an indiscreet individual will lack the strategic judgment to colonize successfully. This type of colonizer, lacking discretion, is considered the least effective.

My teacher asserts that an imprudent colonizer might reveal vulnerabilities in his sponsor, the conqueror. However, Kautilya argues that while such a colonizer might expose these weaknesses, he also paves the way for his own downfall at the hands of the conqueror.

In situations where there is a shortage of suitable individuals for colonizing waste land, the conqueror may arrange for the settlement of such areas as will be discussed in greater detail later under the topic "Capture of an Enemy in the Rear."

The arrangement described above is what is known as a verbal agreement (abhihitasandhi), where the terms are openly communicated. If a powerful king pressures another to sell a portion of land that is fertile and desirable to him, the weaker king might agree to sell under a transparent arrangement. This is referred to as "unconcealed peace" (anibhritasandhi), where the terms are explicitly understood.

If a king of comparable power requests land from another under similar circumstances, the seller should carefully weigh whether he can potentially reclaim the land, maintain control over it, bring his enemy under submission through the transfer, or gain enough wealth or alliances from the sale to strengthen his future endeavors.

This evaluation equally applies when a less powerful king considers buying land, ensuring he gains a strategic advantage.

- In these matters, a king who is skilled in the principles of political science and who manages to secure friends, resources, and land with or without a settled population will strategically position himself to surpass the other rulers aligned with him.

[Thus ends Chapter XI, "Interminable Agreement" in the section of "Agreement for the Acquisition of a Friend, Gold, or Land and Agreement for Undertaking a Work", Book VII, "The End of the Six-fold Policy" of the Arthasástra of Kautilya. End of the hundred and ninth chapter from the beginning.]

CHAPTER XII. AGREEMENT FOR UNDERTAKING A WORK.

When an agreement is made with the terms "Let us have a fort built," it is called an agreement to undertake a specific work. Among two kings, the one who constructs a strong, nearly impenetrable fort on land naturally suited for fortification with minimal labor and expense gains an advantage over the other.

When considering different types of forts—such as those on plains, those surrounded by rivers, and those on mountains—the last type listed is generally superior to the previous. As for irrigation projects, a system that provides a perennial water supply is better than one reliant on diverted sources, and of these perennial sources, the one that can irrigate the most extensive area is most advantageous.

In planting timber forests, the king who establishes a forest producing valuable resources, expanding into wild regions and with a river at its edge, gains an upper hand. A forest with a river is self-sustaining and can serve as a refuge during difficult times. For game forests, the king who cultivates a dense forest of fierce animals near the enemy's animal-filled forests, causing disturbances to the enemy and extending into elephant reserves near the border, is at an advantage.

My teacher argues that between two lands—one densely populated with non-warriors and the other with a small number of brave fighters—the latter is more advantageous since even a few brave soldiers can easily overpower a larger group of timid individuals, leading to the collapse of the enemy's army.

Kautilya disagrees, stating that a larger number of less capable people is preferable. Such a population can perform support tasks in the military camp, assist soldiers actively in the battlefield, and create an intimidating impression simply through sheer numbers. Further, discipline and training can instill courage and motivation in even the timid.

When it comes to mines, the king who can exploit a valuable, easily accessible mine with minimal labor and expense holds an advantage. When comparing a smaller mine yielding high-value materials and a larger mine producing items of lesser value, my teacher argues that the former is preferable. Precious materials such as diamonds, gemstones, pearls, corals, gold, and silver can collectively far outweigh the quantity of common commodities.

Kautilya, however, contends that a large, long-lasting mine yielding lesser-value commodities is more advantageous. The wealth generated from accumulating vast quantities of these items can be used to purchase rare, high-value items as needed, making a large mine with continuous yield a significant asset.

This brings us to the important topic of selecting trade routes. My teacher suggests that between two options—one trade route by water and another by land—the water route is preferable. This is because it tends to be less expensive while also providing the potential for greater profits.

However, Kautilya offers a different perspective, arguing that water routes often face various obstacles, can be unreliable, pose immediate dangers, and lack adequate defenses. In contrast, land routes do not suffer from these disadvantages and are generally more reliable.

When considering water routes, Kautilya points out that a path along the shore is superior to one that runs through the open ocean. The shore route connects numerous trading port towns, making it more accessible. Similarly, river navigation is favorable since it is usually continuous and allows for dangers that can be avoided or managed.

Regarding land routes, my teacher asserts that a route leading toward the Himalayas is better than one heading south. Kautilya, however, disagrees. He explains that aside from items like blankets, animal skins, and horses, many valuable trade goods—such as conch shells, diamonds, precious stones, pearls, and gold—are readily available in the southern regions.

For routes going south, Kautilya emphasizes the importance of selecting a trade route that passes through numerous mines, is well-frequented by people, and is less costly or burdensome. Alternatively, a route that allows for the acquisition of a wide variety of merchandise is also a strong choice.

This leads to considerations for trade routes headed east or west. Between a cart track and a footpath, the cart track is preferred as it allows for larger-scale preparations and transport. Similarly, routes that can accommodate pack animals like donkeys or camels, regardless of the terrain or time of year, are considered beneficial for trade.

Kautilya's analysis also addresses routes intended solely for foot traffic, known as amsa-patha or shoulder-paths, where individuals carry merchandise on their backs. While these paths may have limitations, they can still serve important roles in trade networks, particularly in regions where other forms of transport are impractical.

- It is considered a significant loss for the conqueror to engage in any work that ultimately benefits the enemy, as such endeavors only serve to strengthen his opponent. Conversely, engaging in tasks that hinder the enemy's progress is viewed as a gain for the conqueror. In situations where the benefits from both sides are equal, the conqueror must recognize that his own situation is stagnant, showing no real advancement or improvement.
- Similarly, it is unwise for the conqueror to commit to a project that requires a substantial outlay of resources yet yields minimal returns. On the other hand, a project that reduces costs while enhancing output is deemed beneficial. If the output of a project matches its costs, the conqueror must once again acknowledge that he is in a stagnant condition, neither gaining nor losing ground.
- Therefore, it is crucial for the conqueror to seek out opportunities for fortification and other initiatives that are not only cost-effective but also promise greater profits and enhanced power. This approach ensures that the agreements

made for undertaking various works lead to meaningful progress and improvement rather than stagnation.

[Thus ends Chapter XII, "Agreement for Undertaking a Work," in the section of "Agreement for the Acquisition of a Friend, Gold, or Land and Agreement for Undertaking a Work"' in Book VIII, "The End of the Six-fold Policy" of the Arthasástra of Kautilya. End of the hundred and tenth chapter from the beginning.]

CHAPTER XIII. CONSIDERATIONS ABOUT AN ENEMY IN THE REAR.

When the conqueror and his enemy both attempt to capture the rear of their respective foes, who are preoccupied with attacking others, the one who successfully takes the rear of an opponent with abundant resources gains significant advantages. This is because a king with vast resources must first eliminate his frontal enemy, who is currently under attack, before he can address the threat posed by the rear. In contrast, an enemy lacking resources may not have realized their desired profits and, therefore, poses a lesser threat.

If both enemies are equally resourced, the conqueror who manages to capture the rear of an opponent who has made extensive preparations will also find greater advantages. This is due to the fact that a king who has prepared extensively must deal with his rear enemy only after neutralizing the threat posed by his frontal adversary. Conversely, a king with minimal preparations may find his movements hindered by the broader Circle of States, making him less formidable.

In scenarios where both sides have equal troop strength, capturing the rear of an enemy who has engaged a wandering foe will yield more benefits. A king who has marched against a wandering enemy will likely need to deal with the rear enemy only after securing an easy victory against his initial target. This is unlike a king who confronts a fortified enemy; he may find himself repelled during the assault on the enemy's defenses and, upon retreating, caught between the rear enemy and the frontal adversary, who is protected by strong fortifications.

These principles apply equally to various enemy scenarios discussed previously. When enemies are of similar caliber, the conqueror who targets the rear of a king confronting a virtuous adversary stands to gain more, as the attacking king may lose the support of his own subjects due to the moral implications of his actions. On the other hand, an attack against a wicked king can bolster the attacker's standing with the populace, earning him their goodwill.

Similar reasoning applies when considering those who have marched against an extravagant king or one who lives hand-to-mouth, as well as against a miserly ruler. The dynamics remain consistent when examining confrontations involving allies, where the principles of strategic advantage and resource management continue to hold true.

When two enemies are in play—one focused on attacking a friend and the other targeting an enemy—the one who strikes at the rear of the latter gains significant advantages. This is because a king who has initiated hostilities against a friend can more easily negotiate peace with that friend and subsequently turn his attention toward the rear enemy. It's generally simpler to make amends with a friend than to engage in conflict with an enemy.

In another scenario involving two kings, where one is intent on destroying a friend and the other is focused on an enemy, the king who targets the rear of the first king stands to gain more. A ruler attacking an enemy typically has the backing of his allies, which helps him subdue the rear enemy. In contrast, a king destroying his own allies may find himself isolated and at a disadvantage.

When both the conqueror and his adversary are attacking the rear of an enemy while attempting to enforce the collection of what is not rightfully owed to them, the one whose foe has already suffered significant losses—in terms of both resources and personnel—will benefit more. Conversely, when they aim to collect what is legitimately due to them, the one whose enemy has already lost both profits and troops will reap greater advantages.

If the enemy being targeted is capable of retaliating, and the assailant's rear enemy has fortified himself on one of the assailant's flanks, then the rear enemy has the upper hand. This is because a rear enemy positioned on one of the assailant's sides can not only align with the assailable enemy but also pose a direct threat to the assailant's base. In contrast, a rear enemy situated directly behind the assailant can merely harass the rear without being able to mount a more strategic assault.

- Kings who have the ability to disrupt an enemy's rear and block his movements fall into three categories: those positioned directly behind the enemy and those on either side, each forming a group capable of hampering the enemy's plans.
- A king positioned between a conqueror and his foe is known as an "antardhi," or one who stands between two rulers. If this intermediary king possesses strongholds, alliances with wild tribes, and other types of support, he becomes a formidable barrier, effectively obstructing even the mightiest of forces.

When both the conqueror and his rival are set on capturing a Madhyama king by attacking his rear, the one who manages to sever the Madhyama king's ties with his allies and, in doing so, transforms an enemy into a friend, gains a more favorable position; for a former enemy forced into peace will provide stronger support than an ally coerced to uphold a compromised alliance. This same strategy applies when attempting to win over a neutral king.

Between attacks from the rear and those from the front, the former is often preferable when it enables treacherous warfare (mantrayuddha), where subterfuge and strategy can be more effectively employed.

My teacher believes that in open warfare, both sides ultimately suffer due to heavy losses in men and resources, and even the victor appears weakened because of these costs.

However, Kautilya disagrees, asserting that the enemy's total destruction is worth significant losses of men and money.

When losses of men and resources are equal, the conqueror who first fully annihilates his front-line enemy and then turns to his rear adversary gains a distinct advantage. If both the conqueror and his enemy are each tackling their respective frontal foes, the one who first destroys a deeply antagonistic front-line enemy with abundant resources reaps the greatest benefits.

This approach illustrates the strategy for neutralizing various enemies and wild tribes:

- When an enemy exists both in the rear and front, along with an assailable target ready to be marched against, the conqueror should consider the following plan:
- The rear enemy typically encourages the frontal enemy to strike at the conqueror's ally. To counter this, the conqueror should set the ákranda (the enemy of the rear enemy) against the rear enemy's ally, provoking conflict between them to weaken the rear enemy's plans. Similarly, he should instigate hostilities between the allies of both the ákranda and the rear enemy.
- In parallel, the conqueror should ensure his own ally engages the frontal enemy's friend in conflict, thereby distracting them. To further protect himself, he should enlist the assistance of his ally's ally to counter any threat posed by the friend of his enemy's friend.
- With the support of his ally, the conqueror should keep his rear enemy contained and, using his ally's ally, prevent any attack from his rear enemy against the ákranda (his rear ally).
- By enlisting the help of his allies, the conqueror should bring the Circle of States, both in his rear and front, under his influence. He should place messengers and spies in each state within this Circle, and continually weaken his enemies' strength, all the while maintaining secrecy over his strategies and alliances.
- For the ruler who fails to conceal his strategies, his accomplishments, even if momentarily successful, will ultimately collapse—just as surely as a damaged raft lost on the sea.

[Thus ends Chapter XIII, "Considerations about an Enemy in the Rear," in Book VII, "The End of the Six-fold Policy" of the Arthasástra of Kautilya. End of the hundred and eleventh chapter from the beginning.]

CHAPTER XIV. RECRUITMENT OF LOST POWER.

When the conqueror faces an attack from a united front of enemies, he can approach their leader with a peace proposal: "Let us make peace. I offer you gold, and I am your ally. Your advantage will double, and it's unwise to bolster the power of your allies who now show a friendly face, for as they grow stronger, they will turn on you in time."

Alternatively, he might appeal to the leader's sense of caution to dismantle the coalition: "Just as you now unite to attack someone as harmless as I am, these same allies will target you in your times of prosperity or hardship. The lure of power can change loyalties; it's best to dissolve this alliance."

Once the alliance weakens, the conqueror could direct the leader to focus on the weakest of the enemies or persuade the leader to turn the alliance's weaker members against him. He may use any approach beneficial to his own cause to provoke dissatisfaction among the allied ranks. Offering the leader a more profitable prospect could tempt him into a separate agreement, creating division. Those who serve both states may praise the leader's benefits and subtly mock the unity of the coalition, saying, "It appears you have banded together nicely."

If some of the allies are already unstable, they could be encouraged to break the agreement, and those drawing income from both alliances can remind them of their previous warnings, ensuring further discord. Once disunited, the conqueror can ally himself with any isolated leader.

If there's no primary leader, the conqueror can reach out to the one who initiated the alliance, the most resolute, the people's favorite, the most fearful, the one whose friendship aligns through royal ties, a trusted ally, or even a wandering adversary — in this particular order.

For each type, he must employ suitable tactics: gain favor with the alliance's initiator by showing deference; win over the resolute one through greetings and respect; secure an alliance with the people's favorite by offering twice the expected gains; satisfy the greedy by promising men and money; calm the fearful by presenting a hostage; solidify royal ties by forming closer bonds; please an old friend by extending goodwill and dropping hostilities; and aid and align with the wandering enemy. Using appropriate approaches—conciliation, gifts, sowing discord, or even threats, as detailed under "Troubles"—the conqueror should aim to win over any of these individuals.

He who is facing difficulties and fears an attack from his enemy should, by offering military and financial support, establish a peace agreement with the enemy that includes clear terms on location, timing, and tasks. He should also amend any offenses he may have caused by breaching previous treaties. If lacking in support, he should seek allies among his relatives and friends. Additionally, constructing a well-fortified stronghold can provide him with much-needed defense, as having protection from forts and friends commands respect from both his people and his enemies.

One who lacks the wisdom to deliberate effectively should surround himself with knowledgeable advisors and consult experienced elders with extensive learning. This will help him achieve his objectives.

For someone without a robust treasury and military, his focus should be on fortifying the fundamental elements of his sovereignty. A stronghold is essential, as the land provides the resources to build wealth and support an army, and a secure fort offers refuge for both the king and his forces.

Waterworks, such as irrigation systems, are vital for ensuring a steady supply of crops, as they help provide consistent crop yields regardless of rainfall. Well-maintained trade routes are crucial for strategic advantage over enemies; through these routes, armies and spies move, essential equipment like weapons, armor, chariots, and draft animals are procured, and travel becomes more accessible for both exit and entry.

Mines are a foundational source for resources used in warfare. Similarly, forests rich in timber supply the materials necessary for constructing forts, vehicles, and chariots, all of which are indispensable in sustaining a fortified and well-prepared kingdom.

Elephant forests provide elephants essential for warfare and transportation. Pasturelands support cows, horses, and camels, which are vital for pulling chariots. If he lacks these resources in his own territory, he should seek to acquire them from his relatives or allies. In the absence of a proper army, he should strive to attract brave individuals from guilds, thieves' networks, wild tribes, non-local groups, and spies skilled in causing harm to enemies.

In times of vulnerability, he may need to adopt the approach of a weaker king when dealing with a more powerful one, focusing on diplomacy to avoid threats from both enemies and allies.

- Thus, by leveraging his loyal supporters, wise counsel, treasury, and military, he can escape the grip of his adversaries.

[Thus ends Chapter XIV, "Recruitment of Lost Power," in Book VII, "The End of the Six-fold Policy" of the Arthasástra of Kautilya. End of the hundred and twelfth chapter from the beginning.]

CHAPTER XV. MEASURES CONDUCIVE TO PEACE WITH A STRONG AND PROVOKED ENEMY; AND THE ATTITUDE OF A CONQUERED ENEMY.

When a weaker king is under attack from a stronger foe, he should look for protection from an ally who is more powerful than the enemy and beyond the reach of the enemy's skill in planning intrigues. Among kings equal in strategic abilities, the distinction should be made by assessing stable prosperity and the support of experienced advisors.

If a superior ally isn't available, the weaker king should seek out allies of equal power who, combined, match the strength of the enemy but remain beyond the enemy's influence over wealth, military force, or intrigue. Among kings who are equally equipped with resources, army, and clever tactics, preference should be given to those capable of making substantial preparations.

If allies of equal power are not an option, he should turn to lesser kings who are loyal, enthusiastic, capable of resistance, and also beyond the enemy's sway. In choosing among kings equally enthusiastic and action-oriented, preference should be given to those who can secure strategic battlefields. Among those with equal battlefield advantages, priority should go to those who are consistently prepared for war. Among kings who possess both favorable terrain and readiness, distinction should be based on their weaponry and armor supply.

If no allies can be found, the weaker king should take refuge in a fortified location where the enemy's large army cannot disrupt the steady supply of food, fodder, firewood, and water, thus causing the enemy substantial losses in both men and resources. If multiple forts are available, preference should be given to those well-suited for storing and securing provisions. Kautilya advises that refuge should be taken in a fort populated with loyal inhabitants and stocked with ample supplies. Additionally, the choice of such a fort is supported by the following reasons:

"I shall confront the enemy by aligning with his adversary's ally, or by seeking support from a mediating king or a neutral ruler. With the assistance of a neighboring king, wild tribes, a relative of the enemy, or an imprisoned prince, I will either seize or devastate his kingdom. I will stir up chaos within his fort, land, or camp using my loyal followers already embedded there. When he draws near, I will eliminate him through secret means, whether by weapons, fire, poison, or other hidden strategies as I see fit. I shall exhaust his resources by pushing him into costly undertakings, either initiated by himself or manipulated by my spies. By inflicting significant losses, I will create discord among his allies or sow discontent within his army.

I will cut off his camp's supply lines to weaken him, or I might feign surrender to introduce vulnerabilities within his ranks and eventually overpower him using all my resources. If his spirit wanes, I will impose my terms for peace. If I block his movements, he will encounter hardships from all quarters; and when he is defenseless, I will crush him using my hereditary army, or perhaps with the aid of his own enemies or wild tribes. I will safeguard my extensive domain by fortifying my stronghold, where the united forces of myself and my allies will be unbeatable. My troops, trained to fight from valleys, pits, or under cover of darkness, will create traps for him on his path, particularly if he is engaged in pressing matters.

As he faces continual losses, he will weaken on arrival, reaching this hostile territory in an unfavorable place and at an unfavorable time. With fortifications and wild tribes in his way, he will find access to my lands costly in terms of men and resources. Unable to secure advantageous positions for his or his allies' armies, and afflicted by disease, he will be in a state of distress when he reaches my stronghold—and, once here, he will have no chance of retreat."

In the absence of such favorable conditions, or if the enemy's army proves overwhelmingly strong, one might have to abandon the fort and flee. My teacher argues that, in such a scenario, one could charge toward the enemy like a moth to a flame, as a brave confrontation would lead to one outcome or another—either honorable death or possible victory for one who disregards the risks to life.

Kautilya, however, advises a different approach. If conditions exist that favor a peace agreement, he suggests making peace with the enemy. If no such conditions arise, one may try to achieve peace through strategic threats or secure an ally. Alternatively, a messenger could be sent to the enemy with an invitation for peace. Another method might be to honor and reward the enemy's envoy, conveying to him, "Here is the king's armory, the queen's residence, and the princes; I and this kingdom are yours, with the approval of the royal family."

Once under the protection of the enemy, the king should serve his protector as a loyal subordinate, catering to his protector's occasional needs. Any fortifications, acquisition efforts, marriage alliances, installation ceremonies for an heir, commercial ventures, capturing elephants, setting up secret battle spots, marching campaigns, and festivities must be undertaken only with his protector's approval. Additionally, he should request permission for any treaties with the settlers in his territory and for punishing anyone fleeing his lands. If citizens or villagers turn hostile or unfaithful, he may petition his protector for a new territory or eliminate disloyal individuals through covert means as would befit dealing with traitors. He must refrain from accepting even a favorable offer of territory from a friend without the protector's knowledge, although he may still consult with the protector's ministers, priest, army chief, or heir.

The king should support his protector in every feasible way. During public worship or prayers, he should lead his people in praying for the protector's long life and continuously proclaim his loyalty and dedication to the protector.

- A conquered king, faithfully serving his strong protector, should always avoid associating with people of doubtful loyalty and show full allegiance, serving loyally and diligently within the protector's circle.

[Thus ends Chapter XV, "Measures Conducive to Peace with a Strong and Provoked Enemy and the Attitude of a Conquered Enemy," in Book VII, "The End of the Six-fold Policy" of the Arthasástra of Kautilya. End of the hundred and thirteenth chapter from the beginning.]

CHAPTER XVI. THE ATTITUDE OF A CONQUERED KING.

To create financial strain on his protector, a powerful vassal king who aims to expand his territory may, with the protector's consent, launch a campaign in regions where the land and climate are advantageous for his army's maneuvers. Ideally, this would be against an enemy lacking strongholds or defensive structures, with the vassal having no immediate threats in his rear. However, if there are rear threats, he should take steps to secure his defenses before marching forward.

For weaker kings, he should use conciliation and gifts to bring them under control, while for stronger kings, he should employ tactics like sowing discord and making strategic threats. Depending on the circumstances, he may use one, some, or all of these approaches to subdue both his immediate and distant rivals.

In practicing conciliation, he should offer promises to safeguard villages, protect forest dwellers, secure herds of cattle, and ensure the safety of trade routes. He can also grant pardons to those who have been exiled, fled, or committed transgressions.

The policy of gifting may involve granting land, valuable items, and even daughters in marriage, along with assurances of safety. To instill division among enemies, he could incite a neighboring king, a wild tribal leader, a relative of the enemy, or an imprisoned prince to stir up internal conflicts.

He should confront his enemy directly in an open battle, through a well-coordinated ambush, via conspiracy, or during the upheaval of a strategic capture of the enemy's fortress. Each method provides an opportunity to bring the enemy to submission.

The vassal may reinstate deposed kings who show spirit and can strengthen his forces. Similarly, he may reinstate those who possess strong financial or military resources, as they could bolster his own with funds and forces, or those who are knowledgeable in land management and could provide access to territories.

Among his allies, different types of friends offer various benefits:

- A friend offering diverse resources (chitrabhoga) aids with gems, valuable commodities, raw materials from commercial hubs, resources from villages and mines, or animals for transportation from timber and elephant forests.
- A friend offering abundant support (mahábhoga) provides wealth and military assistance.
- A friend offering comprehensive support (sarvabhoga)

contributes army forces, funds, and land.

- A friend offering limited support (ekatobhogi) provides defense against an enemy on one front.
- A friend offering dual support (ubhayatobhogi) aids both the vassal and the vassal's adversary, as well as their allies.
- Finally, a friend offering complete support on all fronts (sarvatobogi) aids in dealing with the enemy, the enemy's allies, any neighboring threats, and wild tribes, ensuring a stable advantage across all borders.

If he has an enemy in his rear, a wild chief, or a particularly strong enemy who can be appeased by offering land, he should provide each with a strategically chosen piece of territory. To an enemy with fortifications, he should grant land that is disconnected from his own territory; to a wild chief, he should offer land with little means of subsistence; to a relative of the enemy, a piece of land that can easily be reclaimed; to a former enemy held as a prisoner, land that has not been captured from the enemy's territory; to an armed corporation, land constantly troubled by external threats; and to a coalition of such groups, land adjacent to a more powerful ruler. For a military corporation skilled in warfare, he should assign land troubled by both internal strife and external threats. If dealing with a belligerent king who desires conflict, he should give land unsuitable for military maneuvers. To a supporter of his enemy, he should offer barren land; to an exiled prince, land stripped of resources; to a ruler who has recommitted to peace after breaking it, a land that requires considerable resources for settlement; to a deserted prince, land with minimal defenses; and finally, to his own protector, an inhospitable piece of territory.

In continuing relations with these figures, he should maintain his approach toward those most helpful and steady in their support. For those opposed to him, he should work behind the scenes to sway them. To loyal allies, he should provide assistance to enable even more help, rewarding and honoring them generously. If an ally is in difficulty, he should offer support. When receiving visitors, he should accommodate their preferences and make efforts to ensure their satisfaction. He should avoid any dismissive, threatening, slanderous, or harsh language, and he must protect those he has promised safety, as a father would. For the guilty, he should announce their crimes publicly before punishing them, and for minor offenders, he should deliver discreet, secret punishments to avoid any suspicion from his protector.

He must refrain from seizing the lands, possessions, families, or any inheritance of defeated kings. Instead, he should restore these to the slain king's relatives. For a king who has passed away while allied with him, he should place the rightful heir on the throne. By showing such respect, the conqueror will ensure that defeated kings, seeing the protection of their lands and families, will remain loyal and encourage their descendants to support the conqueror's family for generations.

Should he disregard these policies and covet the lands, treasures, or families of those he has conquered or imprisoned, he will incite hostility within the surrounding kingdoms, driving the Circle of States to turn against him. Even his own ministers may grow resentful and seek safety within this circle, harboring plans against his life and rule.

- Therefore, conquered kings who are allowed to remain in their lands under a policy of conciliation will remain faithful to the conqueror, extending their loyalty to his descendants for generations.

[Thus ends Chapter XVI, "The Attitude of a Conquered King," in Book VII, "The End of the Six-fold Policy," of the Arthasástra of Kautilya. End of the hundred and fourteenth chapter from the beginning.]

CHAPTER XVII. MAKING PEACE AND BREAKING IT.

The terms sama (quiet), sandhi (peace agreement), and samádhi (reconciliation) are interchangeable, each referring to an arrangement that nurtures mutual trust and harmony between rulers. The essence of these agreements is to create stability and peace that all parties can rely upon.

One of my teachers holds the view that peace based solely on an honesty pledge or oath is somewhat unreliable and susceptible to change, while peace founded upon a secured pledge, like a hostage or a tangible guarantee, offers stronger stability and is less likely to be broken. However, Kautilya disagrees with this, stating that peace rooted in an honesty pledge or oath is enduring and steadfast, not only in this world but in the spiritual realm as well. The tangible guarantee or hostage is useful only for reinforcing the physical aspects of the agreement in this world and for establishing confidence on both sides.

In the past, kings known for their integrity would often form peace alliances with a simple declaration, "We are joined in peace," signifying a bond that they expected to endure without question. However, if there was any fear of an integrity breach, leaders might enhance the pact's strength with a solemn oath, swearing upon revered items or symbols of significance and strength, such as fire, water, the front of a chariot, the shoulder of an elephant, the sturdy brick of a fort wall, or even materials like precious gold. By invoking these items in their oaths, they bound themselves to a greater degree, pledging that breaking the promise would bring ruin upon the violator, forsaken by these powerful symbols of prosperity and stability.

In cases where the risk of violating an oath remained, peace could be further stabilized with the involvement of prominent figures, such as revered ascetics or high-ranking nobles, acting as guarantors. These guarantors added a layer of trustworthiness and weight to the agreement. Among such guarantors, the one who holds the greatest sway or influence over the enemy's actions provides the most substantial assurance, whereas selecting a figure without much control is ineffective and can even invite deception.

When the treaty requires hostages, especially children, strategic choices come into play. For instance, offering a princess as a hostage can be advantageous, as a princess often brings challenges to her captors due to her potential influence, while a prince may be seen as a more straightforward hostage with fewer implications. If there are multiple sons, choosing which to send is also significant: sending a high-born, brave, wise son who is well-trained in military arts, or an only son, generally benefits the captor more than the family surrendering him. Therefore, sending a lower-born son with limited inheritance rights or a son who lacks intellect and has no training in military arts can reduce the disadvantage to the family giving him. In such cases, a timid or unskilled son, or one of many, is less valuable in political terms, as he is not integral to the continuity of the kingdom.

Among sons, loyalty and wisdom may weigh differently: people are usually loyal to a high-born son, even if he isn't particularly wise, whereas a wise son, though low-born, will generally excel at the practical aspects of governance. However, when it comes to effective statecraft, a high-born prince who collaborates with experienced advisors often outshines a low-born but wise son.

When choosing between a wise prince and a brave prince, the wise prince, despite possibly being less bold, has intellectual strengths that favor him in many situations, while the brave prince, even if not particularly wise, embodies courage and can be invaluable in battle. Yet, in the long run, a wise prince's strategic foresight and planning capabilities enable him to surpass even the most courageous warriors, just as a skilled hunter can ultimately overcome even a formidable elephant through craftiness and cunning.

- This careful approach to alliances and hostages illustrates that true strength and stability in peace agreements come not only from power but from strategic choices about who is pledged, the nature of the pledge, and the intent behind these alliances.

Regarding the comparison between a brave prince and a trained prince, a brave prince, even if untrained, possesses the natural ability and inclination for battle, while a trained prince, though possibly less courageous, can aim accurately and hit his targets. Despite the trained prince's accuracy, a brave prince's strong will and commitment to his principles make him stand out, as bravery often leads to a more determined approach to governance and warfare.

When it comes to a king with multiple sons versus a king with only one son, the former has the advantage of being able to offer one son as a hostage while keeping the others safe, which allows him to break the peace if necessary without endangering his lineage. On the other hand, a king with only one son lacks this flexibility and may need to approach peace agreements with more caution.

In cases where the king hands over all his sons as hostages, it becomes crucial to consider the king's ability to father more sons in the future. If both kings have this potential, the advantage lies with the king who can beget capable sons, as this promises strong heirs to continue his line. If both kings can produce able sons, the advantage then goes to the king likely to have a son sooner, as this reduces the risk posed by having all sons held as hostages.

If a king has only one son who is also brave and lacks the capacity to have more sons, he should consider surrendering himself instead of his only son as an assurance of peace. However, if a king is in a position of rising power, he may consider breaking the peace agreement altogether.

Should the prince be held as a hostage, clever strategies can be employed for his potential escape. Carpenters, artisans, and covert agents stationed with the prince might assist him, creating a secret escape route through an underground tunnel. Additionally, dancers, actors, singers, musicians, entertainers, royal poets, swimmers, and certain individuals skilled in covert operations may be placed within the enemy's service to covertly support the prince. These individuals should have unrestricted access to the palace, allowing them to blend in and move freely, providing the prince with potential opportunities to disguise himself and escape at night.

Similarly, female agents and spies posing as entertainers or other service workers within the enemy's palace might also serve as valuable assets. The prince could slip away, disguised as one of these workers, carrying their tools, dishes, or other belongings as cover. Moreover, cooks, confectioners, attendants, and others assigned to serve the enemy king could assist the prince's escape by concealing him under various items, such as food trays, blankets, or ceremonial objects. Servants responsible for maintaining the palace, handling the king's chariots, preparing his bed, assisting with personal grooming, or drawing bath water may also provide cover for the prince. Using the cover of darkness, he could escape disguised as one of these attendants, blending into the palace's usual routines to slip away unnoticed.

These tactics exemplify the clever methods that can be employed to facilitate the prince's escape and ensure his safety, even when he is held as a hostage.

Or the prince might appear to be in spiritual communion with the god Varuna, secluded in a reservoir connected to the palace by an underground tunnel, or he could be escorted there under cover of night. Spies disguised as traders might then distribute poisoned cooked rice and fruit to the sentinels, incapacitating them. Alternatively, on religious occasions, such as offerings to the gods or ceremonies honoring ancestors, the prince could serve the guards rice and beverages mixed with the juice of the madana plant, inducing them to fall asleep, thus giving him an opening to escape.

He might also secure his freedom by bribing the guards directly. Spies, posing as city officials, court bards, or physicians, could further assist by setting fire to a building filled with valuable items to cause a distraction, or merchants with spy affiliations could set ablaze stores filled with commercial goods, diverting attention. In order to throw off any pursuers, the prince could leave a dummy body in his quarters and set the room on fire, giving the impression he perished in the flames. He might then escape through a loosened house joint, an open window, or a tunnel.

Alternatively, disguised as a carrier of goods like glass beads or pots, the prince could slip away under the cover of night. If he seeks further concealment, he might enter the quarters of ascetics and emerge disguised as one of them, whether shaven-headed or with twisted hair. Another tactic might involve posing as a person with a peculiar illness, a forest-dweller, or even being carried out disguised as a corpse. He could also escape by impersonating a widowed woman following a funeral procession, blending in among mourners.

Spies disguised as forest people could misdirect any pursuers by sending them on the wrong path, while the prince himself would take an alternate route. Hiding among carts and drivers, he might merge into a caravan to avoid detection. If closely trailed, he could lead his followers into an ambush or, in its absence, lay a trail of gold coins or poisoned morsels along the road, prompting his pursuers to pause and investigate while he takes a different path.

Should he be captured, the prince could attempt to win over his captors with offers of conciliation or by serving them poisoned food. Meanwhile, his father, staging a sacrifice for Varuna or exploiting an accidental fire, might place a decoy body as a false martyr, using it to publicly accuse the enemy of murdering his son, thereby creating an opportunity to launch a counter-attack.

- Or, in a final act of defiance, the prince might draw a concealed sword, striking at his guards with swift force and escaping with the help of his previously hidden spies.

[Thus ends Chapter XVII, "Making Peace and Breaking It," in Book VII, "The End of the Six-fold Policy" of the Arthasástra of Kautilya. End of the hundred and fifteenth chapter from the beginning.]

CHAPTER XVIII. THE CONDUCT OF A MADHYAMA KING, A NEUTRAL KING, AND OF A CIRCLE OF STATES.

The third and fifth states from a madhyama king (a king who is a mediator or positioned between other powers) are generally friendly to him, while the second, fourth, and sixth states are usually unfriendly. If this madhyama king shows favor to both the friendly and unfriendly states, the conqueror should align himself amicably with the madhyama. But if the madhyama king does not favor these states, then the conqueror should instead seek friendship directly with those states.

When the madhyama king aims to secure an alliance with a potential ally of the conqueror, the conqueror should act decisively. By mobilizing his own allies and the allies of his friend against the madhyama, and by distancing the madhyama king from his allies, the conqueror can maintain and secure his own alliance. Alternatively, the conqueror might rouse the surrounding Circle of States against the madhyama king by declaring, "This madhyama king has grown overly ambitious and is plotting our ruin; let us unite and thwart his advances."

If this Circle of States is supportive, the conqueror can proceed to enhance his own power by suppressing the ambitions of the madhyama king. But if the Circle of States does not fully support him, the conqueror should instead bolster his friend with men and resources. Then, through conciliation and gifts, he should sway either the leader of the madhyama king's opposition or a nearby ruler who is hostile toward the madhyama, or a ruler who has been in a state of mutual reliance with the other kings, or those who are hesitant to act due to distrust of one another. By winning over a single ally, he doubles his strength; by securing a second, he triples it. With these accumulated allies, the conqueror can then proceed against the madhyama king.

However, if conditions—either of location or timing—are unfavorable for this approach, the conqueror should instead secure peace by allying with an enemy of the madhyama king or by instigating traitorous elements to unify against the madhyama. If the madhyama king threatens the conqueror's allies, the conqueror should step in to prevent this aggression, reassuring his friend with, "I will protect you as long as you remain vulnerable." He must extend tangible support, particularly when his ally's resources are weak or depleted. Should the madhyama king attempt to displace one of the conqueror's friends, the conqueror should immediately offer assistance and either provide new lands to this ally or ensure that they remain under his own protection, thus preventing them from seeking protection elsewhere.

In cases where some of the conqueror's allies, particularly those who are either reducible or vulnerable to the madhyama king, start to side with the madhyama, the conqueror should consider forming a strategic peace with a third king. Likewise, if certain allies of the madhyama king, especially those who are similarly vulnerable to the conqueror, demonstrate a capacity for both offense and defense and turn friendly towards the conqueror, then he should make peace with them as well. By doing so, the conqueror not only achieves his own objectives but also manages to appease and influence the madhyama king.

If the madhyama king is eager to secure the conqueror's potential ally as his own, the conqueror can either make peace with another ruler or try to deter his friend from switching allegiance, advising him with words like, "It is unworthy of you to abandon a friend who values your companionship." Alternatively, the conqueror may choose to remain passive if he believes that the Circle of States might resent the friend's disloyalty. In situations where the madhyama king seeks to ally with the conqueror's enemy, the conqueror should covertly support this enemy with resources and troops, ensuring his assistance is unnoticed by the madhyama.

If the madhyama king aims to befriend the neutral king, the conqueror should attempt to sow discord between them. He should seek the protection of whichever—madhyama or neutral king—is respected by the Circle of States. The behavior of the madhyama king often mirrors that of the neutral king. If the neutral king intends to form an alliance with the madhyama, the conqueror should work to obstruct the neutral king's plans to overpower a foe, support an ally, or secure the services of another neutral king's army. In this way, the conqueror can strengthen his position, suppress his enemies, and extend aid to his allies, even if these allies have acted unfavorably toward him.

The conqueror's potential adversaries include a king of malicious disposition who is generally harmful, a rear-enemy allied with a frontal enemy, a weakened foe facing difficulties, and one who waits for the conqueror to encounter trouble before launching an attack.

Conversely, kings likely to align with the conqueror include those who march alongside him toward a shared goal, those who march with him but for different reasons, those who wish to join forces to attack a mutual enemy, those who march together after forming a peace agreement, those with personal objectives, those rising together with others, those willing to trade armies or treasuries, and those adopting the dual strategy of allying with one while fighting another.

Neighboring kings who may serve the conqueror's interests include a neighboring ruler fearing an attack from a powerful adversary, one positioned between the conqueror and his enemy, the rear-enemy of a dominant ruler, one who has voluntarily submitted to the conqueror, one who surrenders out of fear, and one already subdued. The same holds true for those kings who are positioned next to the immediate foes of the conqueror.

- Among these kings, the conqueror should prioritize supporting the friend who shares the conqueror's objectives in opposing their common enemy, using this alliance to hold the enemy at bay.
- Once the enemy has been subdued and if the friend, having gained in strength, begins to resist the conqueror's influence, the conqueror should take measures to turn neighboring rulers, including those adjacent to the neighbor, against this now unsubmissive friend.
- Alternatively, the conqueror might support a relative of the friend or an imprisoned prince in claiming his lands, or act in a way that keeps the friend dependent on the conqueror's assistance to maintain his loyalty.
- The conqueror should refrain from assisting a friend who is in continuous decline, ensuring instead that the friend remains neither so weak as to require constant help nor so strong as to become a threat. A skilled ruler maintains balance, positioning allies to neither deteriorate nor exceed their assigned influence. When, with the desire of getting wealth, a wandering friend (i.e., a nomadic king) makes an agreement with the conqueror, the latter should so remove the cause of the friend's flight that he never flies again.
- When a friend is equally accessible to both the conqueror and the enemy, the conqueror should first work to sever that stubborn friend's alliance with the enemy. Once the friend is

isolated, he can be subdued, and the conqueror may then turn to defeating the enemy.

- If a friend maintains a neutral stance, the conqueror should subtly arrange for the friend to incur the animosity of his closest adversaries. When the friend is embroiled in conflicts with them, the conqueror can step in and offer assistance, securing loyalty through this aid.

- When a friend, due to his weakness, seeks protection from both the conqueror and the enemy, the conqueror should support him with military forces, ensuring that the friend remains reliant on this aid and refrains from shifting loyalties.

- Alternatively, the conqueror might remove the friend from his current territory, relocating him to a different region. In this way, the conqueror retains control, with the option to administer punishment or reward, depending on the friend's loyalty.

- Alternatively, the conqueror might weaken a friend who has become too powerful, or eliminate him if he fails to support the conqueror in times of danger yet enjoys the conqueror's protection during peaceful times.

- If an enemy aggressively turns against his own adversary (who is the conqueror's ally) when the adversary is already burdened by troubles, the ally should, without exposing his vulnerabilities, take action to suppress this enemy.

- However, if a friend takes no further action after initially opposing a troubled enemy, the enemy will overcome his difficulties and ultimately subdue the inactive friend.

- A strategist well-versed in political science should carefully assess the stages of advancement, decline, stagnation, attrition, and collapse, as well as the application of every form of strategic maneuver.

- One who understands the intricate interdependencies within the sixfold policy can skillfully manipulate and command rulers as if they were bound in a web of alliances and rivalries crafted by his own design.

Book 8

CHAPTER I. THE AGGREGATE OF THE CALAMITIES OF THE ELEMENTS OF SOVEREIGNTY.

When several calamities strike at once, the first consideration should be to assess whether a proactive offense or a strategic defense is more manageable. National calamities, whether they arise from natural events, mismanagement, or external factors, often reflect a blend of bad fortune and poor decision-making. The term vyasana (translated as vices or calamities) encompasses the opposite of virtue, signifying not only a lack of positive qualities but also the escalation of adverse conditions and hardships. Vyasana, in essence, signifies a force that diminishes one's prosperity and stability, undermining well-being at the personal or national level.

My teacher asserts that among various calamities—including distress afflicting the king, his ministers, the general population, fortifications, finances, the army, or allies—the distress of the king is the most consequential, with each subsequent calamity listed in descending order of seriousness.

Bháradvája, however, contends that between the distress of the king and that of his ministers, ministerial distress is more severe. Ministers bear the weight of council deliberations, securing the realization of strategies, overseeing projects, managing finances and expenditures, mobilizing and maintaining the army, defending the kingdom from both internal and external threats, preserving order, protecting the kingdom's heir, ensuring the smooth installation of successors, and enacting solutions to ongoing or anticipated crises. In the absence of capable ministers, these critical duties suffer, and the king—like a bird stripped of its wings—is deprived of effective action, giving rise to unchecked enemy schemes. Ministerial distress poses an immediate threat to the king's life and stability, for ministers are the bedrock of his security and protection.

Kautilya argues differently, prioritizing the king's welfare above all. According to Kautilya, the king is the linchpin of the kingdom's structure. His role encompasses appointing ministers, priests, and administrators; addressing the challenges facing his people; tackling kingdom-wide issues; and driving forward-looking policies to benefit the realm. Should ministers face challenges, the king has the authority to replace them. A just and vigilant king ensures order through merit-based rewards and just punishments, which foster loyalty and balance among his people. The king's character, ultimately, sets a standard that permeates throughout society, shaping whether the people thrive or falter. Hence, the king is the aggregate force that embodies and directs the people's collective strength and progress.

Visálaksha holds a distinct view, asserting that between the distress of ministers and that of the people, the troubles facing the people are more serious. National wealth, military strength, resources, skilled labor, transport networks, and other essentials rely on the vitality of the general populace. Without the people, a kingdom's resources dwindle, second in importance only to the presence of a competent king and ministers.

Kautilya counters this argument by emphasizing that the effective functioning of the kingdom depends heavily on the role of the minister. Ministers coordinate and execute the king's vision, ensuring the public's safety, advancing land development, protecting property from enemies, expanding the army, maintaining financial health, managing resources, and deploying solutions to ongoing crises. Ministers play a foundational role in securing the kingdom's stability and its people's prosperity, ensuring that these functions are consistently and effectively executed.

The school of Parásara argues that, between distress of the people and issues arising from poor fortifications, the latter is far more troubling. Fortified towns serve as repositories for both treasury and military resources, offering a safe haven for the population. These fortifications provide strength beyond what mere citizens or rural people can offer, becoming powerful instruments of defense in times of threat. They afford the king a secure stronghold, while the people themselves are a shared asset, accessible to both the king and his enemy.

Kautilya disagrees, asserting that forts, financial resources, and the military ultimately rely on the populace for support. It is the people who uphold the construction of buildings, facilitate trade, sustain agriculture, manage livestock, and contribute bravery, stability, and other resources. Natural barriers like mountains and islands often serve as defensive structures in inhabited lands, whereas standalone forts become essential only in countries with limited open lands. In regions dominated by agriculture, lack of fortifications can be a source of distress, while in areas with largely martial populations, scarcity of cultivated lands or resources can pose serious challenges.

Pisuna claims that the absence of financial resources outweighs the troubles arising from lack of fortifications. Fort repairs, structural upkeep, and strategic maneuvers—such as funding espionage efforts to capture an enemy's stronghold—are made possible through wealth. Financial resources provide control over people, influence over allies and adversaries, encouragement for outsiders, and means for sustaining and mobilizing an army. Treasure can be relocated in times of crisis, but a fort cannot be so easily moved.

Kautilya counters, emphasizing that the fort itself safeguards both the treasury and the army, while supporting covert operations, controlling loyalists, maintaining the armed forces, receiving allies, and repelling threats, whether from enemies or wild tribes. Without fortifications, treasury resources are at risk of falling into enemy hands. For those who possess a well-fortified base, Kautilya notes, there is a shield against total ruin.

Kaunapadanta argues that of the two—lack of financial resources or the absence of an effective military—lacking a capable army is the greater detriment. A proficient army is vital for maintaining control over friends and enemies alike, for the possibility of swaying enemy forces, and for managing the overall administration of the kingdom. Without a military force, the treasury itself becomes vulnerable to seizure. While financial shortages may be mitigated by harvesting resources from lands, acquiring raw materials, or capturing an adversary's territory, the military's loyalty is paramount, as soldiers might even defect to the enemy or cause instability, endangering the king's life and bringing calamity.

Yet, Kautilya asserts that financial resources remain the key to observing virtuous acts and fulfilling material needs. Depending on shifts in location, timing, and strategic priorities, either finance or the army may momentarily hold more influence. The military can safeguard existing wealth, but wealth is the enduring foundation that secures both the treasury and the military. Given the dependency of all national activities on financial health, Kautilya concludes that financial distress is ultimately the most significant threat.

Vátavyádhi claims that between the distress of the army and that of an ally, it is more serious when an ally faces difficulties. An ally, even if not directly supported with resources or if stationed far away, can still play a crucial role. He fends off both rear and frontal enemies, subdues the allies of enemies, and keeps wild tribes at bay. Moreover, in times of crisis, an ally provides support in the form of funds, troops, and additional lands.

Kautilya, however, disagrees, arguing that a well-maintained and powerful army ensures the loyalty of allies, and can even encourage an enemy to adopt a friendly posture. When a task can be accomplished equally well by the army or by an ally, the choice between the two should depend on the strategic benefits of timing, location, and anticipated gains. During sudden campaigns, or when threats arise from external enemies, wild tribes, or internal rebellions, relying solely on allies can be risky. Friends are generally dependable only when financial support is available; when resources are scarce, alliances may falter, especially if an enemy has grown stronger. Therefore, Kautilya asserts, assessing the severity of various calamities across the elements of sovereignty should involve carefully weighing the current strength of both army and allies.

- When a portion of one element within sovereignty is affected by troubles, the potential to accomplish a task can be assessed based on the extent, loyalty, and strength of the unaffected and serviceable part.

- When two elements of sovereignty experience troubles simultaneously, they should be evaluated according to their trends—whether they are advancing or in decline—assuming that the remaining elements are in stable and positive condition and do not require further assessment.
- However, if the calamities affecting a single element threaten to destabilize or destroy the remaining elements, then these calamities, regardless of whether they impact the foundational or another specific element, are indeed of the utmost severity and urgency.

[Thus ends Chapter I, "The Aggregate of the Calamities of the Elements of Sovereignty," in Book VIII, "Concerning Vices and Calamities" of the Arthasástra of Kautilya. End of the hundred and seventeenth chapter from the beginning.]

CHAPTER II. CONSIDERATIONS ABOUT THE TROUBLES OF THE KING AND OF HIS KINGDOM.

The king and his domain serve as the core elements of any state's foundation, and their stability is essential for the overall strength and prosperity of the realm.

The challenges that a king faces may stem from either internal or external sources. Internal threats, though often less visible, are frequently more dangerous than external ones; they can be likened to the lurking threat of a hidden serpent that quietly waits to strike. Within internal threats, those arising specifically from ministers or close advisors are considered the most hazardous, as they have intimate access to the ruler's trust and influence. For this reason, it is vital that the king personally maintains control over the state's key functions—namely, the treasury and the military forces—to prevent manipulation from within his own court.

When comparing the vulnerabilities of divided rule versus foreign rule, both scenarios pose serious risks to stability. Divided rule—where governance is shared between two kings—often leads to conflict due to rivalry, jealousy, and conflicting loyalties, resulting in inefficiencies and eventual collapse. In contrast, foreign rule, which arises when a foreign power seizes control of a kingdom while the rightful ruler still lives, can be even more damaging. Foreign rulers typically view the conquered territory as an alien possession, exploiting it for its resources while treating it as disposable. Such rulers may strip the country of its wealth, treat it as a commercial asset, and leave it impoverished. When the citizens inevitably lose their loyalty to these foreign rulers, the latter are often quick to abandon the territory, leaving it weakened and destabilized.

In evaluating a blind king—one lacking knowledge in governance—and a king who deviates from wise policies, my teacher argues that a blind king is inherently more dangerous. A blind king, being untrained in the sciences of administration and strategy, acts impulsively, stubbornly, and often at the behest of others. His inability to make informed decisions leads to the downfall of the kingdom. On the other hand, a king who occasionally errs against wisdom can be brought back on course when his actions clearly diverge from sound governance. Kautilya, however, has a different view, asserting that a blind king, despite his limitations, can still be guided by competent advisors who help steer him toward correct policies. An erring king, however, particularly one who chooses to act against established wisdom, poses a graver risk, as his deliberate misjudgments are likely to lead to long-term damage to the state and its people.

When considering a sick king versus a new ruler, my teacher believes that a king suffering from illness may lose his throne due to ministerial conspiracies or may even lose his life due to the physical toll of managing state affairs, especially if he lacks the strength to keep control. A new ruler, on the other hand, often garners immediate support from the populace by performing popular actions such as adhering to his duties, lowering taxes, and bestowing gifts and favors upon the people. Kautilya counters this perspective by emphasizing that a sick king, even amid his illness, continues to uphold his duties out of necessity, knowing that the welfare of the kingdom depends on his role. A new ruler, however, can be unpredictable; assuming that his newly acquired lands are entirely his by right, he may act impulsively without considering the consequences. Such a king is prone to tolerating the aggressions of neighboring kings who seek to exploit his lack of control, or he may find himself overpowered by internal conflicts, as he lacks the same level of authority and established relationships with state elements as an experienced ruler. Furthermore, Kautilya differentiates between various types of kings in this context: there is a distinction between a king who is morally diseased and one who suffers from physical ailments, just as there is a difference between a high-born ruler and one of humble birth.

In comparing a high-born but weak king with a strong but low-born king, my teacher argues that people may be inclined to accept a weak but noble-born ruler out of respect for lineage, but they would ultimately resist an ineffective or unfit ruler, regardless of his birth. Conversely, if they prioritize strength and power, they may more easily accept a strong, low-born leader, allowing him to wield influence and control due to his personal capabilities rather than his heritage.

No, Kautilya says, people will naturally follow a high-born king, even if he is weak, because a thriving people tend to respect a king with noble roots. They also make sure the schemes of a strong but low-born person fail, as there is an old saying that having virtues strengthens friendships.

The loss of crops is more damaging than losing a few handfuls of grain since the hard work that went into it is destroyed. A lack of rain is worse than too much rain.

- The relative seriousness or insignificance of any two types of troubles affecting the key parts of sovereignty, following the order of the different types of distress, determines whether to take an offensive or defensive approach.

[Thus ends Chapter II, "Considerations about the Troubles of the King and of his Kingdom," in Book VIII, "Concerning Vices and

Calamities," of the Arthasástra of Kautilya. End of the hundred and eighteenth chapter from the beginning.]

CHAPTER III. THE AGGREGATE OF THE TROUBLE OF MEN.

Understood! I'll ensure every sentence is translated exactly without any shortening, maintaining a line-by-line structure to preserve the original meaning and length. Here is the expanded version:

Ignorance and lack of discipline are the root causes of a person's troubles. A person without proper training fails to recognize the harm that can come from indulging in vices. Now, we will discuss these vices in detail:

There are three types of vices that stem from anger, while those arising from desire fall into four categories. Between these two types, anger is considered worse, as it drives one to act against all in its path. In most cases, kings who gave in to anger have been reported to fall prey to the rage of the people. On the other hand, kings who were addicted to pleasure have often succumbed to severe illnesses brought about by excess and the depletion of their resources.

No, says Bháradvája, anger is the trait of a righteous person. It is the very foundation of courage; it acts as a force to eliminate despicable individuals, and it instills fear among the people, keeping them under control. Anger is always an essential trait for the prevention of wrongdoing. On the other hand, desire is linked to the pursuit of pleasurable outcomes, the willingness to forgive, acts of generosity, and efforts to endear oneself to others. Desire is necessary for anyone who wishes to enjoy the benefits of their achievements.

No, says Kautilya, anger leads to enmity and stirs up conflict with adversaries, and it is consistently associated with pain. Addiction to pleasure (káma) results in loss of respect, financial ruin, and throws the one addicted into the company of thieves, gamblers, hunters, musicians, and other undesirable characters. Among these issues, enmity is more dangerous than disrespect, as a disrespected person becomes vulnerable to betrayal by both their people and their enemies, while a hated person is actively destroyed. Conflict with enemies is more severe than financial loss, as financial loss causes distress in one's resources, while enmity poses a risk to life itself. Suffering from vices is more significant than keeping poor company, for undesirable company can be abandoned immediately, but suffering from vices brings enduring harm. Therefore, anger is the more serious of the two evils.

Which is worse: the abuse of words, misuse of wealth, or the imposition of oppressive punishment?

Visáláksha argues that, when comparing the abuse of language to the misuse of money, the harm done through harsh words is more severe. For, when harshly spoken to, a brave person is moved to retaliate; harsh words, like a nail that pierces the heart, provoke anger and bring pain to all the senses.

No, says Kautilya, money as a gift can ease the anger caused by harsh words, while the misuse of money itself can lead to the loss of one's means of livelihood. Misuse of money involves giving, taking, losing, or neglecting wealth altogether.

The School of Parásara argues that misuse of money is more harmful than excessive punishment because good deeds and pleasures in life rely on wealth; even the fabric of society is tied to it. Thus, its misuse is a far greater danger.

No, says Kautilya, people would rather risk large sums than their own lives. Excessive punishment not only risks one's well-being but also exposes one to similar punishment from one's enemies.

This completes the set of evils arising from anger.

Next are the four vices rooted in desire: hunting, gambling, women, and drinking.

Pisuna asserts that hunting is the worse of the two vices, compared to gambling. Hunting leads to dangers such as encounters with robbers, enemies, wild animals, and fire, disorientation, fear, hunger, thirst, and even death. In gambling, however, a skilled gambler can achieve success, like Jayatsena and Duryodhana did.

No, says Kautilya, in gambling, one party is always bound to suffer defeat, as seen in the tale of Nala and Yudhishthira. Wealth won in gambling, much like a mere piece of meat, often brings enmity. The harms of gambling include failing to appreciate hard-earned wealth, gaining wealth unethically, losing wealth without enjoying it, ignoring basic needs, and falling ill from irregular meals. In hunting, however, benefits include physical exercise, reduced phlegm, bile, fat, and sweat, the development of skills in aiming at both moving and still targets, learning how animals behave when provoked, and engaging in an occasional journey.

Kaunapadanta argues that addiction to gambling is a worse vice than addiction to women. Gamblers are known to play all hours, even by lamplight at night, disregarding events as grave as the death of a family member. A gambler easily shows anger when spoken to during tough times. In the case of attachment to women, however, conversations about virtue and prosperity are still possible during daily routines like bathing, dressing, or eating. Moreover, it's feasible to manage a woman's behavior in a way that could support the king's welfare or even end the relationship discreetly under the guise of illness if necessary.

No, says Kautilya, it is possible to distract someone from gambling, but much harder from women. The consequences of addiction to women include failing to observe duties, neglecting immediate tasks, inability to focus on political matters, and slipping into the vice of drinking.

Vátavyádhi contends that addiction to women is more harmful than drinking, pointing to various forms of childishness often seen among women, which is elaborated in the section on "The Harem." By contrast, drinking offers sensory enjoyment, pleases others, garners followers' favor, and provides a means of relaxing after hard work.

No, says Kautilya, being involved with women can lead to children, the need for self-defense, changes in relationships within the harem, and can avoid consequences if outside women are deemed unsuitable. Drinking brings both positive and negative results, but its ill effects are striking: loss of wealth, madness in otherwise reasonable men, a lifeless appearance while living, indecency, neglect of sacred knowledge, and the loss of life, assets, and friendships. It severs ties with respectable people, brings suffering, and often leads to wasting wealth on music and singing.

Of the two vices, gambling and drinking, gambling causes gain or loss of stakes for one side or the other. Even animals display divisive tendencies and aggression under its influence. Particularly in assemblies or alliances with unified interests, gambling has been known to divide and ruin them. Worst of all evils is engaging in unworthy activities, as this completely diminishes one's capacity for wise governance and political insight.

- The pursuit of what is generally condemned stems from desire, while anger manifests in acts that oppress those who are good. Since both of these tendencies lead to numerous harms, they are regarded as the most destructive of all vices.
- Therefore, a person with good judgment should seek the company of the wise and, by mastering their own passions, rid themselves of both anger and desire, as these impulses give rise to further evils and undermine the very foundation of a stable life.

[Thus ends Chapter III, "The Aggregate of the Troubles of Men," in Book VIII. "Concerning Vices and Calamities" of the Arthasástra of Kautilya. End of the hundred and nineteenth chapter from the beginning.]

CHAPTER IV. THE GROUP OF MOLESTATIONS, THE GROUP OF OBSTRUCTIONS, AND THE GROUP OF FINANCIAL TROUBLES.

Natural calamities include fires, floods, disease outbreaks, famine, and epidemics like maraka.

My teacher believes that between fires and floods, fire's destruction is worse because it's beyond remedy. In contrast, most troubles, aside from fire, can be alleviated, and flood-related troubles eventually subside.

Kautilya disagrees, arguing that fires typically affect a single village or part of one, while floods can sweep away entire regions, affecting many villages at once.

According to my teacher, of pestilence and famine, pestilence is worse as it disrupts all kinds of work, causes illness and death, and prompts people to flee, leading to a halt in activities, while famine doesn't stop work entirely and still allows for some trade, livestock use, and tax collection.

Kautilya, however, notes that pestilence generally devastates a limited area and can be remedied, while famine affects the whole region, depriving everyone of their means to live.

This view also explains the impact of maraka.

My teacher believes that the loss of common people obstructs everyday work more than the loss of leaders.

Kautilya disagrees, explaining that it is possible to replace common people due to their sheer numbers. For common people's benefit, leaders must be preserved, as they're often one in a thousand— uniquely brave and wise, serving as a foundation for the community.

On troubles within one's own Circle of States versus those of an enemy's, my teacher asserts that internal troubles are more harmful and unmanageable since an external threat can either be fought off or kept away with allies or by negotiating peace.

Kautilya counters, saying that internal problems can be resolved by containing or eliminating problematic leaders, and such issues may impact only parts of a kingdom, whereas an enemy's Circle of States can cause destruction, burning, and devastation across many areas.

My teacher claims that discord among citizens is more damaging, as it can create disunity and invite enemy invasion, whereas disputes between kings bring benefits like better wages and tax relief for the people.

Kautilya has a different view, noting that internal disputes can be quelled by detaining the leaders or removing the causes, and infighting among citizens can actually encourage productivity as they compete, ultimately benefiting the country. However, conflicts between kings lead to widespread suffering, requiring twice as much effort to manage and causing more significant harm to the people.

My teacher believes that of a king who enjoys leisure activities and a people who are also sportive, a populace given to amusements is more damaging to productivity since their playfulness affects the kingdom's work, while a king inclined to enjoyment benefits artisans, entertainers, and merchants.

But Kautilya disagrees, arguing that when a country takes to recreation, it is generally a minor interruption, and after some leisure, the people return to work. In contrast, a king given to indulgence disrupts governance by favoring courtiers, seizing resources, and causing delays in production and industry.

My teacher suggests that between a favored wife and a prince, the prince causes more harm by indulging his followers, extracting resources, and obstructing work, whereas a wife devoted to personal enjoyment only involves herself in such pursuits.

Kautilya sees it differently. He notes that any misbehavior of a prince can be managed through the minister and priest, while the favored wife's influence, often coupled with her willfulness and poor associations, is harder to control.

According to my teacher, trouble from a corporation of people versus that from a leader is harder to manage when dealing with the people's group. Being large in number, they can disrupt through theft and disorder, while a single leader may only interfere with certain tasks.

Kautilya holds a different view, pointing out that a corporation can be controlled or subdued, as it follows the king's fortunes and can be kept in check by detaining a few members or the leader. On the other hand, a leader with strong backing poses greater risks by threatening the well-being and assets of others.

In considering the chamberlain versus the revenue collector, my teacher suggests the chamberlain, with his tendency to meddle in operations and impose fines, is more burdensome, while the collector focuses on the income of his own department.

Kautilya disagrees, arguing that the chamberlain may intercept offerings meant for the treasury, but the collector may prioritize his revenue over the king's or even divert it altogether, interfering with the kingdom's finances.

Regarding the boundary superintendent and a trader, my teacher believes that the superintendent hampers commerce by tolerating theft and overtaxing, whereas a trader benefits the kingdom by creating wealth through fair exchanges.

Kautilya argues the opposite, noting that the boundary superintendent can promote trade by welcoming goods and fostering exchanges, whereas traders often collude to manipulate prices for profit, increasing or decreasing values to their advantage.

Finally, when weighing land held by a noble against land reserved for cattle grazing, which is more beneficial?

My teacher argues that land occupied by a high-born individual is highly productive, supplying manpower to the army. For this reason, it should not be taken over, as the owner might retaliate and cause disturbances. Meanwhile, land used for cattle grazing, which can be cultivated, should be freed up for crops since agricultural land is more valuable than grazing land.

However, Kautilya holds a different view. Though land used by a noble is indeed useful, it should still be reclaimed to prevent potential issues from arising if the noble becomes rebellious. On the other hand, land reserved for cattle grazing generates revenue from livestock and does not need to be confiscated unless it directly interferes with farming activities.

My teacher also says that between robbers and wild tribes, robbers are more troublesome. They are constantly on the lookout for opportunities to abduct people at night, ambush others, and steal substantial amounts of wealth. Wild tribes, on the other hand, are more organized under a leader, generally sticking to nearby forests and only causing limited damage.

Kautilya disagrees, suggesting that robbers typically target only those who are careless, making them easier to identify and catch. In contrast, wild tribes often have fortified bases and are numerous and courageous, willing to launch attacks even in broad daylight. They can seize and devastate large areas, similar to small kingdoms.

Between animal forests and elephant forests, ordinary animals are numerous and provide ample resources, such as meat and hides. They naturally limit the growth of grass and are relatively easy to manage. Elephants, however, are quite the opposite and have been known to cause substantial damage to territories, even after they have been captured and tamed.

Benefits from one's own country, like grains, cattle, gold, and raw materials, are essential for sustaining the population in times of crisis, whereas foreign resources lack the same reliability and accessibility during hardships.

This comprises the group of molestations.

When movement is restricted by a local leader, it's called an internal obstruction; however, restrictions due to an enemy or a wild tribe are external obstructions.

This makes up the group of obstructions.

Financial troubles stemming from these two kinds of obstructions and the molestations listed above include revenue stagnation, loss of wealth through tax exemptions given to leaders, dispersed revenue, inaccurate revenue records, and funds held by neighboring kings or wild tribes.

Thus concludes the group of financial troubles.

- To ensure the country's prosperity, one should strive to prevent the causes of such troubles, address them effectively when they arise, and actively remove both obstructions and financial difficulties.

[Thus ends Chapter IV, "The Group of Molestations, the Group of Obstructions, and the Group of Financial Troubles" in BookVIII, "Concerning Vices and Calamities," of the Arthasástra of Kautilya. End of the hundred and twentieth chapter from the beginning.]

CHAPTER V. THE GROUP OF TROUBLES OF THE ARMY, AND THE GROUP OF TROUBLES OF A FRIEND.

The troubles that weaken an army encompass a wide range of situations, each of which affects the army's ability to fight effectively. These troubles include, but are not limited to: an army that feels disrespected by its leadership, one that suffers from deep humiliation, another that has not been paid, one plagued by illness, one that has just arrived without proper preparation, one exhausted from a prolonged journey, and one physically worn out. Additionally, an army that has suffered recent losses, faced outright defeat, had its front lines broken, or one that is suffering from severe weather or stationed in an unsuited terrain can be seriously impaired. Furthermore, an army can be troubled by frustration over unmet expectations, or can be affected by soldiers who have fled from previous battles, troops preoccupied with family concerns, individuals with divided loyalties, segments angered due to conflicts with the leadership, troops who have previously served in other states, and those that specialize in specific maneuvers or terrains that do not align with the current battlefield.

Among these, there are specific remedies that can improve the condition of an army in some situations but not all. For instance, an army that feels disrespected may recover and become battle-ready if leadership takes steps to restore honor and morale. However, an army that is deeply humiliated and has lost faith in its cause will be harder to rally. In cases where an army is either unpaid or plagued by illness, payment can renew loyalty and readiness, while sick troops are simply unfit for combat, regardless of external efforts. Similarly, when dealing with a freshly arrived army and one that is tired from travel, the newly arrived soldiers can be positioned and integrated, while long-traveled forces require rest before they are battle-ready. An exhausted army can be rejuvenated through adequate sleep, nourishment, and rest, while an army that has suffered significant loss, particularly of its leaders, is greatly weakened and must regroup to restore strength.

When comparing an army repelled in combat with one that has had its front lines broken, the repelled forces may reengage if reinforced with fresh troops, while an army suffering heavy casualties in its front lines will find it difficult to recover morale and strength. Troops weakened by harsh weather conditions may be readied for battle if given proper clothing and gear, whereas those stationed in unsuitable terrain cannot move freely and are likely to suffer in their combat effectiveness. Armies disappointed by unmet expectations can be brought back to readiness if they are satisfied, but soldiers who have previously fled from battle are unreliable.

Furthermore, some soldiers may be deeply attached to their families, causing distractions, and they may be made ready by temporarily separating them from familial ties, while troops who have defected to the enemy or have divided loyalties are inherently unreliable, posing risks similar to those of internal enemies. This array of potential challenges demonstrates the various ways in which an army's strength can be impacted, as well as the necessary measures that might either remedy or fail to address these unique trouble

Among armies facing issues of internal conflict, those with only a faction that is provoked or agitated can still be mobilized if that faction is pacified through careful negotiation, conciliation, or other strategic methods. However, a disunited army, whose members have developed estrangement or hostility toward each other, should not be relied upon in combat due to lack of cohesion. For forces that have resigned from service in one or multiple states, an army that departed from a foreign state without signs of conspiracy can still be led into battle under trusted commanders or spies. In contrast, an army that has resigned from several states carries greater risk and should not be deployed due to its potential for disloyalty or danger.

When considering armies trained in specialized maneuvers, one accustomed to specific strategies in both encampment and battle tactics can be effective. Yet, troops trained only to operate within specific territories or environments are limited and may not be suitable for unfamiliar or varied conditions. Armies facing obstructions are also to be handled with care. Troops blocked in one direction may still be redirected against an enemy from another direction, but an army encircled on all sides lacks the necessary mobility and should be spared from combat until freed.

For armies whose supplies have been disrupted, the specific nature of the shortage determines their readiness. Troops deprived of grain can be supported by acquiring food from alternative sources, either bringing in foodstuffs or supplying the army with movable and immovable provisions like livestock or preserved goods. However, an army cut off entirely from reinforcements and provisions is unsustainable and should not be sent to battle without reestablishing these essential resources.

Armies based domestically, as opposed to those stationed with allies, offer different strategic advantages. Those stationed within one's own country can be more easily disbanded or called back if dangers arise, whereas forces placed under an ally's protection, removed in both time and distance, present challenges in mobilization and may not be effective in immediate threats.

With armies containing traitorous elements or those fearing attack from the rear, troops infiltrated by traitors may still be of use if they are carefully isolated and placed under the command of a trusted leader. However, an army fearing a rear assault is compromised in morale and should not be exposed to the front lines until that threat is addressed. Armies that have lost communications with their central command can regain effectiveness once communication is restored, ideally with the support of civilians and local populations. Yet, a force entirely without leadership, whether that be the king or another figure of authority, lacks direction and should be restructured before deployment.

Finally, for troops that have lost a key leader or lack training, those with missing leaders may recover strength if a new, capable commander is appointed. However, untrained troops lack the necessary discipline and experience to function effectively in battle and should be drilled or properly instructed before any engagement.

- To protect his army from troubles, a king should focus on eliminating vices and challenges within the ranks, recruit capable new men, avoid areas where an enemy could stage an ambush, and ensure harmony among the army's officers.
- A wise king constantly watches for any threats posed by his enemy and remains ready to strike when the opposing army faces difficulties.
- When the king identifies any source of trouble for his people, he must quickly and carefully implement countermeasures to neutralize it.
- A friend who either independently, in alliance with others, or under another ruler's influence has turned against his own ally; a friend who has been left out due to a lack of ability to sustain loyalty, or due to greed or apathy; and
- A friend who has been swayed by another and withdrawn from battle should all be managed with caution.
- A friend who, in adopting a strategy of making peace with one ally and planning an attack against another, has aligned with someone preparing to advance—either alone or in alliance— against his own ally;
- A friend who is unable to overcome his own difficulties due to fear, contempt, or indifference; a friend cornered in his own territory or forced to flee in fear;
- A friend who is discontented because he has paid too much, because he has not received his rightful due, or because he remains dissatisfied even after receiving what was owed to him;
- A friend who has willingly paid excessively or has been compelled by another to pay more than his fair share;
- A friend who is held under undue pressure or who, after breaking ties of loyalty, has sought to establish friendship

elsewhere—each of these scenarios requires careful handling.

- A friend neglected because of a lack of capability to retain his loyalty, or a friend who turns hostile despite an ally's attempts to prevent it—such friends are rarely retained, and even if they are, they often drift away.

- A friend who understands the obligations of friendship, who is honorable, or who may feel disappointed due to lack of communication, or who, despite his enthusiasm, is not equipped for the task, or who retreats in fear from another source of threat;

- Or a friend who becomes fearful at witnessing another ally's downfall, or who fears a coalition of enemies, or who is influenced by traitors to abandon his friendship—this type of friend is likely to be won over, and once gained, is steadfast in loyalty.

- Therefore, one must be careful to avoid causes that could undermine a friendship, and if such causes do arise, they should be resolved by showing a warm and genuine approach to restore and strengthen the bond.

Book 9

CHAPTER I. THE KNOWLEDGE OF POWER, PLACE, TIME, STRENGTH, AND WEAKNESS; THE TIME OF INVASION.

The conqueror should thoroughly assess his own strength and that of his enemy. After carefully considering factors like resources, terrain, timing, march readiness, army recruitment, potential outcomes, as well as expected losses, profits, and risks, he should proceed only if he can mobilize his full force. Otherwise, it's best to remain at rest.

My teacher asserts that enthusiasm surpasses sheer power. A king who is energetic, brave, healthy, skilled in arms, and who drives his army with fervor can overcome even a powerful rival. A smaller force, led by a determined king, is capable of achieving its goals. Conversely, a king lacking in enthusiasm will fail, no matter how strong his army may be.

However, Kautilya disagrees, claiming that strength holds greater importance than enthusiasm alone. Through sheer power, a king can outmaneuver another who relies solely on zeal. By acquiring or allying with an enthusiastic king and brave soldiers, he can leverage the enthusiasm of his armies—be they cavalry, elephants, chariots, or other forces—moving them swiftly and decisively. Throughout history, powerful rulers, regardless of gender, age, or physical limitations, have achieved dominion by enlisting or purchasing the support of passionate allies.

My teacher also holds that power—meaning wealth and army—outweighs skill in intrigue because, while a king may be skilled in strategy, he is powerless without resources. Without power, he is like seeds withering in a drought, vulnerable to losing his kingdom.

Kautilya, however, contends that skill in intrigue is superior. A leader with insight and knowledge of statecraft can achieve success with minimal effort by applying strategies like conciliation, subterfuge, spies, and even chemical methods. This adept use of intrigue enables him to outwit those rulers who rely solely on enthusiasm and brute force. Hence, among enthusiasm, power, and skill for intrigue, the one who possesses the quality ranked later in this sequence has the advantage over those holding the earlier ones.

In terms of territory, or space, it signifies the land itself. A vast stretch of earth—such as the thousand yojanas (a unit of measure) from the Himalayas to the ocean—is the dominion of a true emperor, encompassing varied landscapes like forests, villages, waterfalls, plains, and rugged areas. In this diversity, a king should initiate ventures that reinforce his power and wealth. The best land is one where his army finds strategic maneuverability and that challenges his enemy; the worst is land that offers no advantage, and somewhere in between is a land of mixed characteristics.

Time, as another vital factor, includes the cold, hot, and rainy seasons and periods such as day, night, fortnight, month, season, solstice, year, and five-year cycles (Yuga). In these cycles, a ruler should embark on initiatives that promote his power and success. The most advantageous time is one that benefits his army's movements and disadvantages his enemy; the least favorable is time that reverses this balance, while a time of both advantages and drawbacks is moderate in quality.

My teacher argues that among the three factors—strength, location, and timing—strength is ultimately the most crucial. When a person is endowed with sufficient strength, they are more likely to overcome any hindrance, whether caused by rough terrain or difficult seasonal conditions, such as intense heat, biting cold, or continuous rain. A powerful king can still prevail over obstacles if he possesses adequate strength, as his resources and resilience can carry him through. Some, however, assert that location may be even more critical; they offer the analogy of a dog that, if positioned well on solid ground, can drag even a crocodile, but if that same crocodile pulls the dog into lower ground, it gains the advantage. In this sense, the right setting or advantageous ground can be as valuable as raw strength.

Another school of thought holds that timing is the most vital of the three. Those who prioritize timing often point out that by day, a crow can easily kill an owl, yet as night falls, the owl becomes dominant and can kill the crow. Thus, even the strengths of the most able creature can be influenced or thwarted by timing.

Kautilya, however, disagrees with these singular views, arguing that strength, location, and timing each play vital roles that enhance and complement each other. He contends that whoever can effectively harness all three factors will have a considerable advantage. A ruler should, therefore, take care to secure each element of strength, location, and timing in preparation for an advance. Once these are in place, the conqueror should allocate part of his forces, roughly one-third to one-fourth, to protect his base of operations from potential rear threats posed by enemies or wild tribes in the vicinity. Then, equipped with the remainder of his force and ample resources, he should aim to attack during the month of Mārgaśīrṣa (December). At this time, he can capitalize on the enemy's outdated, stale food supplies, as the opponent is unlikely to have stocked fresh provisions or repaired his fortifications. This timing enables the conqueror to devastate his enemy's most recently harvested crops, which are generally set aside for the rainy season, as well as autumnal reserves.

If his objective is to spoil both autumn harvests and spring stockpiles, the king should initiate his advance during the month of Chaitra (March). This allows him to strike his enemy's autumn crops before they can be fully secured and also attack early preparations for the next season. For further advantage, he might choose to march in Jyestha (May-June), particularly if the enemy's stores of fodder, firewood, and water have already been partially depleted. Since many rulers overlook maintaining adequate supplies during these months, it would also be an ideal time to compromise the enemy's fortifications. By doing so, the conqueror can disrupt both the spring harvests and summer provisions, inflicting a dual loss on his foe.

Alternatively, he could consider a dewy-season campaign, particularly if his opponent's territory is naturally dry, with limited access to fodder and water, making it difficult for the enemy to sustain his forces. A summer march might also be effective if his opponent's territory is prone to mist that could obstruct visibility, and if the terrain is marked by deep valleys, dense thickets, and natural foliage that would serve the conqueror's purposes. Moreover, if his enemy's country has ample water resources that are also suitable for maneuvering his own army while impeding the enemy's, he might choose to strike during the rainy season to use the weather to his advantage.

Planning the length of the march is equally critical. Longer marches are best conducted between Mārgaśīrṣa (December) and Taisha (January), as these are the months when food and weather conditions permit sustained campaigns. Campaigns of medium length may be scheduled between March and April when the climate is moderate, allowing troops to endure without becoming overexposed to extreme weather. Short campaigns are most effectively carried out between May and June, where swift action is essential to capitalize on short bursts of readiness. However, if a ruler finds himself hampered by his own difficulties, it is usually advisable to remain stationary and avoid overextending his resources.

The concept of advancing against an enemy under duress has already been outlined in the context of "Marching After Declaring War," providing additional guidance on timing and readiness.

My teacher suggests that nearly all campaigns should capitalize on any visible struggles faced by an enemy. Yet Kautilya offers a more cautious view, advising that a ruler should advance only when his own resources are sufficiently robust to manage any unexpected turns of events, as it is often difficult to fully ascertain the extent of an enemy's distress. However, if an opportune situation arises, where the conqueror is reasonably certain of reducing or subduing the enemy, a campaign could proceed confidently.

In seasons with mild temperatures, the conqueror should rely predominantly on an elephant-heavy army. Elephants, although invaluable in strength, are highly susceptible to health issues like leprosy if made to work in hot weather without sufficient water for bathing and drinking. Under such circumstances, they tend to become sluggish and resistant to orders. On the other hand, if the opponent's land is abundant in water, the rainy season provides a fitting time for deploying an elephant-centric army. Against an enemy stationed in an area with minimal rainfall or muddy water supplies, an army composed primarily of donkeys, camels, and horses would be most effective. These animals are better suited to such conditions, making them ideal for campaigns where the terrain and climate challenge the enemy's defenses.

When marching against a desert, the rainy season is the ideal time to deploy the full composition of the army—elephants, horses, chariots, and infantry—ensuring each unit is suited to the harsh, arid environment with added rainfall. For the march itself, the conqueror should carefully organize a plan that outlines both short and long stretches of travel, adjusted to match the landscape's various types.

Whether moving across level ground, rough terrain, valleys, or wide plains, each route should account for the challenges unique to each setting, allowing for adaptable progress based on the land's conditions.

When the intended task or objective is minimal, the campaign against any enemy should be brief to avoid unnecessary resource drain. Conversely, if the task is more substantial, requiring considerable effort or larger-scale conquest, the campaign should be proportionately extended, allowing time to accomplish more complex goals effectively. In times of rain, it's wise to establish camps in regions farther afield, where they can safely continue operations without facing setbacks due to weather, enabling the conqueror to maintain readiness and avoid stagnation even amid challenging conditions.

[Thus ends Chapter I, "The Knowledge of Power, Place, Time, Strength and Weakness, the Time of Invasion," in Book IX, "The Work of an Invader," of the Arthasástra of Kautilya. End of the hundred and twenty-second chapter from the beginning.]

CHAPTER II. THE TIME OF RECRUITING THE ARMY; THE FORM OF EQUIPMENT; AND THE WORK OF ARRAYING A RIVAL FORCE.

The best times to recruit different types of troops—such as hereditary soldiers, hired soldiers, corporations of soldiers, allied forces, and wild tribes—are based on the king's careful evaluation of his own resources, the enemy's capabilities, the nature of the mission, and the anticipated conditions. Each type of troop has distinct strengths, and the decision to deploy one over the other should be based on strategic priorities.

For the king, hereditary troops are a valuable asset, especially when he recognizes their reliability and attachment to his rule. If the king finds that his hereditary forces exceed his defensive needs and that having a large group idle could lead to dissatisfaction or even unrest among the ranks, he should opt to use them in action. Their loyalty is a significant advantage, especially if he fears that his enemy's own hereditary forces are large and skilled, requiring a more adept and connected army to counter them. Additionally, if the landscape and weather conditions are generally favorable for the march, hereditary troops are a dependable choice due to their endurance and unity, both crucial in extended or challenging campaigns. Hereditary forces are unlikely to be swayed by the enemy's intrigues, making them preferable when loyalty and unity are essential.

However, if the king's hired army is significantly larger than his hereditary force, and the enemy's army is known to be weaker or smaller in numbers, hired soldiers become an appropriate choice. This option is particularly useful if the campaign relies more on clever tactics than sheer force, as the hired army can bring a distinct flexibility to the strategy. If the journey's path and conditions are manageable, and the king can trust that his hired soldiers won't be swayed by enemy influences, this option allows him to utilize their skills without compromising loyalty. Hired forces work well when the enemy is not especially powerful and when they can perform with minimal risk of subversion by enemy schemes.

In situations where the king relies on corporations of soldiers, these forces serve him well if they are trustworthy and if their primary purpose is to defend his state during his absence. When a campaign is expected to be short, or if the enemy's forces also consist largely of soldier corporations, this force becomes particularly useful. Soldier corporations are cohesive units and thus are not easily divided by the enemy's tactics, making them well-suited for situations requiring solid frontlines and quick adaptability against a similar corporate army.

In certain cases, if the king has a strong alliance with another ruler, an allied army can be particularly effective. This allied force can not only aid in his own country's defense but can also support his campaign when he marches out. If he plans to move against the enemy for a limited period and anticipates more open warfare than tactical skirmishes, then allied forces are advantageous, as they bring additional resources and fresh troops to the effort. The king could place allied forces in territories that need monitoring—wild regions, cities, or open plains—while he advances his own troops to engage the enemy directly. This distribution of forces allows for strategic positioning where his ally's forces engage the enemy's supporters, keeping the main field free for his own army's maneuvers. If the king's success strongly depends on this ally, or if the ally is well-positioned nearby and deserving of the king's favor, the allied forces are a valuable addition, particularly when his friend's army is large and readily available.

In each case, the king should weigh the potential impact of his choice on both the short-term and long-term security of his kingdom. By understanding the strengths, weaknesses, and specific functions of each type of force, he can ensure that his approach is tailored to achieve the greatest advantage in his march against the enemy.

When a king believes that he can skillfully manipulate his strong enemy into fighting another rival over a city, plain, or stretch of wild land, he knows that this conflict will help him achieve one or another of his goals—much like an outcast benefits from a fight between a dog and a pig. Through this confrontation, he might see the disruptive power of his enemy's allies or wild tribes diminished, thus weakening them in the long run. If he assesses that he can redirect his immediate and powerful adversary's focus to another area, this diversion could help him relieve internal unrest, particularly if it's incited by his enemy. If he senses that the right time has come, perhaps with other rivalries heating up or minor kings becoming restless, he can leverage the enemy's forces to serve his ends by stoking such conflicts.

This strategy also sheds light on the best timing to use wild tribes in warfare. When the king sees that the enemy's path leads through areas inhabited by wild tribes, and that the road will be particularly challenging for the enemy's army to traverse, he might decide it's an ideal moment to deploy these native forces. Such wild tribes often prove invaluable in such terrains, and like using one wood-apple to split another, the tribes can be set against a smaller enemy force to weaken or even destroy it.

A well-trained and prepared army—one that is large, composed of various groups, and so devoted that it rises for battle whether paid or unpaid, even seeking plunder when the opportunity arises—is truly a formidable force. This type of force can withstand adverse weather, disband without major consequence, and be nearly impossible for an enemy to overcome. The ideal compact army is one in which all its members share the same homeland, caste, and training background, creating a cohesive and powerful military unit that can function as a united front against enemies.

These are the optimal times for gathering forces to prepare for a campaign. Among these different kinds of armies, payment to wild tribes is best provided through either raw goods or the allowance to claim spoils from conquered areas.

When the enemy's army is nearing, it's essential to obstruct their advance, push them back, delay their progress, or lead them astray with deceptive promises so that their timing becomes misaligned. This way, after the ideal marching period has passed, the enemy may find themselves at a disadvantage. Throughout these maneuvers, one must remain ever-watchful, strengthening one's own resources while ensuring that any efforts the enemy makes to bolster their forces are thwarted.

Among the different types of armies, the first mentioned generally holds the advantage over the next in the sequence. A hereditary army, bound to its master by tradition and consistently trained, offers distinct advantages over a hired force. This loyalty-driven force depends on the welfare of its leader, giving it a unity of purpose and resilience.

Of hired forces, those that remain close, rise quickly, and display unwavering loyalty are more valuable than loosely organized corporations of soldiers.

A company of soldiers, especially one that is native to the land, shares the same goals as the king, and is driven by similar sentiments of rivalry, anger, and hope for victory and reward, is more effective than the forces of an allied king. Even if such a company of soldiers is located further away and needs more time to mobilize, its unity of purpose makes it superior to the allied army.

An enemy's army led by an Arya, a noble or respected leader, is a better force than a wild tribe's army, as both types of forces are motivated by the prospect of plunder. However, in the absence of loot and when faced with difficulties, these armies can become a liability, as unpredictable as a snake in hiding.

My teacher asserts that, among armies composed of different castes—Brahmins, Kshatriyas, Vaishyas, or Shudras—the army led by Brahmins is preferable for its bravery. Each of these castes contributes something unique, yet each subsequent group is less desirable than the previous in this order.

Kautilya, however, disagrees, arguing that an army of Brahmins might be easily swayed by the enemy's flattery and acts of respect, possibly defecting to the enemy's side. Therefore, he suggests that an army of Kshatriyas, trained in the skills of weaponry and combat, is more reliable. Alternatively, an army composed of the numerically strong Vaishyas or Shudras could also be advantageous due to its sheer size.

In preparing his army, the king should assess his forces in relation to his enemy's, thinking strategically: "This is the strength of my enemy's forces; and this is how my army will counter it."

To counter an army that includes elephants, it's essential to have a force equipped with specialized items like large machines, the sakatagarbha (a siege device), wooden rods (kuntas), short dual-handled weapons (prasas), kharvatakas (presumably tactical implements), sturdy bamboo sticks, and heavy iron clubs. Each of these tools and weapons is effective against the massive power of elephants.

To confront an enemy army that relies on chariots, soldiers should be well-supplied with stones, clubs, armor, hooks, and plenty of spears. These can disrupt the momentum of chariot forces and pose serious obstacles to their movement.

For countering cavalry, a similar force equipped with the same weapons is also recommended.

To combat elephants directly, foot soldiers armored with protective gear are effective, as they can withstand the impact and pressure of these formidable animals.

For fighting heavily armored infantry, cavalry is advantageous as it provides speed and agility to outmaneuver the slower, well-protected soldiers.

When preparing to oppose an army composed of all four traditional components—elephants, chariots, cavalry, and infantry—the best approach is to deploy a mix of armored men, chariots, soldiers equipped with defensive weapons, and a well-prepared infantry. This blend of forces can counter each element of a diverse enemy army.

- Therefore, by carefully evaluating the strengths and capabilities within the various branches of one's own four-part army (composed of elephants, chariots, cavalry, and infantry), one should enlist the appropriate men and equip them accordingly. This will ensure that the army is adequately prepared to counter the unique threats and strengths posed by the enemy's forces, positioning the king's forces for successful engagement and defense.
- [Thus ends Chapter II, "The Time of Recruiting the Army, the Form of Equipment, and the Work of Arraying a Rival Force," in Book IX, "The Work of an Invader," of the Arthasástra of Kautilya. End of the hundred and twenty-third chapter from the beginning.]

CHAPTER III. CONSIDERATION OF ANNOYANCE IN THE REAR; AND REMEDIES AGAINST INTERNAL AND EXTERNAL TROUBLES.

Of the two issues—having a minor disturbance in the rear and achieving a significant gain at the front—a minor disturbance in the rear is actually more concerning. This is because any small annoyance at the back can quickly be magnified by traitors, enemies, and hostile tribes, who may exploit it. Meanwhile, members within one's own state may become unsettled by the pursuit of large-scale profit at the front.

If a ruler finds himself in this situation while under the protection of another, he should aim to weaken the influence and resources of the enemy in the rear. To secure the gains at the front, it may be prudent to send either the commander of the army or the heir-apparent to lead the forces. Alternatively, if the ruler himself is confident in his ability to keep the rear secure, he may choose to personally go forward to receive the gain.

Should the ruler fear internal unrest while advancing, it may be wise to bring along any leaders whose loyalty is in question. If the threat lies externally, he should prepare by keeping the families—sons and wives—of suspected traitors within the capital as a precaution. Further, he could split the forces under the officer managing the border territories into smaller units, each led by separate chiefs. If the risk of rebellion is high, it may even be necessary to cancel the march altogether, as internal turmoil is often more perilous than external threats.

The emergence of disloyalty from critical figures like a minister, priest, commander-in-chief, or heir-apparent is regarded as a serious internal issue. Such enemies within should be dealt with—either by resolving the ruler's own faults that may have provoked them or by exposing the risk posed by an external threat. If the priest is gravely treacherous, solutions may include confinement or banishment. If the heir-apparent is guilty, confinement or, if necessary, capital punishment could be considered—particularly if there is another son who can succeed him. Similar measures would apply to cases involving a minister or commander-in-chief.

In situations where a son, brother, or other royal family member attempts to seize control, they may be placated by offering them incentives. If this approach fails, alternative conciliatory measures include allowing them to retain their current holdings, brokering a formal agreement, or creating intrigue through an enemy. Providing them with land acquired from an enemy or involving other hostile figures may also help resolve the issue. Another option is to send them on a mission that aligns them with unfriendly forces, which may result in a fitting outcome. Additionally, enlisting the help of a frontier king or hostile tribe to manage the situation can be effective, as can employing strategies typically used in liberating an imprisoned prince or capturing enemy villages.

Finally, discontent among lower-ranking ministers represents internal ministerial unrest. Even in such cases, appropriate strategic measures should be adopted to prevent or address these challenges effectively.

Provoking unrest among external officials, such as a district chief, the officer in charge of borders, the head of wild tribes, or a recently conquered king, is referred to as external trouble. To manage this, it is strategic to set these figures against one another. If one of them is particularly fortified, he may be neutralized through the intervention of a neighboring king, a tribal chief, a relative, or an imprisoned prince. Alternatively, a friendly ally can be enlisted to prevent this individual from aligning with an enemy. A spy might also discourage the figure from such alliances by presenting a warning: "This enemy manipulates you, merely using you to turn against your own lord. When you've served his purpose, he'll send you to fight others or place you in an inhospitable location, far from your loved ones. Weakened, you'll be cast aside, perhaps even sold back to your lord, or perhaps he'll abandon you entirely after making peace with your own ruler. The wisest course is to join forces with your own lord's most reliable ally."

If he consents to this reasoning, he should be welcomed and rewarded. Should he decline, the spy might then say, "I am here specifically to ensure you don't become an enemy agent." Failing that, covert action may be necessary: the spy could arrange for his assassination through hidden agents or by embedding supposed loyalists around him, who are quietly tasked with eliminating him. This brings external troubles to an end, while encouraging similar disruptions within the enemy's own ranks.

In situations where an individual possesses the influence to either cause or alleviate disturbances, intrigue may be employed to sway them. However, with those who demonstrate reliability, are capable of effective action, and show a proven loyalty to their allies in times of success or adversity, counter-intrigue (pratijápa) may be used to ensure their allegiance. In assessing loyalty, it's crucial to consider whether someone has a cooperative or stubborn temperament.

When a stubborn-minded foreigner begins to sow intrigue among local figures, it often takes the following form: "If he kills his own master and joins me, I gain twice: my enemy's defeat and his land's acquisition. Or, should my enemy kill him, I stand to benefit as well. Those associated with the deceased and others implicated might then, fearing the same fate, disrupt my enemy's peace, especially as he finds himself isolated. Or, if my enemy's suspicions shift to any other compromised individual, I can leverage this to incite internal strife, ultimately targeting and weakening those under his command."

When a local person with a stubborn nature engages in intrigue with a foreign ally, it generally follows this pattern: "I will either loot this king's treasury or dismantle his army. I'll arrange for my master's assassination by using this foreigner's resources. If my master agrees, I'll encourage him to march against an external enemy or a nearby wild tribe, bringing confusion to his Circle of States and stirring up animosity among his neighboring rulers. This will make it easier to dominate and manipulate him—or perhaps I'll even take control of the kingdom myself. Once I have him in chains, I'll claim both his land and any nearby territories. Alternatively, I'll provoke his enemy to march, then arrange for the enemy's assassination under the guise of goodwill, or take over the enemy's capital while it's left unguarded."

When someone with a cooperative nature initiates a plot with the intent of mutual gain, it's wise to form an agreement with him. However, if a person with a stubborn disposition devises such a plan, he should be allowed to proceed on his course and then deceived when the opportunity arises. Thus, each approach should be carefully weighed and chosen accordingly.

- Enemies within one's own enemy's ranks, subjects from among subjects, subjects who may be influenced by enemies, and enemies who have access to subjects—all should be vigilantly monitored. A wise ruler or advisor should always guard against threats, securing both his own person and his interests from dangers posed by both his subjects and his adversaries.

[Thus ends Chapter III, "Consideration of Annoyance in the Rear, and Remedies Against Internal and External Troubles," in Book IX, "The Work of an Invader," of the Arthasástra of Kautilya. End of the hundred and twenty-fourth chapter from the beginning.]

CHAPTER IV. CONSIDERATION ABOUT LOSS OF MEN, WEALTH, AND PROFIT.

A reduction in skilled and loyal soldiers is what is referred to as kshaya, or loss of men, a state that can weaken the operational strength of a kingdom. Similarly, when there is a significant decrease in both gold and grain supplies, it is known as a loss of wealth, which undermines the economic stability and resources available for governance and defense. When the anticipated gain from an undertaking is expected to outweigh these potential losses, only then should a ruler consider advancing against an enemy.

Certain qualities define an anticipated gain. Ideally, it should be both attainable and secure, possibly requiring repayment but with minimal risk, widely acceptable or even favorable to the people, able to withstand the criticisms of opponents, obtainable within a manageable time frame, achievable with minimal loss of life, requiring only modest financial expenditures, large in scale, productive over time, harmless to the people and realm, just and fair in nature, and accessible without excessive delay.

A gain that can be achieved easily and kept securely without the necessity of returning it to others is known as "receivable." On the other hand, a gain that must later be repaid or relinquished to another is termed "repayable," a situation that can be precarious and often leads to misfortune. However, if the ruler considers that by taking on a repayable profit he will diminish his enemy's treasury, drain their army, or weaken their critical resources; or if he sees that the acquisition will exploit his enemy's mines, forests, irrigation systems, and trade routes; or if he anticipates the enemy's people will suffer or begin to migrate, possibly leading to internal rebellion, he may feel justified in moving forward. The condition becomes even more favorable if he can set one of his enemy's allies or other rivals against them, or cause the enemy to flee to a distant ally for protection. Additionally, the ruler may reason that by temporarily managing the enemy's lands and returning them improved, he may ultimately gain a devoted ally. With such reasoning, even a repayable gain may be wisely pursued. In this way, both receivable and repayable profits are considered, each carrying its respective benefits and risks.

A profit acquired from a corrupt ruler by a virtuous king tends to please the king's own people and is often seen favorably by others; but a gain obtained through opposite circumstances, particularly by betraying allies or abandoning virtues, tends to provoke resentment or anger. Profits taken on the advice of ministers who are self-serving or treacherous may also create dissatisfaction among loyal subjects, who may say, "This ruler has damaged our interests and drained our resources." Similarly, a gain acquired without regard for the counsel of honest ministers may lead them to complain, "The king grows wealthy while harming his own supporters." Conversely, a profit acquired through judicious actions that consider both allies and ministers will tend to be pleasing to all, reflecting wise governance and good judgment. In this manner, it is essential to discern between favorable and provoking gains.

A gain obtained by simply mobilizing and marching the army directly to the objective is considered a quick gain, as it does not require lengthy planning or delay. A gain achieved through strategic negotiation and careful planning incurs minimal loss of life and maintains the strength of the army. Likewise, a gain that primarily requires only the expenditure for essential provisions, without depleting the treasury, involves minimal financial risk. A gain that is immediately substantial and clearly beneficial to the kingdom is known as vast.

In making these evaluations, a ruler must carefully assess each type of gain's merits, considering that each advantage should ideally That which provides a stable source of income or assets is considered productive, as it generates wealth and resources continuously. When an undertaking can be achieved without any accompanying issues or risks, it is viewed as harmless, as it does not disrupt the lives or well-being of the people. Any gain acquired through fair and rightful means, without unjust actions or deception, is just. A gain obtained smoothly, without causing friction or obstruction from allies, is regarded as a primary or first profit, as it paves the way for future cooperation and mutual benefit.

When profits from two opportunities seem comparable, a wise ruler should evaluate various factors before deciding. He should weigh the suitability of the location, the season or timing of the action, the required strength, and available means. He must also consider the impact on relations—whether it will strengthen loyalty or provoke discontent—and the level of intrigue or stability involved. Furthermore, he should assess the proximity or remoteness of the profit, its immediate and long-term effects, whether it is of consistent value or likely to fluctuate, its abundance, and its practical utility. After thoroughly examining these elements, he should proceed only with the profit that embodies the most advantageous qualities.

Certain obstructions, however, can hinder the path to profit and must be managed. These include impulsive passion, rash anger, excessive timidity, unwarranted mercy, self-consciousness, or disregard for the traditional values of nobility. Arrogance, misplaced pity, excessive spiritual pursuits, rigid commitment to virtuous behavior, deception, poverty, jealousy, and disregard for immediate gains can also obstruct profit. Additional obstacles include unnecessary generosity, lack of confidence, fear, low tolerance for hardship, and over-reliance on auspicious signs, such as lunar phases and astrological predictions.

- One must realize that wealth eludes those who rely too heavily on omens and stars. In reality, wealth itself is the star that guides other wealth. What power do stars hold over one's prosperity? Those who are skilled and persistent in their efforts will surely amass wealth, even if it requires countless attempts.
- Wealth attracts wealth, just as elephants are subdued and controlled by counter-elephants. In this way, steadfastness and practical action are the true guides to prosperity.

[Thus ends Chapter IV, "Consideration about Loss of Men, Wealth and Profit,' in Book IX, "The Work of an Invader," of the Arthasástra of Kautilya. End of the hundred and twenty-fifth chapter from the beginning.]

CHAPTER V. EXTERNAL AND INTERNAL DANGERS.

When a treaty or settlement is formed improperly, outside the best interest of the state, it leads to weak policies that open doors to various dangers. The types of dangers include: those that originate externally but are supported internally; those that start internally and find external support; those with both origins and backing from external sources; and those that are wholly internal.

When foreign agents conspire with local men, or locals plot with foreigners, the outcome of such combined scheming becomes particularly dangerous. Generally, those who support a scheme have greater leverage than its originators. If the primary instigators are quashed, others will be discouraged from undertaking new plots. Foreigners usually struggle to gain the allegiance of locals through intrigue, just as locals find it difficult to sway foreigners. Foreign efforts typically fail and often end up inadvertently bolstering the king's position.

To handle internal abettors supporting foreign schemes, the king should use conciliation and gifts. Conciliation involves satisfying a person of influence through respect and honor. Gifts might include lowering taxes or offering key roles in the administration.

When foreign entities support internal conspiracies, the king should counter with strategies of division and force. For instance, spies disguised as friends can warn foreign agents that, "This person intends to deceive you through his own spies, who appear as insiders." Spies masquerading as traitors can also join conspiracies to drive a wedge between foreign agents and local traitors. Specialized spies, known as fiery spies, could gain the trust of traitors and then eliminate them using weapons or poison, or even lure foreign agents to gatherings where they can be eliminated.

When foreigners plot with other foreigners or locals with other locals, the unified intent behind such plans poses a grave threat. If wrongdoing is fully eliminated, there will be no guilty parties left to spread discontent; however, if only one guilty individual is removed, their guilt may spread to others. Therefore, if foreign agents carry out a conspiracy, the king should deploy both division and force. Spies posing as friends may tell the foreign conspirators, "Your leader, eager to enrich himself, is bound to turn against you all." Fiery spies might infiltrate the ranks of the foreign conspirators' supporters, striking them down with weapons or poison. Other spies can then reveal or betray the plot's abettor, ensuring the conspiracy collapses.

This strategic approach helps protect the king's state against both foreign and internal dangers that arise from poorly considered alliances and treaties.

When local individuals conspire with others within their own ranks, the king should apply the appropriate strategic methods to suppress the plot. Conciliation should be employed toward those who outwardly appear content or who are either naturally discontented or have shown signs of dissent. Gifts may be extended under the guise of expressing satisfaction with a loyal individual's consistent character or concern for their well-being. A spy, posing as a close ally, could advise the locals, "The king is seeking to understand your true feelings, so be honest with him." Alternatively, conspirators can be turned against one another by insinuating, "This person has been reporting your actions to the king." For conspiracies that persist, more forceful methods may be deployed, following guidelines established in the chapter on "Punishments."

Of the four identified types of dangers, internal threats should be addressed first. It has already been noted that internal dangers, like the stealthy menace of a hidden snake, are generally more severe than external ones.

- One should recognize that within these four types of dangers, those named first tend to be less serious than those mentioned later, especially when influential figures are involved in the threat. If, however, the danger stems from minor players, simpler methods of resolution may be sufficient to eliminate it.

[Thus ends Chapter V, "External and Internal Dangers" in Book IX, "The Work of an Invader," of the Arthasástra of Kautilya. End of the hundred and twenty-sixth chapter from the beginning.]

CHAPTER VI. PERSONS ASSOCIATED WITH TRAITORS AND ENEMIES

There are two categories of individuals who can be considered innocent in relation to conspiracies or conflicts: those who have actively chosen to distance themselves from traitors within the kingdom and those who have intentionally stayed away from any affiliation with external enemies. Recognizing the value of maintaining unity among his people, the king should carefully employ a variety of strategic methods to separate loyal citizens and country folk from traitors. In doing so, he should avoid using force whenever possible, as it is extremely difficult to impose harsh punishments on a group of influential individuals without potentially stirring greater discontent or undesirable consequences. However, when a leader or prominent figure of a rebellious group poses a risk to the unity and safety of the kingdom, the king can take measures against them, as indicated in the guidelines on "Punishments."

To ensure that his people remain uninfluenced by external enemies, the king should rely on strategic methods such as conciliation, persuasion, or careful countermeasures to undermine any attempts by the enemy's principal agents, who may be working to create alliances or gain support within the kingdom. The king's ability to secure and effectively utilize competent agents for such delicate operations largely depends on his skills, but it is equally reliant on the wisdom and support of his ministers, who play a vital role in ensuring these efforts reach the desired outcome. Thus, the success achieved through trusted and capable agents is a collaborative effort between the king and his ministers, and this combined approach provides the stability needed to counter the effects of any conspiracy or faction.

When a victory is achieved despite the presence of both traitors and loyal subjects within the ranks, this is known as "mixed success." In situations where loyalty and disloyalty are blended, success is best pursued by relying on those who are confirmed to be loyal, as it is impossible to accomplish lasting victory with unreliable support. Success, when entangled with the involvement of both allies and enemies, is described as "success contaminated by an enemy." When this occurs, it should be managed with the assistance of trusted allies, as it is far easier to secure a positive outcome with a dependable ally than with an enemy who might have ulterior motives or hidden agendas.

When a friend or ally appears hesitant or uncooperative, intrigue should be deployed to win them over, preferably through repeated strategic influence. Spies can play a crucial role here, as they can subtly work to draw the reluctant ally away from the enemy's influence, gradually encouraging alignment with the king. If the king's allies form a combined alliance, it can also be advantageous to approach the least influential ally first, as this may lead to a fracturing of the group, causing allies in middle or leading positions to reconsider their alignment. Another approach is to focus on winning over a key middle-ranked ally within the alliance; securing a central position ally often weakens the unity of those on either extreme, making it challenging for them to maintain cohesion. In essence, the king should employ any methods that can foster division within the allied ranks of his opponents.

To win the favor of a virtuous king, he may be swayed by appeals to noble qualities, such as acknowledging his high birth, family legacy, learning, and reputation for integrity. Emphasizing the history of relationships his ancestors held with those now seeking his alliance, or reminding him of previous benefits received and the absence of hostility shown toward him, can further secure his cooperation.

Or a king who harbors good intentions, one whose enthusiasm and spirit have waned, or who has exhausted his strategic resources after numerous conflicts, or who has suffered significant losses in men and wealth, or has endured the hardships of traveling far from his kingdom, or who sincerely seeks a dependable friend, or is concerned about potential threats from another, or values friendship above all else—such a king may be brought to form an alliance through conciliation.

In the case of a king driven by greed or weakened by losses in his army, he may be persuaded with carefully chosen gifts delivered through trusted intermediaries, such as ascetics or chiefs, who have been positioned with him for this purpose. Gifts used in this context fall into five categories: the remission of obligations due for payment, continuation of an existing provision, repayment of previously received items, offerings from one's own treasury, and support in carrying out a voluntary raid on another's assets.

If two kings both fear potential hostilities and territorial encroachment from each other, seeds of discord can be effectively planted between them. The more fearful of the two might be threatened with destruction and convinced by statements like, "This other king, while feigning peace with you, is plotting against you; and he has even granted his ally permission to openly pursue peace with your enemies."

Should merchandise or key goods be on their way from either the conqueror's own land or another allied land into an enemy's territory, spies may spread rumors that these supplies are sourced from a person whom the enemy had intended to attack. When such commodities have accumulated in large quantities, a message might be sent to the enemy, saying: "These goods and trade items are being offered by me to you; if you declare war against the coalition of kings or withdraw from their alliance, you will receive the remaining tribute." Spies can then relay to other members of the coalition, "These goods have been offered by your enemy as support for this other king."

To create further discord, the conqueror might obtain unique merchandise specific to his enemy's land, items that are rarely seen or unknown outside of that region. Spies, posing as merchants, could then sell these unique goods to other significant enemies, hinting that this merchandise was a direct gift to the conqueror from the enemy whose land originally produced it.

Or, by providing wealth and honors to those known to be particularly treacherous among the enemy's people, the conqueror can arrange for these individuals to remain close to the enemy, armed with weapons, poison, or fire. One of the enemy's ministers could be eliminated, and the minister's family—his sons and wife—might be influenced to claim that he was murdered at night by a specific person. The enemy's own ministers could then interrogate each family member of the deceased minister to determine the cause of death. If they provide the agreed-upon response, they may be released; otherwise, they would be detained for further questioning. A trusted advisor to the enemy might then privately suggest to the enemy king that he should be wary of another minister who may be plotting against him. An agent, receiving payment from both the conqueror and enemy states, could then secretly encourage the suspicious minister to eliminate the king himself.

Alternatively, enthusiastic and powerful rulers may be subtly encouraged by the conqueror to seize territory from a rival king while keeping their peace treaty intact. Spies could then alert the targeted king to the impending attacks, causing him to retaliate and weaken the invading force's provisions and followers. Meanwhile, additional spies, pretending to be allies, could convince these attacking kings that it's essential to destroy the targeted king entirely.

If an enemy's courageous soldier, prized elephant, or renowned horse dies or is secretly killed or stolen by spies, others could then spread the rumor within the enemy's ranks that this loss resulted from infighting among the enemy's own followers. The person responsible for these covert eliminations might be encouraged to repeat the task, promised payment of any remaining compensation. The payment would come from a dual-state agent, further sowing division within the enemy's ranks and even convincing some members to defect to the conqueror's side.

This tactic also applies to the enemy's commander-in-chief, prince, or military officers, using similar methods to incite internal divisions and mistrust. Furthermore, the conqueror can use this approach to foster distrust among allied states, strategically planting seeds of discord that weaken their cooperation.

Undercover spies might also take direct action against a fortified enemy of low character or one already beset by challenges, executing the target without needing additional support. If any of the concealed spies find an opportune moment, they could act alone, using weapons, poison, or fire to eliminate the target. A fiery spy, who excels in direct action, can often accomplish independently what would otherwise require a full team and resources.

These actions reflect the four strategic forms of diplomacy: conciliation, gift, dissension, and conciliatory coercion. Conciliation, the most straightforward, is a singular strategy. Gifts, which usually follow conciliation, involve two elements. Dissension adds a third layer, as it follows both conciliation and gifts. Conciliatory coercion is the most complex, involving all four elements in a sequence.

These strategies also apply to dealing with internal or local adversaries, with a slight variation. Chief messengers familiar with regional operations could be dispatched to one of these local enemies, either to negotiate a treaty or to instigate the elimination of a specific figure. Upon receiving a positive response, the messengers could inform their master of the progress, and dual-state agents might secretly inform the target's people or other adversaries, saying, "This individual is, in truth, a dangerous ruler."

When one individual fears or dislikes another, spies can heighten this tension by telling one of them, "This person is secretly negotiating with your enemy and may soon betray you; you should secure peace with the king immediately and focus on removing this threat." Spies might also arrange alliances or marriages with individuals who have previously had no affiliation, thus creating new loyalties and separating them from former allies. Through the influence of a neighboring king, a wild tribe leader, a member of an enemy's family, or an imprisoned prince, spies may work to eliminate enemies situated just outside the kingdom.

Spies may also utilize caravans or wild tribes to ambush and kill a local enemy along with his forces. Alternatively, those pretending to support a local adversary and belonging to the same caste can wait for an opportune moment to assassinate him. Hidden spies might also eliminate local threats through fire, poison, or weapons.

- When a country is overrun with local enemies, they can be subdued by having them consume poisoned drinks. A particularly shrewd and stubborn enemy may be dealt with through the use of spies or by offering him food, such as meat, that has been covertly poisoned and given under the guise of goodwill.

[Thus ends Chapter VI, "Persons Associated with Traitors and Enemies," in Book IX, "The Work of an Invader," of the Arthasástra of Kautilya. End of the hundred and twenty-seventh chapter from the beginning,]

CHAPTER VII. DOUBTS ABOUT WEALTH AND HARM; AND SUCCESS TO BE OBTAINED BY THE EMPLOYMENT OF ALTERNATIVE STRATEGIC MEANS.

The intense desires and unchecked passions of a ruler or leader can provoke discontent and disloyalty among their own people, while poor strategies and unwise decisions can ignite hostility from external enemies. These tendencies are seen as the hallmarks of a life driven by reckless or demoniac influences. Anger, in particular, creates discord within the ranks and stirs up frustration, which can lead to a chain of internal issues. Certain types of wealth and resources can also inadvertently empower adversaries if managed poorly. These forms of wealth—dangerous wealth, provocative wealth, and wealth of uncertain outcomes—pose a risk not only to stability but also to overall strength and security.

Dangerous wealth refers to resources or gains that may ultimately fortify an enemy's position or create dependencies that weaken one's own standing. This type of wealth might include assets shared with neighboring kings that could later serve their purposes more than one's own, wealth obtained but repayable to an enemy, or resources that might lead to financial or personnel losses. Examples of dangerous wealth are resources seized like personal property, or profits made at the expense of prior alliances, which might cause the wider Circle of States to view such actions unfavorably. Furthermore, if wealth in the front lines creates vulnerabilities in the rear or if it comes from betraying allies, such acquisitions are dangerous because they invite resentment, potentially from both enemies and former allies alike.

Provocative wealth refers to assets that, when acquired, lead to fear or resentment, either from one's own people or from external forces. Provocative wealth may trigger anger, jealousy, or fear, even within the heart of one's own state, or it may stoke the envy or ambitions of other kings. When contemplating whether a particular form of wealth is provocative or benign, it's crucial to weigh the possibility of it being misinterpreted or feared by others. Questions may arise, such as, "Will acquiring this wealth provoke an adversary or threaten peace? Will this wealth be first provocative, but later harmless? Will providing this wealth as support to an enemy's troops foster ill will among allies?" Such uncertainties reveal that it's often better to question whether acquiring the wealth is wise rather than to accept it and risk potential conflicts or harm.

There are also six varieties of wealth that may ultimately prove harmful: wealth that generates more wealth, wealth that yields no returns, wealth that results in harm, harm that leads to wealth, harm that has no productive outcome, and harm that only worsens over time.

"Wealth that generates more wealth" can refer to situations where neutralizing an enemy in the front eventually allows for a decisive advantage over an adversary at one's rear. This type of wealth builds upon itself by ensuring further stability and security. "Wealth that yields no returns," however, may arise when offering military assistance to a neutral king without any strategic gain in return. In this case, the investment is unreciprocated and produces no tangible benefit, leaving resources and effort expended without reward.

"Wealth that results in harm" may include tactics that undermine an enemy's internal unity, leading to immediate gains but sowing seeds for potential backlash or retaliation. "Harm that leads to wealth" involves offering support, like men or money, to a neighboring adversary of one's primary enemy, as this kind of harm may reduce the enemy's influence and provide indirect gains.

Withdrawing after encouraging a weaker king with limited resources to act against another is termed as "harm that yields no benefit." This type of harm doesn't result in any favorable outcome or profit, as the efforts exerted don't contribute towards one's own advantage. Similarly, if a weaker party provokes a stronger king and then remains inactive, this can lead to further detrimental effects, a scenario known as "harm that yields only more harm." Among these situations, it is better to pursue the first option listed—indirect harm without benefit—than to face the risk of further detrimental consequences. This approach exemplifies a strategic procedure to follow when setting plans in motion.

If the conditions surrounding one's efforts are highly favorable for gaining wealth, it is known as a situation where "wealth flows from all directions." However, if an enemy in the rear obstructs the acquisition of wealth from various directions, the situation shifts, becoming dangerous wealth that is fraught with uncertainties. In either of these cases, success can still be achieved by leveraging support from a friend or an enemy of the rear adversary, thus securing a means to proceed forward.

In cases where fear of surrounding enemies looms from all directions, it can be considered a critical threat, or "dangerous trouble." If, however, a friend steps in to assist in managing this looming threat, the situation may still hold uncertainties, but the danger becomes more manageable. Success in these cases can be pursued by rallying support from a nomadic force or from an enemy who stands opposed to the rear-enemy, thereby diffusing some of the immediate tension from all sides.

When profitable wealth becomes impossible to secure due to formidable blockages posed by enemies, it is termed "dangerous wealth." Whether in such a case of obstruction or when there are favorable conditions for wealth from all directions, one should consider advancing to gain wealth with potential. If there are equal prospects from two sources, the leader should target the wealth source that is both vital, conveniently close, reliable, and obtainable with the least resistance or cost.

When the threat of harm exists from two separate quarters, it is known as wealth endangered by dual opposition. Similar to situations where wealth is endangered from all sides, success is most likely if a network of allies can be engaged. In the absence of friendly support, the leader should attempt to reduce the threat from one side by securing an alliance with a power that can be easily swayed. For dangers coming from two quarters, an alliance with a power of greater strength is advised; and if danger arises on all fronts, all available resources should be deployed to counteract it.

In circumstances where warding off these threats proves impossible, retreat may be the wisest course, abandoning possessions to preserve life. Survival enables a potential return to power at a later stage, as exemplified in the historic cases of Suyátra and Udayana, who regained strength and reestablished power through resilience and timing.

When there's a chance of gaining wealth from one direction and the risk of an attack from another, this is known as a scenario filled with both opportunity and threat. In this case, the leader should advance towards the potential wealth if it will empower him to counter the attack. If this is not feasible, his focus should be on preventing the anticipated attack. This also applies when wealth and threat loom from multiple sides.

If there's a looming threat from one side, while potential wealth from another side is uncertain, this is a situation of doubt involving both wealth and danger from two fronts. Here, it is wise to address the threat first; once this is managed, efforts can shift towards acquiring the uncertain wealth. This approach also applies when similar doubts arise about wealth and harm from multiple directions.

When there is wealth expected from one quarter, but potential harm is uncertain from another, it's known as a scenario involving both wealth and ambiguous harm from two sides. In this case, he should carefully try to neutralize any possible threats against each part of his kingdom in order of importance. It is often better to risk a friend under uncertain threats rather than jeopardize the army; similarly, the army can be sacrificed under uncertain conditions rather than risking the treasury. If all elements of sovereignty cannot be fully protected from harm, he should at least prioritize securing some.

Among these elements, first safeguard those human elements that are most loyal and free from dissenters or opportunistic individuals. For non-human resources, focus on preserving those assets that are highly valuable and essential. Any elements that can be easily secured should be protected through simpler means such as peace agreements, maintaining neutrality, or forming strategic alliances with one side while keeping other adversaries at bay. Resources or elements requiring more effort may call for additional strategies.

Of the three stages—deterioration, stagnation, and progress—focus should be on securing progress first. If, however, the current environment indicates that a stage of deterioration or stagnation may lead to greater long-term gains, reverse this order. This approach can also apply to potential harm and gains, both midway or towards the end of a campaign.

Given that doubts around profit and risk are always present in any campaign, it is wiser to secure wealth that aids in weakening an enemy from the rear, discourages the enemy's allies, replenishes losses of men and resources, funds extended operations abroad, manages obligations, and safeguards the kingdom. Further, any doubts about security or economic prospects within one's own territory should never be tolerated, as they undermine stability directly within the homeland.

This explains the situation of potential harm during the midst of an expedition. However, towards the end of a campaign, it's preferable to gain wealth by either subduing or completely overcoming a weaker or vulnerable enemy rather than finding oneself in a situation of uncertain risk. This is because unresolved threats might allow enemies to create significant disruptions. However, for someone who is not leading a coalition of states, it may be more acceptable to endure uncertain wealth or risk at either the midpoint or the conclusion of an expedition, as they are not bound to carry on with the campaign to the same extent.

In strategic terms, wealth, virtue, and pleasure form a grouping of three kinds of benefits. Among these, the focus should always be on securing the first in the list, as each subsequent element in the order relies on the stability of the former.

In contrast, harm, sin, and sorrow represent the triad of harmful consequences. When addressing these, priority should be given to tackling the first type listed before considering the others, as this sequence best preserves order and minimizes disruption.

Thus, decisions on wealth or harm, virtue or sin, and pleasure or sorrow involve considering three types of uncertainties. When choosing among these, it's wise to prioritize the first option in the list, ensuring that, where feasible, these initial choices support successful outcomes. In this way, the assessment of strategic opportunities comes to completion, marking the end of the discourse on dangers.

As for addressing risks in dangerous situations and times, specific approaches are suggested depending on the source of troubles. In cases where issues arise from sons, brothers, or other family members, the best approach is through conciliation and offering gifts. When dealing with unrest from citizens, local populace, or military chiefs, the most effective methods are distributing gifts and fostering internal divisions. And in situations involving conflicts with neighboring kings or hostile tribes, planting seeds of discord and exerting coercion tend to yield the best results. This hierarchy of methods follows a set order of actions. In other situations, these methods might be used in the opposite sequence.

The complexity of overcoming adversaries and friends alike often demands multiple strategic approaches, as each method complements the others. For suspected ministers within an enemy's ranks, conciliation may suffice without additional measures. Treacherous ministers require gifts; alliances among states call for sowing dissension; and powerful figures must be countered through direct coercion.

When faced with a mix of severe and mild threats, the strategic approach can involve a specific single measure, an alternative among measures, or a combination of methods.

- "By this alone and no other" refers to applying a single, targeted method.
- "By this or that" implies selecting an alternative approach.
- "By this as well as by that" indicates employing multiple strategies together.

In total, these options form 15 distinct types of strategic combinations: four single methods, six pairwise combinations, four combinations of any three methods, and one involving all four methods. Reversing these combinations offers the same number of strategic approaches.

A king achieving success through only one of these methods is known as one of "single success"; using two, he is known as one of "double success"; with three, he attains "treble success"; and with four, he is one of "fourfold success."

Virtue serves as the foundation for wealth, while enjoyment stands as wealth's ultimate purpose. Achieving wealth that fulfills virtue, prosperity, and enjoyment is known as "universal success" (sarvárthasiddhi). These are the various forms of success.

Providential afflictions such as fire, floods, illness, widespread disease (pramara), fever (vidrava), famine, and supernatural disturbances are considered significant threats. Success in preventing these disasters involves performing worship to the gods and honoring Bráhmans.

- Whether supernatural disturbances are nonexistent, abundant, or in normal quantities, the prescribed rites from the Atharvaveda, along with those conducted by skilled ascetics, should be observed for securing success.

Book 10

CHAPTER I. ENCAMPMENT.

On a site deemed most suitable according to architectural science, the leader (náyaka), carpenter (vardhaki), and astrologer (mauhúrtika) should outline a circular, rectangular, or square area for the camp. This camp should ideally have four gates, six roads, and nine sections, aligned according to the available space. For added security, the camp should include ditches, parapets, walls, doors, and watchtowers, all aimed at guarding against potential threats.

The king's quarters should occupy one of the nine divisions, ideally positioned toward the north from the camp's center and spanning a length of 1,000 bows and a width of half that. To the west of this lies the harem, with the harem's own security forces stationed at its edge. Directly before the king's quarters is a space dedicated to worshipping the gods; to the right is where the finance and accounting offices should be placed; and to the left, stables for the elephants and horses used by the king. A perimeter, set 100 bows away from the center, should feature four prominent pillars (sakatamedhi) along with walls.

In the first of the four divisions within this perimeter, accommodations should be arranged for the prime minister and the chief priest. To the right of this, provisions for storage and kitchens are required, while to the left, supplies for raw materials and weaponry should be stored. The second division is designated for the king's hereditary forces, as well as cavalry and chariots. Outside this perimeter, hunters and dog keepers should be stationed with trumpets and controlled fire, alongside spies and sentinels. Additionally, wells, raised mounds, and thorn barriers should be strategically placed to safeguard against enemy attacks.

Eighteen teams of rotating sentinels are responsible for the king's safety, each taking shifts in turn. To monitor the movements of spies, a daily schedule of activities should be maintained. Further regulations include prohibitions on disputes, drinking, social gatherings, and gambling within the camp, with a passport system in place for identification. The boundary officer (in charge of camp borders) should oversee the behavior of the commander-in-chief and ensure that all military protocols are closely followed.

The instructor (prasástá), with his own attendants as well as carpenters and laborers, should travel ahead along the chosen route, preparing the road by digging wells for water to ensure readiness.

Chapter II: The March of the Camp and Protection of the Army During Hardships and Attacks

With a detailed list of villages and forests along the march route, noting each location's capacity to supply grass, firewood, and water, the pace of the army's march should be adjusted according to scheduled short and extended halts. Provisions for food and other necessities must be carried in amounts double that which might be required in an emergency. Should there be no separate means to transport provisions, the army itself should carry these supplies, or they may be stockpiled at a central depot.

The army's formation during the march should follow a specific order: the leader (náyaka) at the forefront, the harem and the king positioned centrally, bodyguards (báhútsára) stationed on the flanks, and at the outer edges, elephants and additional troops. The troops accustomed to forest terrain should flank all sides, ensuring protective coverage. Other sections of the force, including the camp followers, the commissariat, and any allied armies, should independently choose their routes to guarantee tactical advantage. Armies positioned effectively for terrain will have an upper hand over those in poorly suited locations.

The quality of the army determines its daily progress: armies of the lowest quality can advance a single yojana (approximately 5.5 miles), armies of middle quality cover one and a half yojanas, and armies of the highest quality can march up to two yojanas per day. Therefore, the army's pace can be easily determined. The commander should march at the rear and establish his encampment at the forefront of the advancing force.

When encountering an obstacle on the march, the army should adjust its formation according to the terrain and threat level. In situations where the path is clear, the army should arrange itself in a crocodile formation at the front, a cart-like formation at the rear, and a diamond formation along the sides, providing protective layers from all angles. When confined to a narrow path that allows passage for only a single file, the army should adopt a pin-like formation to proceed with minimal risk. When peace has been established with one ally but conflict is expected with another, it is crucial to arrange defenses for allied forces bringing support, especially against potential attacks from a rear enemy, his allies, or other nearby kings who could intervene. Any obstructed paths should be cleared after a thorough inspection to secure a safe route forward. Likewise, a detailed review of financial resources, the army's strength, the power of allied and enemy forces, and wild tribes, along with an assessment of upcoming weather and seasonal conditions, is essential for a well-informed march.

If intelligence suggests that enemy fortifications and supplies are weakening or that unrest is brewing within the enemy's hired troops or allied forces, a cautious, slower approach is warranted. This slower advance may also be appropriate if intrigue and espionage measures require additional time or if there are signs that the enemy might seek negotiations. Conversely, if a swift assault is advantageous, the march should proceed at maximum speed.

Rivers and other bodies of water can be crossed using various methods: elephants, bridges, boats, or makeshift platforms constructed from logs, bamboo clusters, rafts, or even large baskets coated with hides. For a more discreet crossing, the army may also use lightweight items like dried gourds or specialized rafts designed to support the load. Should the enemy obstruct a crossing, the army could consider crossing further upstream or downstream, thus flanking the enemy and setting up an ambush.

The leader should ensure the safety and morale of his forces when they face challenging terrains, such as extended deserts without water or areas lacking sufficient grass, firewood, and water. Provisions should also be made to protect the army when traversing harsh or unfamiliar roads, particularly in mountainous regions marked by muddy ground, waterlogged patches, rivers, and steep hills. The army must also be shielded against enemy harassment when fatigued or weakened by hunger and thirst after a long journey, especially in precarious situations like crowded narrow paths or difficult passages. Protection protocols are equally necessary during halts for rest, meals, or sleep; in times of widespread illness or pestilence; and when soldiers or animals (such as horses and elephants) are weakened or afflicted by disease. Any sign of diminishing strength or morale, whether due to physical hardship or low supplies, requires heightened security and vigilance to keep the army intact and prepared. Furthermore, if the enemy's forces find themselves in any of these distressing situations, they should be swiftly attacked to exploit their vulnerability.

When the enemy's forces are constrained to travel along a single-file route, the invading commander should assess the enemy's true strength by carefully observing the volume of food supplies, grass, bedding, and other essentials they transport, along with tools like fire pots, banners, and weaponry. To maintain strategic advantage, the commander should take steps to conceal his own army's supplies and strength from enemy eyes.

- With a stronghold positioned in a mountainous region or along a river in his own territory, complete with all essential resources, the commander should strategically station his forces or establish his camp. This secure position not only offers natural defenses but also ensures access to necessary provisions and reinforces his ability to defend or advance against the enemy effectively.

[Thus ends Chapter II, "March of the Camp; and Protection of the Army in Times of Distress and Attack" in Book X, "Relating to War" of the Arthasástra of Kautilya. End of the hundred and thirtieth chapter from the beginning.]

CHAPTER III. FORMS OF TREACHEROUS FIGHTS; ENCOURAGEMENT TO ONE'S OWN ARMY AND FIGHT BETWEEN ONE'S OWN AND ENEMY'S ARMIES.

He who commands a strong, well-prepared army, who has succeeded in strategic planning, and who has effectively addressed potential threats can initiate an open confrontation if he holds a position advantageous to his forces; otherwise, he should consider engaging in a more deceptive, tactical assault.

An opportune moment to strike is when the enemy's forces are weakened by internal troubles or are under heavy attack, or if the commander holds a strong position and can strike the enemy while they are trapped in a less favorable setting. A leader who maintains firm control over his state and resources may exploit the enemy's own internal dissidents, foreign enemies, or hostile groups, creating the illusion of his own defeat to lure the enemy out of their secure position and into vulnerability. When the enemy has regrouped tightly, elephants can be employed to scatter their forces; once the enemy pursues, believing the false retreat, the commander can turn back and strike. After a frontal attack, elephants and cavalry can again target the fleeing enemy as they turn their backs. If an attack at the front is not favorable, a strike from behind is wise, and likewise, if a rear attack is unwise, a frontal or side approach should be considered.

By pitting the enemy against their own traitors, hostile factions, or warring tribes, the commander can then advance with his fresh forces and strike when the enemy is exhausted. Or, the enemy can be tricked into thinking victory is within reach through a feigned defeat involving a traitor's forces, leading to an ambush where the confident enemy can be overpowered by the commander's full-strength army. The vigilant commander may surprise the enemy when they are complacent, misled into thinking that their rival's resources—merchants, camps, and carriers—have been devastated. Or, by disguising his formidable forces to appear weak, he can provoke the enemy's bravest fighters into attacking, setting them up for defeat. Capturing enemy livestock or destroying valued assets may lure these brave forces into an ambush.

If an enemy's men are harassed continuously through the night to deprive them of sleep, they can be struck in the daytime when fatigue and sun exposure sap their strength, while the commander's troops rest in shaded areas. For a night assault, he may equip his elephant troops with flame-retardant cloth and leather armor, ensuring protection while engaging the enemy under cover of darkness. Striking in the late afternoon can exploit the enemy's fatigue from morning preparations, while a direct advance against the whole army as they face the sun capitalizes on their visual disadvantage.

A desert, dangerous terrain, marshes, mountains, valleys, unstable boats, cattle obstacles, formations like a cart, mist, and night all serve as strategic lures (sattras) to draw the enemy into a disadvantageous position against the invader. These natural features and formations act as enticing traps that can mislead or hinder the enemy's movement.

The most opportune moment for launching a treacherous assault is at the very beginning of the enemy's advance. As for an open and honorable engagement, a just king should first assemble his troops, specifying the planned location and time for battle, and address them with words of unity and purpose: "I, like you, serve this land and am bound to its defense; together, we are stewards of this country, its protection our shared duty. The enemy before us is yours to confront under my command."

The king's minister and priest should further inspire the soldiers with words of valor and dedication: "The Vedas declare that those who perform sacrifices, giving their best, and those who serve in bravery reach the same sacred destination. Just as the sacrificers achieve a high state after their final ritual ablutions, so too do the courageous find their reward in valor."

Two verses on this matter go as follows:

- Beyond the realms that Bráhmans, in their pursuit of heaven, reach through dedicated sacrifices and penances lie the places reserved for brave warriors who lose their lives in noble battles. These warriors are destined to attain this honored state without delay, their courage earning them an immediate place beyond the earthly.
- Let the fate of a new vessel filled with consecrated water, covered in darbha grass, be denied to the man who does not stand and fight in return for the sustenance given by his master. Such a person, neglecting his duty, faces not honor but the punishment of descent into the depths of suffering.

Astrologers and other close advisors of the king should inspire confidence in the army by emphasizing the unbreakable formation of their array, the king's alignment with divine powers, and his profound wisdom. At the same time, they should work to instill fear in the enemy. The day before the battle, the king should observe a fast, resting on his chariot with his weapons nearby. He should also make offerings into the sacred fire, reciting Atharvaveda mantras, and arrange for prayers both for the victory of his forces and for those who, by their brave death on the battlefield, will ascend to heaven. The king should submit himself humbly to the blessings of Bráhmans and position the core of his forces with warriors distinguished by bravery, skill, noble birth, and loyalty, and who remain content with the honors and rewards they've received.

The king should be positioned among trusted warriors—his father, sons, brothers, and others skilled with weapons, without distinctive flags or headgear for protection. He may ride an elephant or chariot if the army is primarily mounted, or choose to ride the animal most familiar or expertly trained within his forces. An individual disguised as the king should be assigned the task of overseeing the alignment of the troops.

Soothsayers and court poets should praise heaven as the ultimate destination for the courageous and damnation for the cowardly, extolling the caste, clan, lineage, achievements, and virtues of the soldiers. The priest's attendants should announce the favorable outcomes of any protective spells cast. Spies, builders, and astrologers should report on the positive results of their own strategies while declaring the shortcomings of the enemy's efforts.

After ensuring that the troops are well-motivated with rewards and honors, the commander-in-chief should address the soldiers, proclaiming rewards for valor in battle as follows: one hundred thousand panas for killing the enemy king, fifty thousand for killing the enemy's commander-in-chief or heir-apparent, ten thousand for slaying the chief of the brave, five thousand for taking down an elephant or a chariot, one thousand for killing a horse, a hundred panas for slaying the chief of the infantry, twenty panas for presenting an enemy's head, and double pay plus any loot acquired. This incentive structure should be communicated to each group of ten soldiers to inspire their commitment to victory.

The army's support should be close at hand: physicians equipped with surgical tools, ointments, healing oils, and cloth for treating the wounded, along with women prepared with food and drink to nourish the fighters, all encouraging them with words of support from behind the lines.

The army should be arranged in a strategic formation on favorable terrain, ideally facing away from the south and with the sun at their back, ready to advance. If the terrain is unfavorable, horses should be run to test the ground's stability. An army forced into an unsuitable position and pushed into retreat will be vulnerable, either as it stands or as it retreats. On the other hand, if the army stands firm or advances from a favorable position, it is poised to defeat the enemy, whether standing or moving.

The terrain should be carefully assessed: whether it is flat, uneven, or a mix, and whether this applies to the front, sides, or rear of the formation. On level ground, a staff-like or circular formation is ideal, while uneven terrain calls for formations designed for dense movement or maneuverable, separated units.

If the enemy's army is thoroughly broken, the invader should consider negotiating peace. If the armies are equally matched, peace should be made if requested. However, if the enemy's forces are inferior, they should be decisively defeated—except if they hold a strong position and are willing to fight to the last.

- When an enemy's defeated and scattered army regroups with renewed vigor, showing disregard for their own lives, their rage becomes nearly unstoppable; therefore, it's unwise to provoke or further pressure a broken army that is regaining its momentum.

[Thus ends Chapter III, "Forms of Treacherous Fights; Encouragement to One's Own Army, and Fight Between One's Own and Enemy's Armies," in Book X, "Relating to War," of the Arthasástra of Kautilya. End of the hundred and thirty-first chapter from the beginning.]

CHAPTER IV. BATTLEFIELDS; THE WORK OF INFANTRY, CAVALRY, CHARIOTS, AND ELEPHANTS.

Ideal positions for infantry, cavalry, chariots, and elephants are essential in both battle and camp.

The army's different divisions benefit from terrain suited to their training: soldiers practiced in desert terrains, forests, valleys, or open plains; those trained for fighting from ditches or elevated positions, whether in daytime or at night; elephants accustomed to riverine, mountainous, marshy, or lake regions; and horses familiar with specific terrains should each have a battlefield that aligns with their particular strengths.

The best ground for chariots is one that is even and stable, lacking mounds or pits from previous movement of wheels or animals, free from natural obstructions like trees, shrubs, and roots, and clear of any boggy patches, sandy areas, or thorny clusters.

For elephants, horses, and infantry, either even or slightly uneven grounds are suitable, whether for camp or combat.

For horses, an ideal terrain contains minor stones, trees, and small pits that can be leaped over, with minimal thorns.

For infantry, the terrain is best when it has larger stones, a mix of dry and green trees, and natural features like ant-hills.

Elephants perform best on uneven terrain with hills and valleys that can be assaulted, trees that can be uprooted, and soft, muddy soil free from sharp thorny growths.

For infantry, the ideal terrain is slightly uneven yet spacious and free from thorns.

For horses, the terrain should be doubly expansive, dry, and free of tree roots, mud, or gravel that could harm hooves.

Elephants fare well on terrain with soft mud, water, dust, grass, and low-lying weeds, clear of thorny barriers or overhanging branches from large trees.

Chariots need terrain that includes lakes, open spaces, and areas free from mounds and wetlands, providing room to maneuver and turn.

These conditions outline the ideal grounds for each type of military unit in camp or battle, helping each division perform optimally in its element.

Securing occupied positions in camps and forests; holding onto ropes for safe passage while crossing rivers or enduring strong winds; managing or safeguarding supplies and new troops as they arrive; overseeing military discipline; extending the line of troops; protecting flanks; launching the initial assault; dispersing enemy forces; trampling down any remaining threats; setting up defenses; capturing and releasing positions strategically; guiding the army in new directions; transporting treasury assets and royal family members; striking the rear of the enemy's forces; chasing down fleeing opponents; maintaining pursuit; and regrouping when needed—these tasks define the role of horses in battle.

Elephants, meanwhile, have specific responsibilities, such as leading the front line; preparing roads, camps, and water access points; securing flanks; standing firmly or crossing through water obstacles; performing forced entries into fortified positions; managing fire either to start or extinguish it; overpowering one of the enemy's four military divisions; rallying dispersed soldiers; breaking apart tightly formed enemy ranks; providing protection from threats; trampling over opposing forces; intimidating and scattering them; displaying grandeur and might; seizing or abandoning specific points; breaking down walls, gates, and towers; and carrying the treasury—these are all within the domain of elephants.

For chariots, their tasks include shielding the army; defending against assaults from all four divisions of the enemy; capturing and releasing positions during combat; reassembling scattered troops; disrupting and scattering enemy formations; instilling fear with their presence; showcasing majesty and grandeur; and generating a thunderous, intimidating noise—all essential roles of the chariots in battle.

Infantry tasks include the consistent transport of weapons to all locations on the battlefield and engaging in direct combat.

Lastly, free laborers play a vital role in checking camps, clearing roads, constructing and reinforcing bridges, and ensuring safe passage along wells and rivers. They are also tasked with transporting machinery, weaponry, armor, essential tools, and provisions, as well as retrieving fallen soldiers along with their equipment and armor.

This division of labor across each military component ensures that each unit contributes to the army's success in a coordinated and effective manner.

- A king with limited cavalry can bolster his forces by mixing bulls alongside his horses; similarly, if he lacks sufficient elephants, he can strengthen the center of his army by placing mules, camels, and carts strategically to supplement his forces.

[Thus ends Chapter IV, "Battlefields; the Work of Infantry, Cavalry, Chariots and Elephants," in Book X, "Relating to War," of the Arthasástra of Kautilya. End of the hundred and thirty-second chapter from the beginning.]

CHAPTER V. THE DISTINCTIVE ARRAY OF TROOPS IN RESPECT OF WINGS, FLANKS, AND FRONT; DISTINCTION BETWEEN STRONG AND WEAK TROOPS; AND BATTLE WITH INFANTRY, CAVALRY, CHARIOTS AND ELEPHANTS.

Once the camp is securely fortified at a distance of five hundred bows from the enemy's reach, the preparations for engaging in battle can begin. This distance provides a defensive buffer, and fortifications are strategically chosen to ensure that both the position and resources are advantageous for the army. The commander-in-chief, alongside the primary leader of the army, should allocate the elite troops to a favorable and discreet location where they remain hidden from the enemy's view, ready to be deployed at a critical moment. Meanwhile, the main bulk of the army should be arranged in a carefully structured formation to ensure both effective offense and defense.

To maintain the flow and organization of troops, there is a specific spatial arrangement for each unit: infantrymen are spaced at intervals of one sama (14 angulas) to allow for coordinated movement without overcrowding; cavalry units are spaced three samas apart to maneuver freely and effectively in support or attack; chariots are spaced four samas apart to allow for greater mobility; and elephants are given the largest space, at two to three times the distance between chariots, due to their size and need for maneuverability. This systematic spacing ensures that each type of unit can perform optimally without interference from others, allowing a unified and dynamic response during battle.

Each bow, the unit of distance used for positioning, measures five aratnis, which total 120 angulas. To organize forces, archers should be stationed five bows apart to maintain range capabilities without crowding; cavalry should be positioned three bows apart, optimizing for swift and versatile responses to enemy advances or retreats; chariots and elephants should each be placed five bows apart, maximizing the stability and impact of these larger units.

The layout of the army includes spacing known as aníkasandhi between the different sections—wings, flanks, and the central front—measuring five bows between each section to create clear pathways. For effective combat ratios, three infantrymen are assigned to counter one enemy cavalry unit. Fifteen soldiers, or alternatively five horses, are allocated to counter each enemy chariot or elephant, allowing for a targeted opposition that optimizes both resources and tactical effectiveness. In addition, each cavalry unit, chariot, or elephant has fifteen attendants (pádagopa) responsible for maintaining them, which includes handling equipment and preparing them for battle.

The standard chariot array includes a carefully organized formation of three groups (aníka), each consisting of three chariots positioned at the front, with identical group formations positioned along the two flanks and two wings of the army. In total, this creates a unified array comprising forty-five chariots, 225 horses, and 675 soldiers, with an equal number of attendants providing necessary support for these units. This formation, known as an even array, offers balanced strength and allows coordinated movements across all fronts. When circumstances permit, additional chariots may be added in groups of two until the number reaches twenty-one, resulting in a diverse set of ten possible arrangements of odd-numbered arrays.

Any surplus forces, which might be referred to as ávápa, are allocated to areas where their strengths can best be utilized. Two-thirds of these additional chariots should be stationed along the flanks and wings to reinforce vulnerable areas, while the remaining third is placed at the front to support offensive maneuvers. The surplus chariots thus strategically balance both offensive and defensive capabilities, enhancing the overall flexibility of the formation.

Specific terms categorize different configurations of force levels within the army. Ávápa, or surplus, refers to the presence of additional forces beyond the basic requirements; pratyávápa denotes a shortfall in infantry that requires immediate reinforcement; anvávápa describes the situation when there is an excess in one type of military constituent, such as an abundance of chariots or horses; and atyávápa is a term used when there is an undesirable surplus, particularly of traitorous or unreliable troops, which could undermine the army's integrity. Based on the available resources and intelligence on the enemy's numbers, a well-prepared leader should aim to increase their forces from four up to even eight times the enemy's surplus forces or any detected shortfall in the enemy's infantry strength. This careful calculation allows the army to maximize its own potential and secure an advantageous position before engaging in battle, ensuring readiness to meet or even exceed the necessary measures for a successful confrontation.

The arrangement of elephants in battle mirrors the setup used for chariots, yet offers its own distinct configurations. An array combining elephants, chariots, and cavalry can be structured with elephants placed at the circular array's endpoints, horses and primary chariots stationed along the flanks for added force and maneuverability. In an arrangement where elephants hold the front, chariots guard the flanks, and cavalry fills the wings, this configuration is particularly effective for breaching the enemy's central forces; conversely, positioning elephants on the flanks, chariots in front, and horses on the wings will prove advantageous for harassing the enemy's extremities. When organizing a formation solely with elephants, the battle-trained elephants should take the lead, riding-trained elephants are set on the flanks, while rogue elephants occupy the wings to create additional unpredictability.

For a cavalry array, armored horses are positioned upfront to face direct confrontation, with unarmored horses securing the flanks and wings, providing both offense and defense. Infantry formations consist of armored soldiers at the front for durability, archers positioned in the rear for ranged support, and unarmored troops on the wings, or alternatively, cavalry on the wings, elephants on the flanks, and chariots in front to bolster attack versatility. Many other strategic adjustments may be made, adapting to effectively counter the specific strengths and weaknesses of the opposing force.

The strongest army combines robust infantry with elephants and horses distinguished for their lineage, strength, youthfulness, vigor, endurance in older age, combat readiness, skill, resilience, noble spirit, obedience, and disciplined behaviors. To optimize the force's arrangement, one-third of the finest infantry, cavalry, and elephants should be placed at the forefront, while two-thirds of the best troops are distributed across both the flanks and wings. A formation ordered by strength—from strongest to weakest—is arranged in direct order; if interspersing strong and weak units in a mix, the order is then reversed. An understanding of all variations of these configurations is crucial for effective battlefield adaptation.

Positioning weaker troops at the army's ends risks exposing them to the enemy's strongest attacks. Instead, stationing elite forces at the forefront, with equally reinforced wings, offers better protection. By arranging one-third of the best units at the rear and the weaker forces within the center, the formation becomes adept at resisting an enemy's assault. When engaged, this setup allows the commander to strike with one or two units stationed at the wings, flanks, and front, while the rest can converge on and capture the enemy from multiple angles.

If the enemy's force is notably weaker, with limited horses and elephants, and if internal intrigues are disrupting their command, the conqueror should capitalize on this vulnerability by attacking with his strongest divisions. Reinforcing any section of the army that appears weak in numbers will ensure an advantage. Troops should be concentrated along the enemy's weakest side or along areas where danger is anticipated.

There are varied tactical approaches to war when fighting with cavalry, such as direct charges, circling around the enemy, bypassing to attack from behind, and retreating to regroup and disrupt the enemy's halt. Additional methods include amassing forces, using curved and circular maneuvers, diversions, removing the rear guard, attacking from the front, flanks, and rear, rescuing broken ranks, and taking down a disrupted enemy formation.

For elephants, warfare strategies include all but miscellaneous maneuvers, with options like breaking up the enemy's four main divisions either in isolation or collectively, dispersing their flanks, wings, and front, trampling their ranks, and catching them off guard while asleep.

Chariots operate similarly but lack certain tactics, such as disturbing halts, direct charges, tactical retreats, and fighting while stationary. The infantry, in contrast, is adaptable to almost any environment and capable of engaging effectively at all times and locations, excelling particularly in surprise assaults.

In summation, the structured diversity in formations and tactical maneuvers across the different types of troops—whether elephants, cavalry, chariots, or infantry—empowers a well-prepared army to adapt dynamically to any battlefield conditions. The appropriate configuration and use of tactics depend on the type of enemy, terrain, and available resources, ensuring that the army is equipped to handle and adapt to every possible scenario.

- He should arrange formations in both odd and even arrays, ensuring that the strength of the four key components—infantry, cavalry, chariots, and elephants—remains balanced across the setup. The king, once he has reached a distance of approximately 200 bows from the enemy line, should secure his position with the reserve forces of his army.
- He must avoid entering battle without a reserve, as this backup force is crucial for rallying and regrouping any scattered troops and maintaining the coherence and strength of the army during the fight.

[Thus ends Chapter V, "The Distinctive Array of Troops in Respect of Wings, Flanks and Front; Distinction between Strong and Weak Troops; and Battle with Infantry, Cavalry, Chariots and Elephants," in Book X, "Relating to War," of the Arthasástra of Kautilya. End of the hundred and thirty-third chapter from the beginning.]

CHAPTER VI. THE ARRAY OF THE ARMY LIKE A STAFF, A SNAKE, A CIRCLE, OR IN DETACHED ORDER; THE ARRAY OF THE ARMY AGAINST THAT OF AN ENEMY.

Wings and front positioned to enable swift turns against the enemy form what is called a snake-like array, or bhoga. According to the teachings of Brihaspati, an array constructed with two wings, two flanks, a front, and a reserve serves as a foundational setup. The main formations—staff-like, snake-like, circle-like, and detached—are varied applications of this basic structure involving wings, flanks, and front.

When the army is aligned to face forward in a single broad line, this setup is called a staff-like array, or danda. If the arrangement follows a sequential line, where one unit follows directly behind another, it forms a snake-like array, or bhoga. When positioned in a circular arrangement that faces all directions, it is known as a circle-like array, or mandala. And when arranged in smaller, separated units that can act independently, it's called a detached order array, or asamhata.

The staff-like array with equal strength across wings, flanks, and front holds the name danda. If its flanks project forward, it becomes known as pradara, signifying its intent to break through enemy formations. When the wings and flanks are pulled back, making it particularly stable, it's known as dridhaka, or firm. If the wings are extended, creating a resilient formation, the array is called asahya, or irresistible. When the wings are structured and the front bulges outward, this is known as an eagle-like array.

These configurations have additional names when arranged in reverse: "a bow," "the center of a bow," "a hold," and "a strong hold." An array with bow-like wings is termed sanjaya (victory); if the front also projects forward, it is called vijaya (conqueror). When its flanks and wings take on the appearance of a staff, it is referred to as sthúlakarna (big ear); if its front is doubled in strength, it becomes visálavijaya (vast victory). With wings stretched forward, it forms chamúmukha (face of the army), while in a reversed formation, it is named ghashásya (face of the fish).

When the staff-like array positions units one behind the other, it is described as a pin-like array. If two such lines are created, it forms an aggregate, or valaya, and with four lines, it becomes known as an invincible array. These are the variations of the staff-like formation.

The snake-like array, when wings, flanks, and front differ in depth, is identified as sarpasári (serpentine movement) or gomútrika (resembling the winding trail of a cow's path).

When the formation has two lines in front with wings positioned like in the staff-like setup, it's called a cart-like formation; the reverse of this is known as a crocodile-like formation. A cart-like array that includes elephants, horses, and chariots is called váripatantaka. These are the types of the snake-like formations.

In the circle-like formation, where the difference between wings, flanks, and front fades away, it is known as sarvatomukha (facing all directions), or sarvatobhadra (all-auspicious), ashtánika (eight divisions), or vijaya (victory). These represent the variations of the circle-like formation.

When the wings, flanks, and front are each placed separately, it is called a detached-order formation. If five divisions of the army are arranged in this detached way, it is known as vajra (diamond) or godha (alligator). When four divisions are separated, it is called udyánaka (park) or kákapadi (crow's foot). When three divisions are arranged in this style, it is called ardhachandrika (half-moon) or karkátakasringi. These are the variations of the detached-order formation.

The formation where chariots are placed at the front, elephants on the wings, and horses at the rear is known as arishta (auspicious). A formation where infantry, cavalry, chariots, and elephants stand one behind the other is called achala (immovable). The formation where elephants, horses, chariots, and infantry line up in order, one behind the other, is known as apratihata (invincible).

The conqueror should counter the pradara formation with the dridhaka; dridhaka with the asahya; the syena (eagle-like formation) with chápa (bow-like formation); a hold formation with a strong-hold formation; the sanjaya with the vijaya; the sthúlakarna with the visálavijaya; and the váripatantaka with sarvatobhadra. The conqueror may use the durjaya formation to strike at any other types of formations.

Of infantry, cavalry, chariots, and elephants, each is best opposed by the next type listed in order; and a small part of the army should be met by a larger one. For every group of ten members within each part of the army, there should be one commander, called a padika; ten padikas report to a senápati; and ten senápatis report to a náyaka, or leader.

The different sections of the army formations should be named according to trumpet sounds, flags, and signs. Success in organizing the army's formations, gathering forces, setting up camp, marching, retreating, launching attacks, and keeping formations balanced relies on choosing the right time and place for action.

By showing the full strength of his army, using secret tactics, deploying fiery spies to attack the enemy when distracted, employing witchcraft, spreading word of the conqueror's divine favor, using carts, and decorating elephants with impressive ornaments;

By inciting traitors, driving herds of cattle into the enemy's midst, setting the enemy's camp ablaze, targeting the wings and rear of their forces, or sowing seeds of discord through agents posing as servants;

Or by spreading rumors that the enemy's fortress was burned or captured, or that a member of his family, an ally, or a wild chief had rebelled—through these and similar strategies, the conqueror should create panic and confusion within the enemy's ranks.

An arrow shot by an archer may or may not strike down a single man, but a cunning scheme crafted by wise minds can eliminate even those yet unborn.

Book 11

CHAPTER I. CAUSES OF DISSENSION; AND SECRET PUNISHMENT.

Obtaining support from corporate groups is more beneficial than acquiring an army, an ally, or immediate profits. Through conciliation and rewards, the conqueror should secure the loyalty and support of corporations that are either powerful enough to withstand the enemy or are already favorably inclined toward him. As for groups opposing him, he should weaken them by sowing division among them and, if needed, discreetly punishing them.

The warrior corporations, or kshattriyasrení, from regions like Kámbhoja, Suráshtra, and others, sustain themselves through agriculture, trade, and skill with weapons. Other groups, like those from Lichchhivika, Vrijika, Mallaka, Mudraka, Kukura, Kuru, and Pánchála, operate under royal titles.

Spies should be deployed within these groups to observe any existing jealousy, rivalry, or grudges. They should then exploit these tensions, inciting well-crafted dissensions by subtly informing one member, "This person criticizes you." Spies posing as teachers or advisors can encourage conflicts during discussions on subjects like science, arts, or sports. Fiery spies could stir up tension by publicly praising lesser-known leaders in public spaces, such as taverns or theaters, or by discreetly stoking the ambitions of low-born princes with remarks on their lineage. They could interfere with social customs by urging senior members to dine or marry among lower ranks, or they could amplify frustrations by contrasting traditional roles in birth, bravery, and social status.

Additionally, fiery spies might instigate disputes at night by tampering with properties, animals, or individuals entangled in legal issues. In all such disturbances, the conqueror should support the lesser factions with funds and reinforcements, using them to undermine the dominant group. Once these groups are fractured, he could arrange to relocate them, or he might unite and resettle them in fertile areas within their territory under structured "five-household" and "ten-household" units, training them in military tactics as they build up. Established fines should deter any rebellious alliances among these groups.

He may choose to appoint a prince of noble lineage, who is perhaps dethroned or imprisoned, as the heir-apparent to rally loyalty. Spies, acting as astrologers or other trusted figures, should subtly highlight this prince's royal qualities and encourage respected leaders of the corporations to show loyalty to him, framing the prince as the heir ready to hear their concerns. The conqueror should also send funds and supporters to these loyalists to help win over additional backers.

During moments of unrest, spies disguised as tavern-keepers should distribute hundreds of cups of liquor mixed with madana plant juice, under the pretense of celebrating events like a birth, marriage, or death. Around the entrances to temples, altars, and other guarded locations, spies should create the impression that they are discussing deals with the corporations' enemies, including promises of payment, bags of money stamped with the enemy's golden seal, and rewards. When approached by members of the corporations, the spies might confess, "We've sided with your enemy," challenging them to fight.

Another tactic is to seize livestock and valuable items belonging to the corporations, giving the best of these items to their chief, thereby stirring resentment within the group. When the corporations question the missing goods, the spies could reply that the items were gifted to the chief, inciting internal conflict. This strategy outlines how to spark discord in camps and among wild tribes.

Alternatively, a spy might approach a self-assured son of a corporation chief, saying, "You're the son of a noble king, kept here out of fear of enemy threats." Once the young man is convinced, the conqueror can secretly aid him with troops and resources, encouraging him to challenge the corporations. Once his purpose is fulfilled, the conqueror might then exile him.

Spies managing entertainers or dancers, actors, and musicians could also work to sway the corporation chiefs, using alluring women to captivate them. By sending this woman to someone else or spreading rumors that another man has forcefully taken her, spies could provoke conflict between those competing for her attention. During the resulting altercation, fiery spies can incite further strife, declaring, "This man has met his fate because of his infatuation."

A woman who has rejected a suitor but was later forgiven might approach another chief, saying, "That man has been harassing me when my heart belongs to you; I can't stay here while he's around." This can lead the latter to kill the former.

Additionally, if a woman is forcefully taken at night, she might work with fiery spies or use poison herself to bring about her attacker's death in a park or pleasure house, later claiming, "My beloved was murdered by this person."

An undercover spy disguised as an ascetic might apply a special ointment, supposedly a charm to win the affection of a beloved woman, but mixed with poison, to a man eager to impress his lover.

Afterward, the spy would disappear, and other spies would attribute the event to the actions of an enemy.

Women spies, such as widows with covert instructions, might engage in a dispute over a deposit allegedly held by the king. During this quarrel, their beauty would catch the attention of the corporation chiefs as they appeal to the king to resolve their issue.

A harlot, dancer, or singer might arrange to meet a man in a secluded house. When he arrives, hopeful to see her, fiery spies would either kill him or abduct him.

A spy might approach a chief known for his interest in women, saying, "In a nearby village, a poor man has passed away, leaving a beautiful widow who would be a fitting wife for a king. Claim her as your own." After the woman is seized, an ascetic spy could appear before the corporation half a month later, accusing the chief: "This man has wrongfully taken my main wife, sister-in-law, sister, or daughter." If the corporation then punishes the chief, the conqueror should ally with the corporation, encouraging them against corrupt members. Fiery spies should frequently send an ascetic spy to walk at night. Select spies should accuse the chief, saying, "This man has committed the heinous act of killing a Bráhman and has also engaged in adultery with a Bráhman woman."

Another spy disguised as an astrologer might describe a maiden's fortune to a chief, saying, "This young woman is meant to be the wife of a king and will bear a royal son. You should either offer all your wealth for her or take her by force." If she cannot be secured, the spies should provoke a conflict. If she is seized, a quarrel will naturally follow.

A female beggar spy might approach a chief who is devoted to his wife and say, "Another chief, proud of his youth, has sent me to entice your wife and sent this letter and jewelry as a gift for her. Your wife is innocent, but this man must be stopped. I'm deeply concerned for your success in this."

Whether the quarrels arise on their own or are fueled by spies, the conqueror should support the weaker party with men and funds, setting them against the corrupt individuals or prompting them to relocate elsewhere.

By these methods, he should establish himself as the singular ruler of all corporations. Under his singular protection, the corporations should remain vigilant against all forms of betrayal.

- The leader of corporations should gain the trust and affection of all the people by living a life of integrity, mastering his desires, and choosing actions that are respected and valued by everyone under his leadership.

Book 12

CHAPTER I. THE DUTIES OF A MESSENGER.

When a king with limited resources faces an attack from a stronger enemy, he should submit to the enemy along with his sons and yield as a reed bends in flowing water.

Bháradvája argues that surrendering to a more powerful force is like bowing before Indra, the rain god, gaining favor through humility. However, Visálaksha believes a weak king should instead fight with all his resources, for courage can overcome hardships; fighting is the duty of a Kshatriya, even if it leads to either victory or defeat.

Kautilya disagrees, stating that one who constantly bows to the powerful lives without hope, like a crab on a riverbank, and one who fights with a small force against a mighty enemy perishes, much like a man trying to cross the sea without a boat. Therefore, a weak king should either seek protection from a powerful ruler or sustain himself in an unbreakable fortress.

Invaders can be of three types: a just conqueror, a demon-like conqueror, and a greedy conqueror. The just conqueror accepts respect and loyalty as sufficient, so a weak king should seek refuge under such a leader. A greedy conqueror, fearing threats from his own enemies, is content with what he can safely claim in land or wealth; hence, a weak king should satisfy such a conqueror with offerings of wealth. The demon-like conqueror, however, will only be appeased by seizing all—territory, treasure, family, and even the life of the conquered. Therefore, a weak king should keep such a conqueror at bay with both land and wealth.

When any of these types threatens a weak king, he should try to prevent the invasion by negotiating a peace treaty, strategizing through intrigue, or employing covert warfare on the battlefield. The king could sway the enemy's men with diplomacy or gifts and prevent betrayal within his ranks by creating discord among them or punishing dissenters. Spies, working secretly, may be deployed to capture the enemy's fort, territory, or camps using weapons, poison, or fire. Additionally, he may harass the enemy's rear forces or damage their lands with the help of allied wild tribes. An imprisoned prince or a branch of the enemy's family might even be encouraged to seize the enemy's territory.

After causing this damage, the king might then send an envoy to the enemy to negotiate peace. Alternatively, he may seek a peaceful resolution without risking offense. However, if the enemy continues his advance, the weak king could offer peace by pledging a quarter of his wealth and forces, with payment arranged within a day and night.

If the enemy proposes peace on the condition that the weaker king surrenders a portion of his army, the king may send over his wildest elephants and least controllable horses, or those with poison-treated equipment. If the enemy demands the surrender of his chief officers, he could assign his forces that include traitors, rival factions, and hostile wild tribes under a trusted officer's command, ensuring that both his enemy and these disruptive forces are mutually harmed. Alternatively, he might send troops composed of fiery spies, provided he first pacifies his own discontented followers. The king could also strategically transfer his loyal, hereditary forces who can inflict damage on the enemy during vulnerable moments.

If the enemy seeks wealth as a term of peace, the king might offer valuable items that are difficult to sell or raw materials that are ineffective for warfare. If peace hinges on ceding a portion of land, he may yield lands that are recoverable, already exposed to attacks from other enemies, lack natural defenses, or would require substantial investment to settle and maintain. If the demand is for a larger surrender, he could concede all lands except his capital, securing his position in the heart of his domain.

- He should craftily maneuver to make the enemy accept something that is vulnerable to another force's interference. Above all, the king should prioritize his own safety over the preservation of wealth, for wealth that leads to ruin is of little value.

[Thus ends Chapter I, "The Duties of a Messenger, and Request for Peace," in Book XII, "Concerning a Powerful Enemy," of the Arthasástra of Kautilya. End of the hundred and thirty-sixth chapter from the beginning.]

CHAPTER II. BATTLE OF INTRIGUE.

If the enemy insists on disregarding peace, he should be warned:

"Kings have fallen by succumbing to the set of six hostile forces; it is not in your interest to follow the example of these misguided rulers. Take heed of virtue and safeguard your wealth. Those advising you to confront danger, risk sin, and compromise your assets are enemies disguised as friends. Engaging with those who disregard their own lives is hazardous; it's sinful to cause widespread bloodshed, and it's wasteful to abandon reliable wealth and a trustworthy ally in me. That king you face has many allies he could align against you, leveraging resources that he gains through your efforts against me, attacking from all sides. He has not yet lost the favor of the Circle of the madhyama and neutral States, unlike you, who have weakened your influence over them. These states, thus, await the chance to turn against you. Endure temporary losses of men and resources to break ties with this risky ally. We will then be able to undermine his influence in that stronghold over which he has lost authority. So, do not listen to those posing as friends but are actually enemies, nor should you risk your loyal friends' wellbeing, empower your true enemies to succeed, or entangle yourself in dangers that threaten life and property."

If, despite this warning, the enemy disregards the advice, the weaker king should secretly incite disloyalty among the enemy's ranks, using tactics outlined in the sections on "The Conduct of Corporations" and "Enticement of the Enemy through Secret Means." Fiery spies and poison should be employed to destabilize the enemy, especially in matters crucial to the enemy's personal safety as discussed in "Safety of His Own Person." Keepers of courtesans may tempt and captivate key leaders in the enemy's army with youthful and alluring women. Fiery spies could then provoke discord among these leaders if one or more falls in love, sparking conflicts that might lead the defeated to either leave or even support the weak king in his efforts.

Additionally, spies disguised as ascetics could provide a love-struck enemy leader with poison, suggesting it's a medicinal potion to fulfill their romantic desires.

A spy, disguised as a merchant, might lavish gifts upon a close maid-servant of the beautiful queen (of the enemy) under the pretense of courting her, only to abandon her later. Another spy, posed as a servant to this maid-servant, may hand her a medicinal potion, saying it's meant to rekindle the merchant's affection if applied by her to his person. Once the maid-servant finds this effective, she could be persuaded to tell the queen that the same potion would secure the king's affections. The potion could then be substituted with poison for use on the king.

A spy posing as an astrologer may subtly convince the enemy's prime minister that he possesses all the attributes of a king. Meanwhile, a mendicant woman could hint to the minister's wife that she has the traits of a queen and will bear a prince. Or another woman, acting as if she were the minister's wife, might relay to him: "The king has been harassing me, and an ascetic woman has delivered this letter and jewelry to me."

Spies disguised as royal cooks could, under the pretense of following the king's orders, deliver coveted wealth to the minister, purportedly intended for use in an imminent campaign. A spy posing as a merchant could then, by various means, acquire this wealth and notify the minister of the readiness of all preparations for the mission. In this way, by employing one, two, or even three strategic maneuvers, the ministers from each faction among the allied enemies could be lured away from their respective kings on a false expedition, leaving those kings unsupported.

Spies serving under the enemy's officer in charge of waste lands could alert the townsfolk and rural people within the enemy's fortified cities to the officer's perceived alliance with the populace. They might say, "The officer in charge of waste lands warns the warriors and officials, saying, 'The king has barely survived a recent danger and has only just returned alive. Don't hoard wealth or create rivals, or you'll face execution.'" Once a crowd gathers, fiery spies could lure the citizens outside the town and assassinate their leaders, declaring, "This fate awaits anyone who ignores the warnings of the officer overseeing the waste lands." On the waste lands, these spies might scatter weapons, coins, and bloodstained ropes as if a violent struggle occurred. Other spies would then circulate the story that the officer in charge is brutalizing and robbing the people.

Similarly, spies could sow discord between the enemy's collector-general and the local population. By publicly addressing the collector-general's servants in the village square at night, fiery spies could announce, "Anyone who unjustly oppresses the people will be dealt with in this manner." When news of the collector-general's or the waste lands officer's wrongdoings spreads widely, the spies might incite the people to overthrow one of them, installing in his place a family member or an imprisoned figure under the spies' influence.

- Spreading false rumors of impending danger to the enemy, spies could incite panic by setting fire to the royal harem, the town gates, and the storehouses holding grain and other provisions, as well as assassinating the sentinels assigned to guard these places.

[Thus ends Chapter II, "The Duties of a Messenger and Battle of Intrigue," in Book XII, "Concerning a Powerful Enemy," of the Arthasástra of Kautilya. End of "Battle of Intrigue." End of the hundred and thirty-seventh chapter from the beginning.]

CHAPTER III. SLAYING THE COMMANDER-IN-CHIEF AND INCITING A CIRCLE OF STATES.

Spies working for the enemy king or his close allies might, under the guise of friendship, suggest in front of other allies that the king is angry with leaders of the infantry, cavalry, chariots, and elephants. Once these leaders gather with their forces, fiery spies, having avoided the night guards, could pretend to act under the enemy king's orders by summoning these leaders to a particular place, then assassinating them as they depart. Other nearby spies would then declare that this action was indeed an order from the enemy king. Spies could also approach exiles from the kingdom, warning, "This outcome is exactly as we warned; for your safety, you might consider leaving for another place."

Similarly, spies could tell those whose requests have been denied by the king that the officer overseeing the waste lands was instructed by the king to handle them: "This individual has requested something inappropriate from me, which I denied. He is conspiring with my enemy. Find a way to subdue him." After planting this idea, the spies would follow their typical procedures.

In cases where requests were granted, spies could inform such individuals that the king has given secret orders to the officer in charge of the waste lands, stating, "Those people demanded what was owed, so I granted it to win their trust. But they are plotting with my enemy. Make arrangements to suppress them." The spies would then continue with their standard actions.

Spies might also approach those who refrain from asking for what they are due from the king, telling them that the officer in charge of waste lands has been instructed: "These individuals don't make their rightful requests of me. What reason could they have other than a fear that I'm aware of their guilt? Take measures to subdue them." The spies would then proceed with their usual methods.

This illustrates how to handle those aligned with the enemy.

A spy who serves as the enemy king's personal attendant might inform him that certain ministers are meeting secretly with agents of a rival king. Once convinced of this, the king could be shown certain deceptive people as supposed "envoys of the enemy," with spies pointing them out directly.

To weaken the enemy, chief army officers might be persuaded with promises of land and gold to turn against their own forces and defect from their leader. If a son of the commander-in-chief lives in or near the fortress, a spy might tell him, "You are the most capable of your father's sons, yet you're ignored. Why remain passive? Claim your rightful position by force, or risk being eliminated by the heir-apparent."

Alternatively, a family member of the commander or the king, or someone held in captivity, could be bribed with gold and instructed, "Undermine the inner strength of the enemy, or weaken his forces stationed on the border."

Or, wild tribes might be enticed with rewards and incited to pillage the enemy's lands. The enemy's rivals might also be approached with a message: "I am the bridge that links you. If I fall, this king will be your undoing. Let us unite to halt his advance." Further, messages could be sent to various states, individually or collectively, warning: "Once he's finished with me, this king will turn on each of you. Be cautious. I am your strongest ally."

- To avoid the threat posed by a close enemy, a king should regularly send gifts or offerings to a madhyama (mediator) or neutral king that would likely win their favor. Alternatively, the king could offer all his resources to the enemy, placing his entire property under their control.

[Thus ends Chapter III, "Slaying the Commander-in-Chief and Inciting a Circle of States," in Book XII, "Concerning a Powerful Enemy," of the Arthasástra of Kautilya. End of the hundred and thirty-eighth chapter from the beginning.]

CHAPTER IV. SPIES WITH WEAPONS, FIRE, AND POISON; AND DESTRUCTION OF SUPPLY, STORES AND GRANARIES.

Spies working for the conqueror, positioned as traders in the enemy's forts, farmers in the villages, or disguised as cowherds or ascetics along the enemy's borderlands, may discreetly inform a neighboring rival, a wild chieftain, a relative of the enemy, or even an imprisoned prince that the enemy's territory is vulnerable for capture. When these external forces arrive, they should be generously rewarded with wealth and honors and shown the enemy's weaknesses. Using this guidance, the spies can then target the enemy's vulnerable areas with strategic strikes.

Alternatively, a banished prince might be placed within the enemy's camp, and a spy posing as a vintner could distribute large quantities of liquor spiked with madana plant juice. On the first day, the vintner might serve regular or mildly intoxicating liquor, followed in subsequent days by liquor tainted with poison. Or, after offering pure liquor to the enemy's officers, the spy could serve them poisoned drinks while they are intoxicated.

A spy positioned as a senior officer in the enemy's army could also carry out similar strategies to weaken the troops. Spies posing as vendors of cooked meat, rice, liquor, or cakes might publicly boast of selling fresh supplies at low prices, drawing in the enemy's troops and then selling them poisoned goods under the guise of a special deal.

Women and children may receive vessels filled with poisoned liquor, milk, curd, ghee, or oil from traders, then pour these back into the traders' containers, making it seem like they intend to buy all the contents. Spies, disguised as merchants, may buy these items to be sure that enemy servants feed these contaminated supplies to their elephants and horses along with rations and grass. Spies posing as attendants could even sell poisoned grass and water directly. Others, acting as cattle traders over time, might leave herds of cattle, sheep, or goats in plain sight to distract the enemy from an impending attack. Disguised as cowherds, they may release aggressive animals like horses, mules, camels, or buffaloes whose eyes have been smeared with musk-rat blood, making them agitated and dangerous. Spies acting as hunters might release wild beasts from traps, while those pretending to be snake charmers could unleash venomous snakes; elephant keepers might set elephants loose near the enemy's camp, and spies skilled with fire could set the camp ablaze. Hidden agents might ambush enemy leaders from behind or set fires in key residences.

Traitors, enemy sympathizers, or wild tribes can be engaged to disrupt the enemy's rear or block reinforcements. Spies concealed in forests could infiltrate the border areas of the enemy's territory to wreak havoc or target their supplies and other essentials on narrow paths that can only be traversed single-file.

Following a prearranged plan, spies might, during a night raid, enter the enemy's capital and blow trumpets while loudly declaring, "We've taken the capital; the country has been conquered." Amid this chaos, they could infiltrate the palace and assassinate the king. As the king flees from one point to another, hidden Mlechchhas, wild tribes, or army chiefs lying in ambush or concealed by a post or fence might strike him down. Disguised as hunters, spies might eliminate the king while he directs his attack or during the frenzy of a planned ambush.

Taking advantage of strategic terrain, spies could kill the enemy as he marches along a single-file path, on a mountain, near a tree trunk, or under the branches of a banyan tree. Alternatively, they might unleash a torrent by breaking a dam on a river, lake, or pond, sweeping the enemy away with the force of the water. In a fort, forest, valley, or desert, the enemy might be annihilated with an explosive device or a poisonous snake. Fire is most effective against an enemy under a thicket; smoke, when he is stranded in a desert; poison, if he is in a comfortable location; crocodiles or other fierce beasts, if he is in water. Or, he might be attacked while escaping from a burning residence.

- By using methods described in the chapter, "Enticement of the Enemy by Secret Means," or through other strategies, the enemy should be captured either in areas where he is confined or in those from which he is trying to escape.

[Thus ends Chapter IV, "Spies with Weapons, Fire and Poison; and Destruction of Supply, Stores and Granaries," in Book XII, "Concerning a Powerful Enemy," of the Arthasástra of Kautilya. End of the hundred and thirty-ninth chapter from the beginning.]

CHAPTER V. CAPTURE OF THE ENEMY BY MEANS OF SECRET CONTRIVANCES OR BY MEANS OF THE ARMY; AND COMPLETE VICTORY.

Plans to eliminate the enemy may be set up in places of worship or pilgrimage that he regularly visits under religious devotion.

A wall or stone held by a mechanical device can be loosened to fall on the enemy's head when he enters a temple. Stones and weapons can be dropped from the upper stories above him, or a door panel may be released to crash down. A large rod positioned above or partially attached to a wall can be made to fall on him. Hidden weapons inside the statue of a deity might be triggered to strike him, or the floor where he usually stands, sits, or walks can be treated with poison mixed with cow dung or pure water. Poison could also be administered under the pretense of giving him flowers, incense, or perfumed smoke. Another option is to remove the supports of a cot or seat to make him fall into a pit lined with pointed spears.

If he is desperate to escape imprisonment in his country, he may be deceived and led into the hands of a nearby wild tribe or enemy lying in wait. Similarly, if he is eager to flee from his fortress, he could be misled into entering an enemy territory that is about to fall into the conqueror's hands. The enemy's people should also be held under the protection of the conqueror's family—sons or brothers—in fortresses located in mountains, forests, or river islands separated from the enemy's country by wild lands.

Measures to hinder the enemy's movements are covered in the section, "The Conduct of a Conquered King." Grasslands and firewood areas should be set ablaze up to a yojana (about 5.25 miles); water sources should be polluted and diverted; external fort structures like mounds, wells, pits, and thorn barriers should be removed. The mouth of the enemy's underground tunnel can be widened, allowing removal of their supplies and leaders—or even the enemy himself. If the tunnel has been created by the enemy for escape, the ditch outside the fort may be used to flood it. Empty pots or bronze vessels may be placed in suspicious spots along the parapet or around wells outside the fort to detect air movement from the tunnel. Once the tunnel's direction is identified, a counter-tunnel can be dug, or the discovered tunnel can be filled with smoke or water to incapacitate those inside.

Once the enemy has arranged for his fort's defense under a trusted family member, he may flee to a location where he could meet allies, relatives, or friendly wild tribes. He might go to the lands of his enemy's unreliable allies with substantial resources, hoping to split the enemy from these allies, or he may target the enemy's rear guard, territory, or disrupt the enemy's supply lines. He could head to an area where he can attack by using trees or obstacles or move to a region from which he can organize reinforcements for his own army, or he might aim for a place where peace can be negotiated on favorable terms.

The conqueror's allies might then approach this fleeing enemy with a proposal, saying: "This enemy of yours has come into our reach. Under the guise of a trade exchange or as a gift, send gold and a strong force; we will either hand him over to you, bound and chained, or expel him from here." If he accepts this offer, any gold or forces he sends could then be taken over by the conqueror.

The boundary officer of the enemy's country, having gained entry to the enemy's stronghold, may lead a portion of his force to eliminate the enemy in good faith, claiming he is moving in to subdue a local disturbance. He may also divert the enemy to an opposing force, or surround the enemy at a favorable spot and kill him under the guise of defending his own people.

A feigned ally could alert an external party, saying: "The grain, oil, jaggery, and salt supplies in the enemy's fort are nearly depleted; fresh supplies are expected at a specific location and time. Move swiftly to capture it." Traitors, enemies, wild tribes, or other appointed agents may then send in a shipment of poisoned grain, oil, jaggery, or salt to the fort. This tactic exemplifies the capture of all kinds of enemy supplies.

The fleeing enemy, having agreed to a truce with the conqueror, might begin paying the promised gold but only partially, delaying the rest in installments. He may then use this delay to create an impression of weakened defenses and then strike back with fire, poison, or direct attack. Alternatively, he could build trust with the conqueror's officials responsible for collecting tribute, using this opportunity to undermine the conqueror's resources or planning.

If his resources are entirely depleted, he may abandon his fort and flee, either escaping through an existing tunnel, a newly created hole, or by breaking through the parapet. Alternatively, he might challenge the conqueror at night, planning to confront the attack; if this fails, he can escape through a side path. He could disguise himself as a wandering ascetic with a small retinue, or he might be carried off by spies, pretending to be a corpse. Disguised as a grieving woman, he could follow another corpse, as if it were her husband's funeral procession, to the cremation grounds.

During a public event such as a ceremony honoring the gods, the ancestors, or during a local festival, he may use poisoned rice and water to harm the enemy. By collaborating with enemy traitors, he might also ambush his foe with a hidden army. If surrounded in his fort, he could consume sacramental food, set up an altar, and conceal himself in a hidden compartment within an idol. He might also hide in a concealed chamber within a wall or in a carved-out space in an underground idol. After the enemy's guard is down, he could emerge through a tunnel, enter the palace, and attack his enemy while he sleeps. Another strategy might involve loosening the fastenings of a machine to let it fall on the enemy. If the enemy rests in a chamber coated with poisonous or flammable materials, he might ignite it to trap his foe within.

Hidden spies, concealed in an underground chamber, a tunnel, or inside a wall, could ambush the enemy when he is leisurely enjoying a park or another place of relaxation. Other concealed spies might poison him, or women in hiding could throw a snake, poison, fire, or poisonous smoke over him while he sleeps in a confined area. Spies with access to the enemy's harem could seize any opportunities to harm the enemy and then disappear without detection. In these situations, they should use specific signs to indicate their intentions to members of their secret society.

- By using trumpet signals, he could gather the sentinels at the gate, along with older men and other spies placed there by others, allowing him to carry out the remainder of his plans seamlessly.

Book 13

CHAPTER I. SOWING THE SEEDS OF DISSENSION.

When a conqueror seeks to overtake a rival's village, he should actively uplift his own troops' confidence while strategically intimidating the enemy's people. This can be achieved by publicly showcasing his "omniscient" knowledge of events and a seemingly direct connection to divine forces, both of which can be used to instill fear and uncertainty in the enemy.

To showcase his omniscience, he might carry out carefully staged actions that create the impression of uncanny insight into people's private matters. For example, he could publicly dismiss high-ranking officials, revealing that he already knows personal details about their hidden lives, or expose traitors based on information gathered by spies discreetly planted to monitor them. By subtly pointing out the weak spots in any proposals given to him, he demonstrates an uncanny ability to assess the faults in suggestions, which fuels the image of his infallible judgment. Additionally, he might claim insight into far-reaching foreign affairs, attributing this knowledge to his ability to interpret signs and omens, which he could explain as a talent that allows him to foresee even distant matters—such as when a carrier pigeon arrives with a message and he can predict its contents.

To project the image of a divine connection, the conqueror might use concealed spies who stage supernatural appearances, claiming to be gods and performing feats that appear otherworldly. He could, for instance, hold "conversations" with spies dressed as deities in settings designed to look mystical, such as having spies emerge from tunnels to stand in the flames of a sacred altar or within the body of a hollow idol. These spies would pretend to be gods of fire, water, or serpents, as if appearing by divine will to bless or communicate with him. He might also stage scenes by water with spies disguised as spirits of the river or snake-gods who "rise" from the water. Further adding to the spectacle, he might instruct people to place oil and sea foam on water, lighting it at a distance to create what looks like spontaneous fire breaking out across the surface. While on a raft in the water, secretly tethered to a rock, he could put on a "divine performance" for his audience. He might even employ skilled performers who, using underwater devices created from the organs of aquatic animals, would appear to move with ease under the water while speaking in the guise of godly messengers.

Astrologers, soothsayers, and omen-readers, along with various types of spies and informers, should spread tales of the king's powers widely throughout his own land, emphasizing how gods and spirits regularly visit him and how divine beings have personally delivered valuable weapons or treasures to him. The conqueror's agents should ensure that rumors reach foreign territories as well, asserting that he has received supernatural assistance that will guide him to victory. Astrologers could also interpret signs of victory for the king, such as his ability to explain the language of animals or foresee the outcomes of dreams, contrasting this by claiming the opposite for his enemy, painting the rival as bereft of divine favor. His agents could go further by creating ominous signs in the skies of the enemy's territory, such as arranging for flaming firebrands to fall accompanied by the sound of drums on the enemy ruler's birthday, marking it as an inauspicious omen for the enemy.

Through these calculated displays and manipulations, the conqueror carefully builds his reputation, using public perception and spectacle to weaken the morale of the enemy's people, thereby advancing his conquest with psychological as well as military strategy.

The conqueror's main envoys, while pretending to be allies of the enemy, should speak highly of the conqueror's gracious treatment of guests, the formidable strength of his army, and the looming likelihood of the enemy's defeat. They should also communicate that under the conqueror's rule, both ministers and soldiers alike enjoy security and well-being, and that he treats his followers with a genuine, almost parental care in both prosperous and difficult times.

Through these and similar methods, they should gradually sway the enemy's people as previously described and as will be further detailed. They should describe the enemy ruler in unflattering terms, likening him to an "ordinary donkey" in how he treats skilled individuals, and to a "broken branch of lakucha" (Artocarpus Lacucha) in his treatment of his officers. To the frustrated and unappreciated, they should describe the enemy king as nothing more than a crab washed up on the shore. For those treated with disdain, he should be likened to a "storm of lightning," inciting only fear and chaos. To those disappointed by his promises, he should be compared to "a reed, a barren tree, an iron ball, or false clouds." To those loyal despite receiving little reward, he could be described as "the ornaments of an unattractive woman," adding no benefit to the wearer. To those previously favored but now disillusioned, the conqueror's agents should portray the enemy king as dangerous and deceptive—like "the skin of a tiger" or "a trap of death." To those who've sacrificed much on his behalf, they could liken loyalty to the enemy to "chewing on the wood of pílu" (Careya-Arborea), or the fruitless act of "churning a camel's or donkey's milk for butter."

Once the enemy's people are persuaded, the envoys may guide them to seek refuge with the conqueror in exchange for wealth and honor. For those in need of provisions, they should supply them generously with food and money, while those who prefer other support might be given jewelry for their families.

During times of famine or when thieves and wild tribes are oppressing the enemy's lands, the conqueror's spies should sow seeds of discontent, suggesting, "Let's appeal to the king for relief, but if he doesn't respond, we can seek a better place to live."

- When the enemy's people respond to these ideas, they should receive financial support, food, and any necessary aid. In this way, discord among the enemy's people can be effectively fostered.

[Thus ends Chapter I, "Sowing the Seeds of Dissension," in Book XIII, "Strategic Means to Capture a Fortress" of the Arthasástra, of Kautilya. End of the hundred and forty-first chapter from the beginning.]

CHAPTER II. ENTICEMENT OF KINGS BY SECRET CONTRIVANCES.

An ascetic, either with a shaved head or braided hair, dwelling in a cave on a mountain, may pretend to be four hundred years old. This ascetic, accompanied by a group of followers with braided hair, could set up camp near the capital of the enemy. The disciples would then present offerings of roots and fruits to the king and his ministers, inviting them to visit the revered ascetic. When the king arrives, the ascetic may recount stories of ancient kings and the history of their lands. He might say, "Every hundred years, I enter the fire and emerge reborn as a youthful being. Now, in your presence, I am about to undergo this transformation for the fourth time. It would be a great honor to have you present during this sacred event. Please, request three boons." If the king agrees, the ascetic could ask him to remain at the site with his family for seven nights to witness the ritual. Once there, the king could be captured.

Another approach involves an ascetic, either bald or with braided hair, claiming to know the secrets hidden deep within the earth. He could plant a bamboo stick wrapped in cloth stained with blood and dusted with gold, or a hollow golden tube where a snake can coil, inside an ant hill. One of his followers might then tell the king, "This holy man can locate blooming treasures buried in the earth." When the king inquires, the ascetic could confirm this skill by pulling out the bamboo stick. Alternatively, he might place more gold in the ant hill and tell the king, "A snake guards this treasure, and it can only be retrieved after a sacred ritual." Should the king agree, he could be asked to stay at the spot for seven nights, as before.

At night in a secluded area, an ascetic feigning the power to locate hidden treasures might be seated with his body seemingly ignited by magical fire. His followers could then bring the king to witness this remarkable sight, telling him that the ascetic is truly capable of uncovering such treasures. During any task requested by the king, the ascetic could then urge the king to stay for seven nights, just as before.

A skilled ascetic might deceive a king through knowledge of a magical science known as jambhaka, convincing him to stay as outlined earlier.

An ascetic may also claim to have earned the favor of the powerful deity who protects the land. He could mesmerize the king's chief ministers through amazing feats, gradually winning the king's trust.

Any individual disguised as an ascetic, living underwater or hidden within an idol reached through a secret tunnel or chamber, could be presented by his disciples as Varuna, the god of water, or as the king of snakes, and shown to the king. When going forth to fulfill the king's desires, he could again invite the king to remain for seven nights, as before.

An accomplished ascetic, halting in the vicinity of the capital city, may invite the king to witness the person (of his enemy) when he comes to witness the invocation of his enemy's life in the image to be destroyed, he may be murdered in an unguarded place.

Spies, under the, guise of merchants come to sell horses, may invite the king to examine and purchase any of the animals. While attentively examining the horses, he may be murdered in the tumult or trampled down by horses.

At night, in an altar near the enemy's capital, fiery spies could gather, blowing flames from tubes or hollow reeds filled with fire from pots. They would then shout loudly, "We are here to devour the flesh of the king or his ministers; let the gods be worshipped." Disguised as soothsayers and astrologers, other spies might spread these unsettling rumors among the people.

Spies disguised as Nagas, or snake gods, with bodies smeared in blazing oil (tejánataila), could stand in the center of a sacred pool or lake at night, sharpening iron swords or spikes, shouting threats as before. Other spies, wearing cloaks made of bear skins, might create smoky effects from their mouths, acting like demons. They could circle the city three times from right to left, then raise frightening cries in places echoing with the sounds of jackals and other wild animals. Alternatively, spies could ignite an altar or a deity's statue, coated with mica and burning oil, and again cry out as before. Other agents would then spread word of these events throughout the city.

The spies could also make blood appear to flow dramatically from revered statues of gods. Witnesses would spread this eerie news, challenging anyone brave enough to come and see the divine blood. If anyone accepted the challenge, hidden agents would ambush them, beating them to death with rods to make it appear they had been killed by supernatural forces. The spies, along with others, would then report this terrifying incident to the king. Disguised as soothsayers and astrologers, the spies might advise the king to perform auspicious and cleansing rituals to protect himself and his people from the evil consequences. When the king agrees, he might be instructed to conduct special sacrifices and ceremonies using specific mantras each night for seven days. During this time, they would plan to eliminate him as previously arranged.

To set an example and sow further confusion among other rulers, the conqueror could publicly conduct similar rites to avert evil, encouraging others to follow suit.

To ward off the negative effects of unnatural events, the conqueror may also gather funds from his subjects under this pretense.

If the enemy is particularly fond of elephants, spies might lure him with a sighting of a magnificent elephant, supposedly cared for by the officer in charge of the elephant forests. When the enemy shows interest in capturing this creature, he could be led to a remote and deserted part of the forest, where he would either be killed or captured. This demonstrates the dangers that can befall rulers who are overly eager for hunting excursions.

If the enemy has a weakness for wealth or beautiful women, spies could use this against him by presenting him with wealthy and attractive widows, seemingly seeking his help to reclaim a fortune entrusted to a relative. Then, under the guise of a private meeting arranged at night, concealed spies could kill him using weapons or poison.

If the enemy frequently visits ascetics, sacred shrines, religious pillars (stúpa), or statues of deities, spies hiding in underground chambers, secret tunnels, or within walls could take advantage of these private moments to ambush and eliminate him.

- At any location where the king personally goes to view special displays or events, or whenever he engages in activities like playing games or swimming, spies might prepare to strike.
- Similarly, they can take advantage when the king, in moments of distraction, lets out careless words or when he's preoccupied with sacrificial ceremonies, birth events, times of mourning or illness in the palace, or during moments of intimacy, grief, or fright.
- Any gatherings or celebrations held by the king's own people,

where he may attend and remain unguarded, present further opportunities, as do cloudy or stormy days, or when he is amidst large, tumultuous crowds.

- Spies may also target him when he attends Brahman assemblies, goes to inspect the scene of a fire, finds himself in a secluded place, or even while he's dressing, putting on jewelry or floral garlands, resting in bed, or sitting.

- Whether during meals or drinks, or other private moments, spies, accompanied by hidden accomplices stationed there ahead of time, may wait for the signal from trumpets to carry out their mission.

- They can then discreetly leave the scene as inconspicuously as they arrived, blending into the spectators, thereby ensuring that unsuspecting kings and individuals are lured out and taken by surprise.

[Thus ends Chapter II, "Enticement of Kings by Secret Contrivances," in Book XIII, "Strategic means to Capture a Fortress," of the Arthasástra of Kautilya. End of the hundred and forty-second chapter from the beginning.]

CHAPTER III. THE WORK OF SPIES IN A SIEGE.

The conqueror might dismiss a trusted chief from a local corporation, allowing the chief to defect to the enemy as a friendly agent and offer resources like recruits and supplies gathered from the conqueror's own territory. Accompanied by a team of spies, this chief might win the enemy's favor by targeting a rebellious village, a regiment, or an ally of the conqueror, even presenting the enemy with elephants, horses, or disloyal members of the conqueror's forces or those of his allies. Alternatively, a close officer from the conqueror's ranks might request help from a section of the enemy's territory, a guild (sreni), or wild tribes. Once he gains their trust, he can steer them toward the conqueror, where they can be swiftly subdued during a staged event involving elephants or wild tribes.

This strategy illustrates the dual role that ministers and chiefs of wild tribes can play on behalf of the conqueror.

After securing peace with the enemy, the conqueror may let go of his trusted ministers, who then approach the enemy with a plea to restore their loyalty to the conqueror. If the enemy sends an envoy on their behalf, the conqueror can scold this messenger, saying, "Your leader seeks to divide me and my ministers; you should not return here." One of these dismissed ministers, accompanied by spies, traitors, unruly allies, or wild tribes without allegiance, may then offer to serve the enemy, eventually persuading him to dispose of certain leaders like the boundary guard, local chiefs, or the enemy's army commander by claiming, "These individuals are allied with your adversary." Thus, by the enemy's command, these individuals may be eliminated.

The conqueror could also propose to the enemy: "A nearby leader with a formidable army poses a threat to us both; let's join forces to defeat him. You may seize his treasury or lands." If the enemy accepts, he could be ambushed in the chaos of battle or by the conqueror's allies during the clash. Alternatively, the conqueror might extend an invitation to the enemy to attend a staged ceremony for granting new territory, naming an heir, or performing rites. At this gathering, the conqueror could capture or eliminate the enemy. If the enemy resists such events, agents may still attempt to eliminate him through covert methods or by employing the enemy's own foes.

Should the enemy insist on moving alone with his troops, the conqueror may trap him between two forces and destroy him. If the enemy decides to independently capture an unguarded enemy's territory, the conqueror can engage one of his foes or another well-prepared agent to ambush him. Should the enemy seek out his subjugated rival to raise forces, the conqueror could seize his capital in his absence. Alternatively, the conqueror might prompt the enemy to annex the territory of an ally or friend of the conqueror, where the conqueror's ally would act against the enemy, ultimately capturing him.

These strategies and maneuvers, subtle or overt, all ultimately work to the conqueror's advantage.

If the enemy shows interest in capturing the territory of the conqueror's ally, the conqueror might appear cooperative and even lend his army to aid the enemy's pursuit. Behind the scenes, however, he could form a secret alliance with his friend, feigning vulnerability and allowing himself to be attacked by the enemy, now paired with the overlooked ally. Positioned between two forces, the enemy could be cornered, either captured alive or killed, with his lands then divided between the conqueror and his ally.

If the enemy, supported by his own allies, takes refuge in a highly fortified position, nearby foes could be enlisted to devastate his territory. Should the enemy attempt to defend his lands with his forces, those forces might be neutralized in battle. When separating the enemy from his ally is impossible, both may be approached openly, with each offered the chance to make a deal with the conqueror to seize the other's territory. In this case, each would send representatives who serve both sides, relaying the message, "The conqueror, backed by my forces, plans to seize your lands." Consequently, one of the allies, provoked by anger and suspicion, would likely turn on the other.

The conqueror might discharge his own officers responsible for his forests, outlying territories, and army on grounds of alleged conspiracy with the enemy. Once these officers join the enemy's ranks, they could undermine him in moments of war, siege, or other crises. They could also create rifts between the enemy and his supporters, providing coached witnesses to back up claims of discord.

Spies, disguised as hunters, could station themselves near the enemy's fortress gate, selling meat and gradually forming friendships with the guards. By repeatedly alerting the enemy of nearby robberies, they could gain credibility, ultimately convincing him to split his forces and station troops in different parts of his land. During a village raid, they might warn of an imminent threat, suggesting that the robbers are dangerously close and require a substantial force to fend them off. The supplied army could then be handed over to the raiding commander, and later that night, some of the commander's forces could return with the spies to the fortress gate, loudly proclaiming that the robbers have been defeated and the army has triumphed. When the guards, under the enemy's orders or in confidence, open the gate, the returning army could launch a surprise attack, seizing control of the fortress.

Artists, carpenters, heretics, actors, merchants, and various other spies from the conqueror's forces could blend seamlessly into the enemy's fortified city. These agents might live under the guise of simple villagers or craftsmen, quietly preparing to act. Spies disguised as farmers can help covertly supply hidden weapons into the fortress, transporting them under layers of firewood, grass, or grains loaded into carts. Additionally, they may conceal arms and armor within items that appear harmless, such as religious images or flags of gods, allowing them to position these tools strategically within the fort without raising suspicion.

Once these resources are inside, spies posing as holy priests may alert the enemy by blowing conch shells and beating drums, proclaiming that a fierce army, intent on destruction and fully equipped, is closing in on the city. The sudden panic and confusion within the fort may create the ideal opportunity for these disguised spies to seize control of the fortress gate, along with the towers and other strategic points, preparing the way for the conqueror's forces to enter. Alternatively, amidst the uproar, the agents could disperse the enemy's guards and army, hastening the city's fall.

Further, under a pretense of peace or friendly relations with the enemy, the conqueror can have his agents smuggle both troops and weapons into the enemy's stronghold. Spies may arrive disguised as traders in caravans, processions for a bride, merchants selling horses, traveling peddlers, buyers and sellers of grains, or even wandering ascetics. These disguised troops and weapons would be strategically positioned to secure the conqueror's victory. These are the core agents assigned with the critical task of targeting the life of the opposing ruler.

The same undercover agents, along with those previously described in "Elimination of Threats," may use local thieves to destroy the enemy's cattle herds or merchandise in wilderness-adjacent areas.

In addition, spies may lace the food and drink prepared for the enemy's cowherds with the intoxicating juice of the madana plant. Disguised as herders, merchants, or even opportunistic thieves, these agents could strike when the cowherds, weakened and inebriated, are least able to protect their flocks, allowing them to carry off large numbers of cattle.

Moreover, spies disguised as ascetics with shaved heads or braided hair may pretend to be followers of the deity Sankarshana. They might offer cowherds a sacrificial beverage secretly mixed with madana juice, leading to intoxication, which would enable the spies to take the cattle while the cowherds are incapacitated.

An agent posing as a vintner could exploit religious processions, funeral rites, festivals, and other public gatherings to sell liquor to the cowherds, lacing it with madana juice. Once the cowherds succumb to intoxication, other spies lying in wait could take advantage, overpowering the guards and herders to seize the cattle. Through careful preparation and deception, each of these covert operations serves the conqueror's objective of destabilizing and weakening the enemy from within.

- Agents sent into the enemy's territories under the guise of bandits, with the pretense of raiding villages and seizing valuables, yet who abandon this plundering to focus on covertly undermining or eliminating key enemy forces, are classified as spies disguised as thieves. These operatives pose as marauders but are in fact strategically directed by the conqueror to dismantle the enemy's resources and security from within. Their mission is dual-purpose, utilizing the appearance of disorder and theft to mask deliberate actions aimed at destabilizing and weakening the enemy's defenses and morale.

[Thus ends Chapter III, "The Work of Spies in a Siege," in Book XIII, "The Strategic Means to Capture a Fortress," of the Arthasástra of Kautilya. End of the hundred and forty-third chapter from the beginning.]

CHAPTER IV. THE OPERATION OF A SIEGE.

Before laying siege, it's essential to weaken the enemy's resources and morale. Any newly conquered land should be stabilized to the point where its inhabitants feel secure enough to rest without fear. If there is unrest, it can be quelled by granting rewards and reducing taxes—unless the conqueror intends to abandon it. The conqueror should also plan to conduct battles in distant parts of the enemy's territory, away from densely populated areas, as Kautilya advises that a true kingdom or country is defined by its population. If the people resist conquest, then the conqueror can weaken their resolve by targeting their supplies, destroying their crops, and cutting off their trade.

- By disrupting trade, demolishing agricultural outputs and standing crops, forcing the people to flee, and eliminating their leaders through covert actions, the land will gradually be emptied of its population.

When the conqueror sees his advantage—knowing that his army is well-supplied with staple grains, raw materials, equipment, weapons, clothing, laborers, ropes, and similar essentials, and that the season favors his side while his enemy is hampered by unfavorable weather, disease, famine, and dwindling resources—he can consider starting the siege. This is especially favorable if the enemy's forces and any allied troops are weakened and demoralized.

First, he should ensure the security of his camp, transport units, supplies, and communication routes, surrounding his camp with a trench and building a rampart. Then, to weaken the enemy's defenses, he might pollute the water in the ditches around the fort, drain the water if the ditches are full, or fill empty ditches with water to disrupt the enemy's routine. With tunnels and iron rods, he could attack the ramparts and parapets. If the trench is too deep to cross, he might fill it with earth; if it's well-defended, he could use machines to destroy it. His cavalry could attempt to break through the gate and engage the enemy inside. Periodically, amidst the chaos, he could extend an offer to negotiate terms, using one or more strategic approaches to weaken their resolve.

If birds—like vultures, crows, naptris, bhásas, parrots, máinas, or pigeons—are nesting in the fort walls, he might capture these birds, attach combustible powders to their tails, and release them toward the fort to spread fire. When his camp is set at a distance with elevated posts for archers and their flags in view, the enemy fort may be ignited from afar. Spies, disguised as fort watchmen, can secure inflammable powders to the tails of mongooses, monkeys, cats, or dogs and let these animals wander over thatched roofs to ignite them. A small fire hidden within a dried fish may also be carried by a monkey, a crow, or any other bird, delivering fire onto the thatched roofs within the fort.

Small incendiary balls can be made by mixing ingredients like sarala (Pinus Longifolia), devadáru (deodar), pútitrina (stinking grass), guggulu (Bdellium), sriveshtaka (turpentine), the juice of sarja (Vatica Robusta), and láksha (lac) combined with the dung of animals such as an ass, camel, sheep, and goat. These balls are highly inflammable and designed to sustain a flame for long durations.

An alternative incendiary powder can be prepared by blending the powder of priyala (Chironjia Sapida), the charcoal of avalguja (Serratula anthelmintica), madhúchchhishta (wax), and the dung of a horse, ass, camel, and cow. This powder is effective when hurled against the enemy as it is capable of igniting upon impact.

Another mixture involves the powdered form of all common metals, rendered to a fiery red hue, or a blend of powdered kumbhí (Gmelina arborea), sísa (lead), and trapu (zinc) with charcoal from the flowers of páribhadraka (deodar) and palása (Butea Frondosa), mixed with oil, wax, and turpentine. This combination produces another potent incendiary powder.

To create a fire-arrow, a stick coated with visvásagháti and the above mixture can be wrapped with a bark that includes hemp, zinc, and lead. These arrows are highly effective for use against enemy forces.

However, if a fort can be taken by other methods, setting it on fire should be avoided. Fire is unpredictable and dangerous, potentially incurring the wrath of the gods and destroying valuable resources, including grains, cattle, gold, and raw materials. Capturing a fort where everything has been ruined by fire also brings additional losses in terms of upkeep and repairs, making a less destructive method of conquest preferable.

When the conqueror assesses that he is sufficiently stocked with resources, supplies, and skilled workers, while his enemy is weakened, suffering from incompetent or corrupt officers, unprepared with incomplete forts, low on supplies, and isolated or even allied with untrustworthy friends, then he should recognize this as the perfect opportunity to launch a siege and storm the fort with full force.

When fire, whether accidental or set deliberately, erupts; when the enemy's people are occupied with sacrificial rituals, watching performances, involved in a brawl sparked by drunkenness, or when the troops are exhausted from prolonged battles and have suffered significant losses over repeated engagements; when the enemy's people, weary and sleep-deprived, have fallen into a deep slumber; or when there is the cover of cloudy weather, floods, thick fog, or snow — these moments are ideal for launching a full assault.

Alternatively, the conqueror might abandon his camp to hide in a nearby forest, striking at the enemy when they come out in pursuit. Another tactic involves a king pretending to be the enemy's closest friend or ally, deepening their bond and sending a messenger to convey messages like, "Here's your weak point; these are your internal enemies; this is the weakness of the besieging forces; and this person (who appears to have abandoned the conqueror to join you) is now your ally." When this supposed ally returns from the enemy with a second messenger, the conqueror can capture and publicly reveal the "traitor's" actions, banish him, and momentarily withdraw from siege activities. The supposed ally may then suggest to the besieged enemy, "Come out to join me, or let's unite to strike at the besieger." When the enemy is lured out, they can be trapped between two forces — the conqueror's and the ally's — and either killed or captured. The conqueror may then seize the enemy's territory and raze the capital to the ground, drawing out the elite of the enemy's forces to destroy them.

This approach explains the conqueror's handling of a subjugated enemy or a wild chief.

Either a conquered foe or a wild tribal chief working with the conqueror may deceive the besieged by saying, "The conqueror seems to consider retreating from the siege, fearing the spread of disease, vulnerability to a rear attack, or potential rebellion within his ranks." Once the besieged enemy believes this, the conqueror may set fire to his camp as a ruse and pull back. Then, when the enemy comes out, they can be trapped as before.

Alternatively, the conqueror may gather merchandise laced with poison and trick the enemy by sending this tainted merchandise to them. Another approach is to have a supposed ally of the enemy send a message saying, "Come out to attack the conqueror, who has already been struck by me." When the enemy complies and leaves their stronghold, they can be surrounded as before.

Spies disguised as friends or relatives, equipped with appropriate passes and orders, may infiltrate the enemy's fort and assist in its capture. Or, a feigned ally of the enemy could relay to the besieged: "I plan to strike the besieging camp at this specific time and place; when that happens, you should join in the attack with me." Should the enemy decide to attack, or if they come out upon hearing a chaotic uproar from the supposedly threatened besieging army, they may be defeated as before.

The conqueror may also persuade a friendly ally or a wild chief in alliance with the enemy to seize the enemy's land while they're under siege. If such an ally attempts to take the enemy's territory, the conqueror can deploy spies among the enemy's population or recruit leaders from the enemy's defectors to assassinate this ally, or the conqueror himself may secretly administer poison. A second fake friend may then inform the enemy that the murdered ally was acting treacherously, trying to seize the territory of his so-called friend in a time of distress. After building greater trust with the enemy, this feigned friend can sow seeds of discord between the enemy and their officers, possibly leading to their execution. By inciting unrest among the enemy's people, this spy can suppress the uprising without the enemy's knowledge. Then, after gathering a portion of his army, reinforced by fierce wild tribes, the feigned ally can enter the enemy's fort, only to let the conqueror's forces take control.

Lastly, traitors, enemies, wild tribes, or defectors from the enemy's ranks may claim to have been reconciled, honored, and rewarded, then return to the enemy's side and facilitate the fort's capture by the conqueror.

Once he has captured the fort or returned to his camp after its capture, the conqueror should show mercy to the defeated enemy's troops who surrender, whether they lie prostrate in the field, stand with their backs turned, have their hair disheveled, have thrown down their weapons, or are visibly distressed and fearful. After ensuring that the captured fort is secured, with his men guarding it both inside and out and clearing it of any remaining enemy loyalists, he can make his victorious entry.

With the territory of the immediate enemy subdued, the conqueror should next set his sights on that of the madhyama king. Upon securing this, he can then focus on the neutral king's lands, completing the first method of world conquest. If the madhyama and neutral kings are absent, he should instead earn the loyalty and trust of the former enemy's subjects through his own virtues, then turn his attention to conquering other distant enemies. This is the second path to victory. In the absence of a Circle of States to challenge, he may defeat either a friend or an enemy by positioning his forces strategically between his ally and adversary, gaining an advantage through their placement. This is the third approach.

Alternatively, he could start by defeating an almost unconquerable neighboring enemy, thus doubling his own power. With this strength, he can then take on a second enemy, tripling his power upon victory, before setting his sights on a third. This constitutes the fourth way to achieve total conquest.

Once he has conquered the land and its people, each with their own unique castes and ways of religious life, the conqueror should rule and enjoy his kingdom, governing in accordance with the noble responsibilities prescribed for kings.

- The five methods for capturing a fort are as follows: creating intrigue, employing spies, winning over the loyalty of the enemy's people, conducting a siege, and launching a direct assault.

[Thus ends Chapter IV, "The Operation of a Siege and Storming a Fort," in Book XIII, "Strategic Means to Capture a Fortress," of the Arthasástra of Kautilya. End of the hundred and forty-fourth chapter from the beginning.]

CHAPTER V. RESTORATION OF PEACE IN A CONQUERED COUNTRY.

The conqueror's military campaign may target either vast wilderness areas or single villages and small settlements. The territory he gains can be classified into three types: newly acquired land, territory reclaimed from usurpers, and inherited land.

For newly acquired territories, he should outshine the enemy by displaying his own virtues and amplifying them to overshadow any merits of the enemy. This includes adhering to his own duties rigorously, staying focused on his responsibilities, providing rewards, reducing taxes, offering gifts, and bestowing honors. The conqueror should align himself with the local leaders and influential figures. He should also fulfill any promises made to defectors from the enemy's side and continue rewarding their loyalty each time they support him. Failure to keep promises weakens trust with both the conqueror's own people and the enemy's. Acting against the people's wishes or traditions will also damage reliability.

To build rapport, he should adopt the local customs, language, dress, and social norms. Participating in national, religious, and local festivals shows solidarity. His spies should highlight for local leaders, village heads, castes, and guilds how the enemy was punished and, by contrast, how much respect and support the conqueror offers them, aligning his prosperity with theirs. By providing gifts, tax relief, and security, he can win over the people. The conqueror should openly honor religious practices and support scholars, speakers, charitable, and courageous individuals with gifts of land, financial aid, and tax relief.

He should release prisoners and support those who are poor, helpless, or ill. To encourage compassion, animal slaughter could be restricted for two weeks during the monsoon festival (Chaturmasya), four nights around the full moon, and on his birthday or on the national day. Additionally, the killing of young animals and females should be prohibited, as should castration.

Practices or customs that threaten his revenue, military strength, or moral principles should be reformed. Known thieves and certain nomadic groups should frequently change locations, keeping them from consolidating power or influence. Loyal officers in charge of forts, rural areas, and the army, along with ministers and priests who have been caught conspiring with the enemy, should be required to live on the borders of the enemy's territory, thus reducing any internal threat.

Potentially harmful individuals who understand their own fortunes are tied to the conqueror's success should be pacified through private reprimands, while defectors captured with the enemy should be relocated to distant areas. Relatives of the enemy who pose a threat and take refuge in nearby wilderness or border regions should be granted less productive lands or a fourth of a fertile area, in exchange for taxes and soldiers. This arrangement may provoke public discontent, leading to their downfall.

Anyone who disrupts public peace or loses favor with the people should be moved to a precarious area where any actions against the conqueror may ultimately endanger them.

After reclaiming a lost territory, the conqueror should conceal the flaws that led to its loss and amplify the virtues that allowed its recovery.

For an inherited territory, he should mask the weaknesses of his predecessor and highlight his own strengths and virtues.

- He should establish any righteous practices observed in other territories but not yet followed in his own, and he should prevent the adoption of any customs, even if common elsewhere, that are considered unrighteous.

Book 14

CHAPTER I. MEANS TO INJURE AN ENEMY.

To protect the structure of the four castes, the methods discussed in the secret sciences should be used against those who act wickedly. Using individuals of the Mlechchha class skilled in various disguises that fit different regions, trades, or professions—or who can appear as hump-backed, dwarfed, short-statured, mute, deaf, mentally unsound, or blind—poisons such as kálakúta and others should be discreetly applied in the food and other pleasures of the wicked. Spies embedded in the same household or in close proximity may utilize weapons during royal events, sports, musical gatherings, or other festivities. Spies disguised as night wanderers or fire-keepers can set fire to the properties of wrongdoers.

The powder made from specific creatures—like the chitra, bheka (frog), kaundinyaka, krikana (a type of partridge), panchakushtha, and satapadi (centipede)—or from others, such as uchchitinga (crab), kambali, krikalása (lizard), with satakanda (a plant bark), or creatures like grihagaulika (house lizard), andháhika (blind snake), krakanthaka (another partridge), pútikíta (a noxious insect), and gomárika, mixed with the juices of bhallátaka (Semecarpus Anacardium) and valgaka, can produce smoke that causes immediate death when burned.

- If any of these creatures are heated with a black snake and priyangu (panic seed) and then powdered, the mixture, once set aflame, causes instant fatality.

The powder made from the roots of dhámárgava (likely lufta foetida) and yátudhána, when mixed with powder from the flower of bhallátaka (Semecarpus Anacardium), induces death within half a month when administered. The root of vyághata (Cassia fistula), ground with bhallátaka flowers and the essence from an insect (kíta), leads to death within a month. Doses differ by creature: a kalá (1/16 of a tola) for humans, twice that amount for mules and horses, and four times for elephants and camels.

When burned, the smoke from satakardama, uchchitinga (crab), karavira (nerium odorum), katutumbi (a type of bitter gourd), and fish mixed with the chaff from madana and kodrava grains (paspalam scrobiculatum), or with the chaff of hastikarna seeds (castor oil tree) and palása (butea frondosa), kills all life within the reach of the wind.

The smoke from burning pútikita (a stinking insect), fish, katutumbi, satakardama bark, and indragopa (cochineal insect), or a mix of pútikita, kshudrárála resin (shorea robusta), and hemavidári, when combined with goat hoof and horn powder, causes blindness.

Smoke from pútikaranja (guilandina bonducella) leaves, yellow arsenic, realgar, gunja seeds (abrus precatorius), red cotton seed chaff, ásphota (Careya arborea), khácha (possibly salt), along with cow dung and urine, also results in blindness.

Blindness can similarly result from smoke produced by burning snake skin, cow and horse dung, and the head of a blind snake.

To create instant lethality wherever wind carries it, one can burn a mixture of dung and urine from pigeons, frogs, carnivores, elephants, humans, and boars, plus chaff and barley powder combined with kásísa (green sulfate of iron), rice, cotton seeds, kutaja (nerium antidysentericum), and kosátaki (lufta pentandra). Add cow's urine, bhándi root (hydrocotyle asiatica), nimba (neem), sigru (moringa), phanirjaka (tulsi variant), kshíbapíluka (ripe Coreya arborea), and bhánga (a common intoxicant), along with snake and fish skin, elephant nail and tusk powder, chaff from madana and kodravá seeds, or chaff from hastikarna seeds and palása.

For assaults, a combatant may safeguard their eyes with ointment and medicinal water before burning roots like káli (Tragia involucrata), kushtha (costus), nada (a reed), satávari (asparagus racemosus), or a powder of snake skin, peacock tail, krikana (a kind of partridge), and panchakushtha. This mixture, along with previously specified or moist or dry chaff, produces smoke that blinds all exposed animals.

An ointment created by combining the secretions of the sáriká (myna), kapota (pigeon), baka (crane), and baláka (a type of small crane) with the milk of kákshiva (possibly moringa), píluka (a type of Careya arborea), and snuhi (Euphorbia plant) can induce blindness and also poison water sources.

A blend of yavaka (a type of barley), sála root (Achyranthes triandria), fruit of madana (possibly the datura plant), leaves of játí (possibly nutmeg), and human urine, mixed with powdered plaksha root (fig tree) and vidári (liquorice), along with extracts from decoctions of musta (a poisonous plant), udumbara (cluster fig), and kodrava (paspalam scrobiculatum), or with a decoction made from hastikarna (castor oil plant) and palása (Butea frondosa) is known as "madana juice" (madanayoga).

Similarly, a combination of powders made from sringi (atis betula), gaumevriksha, kantakára (solanum xanthocarpum), mayúrapadi, gunja seeds (abrus precatorius), lánguli (possibly Jussiaea repens), vishamúlika, and ingudi (possibly heart-pea), with additional powders from karavira (oleander), akshipiluka (Careya arborea), arka plant, and mrigamáríni, blended with a decoction of madana and kodrava or alternatively with hastikarna and palása, is also termed a "madana mixture" (madanayoga).

Together, these mixtures, when applied, poison grass and water sources.

Smoke produced by burning a blend of krikana (a partridge), krikalása (lizard), grihagaulika (a house lizard), and andháhika (a blind snake) severely damages eyesight and can cause madness.

The smoke from krikalása and grihagaulika alone may induce leprosy.

Adding chitrabheka (a colorful frog) entrails and madhu (possibly Celtis orientalis) to this mixture, when burned, produces smoke that leads to gonorrhea.

The same mixture, when moistened with human blood, can induce consumption.

A combination of dúshívisha, madana (possibly datura), and kodrava (paspalam scrobiculatum) destroys the tongue when applied.

A mix containing the powder of mátriváhaka, jalúka (leech), peacock tail feathers, frog eyes, and píluká (Careya arborea) brings about vishúchika disease.

Finally, a concoction of panchakushtha, kaundinyaka, rájavriksha (Cassia fistula), madhupushpa (bassia latifolia), and madhu (honey) is known to cause fever.

A mixture made from the powdered knot of the tongue of the bhája (?) and nakula (mongoose) blended into a paste with the milk of a she-donkey induces both deafness and muteness.

The doses required to bring about desired deformities in humans or animals within a fortnight or a month follow the prescribed quantities mentioned earlier.

The potency of these mixtures is enhanced considerably: in the case of drugs, by preparing them as a decoction; for animals, by creating them as powders; or, universally, by using the decoction method.

An arrow tipped with a mixture prepared from powdered sálmali (Bombax heptaphyllum) and vidári (liquorice), combined with múlavatsanábha (a type of poison) powder and smeared with musk-rat blood, can induce biting behavior in the victim. This individual bites others, causing a chain reaction where those bitten continue to bite others.

A preparation from the flowers of bhallátaka (Semecarpus anacardium), yátudhána (?), dhámárgava (Achyranthes aspera), and bána (sal tree), mixed with powdered elá (large cardamom), kákshi (red aluminous earth), guggulu (bdellium), and háláhala (a potent poison), along with goat and human blood, induces a violent madness, driving those affected to bite others.

If a half dharana (unit of weight) of this concoction, mixed with flour and oil-cakes, is cast into a reservoir a hundred bows long, it taints the entire body of water. Fish that ingest or even touch this mixture become poisonous; anyone who drinks or touches the water is also poisoned.

A condemned individual who pulls from the earth an alligator or iguana (godhá) with three or five handfuls of both red and white mustard seeds will die upon merely seeing it.

During rituals on days ruled by the stars krittiká or bharaní, if a black cobra, frothing at the mouth from a lightning shock or captured using sticks from a tree struck by lightning, is offered into a fire while performing fearful rites, that fire will continue to burn unquenchably.

- An offering of honey should be made in a fire fetched from the blacksmith's house; of wine in a fire brought from the vintner's house; and of clarified butter in the fire of a sacrificer.
- An offering of a garland should be made in the fire kept by a sacrificer with one wife; of mustard seeds in the fire maintained by an adulterous woman; of curds in the fire kept during a child's birth; and of rice-grain in the fire of a sacrificer.
- An offering of flesh should be made in the fire kept by a chandala; of human flesh in the fire burning in cremation grounds. Additionally, an offering of the serum from goat and human flesh shall be made with a sacrificial ladle in a fire that combines all the above fires.
- Repeating sacred chants to the fire, an offering of wooden pieces from the rájavriksha (cassia fistula) tree should be made

into this same fire. This fire will burn unquenchably, creating illusions and confusion for the enemy.

Greetings to Aditi, greetings to Anumati, greetings to Sarasvati, and greetings to the Sun; an offering to Agni, an offering to Soma, an offering to the Earth, and an offering to the Atmosphere.

[Thus ends Chapter I, "Means to Injure an Enemy," in Book XIV, "Secret Means," of the Arthasástra of Kautilya. End of the hundred and forty-sixth chapter from the beginning.]

CHAPTER II. WONDERFUL AND DELUSIVE CONTRIVANCES.

A dose of powder made from sirisha (mimosa tree), udumbara (glomerous fig-tree), and sami (acacia suma), when mixed with clarified butter, allows a person to sustain fasting for up to half a month. Similarly, a froth concocted from the roots of kaseruka (a type of water-creeper), utpala (costus plant), and sugar cane, combined with bisa (water lily), durva grass, milk, and clarified butter, enables fasting for a month.

A blend of powders from masha (mung beans), yava (barley), kuluttha (horse gram), and the roots of darbha (sacred grass), mixed with milk and clarified butter, also sustains fasting. Milk derived from valli (a kind of vine) and clarified butter made from it, mixed equally with paste from sala (shorea robusta) and prisniparni (hedysarum lagopodioides) roots and consumed with milk, allows one to endure fasting for up to a month. Another option includes drinking a mixture of milk, clarified butter, and a spirit made from the same ingredients to facilitate a month-long fast.

Oil derived from mustard seeds soaked for seven nights in the urine of a white goat will, after being stored in a large bitter gourd for a month and a half, change the color of both bipedal and quadrupedal creatures when applied externally. Oil from white mustard seeds mixed with barley contained in the dung of a white donkey, which has been fed exclusively on butter, milk, and barley for over a week, also induces a color change.

An oil made from mustard seeds previously steeped in the urine and liquid dung of either a white goat or a white donkey results in a white color similar to the fiber of the arka plant or the down feathers of a white bird when applied. A blend of dung from a white rooster and an ajagara (boa constrictor) produces a white coloring effect.

A mixture created from white mustard seeds that have been kept for seven nights in white goat urine, combined with buttermilk, arka plant milk, salt, and grains (dhanya), will, if applied for a period of two weeks, turn the skin white. Finally, a paste made from white mustard seeds kept in a large bitter gourd along with clarified butter from valli creeper milk for half a month will turn hair white.

- A mixture made from bitter gourd, a pungent-smelling insect (putikita), and a white house lizard, when ground into a paste and applied to hair, will turn the hair as white as a conch shell.

If any part of a person's body is rubbed with a paste made from tinduka (glutinosa) and arishta (soap-berry), along with cow dung, and then coated with the juice of bhallataka (marking nut or semecarpus anacardium), that area will develop leprosy within a month.

The application of a paste made from gunja seeds that have been stored for seven nights in the mouth of a white cobra or a house lizard will also cause leprosy. Similarly, external application of the liquid from parrot and cuckoo eggs results in leprosy.

To treat leprosy, one may use a paste or decoction from priyala (possibly chironjia sapida or vitis vinifera). Eating a mixture of powders made from the roots of kukkuta (marsilia dentata), kosataki (duffa pentandra), and satavari (asparagus racemosus) for a month will lighten the skin to white.

Bathing in a decoction of vata (banyan tree) and rubbing the body with a paste from sahachara (yellow barleria) will darken the skin. A mixture of sulphur arsenic and red arsenic, when combined with oil from sakuna (a type of bird) and kanka (vulture), will also cause darkening.

Powder from the khadyota (fire-fly) mixed with mustard oil will make the mixture glow at night. The powder of khadyota (fire-fly) and gandupada (earthworm), or the powder of ocean-dwelling creatures combined with bhringa (malabathrum), kapala (a pot-herb), khadira (mimosa catechu), and karnikara (pentapetes acerifolia), mixed with the oils from sakuna and kanka, becomes tejanachurna (an ignition powder).

Rubbing the body with a powder made from the charcoal of paribhadraka (erythrina indica) bark mixed with frog serum can protect the skin from being harmed by fire. A body coated with a paste from the bark of paribhadraka and sesame seeds will burn when exposed to fire without causing harm to the individual.

A ball made from the powdered charcoal of the bark of pilu (careya arborea) can be held in one's hand while being burned without causing harm.

When a person's body is coated with the serum from frog flesh, it can be exposed to fire without injury. If this serum is combined with oils extracted from the fruits of kusa (ficus religiosa) and amra (mango tree), and if a powder made from an ocean frog (samudra manduki), phenaka (sea foam), and sarjarasa (the resin of vatica robusta) is sprinkled over the body, it will burn with fire but remain unharmed.

Applying sesame oil mixed with equal parts serum from frog flesh, crab, and similar animals to the body enables it to withstand fire. Additionally, if the body is coated in the serum of frog flesh alone, it remains protected from burns.

If the body is rubbed with a mixture containing the powder of bamboo roots and saivala (an aquatic plant) and then coated with frog serum, it will be safe from fire damage.

For someone who applies oil derived from a paste made from the roots of paribhadraka (erythrina indica), pratibala (?), vanjula (a type of rattan or tree), vajra (either andropogon muricatum or euphorbia), and kadali (banana) mixed with frog serum onto their legs, they can walk over fire without harm.

- Oil can be made from a paste using the roots of pratibala, vanjula, and paribhadraka, plants that grow near water, and blending it with serum from frog flesh.
- When this special oil is applied to one's legs, it allows the person to walk across a white-hot bed of fire as effortlessly as if strolling over soft petals.

If large birds like the hamsa (goose), krauncha (heron), and mayura (peacock) are released at night with a burning reed attached to their tails, they create the appearance of a firebrand descending from the sky. Ashes left from a lightning strike can extinguish fire. Placing kidney beans (masha) soaked in menstrual fluid, along with the roots of vajra (a type of grass) and kadali (banana), both soaked in frog serum, in a fireplace prevents grains from being cooked. Cleaning the fireplace will restore its function.

Holding a small ball of pilu (careya arborea) or a knot of the root of suvarchala (linseed tree) filled with fire inside and wrapped with thread and cotton enables a person to exhale smoke and fire. Pouring oil made from kusa (ficus religiosa) and amra (mango) onto fire keeps it burning even during a storm. Sea-foam soaked in oil will burn steadily when floating on water.

A fire started by churning a monkey's bone with a bamboo stick that has both white and black coloring (kalmasavenu) will continue to burn in water instead of being extinguished. If a fire is started by churning the left rib bone of a person who died by weapon or execution using a similarly colored bamboo stick, or by rubbing together bones of two different people, it will prevent any other fire from burning in that place when circled three times counterclockwise.

- A paste made from animals such as the chuchundari (musk-rat), khanjarita (likely a small mammal), and kharakita (unidentified animal) mixed with horse urine, when applied to shackles binding someone's legs, will cause the chains to break apart.

When the ayaskanta (sun-stone) or other similar stones are wetted with the serum from the flesh of animals like kulinda, dardura, and kharakita, they will shatter. A paste made from the powdered rib bones of animals such as naraka, a donkey, kanka (a type of vulture), and bhasa (another bird), combined with water-lily juice, can be applied to the legs of humans and animals during travel.

For long journeys, a person can wear shoes made from camel skin, coated with serum from the flesh of an owl and a vulture, and covered with banyan leaves; this preparation allows a person to walk up to fifty yojanas without tiring. When these shoes are smeared with the marrow, pith, or essence of the birds syena, kanka, kaka, gridhra, hamsa, krauncha, and vichiralla, the traveler can journey up to a hundred yojanas without fatigue.

The fat or serum from roasting a pregnant camel alongside saptaparna (Indian devil tree), or from roasting deceased children in cremation grounds, can also be applied to facilitate a journey of a hundred yojanas.

By displaying such remarkable and awe-inspiring techniques, terror can be instilled in the enemy, utilizing these wonders to evoke fear.

- While anger and terror are common responses, creating terror through such extraordinary means is considered an effective strategy for securing peace.

[Thus ends Chapter II, "Wonderful and Delusive Contrivances," in Book XIV, "Secret Means," of the Arthasástra of Kautilya. End of the hundred and forty-seventh chapter from the beginning.]

CHAPTER III. THE APPLICATION OF MEDICINES AND MANTRAS.

By removing the right and left eye-balls of animals such as a cat, camel, wolf, boar, porcupine, váguli, naptri, crow, and owl—or even from just one, two, three, or multiple animals that are active at night—one can create two types of powder from them. When someone applies the powder from the left eye of one of these animals to their own right eye, and the powder from the right eye to their own left eye, they can see clearly even in the darkest of nights.

- One effective choice is the eye of a boar, or that of a khadyota (fire-fly), a crow, or a mina bird. Applying any of these to one's eyes enables clear vision at night.

After fasting for three nights, on the day marked by the star Pushya, one should obtain the skull of a man who has been executed or killed in combat. This skull should be filled with soil and barley seeds, which are then to be watered with goat and sheep milk. Wearing a garland made from the sprouts of this barley will render the wearer invisible to others.

Similarly, after fasting for three nights, one should remove both the right and left eyes of a dog, cat, owl, and váguli (if available) on the day of Pushya. These should be ground into two types of powder and used as an ointment for one's eyes, allowing the wearer to become unseen.

On another occasion of fasting for three nights, a round-headed pin (saláká) should be crafted from a branch of the purushagháti (punnága tree) on the day of Pushya. This pin, alongside the ointment prepared in the skull of any nocturnal animal, should be inserted into the reproductive organ of a deceased woman, then burned. The extracted ointment, when applied to one's eyes, allows one to walk undetected.

If one encounters the burnt or partially burnt corpse of a Bráhman who kept sacrificial fire, fasting for three nights there and then gathering ashes in a sack made from the clothes of a naturally deceased person on the Pushya star day can be an effective way to achieve invisibility. Wearing this sack on the back renders one unseen.

The dried skin of a snake, packed with the powdered bones and marrow or fat of a cow sacrificed for a Bráhman's funeral rites, when placed on the back of cattle, will render them invisible.

The slough of a prachaláka (a type of bird) filled with the ashes of a snake-bite victim's corpse will make wild animals invisible.

A snake's skin filled with the powdered bone from the knee-joint, combined with that of the tail and the excrement of an owl and a váguli, can make birds invisible.

These are the eight specific methods known to achieve invisibility.

- I bow to Bali, son of Virochana; to Sambara, master of a hundred magical arts; to Bhandírapáka, Naraka, Nikumbha, and Kumbha.
- I bow to Devala and Nárada; I bow to Sávarnigálava. With their permission, I bring upon thee a profound sleep.
- As the boa-constrictor known as *ajagara* drifts into a deep slumber, so may the guards of this village, restless and vigilant, fall into a deep, unbreakable sleep.
- With thousands of guard dogs, hundreds of watchful geese, and donkeys all lulled into a deep, tranquil sleep, I shall step quietly into this place, and may the dogs remain calm and silent.
- Bowing to Manu and securing the roguish dogs, I also bow to the gods in the heavens and to the Bráhmans among men;
- To those skilled in Vedic wisdom, those who have reached the heights of Kailása through penance, and to all sages and prophets, I bring deep slumber to thee.

The fan of Chamari waves, and may all obstacles withdraw. I offer my respects to Manu, to you, O Aliti and Paliti.

The usage of the above mantra is as follows:—

After fasting for three nights, on the fourteenth day of the dark half of the month, specifically on the day marked by the star Pushya, one should obtain vilikhávalekhana (possibly fingernails) from a low-caste woman (svapáki). Keeping them in a small basket, one should bury them alone in a cremation ground. On the next fourteenth day, they are to be unearthed and ground into a paste with kumári (possibly aloe). Small pills are then formed from the paste. When any of these pills is placed in a location while chanting the above mantra, all living creatures in that area will fall into a deep sleep.

Following a similar ritual, three white and three black dart-like hairs (salyaka) of a porcupine should be buried separately in a cremation ground. When these are retrieved on the next fourteenth day, and scattered along with ashes from a burnt corpse while chanting the above mantra, all living creatures in that area will fall into deep sleep.

- Oblation to thee, O Amile, Kimile, Vayujáre, Prayoge, Phake, Kavayusve, Vihále, and Dantakatake, oblation to thee.
- May the vigilant dogs guarding the village fall into a deep, restful slumber; these three white dart-like hairs of the porcupine are the creation of Bráhma.

All prophets have fallen into deep slumber. I cast sleep over the entire village up to its borders until the sun rises. Oblation!

- May the dogs that vigilantly guard the village fall into a deep, peaceful slumber; these three white, dart-like hairs from the porcupine are creations of Bráhma.
- All enlightened sages have fallen into profound sleep. I cast sleep over the entire village, reaching every corner and boundary, until the sun rises. Oblation!

To apply the mantra above:

After fasting for seven nights, a person should obtain three white, dart-like hairs from a porcupine. On the fourteenth day of the dark half of the month, they must make 108 oblations into a sacred fire using sacrificial wood from khadira (mimosa catechu) and similar trees, adding honey and clarified butter while chanting the mantra. Then, chanting the mantra again, they should bury one of the hairs at the entrance of a village or any house within it. This will cause all animal life inside to fall into a deep sleep.

- I offer my respects to Bali, son of Vairochana; to S'atamáya, S'ambara, Nikumbha, Naraka, Kumbha, Tantukachchha, and the mighty demon.
- I honor Armálava, Pramíla, Mandolúka, Ghatodbala, Krishna with his followers, and the renowned woman, Paulomi.

- Reciting the sacred mantras, I retrieve the essence or bone of the corpse (savasárika) that fulfills my desired intentions—may the S'alaka demons be triumphant; I bow to them with offerings. May the vigilant dogs guarding the village enter a deep and peaceful sleep.
- May all enlightened ones (siddhártháh) rest in contentment regarding our goal from dusk to dawn, until my aim is achieved. Oblation!

The method of applying the above mantra is as follows:

After fasting for four nights, on the fourteenth day of the dark half of the month, perform an animal sacrifice (bali) in the cremation grounds. While chanting the above mantra, gather the essence (savasárika) of a corpse and place it in a basket made from leaves (pattrapauttaliká). When this basket is pierced in its center with a dart-like hair of a porcupine and buried while reciting the mantra, all animal life in that area will fall into a deep slumber.

- I seek protection from the god of fire and all goddesses in the ten directions; may all obstacles be removed, and may everything come under my control. Oblation.

The application of the above mantra is as follows:--

Having fasted for three nights and having on the day of the star of Pushya prepared twenty-one pieces of sugar-candy, one should make oblation into the fire with honey and clarified butter; and having worshipped the pieces of sugar-candy with scents and garlands of flowers, one should bury them. When, having on the next day of the star of Pushya unearthed the pieces of sugar-candy, and chanting the above mantra, one strikes the door-panel of a house with one piece and throws four pieces in the interior, the door will open itself.

Having fasted for four nights, one should on the fourteenth day of the dark half of the month get a figure of a bull prepared from the bone of a man, and worship it, repeating the above mantra. Then a cart drawn by two bulls will be brought before the worshipper who can (mount it and) drive in the sky and tell all that is connected with the sun and other planets of the sky.

O, Chandáli Kumbhi, Tumba Katuka, and Sárigha, thou art possessed of the bhaga of a woman, oblation to thee.

When this mantra is repeated, the door will open and the inmates fall into sleep.

Having fasted for three nights, one should on the day of the star of Pushya fill with soil the skull of a man killed with weapons or put to the gallows, and, planting in it valli (vallari ?) plants, should irrigate them with water. Having taken up the grown-up plants on the next day of the star of Pushya (i.e., after 27 days), one should manufacture a rope from them. When this rope is cut into two pieces before a drawn bow or any other shooting machine, the string of those machines will be suddenly cut into two pieces.

When the slough of a water-snake (udakáhi) is filled with the breathed-out dirt (uchchhvásamrittika?) of a man or woman (and is held before the face and nose of any person), it causes those organs to swell.

When the sack-like skin of the abdomen of a dog or a boar is filled with the breathed-out dirt (uchchhvásamrittika) of a man or woman and is bound (to the body of a man) with the ligaments of a monkey, it causes the man's body to grow in width and length (ánáha),

When a figure of an enemy carved from the rájavriksha (cassia fistula) tree is coated with the bile of a brown cow that was sacrificed on the fourteenth day of the dark half of the month, it induces blindness in the enemy.

After fasting for four nights and performing an animal sacrifice (bali) on the fourteenth day of the dark half of the month, create several bolt-like pieces from the bone of a man who was executed on the gallows. If one of these pieces is placed in the feces or urine of an enemy, it will cause the enemy's body to swell (ánáha). If the piece is buried beneath the enemy's feet or seat, it will cause him to suffer a wasting illness, leading to death. If it is buried in the enemy's shop, fields, or house, it will cause him financial ruin and a loss of livelihood.

This method of smearing and burying also applies to bolt-like pieces (kílaka) crafted from the vidyuddanda tree.

- If the nail of the little finger, along with nimba (neem), káma (bdellium), madhu (celtis orientalis), a monkey's hair, and a human bone,
- Is wrapped in a garment of the deceased and buried in a person's house or trodden underfoot by them, that individual and their family—including spouse, children, and wealth—will not survive beyond three fortnights.
- Similarly, if the little finger nail, along with nimba, káma, madhu, and the bone of a person who died of natural causes, is buried under a person's feet or close to their residence,
- Or near the camp of an army, village, or city, the affected person (or community) along with their spouse, children, and possessions will not endure beyond three fortnights
- Collecting the hairs of a sheep, monkey, cat, and mongoose, as well as the hair of Bráhmans, those of low caste (svapáka), and of a crow and owl, can bring about specific outcomes.
- When the collected hairs of a sheep, monkey, cat, mongoose, Bráhmans, those of low caste (svapáka), and of a crow and owl are ground into a paste with feces, its application causes instantaneous death.

If a garland taken from a deceased person, the ashes from a burnt corpse, the hair of a mongoose, and the skins of a scorpion, bee, and snake are buried under a person's feet, that person will lose all human appearance As long as these items remain in place, the effect continues.

After fasting for three nights and, on the day of the star of Pushya, planting gunja seeds in the soil-filled skull of a man who was executed or killed by weapons, one should water them. On the next new or full moon day under the star of Pushya, the grown plants can be removed and used to create circular pedestals (mandaliká). Any food or water vessels placed on these pedestals will remain undiminished in quantity.

During a grand night procession, cut off the nipples from a deceased cow's udder and burn them in a torch flame. The ashes should be mixed with bull urine to coat a fresh vessel. When this vessel is carried around the village in a counterclockwise direction and then set down, it will attract all the butter produced by the cows in the village to itself.

On the fourteenth day of the dark half of the month aligned with the star of Pushya, insert an iron seal into the reproductive organ of a dog, and retrieve it once it falls out on its own. When this seal is held and the magician calls for a collection of fruits, they will arrive of their own accord.

• By using mantras, specific substances, and other magical practices, one can safeguard their own people and bring harm to the enemy.

[Thus ends Chapter III, "The Application of Medicine and Mantras," in Book XIV, "Secret Means," of the Arthasástra of Kautilya. End of the hundred and forty-eighth chapter from the beginning.]

CHAPTER IV. REMEDIES AGAINST THE INJURIES OF ONE'S OWN ARMY.

To counteract the effects of poisons and toxic compounds used by enemies against one's own army or people:

When items intended for the king's use, including parts of the body of his consorts, as well as military equipment, are cleansed in warm water made from a decoction containing sleshmátaki (sebesten or cordia myk), kapi (emblica officinalis), madanti, danta (ivory), satha (Citron tree), gojigi (gojihva or elephantophus scaber), visha (aconitum ferox), pátali (bignonia suaveolens), bala (lida cardifolia and rombifolia), syonáka (bignonia indica), punarnava, sveta (andropogon aciculatum), and tagara (tabernæmontana coronaria), mixed with sandalwood (chandana) and the blood of a jackal (salávriki), it neutralizes the harmful effects of poison.

A compound made from the bile of prishata (red-spotted deer), nakula (mongoose), nílakantha (peacock), and godhá (alligator), mixed with charcoal powder (mashíráji) and the young shoots (agra) of sinduvára (vitex trifolia), tagara (tabernæmontana coronaria), varuna (teriandium indicum), tandulíyaka (amaranthus polygamus), and sataparva (convolvulus repens), along with pindítaka (vangueria spinosa), can counteract the effects of a madana poison mixture.

Decoctions made from the roots of srigála (bignonia indica), vinna, madana, sinduvára (vitex trifolia), tagara (tabernæmontana coronaria), and valli (a type of creeper) can be taken individually or together with milk to neutralize madana poison.

The pungent oil extracted from kaidarya (vangueria spinosa) acts as an antidote to madness.

A blend made from priyangu (panic seed) and naktamála (galedupa arborea) alleviates leprosy when applied nasally.

For consumption (a wasting disease), a preparation from kushtha (costus) and lodhra (symplocus) is beneficial.

A combination of katuphala (glelina arborea), dravanti (anthericum tuberosum), and vilanga (a type of seed) can relieve headache and other head-related ailments when applied through the nose.

The application of a mixture made from priyangu (panic seed), manjishtha (rubia manjit), tagara (tabernæmontana coronaria), lákshárasa (lac essence), madhuka, haridrá (turmeric), and kshaudra (honey) revives individuals who have lost consciousness due to incidents like being struck with a rope, falling into water, ingesting poison, being whipped, or taking a fall.

The recommended dose is approximately one aksha for humans, double for cows and horses, and quadruple for elephants and camels.

A spherical amulet (mani) prepared from this mixture and embedded with a core of gold (rukma) serves as an antidote for any poison.

An amulet made from the wood of asvattha (sacred fig tree) entwined with medicinal plants such as jívantí, sveta (andropogan aciculatum), mushkaka flowers, and vanadáka (epidendrum tesseloides) also neutralizes any form of poison.

- The sound of trumpets coated with the above mixture neutralizes poison, while anyone who gazes upon a flag or banner smeared with this mixture will be protected from poison.
- Once a king has employed these remedies to ensure his and his army's safety, he may proceed to use toxic smokes and other preparations to contaminate the enemy's water supply.

Book 15

CHAPTER I. PARAGRAPHICAL DIVISIONS OF THIS TREATISE.

The term artha, or wealth, refers to the foundation of human livelihood; the earth that sustains human life is also termed artha, or wealth. The science that explores the methods to acquire and sustain this earth is the Arthasástra, the Science of Polity.

This science is divided into thirty-two sections: the book (adhikarana), contents (vidhána), reference to similar cases (yoga), the meaning of a term (padártha), the purpose behind reasoning (hetvartha), summary (uddesa), detailed explanation (nirdesa), instruction (upadesa), quotation (apadesa), application (atidesa), place of reference (pradesa), analogy (upamána), implication (arthápatti), doubt (samsaya), reference to similar practice (presanga), contradiction (viparyaya), ellipsis (vakyasesha), approval (anumata), explanation (vyákhayána), etymology (nirvachana), example (nidarsana), exception (apavarga), special terms by the author (svasanjá), preliminary view (púrva paksha), counterview (uttrapaksha), conclusion (ekánta), future reference (anágatávekshana), previous reference (atikrantávekshana), command (niyoga), alternative (vikalpa), compilation (samuchchaya), and deduction (úhya).

A book is the portion of a work in which a particular subject or topic is addressed. For example, the Arthasástra is presented as a condensed guide of all Arthasástras, serving as a manual for kings in acquiring and sustaining the earth, as written by the teachers of old.

The contents of a book provide a concise outline of its topics, such as: "The purpose of learning; association with elders; control over the senses; selection of ministers, and similar topics."

Suggestion of similar facts is achieved by using phrases like "These and the like" to point out comparable instances; for example, "The world comprising the four castes and the four religious divisions, and the like."

The meaning of a word refers to its intended sense; for instance, in the term múlahara: "One who squanders wealth inherited from father and grandfather is known as a múlahara, or prodigal."

The purport of reason conveys the purpose behind an assertion; for example: "Charity and the enjoyment of life rely on the possession of wealth."

Mentioning a fact in brief expresses an idea in a single word or phrase; for instance: "Control over the senses is foundational to success in learning and discipline."

Detailing a fact provides an expanded explanation; for example: "The restraint of the senses refers to harmonious perception through hearing, touch, sight, taste, and smell via the ears, skin, eyes, tongue, and nose."

Guidance is conveyed through statements like, "Thus, one should live," as in: "One should live without violating the principles of righteousness and economy."

Quotation uses phrases like "he says thus" to reference other teachings; for example: "The school of Manu suggests that a king's council should have twelve ministers; Brihaspati's school advises sixteen; Usanas' school recommends twenty; Kautilya holds that the council size should suit the kingdom's needs."

Application refers to extending a discussed rule to another matter; for instance: "What applies to an unpaid debt also applies to the failure to fulfill a promised gift."

Place of reference is a method of establishing a fact or principle based on a point to be covered in greater detail later. This approach creates a preparatory context for ideas that will soon follow, offering readers a way to anticipate future discussions. For example: "Utilizing strategic methods like conciliation, bribery, dissension, and coercion, as we'll explain fully in our section on calamities." This points forward, promising further elaboration and depth regarding these tactics.

Simile is used to clarify an unseen or abstract situation by drawing a parallel with a familiar, visible circumstance. It's a way of illuminating complexities by highlighting similar, known instances. For example: "Just as a father provides guidance and security for his son, so should the ruler protect subjects who have outgrown exemptions from taxes." This analogy encourages readers to understand leadership as an extension of familial care, lending insight into the protective duties expected of a ruler.

Implication occurs when facts lead logically to an unstated, inferred truth. It's a way of suggesting principles or rules indirectly by presenting context and letting readers recognize what logically follows. For example: "A knowledgeable person, well-experienced in worldly matters, should gain the favor of a worthy and ethical king through friends and trusted advisors, implying that it is unwise and even dangerous to seek favor through those who oppose the king." Here, the underlying idea is the strategic importance of approaching a leader via trusted channels rather than through adversaries.

Doubt presents a situation where reasoning could apply to multiple options, creating an intentional ambiguity that reflects the complex nature of certain choices. It highlights scenarios where decision-making isn't straightforward but rather subject to thoughtful consideration. For example: "When deciding on a military campaign, which is more strategically sound: should a conqueror focus on an adversary whose subjects are impoverished and inclined to defect, or one whose subjects feel oppressed and resentful?" This showcases situations requiring critical evaluation without clear, singular answers.

Reference to similar procedure applies a previously discussed method or action to new and different circumstances, allowing a familiar process to serve as a guide for consistency. It extends established procedures to similar scenarios for simplicity and coherence. For example: "In cultivating lands newly allotted for agricultural use, he should follow the methods and processes already established, as before." This maintains continuity, applying proven approaches in new areas for dependable results.

Contrariety is inferred by taking the opposite meaning from a positive statement, providing insight by suggesting an alternative outcome. It's a way of deducing what could happen under contrasting conditions. For example: "When a king shows displeasure with the messenger, it implies that his response will contrast sharply with the respectful reception given to a valued emissary." This gives context by revealing likely behavior based on emotional signals.

Ellipsis omits a portion of a sentence that's implied, completing the sense in the reader's mind. This form creates a space for interpretation while conveying a complete idea. For example: "Once stripped of his feathers, he will lose his power to move." Here, "like a bird" is implied but omitted, enhancing the image by assuming familiarity with the analogy.

Acceptance acknowledges another's perspective or teaching without challenge, representing open acknowledgment of varied viewpoints. It's a way of presenting ideas within a neutral context. For instance: "The structure of an army formation, with wings, front, and reserve, is an arrangement as recommended by the school of Usanas." This citation honors a viewpoint without necessarily aligning with it, leaving space for differing interpretations.

Detailed description, known as explanation, refers to an expanded discussion of a topic, clarifying its nature and implications. It deepens understanding by breaking down complex ideas. For instance: "In assemblies of kings or confederacies marked by the characteristics of such gatherings, quarrels frequently arise due to gambling, leading to the potential downfall of individuals involved in these disputes. This is why gambling stands as the most dangerous vice, as it deprives the king of his capacity for effective leadership and action." This explanation sheds light on gambling's destabilizing effect on governance.

Derivation involves breaking down a word to reveal its core meaning or purpose, often pointing to the word's etymological or functional essence. For example: "That which diverts (vyasyati) a king from his successful path is termed propensity (vyasana)." This offers a linguistic insight that clarifies the underlying purpose or consequence of the word.

Illustration provides a concrete example to support a concept, helping readers to visualize or understand the principle being discussed. For example: "In a battle against a far superior force, an inferior army is much like a lone foot soldier facing an elephant—it's likely to be overwhelmed." This illustration reinforces the concept of power imbalance.

Exception is applied to limit or clarify a general statement by introducing specific conditions under which the rule doesn't apply. It removes potential misconceptions. For example: "A king may allow his enemy's forces to camp near his borders unless there's a reason to suspect internal dissent or disloyalty." This clarifies that, while proximity can be tolerated, signs of internal unrest could make such proximity risky.

Technical terms, unique to an author's framework, are words or phrases used in a particular, specialized way that may not be common in broader discourse. They are essential for understanding the author's intent. For example: "The term 'first member' refers to the territory closest to the conqueror's, followed by 'second member' for the next in line, and so forth." This terminology specifically organizes the geopolitical landscape for the author's analysis.

Prima facie view is the initial stance or argument introduced for scrutiny, serving as a hypothesis to test or refute. For example:

"Between the king's distress and his minister's, the minister's distress is viewed as the greater harm." This opens a line of reasoning that can be evaluated in subsequent discussion.

Rejoinder is a settled opinion that follows a prima facie view, clarifying the author's stance on the issue. For example: "The king's distress is ultimately more consequential, as the kingdom's stability pivots on his leadership." This counters the previous view with a final conclusion emphasizing the king's central role.

Conclusion or established fact refers to a universal or broadly applicable statement that forms a foundational principle. For example: "A king must always be prepared for diligent and vigorous action." This reflects a general truth about the nature of kingship.

Reference to a subsequent portion signals where a concept will be expanded upon later, helping the reader anticipate a more comprehensive discussion. For example: "The topic of balance and weights will be discussed in full in the upcoming chapter, 'The Superintendent of Weights and Measures.'" This directs readers forward for further elaboration.

Reference to a previous portion points back to an earlier discussion, reminding the reader of groundwork already covered. For example: "As previously discussed, a minister's qualifications have already been outlined."

Command indicates a directive that leaves no room for deviation. It mandates specific behavior or choices. For example: "Thus, he should be taught the principles of righteousness and wealth, and never unrighteousness or unproductive paths."

Alternative provides options, showing the existence of more than one possible route. For example: "Or daughters may be born from an approved (dharmaviváha) marriage."

Compounding together brings together elements from different origins or paths to form a cohesive idea. For instance: "A child born to a man and his wife is considered agnatic both to the father and the father's kin."

Finally, determinable fact highlights areas requiring careful assessment before reaching a judgment, especially in cases where various factors influence the outcome. For example: "Gifts' validity or invalidity shall be evaluated by experts to ensure fairness, safeguarding the interests of both giver and recipient." This underscores the need for expertise and careful judgment.

- Thus, this Sástra, adhering to these structured divisions, is composed to serve as a comprehensive guide for acquiring and safeguarding success in both this world and the world beyond.
- In the context provided by this Sástra, one can initiate and sustain actions rooted in righteousness, economic prudence, and aesthetic value while effectively curtailing actions that are unrighteous, wasteful, and unappealing.
- This Sástra was created by him who, motivated by an aversion to injustice and misrule, swiftly reclaimed the sacred scriptures, the science of warfare, and the realm itself, which had fallen under the control of the Nanda king. Through his efforts, order, wisdom, and prosperity were restored, and this work stands as a testament to that enduring vision of governance.

The Art of War

Sun Tzu

Introduction

I. Brief Biography of Sun Tzu

Origins and Early Life

Sun Tzu, originally named Sun Wu, was born around 544 BCE in the state of Qi, which is now part of Shandong, China. The name Sun Tzu, by which he is better known, is a title meaning "Master Sun." Though much of his early life is still unknown, historical evidence suggests he came from a family with strong roots in military strategy and learning. This background likely helped shape his extraordinary skills in warfare and tactics, setting him up for the distinguished career he would later have.

As a young man, Sun Tzu began gaining a reputation for his sharp mind in strategy, though historical records about him are somewhat scarce. The lack of solid information has only made his life more fascinating, with parts of his story seeming like a mix of history and legend. His eventual rise to fame as a general and thinker was based not just on his practical knowledge of warfare, but also his ability to apply general ideas to real-life situations. His famous work, *The Art of War*, would form the foundation of his lasting influence, even though much of his life story has been blended with myths.

Military Career and Rise to Prominence

Sun Tzu's skills in military strategy didn't go unnoticed. He served under King Helü of the state of Wu, a role that gave him the chance to show his expertise on a larger stage. His ability to turn hopeless situations into victories earned him respect across the region. One of the biggest examples of his brilliance was when he defeated the state of Chu, which was much bigger and had more resources. This win highlighted his talent for outsmarting opponents with greater numbers and supplies.

The defeat of Chu was more than just a military win; it strengthened Wu's power and stability during a time when warfare between Chinese states was constant. Sun Tzu's strategies often used psychological tricks and deception, with clever tactics to weaken his enemies' morale before any fighting began. His deep understanding of terrain, human nature, and the use of deception made him stand out among other military minds of his time. These achievements earned him lasting fame and confirmed his place as one of the greatest military strategists in Chinese history.

Creation of The Art of War

It was during this period of political upheaval and near-constant warfare that Sun Tzu is believed to have authored The Art of War. The Warring States period (475–221 BCE) was a time of great instability, with various factions vying for control of China. In this context, Sun Tzu's strategies and insights were not only revolutionary but essential for survival.

Rather than a theoretical treatise, The Art of War is a distilled collection of Sun Tzu's accumulated experiences and the military wisdom passed down from generations before him. The text, composed of concise aphorisms and principles, is a practical guide intended for military leaders facing the challenges of warfare. Sun Tzu's approach to warfare emphasized the importance of strategy over brute force, and many of his insights remain highly applicable even in the modern world. His genius lay in his ability to condense complex concepts into simple, memorable phrases that have stood the test of time.

Even today, The Art of War continues to influence a wide array of fields beyond the battlefield, from business to sports, and remains a touchstone for anyone seeking to understand the nature of conflict and strategy. The timelessness of Sun Tzu's work speaks to his mastery of the art of warfare and his ability to provide wisdom that transcends the ages.

II. Historical Context

Sun Tzu lived during one of the most chaotic times in Chinese history, a period historians call the Spring and Autumn period, which later became the Warring States period (around 771–221 BCE). This era saw the weakening of the Zhou Dynasty's power, leading to constant wars between rival states. Regional leaders fought for control, with alliances constantly shifting and battles happening frequently. The political scene was unstable, and military skill was vital not just for winning but for survival.

As states competed for dominance, warfare was about more than just expanding territories; it was necessary for keeping sovereignty. Even small mistakes could lead to the complete destruction of a state, making military leaders crucial to the survival of nations. It was in this intense environment that Sun Tzu's strategies developed. He created his tactics not only to secure victories but to ensure long-term survival in a world where states were often annexed or destroyed. His strategies responded to a reality where the stakes were incredibly high, offering insights that went beyond war and into the political dynamics of the time.

The fierce competition for power among Chinese states during the Warring States period required new approaches to warfare, focusing on cunning, intelligence, and strategy rather than just raw strength. Sun Tzu's writings came out of this era of near-constant conflict, where he understood that success depended on outsmarting the opponent, not just overpowering them. His methods were designed for a time when a single wrong move could lead to disaster, stressing careful planning and the need for preparation in an unpredictable and dangerous world.

The Role of Warfare in Ancient China

In ancient China, warfare was much more than just battles fought on the field; it was closely connected with politics, philosophy, and governance. Leaders during this time were expected not only to be skilled in battle but also to be strong in diplomacy and statecraft. Military action was often a tool used to achieve political goals, and leaders had to balance the challenges of internal governance while also preparing for outside threats. Sun Tzu's approach to warfare reflects this larger understanding, as he constantly stressed the importance of planning ahead, being flexible, and understanding both the enemy and one's own forces.

Warfare during this period was all-encompassing. It involved logistics, governance, and diplomacy, areas where military leaders needed to show not only strength but also wisdom. Sun Tzu's strategies, which often focused on winning without fighting, came from this broader view of conflict, where preserving resources and maintaining the stability of the state were as crucial as defeating the enemy. His well-known principle, "The supreme art of war is to subdue the enemy without fighting," demonstrates his understanding of the long-term effects of war. Instead of seeking short-term victories at great costs, he promoted strategies that would protect the state's power while weakening the opponent's will.

During Sun Tzu's era, military leaders were expected to grasp the moral and philosophical sides of warfare. Confucian values influenced Chinese society deeply, shaping how rulers led and how they fought. Leaders were judged not just by their military successes but by their ability to keep order and promote justice. Sun Tzu's work reflects this, as it puts great importance on the qualities of leadership and the ethical aspects of warfare. He supported the idea of a wise and virtuous leader, one who could inspire loyalty among soldiers while staying calm and focused in the chaos of battle.

The political landscape was always changing, with alliances breaking as quickly as they were formed. Espionage, deception, and psychological warfare became key tools for staying ahead. Sun Tzu's contributions to the art of war went beyond just battlefield tactics; they involved understanding the enemy's mind and manipulating both physical and mental conditions to achieve victory. He understood that sometimes the best battle is the one that's won before it even starts. His insights into psychological manipulation, deception, and moral unity within an army were direct responses to the complex and high-stakes world of ancient Chinese warfare.

In this world of shifting power and constant conflict, Sun Tzu developed his principles not as abstract ideas but as practical tools for survival and dominance. His belief that victory could be achieved in ways other than battle was groundbreaking in a time when brute strength often ruled. His strategies focused on flexibility, intelligence, and the power of unpredictability. By continuously adjusting to changing situations, he believed a general could turn even the most desperate circumstances into opportunities for success. In this way, his work is not only a reflection of his era but a timeless guide for those looking to navigate conflict with wisdom and precision.

III. Philosophical Background

Sun Tzu's ideas didn't develop in isolation; they were influenced by the major philosophical traditions of ancient China, especially Daoism and Confucianism. Daoism, which emphasizes balance, harmony, and non-contention, had a deep impact on his strategic thinking. At its core, Daoism teaches that one should move with the natural flow of the universe, rather than resist it. This belief in flexibility and adaptability is reflected in Sun Tzu's view that a good leader must be flexible in both thought and action, ready to adapt to changing situations instead of sticking rigidly to a set plan. The idea of winning with minimal force—ideally without fighting at all— embodies the Daoist principle of achieving results with the least effort, which is central to The Art of War.

Moreover, Daoism's focus on harmony is seen in Sun Tzu's approach to warfare as an art where the best outcomes are those that avoid conflict altogether. He recognized that forcing a victory often brings about unnecessary destruction and loss, not just in terms of lives but also resources and morale. Instead, he advocated for strategies that involved subtlety, psychological manipulation, and careful planning, all aligned with the natural course of events. Sun Tzu's famous saying, "The supreme art of war is to subdue the enemy without fighting," reflects Daoist wisdom, where the soft overcomes the hard, and the flexible triumphs over the rigid.

Confucianism also played a key role in shaping Sun Tzu's philosophy. Confucian values like duty, ethical conduct, and governing with moral integrity are present in his view of leadership.

In Confucian thought, a leader's role is not just about winning; it includes the well-being of the people and the pursuit of order and justice. Sun Tzu's writings, although focused on military strategy, emphasize that a good general must also be a wise and virtuous leader. This aligns with the Confucian ideal of the "Junzi," or the gentleman, who leads by moral virtue and serves as a role model. Sun Tzu believed that an effective leader earns loyalty and trust, not through fear or force, but through wisdom, fairness, and calm decision-making. The combination of Confucian ethics and Daoist practicality creates a balanced framework for Sun Tzu's strategies, making The Art of War not just a guide to military success but also a blueprint for ethical leadership.

Core Principles of Sun Tzu's Philosophy

The Importance of Strategy Over Force

At the core of Sun Tzu's philosophy is the belief that strategic insight is more valuable than brute strength. He argues that the best victories are those achieved without fighting, highlighting the need for careful planning, foresight, and the use of intelligence rather than relying solely on physical power. For Sun Tzu, a leader's role is to outthink their opponent instead of outfight them. He advocated for a strategic approach that reduces the costs of war, both in terms of human lives and resources. Instead of direct conflict, Sun Tzu advises military leaders to disorient their enemies, target their weaknesses, and use deception to gain an advantage. To him, a well-fought battle is one that ends before it even starts, with the enemy defeated by the unseen forces of superior strategy.

Flexibility and Adaptability in Warfare

One of Sun Tzu's key principles is that rigid plans often lead to failure. Success on the battlefield depends on the ability to adapt and respond to constantly changing conditions. He teaches that no two battles are the same, so no single strategy can work for every situation. Instead, Sun Tzu emphasizes the need for flexibility, urging generals to stay fluid in both thought and action. In his view, the best leaders are those who can read the terrain, understand their troops' morale, anticipate their enemy's moves, and adjust their tactics as needed. By avoiding predictable patterns, a leader can keep their opponents off balance, staying one step ahead.

Flexibility goes beyond just physical movements on the battlefield. It includes mental agility, the ability to think quickly, and the willingness to abandon a failing plan for a better one. Sun Tzu believed that sticking stubbornly to a plan, no matter how well thought out, could lead to disaster if it didn't fit the situation. His philosophy encourages leaders to be like water, adapting to the shape of their environment, changing form as conditions change, and always finding a way to move forward. This principle of adaptability has made The Art of War highly relevant in many areas beyond the military, including business and sports, where the ability to pivot in response to new challenges is often the key to success.

Psychological Warfare

Another core element of Sun Tzu's philosophy is his deep understanding of the human mind, both in terms of the enemy and one's own troops. He places great emphasis on psychological warfare, believing that many battles are won or lost in the mind long before they are fought on the battlefield. A leader who can demoralize the enemy, spread confusion, or instill doubt has already set the stage for victory. Sun Tzu advocates using tactics such as deception, misinformation, and surprise to weaken the enemy's confidence and will to fight. By showing strength when weak or pretending to be disorganized when ready to attack, a leader can manipulate the enemy into making costly errors. To Sun Tzu, deception is not just a tactic— it is the essence of warfare.

Equally important is understanding the psychology of one's own troops. Sun Tzu teaches that a successful leader must know how to keep their forces united and their morale high. Soldiers who trust their commander, believe in their cause, and feel confident in the strategy are far more likely to fight bravely and with determination. Sun Tzu believed that a wise general knows how to inspire and motivate, how to reward loyalty, and how to manage fear and uncertainty within the ranks. In his view, leadership is just as much about fostering the right mindset as it is about military skill.

The Role of Leadership

At the core of Sun Tzu's strategic thought lies Sun Tzu believed that leadership is essential to the success of any endeavor, whether military or otherwise. The qualities of a great leader, in his view, go beyond tactical skill. A leader must possess wisdom, remain calm under pressure, be decisive, and uphold moral integrity. For Sun Tzu, leadership isn't just about giving orders; it's about guiding one's people with a steady hand and clear vision. The ability of a leader to inspire trust and unity among their troops is often the key to determining the outcome of a battle.

In The Art of War, Sun Tzu stresses that a leader must deeply understand human nature and manage both resources and emotions wisely. A good leader knows when to be strict and when to show compassion, when to give rewards and when to administer punishment, always balancing authority with wisdom. The leader's role is to create harmony within the ranks, ensuring that everyone, from the highest officers to the lowest soldiers, works together as a unified team. Sun Tzu believed that leadership was the ultimate factor in determining success, and that no amount of strength or resources could make up for a lack of vision and guidance from the top.

For Sun Tzu, leadership is both an art and a responsibility. It requires not only the skill to create great strategies but also the wisdom to carry them out with compassion and integrity. His insights elevate the role of a leader to that of a moral authority, making it clear that true power comes not from dominance but from understanding and mastering oneself, the situation, and those who follow.

IV. Key Themes and Structure of The Art of War

The Art of Strategy

At the core of The Art of War is the idea that victory is achieved through careful planning and strategic foresight. Instead of depending on brute force or sheer numbers, Sun Tzu highlights the importance of intelligence, preparation, and the thoughtful management of resources. To him, a successful campaign begins long before the actual battle. It requires a leader to evaluate not only their own strengths and weaknesses but also those of their enemy. This involves understanding the terrain, the morale of the troops, and the timing of actions. A well-planned strategy, in Sun Tzu's view, allows one to control the battlefield before the enemy even realizes they are being outmaneuvered.

Sun Tzu explains that strategy is the key to using minimal resources for maximum effect. It's not enough to simply fight well; one must fight smart, knowing when to strike and when to hold back. His focus on strategic thinking teaches that victory often belongs to those who understand when to avoid fighting altogether. For Sun Tzu, the greatest generals are those who can win wars without engaging in combat. His insights encourage readers to look at the bigger picture of their challenges, whether in warfare or life, and to approach them with deliberate, calculated actions rather than reacting on impulse.

The Principle of Deception

One of the most enduring and thought-provoking principles in The Art of War is the role of deception. Sun Tzu's famous statement, "All warfare is based on deception," sums up his belief that a commander's true strength lies in their ability to mislead and outsmart the enemy. Deception isn't just a tactic—it's a fundamental part of strategy, allowing a leader to shape the enemy's perceptions and decisions. By creating a false sense of security or concealing one's true intentions, a skilled leader can manipulate their adversary into making costly errors. Misinformation, fake retreats, and surprise attacks are all tools in the strategist's toolkit.

In Sun Tzu's philosophy, deception is about gaining the upper hand through psychological means. The aim is to make the opponent feel secure where they are weak and vulnerable where they are strong. By hiding one's true strengths and revealing only what is necessary, a general can keep the enemy in a constant state of doubt. This unpredictability, according to Sun Tzu, is essential for achieving success. His teachings on deception go far beyond the battlefield and have proven valuable in many areas of modern life, including business negotiations, competitive sports, and political strategy.

Adaptability and Flexibility

Throughout The Art of War, Sun Tzu consistently emphasizes the importance of adaptability in the face of changing circumstances. A leader who clings to a single plan or strategy, regardless of the evolving situation, is bound to fail. Instead, Sun Tzu advocates for a flexible approach, where a commander can pivot quickly and seize opportunities as they arise. In his view, the ability to adapt is a defining quality of a great general. Sun Tzu compares the ideal leader to water, which conforms to the shape of whatever contains it. Just as water flows around obstacles, a successful commander must move with the ever-changing conditions of warfare.

This principle of adaptability aligns with Sun Tzu's belief that no two battles are alike. The unpredictable nature of conflict requires a mindset open to change, whether in tactics, alliances, or terrain. Leaders must be able to set aside preconceived notions and embrace the fluid nature of their surroundings. Sun Tzu's insight extends beyond military situations to modern leadership challenges, reminding readers that success often depends on staying flexible, innovative, and responsive to new information.

The Role of Morale and Unity

For Sun Tzu, victory is not merely about having the largest army or the most skilled fighters. The morale of the troops and the unity of the command structure are just as vital to success as any weapon or strategy. Soldiers who trust their leader and believe in their cause are much more likely to perform well under pressure than those who are demoralized or divided. Sun Tzu places significant importance on treating soldiers with respect, addressing their needs, and inspiring them with a sense of purpose. A general who can command loyalty and cultivate unity within the ranks is far better prepared to face the challenges of war.

Additionally, Sun Tzu underscores the need for clear and consistent leadership. A general must be decisive and fair, maintaining discipline while also knowing when to show compassion. The bond between a leader and their soldiers is a crucial element in creating a cohesive and effective fighting force. Internal harmony can often be the deciding factor in battle, especially when facing difficult circumstances. Sun Tzu's teachings on morale and unity go beyond the battlefield, offering valuable insights for modern leaders in business, politics, or personal endeavors. They remind us that a team's success often hinges as much on its internal dynamics as it does on external factors.

V. Influence and Legacy of The Art of War

Influence in East Asia

The Art of War has been a foundational text in East Asia for centuries, deeply influencing the philosophies and practices of military leaders, scholars, and political strategists. From China to Japan and Korea, its principles have shaped the ways wars were fought and how empires were governed. In China, where Sun Tzu first developed his strategies, dynasties studied the text to refine their military tactics, using its teachings to defend and expand their territories. Beyond the battlefield, The Art of War guided Chinese governance, diplomacy, and statecraft, serving as a manual for leaders who sought to balance power, strategy, and ethics.

In Japan, The Art of War became prominent during the Samurai era, especially in the development of Bushido, the warrior's code of honor. Japanese military leaders, including figures like Oda Nobunaga and Tokugawa Ieyasu, drew inspiration from Sun Tzu's principles. His teachings on discipline, adaptability, and the importance of psychological warfare resonated deeply with the samurai ethos, further embedding The Art of War into Japan's cultural and military traditions. The text's influence reached beyond warfare, shaping how political leaders approached negotiations and alliances.

Korea also embraced Sun Tzu's strategies, applying them in times of internal conflict and external threats, particularly during struggles with neighboring states. For centuries, Korean scholars and military generals turned to The Art of War when planning defenses and military campaigns, finding in its pages the strategic insight and adaptability needed to navigate complex geopolitical landscapes. Sun Tzu's focus on intelligence, deception, and strategic positioning over brute force made his work a vital resource in East Asia's long history of warfare and statecraft.

Influence in Modern Warfare

As the centuries went by, The Art of War spread beyond East Asia and started to influence military strategies around the world. Its ideas were eventually adopted by Western military leaders and strategists, especially during the 19th and 20th centuries when warfare became more complicated. For example, Napoleon Bonaparte is said to have been greatly influenced by Sun Tzu's teachings. His military campaigns across Europe showed how effective it was to use strategic surprise, careful planning, and taking advantage of the enemy's weaknesses— all key elements of Sun Tzu's approach.

In the 20th century, Sun Tzu's influence could be seen especially in guerrilla warfare tactics. Revolutionary leaders like Mao Zedong in China and Ho Chi Minh in Vietnam used The Art of War's focus on psychological warfare, deception, and asymmetrical tactics to defeat stronger and better-equipped enemies. In Vietnam, during the conflict with the United States, Ho Chi Minh and his generals applied Sun Tzu's strategies very effectively, using the jungle terrain and psychological endurance to weaken their enemy's determination and eventually force their withdrawal.

Today, The Art of War is often studied in military academies alongside other classic works on strategy and tactics. Its ideas have shaped both the theoretical and practical education of military officers around the world. From Sandhurst in the UK to West Point in the United States, Sun Tzu's teachings still provide important lessons about leadership, intelligence gathering, and the moral aspects of warfare. His belief that the best victories are those won without fighting connects well with modern military thinking, where political and economic strategies often work alongside or instead of traditional battles.

Beyond the Battlefield: Business, Sports, and Politics

While The Art of War started as a military guide, its influence has spread far beyond the battlefield. In the business world, leaders and entrepreneurs have used Sun Tzu's principles to navigate competitive markets, secure good deals, and manage teams effectively. The strategic use of resources, understanding the competition, and adapting to changes are all ideas from The Art of War that have been applied to the corporate world. Today, it's common for business executives to look to Sun Tzu for advice on everything from launching new products to negotiating mergers.

Likewise, sports coaches and athletes have found value in Sun Tzu's focus on preparation, adaptability, and mental strength. Competitive sports, like warfare, require knowing your opponent, anticipating their moves, and adjusting strategies as the game goes on. Whether in battle or in sports, the ability to stay calm and outsmart the competition is universally important.

In politics, The Art of War has also left its mark. Leaders use its ideas when approaching diplomacy, forming alliances, and even running election campaigns. Politicians often apply Sun Tzu's tactics to influence public perception, undermine rivals without direct conflict, and take advantage of timing and positioning. The text's focus on intelligence gathering and strategic alliances is especially relevant in modern politics, where behind-the-scenes efforts can determine the outcome of public contests.

A Lasting Legacy

The Art of War remains a timeless resource, providing guidance that transcends time, culture, and discipline. Whether on the battlefield, in the boardroom, or in everyday life, Sun Tzu's strategies have endured because they are rooted in a deep understanding of human nature and the complexities of conflict. His ability to simplify the chaotic and often harsh realities of war into clear, actionable principles continues to inspire leaders across various fields.

As we move further into an age where technology and information play increasingly larger roles in conflict and competition, Sun Tzu's teachings on deception, intelligence, and adaptability feel more relevant than ever. His insights remind us that victory is not always achieved through strength alone, but through careful thought, ethical leadership, and a deep understanding of the human element in every pursuit.

Sun Tzu's influence on both ancient and modern warfare, along with his broader impact on business, politics, and leadership, solidifies The Art of War as one of the most important and lasting texts on strategy. His legacy continues to shape how people approach conflict, competition, and success, offering timeless wisdom that resonates with each generation.

Chapter 1 - Laying Plans

Sun Tzu said: The art of war is critically important to the State. It can be the difference between life and death, leading to either safety or ruin. Therefore, it must always be carefully studied and never ignored.

The art of war is based on five key factors that must be considered in every military decision. These factors are: (1) The Moral Law; (2) Heaven; (3) Earth; (4) The Commander; (5) Method and discipline.

The Moral Law ensures that the people are fully united with their ruler, making them willing to follow him, even risking their lives without fear of danger.

Heaven refers to the natural conditions, like day and night, cold and heat, and the changing of seasons.

Earth involves distances, both large and small, areas of safety and danger, wide open spaces and narrow paths, and the possibilities of survival or death.

The Commander represents the qualities of wisdom, honesty, kindness, courage, and strictness.

Method and discipline cover the organization of the army, the ranks, the roles assigned to each soldier, and the control of supplies and resources.

These five factors must be studied in depth by those who seek to understand the art of war. By mastering them, a ruler can win the loyalty of the people and command a strong, unified army capable of facing any challenge.

The Moral Law creates harmony between the ruler and the people, inspiring them to follow without hesitation, even in the face of great danger.

Heaven includes the cycles of day and night, the changes in temperature, and the timing of seasons. Some interpret this as a reflection of the broader workings of nature, like the balance of forces or natural elements.

Earth includes not just physical distances but also the dangers and safety that different terrains bring, whether they are wide open plains or narrow mountain passes. These elements can determine the chances of survival or death.

The Commander stands for qualities that inspire trust and loyalty—wisdom, honesty, kindness, bravery, and firmness in discipline. These virtues are essential for strong leadership.

Finally, Method and discipline ensure that the army is well-organized, with clear roles and responsibilities, and that resources are well-managed. These elements ensure that the military is prepared for anything and that chaos is avoided during battle.

Method and discipline mean organizing the army into its proper divisions, assigning ranks among the officers, maintaining roads to ensure supplies can reach the army, and controlling military spending.

These five principles should be well-known to every general: the one who knows them will be victorious; the one who does not will fail.

Therefore, in your planning, when trying to understand the military situation, use these principles as the basis of comparison, in this way:

Which of the two rulers follows the Moral Law? (That is, who is in harmony with their people?)

Which of the two generals is more skilled?

Who has the advantage of favorable conditions from Heaven and Earth?

On which side is discipline enforced the most strictly? (There is a story about Ts'ao Ts'ao, a strict disciplinarian who once followed his own rule so closely that he sentenced himself to death for letting his horse damage crops. Instead of execution, he was convinced to cut off his hair as punishment.)

Which army is stronger, both in physical strength and spirit?

Which side has officers and soldiers who are better trained? (Wang Tzŭ once said that without constant practice, officers will hesitate when forming for battle, and without constant practice, the general will be uncertain when a crisis comes.)

Which side has greater consistency in rewarding good actions and punishing bad behavior?

By considering these seven points, I can predict who will win or lose.

The general who listens to my advice and acts on it will win: such a person should be kept in command! The general who ignores my advice and does not act on it will be defeated: such a person should be dismissed!

While you follow my advice for success, also take advantage of any favorable circumstances that go beyond the usual rules.

As circumstances change, you should adjust your plans accordingly. (Sun Tzu, as a practical soldier, rejects rigid reliance on theoretical principles. He warns us not to rely too heavily on abstract rules because, as Chang Yu says, while the basic principles of strategy can be explained clearly, you must adapt to the enemy's actions to secure a favorable position in battle. Before the Battle of Waterloo, Lord Uxbridge, commanding the cavalry, went to the Duke of Wellington to ask about his plans for the next day. He explained that if he suddenly had to take command, he would need to know the plans. The Duke listened quietly and asked, "Who will attack first tomorrow—me or Bonaparte?" Uxbridge answered, "Bonaparte." "Well," replied the Duke, "Bonaparte hasn't told me his plans, and since my strategy depends on his, how can you expect me to tell you mine?")

All warfare is based on deception. (This wise and profound statement is acknowledged by all soldiers. Col. Henderson notes that Wellington, known for many military qualities, was especially skilled in hiding his movements and deceiving both friend and foe.)

When we are able to attack, we must make it seem as though we are not ready; when using our forces, we must appear inactive; when we are near, we must make the enemy believe we are far away; and when we are far away, we must make him believe we are close by.

Lure the enemy with baits. Pretend to be in disarray, and then crush him. (Most commentators, except Chang Yu, interpret this as "when he is disorganized, crush him," but it's more natural to understand this as another example of how deception works in war.)

If the enemy is well-prepared at all points, be ready for him. If he is stronger, avoid him.

If your opponent has a bad temper, provoke him. Pretend to be weak so that he becomes overconfident. (Wang Tzŭ, as quoted by Tu Yu, compares this tactic to how a cat plays with a mouse, pretending to be weak before suddenly striking.)

If the enemy is resting, don't let him have peace. (This likely means to keep up pressure on the enemy, although Mei Yao-ch'en suggests it could mean "while we rest, let the enemy exhaust himself." The Yu Lan interprets it as "lure him on and tire him out.")

If his forces are united, divide them. (Many commentators offer an alternative explanation: "If the ruler and his subjects are in harmony, cause division between them.")

Attack the enemy where he is unprepared; appear in places where you are not expected.

These military strategies that lead to victory must not be revealed in advance.

A general who wins a battle makes many calculations in his temple before the battle begins. (Chang Yu notes that in ancient times, a temple was set aside for a general about to lead an army, where he could carefully plan his campaign.)

On the other hand, a general who loses a battle makes few calculations ahead of time. Thus, many calculations lead to victory, while few calculations lead to defeat. How much worse it is when no calculations are made at all! It is through understanding this that I can predict who is likely to win or lose.

Chapter 2 - Waging War

[Ts'ao Kung comments: "He who wishes to fight must first calculate the cost," which prepares us for the realization that this chapter is not primarily about what we might expect from its title, but is instead focused on the planning of resources and strategies.

Sun Tzu said: In warfare, when there are in the field a thousand swift chariots, an equal number of heavy chariots, and a hundred thousand soldiers clad in armor (the swift chariots were lightly built and, according to Chang Yu, were used for attack; the heavy chariots were stronger and designed for defense. Li Ch'uan suggests that the heavy chariots were also light, but this seems unlikely. It's interesting to note the similarities between early Chinese warfare and that of the Homeric Greeks. In both cases, the war chariot was central to military formation, surrounded by groups of foot soldiers. As for the numbers here, it is said that each swift chariot was accompanied by 75 footmen, and each heavy chariot by 25 footmen, dividing the army into a thousand battalions, each consisting of two chariots and a hundred men), with provisions sufficient to sustain them for a thousand li (2.78 modern li make up a mile, though the length may have varied somewhat since Sun Tzu's time), the total daily expenditure, both at home and at the front—including the entertainment of guests, small items like glue and paint, and the sums spent on chariots and armor—will amount to a thousand ounces of silver per day. This is the cost of maintaining an army of 100,000 men.

When you engage in actual combat, if victory is slow to come, the soldiers' weapons will grow dull, and their enthusiasm will fade. If you lay siege to a town, you will drain your strength.

Additionally, if the campaign is prolonged, the state's resources will not be able to bear the strain.

Now, when your weapons are dulled, your enthusiasm has waned, your strength is drained, and your resources are depleted, other leaders will rise to exploit your vulnerability. At that point, no one, no matter how wise, will be able to prevent the inevitable consequences.

Thus, while we have heard of foolish haste in war, cleverness has never been associated with long delays. (This brief and challenging sentence has puzzled commentators. Ts'ao Kung, Li Ch'uan, Meng Shih, Tu Yu, Tu Mu, and Mei Yao-ch'en all comment that a general, though typically unwise, might still win by sheer speed. Ho Shih adds that while haste may be foolish, it at least saves energy and resources, whereas prolonged campaigns, even if skillful, lead to disaster. Wang Hsi avoids the difficulty by saying that lengthy operations age the army, drain wealth, empty the treasury, and bring suffering to the people; true cleverness avoids these pitfalls. Chang Yu argues that as long as victory is possible, even hasty actions are preferable to overly cautious delays. However, Sun Tzu does not explicitly suggest that ill-considered haste is better than well-thought-out but prolonged strategies. Instead, his point is more cautious: while speed may sometimes be unwise, delays are always foolish, if only because they lead to national impoverishment. When considering Sun Tzu's point, the example of Fabius Cunctator inevitably comes to mind. Fabius deliberately measured the endurance of Rome against Hannibal's isolated army, reasoning that Hannibal would suffer more in a prolonged campaign in foreign territory. However, whether Fabius' strategy would have worked in the long run is debatable. Though the reversal of his approach led to the disaster at Cannae, this only suggests a negative presumption in favor of his tactics.)

Only someone who fully understands the horrors of war can fully comprehend the value of conducting it in a profitable manner. (That is, with speed. Only those who recognize the devastating consequences of a long war can truly grasp the supreme importance of bringing it to a swift conclusion. Although only two commentators favor this interpretation, it fits the logic of the context better than the alternative rendering, "He who does not know the evils of war cannot appreciate its benefits," which is clearly pointless.)

The skillful commander does not call for a second levy, nor are his supply wagons loaded more than twice. (Once war begins, he will not waste valuable time waiting for reinforcements, nor will he retreat to gather fresh supplies, but will instead cross the enemy's border without delay. While this may seem like a bold strategy, history's greatest military leaders, from Julius Caesar to Napoleon Bonaparte, have all emphasized the importance of time—that is, being slightly ahead of the enemy—over numerical superiority or careful logistical calculations.)

Bring war materials from home, but rely on the enemy for provisions. In this way, the army will always have enough food to meet its needs. (The Chinese word translated here as "war material" literally means "things to be used" and is understood in the broadest sense. It includes everything needed by the army, except for food.)

When the state treasury is poor, the army must be supported by contributions from far-off places. Relying on distant sources to sustain the army leads to impoverishment of the people.

The beginning of this sentence does not connect smoothly with the next, though it is clearly meant to do so. The arrangement is so awkward that it suggests some corruption in the text. It rarely occurs to Chinese commentators that an amendment might be needed to clarify the meaning, so they offer no help here. The Chinese words Sun Tzu used to indicate the cause of the people's impoverishment refer to a system where farmers sent their corn directly to the army. But why would it fall to them to maintain the army in this way, unless the State or Government was too poor to do so?

On the other hand, the presence of an army nearby causes prices to rise, and high prices lead to the people's wealth being drained. (Wang Hsi says that prices increase even before the army leaves its own territory. Ts'ao Kung believes this applies to an army that has already crossed the frontier.)

When the people's wealth is drained, the farmers will suffer from heavy demands placed upon them.

As their wealth is lost and their strength is exhausted, the homes of the people will be left bare, and three-tenths of their income will be consumed. (Tu Mu and Wang Hsi argue that the people are actually deprived of seven-tenths of their income, but this is difficult to extract from the text. Ho Shih adds a characteristic note: "The people are the essential part of the State, and food is their heaven, so is it not right that those in authority should take care to protect both?")

Meanwhile, government expenses for damaged chariots, worn-out horses, breastplates, helmets, bows and arrows, spears and shields, protective coverings, oxen for transportation, and heavy wagons will consume four-tenths of the total revenue.

Thus, a wise general makes it a priority to forage from the enemy. One cartload of the enemy's provisions is worth twenty of one's own, and similarly, a single picul of their supplies is worth twenty from one's own stores. (This is because twenty cartloads of provisions will be consumed during the transportation of one cartload to the front. A picul is a unit of measure equal to 133.3 pounds, or 65.5 kilograms.)

Now, to defeat the enemy, our soldiers must be stirred to anger; and to gain any benefit from defeating the enemy, they must receive rewards. (Tu Mu explains: "Rewards are necessary so the soldiers understand the benefit of beating the enemy. When spoils are captured from the enemy, they should be distributed as rewards, so that all the men will have a strong desire to fight, each for his own gain.")

Therefore, in chariot warfare, when ten or more chariots are captured, the soldiers who take the first one should be rewarded. Our flags should be substituted for the enemy's, and the captured chariots should be integrated and used alongside our own. Captured enemy soldiers should be treated kindly and kept.

This is called using the enemy's resources to strengthen one's own forces.

In war, your main objective should always be victory, not prolonged campaigns. (As Ho Shih remarks: "War is not something to be treated lightly." Sun Tzu reiterates here the central lesson of this chapter.)

Thus, it is clear that the leader of armies holds the fate of the people in his hands, and it is his actions that determine whether the nation will be at peace or in danger.

Chapter 3 - Attack By Stratagem

Sun Tzu said: In the practical art of war, the best course of action is to take the enemy's country whole and intact; to shatter and destroy it is not as good. Likewise, it is better to capture an entire army than to destroy it, better to capture an entire regiment, detachment, or company than to destroy them. (According to Ssu-ma Fa, an army corps consisted of 12,500 men; Ts'ao Kung says a regiment contained 500 men, a detachment could consist of any number between 100 and 500, and a company could range from 5 to 100 men. However, Chang Yu gives the exact figures of 100 for a detachment and 5 for a company.)

Therefore, to fight and win in all your battles is not the highest excellence; the highest excellence consists in breaking the enemy's resistance without having to fight. (Once again, no modern strategist would disagree with these words. Moltke's greatest victory, the surrender of the enormous French army at Sedan, was achieved virtually without bloodshed.)

Thus, the highest form of generalship is to thwart the enemy's plans. (Perhaps the word "thwart" does not fully capture the meaning of the original Chinese, which implies not merely defending by countering each of the enemy's strategies, but actively attacking. Ho Shih explains this clearly in his note: "When the enemy plans to attack us, we must anticipate him by launching our attack first.")

The next best course is to prevent the enemy's forces from combining. (This involves isolating him from his allies. We must remember that Sun Tzu is referring to the many states or principalities into which China was divided in his time.)

After that, the next best option is to attack the enemy's army in the field. (That is, when his forces are already gathered and at full strength.)

The worst course of action is to besiege walled cities.

The rule is not to attack cities with walls unless it is absolutely necessary.

(Another good piece of military advice. If the Boers had followed this in 1899 and not spread their forces thin around places like Kimberley, Mafeking, or even Ladysmith, they likely would have had the upper hand before the British were really ready to fight back.)

Building mantlets, movable shelters, and other war tools will take up three whole months.

(It's not completely clear what the Chinese term translated as "mantlets" really meant. Ts'ao Kung says they were "large shields," but Li Ch'uan gives us a better idea, describing them as protection for soldiers attacking the walls of a city up close. This suggests they might have been like the Roman testudo, a formation where soldiers would use their shields to form a shell. Tu Mu claims they were wheeled vehicles for defense, but Ch'en Hao disagrees. See earlier, II.14. The term also referred to turrets on city walls. The "movable shelters" were more clearly described by various commentators: they were wooden, missile-proof structures with four wheels, covered with raw hides, used in sieges to transport soldiers safely to and from the city walls, often to fill up moats with dirt. Tu Mu adds that nowadays they are called "wooden donkeys.")

Building up ramps against the walls will take another three months.

(These were large mounds or earth ramps built up to the height of the enemy's walls to spot weak points in the defenses and to tear down the fortified turrets mentioned earlier.)

The general, unable to keep his anger in check, will send his men to attack like a swarm of ants.

(This vivid image from Ts'ao Kung comes from the sight of an army of ants climbing up a wall. It means the general, losing patience due to the delay, may order an attack before his war machines are ready.)

As a result, one-third of his men will be killed, and the city will still not be taken. These are the terrible outcomes of a siege.

(We are reminded of the heavy losses suffered by the Japanese in their recent siege of Port Arthur.)

A skilled leader defeats the enemy's troops without ever having to fight; he takes their cities without needing to lay siege; he brings down their kingdom without long, drawn-out battles.

(Chia Lin points out that the leader only removes the government but does not harm individuals. A classic example of this is Wu Wang, who, after ending the Yin dynasty, was celebrated as the "Father and mother of the people.")

With his army fully intact, he will challenge for control of the Empire, and by doing so, without losing a single man, his victory will be complete.

(Because of the double meanings in the Chinese text, the second part of this sentence could also mean: "And thus, since the weapon has not been dulled by overuse, its sharpness remains perfect.")

This is how to conquer through strategy.

In war, if our forces outnumber the enemy ten to one, we surround him; if five to one, we attack him.

(Immediately, without waiting for any further advantages.)

If we are twice as numerous, we split our army into two.

(Tu Mu disagrees with this advice, and at first glance, it seems to go against a basic rule of warfare. However, Ts'ao Kung offers an explanation: "When we are two to one against the enemy, one part of our army can be used in the regular way, and the other can be used for a special maneuver." Chang Yu adds more clarity: "If our army is twice the size of the enemy's, we should split it into two groups—one to face the enemy head-on, and the other to attack from behind. If the enemy responds to the front attack, he can be crushed from behind; if he reacts to the rear attack, he can be defeated from the front." This is what is meant by saying that 'one part may be used in the regular way, and the other for a special maneuver.' Tu Mu doesn't understand that splitting the army is an irregular strategy, just as concentrating the army is the regular strategy, and he is too quick to call this a mistake.)

If we are evenly matched, we can engage in battle.

(Li Ch'uan, supported by Ho Shih, rephrases this as: "If both sides are equal in strength, only a skilled general will choose to fight.")

If we are slightly weaker, we can avoid the enemy.

(The meaning "we can watch the enemy" is an improvement on this, but there isn't much solid backing for this version. Chang Yu reminds us that this advice only holds if other factors are equal. A small difference in numbers can often be balanced out by greater energy and discipline.)

If we are greatly outmatched, we can retreat.

Even though a small force may put up a stubborn fight, in the end, it will be overcome by a larger force.

The general is the foundation of the State: if the foundation is solid in all areas, the State will be strong; if the foundation has weaknesses, the State will be weak.

(As Li Ch'uan puts it briefly: "A gap shows a weakness; if the general's ability is not perfect—if he isn't fully skilled in his role—his army will lack strength.")

There are three ways a ruler can bring disaster to his army:

(1) By ordering the army to advance or retreat without knowing that it cannot follow those orders. This is called crippling the army.

(Li Ch'uan adds: "It's like tying the legs of a racehorse so it can't run." You might think "the ruler" in this case is far away, trying to direct the army from a distance. However, the commentators interpret it the opposite way, quoting T'ai Kung: "A kingdom shouldn't be ruled from the outside, and an army shouldn't be commanded from within." Naturally, during a battle or when close to the enemy, the general shouldn't be right in the middle of his own troops, but should stay a little apart. Otherwise, he might misread the situation and give wrong orders.)

(2) By trying to govern an army in the same way he runs a kingdom, without understanding the conditions within an army, a ruler causes unrest in the soldiers' minds.

(Ts'ao Kung notes: "The military and civil spheres are entirely different; you can't handle an army with soft, delicate treatment." Chang Yu adds: "Humanity and justice are the foundations for governing a state, but not for leading an army. Opportunism and flexibility are military virtues, not civil ones.")

(3) By using officers without making distinctions between them,

(This means the ruler doesn't carefully assign the right person to the right role.)

because he doesn't understand the military principle of adapting to circumstances, he undermines the soldiers' trust.

(I follow Mei Yao-ch'en here. Other commentators refer to the officers employed, not the ruler as in the previous sections. Tu Yu says: "If a general doesn't understand adaptability, he should not be put in charge." Tu Mu quotes: "A skilled leader will employ the wise, the brave, the greedy, and the foolish. The wise man enjoys proving his merit, the brave man seeks to show his courage in action, the greedy man quickly seizes opportunities, and the foolish man fears nothing, even death.")

But when the army is restless and distrustful, conflict will arise from the other feudal princes. This brings chaos into the army and throws away any chance of victory.

From this, we know that there are five key factors for victory: (1) He will win who knows when to fight and when not to fight.

(Chang Yu says: If he can fight, he moves forward and attacks; if he cannot fight, he retreats and defends. Victory is certain for the one who understands when to attack and when to defend.)

(2) He will win who knows how to manage both larger and smaller forces.

(This isn't just about the general's ability to count numbers accurately, as Li Ch'uan and others suggest. Chang Yu explains this better: "By using the art of war, a smaller force can defeat a larger one, and vice versa. The secret is understanding the terrain and seizing the right moment. As Wu Tzǔ says: 'With a larger force, move on easy ground; with a smaller force, seek difficult ground.'")

Chapter 4 - Tactical Dispositions

Ts'ao Kung explains the meaning behind the title of this chapter: "marching and countermarching by the two armies to find out each other's condition." Tu Mu adds: "It is through the positioning of an army that its state can be revealed. Hide your positioning, and your condition remains secret, leading to victory; expose your positioning, and your condition becomes clear, leading to defeat." Wang Hsi comments that a good general "ensures success by adapting his tactics to those of the enemy."

Sun Tzŭ said: The skilled fighters of the past first made sure they could not be defeated, then waited for the right moment to defeat the enemy.

The power to avoid defeat is in our own hands, but the chance to defeat the enemy comes from the enemy himself.

(That is, of course, due to a mistake on the enemy's part.)

Thus, a skilled fighter can always protect himself from defeat,

(Chang Yu explains that this is done by "concealing the positioning of the troops, covering up tracks, and taking constant precautions.")

but he cannot always ensure he will defeat the enemy.

Hence the saying: One may know how to win but still not be able to achieve it.

Protecting oneself from defeat involves defensive tactics, while defeating the enemy involves taking the offensive.

(I keep the meaning found in a similar passage in §§ 1-3, despite the fact that the commentators disagree with me. Their interpretation, "He who cannot conquer takes the defensive," is reasonable, but this version seems clearer.)

Being on the defensive suggests a lack of strength, while attacking shows an abundance of strength.

A general skilled in defense hides in the deepest recesses of the earth;

(Literally, "hides under the ninth earth," a metaphor for complete secrecy and concealment, so the enemy doesn't know his location.)

while a general skilled in attack strikes from the highest heavens.

(Another metaphor, meaning he falls upon his enemy like a sudden thunderbolt, against which there is no time to prepare. Most commentators agree with this interpretation.)

Thus, on one hand, we have the ability to protect ourselves; on the other, the ability to achieve a complete victory.

To see victory only when it is clear to everyone is not the height of excellence.

(As Ts'ao Kung says, "the key is to see the plant before it has sprouted," meaning to foresee the outcome before the action begins. Li Ch'uan mentions the story of Han Hsin, who, before attacking the much larger army of Chao, which was heavily fortified in the city of Ch'eng-an, told his officers, "Gentlemen, we are going to destroy the enemy and will meet again at dinner." His officers didn't take him seriously and gave doubtful replies. But Han Hsin had already devised a clever plan, and as he predicted, he captured the city and crushed his enemy.)

It is also not the height of excellence if you fight and win, and the whole world says, "Well done!"

(True excellence, as Tu Mu says, lies in planning secretly, moving quietly, and outsmarting the enemy's plans so that victory is achieved without a drop of blood being shed. Sun Tzŭ praises achievements that "the world's clumsy thumb and finger cannot grasp.")

Lifting an autumn hair is not a sign of great strength;

("Autumn hair" refers to the fine fur of a hare, which is softest in autumn when it starts growing back. This phrase is commonly used by Chinese writers.)

Seeing the sun and moon is not a sign of sharp vision, and hearing the sound of thunder is not a sign of quick hearing.

(Ho Shih provides examples of true strength, sharp vision, and quick hearing: Wu Huo, who could lift a 250-stone tripod; Li Chu, who could see objects as small as mustard seeds from a hundred paces;

and Shih K'uang, a blind musician who could hear a mosquito's footsteps.)

What the ancients called a clever fighter is someone who not only wins, but wins with ease.

(The second part literally means "one who, while conquering, excels in conquering easily." Mei Yao-ch'en explains: "He who only notices the obvious wins his battles with difficulty; but he who sees beneath the surface wins with ease.")

For this reason, his victories bring him neither a reputation for wisdom nor credit for bravery.

(Tu Mu explains this well: "Since his victories are achieved under circumstances that remain hidden, the world at large knows nothing of them, and he gains no reputation for wisdom. Since the enemy surrenders without bloodshed, he gets no credit for bravery.")

He wins his battles by making no mistakes.

(Ch'en Hao says: "He avoids unnecessary marches and pointless attacks." Chang Yu explains the connection: "One who tries to win by brute force, even if skilled in fighting pitched battles, may sometimes be defeated. But one who can foresee the future and understand conditions before they arise will never make a mistake, and thus always win.")

Making no mistakes ensures victory because it means defeating an enemy who is already defeated.

Thus, the skilled fighter places himself in a position where defeat is impossible and never misses the moment to defeat the enemy.

(A "counsel of perfection," as Tu Mu notes. "Position" isn't just about the physical location of troops; it includes all the preparations and arrangements that a wise general makes to ensure the safety of the army.)

In war, the victorious strategist seeks battle only after victory is already assured, while the one destined for defeat fights first and then looks for victory.

(Ho Shih explains this paradox: "In warfare, first make plans that will guarantee victory, then lead your army into battle. If you rely on brute strength alone without first using strategy, victory will no longer be guaranteed.")

The ideal leader follows the moral law and adheres strictly to method and discipline; by doing so, he can control success.

In terms of military methods, there are: first, Measurement; second, Estimation of quantity; third, Calculation; fourth, Balancing of chances; and fifth, Victory.

Measurement depends on the Earth; Estimation of quantity comes from Measurement; Calculation comes from Estimation of quantity; Balancing of chances comes from Calculation; and Victory comes from Balancing of chances.

(It's hard to distinguish the four terms clearly in Chinese. The first seems to refer to surveying and measuring the ground, which allows us to estimate the enemy's strength and make calculations from that information. This leads to a weighing of chances—comparing the enemy's chances with our own. If the scale tips in our favor, victory follows. The difficulty lies in the third term, which some commentators interpret as a calculation of numbers, making it nearly synonymous with the second term. Perhaps the second refers to considering the enemy's general situation, while the third refers to estimating his numerical strength. Tu Mu suggests that once relative strength is known, we can apply cunning strategies. Ho Shih supports this, but with a weaker interpretation, indicating that the third term points to calculating numbers.)

A victorious army facing a defeated one is like a pound's weight against a single grain.

(Literally, "a victorious army is like an i (20 ounces) weighed against a shu (1/24 of an ounce); a defeated army is a shu weighed against an i." This illustrates the huge advantage a disciplined, victorious force has over one demoralized by defeat. Legge, in his note on Mencius, I.2.ix.2, defines the i as 24 Chinese ounces and corrects

Chu Hsi's claim that it equals only 20 ounces. However, Li Ch'uan of the T'ang dynasty supports Chu Hsi's figure.)

The rush of a victorious force is like water bursting through a dam into a chasm a thousand fathoms deep. This concludes the section on tactical dispositions.

Chapter 5 - Energy

Sun Tzŭ said: Controlling a large army is based on the same principles as controlling a small group; it is simply a matter of dividing them into smaller units.

(This means splitting the army into regiments, companies, etc., each with its own subordinate officers. Tu Mu reminds us of the famous conversation between Han Hsin and the first Han Emperor. The Emperor asked, "How large an army do you think I could lead?" Han Hsin replied, "No more than 100,000 men, Your Majesty." "And how about you?" asked the Emperor. Han Hsin responded, "Oh, the more, the better.")

Fighting with a large army under your command is no different from fighting with a small one; it's just about using signs and signals to communicate.

To ensure that your entire force can withstand the enemy's attack without breaking, you need to use both direct and indirect maneuvers.

(Now we come to one of the most interesting parts of Sun Tzŭ's teachings: the discussion of cheng (direct) and ch'i (indirect). These two terms are tricky to fully grasp or consistently translate into English, so it's helpful to consider what various commentators have said. Li Ch'uan explains that cheng is a frontal confrontation, while ch'i is a diversion to the side. Chia Lin says: "When facing the enemy, your troops should be arranged in a conventional way, but victory comes from using unconventional maneuvers." Mei Yao-ch'en adds: "Ch'i is active, while cheng is passive; waiting for the right moment is passive, but action itself brings victory." Ho Shih explains: "We must make the enemy think our straightforward attack is secretly planned, and vice versa. Thus, cheng can become ch'i and ch'i can become cheng." He uses the example of Han Hsin, who marched his army toward Lin-chin but suddenly sent a large force across the Yellow River in wooden tubs, catching the enemy off guard. In this case, the march on Lin-chin was cheng, and the surprise maneuver across the river was ch'i."

Chang Yu summarizes these ideas by noting that military writers disagree on the definitions of cheng and ch'i. Wei Liao Tzŭ says, "Direct warfare favors frontal attacks, while indirect warfare favors attacks from behind." Ts'ao Kung says, "Going directly into battle is cheng, while appearing behind the enemy is ch'i." Li Wei-kung adds, "In war, marching straight ahead is cheng; turning movements are ch'i." These writers treat cheng and ch'i as separate and fixed, but they don't realize that the two can blend together and switch, like two sides of a circle. A comment on the T'ang Emperor T'ai Tsung goes deeper: "A ch'i maneuver becomes cheng if we make the enemy believe it is cheng; then our real attack will be ch'i, and vice versa. The secret lies in confusing the enemy so they cannot understand our true intentions."

In simpler terms, any operation is cheng if it draws the enemy's attention, and ch'i if it catches them by surprise. If the enemy recognizes a movement meant to be ch'i, it becomes cheng.)

The impact of your army should be like a grindstone smashing against an egg—this is achieved through understanding weak points and strong ones.

In all battles, the direct method may be used to engage the enemy, but indirect methods are necessary to secure victory.

(Chang Yu explains: "Develop indirect tactics steadily, either by striking at the enemy's flanks or attacking from behind." A brilliant example of indirect tactics deciding a campaign was Lord Roberts' night march around Peiwar Kotal during the second Afghan war.)

Indirect tactics, when applied efficiently, are as limitless as Heaven and Earth, as unceasing as the flow of rivers and streams. Like the sun and moon, they end only to begin again; like the four seasons, they pass and return.

(Tu Yu and Chang Yu see this as referring to the changing use of ch'i and cheng. However, Sun Tzŭ isn't specifically talking about cheng here, unless, as Cheng Yu-hsien suggests, a part of the text about cheng was lost. As mentioned before, ch'i and cheng are so interconnected in military operations that they cannot be considered separately. This passage expresses the almost endless resourcefulness of a great leader.)

There are only five musical notes, yet their combinations create more melodies than can ever be heard.

There are only five primary colors—blue, yellow, red, white, and black—yet their combinations produce more hues than can ever be seen.

There are only five basic tastes—sour, acrid, salty, sweet, and bitter—but their combinations yield more flavors than can ever be tasted.

In battle, there are only two methods of attack—the direct and the indirect—yet their combination creates an infinite number of maneuvers.

The direct and the indirect lead into each other, like a circle that has no end. Who can exhaust the possibilities of their combination?

The advance of troops is like the rush of a torrent, powerful enough to carry stones along its path.

The quality of decision is like the well-timed swoop of a falcon that enables it to strike and destroy its target.

(The Chinese here is tricky, and a certain key word in this context resists the best efforts of translation. Tu Mu defines this word as "the measurement or estimation of distance." But applying this meaning to the falcon, it seems to refer to the instinct of self-restraint, which prevents the bird from swooping down on its prey until the right moment, along with the ability to judge when that moment has come.

The analogous quality in soldiers is the important skill of holding back their fire until the exact moment when it will be most effective. When the Victory went into action at Trafalgar, moving at hardly more than a drifting pace, it was under heavy fire for several minutes without returning a single shot. Nelson waited coolly until he was in close range, at which point the broadside he unleashed inflicted devastating damage on the enemy's nearest ships.)

Therefore, the skilled fighter will be fearsome in his attack and prompt in his decision.

(The word "decision" likely refers to the measurement of distance mentioned earlier, holding off until the enemy is close enough to strike. However, I also believe that Sun Tzŭ meant this word figuratively, similar to our own expression "short and sharp." Wang Hsi's note expands on the falcon's method of attack, adding: "This is how the 'psychological moment' should be seized in war.")

Energy may be compared to the bending of a crossbow; decision, to the release of the trigger.

(None of the commentators seem to grasp the true meaning of this simile. The key point is that energy, like the force stored in a bent crossbow, only becomes effective when released by the decision to pull the trigger.)

Amid the turmoil and chaos of battle, there may seem to be disorder, yet there is no real disorder; amid confusion, your formation may appear to lack head or tail, yet it remains unshakable against defeat.

(Mei Yao-ch'en says: "When the subdivisions of the army have been arranged in advance, and the various signals have been agreed upon, the separating, joining, dispersing, and regrouping that occurs during battle may give the appearance of disorder, but true disorder is impossible. Even if your formation seems headless and without direction, your forces will not be routed.")

Simulated disorder requires perfect discipline; simulated fear requires courage; simulated weakness requires strength.

(To make this translation clearer, the sharp paradox of the original needs to be softened. Ts'ao Kung hints at the meaning in his brief note: "These things are all meant to disrupt the enemy's formation and conceal one's true condition." Tu Mu explains it plainly: "If you want to appear confused to lure the enemy, you must first have perfect discipline; if you want to display fear to trap the enemy, you must have great courage; if you want to show weakness to make the enemy overconfident, you must have great strength.")

Hiding order beneath the appearance of disorder is simply a matter of dividing the army into smaller units.

(See earlier, § 1.)

Concealing courage under a display of timidity requires a reservoir of hidden energy.

(The commentators interpret a specific Chinese word here differently than elsewhere in the chapter. Tu Mu says: "When the enemy sees that we are in a favorable position but make no move, they will believe we are truly afraid.")

Masking strength with weakness is accomplished through strategic positioning.

(Chang Yu recounts the story of Kao Tsu, the first Han Emperor. He wanted to attack the Hsiung-nu, so he sent spies to gather intelligence on their condition. However, the Hsiung-nu, anticipating this, hid all their strong soldiers and healthy horses, and only allowed the spies to see old soldiers and weak animals. As a result, all the spies advised the Emperor to attack. Only Lou Ching opposed them, saying: "When two countries prepare for war, they naturally try to show their strength. Since our spies have only seen old and weak forces, this must be a trick, and attacking would be unwise." The Emperor ignored this advice, fell into the trap, and was surrounded at Po-teng.)

Thus, one who is skilled at keeping the enemy on the move uses deceptive appearances, to which the enemy will respond.

(Ts'ao Kung notes: "Create the appearance of weakness and need." Tu Mu adds: "If our forces are stronger than the enemy's, we can pretend to be weak to lure them in; but if we are weaker, we must make the enemy believe we are strong so they stay away. In fact, the enemy's actions should always be based on the signals we choose to give." There is an anecdote about Sun Pin, a descendant of Sun Wu: In 341 B.C., the state of Ch'i was at war with Wei, and Sun Pin was sent to face the general P'ang Chuan, who was his personal enemy. Sun Pin said: "The Ch'i state is known for cowardice, so our enemy will underestimate us. Let's take advantage of this." When their army crossed into Wei territory, Sun Pin ordered 100,000 campfires on the first night, 50,000 on the second night, and only 20,000 on the third night. P'ang Chuan, in pursuit, thought: "I knew these Ch'i soldiers were cowards; their numbers are already less than half." Sun Pin retreated to a narrow pass, knowing that P'ang Chuan would arrive after dark. There, Sun Pin had a tree stripped of its bark and inscribed: "Under this tree, P'ang Chuan will die." As night fell, Sun Pin hid archers nearby, instructing them to shoot when they saw light. When P'ang Chuan arrived, he struck a light to read the inscription on the tree, and was immediately shot down by arrows, throwing his army into confusion. [Tu Mu's version of the story is more dramatic, though the Shih Chi suggests that after the defeat of his army, P'ang Chuan committed suicide in despair.])

He sacrifices something, knowing the enemy will snatch at it.

By offering baits, he keeps the enemy on the move; then, with a group of carefully chosen men, he waits to ambush him.

(With an adjustment suggested by Li Ching, this reads: "He lies in wait with the main body of his troops.")

The clever combatant relies on the effect of combined energy and does not demand too much from individuals.

(Tu Mu explains: "First, he assesses the overall power of his army as a whole; then he takes individual abilities into account and uses each person according to their talents. He does not expect perfection from those who lack it.")

This is why he can select the right men and make use of their combined strength.

When he employs combined energy, his fighters become like rolling logs or stones. A log or stone remains still on level ground but moves when placed on a slope. If it is square, it stops, but if it is round, it rolls down.

(Ts'ao Kung refers to this as "the use of natural or inherent power.")

Thus, the energy generated by skilled fighters is like the momentum of a round stone rolling down a mountain thousands of feet high. This concludes the discussion on energy.

(Tu Mu points out that the main lesson of this chapter is the critical importance of rapid maneuvers and sudden charges in warfare. "With such tactics," he adds, "great results can be achieved with even small forces.")

Chapter 6 - Weak Points and Strong

[Chang Yu tries to explain the sequence of the chapters in this way: "Chapter IV, on Tactical Dispositions, dealt with offense and defense; Chapter V, on Energy, covered direct and indirect methods. The skilled general first familiarizes himself with the theory of attack and defense, and then focuses on direct and indirect methods. He learns how to vary and combine these two methods before moving on to the topic of weak and strong points. The use of direct or indirect methods arises from attack and defense, and recognizing weak and strong points depends on understanding these methods. Therefore, this chapter follows directly after the one on Energy."]

Sun Tzŭ said: Whoever is first to arrive on the battlefield and waits for the enemy will be well-prepared for the fight; whoever arrives second and has to rush into battle will be tired and worn out.

Therefore, the clever combatant imposes his will on the enemy and never allows the enemy to impose his will on him.

(A mark of a great soldier is that he fights on his own terms or not at all.)

By offering advantages, he can lure the enemy to approach; or by causing harm, he can prevent the enemy from drawing near.

(In the first case, he entices with bait; in the second, he strikes a key point the enemy will be forced to defend.)

If the enemy is resting, he can harass him;

(This passage can be cited as evidence against Mei Yao-ch'en's interpretation of I. § 23.)

if the enemy has plenty of food, he can starve him out; if the enemy is quietly encamped, he can force him to move.

Appear at points the enemy must rush to defend; march quickly to places where you are not expected.

An army can cover great distances without suffering if it travels through areas where the enemy is absent.

(Ts'ao Kung summarizes this well: "Emerge from the void—like a surprise attack—and strike at vulnerable spots, avoid defended places, and attack where you are least expected.")

You can be certain of success in your attacks if you only strike at places that are undefended.

(Wang Hsi explains "undefended places" as weak points, meaning areas where the general is lacking in ability, the soldiers lack morale, the walls are not strong enough, precautions are too lax, reinforcements arrive too late, supplies are insufficient, or the defenders are in conflict among themselves.)

You can ensure the safety of your defense if you only hold positions that cannot be attacked.

(That is, where none of the weaknesses mentioned above exist. There's an interesting nuance in interpreting this line. Tu Mu, Ch'en Hao, and Mei Yao-ch'en suggest it means: "To make your defense completely secure, you must even defend places that are unlikely to be attacked," and Tu Mu adds, "How much more so for places that are likely to be attacked." However, this interpretation doesn't balance well with the preceding clause, which is important in the highly antithetical style typical of Chinese writing. Chang Yu seems closer to the point by saying: "The skilled attacker strikes from the topmost heights of heaven [see IV. § 7], making it impossible for the enemy to defend. Thus, the places I will attack are exactly those the enemy cannot defend. The skilled defender hides in the deepest recesses of the earth, making it impossible for the enemy to locate him. Thus, the places I will hold are precisely those the enemy cannot attack.")

Therefore, the general who is skilled in attack confuses the enemy, so they do not know what to defend; the general who is skilled in defense confounds the enemy, so they do not know what to attack.

(An aphorism that sums up the essence of the art of war.)

O divine art of subtlety and secrecy! Through you, we learn to be invisible, through you, we learn to be inaudible;

(Literally, "without form or sound," in reference to the enemy.)

and thus, we hold the enemy's fate in our hands.

You can advance and be absolutely unstoppable if you strike at the enemy's weak points; you can retreat safely and avoid pursuit if your movements are quicker than the enemy's.

If we want to engage in battle, we can force the enemy to fight, even if he is hiding behind a high wall and a deep trench. All we need to do is attack another place that he will be forced to defend.

(Tu Mu explains: "If the enemy is the invader, we can cut off his supply lines and seize the roads he must use to retreat; if we are the invaders, we can aim our attack at the ruler himself." It's clear that Sun Tzŭ, unlike certain generals in later conflicts such as the Boer War, did not believe in frontal assaults.)

If we do not wish to fight, we can prevent the enemy from engaging us, even if our encampment is only outlined on the ground.

All we need to do is confuse him with something strange and unexpected.

(This concise phrase is paraphrased by Chia Lin as: "even though we have constructed neither walls nor ditches." Li Ch'uan adds: "we bewilder him with strange and unusual tactics," and Tu Mu illustrates with three anecdotes. One example is Chu-ko Liang, who, when stationed at Yang-p'ing and about to be attacked by Ssu-ma I, unexpectedly struck his flags, silenced his drums, and opened the city gates, showing only a few men sweeping the grounds. This strange move made Ssu-ma I suspect a trap, causing him to withdraw his army. What Sun Tzŭ is advocating here, therefore, is nothing less than the skillful use of "bluff.")

By discovering the enemy's plans while keeping our own concealed, we can concentrate our forces, while the enemy is forced to divide his.

(The conclusion may not seem obvious at first, but Chang Yu, following Mei Yao-ch'en, explains: "If the enemy's plans are visible, we can attack him with a united force; meanwhile, if our plans are kept secret, the enemy will have to split his forces to guard against attacks from multiple directions.")

We can form a single, united force, while the enemy must divide into smaller parts. Thus, we will have a whole army against only fragments of the enemy's force, meaning we will be many against their few.

If we are able to attack an inferior force with a superior one in this way, the enemy will find themselves in great difficulty.

The location where we intend to fight must not be revealed, because this will force the enemy to prepare for possible attacks at several different points.

(Sheridan once explained General Grant's victories by saying that "while his opponents were kept fully occupied wondering what he was going to do, he was focused mainly on what he was going to do.")

With the enemy's forces scattered in many directions, the number of troops we face at any given point will be relatively small.

For if the enemy strengthens his front lines, he will weaken his rear; if he strengthens his rear, he will weaken his front. If he strengthens his left, he will weaken his right, and if he strengthens his right, he will weaken his left. If he sends reinforcements everywhere, he will be weak everywhere.

(Frederick the Great, in his Instructions to his Generals, wrote: "A defensive war tends to lead us into making too many detachments. Generals with little experience try to defend every point, while those who understand their profession focus only on the main objective, allowing small losses to avoid greater ones.")

Numerical weakness arises from having to prepare against possible attacks, while numerical strength comes from forcing the enemy to make such preparations.

(Colonel Henderson described the highest form of generalship as "compelling the enemy to disperse his army, then concentrating a superior force against each fraction in turn.")

If we know the place and time of the coming battle, we can gather our forces from even the greatest distances to fight.

(Sun Tzŭ is referring to the careful calculation of distances and the expert use of strategy that allow a general to divide his army for a long and rapid march, then bring them together at precisely the right place and time to confront the enemy with overwhelming strength. A dramatic example of this in military history is the appearance of Blücher at the critical moment during the Battle of Waterloo.)

But if neither the time nor place of battle is known, then the left wing will be powerless to help the right, the right will be equally unable to help the left, the front will not be able to relieve the rear, and the rear won't be able to support the front. This is even more true if the furthest parts of the army are separated by over a hundred li and the nearest by several li.

(The Chinese text here lacks precision, but the idea is likely that of an army advancing toward a rendezvous in separate columns, each with orders to meet on a specific date. If the general lets the detachments march haphazardly without precise instructions on when and where to meet, the enemy could destroy the army piece by piece. Chang Yu's note clarifies: "If we do not know the enemy's concentration point or the day they plan to engage, our unity will be lost as we prepare for defense, and the positions we hold will be insecure. If we suddenly encounter a strong enemy, we will be forced into battle in a disorganized state, with no mutual support between wings, vanguard, or rear, especially if there is a great distance between the leading and rear divisions of the army.")

Even though, by my estimation, the soldiers of Yüeh outnumber us, that will not give them any advantage in achieving victory. I say, then, that victory can be achieved.

(Unfortunately, this confident claim was not borne out. The long-standing feud between Wu and Yüeh ended in 473 B.C. with the complete defeat of Wu by Kou Chien, and Wu was absorbed into Yüeh. This likely occurred long after Sun Tzŭ's death. Chang Yu is the only commentator to note the apparent contradiction here, which he explains: "In the chapter on Tactical Dispositions, it is said, 'One may know how to conquer without being able to do it,' whereas here, it says that victory can be achieved. The difference is that in the former chapter, discussing offense and defense, it is acknowledged that if the enemy is fully prepared, victory is not guaranteed. But this passage refers specifically to the soldiers of Yüeh, who, according to Sun Tzŭ's calculations, would remain unaware of the time and place of the impending battle. That's why he says here that victory is possible.")

Though the enemy may have greater numbers, we can prevent him from engaging in battle. Devise schemes to uncover his plans and assess the likelihood of their success.

(An alternate reading offered by Chia Lin is: "Know beforehand all strategies that will lead to our success and the enemy's failure.")

Provoke him, and observe the principle behind his activity or inactivity.

(Chang Yu explains that by noting the enemy's emotional reactions—whether joy or anger—when disturbed, we can deduce whether his strategy is to remain passive or take action. He gives the example of Cho-ku Liang, who sent a woman's head-dress as an insulting gift to Ssu-ma I, provoking him to abandon his cautious, passive tactics.)

Force the enemy to reveal himself, so you can discover his weak points.

Carefully compare the enemy's army with your own, so you will know where strength is abundant and where it is lacking.

(See also IV. § 6.)

In making tactical plans, the highest achievement is to keep them hidden.

(The paradox loses some sharpness in translation. Concealment here doesn't necessarily mean literal invisibility (see § 9 above), but rather not showing any signs of what you intend to do—keeping your thoughts and plans completely veiled.)

Hide your dispositions, and you will be protected from the prying eyes of even the most clever spies and the schemes of the wisest minds.

(Tu Mu explains: "Even if the enemy has intelligent and capable officers, they will not be able to make any effective plans against us.")

How victory is brought about using the enemy's own tactics is something the masses cannot understand.

Everyone can see the tactics by which I win, but no one can see the strategy behind that victory.

(That is, people can observe the outward methods used in winning a battle, but they cannot see the long process of planning and the combinations of strategies that precede it.)

Do not simply repeat the tactics that won you a previous victory; instead, let your methods be shaped by the infinite variety of circumstances.

(Wang Hsi wisely notes: "There is only one core principle of victory, but the tactics leading to it are countless." Compare this to Colonel Henderson's view: "The rules of strategy are few and simple, and can be learned in a week. However, knowing them will not teach a person to lead an army like Napoleon any more than knowing grammar will teach someone to write like Gibbon.")

Military tactics are like water; for just as water flows away from high ground and moves quickly downhill,

so in war, the way is to avoid the strong and strike at the weak.

(Like water, which follows the path of least resistance.)

Water shapes its course according to the nature of the ground over which it flows; in the same way, a soldier works out his victory in relation to the enemy he is facing.

Therefore, just as water has no constant shape, so there are no constant conditions in warfare.

He who can adjust his tactics to match the situation and succeed in winning may be called a captain born of heaven.

The five elements (water, fire, wood, metal, earth) are not always equally dominant;

(Wang Hsi notes: "They dominate in turn.")

The four seasons give way to each other in succession.

(Literally, "they do not always remain in the same place.")

There are short days and long days; the moon waxes and wanes.

(See also V. § 6. The point here is to illustrate the ever-changing nature of war by comparing it to the constant shifts in nature. The comparison is not entirely perfect, however, since the regularity of natural phenomena differs from the unpredictability of war.)

Chapter 7 - Manoeuvering

Sun Tzŭ said: In war, the general receives his orders from the sovereign.

After gathering an army and concentrating his forces, he must blend and harmonize the various elements within it before setting up camp.

(Chang Yu explains: "This refers to creating harmony and trust between the higher and lower ranks before going to battle." He also quotes Wu Tzŭ: "Without harmony in the State, no military campaign can be undertaken; without harmony in the army, no battle formation can be made." In a historical romance, Sun Tzŭ is portrayed telling Wu Yuan: "In general, those who wage war must resolve all internal issues before attacking an external enemy.")

After that comes tactical maneuvering, which is more difficult than anything else.

(I've slightly adjusted the traditional interpretation of Ts'ao Kung, who says: "From the time we receive the sovereign's instructions until we set up camp opposite the enemy, the tactics are the most challenging." It seems more accurate to say that tactics and maneuvers truly begin after the army has marched out and encamped. Ch'ien Hao's note supports this view: "For recruiting, concentrating, harmonizing, and fortifying an army, there are many established rules. The real challenge comes when we start tactical operations." Tu Yu also remarks that "the greatest difficulty is in seizing favorable positions before the enemy does.")

The difficulty of tactical maneuvering lies in turning the indirect into the direct, and transforming misfortune into advantage.

(This sentence is one of Sun Tzŭ's typically condensed and somewhat cryptic expressions. Ts'ao Kung explains: "Make it seem as though you are far away, then cover the distance quickly and arrive before your opponent." Tu Mu says: "Deceive the enemy so that he becomes relaxed and slow while you advance with utmost speed." Ho

Shih offers another perspective: "Even if you have difficult terrain to cross or natural obstacles in your way, this disadvantage can be turned into an advantage through rapid movement." Famous examples include Hannibal's crossing of the Alps, which put Italy at his mercy, and Napoleon's similar feat two thousand years later, resulting in the victory at Marengo.)

Thus, taking a long and circuitous route, while luring the enemy out of position, and although starting later than him, managing to reach the goal before him, demonstrates skill in the art of deviation.

(Tu Mu references the famous march of Chao She in 270 B.C. to relieve the town of O-yu, which was under siege by a Ch'in army. The King of Chao initially sought advice from Lien P'o, who considered the distance too far and the terrain too difficult for a relief mission. However, Chao She, acknowledging the risk, boldly stated: "We will be like two rats fighting in a hole—the braver one will win!" After setting out with his army, Chao She marched only 30 li before stopping to build fortifications for 28 days, ensuring the enemy's spies would report this delay. The Ch'in general, thinking Chao She was unwilling to save a city outside Chao's direct control, relaxed. But as soon as the spies left, Chao She launched a forced march, covering two days and one night, and arrived so swiftly that he seized the advantageous North hill before the enemy knew of his movements. The result was a decisive defeat for the Ch'in, forcing them to abandon the siege and retreat.)

Maneuvering with a disciplined army is advantageous; with an undisciplined multitude, it is most dangerous.

(I adopt the reading of the T'ung Tien, Cheng Yu-hsien, and the T'u Shu for clarity. The commentators using the standard text suggest that maneuvering can be either profitable or dangerous, depending on the general's skill.)

If you march a fully equipped army to seize an advantage, chances are you will be too late. However, sending a flying column for the task often requires sacrificing baggage and supplies.

(Some of the Chinese text is unclear even to the commentators, who paraphrase it. I offer my own translation cautiously, as there seems to be some deeper corruption in the text. Nonetheless, it is apparent that Sun Tzŭ disapproves of undertaking a long march without proper supplies. See § 11 below.)

If you order your soldiers to roll up their coats and make forced marches without stopping day or night, covering twice the usual distance in one go, traveling a hundred li to gain an advantage, the leaders of all your three divisions will end up in the hands of the enemy.

The strongest men will be at the front, while the exhausted ones will fall behind, and following this plan, only one-tenth of your army will reach the destination.

The moral of this, as Ts'ao Kung and others have pointed out, is that you should not march a hundred li to gain a tactical advantage, whether with or without your baggage train. Maneuvers like this should be limited to shorter distances. Stonewall Jackson said: "The hardships of forced marches are often more painful than the dangers of battle." He rarely asked his troops for extraordinary efforts. It was only when he planned a surprise attack or when a rapid retreat was urgently needed that he sacrificed everything for speed.

If you march fifty li to outmaneuver the enemy, the leader of your first division will be lost, and only half of your army will reach the goal.

If you march thirty li for the same purpose, two-thirds of your army will arrive.

From this, we can understand how difficult tactical maneuvers can be.

An army without its baggage train is lost; without provisions, it is lost; without supply bases, it is lost.

I think Sun Tzŭ meant "stores accumulated in depots." But Tu Yu says "fodder and the like," Chang Yu says "goods in general," and Wang Hsi says "fuel, salt, foodstuffs, etc."

We cannot form alliances until we understand the plans of our neighbors.

We are not fit to lead an army on the march unless we are familiar with the terrain—its mountains and forests, its pitfalls and cliffs, its marshes and swamps.

We will not be able to take advantage of natural terrain unless we make use of local guides.

In war, practice deception, and you will succeed. In the tactics of Turenne, deceiving the enemy, especially about the number of his troops, played a very important role.

Only move when there is a real advantage to be gained.

Whether to concentrate or divide your troops must be determined by the circumstances.

Let your speed be as swift as the wind,

(The simile is especially fitting because the wind is not only fast but, as Mei Yao-ch'en notes, "invisible and leaves no trace behind.")

and your formations as dense as a forest.

(Meng Shih's comment comes closer to the meaning: "When marching slowly, order and ranks must be preserved" to guard against surprise attacks. Natural forests don't grow in rows, but they do have the quality of compactness and density.)

When raiding and plundering, be like a raging fire,

(Compare with the Shih Ching: "Fierce as a blazing fire that no one can stop.")

and when holding your position, be as immovable as a mountain.

(This applies when defending a position from which the enemy tries to dislodge you or, as Tu Yu suggests, when the enemy is trying to lure you into a trap.)

Let your plans be as dark and impenetrable as night, and when you strike, hit like a thunderbolt.

(Tu Yu quotes a proverb from T'ai Kung: "You cannot close your ears to thunder or your eyes to lightning—they are too fast." Similarly, an attack should be so swift that it cannot be countered.)

When plundering the countryside, divide the spoils among your men,

(Sun Tzǔ aims to curb the abuses of indiscriminate looting by ensuring that all booty is placed in a common stock and fairly distributed among the troops.)

and when you capture new territory, divide it into allotments for the soldiers.

(Ch'en Hao advises: "Quarter your soldiers on the land and let them sow and cultivate it." By following this principle, harvesting the land they invaded, the Chinese succeeded in carrying out some of their most memorable expeditions, such as Pan Ch'ao's march to the Caspian, and, in more recent times, the campaigns of Fu-k'ang-an and Tso Tsung-t'ang.)

Think carefully and plan before taking any action.

(Chang Yu quotes Wei Liao Tzǔ, saying that we should not leave our camp until we understand the enemy's strength and the intelligence of their general. See the "seven comparisons" mentioned earlier.)

The one who masters the art of deception will win.

(Refer to previous sections for more on this.)

This is the essence of maneuvering.

(These words would naturally end the section, but what follows is an excerpt from an older book on war, which no longer exists but was still known during Sun Tzǔ's time. The style of the passage isn't noticeably different from Sun Tzǔ's own writing, and no commentators question its authenticity.)

The Book of Army Management says:

(It's worth noting that earlier commentators don't provide much information about this book. Mei Yao-ch'en calls it "an ancient military classic," and Wang Hsi refers to it as "an old book on war." Considering the centuries of warfare between different kingdoms in China before Sun Tzŭ's time, it's likely that military wisdom had already been written down in earlier times.)

On the battlefield,

(This is implied but not directly stated in the text.)

spoken commands don't carry far enough, so gongs and drums were introduced. Similarly, normal objects can't be seen clearly in the chaos, which is why banners and flags are used.

Gongs and drums, banners and flags, are used to focus the ears and eyes of the army on a single point.

(Chang Yu explains: "When sight and hearing are concentrated on the same object, the movements of as many as a million soldiers will be as coordinated as those of a single man.")

When the army forms a united body, it becomes impossible for the brave to advance alone or for the cowardly to retreat alone.

(Chuang Yu quotes: "Equally guilty are those who advance without orders and those who retreat without orders." Tu Mu tells a story of Wu Ch'i, who was fighting the Ch'in State. Before the battle began, one of his soldiers, renowned for his daring, went out on his own, captured two enemy heads, and returned to camp. Wu Ch'i had the man executed immediately. When an officer protested, saying, "This man was a good soldier and shouldn't have been beheaded," Wu Ch'i replied, "I know he was a good soldier, but I had him executed because he acted without orders.")

This is the art of managing large masses of men.

In night fighting, use signal fires and drums, and in daytime battles, use flags and banners to influence the ears and eyes of your soldiers.

(Ch'en Hao mentions Li Kuang-pi's night march to Ho-yang with 500 mounted men. They made such an impressive display with torches that the rebel leader Shih Ssu-ming, despite having a large army, didn't dare oppose their passage.)

An entire army can be robbed of its spirit.

(Chang Yu says: "In war, if a spirit of anger can fill the entire army at once, its attack will be unstoppable. The enemy's soldiers will be most eager when they first arrive, so we should not fight right away. Instead, we should wait until their enthusiasm fades before striking. This is how their spirit can be taken from them." Li Ch'uan and others tell a story from the Tso Chuan about Ts'ao Kuei, an advisor to Duke Chuang of Lu. When Lu was attacked by Ch'i, the duke prepared to fight at Ch'ang-cho after hearing the enemy's first drumbeat. Ts'ao said, "Not yet." Only after the enemy's drums sounded a third time did he give the order to attack. The army of Ch'i was defeated. When asked why he delayed, Ts'ao Kuei explained: "In battle, a courageous spirit is everything. The first drumbeat raises this spirit, but with the second it weakens, and by the third it's gone. I attacked when their spirit was gone and ours was at its peak." Wu Tzŭ lists "spirit" as the first of the "four important influences" in war, adding, "The value of an entire army—a mighty host of a million men—depends on one person: such is the power of spirit!")

A commander-in-chief can also lose his presence of mind.

(Chang Yu notes: "Presence of mind is the most vital quality for a general. It enables him to restore order from chaos and give courage to those who are panicking." The great general Li Ching once said, "Attacking does not simply mean assaulting walled cities or striking an army in battle. It also involves shaking the enemy's mental balance.")

A soldier's spirit is at its highest in the morning,

(As long as he has had breakfast, I suppose. At the Battle of the Trebia, the Romans made the mistake of fighting on an empty stomach, while Hannibal's men ate at their leisure. See Livy, XXI, liv. 8, lv. 1 and 8.)

by noon, it starts to fade; and by evening, his only thought is to return to camp.

A wise general, therefore, avoids fighting an army when its spirit is high, but attacks when it is sluggish and ready to retreat. This is the art of studying moods.

To remain disciplined and calm while waiting for disorder and confusion to arise among the enemy: this is the art of maintaining self-possession.

To be close to the goal while the enemy is still far, to wait in comfort while the enemy struggles, to be well-fed while the enemy is hungry: this is the art of conserving strength.

To refrain from attacking an enemy whose banners are in perfect order, or from engaging an army that is calm and confident: this is the art of understanding circumstances.

It is a basic military principle not to advance uphill against the enemy, nor to confront him when he is descending.

Do not chase an enemy who pretends to flee; do not engage soldiers whose spirits are high.

Do not take a bait offered by the enemy.

(Li Ch'uan and Tu Mu, showing a surprising lack of insight, take this literally as food or drink that might be poisoned by the enemy. Ch'en Hao and Chang Yu point out that the saying applies more broadly.)

Do not obstruct an army that is returning home.

(The commentators explain that a soldier whose heart is set on returning home will fight with extreme determination against anyone who tries to stop him, making him too dangerous to oppose. Chang Yu quotes Han Hsin: "Unbeatable is the soldier who desires nothing but to return home." A remarkable story is told of Ts'ao Ts'ao's resourcefulness in San Kuo Chi, chapter 1. In 198 A.D., Ts'ao was besieging Chang Hsiu in Jang, when Liu Piao sent reinforcements to cut off his retreat. Ts'ao was forced to withdraw but found himself trapped between two enemies guarding each exit of a narrow pass. In this desperate situation, he waited until nightfall, dug a tunnel into the mountainside, and set an ambush. Once the entire enemy army had passed, Ts'ao's hidden troops attacked from behind, while he turned to confront them from the front, throwing them into chaos and defeating them. Ts'ao later remarked, "The bandits tried to stop my retreat and forced me into a desperate fight; that's how I knew how to defeat them.")

When you surround an army, leave an opening for escape.

(This doesn't mean you should let the enemy flee. The purpose, as Tu Mu explains, is to make the enemy believe there is a way to escape, preventing them from fighting with the desperation of those with no hope. As Tu Mu adds, "Once they believe they have a way out, you can then crush them.")

Do not press a desperate enemy too hard.

(Ch'en Hao cites the saying: "When birds and beasts are cornered, they will use their claws and teeth." Chang Yu advises: "If your enemy has burned his boats and destroyed his cooking pots, fully committed to the outcome of the battle, you must not push them to the extreme." Ho Shih illustrates this with a story about the general Fu Yen-ch'ing. In 945 A.D., he and his colleague Tu Chung-wei were surrounded by a much larger Khitan army in a barren, desert-like area. Their small Chinese force was suffering due to a lack of water. The wells they dug ran dry, and the soldiers were reduced to squeezing moisture from lumps of mud. Their numbers dwindled rapidly, and Fu Yen-ch'ing declared, "We are desperate men. It is better to die for our country than to be taken captive with our hands tied." A strong wind was blowing from the northeast, filling the air with dense clouds of sand. Tu Chung-wei wanted to wait for the storm to pass before launching their final attack, but another officer, Li Shou-cheng, saw an opportunity and said, "They are many, and we are few, but in this sandstorm, our numbers won't be clear. Victory will go to those who fight hardest, and the wind will be our ally." Fu Yen-ch'ing then led a sudden and unexpected cavalry charge, routing the barbarians and breaking through to safety.)

Chapter 8 - Variation of Tactics

The heading literally means "The Nine Variations," but since Sun Tzŭ doesn't enumerate them specifically and has already stated (V §§ 6-11) that deviations in strategy are practically limitless, we are inclined to agree with Wang Hsi, who explains that "Nine" represents an indefinitely large number. It simply means that in warfare, tactics should be varied to the greatest extent possible. I am unsure how Ts'ao Kung interprets these Nine Variations, but it's suggested they are related to the Nine Situations discussed in chapter XI. This view is also supported by Chang Yu. Another possibility is that something has been lost, which is suggested by the unusual brevity of the chapter.

Sun Tzŭ said: In war, the general receives his commands from the sovereign, assembles his army, and concentrates his forces.

(This is repeated from VII. § 1, where it fits better. It may have been included here simply to provide a start for the chapter.)

When in difficult terrain, do not set up camp. In areas where main roads intersect, join hands with your allies. Do not remain in dangerously isolated positions.

(This situation is not one of the Nine Situations listed in the beginning of chapter XI, but it does appear later on (§ 43). Chang Yu defines it as being located across the border in enemy territory. Li Ch'uan says it refers to land where there are no springs, wells, flocks, or firewood. Chia Lin describes it as a region of gorges, cliffs, and steep terrain with no clear roads forward.)

In situations where you are trapped, rely on strategy. In a desperate position, you must fight.

There are roads that should not be followed,

(Li Ch'uan says this applies especially to narrow passes where ambushes are likely.)

armies that must not be attacked,

(It might be more accurate to say "there are times when an army should not be attacked." Ch'en Hao explains: "When you have an opportunity for a small advantage but cannot achieve a decisive victory, it is better not to attack, to avoid exhausting your troops.")

towns that should not be besieged,

(Compare III. § 4. Ts'ao Kung shares an example from his own experience. While invading Hsu-chou, he bypassed the city of Hua-pi, which lay in his path, and advanced deeper into the country. This strategy paid off with the capture of fourteen key cities. Chang Yu advises: "Do not attack a town that, even if captured, cannot be held or, if left alone, will not pose a threat." Hsun Ying, when urged to attack Pi-yang, responded: "The city is small and well-fortified; even if I succeed in taking it, it won't be a great achievement, but if I fail, I will be ridiculed." Sieges made up a significant part of warfare in the seventeenth century, but Turenne emphasized the value of marches, countermarches, and maneuvers. He remarked, "It is a great error to waste soldiers on capturing a town when the same effort could win an entire province.")

positions that should not be contested, and commands from the sovereign that should not be obeyed.

(This is difficult for the Chinese, given their strong respect for authority. Wei Liao Tzǔ, as quoted by Tu Mu, states: "Weapons are instruments of evil, conflict opposes virtue, and a military commander stands against civil order." Nonetheless, the reality remains that even the emperor's wishes must yield to military necessity.)

The general who thoroughly understands the advantages that come from varying tactics knows how to manage his troops.

The general who does not grasp these advantages, even if he is well aware of the terrain, will not be able to make effective use of his knowledge.

(Literally, "to get the advantage of the ground," meaning not only securing favorable positions but also making the most of natural advantages in every way possible. Chang Yu explains: "Every kind of terrain has its own natural features and also offers room for variation in plans. How can these natural features be used to their full potential unless topographical knowledge is combined with a flexible mind?")

Thus, a student of war who has not mastered the art of varying his strategies, even if he knows the Five Advantages, will fail to make the best use of his soldiers.

(Chia Lin explains that these Five Advantages refer to obvious and generally beneficial courses of action, such as: "if a road is short, it should be taken; if an army is isolated, it should be attacked; if a town is in a precarious state, it should be besieged; if a position can be stormed, it should be attempted; and if consistent with military operations, the ruler's orders should be obeyed." However, there are circumstances in which these advantages may not be used. For instance, "a certain road may be the shortest route, but if it is filled with natural obstacles or if the enemy has laid an ambush there, it should not be followed. A hostile force may be vulnerable to attack, but if it is desperate and ready to fight to the last, it is better not to strike.")

Therefore, in the wise leader's plans, considerations of both advantage and disadvantage are combined.

("Whether in an advantageous or disadvantageous situation," says Ts'ao Kung, "the opposite state should always be kept in mind.")

If we balance our expectation of advantage with awareness of possible disadvantages, we may successfully accomplish the most important part of our plans.

(Tu Mu comments: "If we want to gain an advantage over the enemy, we must not focus only on that goal. We must also consider the possibility of the enemy inflicting harm on us and include that in our calculations.")

If, on the other hand, we are always ready to seize an advantage even in difficult situations, we can free ourselves from misfortune.

(Tu Mu explains: "If I want to escape from a dangerous position, I must not only consider the enemy's ability to harm me but also my own ability to gain an advantage over them. If my plans balance both considerations, I will succeed in getting out of danger. For example, if I am surrounded by the enemy and only focus on escaping, the weakness of my strategy will encourage the enemy to pursue and crush me. It would be much better to encourage my troops to launch a bold counterattack and use the advantage gained to break free from the enemy's grasp." See the story of Ts'ao Ts'ao in VII. § 35, note.)

Reduce the enemy's leaders by causing harm to them.

(Chia Lin lists several ways to harm the enemy, some of which are quite unique: "Entice away the enemy's best and wisest men, leaving him without good advisors. Plant traitors in his country to disrupt government policies. Stir up intrigue and deceit, sowing discord between the ruler and his ministers. Use cunning tricks to weaken his men and drain his resources. Corrupt his morals with insidious gifts that lead him into indulgence. Unsettle his mind by presenting him with beautiful women." Chang Yu, following Wang Hsi, offers a different interpretation: "Force the enemy into a position where he is bound to suffer harm, and he will eventually submit on his own.")

Create difficulties for them,

(Tu Mu explains that this phrase means to create problems that affect the enemy's "assets"—things like a large army, a rich treasury, harmony among soldiers, and the consistent execution of orders. These are what give us leverage over the enemy.)

and keep them constantly occupied.

(Literally, "make servants of them." Tu Yu says: "Deny them any opportunity to rest.")

Offer deceptive attractions and lure them into rushing to a specific point.

(Meng Shih provides a great example of this idiom: "Make them forget pien (the reasons for acting cautiously) and hasten in our direction.")

The art of war teaches us to depend not on the chance that the enemy will not come, but on our own readiness to meet him; not on the hope that he won't attack, but on the certainty that we have made our position unassailable.

There are five dangerous flaws that may affect a general:

(1) Recklessness, which leads to destruction.

("Bravery without forethought," as Ts'ao Kung puts it, causes a man to fight blindly, like a mad bull. Chang Yu says, "Such an opponent should not be met with brute force but can be lured into an ambush and killed." Wu Tzŭ also points out that too much emphasis is often placed on a general's courage, forgetting that courage is just one of the qualities a general should have. A brave man who fights recklessly, without understanding what is truly advantageous, must be condemned. Ssu-ma Fa adds that "simply rushing to one's death does not guarantee victory.")

(2) Cowardice, which leads to capture.

(Ts'ao Kung explains that the word "cowardice" refers to someone "who is too timid to advance and seize an advantage." Wang Hsi adds that it describes someone who flees at the first sight of danger. Meng Shih gives a more detailed interpretation: "He is focused on surviving at all costs," meaning someone who avoids taking risks. But, as Sun Tzŭ knew, success in war often requires risk. T'ai Kung noted: "He who lets an advantage slip will eventually face real disaster." In 404 A.D., Liu Yu chased the rebel Huan Hsuan up the Yangtsze River. Though Liu Yu's forces were much smaller, Huan Hsuan, fearing the consequences of defeat, prepared a small boat attached to his warship for a quick escape. This lack of resolve destroyed his soldiers' morale. When the loyalists launched a determined attack using fireships, Huan Hsuan's forces were completely routed. They had to burn all their supplies and fled for two days without stopping. Chang Yu also tells a similar story of Chao Ying-ch'i, a general of the Chin State, who kept a boat ready during a battle with the Ch'u army in 597 B.C., so he could escape first if defeated.)

(3) A quick temper, which can be provoked by insults.

(Tu Mu tells the story of Yao Hsing, who in 357 A.D. was opposed by Huang Mei, Teng Ch'iang, and others. Yao Hsing shut himself inside his walls, refusing to engage. Teng Ch'iang, knowing Yao's fiery temper, suggested launching constant attacks to provoke him. He believed that Yao, once angered, would come out to fight. This strategy worked—Yao Hsiang left his defenses, was drawn into a trap as far as San-yuan by the enemy's fake retreat, and was ultimately defeated and killed.)

A delicate sense of honor that is easily wounded by shame is another potential fault.

This doesn't mean that a sense of honor is a flaw in a general. What Sun Tzŭ criticizes is being overly sensitive to slander or criticism, the kind of person who is too easily hurt by insults, even when they are undeserved. Mei Yao-ch'en wisely notes, though it may sound contradictory: "Those who seek glory should not worry too much about public opinion."

The fifth fault is being too concerned for the well-being of his men, which causes unnecessary worry and trouble.

Again, Sun Tzŭ isn't suggesting that a general should neglect the welfare of his soldiers. He simply means that focusing too much on their comfort can lead to poor decisions and lost opportunities. This short-term thinking can ultimately cause greater suffering for the troops in the long run because defeat, or a longer war, will be the result. A misguided sense of pity can lead a general to make choices that go against his better judgment, such as relieving a city under siege or sending reinforcements to a detachment under heavy pressure. In the South African War, it's now accepted that our repeated attempts to relieve Ladysmith were strategic errors that failed to achieve their goal. In the end, it was the general who decided to stop letting sentiment for a small part of the army override the needs of the whole who finally succeeded. I recall an old soldier trying to defend one of our generals, who had notably failed during this war, by saying that he was "so kind to his men." In saying this, though he didn't realize it, he was actually condemning the general according to Sun Tzŭ's principles.

These are the five dangerous flaws in a general, which can ruin the conduct of war.

When an army is defeated and its leader is killed, the cause can almost always be traced back to one of these five flaws. Keep them in mind.

Chapter 9 - The Army on The March

Sun Tzu said: Now we turn to the important task of setting up camp and keeping a close eye on the enemy. When traveling through mountainous areas, it's important to move quickly across the mountains and stay near the valleys.

(This is because the dry, barren highlands can leave your troops without enough food or water. It's better to stay near places where water and grass are plentiful. Wu Tzu, an ancient military strategist, once said, "Don't camp in natural ovens," which means avoiding the entrances of valleys where the heat can become unbearable and where you could easily be trapped. Chang Yu provides a historical example: During the Later Han dynasty, a bandit named Wu-tu Ch'iang hid his troops in the hills. Instead of attacking directly, General Ma Yuan, who was sent to capture him, took control of the areas with water and other supplies. Ch'iang's troops soon ran out of provisions because they hadn't secured the valleys. With no access to resources, they were eventually forced to surrender.)

When choosing a campsite, always pick slightly higher ground.

(This doesn't mean the highest mountain peaks, but rather low hills that give you an advantage over the surrounding area. High ground lets you see the battlefield more easily and makes your camp less vulnerable to surprise attacks.)

It is also important to set up your camp so that it faces the sun.

(Some commentators, like Tu Mu, believed this meant facing south, while others, like Ch'en Hao, thought it meant facing east. Either way, the idea is that facing the sun gives your camp better visibility and warmth, making it more comfortable and easier to defend.)

In mountain warfare, one of the key rules is to never climb uphill to attack the enemy. It's better to hold the high ground and force the enemy to come to you. After crossing a river, always move away from it quickly.

(Ts'ao Kung explained this as a strategy to lure the enemy into crossing the river after you, where they will be more vulnerable. Chang Yu added that moving away from the river ensures that you have the freedom to maneuver, preventing the enemy from blocking your retreat or cutting off your supply lines.)

If the enemy is crossing a river, don't attack them while they're in the middle of the crossing. Wait until half of their forces have crossed, then strike.

(Li Ch'uan refers to Han Hsin's famous victory over Lung Chu at the Wei River as an example of this tactic. Han Hsin's forces built a dam upstream at night and crossed the river to fake a retreat. Lung Chu, thinking Han Hsin's army was retreating in defeat, followed him across the river. At that moment, Han Hsin's troops broke the dam, sending a flood downstream that cut off Lung Chu's army. In the resulting chaos, Han Hsin's forces attacked decisively, killing Lung Chu and routing his army.)

If you're preparing to fight near a river the enemy hasn't crossed yet, don't position your troops too close to the river.

(Doing so could give the enemy the chance to plan a better crossing or force you into a defensive position when you could have set up an ambush instead.)

If you're stationed near a river, make sure to place your boats upstream from the enemy, and always keep your camp facing the sun.

(As mentioned before, being upstream gives you a tactical advantage, allowing you to control the flow of water. This applies whether your forces are on the riverbank or in boats. Facing the sun provides better visibility and can also give you a psychological advantage.)

Never move upstream to meet the enemy.

(Tu Mu warns that, since water flows downward, camping in a lower position is dangerous because the enemy could flood the river or poison the water and send it downstream to your camp. Chu-ko Wu-hou also advised against moving against the current in river warfare, as this would allow the enemy to use the natural flow of the river to their advantage.)

When it comes to river warfare, that's all you need to keep in mind. However, when crossing salt marshes, your only goal should be to get through them as quickly as possible.

(Salt marshes are inhospitable. They have little fresh water, the grass is scarce and not nutritious for animals, and the flat, open terrain leaves your forces vulnerable to attack.)

If you must fight in a salt marsh, camp near a source of fresh water and grass, and position your back against a group of trees.

(Li Ch'uan mentions that trees can signal safer ground, while Tu Mu points out that trees can protect your rear and reduce the chances of a surprise attack from the enemy.)

This concludes the rules for fighting in salt marshes. When fighting on flat, dry land, choose a position that is easy to access, with slightly rising ground on your right and behind you.

(Tu Mu quotes T'ai Kung, who recommended positioning your army with a stream or marsh on the left and a hill on the right. This setup offers natural defenses and strategic advantages.)

By following this rule, you will have danger in front of you and safety behind. This concludes the guidelines for warfare on flat land.

These principles of terrain management are the four essential branches of military strategy: (1) mountains, (2) rivers, (3) marshes, and (4) plains. Understanding these principles helped the Yellow Emperor defeat four kings.

(Some scholars question whether the Yellow Emperor truly defeated four kings, as historical records like the Shih Chi only mention his victories over Yen Ti and Ch'ih Yu. However, the Liu T'ao suggests he fought and won seventy battles, ultimately uniting the empire. Ts'ao Kung speculates that the Yellow Emperor established a feudal system with four princes holding the title of emperor. Meanwhile, Li Ch'uan believes that the art of war began with the Yellow Emperor, who learned it from his wise minister, Feng Hou.)

All armies prefer to occupy high ground rather than low ground because high ground offers advantages for both health and combat. Low ground, on the other hand, is often damp and unhealthy for troops.

(Ts'ao Kung advises generals to prioritize finding fresh water and good pasture for their animals to maintain the health and well-being of their forces.)

When choosing a campsite, look for hard, dry ground. This will help keep your soldiers healthy and reduce the risk of illness.

(Chang Yu adds that dry conditions help prevent diseases from spreading, which can be as dangerous as any enemy.)

Whenever possible, position yourself on the sunny side of a hill or slope, with the incline behind you and to your right. This will benefit your soldiers and allow you to make the best use of the natural terrain.

After heavy rains in higher regions, if you encounter a swollen river covered with foam, you must wait for the water to recede before attempting to cross.

Avoid areas with steep cliffs, narrow passes, or deep gorges with fast-flowing streams. These are natural traps—easy to enter but difficult to escape from. Places surrounded by steep banks or filled with water at the bottom should be avoided at all costs, as they are like natural prisons where you could easily be trapped.

(Dense forests with thick undergrowth, where spears cannot be used, should also be avoided, as well as quagmires and other soft ground that makes it difficult for chariots or horsemen to pass.)

While you should avoid such places, try to lead the enemy into them. If you face the enemy in such terrain, position them so that the natural obstacles are behind them, limiting their ability to maneuver.

If your camp is near hilly terrain, ponds surrounded by tall grasses, or woods with dense undergrowth, these areas must be thoroughly searched, as they are ideal hiding spots for enemy spies or ambushes.

When the enemy is nearby but remains still, it is a sign they are relying on the natural strength of their position. When they are distant and try to provoke a battle, they are likely trying to lure you out of your defensive position and into a trap.

If the enemy's camp seems easy to approach, be cautious—it may be a trap. Movement among trees in a forest is a sign that the enemy is advancing, likely cutting down trees to clear a path for their troops.

Birds suddenly taking flight may indicate an ambush. Startled animals could signal an impending attack.

If dust rises in a high column, it means chariots are approaching. If the dust is lower and spread out, infantry is on the move. Dust that moves in several directions suggests soldiers are gathering firewood, while small amounts of dust moving back and forth indicate the army is setting up camp.

When the enemy uses humble words but increases their preparations, it's a sign they are planning an attack. They may be pretending to be weak to make you feel secure.

If the enemy's camp looks humble but their preparations are intensifying, they are likely preparing for an assault. In one case, an army tried to demoralize its enemy by mutilating prisoners and desecrating graves, but this only strengthened the defenders' resolve.

The defenders launched a clever counterattack by sending oxen with burning torches tied to their tails into the enemy's camp, causing chaos and helping them reclaim lost cities.

Aggressive words and forward movements often mean the enemy is preparing to retreat.

When light chariots are positioned on the flanks, it signals the enemy is getting ready for battle.

Peace offers that come without a sworn agreement usually signal a trap.

If the enemy's soldiers are running about and quickly forming up, the decisive moment is near.

If some soldiers advance while others retreat, it is likely a trick designed to confuse and mislead you.

Soldiers leaning on their spears are likely weak from hunger, and if they drink water immediately after getting it, the army is suffering from thirst.

If the enemy hesitates to act even when given an opportunity, it is a sign their troops are exhausted.

If birds are gathering in a specific area, it means that spot is unoccupied.

Noise at night suggests the enemy is anxious, while disorder in their camp indicates the general has lost control.

If the enemy's banners are being moved around frequently, it could mean there is rebellion in the ranks. Anger among the officers suggests that the soldiers are worn out.

When an army begins feeding its horses with grain, slaughtering cattle for food, and not hanging up its cooking pots, it means they are prepared to fight to the death.

When soldiers whisper in small groups, it indicates unrest in the ranks. Frequent rewards suggest the enemy is running low on resources, while excessive punishments point to severe internal problems.

If a general talks boldly but then hesitates out of fear of the enemy's numbers, it reveals a lack of intelligence. When envoys come with polite words, it usually means the enemy is seeking a truce.

If the enemy's troops stand facing yours for a long time without fighting or retreating, they may be preparing a surprise attack. Stay alert.

If your forces are roughly equal to the enemy's, you should be able to hold your position, but attacking head-on would be risky. Instead, gather your strength, watch the enemy closely, and wait for reinforcements.

A leader who underestimates the enemy and doesn't plan ahead will ultimately be defeated.

Punishing soldiers before they are loyal to you will lead to disobedience. However, if they are not disciplined after they become loyal, they will be ineffective in battle.

That's why it's important to first treat soldiers with kindness, then later enforce strict discipline. This is the path to victory.

If commands are enforced consistently, the army will be disciplined. If not, the soldiers will become disorderly. A general who trusts his men while making sure his orders are followed will strengthen both his leadership and his army.

Chapter 10 - Terrain

Sun Tzŭ said: We can identify six kinds of terrain:

(1) Accessible ground;

(Mei Yao-ch'en explains this as ground that is well-supplied with roads and ways of communication.)

(2) Entangling ground;

(Mei Yao-ch'en describes this as "net-like" terrain, where if you enter, you may become entangled.)

(3) Temporizing ground;

(This is ground where you can delay or hold off.)

(4) Narrow passes; (5) Steep heights; (6) Positions far from the enemy.

(It is hardly necessary to point out the issues with this classification. There is a strange lack of logical reasoning in the unquestioning acceptance of these overlapping categories.)

Ground that both sides can freely move across is called accessible.

On this type of terrain, you should arrive before the enemy, take the higher, sunnier spots, and carefully guard your supply lines.

(The general meaning of this last phrase, as Tu Yu explains, is "not to allow the enemy to cut your communications." In view of Napoleon's statement, "the secret of war lies in the communications," it would have been helpful if Sun Tzŭ had elaborated more on this important subject here and in other sections. Col. Henderson says: "The line of supply is as vital to the life of an army as the heart is to a human being. Just as a duelist who finds his opponent's weapon threatening his life and his own guard out of place must adjust to his opponent's movements, the commander whose communications are suddenly threatened finds himself in a bad position. He may be forced to change all his plans, divide his forces into isolated groups, and fight with fewer troops on unprepared ground. In such a situation, defeat could mean the ruin or surrender of his entire army.")

If you follow these steps, you will be able to fight with an advantage.

Ground which can be abandoned but is hard to re-occupy is called entangling ground.

From a position of this sort, if the enemy is unprepared, you may sally forth and defeat him. But if the enemy is prepared for your coming, and you fail to defeat him, then, return being impossible, disaster will ensue.

When the position is such that neither side will gain by making the first move, it is called temporizing ground.

(Tu Mu says: "Each side finds it inconvenient to move, and the situation remains at a deadlock.")

In a position of this sort, even though the enemy should offer us an attractive bait,

(Tu Yu says, "turning their backs on us and pretending to flee." But this is only one of the lures which might induce us to quit our position.)

it will be advisable not to stir forth, but rather to retreat, thus enticing the enemy in his turn; then, when part of his army has come out, we may deliver our attack with advantage.

With regard to narrow passes, if you can occupy them first, let them be strongly garrisoned and await the advent of the enemy.

(Because then, as Tu Yu observes, "the initiative will lie with us, and by making sudden and unexpected attacks we shall have the enemy at our mercy.")

Should the enemy forestall you in occupying a pass, do not go after him if the pass is fully garrisoned, but only if it is weakly garrisoned.

With regard to precipitous heights, if you are beforehand with your adversary, you should occupy the raised and sunny spots, and there wait for him to come up.

(Ts'ao Kung says: "The particular advantage of securing heights and defiles is that your actions cannot then be dictated by the enemy." [For the enunciation of the grand principle alluded to, see VI. § 2]. Chang Yu tells the following anecdote of P'ei Hsing-chien (A.D. 619-682), who was sent on a punitive expedition against the Turkic tribes. "At night he pitched his camp as usual, and it had already been completely fortified by wall and ditch, when suddenly he gave orders that the army should shift its quarters to a hill nearby. This was highly displeasing to his officers, who protested loudly against the extra fatigue which it would entail on the men. P'ei Hsing-chien, however, paid no heed to their remonstrances and had the camp moved as quickly as possible. The same night, a terrific storm came on, which flooded their former place of encampment to the depth of over twelve feet. The recalcitrant officers were amazed at the sight and owned that they had been in the wrong. 'How did you know what was going to happen?' they asked. P'ei Hsing-chien replied: 'From this time forward be content to obey orders without asking unnecessary questions.' From this it may be seen," Chang Yu continues, "that high and sunny places are advantageous not only for fighting, but also because they are immune from disastrous floods.")

If the enemy has occupied the high ground before you, do not pursue him, but instead retreat and try to lure him away.

(Li Shih-min's turning point in his campaign in 621 A.D. against the rebels Tou Chien-te, King of Hsia, and Wang Shih-ch'ung, Prince of Cheng, was his capture of the heights of Wu-lao. Despite this, Tou Chien-te still tried to help his ally in Lo-yang and was defeated and captured. See Chiu T'ang Shu, ch. 2, fol. 5 verso, and also ch. 54.)

If you are far from the enemy and the strength of both armies is equal, it is not easy to provoke a battle,

(The key is that you shouldn't undertake a long, tiring march, which would leave you exhausted while the enemy remains fresh and alert, as Tu Yu explains.)

and fighting in such conditions will put you at a disadvantage.

These six are the principles related to the terrain.

(Or, "principles relating to the ground." See I. § 8.)

A general in a position of responsibility must carefully study them.

Now, an army can face six different calamities, not due to natural causes, but because of the general's mistakes. These are: (1) Flight; (2) Insubordination; (3) Collapse; (4) Ruin; (5) Disorganization; (6) Rout.

If one force is thrown against another ten times its size, the outcome will be the flight of the smaller force.

When the common soldiers are too strong, and their officers are too weak, the result is insubordination.

(Tu Mu refers to the case of T'ien Pu [Hsin T'ang Shu, ch. 148], who was sent to Wei in 821 A.D. to lead an army against Wang T'ing-ts'ou. While he was in command, his soldiers treated him with disdain, openly disrespecting him by riding donkeys around the camp in large numbers. T'ien Pu couldn't control this behavior, and when he finally tried to engage the enemy, his troops scattered in all directions. Afterward, he tragically committed suicide.)

When the officers are too strong and the common soldiers too weak, the result is collapse.

(Ts'ao Kung says: "The officers are eager to advance, but the soldiers are weak and suddenly collapse.")

When higher-ranking officers act out of anger and fight the enemy on their own initiative, without waiting for the commander-in-chief to assess whether they are ready for battle, the result is ruin.

(Wang Hsi comments: "This refers to a general who becomes angry without reason and fails to recognize the capabilities of his subordinate officers. This leads to intense resentment and ultimately brings disaster upon him.")

When the general is weak and lacks authority, and when his orders are not clear or precise,

(Wei Liao Tzŭ in chapter 4 says: "If the commander gives his orders decisively, the soldiers will not need to hear them twice. If his actions are carried out without hesitation, the soldiers will not have doubts about following them." General Baden-Powell also emphasizes, saying: "The key to getting good results from your trained men lies in clear instructions." Wu Tzŭ, in chapter 3, adds: "The worst flaw in a military leader is indecision; the greatest disasters in an army come from hesitation.")

when officers and men are not given specific duties,

(Tu Mu explains: "Neither the officers nor the soldiers have any set routines.")

and when the troops are assembled in a careless and disorganized manner, the result is complete chaos.

When a general fails to properly assess the enemy's strength and sends a smaller force against a much larger one, or orders a weak unit to engage a stronger force without placing the best soldiers at the front, the outcome will be a disastrous defeat.

(Chang Yu explains this by saying: "Whenever there is fighting, the most determined soldiers should be placed at the front, both to inspire confidence in our own troops and to intimidate the enemy." This concept aligns with Caesar's use of the primi ordines in "De Bello Gallico," V. 28, 44, and elsewhere.)

These are six ways to invite defeat, and they must be carefully observed by any general who holds a position of responsibility.

(See earlier discussion in § 13.)

The natural landscape is the soldier's greatest ally;

(Ch'en Hao notes: "The advantages of weather and timing are not as significant as those related to the terrain.")

but the ability to assess the enemy, control the factors that lead to victory, and accurately judge difficulties, dangers, and distances is what defines a truly great general.

He who knows these principles and in fighting puts his knowledge into practice, will win his battles. He who knows them not, nor practises them, will surely be defeated.

If fighting is sure to result in victory, then you must fight, even though the ruler forbids it; if fighting will not result in victory, then you must not fight even at the ruler's bidding.

(Chang Yu also quotes the saying: "Decrees from the Son of Heaven do not penetrate the walls of a camp." Huang Shih-kung of the Ch'in dynasty, who is said to have been the patron of Chang Liang and to have written the San Lueh, has these words attributed to him: "The responsibility of setting an army in motion must devolve on the general alone; if advance and retreat are controlled from the Palace, brilliant results will hardly be achieved. Hence the god-like ruler and the enlightened monarch are content to play a humble part in furthering their country's cause [literally, kneel down to push the chariot wheel]." This means that "in matters lying outside the zenana, the decision of the military commander must be absolute.")

The general who advances without coveting fame and retreats without fearing disgrace,

(It was Wellington, I think, who said that the hardest thing of all for a soldier is to retreat.)

whose only thought is to protect his country and do good service for his sovereign, is the jewel of the kingdom.

(A noble presentiment, in few words, of the Chinese "happy warrior." Such a man, says Ho Shih, "even if he had to suffer punishment, would not regret his conduct.")

Regard your soldiers as your children, and they will follow you into the deepest valleys; look on them as your own beloved sons, and they will stand by you even unto death.

(Cf. I. § 6. In this connection, Tu Mu draws for us an engaging picture of the famous general Wu Ch'i, from whose treatise on war I have frequently had occasion to quote: "He wore the same clothes and ate the same food as the meanest of his soldiers, refused to have either a horse to ride or a mat to sleep on, carried his own surplus rations wrapped in a parcel, and shared every hardship with his men. One of his soldiers was suffering from an abscess, and Wu Ch'i himself sucked out the virus. The soldier's mother, hearing this, began wailing and lamenting. Somebody asked her, saying: 'Why do you cry? Your son is only a common soldier, and yet the commander-in-chief himself has sucked the poison from his sore.' The woman replied, 'Many years ago, Lord Wu performed a similar service for my husband, who never left him afterwards, and finally met his death at the hands of the enemy. And now that he has done the same for my son, he too will fall fighting I know not where.'")

Li Ch'uan mentions the Viscount of Ch'u, who invaded the small state of Hsiao during the winter. The Duke of Shen said to him: "Many of the soldiers are suffering severely from the cold." So he made a round of the whole army, comforting and encouraging the men; and straightway they felt as if they were clothed in garments lined with floss silk.

If, however, you are lenient but unable to assert your authority; kind-hearted but unable to enforce your commands; and also incapable of maintaining order, then your soldiers will be like spoiled children—they will be useless in any real situation.

[Li Ching once said that if you could make your soldiers fear you, they wouldn't be afraid of the enemy. Tu Mu recounts a strict example of military discipline from 219 A.D., when Lu Meng was holding the town of Chiang-ling. He had ordered his army not to bother the local people or take anything from them by force. However, one officer under his command, who happened to be from the same town, took a bamboo hat from a villager to wear over his helmet in the rain. Despite being a fellow townsman, Lu Meng didn't excuse the breach of discipline. He ordered the officer's execution, though tears fell down his face as he gave the command. This strict action instilled a healthy sense of fear in the army, and from that point on, even items left in the road were not touched.]

If we know our own men are ready to attack but don't know that the enemy is not vulnerable to attack, we've only come halfway to victory.

[As Ts'ao Kung says, "in this case, the outcome is uncertain."]

If we know the enemy is vulnerable but don't realize that our own men aren't ready to attack, we've again only come halfway to victory.

If we know the enemy is vulnerable, and we know our men are ready to attack, but we don't realize that the terrain makes fighting impossible, we're still only halfway to victory.

Hence, the seasoned soldier, once on the move, is never confused; once he breaks camp, he is never lost.

[According to Tu Mu, this is because he has planned everything so thoroughly that victory is ensured before any action is taken. Chang Yu adds, "He doesn't act rashly, so when he does move, he makes no mistakes."]

Thus the saying goes: If you know the enemy and know yourself, you won't have to worry about the outcome of a hundred battles; if you know both Heaven and Earth, your victory will be complete.

[Li Ch'uan concludes: "If you understand three things—the affairs of men, the seasons of Heaven, and the natural advantages of Earth—, you will always win your battles."]

Chapter 11 - The Nine Situations

Sun Tzu said: The art of war recognizes nine types of ground: (1) Dispersive ground; (2) facile ground; (3) contentious ground; (4) open ground; (5) ground of intersecting highways; (6) serious ground; (7) difficult ground; (8) hemmed-in ground; (9) desperate ground.

When a leader is fighting in his own territory, it is called dispersive ground. This is because the soldiers, being near their homes and eager to see their wives and children, are likely to seize the opportunity of a battle to scatter in every direction. As Tu Mu explains, "They will lack the desperation needed to fight with full valor, and when they retreat, they will find places of refuge."

When the army has crossed into enemy territory, but not deeply, it is called facile ground. Li Ch'uan and Ho Shih say this is because retreat is still easy, and other commentators give similar explanations. Tu Mu adds, "When your army has crossed the border, you should burn your boats and bridges to show everyone there is no turning back."

Ground that offers great advantage to either side is called contentious ground. Tu Mu defines this as ground "worth fighting for." Ts'ao Kung says it is ground "on which the few and weak can defeat the many and strong," such as "the neck of a pass," which Li Ch'uan mentions as an example. Thermopylae fits this description because holding it for even a short time delayed an entire invading army, providing invaluable time. As Wu Tzu says in his writings: "When facing odds of one against ten, there is nothing better than a narrow pass."

When Lu Kuang was returning from his successful expedition to Turkestan in 385 A.D., and had reached I-ho with many spoils, Liang Hsi, the administrator of Liang-chou, took advantage of the death of Fu Chien, King of Ch'in, to plot against him. Yang Han, governor of Kao-ch'ang, advised him, saying, "Lu Kuang has just won victories in the west, and his soldiers are strong and confident. If we face him in the desert sands, we will not stand a chance. Instead, let's take control of the defile at the mouth of the Kao-wu pass. By cutting off his water supply, we can wait until his troops are weakened by thirst and then dictate our terms. Or, if that pass is too far, we could confront him at the I-wu pass, which is closer. Even a skilled strategist like Tzŭ-fang could not overcome the strength of these two positions." Liang Hsi, however, refused this advice and was overwhelmed and defeated by the invader.

Ground where both sides can move freely is called open ground.

[There are different interpretations of the word used for this type of ground. Ts'ao Kung says it means "ground covered with roads, like a chessboard." Ho Shih suggests it means "ground where communication is easy."]

Ground that forms the key to three neighboring states is ground of intersecting highways.

[Ts'au Kung defines this as "our country next to the enemy's, with a third country adjoining both." Meng Shih uses the example of Cheng, a small state bordered by Ch'i to the northeast, Chin to the west, and Ch'u to the south.]

Whoever takes control of this area first has a strategic advantage over most of the region.

[The one who holds this important position can force many neighboring states to become allies.]

When an army has moved deep into enemy territory, leaving fortified cities behind, it is on serious ground.

[Wang Hsi says it is called serious ground because "the army's situation becomes serious when it reaches this point."]

Mountain forests, steep terrain, marshes, and fens—all areas that are difficult to pass—are called difficult ground.

Ground that is reached through narrow gorges, where retreat can only happen through winding paths, and where a small enemy force could easily defeat a large army, is called hemmed-in ground.

Ground where the only way to avoid destruction is to fight immediately is called desperate ground.

[The situation, as described by Ts'ao Kung, is much like hemmed-in ground but worse, with no way out: "A tall mountain in front, a large river behind, no way to advance, no way to retreat." Ch'en Hao says being on desperate ground is "like sitting in a sinking boat or standing in a burning house." Tu Mu shares a vivid description from Li Ching of an army caught in this type of trap: "Imagine an army in enemy territory with no local guides. The army stumbles into a deadly trap, at the enemy's mercy. A ravine on the left, a mountain on the right, and a path so dangerous that horses must be tied together and chariots lifted with slings. There's no way forward, and retreat is blocked. The soldiers move in single file, barely forming ranks before an overwhelming enemy force appears. There's no time to rest, no escape. We try to fight, but there's no space; we try to defend ourselves, but there's no respite. Staying put means wasting time, but any move invites enemy attacks from the front and rear. The land is wild, with no food or water. The soldiers are exhausted, the horses worn out, and every effort seems hopeless. The path is so narrow that one person could stop an army of ten thousand. The enemy controls all the advantages, while we have lost all our options. Even with the bravest soldiers and sharpest weapons, how could they possibly be effective?" Students of Greek history may recall the tragic end of the Sicilian expedition and the suffering of the Athenians under Nicias and Demosthenes. [See Thucydides, VII. 78 sqq.]]

Do not fight on ground where you're scattered. Do not stop on easy ground. Do not attack when there's a lot of opposition.

[Instead, focus all your energy on getting the upper hand first. So says Ts'ao Kung. However, Li Ch'uan and others believe this means the enemy has already beaten us to it, so attacking would be foolish. In the Sun Tzŭ Hsu Lu, when the King of Wu asks what to do in this situation, Sun Tzŭ responds: "The rule for contested ground is that whoever holds the ground first has the advantage. If the enemy has secured this type of position, do not attack. Trick them into moving by pretending to flee—show your flags and beat your drums—rush to other spots they can't afford to lose—drag branches and kick up dust—confuse their senses—send your best troops to secretly ambush them. Then your enemy will rush out to save the situation."]

On open ground, don't try to block the enemy's path.

[Because it would be pointless and would put the blocking force in danger. There are two interpretations here. I follow Chang Yu's view. The other is found in Ts'ao Kung's short note: "Come closer together"—which means making sure part of your army isn't cut off.]

On ground with crossing roads, join up with your allies.

[Or perhaps, "make alliances with neighboring states."]

On serious ground, take what you need.

[Li Ch'uan adds an interesting note: "When an army moves deep into enemy territory, it's important not to anger the local people by treating them unfairly. Follow the example of the Han Emperor Kao

Tsu, who during his march into Ch'in territory didn't harm women or steal valuables. [Note: this was in 207 B.C., a lesson that could embarrass Christian armies that marched into Peking in 1900 A.D.] This is how he won the hearts of the people. In this passage, I think the right reading is not 'take what you need,' but 'don't take what you don't need.' Sadly, the commentator's emotions may have clouded his judgment. Tu Mu, at least, isn't under any such illusions. He says: 'When camped on serious ground, where there's no reason to advance and no chance to retreat, one should prepare for a long defense by gathering supplies from all around, while keeping a close watch on the enemy.'"]

In tough terrain, keep moving steadily forward.

[Or, in the words of VIII. § 2, "don't stop and make camp."]

When trapped, use a clever strategy.

[Ts'ao Kung says, "Try something unusual or unexpected," and Tu Yu adds, "In such situations, you must come up with a plan that fits the moment. If you can trick the enemy, you might escape the danger." This is exactly what happened when Hannibal was trapped in the mountains on the road to Casilinum, seemingly caught by the dictator Fabius. Hannibal came up with a clever trick, similar to one used by T'ien Tan 62 years earlier. [See IX. § 24, note.] At nightfall, they tied bundles of twigs to the horns of around 2,000 oxen and set them on fire. The terrified animals were driven towards the mountain passes held by the enemy. The sight of these fast-moving lights frightened the Romans, causing them to retreat, and Hannibal's army safely passed through the narrow pass. [See Polybius, III. 93, 94; Livy, XXII. 16, 17.]]

When in desperate situations, fight.

[As Chia Lin notes, "If you fight with everything you've got, you have a chance to survive. But if you just stay in your corner, death is certain."]

In the past, skilled leaders knew how to divide the enemy's front from their rear;

[In more exact terms, "They would make sure the front and rear were no longer in touch with each other."]

They knew how to stop the enemy's big and small divisions from working together, and how to prevent strong troops from saving the weak, and officers from rallying their soldiers.

When the enemy's troops were scattered, they made sure the enemy couldn't regroup. Even when the enemy's forces were united, they still managed to keep them disorganized.

When it was to their advantage, they moved forward; if not, they stayed put.

[Mei Yao-ch'en links this to the previous point: "After successfully disrupting the enemy, they would advance to secure any advantage; if there was no advantage, they would stay where they were."]

If asked how to handle a large, organized enemy force about to launch an attack, I would say: "Start by capturing something your opponent values; this will force him to act according to your will."

[There are different views on what Sun Tzŭ meant here. Ts'ao Kung thinks it refers to "some strategic advantage the enemy relies on." Tu Mu says: "The three things an enemy is eager to do, and on which his success depends, are: (1) to capture our key positions; (2) to destroy our farmlands; and (3) to protect his own supply lines." Our goal should be to disrupt his plans in these three areas, rendering him powerless. [Cf. III. § 3.] By boldly seizing the initiative, you force the enemy into a defensive position.]

Speed is the essence of war.

[Tu Mu explains, "This is a summary of the main principles of warfare," and adds, "These are the deepest truths of military science, and the general's most important duty." The following stories, told by Ho Shih, show how important speed was to two of China's greatest generals. In 227 A.D., Meng Ta, governor of Hsin-ch'eng under the Wei Emperor Wen Ti, was planning to defect to the House of Shu, and had begun communicating with Chu-ko Liang, the Prime Minister of that state. The Wei general Ssu-ma I, who was then the military governor of Wan, heard about Meng Ta's treachery and immediately set out with an army to stop him, after having tricked him with a friendly message. Ssu-ma's officers suggested that they should investigate more thoroughly before making a move. Ssu-ma I replied, "Meng Ta is an unreliable man, and we should go and punish him right away, while he is still uncertain and before he has fully betrayed us." Then, with a series of forced marches, he brought his army to the walls of Hsin-ch'eng in just eight days. Now, Meng Ta had earlier written in a letter to Chu-ko Liang: "Wan is 1,200 li from here. When news of my revolt reaches Ssu-ma I, he will inform the emperor, but it will take a whole month before any action is taken. By that time, my city will be well fortified. Besides, Ssu-ma I is not likely to come himself, and the generals that will be sent are not worth worrying about." But his next letter was full of panic: "Though only eight days have passed since I revolted, an army is already at the gates. What incredible speed!" Two weeks later, Hsin-ch'eng fell, and Meng Ta was executed. [See Chin Shu, ch. 1, f. 3.] In 621 A.D., Li Ching was sent from K'uei-chou in Ssu-ch'uan to defeat the rebel Hsiao Hsien, who had declared himself Emperor in the modern-day Ching-chou Fu in Hupeh. It was autumn, and the Yangtze River was in flood, so Hsiao Hsien did not expect Li Ching to risk coming down through the gorges, and as a result made no preparations. But Li Ching immediately prepared his army and was about to set off when the other generals begged him to delay his departure until the river was less dangerous to navigate. Li Ching replied, "For a soldier, overwhelming speed is of the utmost importance, and he must never miss an opportunity. Now is the time to strike, before Hsiao Hsien even knows we have gathered an army. If we attack while the river is in flood, we will reach his capital with such unexpected speed, like thunder that is heard before you have time to cover your ears." [See VII. § 19, note.] This is a key principle of war. Even if Hsiao Hsien hears of our approach, he will have to raise his soldiers in such a rush that they will not be fit to fight us. This way, we will secure total victory." Everything happened as predicted, and Hsiao Hsien was forced to surrender, nobly asking that his people be spared and he alone face death.]

Take advantage of the enemy's lack of readiness, move by unexpected routes, and attack where they are not guarded.

Here are the principles for an invading force to follow: The deeper you go into a country, the stronger the unity among your troops will become, and the defenders will struggle to defeat you.

Make raids in fertile lands to provide your army with food.

[Cf. § 13. Li Ch'uan does not provide a note here.]

Pay close attention to the well-being of your soldiers,

[By "well-being," Wang Hsi means, "Take good care of them, indulge them, make sure they have enough food and drink, and generally keep them in good condition."]

and do not overwork them. Focus your energy and save your strength.

[Ch'en recalls the approach used in 224 B.C. by the brilliant general Wang Chien, whose leadership was key to the First Emperor's success. He invaded the Ch'u State, where a mass mobilization had been raised against him. However, uncertain about the mood of his troops, he refused to engage in battle and stayed strictly on the defensive. The Ch'u general tried repeatedly to provoke a fight, but day after day, Wang Chien remained inside his fortifications. Instead of rushing into battle, he focused on winning the trust and loyalty of his soldiers. He ensured they were well-fed, even sharing meals with them, provided opportunities for bathing, and used every possible method to keep them content and united. After some time, he sent people to check on how his soldiers were spending their free time. The report came back that they were competing in activities like weightlifting and long jumping. When Wang Chien heard this, he knew their morale was high, and they were ready for battle. By then, the Ch'u army, frustrated by their unanswered challenges, had marched away to the east. At that moment, Wang Chien broke camp and pursued them. In the battle that followed, the Ch'u forces were crushed, and shortly after, the entire state of Ch'u was conquered by Ch'in, with their king, Fu-ch'u, taken captive.]

Keep your army constantly on the move,

[So the enemy never knows where you are. However, it has occurred to me that the true meaning might be "link your army together."]

and develop plans that are impossible for the enemy to understand.

Put your soldiers in positions where there is no escape, and they will choose death over retreat. If they are ready to face death, there is nothing they cannot accomplish.

[Chang Yu quotes Wei Liao Tzŭ (ch. 3): "If a single man ran wild with a sword in a marketplace, and everyone else fled from him, it wouldn't mean that he alone was brave and the rest were cowards. The truth is, a man with nothing to lose and a man who values his life are not in the same position."]

Both officers and soldiers will give their full strength.

[Chang Yu says: "If they find themselves in a difficult situation together, they will definitely combine their strength to get out of it."]

When soldiers are in desperate situations, they lose all sense of fear. If they have nowhere to run, they will stand firm. If they are deep in enemy territory, they will fight with determination. If there is no other option, they will fight fiercely.

Thus, without needing to be organized, soldiers will always be alert; without needing to be asked, they will follow your orders.

[Literally, "Without asking, you will receive."]

Without strict rules, they will stay loyal; without needing commands, they can be trusted.

Ban the taking of omens, and eliminate superstitious doubts. Then, until the moment of death, no disaster will be feared.

[Superstition and fear can turn men into cowards who "die many times before their deaths." Tu Mu quotes Huang Shih-kung: "Spells and incantations should be strictly forbidden, and no officer should inquire about the fate of the army through divination, as this can unsettle the soldiers' minds." He continues, "If all doubts and superstitions are cast aside, your soldiers will remain resolute until the very end."]

If our soldiers are not burdened with wealth, it is not because they dislike riches; if their lives are not overly long, it is not because they do not want longevity.

[Chang Yu explains this well: "Wealth and long life are natural desires for all men. So, if soldiers burn or throw away valuables and give up their lives, it is not because they hate them, but because they have no choice." Sun Tzŭ hints that since soldiers are only human, it is the general's responsibility to make sure they are not tempted to avoid battle and seek riches instead.]

On the day your soldiers are ordered to battle, they may cry,

[The word used here is "snivel," which suggests deeper sorrow than just tears.]

some of them sitting up and soaking their clothes with tears, while others lying down let the tears roll down their faces.

[This isn't because they are afraid, but because, as Ts'ao Kung says, "they have all made a firm decision to fight to the death." We can also remember that the heroes of the Iliad were similarly open in showing their emotions. Chang Yu references the sad farewell at the I River between Ching K'o and his friends, when Ching K'o was sent to assassinate the King of Ch'in (who would later become the First Emperor) in 227 B.C. As he said goodbye, tears flowed like rain, and he recited these lines: "The wind blows sharp, the river is cold; Your hero goes forth—never to return."]

But when they are cornered, they will show the courage of a Chu or a Kuei.

[Chu was the personal name of Chuan Chu, a native of the Wu State and a contemporary of Sun Tzŭ. He was hired by Kung-tzu Kuang, also known as Ho Lu Wang, to assassinate the king Wang Liao with a dagger hidden inside a fish at a banquet. He succeeded, but was immediately cut down by the king's guards. This happened in 515 B.C.

The other hero, Ts'ao Kuei (also known as Ts'ao Mo), became famous 166 years earlier, in 681 B.C. After Lu had been defeated three times by Ch'i, they were about to sign a treaty giving up a large part of their territory. At that moment, Ts'ao Kuei grabbed Huan Kung, the Duke of Ch'i, at the altar and held a dagger to his chest. None of the Duke's men dared move, and Ts'ao Kuei demanded that all of Lu's territory be returned, arguing that Lu was unfairly treated because it was smaller and weaker. Fearing for his life, Huan Kung agreed. Ts'ao Kuei then calmly put away his dagger and sat back down, showing no fear. Although the Duke wanted to break the agreement later, his wise counselor Kuan Chung advised him that it would be unwise to go back on his word. As a result, Lu regained all the land they had lost in the three battles.]

A skilled strategist can be compared to the shuai-jan. The shuai-jan is a snake found in the Ch'ang mountains.

["Shuai-jan" means "suddenly" or "rapidly," and the snake got this name because of how quickly it moves. Over time, the term came to refer to military maneuvers.]

If you strike at its head, its tail will attack you; if you strike at its tail, its head will attack you; if you strike at its middle, both head and tail will attack you together.

If asked whether an army can be made to act like the shuai-jan,

[As Mei Yao-ch'en says, "Is it possible to make the front and rear of an army respond quickly to an attack on the other, just as if they were parts of one living body?"]

I would answer, Yes. The men of Wu and the men of Yüeh are enemies;

[Cf. VI. § 21.]

yet if they are crossing a river in the same boat and a storm strikes, they will help each other, just as the left hand helps the right.

[The meaning is: If two enemies will cooperate when faced with a shared danger, how much more should two parts of the same army, bound together by shared interests and camaraderie, work together? Still, it is well known that many campaigns have been lost because of a lack of cooperation, especially when allied armies are involved.]

Therefore, it is not enough to rely on tethering horses or burying chariot wheels in the ground to keep an army from fleeing.

[These strange methods, meant to stop soldiers from running away, remind us of the Athenian hero Sophanes, who carried an anchor into battle at Plataea and used it to tie himself to one spot. [See Herodotus, IX. 74.] Sun Tzŭ is saying that merely making flight impossible through such mechanical means is not enough. You will only succeed if your men have strong willpower, unity of purpose, and, most importantly, a spirit of cooperation. This is the lesson we can learn from the shuai-jan.]

The way to manage an army is to set one standard of courage that everyone must meet.

[Literally, "make the courage of all equal as if it were that of one." If the ideal army is to act as one cohesive unit, then the determination and spirit of its members must be of the same quality, or at least not below a certain level. Wellington's comment about his army at Waterloo, calling it "the worst he had ever commanded," was likely a reflection of its lack of this essential trait—unity of courage and spirit. If he hadn't anticipated the Belgian defections and kept those troops in the background, he almost certainly would have lost the battle.]

How to make the best use of both strong and weak soldiers is a matter of how you use the terrain.

[Mei Yao-ch'en explains: "The way to erase the differences between strong and weak and make both useful is by using the natural features of the ground." Weaker troops, if placed in strong defensive positions, can hold out as effectively as better troops on more vulnerable ground. A good position can make up for a lack of stamina and courage. Col. Henderson comments: "With all due respect to textbooks and standard tactics, I believe the study of terrain is often neglected, and that too little attention is given to the selection of positions and the great benefits that come from using natural features, whether attacking or defending." [2]]

Thus, the skillful general leads his army as easily as if he were leading a single person by the hand, whether they want to follow or not.

[Tu Mu says: "The comparison refers to how easily this is done."]

A general must stay calm to ensure secrecy and be upright and just to maintain order.

He must be able to confuse his officers and soldiers with false reports and deceptive appearances,

[Literally, "to deceive their eyes and ears."]

so that they remain in complete ignorance of his true plans.

[Ts'ao Kung gives a wise saying: "Troops should not be allowed to know your plans at the beginning; they may only share in your success when it is achieved." One of the key principles of war is "to mystify, mislead, and surprise the enemy." But how about deceiving your own troops? Those who think Sun Tzŭ overstates this would benefit from reading Col. Henderson's comments on Stonewall Jackson's Valley campaign: "The great care Jackson took to hide his movements, intentions, and thoughts, even from his most trusted staff officers, would have been seen as unnecessary by a less meticulous commander." [3] In 88 A.D., according to ch. 47 of the Hou Han Shu, Pan Ch'ao led 25,000 men from Khotan and other Central Asian states to attack Yarkand. The King of Kutcha sent his commander with 50,000 troops from Wen-su, Ku-mo, and Wei-t'ou to defend it. Pan Ch'ao called a war council with his officers and the King of Khotan and said, 'We are outnumbered and cannot defeat the enemy directly. The best plan is to split up and go in different directions. The King of Khotan will march east, and I will head west. We will leave after the evening drum sounds.' Pan Ch'ao secretly released some prisoners, who informed the King of Kutcha of these plans. Feeling confident, the King of Kutcha took 10,000 horsemen to block Pan Ch'ao's retreat in the west, while the King of Wen-su led 8,000 cavalry east to intercept the King of Khotan. Once Pan Ch'ao knew the enemy leaders had left, he quickly reunited his troops and launched a surprise attack at dawn on Yarkand's camp. The enemy fled in confusion, and Pan Ch'ao pursued them, killing over 5,000 and seizing many horses, cattle, and other valuables. After Yarkand surrendered, Kutcha and the other states withdrew their forces. From then on, Pan Ch'ao's influence dominated the western regions." In this case, the Chinese general not only kept his officers in the dark about his real plans, but also used the bold tactic of splitting his army to deceive the enemy.]

By altering his tactics and changing his plans,

[Wang Hsi believes this means not using the same strategy twice.]

he keeps the enemy unsure and without clear information.

[Chang Yu, in a quote from another work, says: "The idea that war is based on deception doesn't only apply to tricking the enemy. You must also deceive your own soldiers. Make them follow you without letting them know the reasons behind your decisions."]

By shifting his camp and taking indirect routes, he prevents the enemy from predicting his intentions.

At the crucial moment, the leader of an army acts like someone who has climbed a high wall and then kicks away the ladder behind him. He takes his soldiers deep into enemy territory before revealing his true plans.

[Literally, "releases the spring" (see V. § 15), meaning that he takes a decisive action that makes retreat impossible—similar to Hsiang Yu, who sank his ships after crossing a river. Ch'en Hao, followed by Chia Lin, interprets this less clearly as "uses every trick at his disposal."]

He burns his boats and destroys his cooking pots; like a shepherd driving a flock of sheep, he directs his soldiers this way and that, and no one knows where they are headed.

[Tu Mu says: "The army only understands orders to advance or retreat; it doesn't know the true goals of attacking or conquering."]

To gather his forces and lead them into danger—this is the duty of a general.

[Sun Tzŭ means that once the army is mobilized, there should be no delay in striking at the enemy's core. Note how he returns to this idea again and again. In the warring states of ancient China, desertion was likely a much more immediate and serious threat than in today's armies.]

The different strategies suitable for the nine types of ground;

[Chang Yu says: "One should not rigidly apply the rules for the nine types of ground."]

the need for either aggressive or defensive tactics, and the basic laws of human nature: these are things that must absolutely be studied.

When invading hostile territory, the general principle is that penetrating deeply creates unity, while penetrating only a little leads to division.

[Cf. § 20.]

When you leave your homeland and lead your army into neighboring lands, you are on critical ground.

This kind of ground is mentioned earlier, but it is not listed among the Nine Situations or the Six Calamities in another chapter. At first glance, you might think it means "distant ground," but according to commentators, this is not correct. Mei Yao-ch'en explains that it's ground that is neither far enough to be called "easy" nor close enough to be "scattered." It is somewhere in between. Wang Hsi says that it is ground separated from home by a state whose territory we had to cross to reach it, so it is important to finish our task there quickly. He adds that this situation is rare, which is why it is not included among the Nine Situations.

When you have roads in all directions, it is ground of intersecting highways.

When you go deep into enemy territory, it is serious ground. When you advance only a little, it is easy ground.

When the enemy's strongholds are behind you, and narrow paths are in front, it is hemmed-in ground. When there is no place to retreat, it is desperate ground.

Therefore, on scattered ground, I would unite my men under a common goal.

To achieve this, Tu Mu suggests staying on the defensive and avoiding battle.

On easy ground, I would keep all parts of my army closely connected.

Tu Mu explains that this is to prevent two dangers: the possibility of soldiers deserting or a sudden enemy attack. Mei Yao-ch'en adds that during the march, the troops should stay close together, and in camp, the fortifications should be continuous.

On contested ground, I would hurry to bring up my rear forces.

Ts'ao Kung offers this view, and Chang Yu agrees, saying that the head and tail of the army must reach their destination together without straggling. Mei Yao-ch'en suggests another view: If the enemy hasn't yet reached the desired position and we are behind them, we should move quickly to claim it. Ch'en Hao takes another approach, thinking the enemy may have already chosen their ground. He quotes a passage where Sun Tzŭ warns against attacking when exhausted. If a favorable position lies ahead, Ch'en Hao advises sending a strong unit to secure it, and if the enemy tries to fight for it, the main force can strike their rear, leading to victory.

On open ground, I would stay alert and defend carefully. On ground of intersecting highways, I would strengthen my alliances.

On serious ground, I would make sure to maintain a steady flow of supplies.

Commentators believe this refers to gathering forage and plunder, not maintaining a connection with home, as you might expect.

On difficult ground, I would keep moving forward.

On hemmed-in ground, I would block any escape routes.

Meng Shih explains that this would make it seem like I am defending the position, but my real plan is to break through the enemy's lines unexpectedly. Mei Yao-ch'en adds that this would make my soldiers fight with desperation. Wang Hsi suggests that this would prevent my men from being tempted to flee. Tu Mu points out that this is the opposite of a previous situation, where it is the enemy who is surrounded. An example of this is from 532 A.D., when Kao Huan, who later became Emperor, was surrounded by a much larger army led by Erh-chu Chao and others. Despite his smaller force, which included only 2000 horsemen and fewer than 30,000 foot soldiers, Kao Huan blocked all remaining escape routes by driving oxen and donkeys into the gaps. When his officers and men saw there was no escape, they fought with extraordinary bravery and broke through the enemy ranks with fierce determination.

On desperate ground, I would tell my soldiers there is no hope of survival.

Tu Yu suggests making it clear to the soldiers that survival is impossible by burning their baggage, throwing away supplies, blocking wells, and destroying cooking stoves. The only way to live is to fight as if they expect to die. Mei Yao-ch'en adds that their only chance of survival is to abandon all hope of it.

This concludes what Sun Tzŭ says about "grounds" and their corresponding "variations." Reviewing these passages, it is clear that the subject is treated in a somewhat scattered and unstructured manner. Sun Tzŭ begins by listing a few variations before discussing "grounds" but only mentions five variations, which are later expanded. Some types of ground are addressed earlier, while chapter X introduces six new types of ground, each with a variation to match. However, none of these six types are revisited, and one closely resembles a type of ground described later. In chapter XI, we encounter the Nine Grounds, followed by a list of their variations. By sections 43-45, new definitions for several of these grounds are provided, as well as for another type not previously mentioned. Finally, the nine variations are listed again, though many of them differ from earlier versions.

Although we cannot definitively explain the current state of Sun Tzŭ's text, a few interesting observations stand out: (1) Chapter VIII is titled "Nine Variations," but only five are listed. (2) This chapter is unusually short. (3) Chapter XI is called "The Nine Grounds," but some of the grounds are defined more than once, and two separate lists of variations are given. (4) This chapter is much longer than any other, except chapter IX. While no specific conclusions can be drawn from these facts, it seems likely that Sun Tzŭ's work has not reached us exactly as he originally wrote it. Chapter VIII appears incomplete and possibly out of place, while chapter XI contains material that may have been added later or misplaced from another part of the text.

For it is the soldier's nature to offer a determined resistance when surrounded, to fight fiercely when there is no way out, and to follow orders quickly when faced with danger. Chang Yu refers to the actions of Pan Ch'ao's loyal followers in 73 A.D. The story is found in the Hou Han Shu, chapter 47: "When Pan Ch'ao arrived at Shan-shan, the king, Kuang, initially treated him with great politeness and respect; but soon after, his attitude changed abruptly, and he became negligent and indifferent. Pan Ch'ao spoke of this to the officers with him: 'Have you noticed,' he said, 'that Kuang's courtesy is fading? This must mean that envoys from the Northern barbarians have arrived, leaving him uncertain about which side to support. That is surely the reason. The wise man, we are told, can foresee events before they happen; how much more easily can he observe what is already taking place!' Then he called one of the locals assigned to his service and set a trap by asking, 'Where are those envoys from the Hsiung-nu who arrived a few days ago?' The man, startled and afraid, quickly revealed the whole truth. Pan Ch'ao, having secured the man, then summoned a meeting with his officers, thirty-six in all, and began drinking with them. As the wine took effect, he encouraged their spirits further by saying: 'Gentlemen, here we are in a remote region, eager to achieve riches and honor through a great deed. Recently, an ambassador from the Hsiung-nu has arrived, and because of this, the respectful treatment we've received from the king has faded. If this envoy persuades him to capture us and deliver us to the Hsiung-nu, our bones will be left for the wolves of the desert. What are we to do?' The officers, as one, replied, 'With our lives at risk, we will follow you through life and death.' The rest of this story can be found in chapter twelve, section one."

We cannot form alliances with neighboring rulers until we understand their intentions. We are not fit to lead an army on the march unless we know the landscape—its mountains and forests, its traps and cliffs, its marshes and swamps. We cannot make use of the land's advantages unless we employ local guides. These three statements are repeated from chapter seven to stress their importance, according to the commentators. However, I believe they are placed here as a lead-in to the next statements. Regarding local guides, Sun Tzŭ might have added that there is always a risk of error, either due to their betrayal or through misunderstanding. Livy, for instance, recounts a case where Hannibal ordered a guide to take him near Casinum, where an important pass was to be secured; but Hannibal's Carthaginian accent, not well-suited to Latin names, led the guide to mishear Casilinum instead of Casinum. The mistake was not discovered until the army had nearly reached the wrong location.

To be ignorant of any one of the following four or five principles is unworthy of a warlike leader.

When a prince who is ready for war attacks a strong nation, his skill as a leader comes from stopping the enemy from gathering their forces. He intimidates his opponents, and their allies are scared off from uniting against him.

[Mei Tao-ch'en offers one of the logical chains of thought that the Chinese are fond of: "When attacking a strong state, if you can separate its forces, you gain the advantage in strength; if you have the advantage in strength, you can intimidate the enemy; if you intimidate the enemy, neighboring states will become fearful; and if neighboring states are fearful, the enemy's allies will be stopped from joining her." The following interpretation gives an even stronger meaning: "If the powerful state is defeated before they can call on their allies, then the smaller states will hesitate and avoid bringing their forces together." Ch'en Hao and Chang Yu understand this in a very different way. Ch'en Hao says: "Even though a prince may be strong, if he attacks a large state, he won't have enough troops and will have to rely on outside help. If he ignores this and, with too much confidence in his own strength, tries to scare the enemy, he will certainly lose." Chang Yu explains it this way: "If we recklessly attack a large state, our own people will be unhappy and hesitant. And if our military power is clearly weaker than the enemy's, other leaders will be too scared to join us."]

So, he does not try to form alliances with everyone, nor does he help other states become stronger. He carries out his secret plans, keeping his enemies in fear.

[Li Ch'uan explains the thinking like this: Confident that his enemies won't join forces, "he can afford to turn down risky alliances and just focus on his own secret plans, with his reputation allowing him to do without external friendships."]

In this way, he can capture their cities and bring down their kingdoms.

[Even though this paragraph was written long before the state of Ch'in became a serious threat, it sums up well the strategy that the Six Chancellors used to pave the way for Ch'in's final victory under Shih Huang Ti. Chang Yu, expanding on his earlier note, thinks that Sun Tzŭ is criticizing this cold, selfish, and isolated approach.]

Bestow rewards without regard to rules,

[Wu Tzŭ, less wisely, says: "Let advancement be richly rewarded and retreat be heavily punished."]

issue orders

[Literally, "hang" or post them up.]

without regard to previous arrangements;

["In order to prevent treachery," says Wang Hsi. The general meaning is made clear by Ts'ao Kung's quotation from the Ssu-ma Fa: "Give instructions only upon sighting the enemy; give rewards when you see worthy deeds." Ts'ao Kung paraphrases: "The final instructions you give to your army should not match those that were previously posted." Chang Yu simplifies this to "your plans should not be revealed in advance." And Chia Lin adds: "There should be no fixed rules in your arrangements." Not only is there risk in letting your plans be known, but war often requires reversing them at the last moment.]

and you will be able to manage a whole army as though you were dealing with just one man.

[Cf. supra, § 34.]

Confront your soldiers with the action itself; never let them know your plan.

[Literally, "do not tell them words," meaning do not give reasons for any order. Lord Mansfield once told a junior colleague to "give no reasons" for his decisions, and this rule applies even more to a general than to a judge.]

When the situation looks promising, show it to them; but when the outlook is bleak, tell them nothing.

Place your army in deadly peril, and it will survive; throw it into desperate situations, and it will come out safely.

[These words of Sun Tzŭ were once quoted by Han Hsin to explain the tactics he used in one of his most brilliant battles, mentioned earlier. In 204 B.C., Han Hsin was sent against the army of Chao, halting ten miles from the Ching-hsing pass, where the enemy had gathered in full strength. At midnight, he sent out 2000 light cavalry, each equipped with a red flag. Their orders were to pass through narrow defiles and secretly observe the enemy. "When the men of Chao see me retreating in full flight," Han Hsin said, "they will abandon their defenses and chase us. This will be your signal to rush in, pull down the Chao banners, and raise the red flags of Han instead." He then told his other officers: "The enemy holds a strong position and won't attack us until they see the standard and drums of the commander-in-chief, fearing I might retreat through the mountains." With this, he sent out a division of 10,000 men, ordering them to form a line of battle with their backs to the River Ti. Upon seeing this maneuver, the entire Chao army burst into laughter. By morning, Han Hsin raised his general's flag and marched out of the pass with drums beating, quickly engaging the enemy. A fierce battle followed, lasting for some time, until Han Hsin and his colleague, Chang Ni, left the drums and flag on the battlefield and fled to the division by the river, where another intense fight was underway. The enemy rushed after them to claim the trophies, leaving their defenses exposed, but the two generals managed to join their army, which was fighting desperately. Now it was time for the 2000 horsemen to act. When they saw the men of Chao pursuing the fleeing forces, they galloped behind the abandoned fortifications, tore down the enemy's flags, and replaced them with the banners of Han. When the Chao army looked back during the chase and saw the red flags, they were struck with terror. Convinced that the Hans had overpowered their king, they panicked and scattered, despite their leader's attempts to stop them. Then the Han forces attacked from both sides, completely routing the Chao army, killing many and capturing the rest, including King Ya himself. After the battle, some of Han Hsin's officers approached him and said: "In the Art of War, we are taught to position troops with a hill or mound on the right rear and a river or marsh on the left front. Yet you ordered us to draw up with the river at our backs. How did you manage to win under such conditions?" The general replied: "I'm afraid you haven't studied the Art of War carefully enough. Does it not say, 'Plunge your army into desperate straits, and it will come off in safety; place it in deadly peril, and it will survive'? Had I followed the usual methods, I wouldn't have been able to bring my colleague around. As the Military Classic says, 'Swoop down on the marketplace and drive the men off to fight.' If I hadn't placed my troops where they had no choice but to fight for their lives, and instead allowed them to act freely, they would have scattered, and we couldn't have accomplished anything." The officers acknowledged the wisdom of his argument and said: "These are tactics beyond our own abilities."]

For it is precisely when a force finds itself in danger that it becomes capable of striking a blow for victory.

[Danger has a motivating effect.]

Success in warfare is achieved by carefully adapting to the enemy's intentions.

[Ts'ao Kung says: "Feign ignorance" by appearing to comply with the enemy's wishes. Chang Yu explains: "If the enemy shows a desire to advance, encourage him to do so; if he wishes to retreat, delay deliberately to allow him to carry out his plan." The goal is to make him overconfident and careless before launching our attack.]

By constantly keeping pressure on the enemy's flank,

[I understand this to mean "moving alongside the enemy in the same direction." Ts'ao Kung says: "Unite the troops and advance towards the enemy." But such a rearrangement of words is not defensible.]

we will eventually succeed,

[Literally, "after a thousand li."]

in killing the enemy's commander.

[This was always a significant aim in Chinese warfare.]

This is what it means to achieve something through sheer strategy.

On the day you take command, block the frontier passes, destroy the official tallies,

[These were tablets of bamboo or wood, half of which was used as a permit by an official. When returned within a set period, the gate could be opened for the traveler.]

and stop all communication,

[Whether to or from the enemy's territory.]

Be firm in the council-chamber,

[Show no weakness, and ensure your plans are approved by the ruler.]

so that you can maintain control over the situation.

[Mei Yao-ch'en interprets this to mean: Take the strictest measures to maintain secrecy in your discussions.]

If the enemy leaves an opening, you must charge through it.

Outsmart your opponent by seizing what he values most,

[See earlier, § 18.]

and subtly manipulate the timing of his arrival at the battlefield.

[Ch'en Hao explains: "If I seize a favorable position but the enemy doesn't show up, the advantage gained is meaningless. To control an important position, you must create a kind of 'appointment' with the enemy, tricking him into arriving there as well." Mei Yao-ch'en says this "appointment" can be made by using the enemy's own spies, who will bring back only the information we want them to have. Once we've cunningly revealed our plans, we can make sure, by starting after the enemy, that we arrive before him (VII. § 4). Starting later forces him to move there; arriving first allows us to capture the position without resistance. This supports Mei Yao-ch'en's reading of § 47.]

Walk the path guided by strategy,

[Chia Lin says: "Victory is all that matters, and this cannot be won by strictly following conventional rules." Unfortunately, this interpretation relies on weak authority, though it makes much more sense. As we know, Napoleon, according to the veterans of the old school whom he defeated, won his battles by breaking all the traditional rules of warfare.]

and adapt to the enemy until the moment comes for a decisive battle.

[Tu Mu says: "Follow the enemy's tactics until a favorable moment arises; then engage in a battle that will be conclusive."]

At first, show the reserve of a shy maiden until the enemy gives you an opening; then strike with the speed of a running hare, and it will be too late for the enemy to resist you.

[Though the hare is known for its timidity, Sun Tzǔ was clearly referring to its speed. The words have sometimes been interpreted to mean fleeing from the enemy as fast as a hare, but Tu Mu rightly rejects this idea.]

Chapter 12 - The Attack by Fire

Sun Tzǔ said: There are five ways to attack using fire. The first is to set fire to soldiers in their camp.

[Tu Mu agrees. Li Ch'uan adds: "Set the camp on fire, and kill the soldiers as they try to escape from the flames." Pan Ch'ao, on a diplomatic mission to the King of Shan-shan, found himself in great danger when an envoy from the Hsiung-nu, China's mortal enemies, unexpectedly arrived. During a meeting with his officers, he declared: "Nothing ventured, nothing gained! Our only option now is to attack the barbarians with fire under the cover of night, when they won't be able to see how many we are. Taking advantage of their panic, we can wipe them out, discourage the King, and achieve glory, ensuring the success of our mission." The officers suggested discussing the plan with the Intendant first, but Pan Ch'ao was outraged: "Today is the day our fate will be decided! The Intendant is a mere civilian and will be too scared when he hears our plan, leading to its exposure. Dying ingloriously is not the fate for brave warriors." The officers then agreed to follow his lead. That night, Pan Ch'ao and his small group approached the barbarian camp. A strong wind was blowing. Pan Ch'ao ordered ten men to hide behind the enemy barracks with drums, ready to make a loud noise when they saw the fire. The rest of his men, armed with bows and crossbows, were placed in ambush at the camp's gate. Pan Ch'ao set the camp on fire from the windward side, and immediately, the drums began to beat, and shouts filled the air. The Hsiung-nu ran out in panic. Pan Ch'ao personally killed three of them, while his men beheaded the envoy and thirty others. More than a hundred of the enemy perished in the flames. The next day, Pan Ch'ao, aware of the Intendant's concerns, assured him, "Although you didn't join us last night, I won't take sole credit for the success." This satisfied Kuo Hsun, and Pan Ch'ao presented the head of the barbarian envoy to the King of Shan-shan, causing fear throughout the kingdom. Pan Ch'ao calmed the situation by issuing a public proclamation, took the king's sons as hostages, and then reported his success to Tou Ku." *Hou Han Shu,* ch. 47, ff. 1, 2.]

The second is to burn stores.

[Tu Mu says: "Food, fuel, and fodder." During the Sui dynasty, to subdue the rebellious population of Kiangnan, Kao Keng advised Emperor Wen Ti to make periodic raids and burn their grain stores, a strategy that ultimately succeeded.]

The third is to burn baggage trains.

[An example is Ts'ao Ts'ao's destruction of Yuan Shao's wagons and supplies in 200 A.D.]

The fourth is to burn arsenals and magazines.

[Tu Mu explains that arsenals and magazines contain the same items, listing weapons, bullion, and clothing. See VII. § 11 for comparison.]

The fifth is to hurl fire into the enemy's camp.

[Tu Yu mentions in the *T'ung Tien*: "To drop fire into the enemy camp, dip arrowheads into a brazier to set them alight and then shoot them from powerful crossbows into the enemy's lines."]

In order to carry out an attack, we must have the necessary means available.

[T'sao Kung believes this refers to "traitors in the enemy's camp." However, Ch'en Hao more likely means: "We must have favorable circumstances in general, not just rely on traitors." Chia Lin adds: "We should take advantage of wind and dry weather."]

The material for raising fire should always be kept ready.

[Tu Mu suggests materials for starting a fire like "dry vegetation, reeds, brushwood, straw, grease, oil, etc." This is the material cause. Chang Yu adds: "Containers for hoarding fire and things for lighting fires."]

There is a proper season for making attacks with fire and specific days for starting a blaze.

The proper season is during very dry weather, and the specific days are when the moon is in the constellations of the Sieve, the Wall, the Wing, or the Cross-bar;

[These correspond roughly to the 7th, 14th, 27th, and 28th of the Twenty-eight Stellar Mansions, which are Sagittarius, Pegasus, Crater, and Corvus.]

because these four are all days when the wind rises.

When attacking with fire, you must be prepared for five possible outcomes:

(1) When fire breaks out inside the enemy's camp, immediately launch an attack from outside.

(2) If a fire starts but the enemy's soldiers remain calm, wait and do not attack.

[The main goal of attacking with fire is to create confusion among the enemy. If that doesn't happen, it means the enemy is prepared for you. Therefore, caution is necessary.]

(3) When the flames reach their peak, follow up with an attack if possible; if not, stay where you are.

[Ts'ao Kung advises: "If you see an opportunity, advance; but if the difficulties seem too great, retreat."]

If it is possible to make an assault with fire from the outside, do not wait for it to break out within, but launch your attack at a favorable moment.

[Tu Mu explains that the previous sections referred to fire breaking out inside the enemy's camp, either by accident or through arson. He adds: "But if the enemy is camped in a waste area filled with grass, or if he has set up camp in a location that can easily be burned, we should attack with fire at any good opportunity instead of waiting for a fire to start within. Otherwise, the enemy might burn the surrounding vegetation themselves, rendering our efforts useless." The famous Li Ling once outsmarted a leader of the Hsiung-nu this way. The latter, taking advantage of a favorable wind, attempted to set fire to the Chinese general's camp, but found that all combustible vegetation had already been burned down. On the other hand, Po-ts'ai, a general of the Yellow Turban rebels, was badly defeated in 184 A.D. for neglecting this basic precaution. While leading a large army, he was besieging Ch'ang-she, which was defended by Huang-fu Sung. Although the garrison was small and nervous, Huang-fu Sung called his officers together and said: "In war, there are various indirect ways to attack, and numbers are not everything." [Here the commentator quotes Sun Tzŭ, V. §§ 5, 6, and 10.] "The rebels have set up camp in thick grass that will easily catch fire when the wind blows. If we set fire to it at night, they will panic, and we can attack from all sides, just like T'ien Tan did." [See page 90.] That night, a strong breeze arose, so Huang-fu Sung ordered his soldiers to bind reeds into torches and guard the city walls. Then, he sent out a group of brave men who sneaked through the enemy lines and started the fire with loud shouts and yells. At the same time, a bright light flared up from the city walls, and Huang-fu Sung, sounding the drums, led a swift charge, throwing the rebels into confusion and sending them fleeing." *Hou Han Shu,* ch. 71.]

When you start a fire, make sure you are upwind from it. Do not attack from the downwind side.

[Chang Yu, following Tu Yu, explains: "When you start a fire, the enemy will retreat away from it; if you block their retreat and attack, they will fight desperately, which will not lead to your success." Tu Mu offers a simpler explanation: "If the wind is blowing from the east, begin burning to the east of the enemy and follow up your attack from that direction. If you start the fire on the east side and attack from the west, both you and the enemy will suffer."]

A wind that rises during the day lasts long, but a night breeze dies down quickly.

[Lao Tzŭ says: "A violent wind does not last the space of a morning." (Tao Te Ching, chap. 23.) Mei Yao-ch'en and Wang Hsi explain: "A daytime breeze fades at nightfall, and a night breeze ends at daybreak. This is usually the case." While this observation may be accurate, how this applies in the context is not immediately clear.]

In every army, the five developments related to fire must be understood, the movements of the stars calculated, and attention paid to the proper days.

[Tu Mu says: "We must calculate the paths of the stars and watch for the days when wind will rise before launching a fire attack." Chang Yu seems to interpret the text differently, suggesting: "We must not only know how to attack our opponents with fire but also guard against similar attacks from them."]

Those who use fire as a tool for attacking show intelligence, while those who use water as a tool for attacking gain additional strength.

By means of water, an enemy may be intercepted, but not stripped of all his possessions.

[Ts'ao Kung comments: "We can only obstruct the enemy's path or divide his forces, but we cannot wipe out all his stores." Water can be helpful, but it lacks the overwhelming destructive power of fire. This, Chang Yu concludes, is why water is dismissed in just a few lines, while fire attacks are discussed in detail. Wu Tzŭ (ch. 4) remarks: "If an army is camped on low-lying marshy ground, where water can't drain away, and where rainfall is heavy, it may be flooded. If an army is camped in wild marshlands overgrown with weeds and brambles, and frequently visited by gales, it may be wiped out by fire."]

Unhappy is the fate of one who tries to win his battles and succeed in his attacks without fostering a spirit of initiative; for the result is wasted time and general stagnation.

[This is one of the most puzzling passages in Sun Tzŭ. Ts'ao Kung says: "Rewards for good service should not be delayed even for a single day." Tu Mu adds: "If you don't seize the opportunity to advance and reward those who deserve it, your subordinates will not follow your orders, and disaster will follow." However, I prefer the interpretation suggested by Mei Yao-ch'en, whose words I will quote: "Those who want to ensure success in their battles and attacks must seize favorable opportunities when they arise and not shy away from bold measures. That means they must use such means of attack as fire, water, and the like. What they must avoid, which will lead to failure, is sitting still and merely holding on to the advantages they have already gained."]

Hence the saying: The enlightened ruler plans well in advance; the capable general builds up his resources.

[Tu Mu quotes from the *San Lueh,* ch. 2: "The warlike prince controls his soldiers through his authority, unites them through trust, and makes them serve through rewards. If trust fades, there will be disorder; if rewards are insufficient, orders will not be obeyed."]

Move not unless you see an advantage; use not your troops unless there is something to be gained; fight not unless the position is critical.

[Sun Tzŭ may seem overly cautious at times, but he never goes as far as the passage in the *Tao Te Ching,* ch. 69: "I dare not take the initiative but prefer to act defensively; I dare not advance an inch but prefer to retreat a foot."]

No ruler should send troops into the field merely to satisfy personal anger; no general should fight a battle out of resentment.

If it benefits you, make a forward move; if not, stay where you are.

[This repeats from XI. § 17. It feels like an interpolation here because § 20 clearly follows from § 18.]

Anger may eventually turn into gladness; frustration may be replaced by contentment.

But a kingdom once destroyed can never be restored;

[The Wu State serves as a sad example of this saying.]

nor can the dead ever be brought back to life.

Therefore, the enlightened ruler is cautious, and the wise general is full of care. This is the way to keep a country at peace and an army intact.

["Unless you enter the tiger's lair, you cannot catch its cubs."]

Chapter 13 - The Use of Spies

Sun Tzŭ said: Raising an army of a hundred thousand men and marching them over long distances causes heavy losses to the people and drains the State's resources. The daily cost will amount to a thousand ounces of silver.

[Cf. II. §§ 1, 13, 14.]

There will be unrest both at home and abroad, and men will collapse from exhaustion along the highways.

[Cf. *Tao Te Ching,* ch. 30: "Where troops have been stationed, thorns and brambles spring up." Chang Yu notes: "We are reminded of the saying: 'On serious ground, gather in plunder.' So why does transport cause such exhaustion on the highways?—The answer lies in the fact that it is not just food but all sorts of munitions that must be transported to the army. Additionally, the command to 'forage on the enemy' means that, when deeply engaged in enemy territory, food shortages must be anticipated. Therefore, while not entirely dependent on the enemy for supplies, we must forage to ensure a continuous flow. Moreover, in places like salt deserts, where provisions are unavailable, supplies from home become indispensable."]

As many as seven hundred thousand families will be hindered in their work.

[Mei Yao-ch'en comments: "There will be a shortage of men to work the fields." The reference is to the system of dividing land into nine parts, with the central plot farmed for the State by the tenants of the other eight plots. It was here, as Tu Mu notes, that the families built their cottages and shared a common well. [See II. § 12, note.] During wartime, one family had to serve in the army, while the other seven provided support. Therefore, when 100,000 men were conscripted (with one able-bodied soldier per family), the agricultural work of 700,000 families would be affected.]

Hostile armies may face each other for years, striving for a victory that is decided in a single day. Given this, to remain ignorant of the enemy's condition simply because one begrudges the cost of a hundred ounces of silver for rewards and payments

["For spies" is implied here, though it is not explicitly mentioned to maintain the effect of this elaborate introduction.] is the height of inhumanity.

[Sun Tzŭ's argument is quite clever. He starts by acknowledging the immense misery and staggering cost in lives and resources that war brings. If you remain uninformed about the enemy's situation and fail to strike at the right moment, a war can drag on for years. The only way to get this information is by employing spies, and reliable spies cannot be found unless they are well paid. It is false economy to begrudge such a small amount when each additional day of war costs vastly more. This burden falls hardest on the poor, so neglecting the use of spies is, in Sun Tzŭ's view, nothing less than a crime against humanity.]

One who acts in this way is no leader of men, no true support to his sovereign, and no master of victory.

[This notion, that the ultimate goal of war is peace, has deep roots in the Chinese national temperament. Even as far back as 597 B.C., Prince Chuang of the Ch'u State said: "The [Chinese] character for 'prowess' is formed by the characters for 'to stay' and 'a spear' (the cessation of hostilities). Military prowess is seen in the suppression of cruelty, the laying down of weapons, upholding the mandate of Heaven, establishing merit, bringing happiness to the people, promoting harmony among the princes, and spreading wealth."]

Thus, what enables the wise sovereign and the good general to strike and conquer, achieving things beyond the reach of ordinary men, is foreknowledge.

[That is, understanding the enemy's plans and intentions.]

Now, this foreknowledge cannot be gained from spirits; it cannot be derived from experience,

[Tu Mu explains: "[Knowledge of the enemy] cannot be obtained by reasoning from similar cases."]

nor can it be deduced through calculation.

[Li Ch'uan notes: "Quantities like length, breadth, distance, and magnitude can be determined mathematically, but human actions cannot be calculated in the same way."]

Knowledge of the enemy's plans can only be obtained from other men.

[Mei Yao-ch'en adds an interesting point: "Divination can provide knowledge of the spirit-world; inductive reasoning can reveal truths in natural science; and mathematical calculation can verify the laws of the universe. But the enemy's plans can only be learned through spies, and spies alone."]

Hence the use of spies, of whom there are five types: (1) Local spies; (2) inward spies; (3) converted spies; (4) doomed spies; (5) surviving spies.

When all five types of spies are working together, no one can unravel the secret system. This is called "divine manipulation of the threads." It is the sovereign's most valuable skill.

[Cromwell, one of the greatest and most practical cavalry leaders, had officers called 'scout masters,' whose task was to gather all possible intelligence regarding the enemy through scouts and spies. Much of his success in warfare was due to the prior knowledge of the enemy's movements gained in this way.]

Having local spies means using the inhabitants of a region.

[Tu Mu advises: "In the enemy's country, win people over through kind treatment and use them as spies."]

Having inward spies means using officials of the enemy.

[Tu Mu lists several groups likely to be useful in this regard: "Worthy men who have been disgraced, criminals who have been punished, favorite concubines greedy for gold, men frustrated with being in subordinate positions or passed over for promotions, others hoping for their side's defeat so they can showcase their talents, and turncoats who always try to keep a foot in both camps. Officials of these types should be secretly approached and won over with rich gifts. In this way, you can discover the state of affairs in the enemy's country, learn their plans, and also cause discord between the ruler and his ministers." However, dealing with inward spies requires extreme caution, as illustrated by an incident related by Ho Shih: "Lo Shang, Governor of I-Chou, sent his general Wei Po to attack the rebel Li Hsiung of Shu in his stronghold at P'i. After several victories and defeats on both sides, Li Hsiung employed the services of a certain P'o-t'ai, a native of Wu-tu. He had P'o-t'ai whipped until blood flowed, then sent him to deceive Lo Shang by pretending to cooperate from inside the city and promising to light a fire signal for a coordinated assault. Lo Shang trusted these promises, sent out his best troops, and ordered Wei Po and others to attack when P'o-t'ai signaled. Meanwhile, Li Hsiung's general, Li Hsiang, prepared an ambush along their path. P'o-t'ai then raised long scaling ladders against the city walls and lit the signal fire. Wei Po's men rushed in upon seeing the signal, climbed the ladders, and were pulled up by ropes. More than a hundred of Lo Shang's soldiers entered the city, where they were immediately beheaded. Li Hsiung then charged with his full forces, both inside and outside the city, and completely routed the enemy." This occurred in 303 A.D. Though Ho Shih does not provide his source, it is not mentioned in the biographies of Li Hsiung or his father, Li T'e, in *Chin Shu,* ch. 120, 121.]

Having converted spies means capturing the enemy's spies and using them for our own purposes.

[This involves offering them large bribes and making generous promises to turn them against their original side, so they will send false information back to the enemy and spy on their own people. Another approach, mentioned by Hsiao Shih-hsien, is to pretend that we haven't caught on to the spy, allowing him to leave with a false understanding of what is happening. Some commentators accept this as an alternative interpretation, but it's not what Sun Tzǔ intended, as shown by his later comments on treating the converted spy well. Ho Shih gives three examples of successful use of converted spies: (1) T'ien Tan in his defense of Chi-mo, (2) Chao She on his march to O-yu, and (3) Fan Chu in 260 B.C., when Lien P'o was conducting a defensive campaign against Ch'in. The King of Chao, unhappy with Lien P'o's slow and cautious methods, listened to reports from spies who had secretly switched sides and were already being paid by Fan Chu. The spies said, "The only concern Ch'in has is if Chao Kua becomes general. They see Lien P'o as an easy target who will be defeated eventually." Chao Kua, the son of the famous general Chao She, had been obsessed with war and strategy since childhood, believing no one could defeat him. His father, worried about his arrogance, warned that if Kua ever became a general, he would ruin the army of Chao. Despite warnings from his mother and the statesman Lin Hsiang-ju, Chao Kua was appointed to replace Lien P'o. He proved no match for the skilled general Po Ch'i and the mighty Ch'in army. His army was split, his supply lines were cut, and after a 46-day resistance, during which his starving soldiers resorted to cannibalism, he was killed by an arrow, and his entire force, reportedly 400,000 men, was slaughtered.]

Having doomed spies means openly doing certain things to deceive the enemy and letting our own spies know about it so they can report back.

[Tu Yu explains it best: "We deliberately do things to fool our own spies into thinking they've uncovered real secrets. When they are caught by the enemy, they will give false reports, causing the enemy to prepare for something that won't happen." Once the enemy realizes the deception, the spies will be executed. Ho Shih gives the example of prisoners released by Pan Ch'ao during his campaign against Yarkand. He also mentions T'ang Chien, who was sent by T'ai Tsung in 630 A.D. to lull the Turkish Kahn Chieh-li into a false sense of security until Li Ching could launch a surprise attack. Some say the Turks killed T'ang Chien in revenge, but both the old and new T'ang histories record that he escaped and lived until 656. Li I-chi played a similar role in 203 B.C., when sent by the King of Han to negotiate with Ch'i. Li I-chi may be a more fitting example of a doomed spy, as the King of Ch'i, feeling betrayed after an unexpected attack by Han Hsin, had Li I-chi boiled alive.]

Surviving spies are those who return with information from the enemy's camp.

[These are the typical spies, forming a regular part of the army. Tu Mu says: "A surviving spy must be intelligent but appear foolish; he should look shabby on the outside but possess a strong will. He must be active, tough, physically strong, and brave; accustomed to doing dirty work, able to endure hunger and cold, and capable of handling shame and humiliation." Ho Shih tells a story about Ta'hsi Wu of the Sui dynasty: "When he was governor of Eastern Ch'in, Shen-wu of Ch'i launched an attack on Sha-yuan. Emperor T'ai Tsu sent Ta'hsi Wu to spy on the enemy, accompanied by two others. They rode on horseback, wearing the enemy's uniform. After nightfall, they dismounted a few hundred feet from the enemy's camp and sneaked closer to listen. They managed to overhear the army's passwords. Then they got back on their horses and, pretending to be night watchmen, boldly rode through the camp. Several times, they even punished soldiers who were breaking the rules, beating them as if they were enforcing discipline! This way, they gathered detailed information about the enemy's position and returned to report. The Emperor was so impressed by their intelligence that he used it to achieve a major victory over the enemy."]

Hence, none in the entire army should be more closely connected with than spies.

[Tu Mu and Mei Yao-ch'en note that spies have the privilege of entering even the general's private tent.]

No one should be rewarded more generously, and no other work should be kept more secret.

[Tu Mu adds that all communication with spies should be done "mouth-to-ear," in utmost secrecy. The following advice on spies can be quoted from Turenne, who used them more than any previous commander: "Spies work for those who pay them the most. A commander who pays poorly will never be well-served. They should remain unknown to others, and they should not know one another. When they propose something important, secure their loyalty by holding them or their families as hostages for their faithfulness. Only share with them what is absolutely necessary for them to know."]

Spies cannot be effectively used without a certain intuitive sagacity.

[Mei Yao-ch'en says: "To use them well, you must be able to distinguish truth from lies and recognize honesty from deceit." Wang Hsi interprets this more as "intuitive perception" and "practical intelligence." Tu Mu, however, strangely attributes these qualities to the spies themselves: "Before employing spies, we must confirm their integrity and assess their experience and skills." But he adds: "A bold face and a cunning mind are more dangerous than mountains or rivers; it takes a genius to see through them." This leaves some uncertainty as to his true view of the passage.]

They cannot be properly managed without benevolence and straightforwardness.

[Chang Yu says: "After attracting spies with good offers, you must treat them with complete sincerity, so they will serve you with full dedication."]

Without subtle ingenuity, one cannot be sure of the accuracy of their reports.

[Mei Yao-ch'en warns: "Beware of the possibility that spies might defect to the enemy."]

Be subtle! Be subtle! And use your spies for all kinds of tasks.

If a spy leaks a secret before the time is right, he must be executed along with the person who received the information.

[The literal translation is: "If spy matters are heard before [our plans] are carried out," etc. Sun Tzŭ's point is that the spy is executed as punishment for revealing the secret, while the other person is killed, as Ch'en Hao explains, "to keep his mouth shut" and prevent further leaks. If the information has already been shared with others, this would be ineffective. Sun Tzŭ's advice may seem harsh, though Tu Mu defends it, saying the recipient deserves punishment because he must have pressured the spy into revealing the secret.]

Whether the goal is to defeat an army, storm a city, or assassinate a leader, it is crucial to start by learning the names of the attendants, aides-de-camp,

[Literally "visitors," referring to those who supply the general with information, requiring regular meetings with him.]

the doorkeepers, and sentries of the general in command. Our spies must be assigned to find out these details.

[This would be the first step toward determining whether any of these key figures can be bribed.]

The enemy's spies who come to spy on us must be identified, tempted with bribes, and then won over and treated well. This way, they become converted spies and can work for us.

It is through the information provided by the converted spy that we can recruit and use local and inward spies.

[Tu Yu explains: "By converting the enemy's spies, we learn the true state of the enemy." Chang Yu adds: "We must entice the converted spy into our service because he knows which local inhabitants are greedy for profit and which officials are open to corruption."]

It is also through the converted spy's information that we can use doomed spies to send false reports to the enemy.

[Chang Yu says, "The converted spy knows the best ways to deceive the enemy."]

Finally, the converted spy's information allows us to use the surviving spy on special occasions.

The ultimate purpose of all five types of spies is to gain knowledge of the enemy; and this knowledge primarily comes from the converted spy.

[As outlined in §§ 22-24. The converted spy not only provides direct information but also makes it possible to effectively employ the other types of spies.]

Therefore, it is crucial to treat the converted spy with the greatest generosity.

Of old, the rise of the Yin dynasty

[Sun Tzŭ is referring to the Shang dynasty, founded in 1766 B.C., which was later renamed Yin by P'an Keng in 1401.]

was due to I Chih

[Also known as I Yin, the famous general and statesman who played a key role in Ch'eng T'ang's campaign against Chieh Kuei.]

who had served under the Hsia. Likewise, the rise of the Chou dynasty was due to Lü Ya

[Lü Shang, who rose to prominence under the tyrant Chou Hsin, later helped to overthrow him. He is widely known as T'ai Kung, a title given to him by Wen Wang, and is said to have authored a treatise on war, though it has been wrongly identified with the *Liu T'ao.*]

who had served under the Yin.

[The Chinese wording here is less precise than this translation, and the commentaries are not clear. However, in the context, it seems likely that Sun Tzŭ is presenting I Chih and Lü Ya as examples of converted spies or something similar. His point is that the Hsia and Yin dynasties fell because these former ministers had intimate knowledge of their weaknesses, which they shared with the opposing side. Mei Yao-ch'en objects to this interpretation, saying: "I Yin and Lü Ya were not traitors. The Hsia dynasty failed to employ I Yin, so the Yin did. The Yin dynasty failed to employ Lü Ya, so the Chou did. Their great deeds were for the benefit of the people." Ho Shih is also offended: "How could divinely inspired men like I and Lü have been mere spies? Sun Tzŭ is not suggesting that they were spies, but rather that using spies requires the highest level of intelligence, which people like I and Lü possessed. That is why they are mentioned here." Ho Shih believes they are referenced for their wisdom in using spies, but this interpretation is weak.]

Hence, only the enlightened ruler and the wise general will use the highest intelligence in the army for spying, and by doing so, they achieve great results.

[Tu Mu concludes with a note of caution: "Just as water, which can carry a boat across a river, can also sink it, so relying on spies can bring great success but also lead to disaster."]

Spies are a crucial part of warfare because the movement of the army depends on them.

Thank You for Reading

Dear Reader,

We hope this timeless classic has sparked your imagination and enriched your literary journey. Now that you've turned the final page, we want to share a vision for the future of reading—one where every classic you've ever wanted to explore is at your fingertips, in a format that best suits your life.

We'd like to invite you to gain immediate, unlimited digital & audiobook access to hundreds of the most treasured literary classics ever written—along with the option to secure deluxe paperback, hardcover & box set editions at printing cost. Together, we can spark a new global literary renaissance alongside our small, independent publishing house called "The Library of Alexandria."

Thousands of years ago, the Library of Alexandria stood as a beacon of knowledge—until it was lost to history. We aim to reignite that spirit of preservation and discovery right now, in the modern age—only this time, it's accessible to all, in every language and every format.

Picture a world where every timeless classic, novel, poem, or philosophical treatise is not only available to read but also updated for today's readers—modernized, translated into any language or dialect, and ready to enjoy in any format you choose, whether that is in an eBook, audiobook, paperback, or deluxe hardcover & box set version a printing cost.

By joining our movement to rebuild the modern Library of Alexandria, you become part of an unprecedented mission to offer:

- **Unlimited Audiobook & eBook Access to the Greatest Classics of All Time**

  Instantly explore thousands of legendary works, from Plato and Shakespeare to Jane Austen and Leo Tolstoy. All are instantly ready to read or listen to, giving you a complete literary universe at your fingertips.

- **Paperback & Deluxe Editions at Printing Costs:**

  Purchase any title in a paperback, deluxe hardbound, or deluxe boxset edition at printing costs, shipped right to your doorstep. Curate your personal library of Alexandria with editions worthy of display—crafted to last, designed to captivate, and delivered straight to your door.

- **Modern translations for Contemporary Readers in all languages and dialects**

  Discover a vast selection of classics reimagined in clear, current language—no more struggling with outdated phrases or obscure references. Next to the original versions, we aim to offer translations in as many languages and dialects as possible.

  As we continue our translation efforts and add new languages, readers everywhere can connect with these works as if they were written today. By bridging linguistic divides, you're contributing to ensuring that these timeless stories become more meaningful, accessible, and inspiring for people across the globe.

- **Your Personal Library of Alexandria:**

  Over the months and years, you'll curate a unique physical archive of classics—each volume a testament to your taste, curiosity, and love of knowledge. It's not just about owning books—it's about curating a cultural legacy you'll cherish and pass down for generations to come.

- **Join a Global Literary Renaissance:**

  Your support fuels an ongoing mission: allowing us to reinvest in offering deluxe print editions (including special boxsets) at their true cost, broaden the range of available formats and translations, and extend the reach of these works to new audiences worldwide. By joining today, you're not just preserving a legacy of masterpieces; you set in motion a powerful wave of literary accessibility.

We are more than a publisher—we're a movement, and we can't do it alone. Your support lets us scale our mission, preserving and reimagining history's greatest works for tomorrow's readers.

Become a Torchbearer of knowledge.

Thank you for picking up this book and allowing us into your literary journey. As you turn the pages, know that you're part of something larger: a global effort to keep these stories alive, share their wisdom across borders and generations, and spark a true cultural revival for the modern era.

If this resonates with you—please consider taking the next step by visiting:

www.libraryofalexandria.com

With gratitude and a shared love of knowledge,

The Modern Library of Alexandria Team

Visit:

www.libraryofalexandria.com

Or scan the code below: